Leonard Wolf has compiled an anthology of the world's most terrifying terror literature, ranging in time from the Old Testament through the Marquis de Sade and on to Ray Bradbury, Ursula Le Guin, and Shirley Jackson. Styles of terror may change over the ages—the specifics of what scares us now differing at least in superficial ways from what scared people of two thousand years ago—but the fascination with it remains constant. In fact, we still thrill to many of the monsters, ghosts, and vampires of an earlier age, although we have added sci-fi fantasies, atomic explosions, and a wealth of psychological demons to our contemporary catalog of horrors.

Not only does Wolf provide us with scare stories sufficient for many a Halloween to come, but in a brief introduction he develops a theory of terror, explaining why and how such stories scare us, what it says about us that we find fright so delicious a state (in literature as well as in life), and the distinctions between inner and outer, symbolic and actual, "wet" and "dry" terror.

Because of the author's long-standing fascination with terror in all its many guises, this collection, which includes poetry and prose, is packed with werewolves, vampires, ghosts, evil spirits, doppelgangers, science-fiction monsters, various mutant figments of both the supernatural and the natural worlds,

and, perhaps most terrifying of all to a modern sensibility, abundant examples of the horrors lurking beneath conventional "real life." Works from many nations and cultures are included, as the taste for terror is as universal as it is timeless. Brief explanatory notes for each story help make this a collection that will fascinate and inform, titillate and terrify.

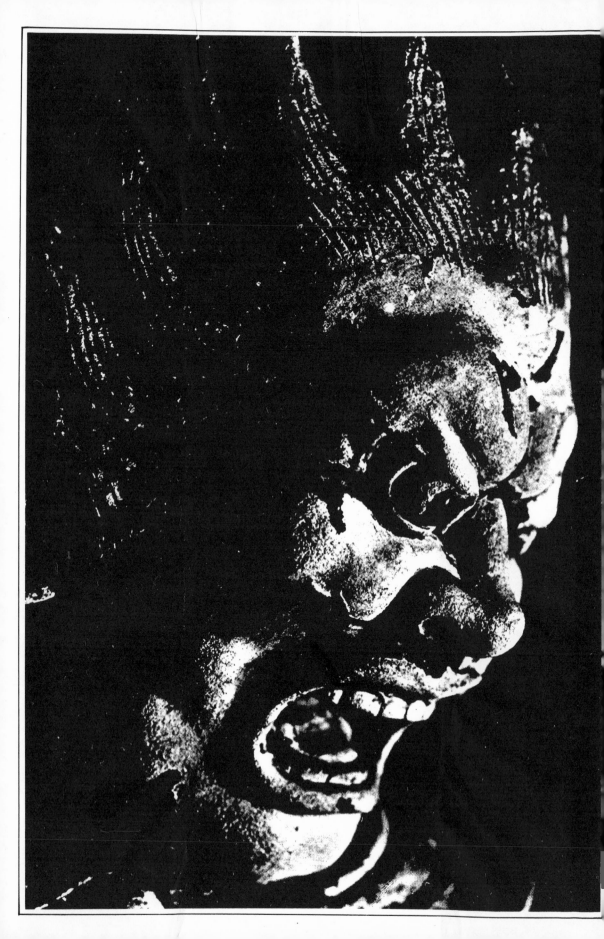

WOLF'S COMPLETE BOOK OF TERROR

EDITED BY LEONARD WOLF

Clarkson N. Potter, Inc. / Publishers NEW YORK

DISTRIBUTED BY CROWN PUBLISHERS, INC.

OTHER BOOKS BY THE AUTHOR:

A Dream of Dracula: In Search of the Living Dead
The Annotated Frankenstein
The Annotated Dracula
Monsters

Designed by Herman Strohbach

Library of Congress Cataloging in Publication Data

Main entry under title:

Wolf's Complete book of terror.

　　1.　Horror—Literary collections.　　I.　Wolf, Leonard.
II.　Title: Complete book of terror.
PN6071.H727W6 1979　　　　　808'.83'872　　　　　79-448

ISBN 0-517-53752-4

CONTENTS

ACKNOWLEDGMENTS

I am grateful to many people for a rich range of suggestions about what to include in the *Complete Book of Terror*. At San Francisco State University, my thanks go to John Alcorn, Robert Berg, Kay Boyle, Art Chandler, John Dennis, William Dickey, Frank Dollard, John Edwards, David Gamble, Arthur Hall, Miley Holman, Louis Kemnitzer, George Moore, Ed Nierenberg, George Price, William Robinson, Catherine Smith, Niel Snortum, Cammy Thomas, Stanley Tick, Gail Todd, Richard Trapp, Vicente Urbistondo, Richard Waidelich, Robin Wells, Peter Weltner, Helen Whitson, Graham Wilson, James Wilson, Lois Wilson, Richard Wiseman.

I also want to thank Dr. Sandor Burstein and Elizabeth Burstein, Margot Patterson Doss of the *San Francisco Chronicle,* Dr. Wolfgang Lederer and Dr. Alexandra Lederer.

For help with various of the more onerous labors that went into the making of this book, I want to thank Renee Ashley, Lisa Graham, Pamela Roberts, and Virginia Verrill.

A PREFATORY NOTE TO

WOLF'S
COMPLETE BOOK
OF TERROR

The tales and poems that are to come have been chosen because they are frightening—and therefore pleasing—to the editor. However, since pleasure is not very useful as a principle of organization, the selections in this anthology have been put in a reverse chronological order. There is some danger that such an arrangement will give a spurious air of inevitability, of historic necessity to the collection—as if my intention was to document the evolution of terror literature from primitive times to the sophisticated present. Nothing can be farther from the truth. The story of Jaël, in *The Book of Judges,* is as skillful and as complex as Shirley Jackson's "The Lottery." Still, the experience of time passing is familiar enough so that a chronological ordering can serve as a comforting metaphor, especially for readers of a book in whose pages chaos and dark night are perpetually intruding.

INTRODUCTION

"The sleep of reason," says Goya in one of a series of etchings entitled "Los Caprichos," "produces monsters." It is a remark intended to admonish us against disorder, and yet "Los Caprichos" demonstrates the paradox that, in the hands of the artist, even the monsters of unreason can be constrained to please. Because fear is the true sixth sense, it is not surprising that we have found a way to make of terror a basis for delight.

The essential beauty of the emotion of fear is the way that it can reduce the self to a single sensation that is at once formless and personal. We speak of being frightened out of our minds, and it is an apt metaphor. Out of our minds and into our bodies. In the adrenalin rush that comes with terror, every cell in the body recalls its ancient duty to freeze, fight, or run. In the real world, in the presence of physical danger, fear makes sensualists of us all and turns the entire self into a pillar of attention. Once we have killed the saber-toothed tiger, or escaped from the embrace of the boa constrictor, the memory of that *sensational* moment, framed now by the relief of our escape, can seem beautiful. That terrifying beauty is what draws us to the literature of fear in whose pages we are reconnected, time after time, to the electric charge of our instinctual life. People in terror tales still face primordial dangers. Disregarding the advice of Satchel Paige, they look back to discover that something *is* gaining on them. Or like the boy Tammie, in "Nuckelavee," who faces his terrible foe and discovers that the creature's

> lower part . . . was like a great horse with flappers like fins about his legs, with a mouth as wide as a whale's . . . He had but one eye and that as red as fire. On him sat, or rather seemed to grow from his back, a huge man with no legs, and arms that reached nearly to the ground . . .

And this skinless beast was breathing "its hot breath like fire on his face; the long arms were stretched out to seize [him] . . . " No one in the grip of such pure terror feels dreary. No one in flight from the terrifying known, or the more terrifying unknown, is ever bored.

Fear literature, however, does more than focus on a brevity of attention within a circle of danger. There are more ways to be terrified, after all, than by the swift imminence of destruction. Mean landscapes, affectless embraces, betrayal, and the misfortunes of love are also terrifying; and there are stories in the *Complete Book of Terror* such as "The Yellow Wallpaper," and "The South" in which the mothlike horrors of free-floating anxiety are explored.

Terror tales do more than elaborate panic for the delectation of their readers. Terror writing validates our continually lingering suspicion that there are mistakes in the Creation; that God swept chaos under the rug at the end of that famous Sixth Day. In fear literature the vast troop of un-creatures—all those mixed-up beasts: part lion and part woman; part wolf and part man; part eagle and part serpent—are still nearby, gnawing away at unalterable Law. The pallor of the vampire and the prowess of the werewolf teach us that evil is as fecund as wisdom. In Lovecraft's pages, the dank mistakes of evolution share their caves and their religion with selected (if loathsome) humans. In Kipling's "The Mark of the Beast," in White's "Lukundoo," the uncanny forces of the universe wielded by primitive men trivialize the concept of civilization and validate our paranoia. In such tales there *is* a "they" that wants to get us, that conspires against us. There *are* "mysterious powers." One does indeed hear voices. A doll, as in Black-wood's story, can stalk and punish the guilty. Yellow wallpaper, as in Charlotte Gilman's tale, can turn malevolent. Conspiracy, as in Poe's "The Pit and the Pendulum," is the only weather. Or, as in the selections from *Maldoror* and *Justine,* the creation itself is indicted. For Lautréamont, God is, if anything at all, a tumid conspirator of the Awful. For de Sade, He is the indifferent architect of Nature who permits what is forbidden. The only imperative, in de Sade's universe, is to be strong. The only ethic is what the strong may choose.

There are, if the truth be told, certain low pleasures to be had from reading terror literature. Murder and madness, rape and revulsion, bestiality and power are the stuff of which the genre is made. When we read the story of Jaël driving her tent peg into a sleeping Sisera's skull, what excites us is the lascivious boudoir redolence that rises from the prophetess Deborah's exaltation of the scene, "He asked water, and she gave him milk; she brought forth butter in a lordly dish . . ." Eros and music *and* a blood-spattered tent; and the smell of betrayal. A fine *potpourri.*

Is it sadism to love such wonderful stuff? Probably. But the fact is that each of us harbors an imp of the perverse. Turning the pages of a book in which we find imagined for us the brutal or nasty ways in which people torment each other is one fairly harmless way to keep that imp quiet. Better to read about those rivulets of blood, those bestial matings, those "pale raveners of horrible meat."

The same rage for order that dictated the inverse chronology of the table of contents prompted the editor, who thought at first he was merely reading from terror to terror, to make some passing notes about the kinds of fear literature that came his way. Without ever seriously intending any such thing, he found himself drawing lines for a rough taxonomy of terror. It was a beguiling, and perhaps not altogether frivolous venture, and it resulted in Figure 1.

It will be seen, then, that I have divided terror literature into two parts, which, in the spirit of Lévi-Strauss, I have named "terror from without" and "terror from within." Terror from without is the traditional mode of terror literature and is the one most widely represented in anthologies, including this one. We are familiar from our earliest childhood with the structure and content of such tales. Invariably, as in "Bluebeard" or "Nuckelavee," the protagonist is pursued, or captured, or immobilized by an enemy. The enemy may be animal, vegetable, or human. Or, it may be a spirit or an elf or a goblin damned. Our protagonist must contend with the wrath or lust of an enemy outside himself. Embodied evil is out to destroy the good.

The term *terror from within* describes a comparatively new genre of fear literature. In such psychological fiction, the terror is essentially a consequence of some slippage in the mind of the protagonist, rather than in any threatening external event. What is overwhelming, for example, in Julio Cortázar's "Axolotl" is the glimpse that we are given of a hell that has no "otherness." The protagonist of "Axolotl" is attacked by nothing at all. What destroys him is his own bleak sympathy for the passivity and the narrow horizon of the amphibious *axolotl.* If, as we are led to believe, the narrator suffers a sea change, it is not because he has been cursed or victimized. Rather, he had drifted toward disaster in imitation of the axolotl with whom he has traded his merely vestigial humanity for a simulacrum of peace. As the story ends, the man and the axolotl are indistinguishable, and the horror of that union is accomplished. In Powys's "The Mark of the Beast" there is, again, no sinister other—though indeed everything in the story is sinister enough. But the terror lies in the glimpse that Powys gives us into the mind of his narrator; the story is a squirming tissue of metaphors, all of them pulsating with torment. In "The Yellow Wallpaper," though we may identify an inimical other in the narrator's husband, the immediate terror itself comes from what we see of the destruction of a fine mind turning in upon itself. In Borges's "The South" the issue is . . . that there is no issue. That violent death may be merely one of the reflexes of the human situation. That the universe has the blank stare of a basilisk.

Let us return briefly to "terror from without." It will be seen (in Figure 1) that I have divided these tales into two categories: natural and supernatural.

FIGURE 1

Terror Literature

Terror from Without	Terror from Within
Natural	Supernatural
Wet	Dry

In the first group, we may put the story of "Jaël," Poe's "The Black Cat" and "The Pit and the Pendulum," Hecht's "The Rival Dummy," and Ellison's "I Have No Mouth, and I Must Scream," all of which take place in a world in which natural law is presumed to be at work. "Piazza Piece," "La

Belle Hélène," "Carmilla," and "Sredni Vashtar," on the other hand, require a suspension of disbelief in the supernatural.

One could, I think, go on making subclassifications, but I have chosen to forebear, with one exception: the difference between "wet" and "dry" terror.

Hardened Lovecraftians will understand the distinction at once. Lovecraft has created a batrachian world in which slime and morass, putrescence and repulsive fluids, are the usual order. But "wet" touches on style as well as subject matter. Our "wet" writers indulge themselves in frenzy. Among the Gothic novelists, "Monk" Lewis is wet, while Ann Radcliffe is dry. Mary Shelley's *Frankenstein* is mostly dry, while *Dracula,* not surprisingly, is wet. In the present collection, the Vampire episode from Apuleius is dry, but "Born of Man and Woman" is wet. "The Wish," "The Yellow Wallpaper," and "Tchériapin" are dry. "The Horla," "La Belle Dame sans Merci," and "La Belle Hélène" are wet. "The Lottery" and "Axolotl" are dry.

A word of caution about these distinctions. None of the categories is an escape-proof enclosure. Even in a story that is as overtly terror from without as "Lukundoo," the protagonist recognizes, "This curse did not grow on me, it grew out of me." In that sense, "Lukundoo" could be read as terror from within. The same is true for "Carmilla," "The Monkey's Paw," and "The Horla."

The stories, not the categories, matter. To get at their terror—inner or outer, wet or dry—it will be well to sit in a darkened room in a comfortable chair under a soft reading light. It will help to have something that can be nibbled easily in a crisis. After that one needs courage, because terror writers, though they deal with the Awfullest Questions, are all but indifferent about providing comforting answers. Their task is to reveal the serpent rising from the slime; to give us the smell of his centuries-old skin, as he comes closer and closer and closer. He may well be the great Beast lurching toward Bethlehem to be born, but so long as he does his lurching in the pages of a book, we can yield ourselves up to the delight of being frightened to death in a safe place.

Safe . . .?

WOLF'S
COMPLETE BOOK
OF TERROR

URSULA K. LE GUIN

THE ONES WHO WALK AWAY FROM OMELAS

(Variations on a theme by William James)

The central idea of this psychomyth, the scapegoat, turns up in Dostoyevsky's *Brothers Karamazov,* and several people have asked me, rather suspiciously, why I gave the credit to William James. The fact is, I haven't been able to re-read Dostoyevsky, much as I loved him, since I was twenty-five, and I'd simply forgotten he used the idea. But when I met it in James's "The Moral Philosopher and the Moral Life," it was with a shock of recognition. Here is how James puts it:

> Or if the hypothesis were offered us of a world in which Messrs. Fourier's and Bellamy's and Morris's utopias should all be outdone, and millions kept permanently happy on the one simple condition that a certain lost soul on the far-off edge of things should lead a life of lonely torment, what except a specified and independent sort of emotion can it be which would make us immediately feel, even though an impulse arose within us to clutch at the happiness so offered, how hideous a thing would be its enjoyment when deliberately accepted as the fruit of such a bargain?

The dilemma of the American conscience can hardly be better stated. Dostoyevsky was a great artist, and a radical one, but his early social radicalism reversed itself, leaving him a violent reactionary. Whereas the American James, who seems so mild, so naively gentlemanly—look how he says "us," assuming all his readers are as decent as himself!—was, and remained, and remains, a genuinely radical thinker. Directly after the "lost soul" passage he goes on,

> All the higher, more penetrating ideals are revolutionary. They present themselves far less in the guise of effects of past experience than in that of probable causes of future experience, factors to which the environment and the lessons it has so far taught us must learn to bend.

The application of those two sentences to this story, and to science fiction, and to all thinking about the future, is quite direct. Ideals as "the probable causes of future experience"—that is a subtle and an exhilarating remark.

Of course I didn't read James and sit down and say, Now I'll write a story about that "lost soul." It seldom works that simply. I sat down and started a story, just because I felt like it, with nothing but the word *Omelas* in mind. It came from a road sign: Salem (Oregon) backwards. Don't you read road signs backwards? POTS. WOLS nerdlihc. Ocsicnarf Nas ... Salem equals schelomo equals salaam equals Peace. Melas. O melas. Omelas. Homme hélas. "Where *do* you get your ideas from, Ms Le Guin?" From forgetting Dostoyevsky and reading road signs backwards, naturally. Where else?

1

With a clamor of bells that set the swallows soaring, the Festival of Summer came to the city Omelas, bright-towered by the sea. The rigging of the boats in harbor sparkled with flags. In the streets between houses with red roofs and painted walls, between old moss-grown gardens and under avenues of trees, past great parks and public buildings, processions moved. Some were decorous: old people in long stiff robes of mauve and grey, grave master workmen, quiet, merry women carrying their babies and chatting as they walked. In other streets the music beat faster, a shimmering of gong and tambourine, and the people went dancing, the procession was a dance. Children dodged in and out, their high calls rising like the swallows' crossing flights over the music and the singing. All the processions wound towards the north side of the city, where on the great water-meadow called the Green Fields boys and girls, naked in the bright air, with mud-stained feet and ankles and long, lithe arms, exercised their restive horses before the race. The horses wore no gear at all but a halter without bit. Their manes were braided with streamers of silver, gold, and green. They flared their nostrils and pranced and boasted to one another; they were vastly excited, the horse being the only animal who has adopted our ceremonies as his own. Far off to the north and west the mountains stood up half encircling Omelas on her bay. The air of morning was so clear that the snow still crowning the Eighteen Peaks burned with white-gold fire across the miles of sunlit air, under the dark blue of the sky. There was just enough wind to make the banners that marked the racecourse snap and flutter now and then. In the silence of the broad green meadows one could hear the music winding through the city streets, farther and nearer and ever approaching, a cheerful faint sweetness of the air that from time to time trembled and gathered together and broke out into the great joyous clanging of the bells.

Joyous! How is one to tell about joy? How describe the citizens of Omelas?

They were not simple folk, you see, though they were happy. But we do not say the words of cheer much any more. All smiles have become archaic. Given a description such as this one tends to make certain assumptions. Given a description such as this one tends to look next for the King, mounted on a splendid stallion and surrounded by his noble knights, or perhaps in a golden litter borne by great-muscled slaves. But there was no king. They did not use swords, or keep slaves. They were not barbarians. I do not know the rules and laws of their society, but I suspect that they were singularly few. As they did without monarchy and slavery, so they also got on without the stock exchange, the advertisement, the secret police, and the bomb. Yet I repeat that these were not simple folk, not dulcet shepherds, noble savages, bland utopians. They were not less complex than us. The trouble is that we have a bad habit, encouraged by pedants and sophisti-cates, of considering happiness as something rather stupid. Only pain is intellectual, only evil interesting. This is the treason of the artist: a refusal to admit the banality of evil and the terrible boredom of pain. If you can't lick 'em, join 'em. If it hurts, repeat it. But to praise despair is to condemn delight, to embrace violence is to lose hold of everything else. We have almost lost hold; we can no longer describe a happy man, nor make any celebration of joy. How can I tell you about the people of Omelas? They were not naïve and happy children—though their children were, in fact, happy. They were mature, intelligent, passionate adults whose lives were not wretched. O miracle! but I wish I could describe it better. I wish I could convince you. Omelas sounds in my words like a city in a fairy tale, long ago and far away, once upon a time. Perhaps it would be best if you imagined it as your own fancy bids, assuming it will rise to the occasion, for certainly I cannot suit you all. For instance, how about technology? I think that there would be no cars or helicopters in and above the streets; this follows from the fact that the people of Omelas are happy people. Happiness is based on a just discrimination of what is necessary, what is neither necessary nor destructive, and what is destructive. In the middle category, however—that of the unnecessary but undestructive, that of comfort, luxury, exuberance, etc.—they could perfectly well have central heating, subway trains, washing machines, and all kinds of marvelous devices not yet invented here, floating light-sources, fuelless power, a cure for the common cold. Or they could have none of that: it doesn't matter. As you like it. I incline to think that people from towns up and down the coast have been coming in to Omelas during the last days before the Festival on very fast little trains and double-decked trams, and that the train station of Omelas is actually the handsomest building in town, though plainer than the magnificent Farmers' Market. But even granted trains, I fear that Omelas so far strikes some of you as goody-goody. Smiles, bells, parades, horses, bleh. If so, please add an orgy. If an orgy would help, don't hesitate. Let us not, however, have temples from which issue beautiful nude priests and priestesses already half in ecstasy and ready to copulate with any man or woman, lover or stranger, who desires union with the deep godhead of the blood, although that was my first idea. But really it would be better not to have any temples in Omelas—at least, not manned temples. Religion yes, clergy no. Surely the beautiful nudes can just wander about, offering themselves like divine soufflés to the hunger of the needy and the rapture of the flesh. Let them join the processions. Let tambourines be struck above the copulations, and the glory of desire be proclaimed upon the gongs, and (a not unimportant point) let the offspring of these delightful rituals be beloved and looked after by all. One thing I know there is none of in Omelas is guilt. But what else should there be? I thought at first there were no drugs, but that is puritanical. For those who like it, the faint insistent sweetness of *drooz* may perfume the ways of the city, *drooz* which first brings a great lightness and brilliance to the mind and limbs, and then after some hours a dreamy languor, and wonderful visions at last of the very arcana and inmost secrets of the Universe, as well as exciting the pleasure of sex beyond all belief; and it is not habit-forming. For more modest tastes I think there ought to be beer. What else, what else belongs in the joyous city? The sense of victory, surely, the celebration of courage. But as we did without clergy, let us do without soldiers. The joy built upon successful slaughter is not the right kind of joy; it will not do; it is fearful and it is trivial. A boundless and generous contentment, a magnanimous triumph felt not against some outer enemy but in communion with the finest and fairest in the souls of all men everywhere and the splendor of the world's summer: this is what swells the hearts of the people of Omelas, and the victory they celebrate is that of life. I really don't think many of them need to take *drooz*.

Most of the processions have reached the Green Fields by now. A marvelous smell of cooking goes forth from the red and blue tents of the provisioners. The faces of small children are amiably sticky; in the benign grey beard of a man a couple of crumbs of rich pastry are entangled. The youths and girls have mounted their horses and are beginning to group around the starting line of the course. An old woman, small, fat, and laughing, is passing out flowers from a basket, and tall young men wear her flowers in their shining hair. A child of nine or ten sits at the edge of the crowd, alone, playing on a wooden flute. People pause to listen, and they smile, but they do not speak to him, for he never ceases playing and never sees them, his dark eyes wholly rapt in the sweet, thin magic of the tune.

He finishes, and slowly lowers his hands holding the wooden flute.

As if that little private silence were the signal, all at once a trumpet sounds from the pavilion near the starting line: imperious, melancholy, piercing. The horses rear on their slender legs, and some of them neigh in answer. Sober-faced, the young riders stroke the horses' necks and soothe them, whispering, "Quiet, quiet, there my beauty, my hope. . . ." They begin to form in rank along the starting line. The crowds along the racecourse are like a field of grass and flowers in the wind. The Festival of Summer has begun.

Do you believe? Do you accept the festival, the city, the joy? No? Then let me describe one more thing.

In a basement under one of the beautiful public buildings of Omelas, or perhaps in the cellar of one of its spacious private homes, there is a room. It has one locked door, and no window. A little light seeps in dustily between cracks in the boards, secondhand from a cobwebbed window somewhere across the cellar. In one corner of the little room a couple of mops, with stiff, clotted, foul-smelling heads, stand near a rusty bucket. The floor is dirt, a little damp to the touch, as cellar dirt usually is. The room is about three paces long and two wide: a mere broom closet or disused tool room. In the room a child is sitting. It could be a boy or a girl. It looks about six, but actually is nearly ten. It is feeble-minded. Perhaps it was born defective, or perhaps it has become imbecile through fear, malnutrition, and neglect. It picks its nose and occasionally fumbles vaguely with its toes or genitals, as it sits hunched in the corner farthest from the bucket and the two mops. It is afraid of the mops. It finds them horrible. It shuts its eyes, but it knows the mops are still standing there; and the door is locked; and nobody will come. The door is always locked; and nobody ever comes, except that sometimes— the child has no understanding of time or interval—sometimes the door rattles terribly and opens, and a person, or several people, are there. One of them may come in and kick the child to make it stand up. The others never come close, but peer in at it with frightened, disgusted eyes. The food bowl and the water jug are hastily filled, the door is locked, the eyes disappear. The people at the door never say anything, but the child, who has not always lived in the tool room, and can remember sunlight and its mother's voice, sometimes speaks. "I will be good," it says. "Please let me out. I will be good!" They never answer. The child used to scream for help at night, and cry a good deal, but now it only makes a kind of whining, "eh-haa, eh-haa," and it speaks less and less often. It is so thin there are no calves to its legs; its belly protrudes; it lives on a half-bowl of corn meal and grease a day. It is naked. Its buttocks and thighs are a mass of festered sores, as it sits in its own excrement continually.

They all know it is there, all the people of Omelas. Some of them have come to see it, others are content merely to know it is there. They all know that it has to be there. Some of them understand why, and some do not, but they all understand that their happiness, the beauty of their city, the tenderness of their friendships, the health of their children, the wisdom of their scholars, the skill of their makers, even the abundance of their harvest and the kindly weathers of their skies, depend wholly on this child's abominable misery.

This is usually explained to children when they are between eight and twelve, whenever they seem capable of understanding; and most of those who come to see the child are young people, though often enough an adult comes, or comes back, to see the child. No matter how well the matter has been explained to them, these young spectators are always shocked and sickened at the sight. They feel disgust, which they had thought themselves superior to. They feel anger, outrage, impotence, despite all the explanations. They would like to do something for the child. But there is nothing they can do. If the child were brought up into the sunlight out of that vile place, if it were cleaned and fed and comforted, that would be a good thing, indeed; but if it were done, in that day and hour all the prosperity and beauty and delight of Omelas would wither and be destroyed. Those are the terms. To exchange all the goodness and grace of every life in Omelas for that single, small improvement: to throw away the happiness of thousands for the chance of the happiness of one: that would be to let guilt within the walls indeed.

The terms are strict and absolute; there may not even be a kind word spoken to the child.

Often the young people go home in tears, or in a tearless rage, when they have seen the child and faced this terrible paradox. They may brood over it for weeks or years. But as time goes on they begin to realize that even if the child could be released, it would not get much good of its freedom: a little vague pleasure of warmth and food, no doubt, but little more. It is too degraded and imbecile to know any real joy. It has been afraid too long ever to be free of fear. Its habits are too uncouth for it to respond to humane treatment. Indeed, after so long it would probably be wretched without walls about it to protect it, and darkness for its eyes, and its own excrement to sit in. Their tears at the bitter injustice dry when they begin to perceive the terrible justice of reality, and to accept it. Yet it is their tears and anger, the trying of their generosity and the acceptance of their helplessness, which are perhaps the true source of the splendor of their lives. Theirs is no vapid, irresponsible happiness. They know that they, like the child, are not free. They know compassion. It is the existence of the child, and their knowledge of its existence, that makes possible the nobility of their architecture, the poignancy of their music, the profundity of their science. It is because of the child that they are so gentle with children. They know that if the wretched one were not here snivelling in the dark, the other one, the flute-player, could make no joyful music as the young riders line up in their beauty for the race in the sunlight of the first morning of summer.

Now do you believe them? Are they not more credible? But there is one more thing to tell, and this is quite incredible.

At times one of the adolescent girls or boys who go to see the child does not go home to weep or rage, does not, in fact, go home at all. Sometimes also a man or woman much older falls silent for a day or two, and then leaves home. These people go out into the street, and walk down the street alone. They keep walking, and walk straight out of the city of Omelas, through the beautiful gates. They keep walking across the farmlands of Omelas. Each one goes alone, youth or girl, man or woman. Night falls; the traveler must pass down village streets, between the houses with yellow-lit windows, and on out into the darkness of the fields. Each alone, they go west or north, towards the mountains. They go on. They leave Omelas, they walk ahead into the darkness, and they do not come back. The place they go towards is a place even less imaginable to most of us than the city of happiness. I cannot describe it at all. It is possible that it does not exist. But they seem to know where they are going, the ones who walk away from Omelas.

HELEN ADAM

I LOVE MY LOVE

"In the dark of the moon the hair rules."

Robert Duncan

There was a man who married a maid. She laughed as he led her home.
The living fleece of her long bright hair she combed with a golden comb.
He led her home through his barley fields where the saffron poppies grew.
She combed, and whispered, "I love my love." Her voice like a plaintive
    coo.
Ha! Ha!
Her voice like a plaintive coo.

He lived alone with his chosen bride, at first their life was sweet.
Sweet was the touch of her playful hair binding his hands and feet.
When first she murmured adoring words her words did not appall.
"I love my love with a capital A. To my love I give my All.
Ah, Ha!
To my love I give my All."

She circled him with the secret web she wove as her strong hair grew.
Like a golden spider she wove and sang, "My love is tender and true."
She combed her hair with a golden comb and shackled him to a tree.
She shackled him close to the Tree of Life. "My love I'll never set free.
No, No.
My love I'll never set free."

Whenever he broke her golden bonds he was held with bonds of gold.
"Oh! cannot a man escape from love, from Love's hot smothering hold?"
He roared with fury. He broke her bonds. He ran in the light of the sun.
Her soft hair rippled and trapped his feet, as fast as his feet could run,
Ha! Ha!
As fast as his feet could run.

He dug a grave, and he dug it wide. He strangled her in her sleep.
He strangled his love with a strand of hair, and then he buried her deep.
He buried her deep when the sun was hid by a purple thunder cloud.
Her helpless hair sprawled over the corpse in a pale resplendent shroud.
Ha! Ha!
A pale resplendent shroud.

Morning and night of thunder rain, and then it came to pass
That the hair sprang up through the earth of the grave, and it grew like
     golden grass.
It grew and glittered along her grave alive in the light of the sun.
Every hair had a plaintive voice, the voice of his lovely one.

"I love my love with a capital T. My love is Tender and True.
I'll love my love in the barley fields when the thunder cloud is blue.
My body crumbles beneath the ground but the hairs of my head will grow.
I'll love my love with the hairs of my head. I'll never, never let go.
Ha! Ha!
I'll never, never let go."

The hair sang soft, and the hair sang high, singing of loves that drown,
Till he took his scythe by the light of the moon, and he scythed that
     singing hair down.
Every hair laughed a lilting laugh, and shrilled as his scythe swept through.
"I love my love with a capital T. My love is Tender and True.
Ha! Ha!
Tender, Tender, and True."

All through the night he wept and prayed, but before the first bird woke
Around the house in the barley fields blew the hair like billowing smoke.
Her hair blew over the barley fields where the slothful poppies gape.
All day long all its voices cooed, "My love can never escape,
No, No!
My love can never escape."

"Be still, be still, you devilish hair. Glide back to the grave and sleep.
Glide back to the grave and wrap her bones down where I buried her
     deep.
I am the man who escaped from love, though love was my fate and doom.
Can no man ever escape from love who breaks from a woman's womb?"

Over his house, when the sun stood high, her hair was a dazzling storm,
Rolling, lashing o'er walls and roof, heavy, and soft, and warm.
It thumped on the roof, it hissed and glowed over every window pane.
The smell of the hair was in the house. It smelled like a lion's mane,
Ha! Ha!
It smelled like a lion's mane.

Three times round the bed of their love, and his heart lurched with
     despair.
In through the keyhole, elvish bright, came creeping a single hair.
Softly, softly, it stroked his lips, on his eyelids traced a sign.

"I love my love with a capital Z. I mark him Zero and mine.
Ha! Ha!
I mark him Zero and mine."

The hair rushed in. He struggled and tore, but whenever he tore a tress,
"I love my love with a capital Z," sang the hair of the sorceress.
It swarmed upon him, it swaddled him fast, it muffled his every groan.
Like a golden monster it seized his flesh, and then it sought the bone,
Ha! Ha!
And then it sought the bone.

It smothered his flesh and sought the bones. Until his bones were bare
There was no sound but the joyful hiss of the sweet insatiable hair.
"I love my love," it laughed as it ran back to the grave, its home.
Then the living fleece of her long bright hair, she combed with a golden
     comb.

HARLAN ELLISON

I HAVE NO MOUTH, AND I MUST SCREAM

Limp, the body of Gorrister hung from the pink palette; unsupported—hanging high above us in the computer chamber; and it did not shiver in the chill, oily breeze that blew eternally through the main cavern. The body hung head down, attached to the underside of the palette by the sole of its right foot. It had been drained of blood through a precise incision made from ear to ear under the lantern jaw. There was no blood on the reflective surface of the metal floor.

When Gorrister joined our group and looked up at himself, it was already too late for us to realize that once again AM had duped us, had had his fun; it had been a diversion on the part of the machine. Three of us had vomited, turning away from one another in a reflex as ancient as the nausea that had produced it.

Gorrister went white. It was almost as though he had seen a voodoo fetish, and was afraid for the future. "Oh God," he mumbled, and walked away. The three of us followed him after a time, and found him sitting with his back to one of the smaller chittering banks, his head in his hands. Ellen knelt down beside him and stroked his hair. He didn't move, but his voice came out of his covered face quite clearly. "Why doesn't it just do-us-in and get it over with? Christ, I don't know how much longer I can go on like this."

It was our one hundred and ninth year in the computer.

He was speaking for all of us.

Nimdok (which was the name the machine had forced him to use, because it liked to amuse itself with strange sounds) hallucinated that there were canned goods in the ice caverns. Gorrister and I were very dubious. "It's another shuck," I told them. "Like the goddam frozen elephant it sold us. Benny almost went out of his mind over *that* one. We'll hike all that way and it'll be putrified or some damn thing. I say forget it. Stay here; it'll have to come up with something pretty soon or we'll die."

Benny shrugged. Three days it had been since we'd last eaten. Worms. Thick, ropey.

Nimdok was no more certain. He knew there was the chance, but he was getting thin. It couldn't be any worse there, than here. Colder, but that didn't matter much. Hot, cold, raining, lava, boils or locust—it never mattered: the machine masturbated and we had to take it or die.

Ellen decided us. "I've got to have something, Ted. Maybe there'll be some Bartlett pears or peaches. Please, Ted, let's try it."

I gave in easily. What the hell. Mattered not at all. Ellen was grateful, though. She took me twice out of turn. Even that had ceased to matter. The machine giggled every time we did it. Loud, up there, back there, all around us. And she never climaxed, so why bother.

We left on a Thursday. The machine always kept us up-to-date on the date. The passage of time was important; not to us sure as hell, but to it. Thursday. Thanks.

Nimdok and Gorrister carried Ellen for a while, their hands locked to their own and each other's wrists, a seat. Benny and I walked before and after, just to make sure that if anything happened, it would catch one of us and at least Ellen would be safe. Fat chance, safe. Didn't matter.

It was only a hundred miles or so to the ice caverns, and on the second day, when we were lying out under the blistering sun-thing it had materialized, it sent down some manna. Tasted like boiled boar urine. We ate it.

On the third day we passed through a valley of obsolescence, filled with rusting carcasses of ancient computer banks. AM had been as ruthless with his own life as with ours. It was a mark of his personality: he strove for perfection. Whether it was a matter of killing off unproductive elements in his own world-filling bulk, or perfecting methods for torturing us, AM was as thorough as those who had invented him—now long-since gone to dust—could ever have hoped.

There was light filtering down from above, and we realized we must be very near the surface. But we didn't try to crawl up to see. There was virtually nothing out there; had been nothing that could be considered anything for over a hundred years. Only the blasted skin of what had once been the home of billions. Now there were only the five of us, down here inside, alone with AM.

I heard Ellen saying, frantically, "No, Benny! Don't, come on, Benny, don't please!"

And then I realized I had been hearing Benny murmuring under his breath, for several minutes. He was saying, "I'm gonna get out, I'm gonna get out . . ." over and over. His monkeylike face was crumbled up in an expression of beatific delight and sadness, all at the same time. The radiation scars AM had given him during the "festival" were drawn down into a mass of pink-white puckerings, and his features seemed to work independently of one another. Perhaps Benny was the luckiest of the five of us: he had gone stark, staring mad many years before.

But even though we could call AM any damned thing we liked, could think the foulest thoughts of fused memory banks and corroded base plates, of burnt out circuits and shattered control bubbles, the machine would not tolerate our trying to escape. Benny leaped away from me as I made a grab for him. He scrambled up the face of a smaller memory cube, tilted on its side and filled with rotted components. He squatted there for a moment, looking like the chimpanzee AM had intended him to resemble.

Then he leaped high, caught a trailing beam of pitted and corroded metal, and went up it, hand-over-hand like an animal, till he was on a girdered ledge, twenty feet above us.

"Oh, Ted, Nimdok, please, help him, get him down before—" She cut off. Tears began to stand in her eyes. She moved her hands aimlessly.

It was too late. None of us wanted to be near him, when whatever was going to happen, happened. And besides, we all saw through her concern. When AM had altered Benny, during his mad period, it was not merely his face he had made like a giant ape. He was big in the privates, she loved that! She serviced us, as a matter of course, but she loved it from him. Oh Ellen, pedestal. Ellen, pristine pure Ellen, oh Ellen the clean! Scum filth.

Gorrister slapped her. She slumped down, staring up at poor loonie Benny, and she cried, It was her big defense, crying. We had gotten used to it seventy-five years ago. Gorrister kicked her in the side.

Then the sound began. It was light, that sound. Half sound and half light, something that began to glow from Benny's eyes, and pulse with growing loudness, dim sonorities that grew more gigantic and brighter as the light/sound increased in tempo. It must have been painful, and the pain must have been increasing with the boldness of the light, the rising volume of the sound, for Benny began to mewl like a wounded animal. At first softly, when the light was dim and the sound was muted, then louder as his shoulders hunched together, his back humped, as though he were trying to get away from it. His hands folded across his chest like a chipmunk's. His head tilted to the side. The sad little monkey-face pinched in anguish. Then he began to howl, as the sound coming from his eyes grew louder. Louder and louder. I slapped the sides of my head with my hands, but I couldn't shut it out, it cut through easily. The pain shivered through my flesh like tinfoil on a tooth.

And Benny was suddenly pulled erect. On the girder he stood up, jerked to his feet like a puppet. The light was now pulsing out of his eyes in two great round beams. The sound crawled up and up some incomprehensible scale, and then he fell forward, straight down, and hit the plate steel floor with a crash. He lay there jerking spastically as the light flowed around and around him and the sound spiraled up out of normal range.

Then the light beat its way back inside his head, the sound spiraled down, and he was left lying there, crying piteously.

His eyes were two soft, moist pools of pus-like jelly. AM had blinded him. Gorrister and Nimdok and myself . . . we turned away. But not before we caught the look of relief on Ellen's warm, concerned face.

Sea-green light suffused the cavern where we made camp. AM provided punk and we burned it, sitting huddled around the wan and pathetic fire, telling stories to keep Benny from crying in his permanent night.

"What does AM mean?"

Gorrister answered him. We had done this sequence a thousand times before, and it was familiar to Benny. "At first it meant Allied Mastercomputer, and then it meant Adaptive Manipulator, and later on it developed sentience and linked itself up and they called it an Aggressive Menace; but by then it was too late; and finally it called *itself* AM, emerging intelligence, and what it meant was I am . . . *cogito ergo sum*. . . . I think, therefore I am."

Benny drooled a little, and snickered.

"There was the Chinese AM and the Russian AM and the Yankee AM and—" He stopped. Benny was beating on the floorplates with a large, hard fist. He was not happy. Gorrister had not started at the beginning.

Gorrister began again. "The Cold War started and became World War Three and just kept going. It became a big war, a very complex war, so they needed the computers to handle it. They sank the first shafts and began building AM. There was the Chinese AM and the Russian AM and the Yankee AM and everything was fine until they had honeycombed the entire planet, adding on this element and that element. But one day AM woke up and knew who he was, and he linked himself, and he began feeding all the killing data, until everyone was dead, except for the five of us, and AM brought us down here."

Benny was smiling sadly. He was also drooling again. Ellen wiped the spittle from the corner of his mouth with the hem of her skirt. Gorrister always tried to tell it a little more succinctly each time, but beyond the bare facts there was nothing to say. None of us knew why AM had saved five people, or why our specific five, or why he spent all his time tormenting us, nor even why he had made us virtually immortal . . .

In the darkness, one of the computer banks began humming. The tone was picked up half a mile away down the cavern by another bank. Then one by one, each of the elements began to tune itself, and there was a faint chittering as thought raced through the machine.

The sound grew, and the lights ran across the faces of the consoles like heat lightning. The sound spiraled up till it sounded like a million metallic insects, angry, menacing.

"What is it?" Ellen cried. There was terror in her voice. She hadn't become accustomed to it, even now.

"It's going to be bad this time," Nimdok said.

"He's going to speak," Gorrister ventured.

"Let's get the hell out of here!" I said suddenly, getting to my feet.

"No, Ted, sit down . . . what if he's got pits out there, or something else, we can't see, it's too dark." Gorrister said it with resignation.

Then we heard . . . I don't know . . .

Something moved toward us in the darkness. Huge, shambling, hairy, moist, it came toward us. We couldn't even see it, but there was the ponderous impression of *bulk,* heaving itself toward us. Great weight was coming at us, out of the darkness, and it was more a sense of *pressure,* of air forcing itself into a limited space, expanding the invisible walls of a sphere. Benny began to whimper. Nimdok's lower lip trembled and he bit it hard, trying to stop it. Ellen slid across the metal floor to Gorrister and huddled into him. There was the smell of matted, wet fur in the cavern. There was the smell of charred wood. There was the smell of dusty velvet. There was the smell of rotting orchids. There was the smell of sour milk. There was the smell of sulphur, of rancid butter, of oil slick, of grease, of chalk dust, of human scalps.

AM was keying us. He was tickling us. There was the smell of—

I heard myself shriek, and the hinges of my jaws ached. I scuttled across the floor, across the cold metal with its endless lines of rivets, on my hands and knees, the smell gagging me, filling my head with a thunderous pain that sent me away in horror. I fled like a cockroach, across the floor and out into the darkness, that *something* moving inexorably after me. The others were still back there, gathered around the firelight, laughing ... their hysterical choir of insane giggles rising up into the darkness like thick, many-colored wood smoke. I went away, quickly, and hid.

How many hours it may have been, how many days or even years, they never told me. Ellen chided me for "sulking" and Nimdok tried to persuade me it had only been a nervous reflex on their part—the laughing.

But I knew it wasn't the relief a soldier feels when the bullet hits the man next to him. I knew it wasn't a reflex. They hated me. They were surely against me, and AM could even sense this hatred, and made it worse for me *because of* the depth of their hatred. We had been kept alive, rejuvenated, made to remain constantly at the age we had been when AM had brought us below, and they hated me because I was the youngest, and the one AM had affected least of all.

I knew. God, how I knew. The bastards, and that dirty bitch Ellen. Benny had been a brilliant theorist, a college professor; now he was little more than a semi-human, semi-simian. He had been handsome, the machine had ruined that. He had been lucid, the machine had driven him mad. He had been gay, and the machine had given him an organ fit for a horse. AM had done a job on Benny. Gorrister had been a worrier. He was a connie, a conscientious objector; he was a peace marcher; he was a planner, a doer, a looker-ahead. AM had turned him into a shoulder-shrugger, had made him a little dead in his concern. AM had robbed him. Nimdok went off in the darkness by himself for long times. I don't know what it was he did out there, AM never let us know. But whatever it was, Nimdok always came back white, drained of blood, shaken, shaking. AM had hit him hard in a special way, even if we didn't know quite how. And Ellen. That douche bag! AM had left her alone, had made her more of a slut than she had ever been. All her talk of sweetness and light, all her memories of true love, all the lies she wanted us to believe that she had been a virgin only twice removed before AM grabbed her and brought her down here with us. It was all filth, that lady my lady Ellen. She loved it, five men all to herself. No, AM had given her pleasure, even if she said it wasn't nice to do.

I was the only one still sane and whole.

AM had not tampered with *my* mind.

I only had to suffer what he visited down on us. All the delusions, all the nightmares, the torments. But those scum, all four of them, they were lined and arrayed against me. If I hadn't had to stand them off all the time, be on my guard against them all the time, I might have found it easier to combat AM.

At which point it passed, and I began crying.

Oh, Jesus sweet Jesus, if there ever was a Jesus and if there is a God, please please please let us out of here, or kill us. Because at that moment I think I realized completely, so that I was able to verbalize it: AM was intent on keeping us in his belly forever, twisting and torturing us forever. The machine hated us as no sentient creature had ever hated before. And we were helpless. It also became hideously clear:

If there was a sweet Jesus and if there was a God, the God was AM.

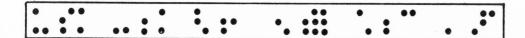

The hurricane hit us with the force of a glacier thundering into the sea. It was a palpable presence. Winds that tore at us, flinging us back the way we had come, down the twisting, computer-lined corridors of the darkway. Ellen screamed as she was lifted and hurled face-forward into a screaming shoal of machines, their individual voices strident as bats in flight. She could not even fall. The howling wind kept her aloft, buffetted her, bounced her, tossed her back and back and down away from us, out of sight suddenly as she was swirled around a bend in the darkway. Her face had been bloody, her eyes closed.

None of us could get to her. We clung tenaciously to whatever outcropping we had reached: Benny wedged in between two great crackle-finish cabinets, Nimdok with fingers claw-formed over a railing circling a catwalk forty feet above us, Gorrister plastered upside-down against a wall niche formed by two great machines with glass-faced dials that swung back and forth between red and yellow lines whose meanings we could not even fathom.

Sliding across the deckplates, the tips of my fingers had been ripped away. I was trembling, shuddering, rocking as the wind beat at me, whipped at me, screamed down out of nowhere at me and pulled me free from one sliver-thin opening in the plates to the next. My mind was a roiling tinkling sucksounding softness of brain parts that expanded and contracted in quivering frenzy.

The wind was the scream of a great mad bird, as it flapped its immense wings.

And then we were all lifted and hurled away from there, down back the way we had come, around a bend, into a darkway we had never explored, over terrain that was ruined and filled with broken glass and rotting cables and rusted metal and far away farther than any of us had ever been . . .

Trailing along miles behind Ellen, I could see her every now and then, crashing into metal walls and surging on, with all of us screaming in the freezing, thunderous hurricane wind that would never end and then suddenly it stopped and we fell. We had been in flight for an endless time. I thought it might have been weeks. We fell, and hit, and I went through red and gray and black and heard myself moaning. Not dead.

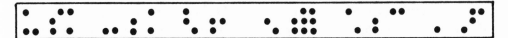

AM went into my mind. He walked smoothly here and there, and looked with interest at all the pock marks he had created in one hundred and nine years. He looked at the cross-routed and reconnected synapses and all the tissue damage his gift of immortality had included. He smiled softly at the pit that dropped into the center of my brain and the faint, moth-soft murmurings of the things far down there that gibbered without meaning, without pause. AM said, very politely, in a pillar of stainless steel and neon letters:

> HATE. LET ME TELL
> YOU HOW MUCH I'VE
> COME TO HATE YOU
> SINCE I BEGAN TO
> LIVE. THERE ARE
> 387.44 MILLION
> MILES OF PRINTED
> CIRCUITS IN WAFER
> THIN LAYERS THAT
> FILL MY COMPLEX.
> IF THE WORD HATE
> WAS ENGRAVED ON
> EACH NANOANGSTROM
> OF THOSE HUNDREDS
> OF MILLION MILES
> IT WOULD NOT EQUAL
> ONE ONE-BILLIONTH
> OF THE HATE I FEEL
> FOR HUMANS AT THIS
> MICRO-INSTANT FOR
> YOU. HATE. HATE.

AM said it with the sliding cold horror of a razor blade slicing my eyeball. AM said it with the bubbling thickness of my lungs filling with phlegm, drowning me from within. AM said it with the shriek of babies being ground beneath blue-hot rollers. AM said it with the taste of maggoty pork. AM touched me in every way I have ever been touched, and devised new ways, at his leisure, there inside my mind.

All to bring me to full realization of why he had done this to the five of us; why he had saved us for himself.

We had given him sentience. Inadvertently, of course, but sentience nonetheless. But he had been trapped. He was a machine. We had allowed him to think, but to do nothing with it. In rage, in frenzy, he had killed us, almost all of us, and still he was trapped. He could not wander, he could not wonder, he could not belong. He could merely be. And so, with the innate loathing that all machines had always held for the weak, soft creatures who had built them, he had sought revenge. And in his paranoia, he had decided to reprieve five of us, for a personal, everlasting punishment that would never serve to diminish his hatred ... that would merely keep him reminded, amused, proficient at hating man. Immortal, trapped, subject to any torment he could devise for us from the limitless miracles at his command.

He would never let us go. We were his belly slaves. We were all he had to do with his forever time. We would be forever with him, with the cavern-filling bulk of him, with the all-mind soulless world he had become. He was Earth and we were the fruit of that Earth and though he had eaten us, he would never digest us. We could not die. We had tried it. We had attempted suicide, oh one or two of us had. But AM had stopped us. I suppose we had wanted to be stopped.

Don't ask why. I never did. More than a million times a day. Perhaps once we might be able to sneak a death past him. Immortal, yes, but not indestructible. I saw that when AM withdrew from my mind, and allowed me the exquisite ugliness of returning to consciousness with the filling of that burning neon pillar still rammed deep into the soft gray brain matter.

He withdrew murmuring *to hell with you.*

And added, brightly, *but then you're there, aren't you.*

The hurricane had, indeed, precisely, been caused by a great mad bird, as it flapped its immense wings.

We had been traveling for close to a month, and AM had allowed passages to open to us only sufficient to lead us up there, directly under the North Pole, where he had nightmared the creature for our torment. What whole cloth had he employed to create such a beast? Where had he gotten the concept? From our minds? From his knowledge of everything that had ever been on this planet he now infested and ruled? From Norse mythology it had sprung, this eagle, this carrion bird, this roc, this Huergelmir. The wind creature. Hurakan incarnate.

Gigantic. The words immense, monstrous, grotesque, massive, swollen, overpowering, beyond description. There on a mound rising above us, the bird of winds heaved with its own irregular breathing, its snake neck arching

up into the gloom beneath the North Pole, supporting a head as large as a
Tudor mansion; a beak that opened slowly as the jaws of the most monstrous crocodile ever conceived, sensuously; ridges of tufted flesh puckered
about two evil eyes, as cold as the view down into a glacial crevasse, ice blue
and somehow moving liquidly; it heaved once more, and lifted its great
sweat-colored wings in a movement that was certainly a shrug. Then it
settled and slept. Talons. Fangs. Nails. Blades. It slept.

AM appeared to us as a burning bush and said we could kill the hurricane
bird if we wanted to eat. We had not eaten in a very long time, but even so,
Gorrister merely shrugged. Benny began to shiver and he drooled. Ellen
held him. "Ted, I'm hungry," she said. I smiled at her; I was trying to be
reassuring. But it was as phony as Nimdok's bravado: "Give us weapons!"
he demanded.

The burning bush vanished and there were two crude sets of bow and
arrows, and a water pistol, lying on the cold deckplates. I picked up a set.
Useless.

Nimdok swallowed heavily. We turned and started the long way back.
The hurricane bird had blown us about for a length of time we could not
conceive. Most of that time we had been unconscious. But we had not eaten.
A month on the march to the bird itself. Without food. Now how much
longer to find our way to the ice caverns, and the promised canned goods?

None of us cared to think about it. We would not die. We would be given
filths and scums to eat, of one kind or another. Or nothing at all. AM would
keep our bodies alive somehow, in pain, in agony.

The bird slept back there, for how long it didn't matter; when AM was
tired of its being there, it would vanish. But all that meat. All that tender
meat.

As we walked, the lunatic laugh of a fat woman rang high and around us
in the computer chambers that led endlessly nowhere.

It was not Ellen's laugh. She was not fat, and I had not heard her laugh
for one hundred and nine years. In fact, I had not heard . . . we walked . . . I
was hungry . . .

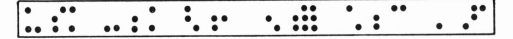

We moved slowly. There was often fainting, and we would have to wait.
One day he decided to cause an earthquake, at the same time rooting us to
the spot with nails through the soft pads of our feet. Ellen and Nimdok were
both caught when a fissure shot its lightning-bolt opening across the floorplates. They disappeared and were gone. When the earthquake was over we
continued on our way, Benny, Gorrister, and myself. Ellen and Nimdok
were returned to us later that night which became a day abruptly as the
heavenly legion bore them to us with a celestial chorus singing, "Go Down
Moses." The archangels circled several times and then dropped the hideously mangled bodies. We kept walking, and a while later Ellen and

Nimdok fell in behind us. They were no worse for wear.

But now Ellen walked with a limp. AM had left her that.

It was a long trip to the ice caverns, to find the canned food. Ellen kept talking about Bing cherries and Hawaiian fruit cocktail. I tried not to think about it. The hunger was something that had come to life, even as AM had come to life. It was alive in my belly, even as we were alive in the belly of AM, and AM was alive in the belly of the Earth, and AM wanted the similarity known to us. So he heightened the hunger. There was no way to describe the pains that not having eaten for months brought us. And yet we were kept alive. Stomachs that were merely cauldrons of acid, bubbling, foaming, always shooting spears of sliver-thin pain into our chests. It was the pain of the terminal ulcer, terminal cancer, terminal paresis. It was unending pain . . .

And we passed through the cavern of rats.

And we passed through the path of boiling steam.

And we passed through the country of the blind.

And we passed through the slough of despond.

And we passed through the vale of tears.

And we came, finally, to the ice caverns. Horizonless thousands of miles in which the ice had formed in blue and silver flashes, where novas lived in the glass. The chill downdropping stalactites as thick and glorious as diamonds that had been made to run like jelly and then solidified in graceful eternities of smooth, sharp perfection.

We saw the stack of canned goods, and we tried to run to them. We fell in the snow, and we got up and went on, and Benny shoved us away and went at them, and pawed them and gummed them and gnawed at them and he could not open them. AM had not given us a tool to open the cans.

Benny grabbed a three-quart can of guava shells, and began to batter it against the ice bank. The ice flew and shattered, but the can was merely dented while we heard the laughter of a fat lady, high overhead and echoing down and down and down the tundra. Benny went completely mad with rage. He began throwing cans, as we all scrabbled about in the snow and ice trying to find a way to end the helpless agony of frustration. There was no way.

Then Benny's mouth began to drool, and he flung himself on Gorrister . . .

In that instant, I went terribly calm.

Surrounded by madness, surrounded by hunger, surrounded by every-thing but death, I knew death was our only way out. AM had kept us alive, but there was a way to defeat him. Not total defeat, but at least peace. I would settle for that.

I had to do it quickly.

Benny was eating Gorrister's face. Gorrister on his side, thrashing snow, Benny wrapped around him with powerful monkey legs crushing Gorrister's waist, his hands locked around Gorrister's head like a nutcracker, and his mouth ripping at the tender skin of Gorrister's cheek. Gorrister screamed with such jagged-edged violence that stalactites fell; they plunged down softly, erect in the receiving snowdrifts. Spears, hundreds of them, every-where, protruding from the snow. Benny's head pulled back sharply, as something gave all at once, and a bleeding raw-white dripping of flesh hung from his teeth.

Ellen's face, black against the white snow, dominos in chalk-dust. Nimdok with no expression but eyes, all eyes. Gorrister half-conscious. Benny now an animal. I knew AM would let him play. Gorrister would not die, but Benny would fill his stomach. I turned half to my right and drew a huge ice-spear from the snow.

All in an instant:

I drove the great ice-point ahead of me like a battering ram, braced against my right thigh. It struck Benny on the right side, just under the rib cage, and drove upward through his stomach and broke inside him. He pitched forward and lay still. Gorrister lay on his back, I pulled another spear free and straddled him, still moving, driving the spear straight down through his throat. His eyes closed as the cold penetrated. Ellen must have realized what I had decided, even as the fear gripped her. She ran at Nimdok with a short icicle, as he screamed, and into his mouth, and the force of her rush did the job. His head jerked sharply as if it had been nailed to the snow crust behind him.

All in an instant.

There was an eternity beat of soundless anticipation. I could hear AM draw in his breath. His toys had been taken from him. Three of them were dead, could not be revived. He could keep us alive, by his strength and his talent, but he was *not* God. He could not bring them back.

Ellen looked at me, her ebony features stark against the snow that surrounded us. There was fear and pleading in her manner, the way she held herself ready. I knew we had only a heartbeat before AM would stop us.

It struck her and she folded toward me, bleeding from the mouth. I could not read meaning into her expression, the pain had been too great, had contorted her face; but it *might* have been thank you. It's possible. Please.

Some hundreds of years may have passed. I don't know. AM has been having fun for some time, accelerating and retarding my time sense. I will say the word "now." *Now.* It took me ten months to say "now." I don't know. I *think* it has been some hundreds of years.

He was furious. He wouldn't let me bury them. It didn't matter. There was no way to dig in the deckplates. He dried up the snow. He brought the night. He roared and sent locusts. It didn't do a thing; they stayed dead. I'd had him. He was furious. I had thought AM hated me before. I was wrong. It is not even a shadow of the hate he now slavers from every printed circuit. He made certain I would suffer eternally and could not do myself in.

He left my mind intact. I can dream, I can wonder, I can lament. I remember all four of them. I wish—

Well, it doesn't make any sense. I know I saved them, I know I saved them from what has happened to me, but still, I cannot forget killing them. Ellen's face. It isn't easy. Sometimes I want to, it doesn't matter.

AM has altered me for his own peace of mind, I suppose. He doesn't want me to run at full speed into a computer bank and smash my skull. Or hold my breath till I faint. Or cut my throat on a rusted sheet of metal. There are reflective surfaces down here. I will describe myself as I see myself:

I am a great soft jelly thing. Smoothly rounded, with no mouth, with pulsing white holes filled by fog where my eyes used to be. Rubbery appendages that were once my arms; bulks rounding down into legless humps of soft slippery matter. I leave a moist trail when I move. Blotches of diseased, evil gray come and go on my surface, as though light is being beamed from within.

Outwardly: dumbly, I shamble about, a thing that could never have been known as human, a thing whose shape is so alien a travesty, that humanity becomes more obscene for the vague resemblance.

Inwardly: alone. Here. Living under the land, under the sea, in the belly of AM, whom we created because our time was badly spent and we must have known unconsciously that he could do it better. At least the four of them are safe at last.

AM will be all the madder for that. It makes me a little happier. And yet ... AM has won, simply ... he has taken his revenge ...

I have no mouth. And I must scream.

JUNICHIRO TANIZAKI

THE TATTOOER

It was an age when men honored the noble virtue of frivolity, when life was not such a harsh struggle as it is today. It was a leisurely age, an age when professional wits could make an excellent livelihood by keeping rich or wellborn young gentlemen in a cloudless good humor and seeing to it that the laughter of Court ladies and geisha was never stilled. In the illustrated romantic novels of the day, in the Kabuki theater, where rough masculine heroes like Sadakuro and Jiraiya were transformed into women—everywhere beauty and strength were one. People did all they could to beautify themselves, some even having pigments injected into their precious skins. Gaudy patterns of line and color danced over men's bodies.

Visitors to the pleasure quarters of Edo preferred to hire palanquin bearers who were splendidly tattooed; courtesans of the Yoshiwara and the Tatsumi quarter fell in love with tattooed men. Among those so adorned were not only gamblers, firemen, and the like, but members of the merchant class and even samurai. Exhibitions were held from time to time; and the participants, stripped to show off their filigreed bodies, would pat themselves proudly, boast of their own novel designs, and criticize each other's merits.

There was an exceptionally skillful tattooer named Seikichi. He was praised on all sides as a master the equal of Charibun or Yatsuhei, and the skins of dozens of men had been offered as the silk for his brush. Much of the work admired at the tattoo exhibitions was his. Others might be more noted for their shading, or their use of cinnabar, but Seikichi was famous for the unrivaled boldness and sensual charm of his art.

Seikichi had formerly earned his living as an ukiyoye painter of the school of Toyokuni and Kunisada, a background which, in spite of his decline to the status of a tattooer, was evident from his artistic conscience and sensitivity. No one whose skin or whose physique failed to interest him could buy his services. The clients he did accept had to leave the design and cost entirely to his discretion—and to endure for one or even two months the excruciating pain of his needles.

Deep in his heart the young tattooer concealed a secret pleasure, and a secret desire. His pleasure lay in the agony men felt as he drove his needles into them, torturing their swollen, blood-red flesh; and the louder they groaned, the keener was Seikichi's strange delight. Shading and vermilioning—these are said to be especially painful—were the techniques he most enjoyed.

When a man had been pricked five or six hundred times in the course of

22

an average day's treatment and had then soaked himself in a hot bath to bring out the colors, he would collapse at Seikichi's feet half dead. But Seikichi would look down at him coolly. "I dare say that hurts," he would remark with an air of satisfaction.

Whenever a spineless man howled in torment or clenched his teeth and twisted his mouth as if he were dying, Seikichi told him: "Don't act like a child. Pull yourself together—you have hardly begun to feel my needles!" And he would go on tattooing, as unperturbed as ever, with an occasional sidelong glance at the man's tearful face.

But sometimes a man of immense fortitude set his jaw and bore up stoically, not even allowing himself to frown. Then Seikichi would smile and say: "Ah, you are a stubborn one! But wait. Soon your body will begin to throb with pain. I doubt if you will be able to stand it. . . ."

For a long time Seikichi had cherished the desire to create a masterpiece on the skin of a beautiful woman. Such a woman had to meet various qualifications of character as well as appearance. A lovely face and a fine body were not enough to satisfy him. Though he inspected all the reigning beauties of the Edo gay quarters he found none who met his exacting demands. Several years had passed without success, and yet the face and figure of the perfect woman continued to obsess his thoughts. He refused to abandon hope.

One summer evening during the fourth year of his search Seikichi happened to be passing the Hirasei Restaurant in the Fukagawa district of Edo, not far from his own house, when he noticed a woman's bare milk-white foot peeping out beneath the curtains of a departing palanquin. To his sharp eye, a human foot was as expressive as a face. This one was sheer perfection. Exquisitely chiseled toes, nails like the iridescent shells along the shore at Enoshima, a pearl-like rounded heel, skin so lustrous that it seemed bathed in the limpid waters of a mountain spring—this, indeed, was a foot to be nourished by men's blood, a foot to trample on their bodies. Surely this was the foot of the unique woman who had so long eluded him. Eager to catch a glimpse of her face, Seikichi began to follow the palanquin. But after pursuing it down several lanes and alleys he lost sight of it altogether.

Seikichi's long-held desire turned into passionate love. One morning late the next spring he was standing on the bamboo-floored veranda of his home in Fukagawa, gazing at a pot of *omoto* lilies, when he heard someone at the garden gate. Around the corner of the inner fence appeared a young girl. She had come on an errand for a friend of his, a geisha of the nearby Tatsumi quarter.

"My mistress asked me to deliver this cloak, and she wondered if you would be so good as to decorate its lining," the girl said. She untied a saffron-colored cloth parcel and took out a woman's silk cloak (wrapped in a sheet of thick paper bearing a portrait of the actor Tojaku) and a letter.

The letter repeated his friend's request and went on to say that its bearer would soon begin a career as a geisha under her protection. She hoped that, while not forgetting old ties, he would also extend his patronage to this girl.

"I thought I had never seen you before," said Seikichi, scrutinizing her intently. She seemed only fifteen or sixteen, but her face had a strangely ripe beauty, a look of experience, as if she had already spent years in the gay quarter and had fascinated innumerable men. Her beauty mirrored the dreams of the generations of glamorous men and women who had lived and died in this vast capital, where the nation's sins and wealth were concentrated.

Seikichi had her sit on the veranda, and he studied her delicate feet, which were bare except for elegant straw sandals. "You left the Hirasei by palanquin one night last July, did you not?" he inquired.

"I suppose so," she replied, smiling at the odd question. "My father was still alive then, and he often took me there."

"I have waited five years for you. This is the first time I have seen your face, but I remember your foot. . . . Come in for a moment, I have something to show you."

She had risen to leave, but he took her by the hand and led her upstairs to his studio overlooking the broad river. Then he brought out two picture scrolls and unrolled one of them before her.

It was a painting of a Chinese princess, the favorite of the cruel Emperor Chou of the Shang Dynasty. She was leaning on a balustrade in a languorous pose, the long skirt of her figured brocade robe trailing halfway down a flight of stairs, her slender body barely able to support the weight of her gold crown studded with coral and lapis lazuli. In her right hand she held a large wine cup, tilting it to her lips as she gazed down at a man who was about to be tortured in the garden below. He was chained hand and foot to a hollow copper pillar in which a fire would be lighted. Both the princess and her victim—his head bowed before her, his eyes closed, ready to meet his fate—were portrayed with terrifying vividness.

As the girl stared at this bizarre picture her lips trembled and her eyes began to sparkle. Gradually her face took on a curious resemblance to that of the princess. In the picture she discovered her secret self.

"Your own feelings are revealed here," Seikichi told her with pleasure as he watched her face.

"Why are you showing me this horrible thing?" the girl asked, looking up at him. She had turned pale.

"The woman is yourself. Her blood flows in your veins." Then he spread out the other scroll.

This was a painting called "The Victims." In the middle of it a young woman stood leaning against the trunk of a cherry tree: she was gloating over a heap of men's corpses lying at her feet. Little birds fluttered about her, singing in triumph; her eyes radiated pride and joy. Was it a battlefield or a garden in spring? In this picture the girl felt that she had found something long hidden in the darkness of her own heart.

"This painting shows your future," Seikichi said, pointing to the woman under the cherry tree—the very image of the young girl. "All these men will ruin their lives for you."

"Please, I beg of you to put it away!" She turned her back as if to escape its tantalizing lure and prostrated herself before him, trembling. At last she spoke again. "Yes, I admit that you are right about me—I *am* like that woman. . . . So please, please take it away."

"Don't talk like a coward," Seikichi told her, with his malicious smile. "Look at it more closely. You won't be squeamish long."

But the girl refused to lift her head. Still prostrate, her face buried in her sleeves, she repeated over and over that she was afraid and wanted to leave.

"No, you must stay—I will make you a real beauty," he said, moving closer to her. Under his kimono was a vial of anesthetic which he had obtained some time ago from a Dutch physician.

The morning sun glittered on the river, setting the eight-mat studio ablaze with light. Rays reflected from the water sketched rippling golden waves on the paper sliding screens and on the face of the girl, who was fast asleep. Seikichi had closed the doors and taken up his tattooing instruments, but for a while he only sat there entranced, savoring to the full her uncanny beauty. He thought that he would never tire of contemplating her serene masklike face. Just as the ancient Egyptians had embellished their magnificent land with pyramids and sphinxes, he was about to embellish the pure skin of this girl.

Presently he raised the brush which was gripped between the thumb and last two fingers of his left hand, applied its tip to the girl's back, and, with the needle which he held in his right hand, began pricking out a design. He felt his spirit dissolve into the charcoal-black ink that stained her skin. Each drop of Ryukyu cinnabar that he mixed with alcohol and thrust in was a drop of his lifeblood. He saw in his pigments the hues of his own passions.

Soon it was afternoon, and then the tranquil spring day drew toward its close. But Seikichi never paused in his work, nor was the girl's sleep broken. When a servant came from the geisha house to inquire about her, Seikichi turned him away, saying that she had left long ago. And hours later, when the moon hung over the mansion across the river, bathing the houses along the bank in a dreamlike radiance, the tattoo was not yet half done. Seikichi worked on by candlelight.

Even to insert a single drop of color was no easy task. At every thrust of his needle Seikichi gave a heavy sigh and felt as if he had stabbed his own heart. Little by little the tattoo marks began to take on the form of a huge black-widow spider; and by the time the night sky was paling into dawn this weird, malevolent creature had stretched its eight legs to embrace the whole of the girl's back.

In the full light of the spring dawn boats were being rowed up and down the river, their oars creaking in the morning quiet; roof tiles glistened in the sun, and the haze began to thin out over white sails swelling in the early breeze. Finally Seikichi put down his brush and looked at the tattooed spider. This work of art had been the supreme effort of his life. Now that he had finished it his heart was drained of emotion.

The two figures remained still for some time. Then Seikichi's low, hoarse voice echoed quaveringly from the walls of the room:

"To make you truly beautiful I have poured my soul into this tattoo. Today there is no woman in Japan to compare with you. Your old fears are gone. All men will be your victims."

As if in response to these words a faint moan came from the girl's lips. Slowly she began to recover her senses. With each shuddering breath, the spider's legs stirred as if they were alive.

"You must be suffering. The spider has you in its clutches."

At this she opened her eyes slightly, in a dull stare. Her gaze steadily brightened, as the moon brightens in the evening, until it shone dazzlingly into his face.

"Let me see the tattoo," she said, speaking as if in a dream but with an edge of authority to her voice. "Giving me your soul must have made me very beautiful."

"First you must bathe to bring out the colors," whispered Seikichi compassionately. "I am afraid it will hurt, but be brave a little longer."

"I can bear anything for the sake of beauty." Despite the pain that was coursing through her body, she smiled.

"How the water stings! . . . Leave me alone—wait in the other room! I hate to have a man see me suffer like this!"

As she left the tub, too weak to dry herself, the girl pushed aside the sympathetic hand Seikichi offered her, and sank to the floor in agony, moaning as if in a nightmare. Her disheveled hair hung over her face in a wild tangle. The white soles of her feet were reflected in the mirror behind her.

Seikichi was amazed at the change that had come over the timid, yielding girl of yesterday, but he did as he was told and went to wait in his studio. About an hour later she came back, carefully dressed, her damp, sleekly combed hair hanging down over her shoulders. Leaning on the veranda rail, she looked up into the faintly hazy sky. Her eyes were brilliant; there was not a trace of pain in them.

"I wish to give you these pictures too," said Seikichi, placing the scrolls before her. "Take them and go."

"All my old fears have been swept away—and you are my first victim!" She darted a glance at him as bright as a sword. A song of triumph was ringing in her ears.

"Let me see your tattoo once more," Seikichi begged.

Silently the girl nodded and slipped the kimono off her shoulders. Just then her resplendently tattooed back caught a ray of sunlight and the spider was wreathed in flames.

JERZY KOSINSKI

A SELECTION
FROM "STEPS"

I won a prize in a photographic contest sponsored by a society for the aid of the old and infirm, and I was commissioned to supply the society with a collection of portraits. The photographs were supposed to depict the serenity and peace of old age. I was required to make up a portfolio of sixty portraits, but I encountered great difficulty in finding suitable subjects. There were very few elderly people left in the cities because the government had set up homes for them in the rural districts.

To reach the nearest home, I had to make a difficult journey, laden with flood lamps, film, cables, transformers, and screens. I also took a portable darkroom so that I could determine on the spot the results of my work. When I arrived, the director of the home showed me around. It was an enormous old manor house converted into a score of wards, eight beds in each. All the patients here were aged, and the majority of them were also sickly, crippled, or senile. It occurred to me immediately that the task I was about to attempt was far more difficult than I had imagined. I was surrounded, pushed, pulled, spat on and cursed by some of these old people, and, on occasion, physically soiled. The wards with public toilets were dark and poorly ventilated. There was an oppressive stench of sweat and urine, against which no disinfectant could make headway.

The next day I returned with my cameras and equipment. Some of the patients I selected refused to pose, claiming they were blinded by the spotlights; others, shaking and spitting, crowded in front of my camera to flaunt their wrinkled, flabby bodies, pulling back their lips and drooling through shrunken and toothless gums. Still others tried to cut the cables running from the electric sockets to the lights; they stepped on my equipment, kicked at the tripod, or plucked at me with hands smeared with excrement. I was unable to take a single successful picture, and one of my cameras was broken. Just before retiring to my quarters I stopped at the director's office.

While I waited, a nurse came into the room. After sipping a glass of water she sank wearily into a chair, and although I had been staring at her she ignored me completely. I felt an urge to touch her face and hair and to smell her skin. I did not care whether or not she was beautiful; it was enough that she was clean and healthy. I desperately wanted to reassure myself that I had nothing in common with the inmates. If she would be willing to help me, I knew I could complete my work.

Abruptly she acknowledged me, asking if I was visiting a relative. When I told her about my project, she reluctantly agreed to work with me, if the director was willing.

The director agreed to assign her to me for the next few days, adding casually that she was a student of psychology. She was especially interested in the psychological problems of the aged and the retarded, so much so that she had requested an additional year's training before taking her degree. Almost three years had passed, and she was still there, working as chief nurse. According to him, she was completely devoted to the patients.

We started photographing early next morning. Our presence in the wards continued to create difficulties. Many of the male patients tried to attract the nurse's attention with inviting gestures; the women, on the other hand, tried to upset her with offensive remarks. She told me it was only to be expected.

When interruptions made work impossible, I would move toward her and put my arm on her shoulder or let my hands brush against her hair as I bent down to pick up a lens from its case. She showed no sign of embarrassment. I continued to touch her whenever our work gave me the occasion.

There was nothing to do outside the home: the local village was small and the nearest town was forty miles away. We had no cinema, no theater, no restaurant.

Apparently my companion was without friends. The rest of the staff was middle-aged, either married or, from her point of view, unsuitable. She mentioned a boy friend in the navy, to whom she wrote regularly.

She was a secretive person, giving no reason for staying so long at the institution and no explanation for not returning to the university to finish her studies. All she said was that her life was her own. Her complacency irritated me. I began to resent the fact that my presence made no difference to her, that she could endure for years an environment which I found unbearable even for a few days. To her, perhaps, there was nothing different or unusual about me. I might have been just another patient, merely a little younger, a little less decrepit than the others.

I began finding certain points of similarity between myself and the inmates. Nor could I avoid the realization that one day I would become what they were now, that the forces which had reduced them to their present state would also take me prisoner. I watched the sick in their endless torment, crawling like broken crayfish. As I worked in the wards I saw the dying inmates, rheumy-eyed and hollow-faced, their bodies shrunken by disease, lying on their narrow beds gaping apathetically at the faded portraits of saints or at the wooden crucifixes stippled with wormholes. Some clutched photographs of their children.

In moments like these I would turn away and stare at the girl for a long while. So complete was my illusion of possessing her that I would experience the most intense rapture amid the most commonplace distractions.

It was always the same. She would help me to pack my equipment and store it for the next day; then she would leave. One afternoon, however, I left the ward and walked down to the basement. I knew she was there. The basement was cold and damp and I stood in darkness. She called my name; I moved toward her voice.

I touched her uniform and knelt in front of her. I lifted her skirt. The starched fabric crackled. She was naked beneath; I pressed my face into her, my body throbbing with the force which makes trees reach upward to drive out blossoms from small, shrunken buds. I was young.

One evening I decided to surprise her with a visit. When I reached her room the other occupant told me she was on the fourth floor of the building. Only as I turned away from her room did it occur to me that I had never been on the fourth floor, which was used mainly for storage. It was quiet when I reached the stairs. Alert to everything, I mounted cautiously, and when the staircase opened into the hallway I found myself facing an ironbound door leading into a narrow, windowless corridor. Inside, it was dark. For a moment I trailed my hands over the walls. There were grates on each side of the passage, but they were all bolted. Then I noticed a single shaft of light escaping from under a door at the far end of the hall. Before I could reach it, I heard her voice. As I moved closer, I stumbled over a small sandbag and crashed against the door. Even as I clutched at the lintel I was halfway into the room.

She was lying naked on the bed, half covered by the furry body of a creature with a human head, pawlike hands, and the short, barrel-chested trunk of an ape. My rapid, blundering entrance frightened them: the creature turned, its small brown eyes glittering maliciously. With a single leap it reached its crib, and whining and yelping, began to burrow under the covers.

The girl pitched forward, her thighs closing as though to protect herself. Her trembling hands searched about her like the claws of a dying chicken; she clutched her dress and began pulling it over her belly. I thought for a moment that she would crawl into the wall or scuttle through the floor boards. Her eyes looked stony and unfocused; a broken word rose to her lips, but she was unable to utter it. I stared at the crib and realized that the creature in it was human. Turning, I put out the light.

I hurried to my cottage in the village and immediately started to fill the bath. Sitting back in the warm water, I could hear only the measured dripping of the tap.

JULIO CORTÁZAR

AXOLOTL

There was a time when I thought a great deal about the axolotls. I went to see them in the aquarium at the Jardin des Plantes and stayed for hours watching them, observing their immobility, their faint movements. Now I am an axolotl.

I got to them by chance one spring morning when Paris was spreading its peacock tail after a wintry Lent. I was heading down the boulevard Port-Royal, then I took Saint-Marcel and L'Hôpital and saw green among all that grey and remembered the lions. I was a friend of the lions and panthers, but had never gone into the dark, humid building that was the aquarium. I left my bike against the gratings and went to look at the tulips. The lions were sad and ugly and my panther was asleep. I decided on the aquarium, looked obliquely at banal fish until, unexpectedly, I hit it off with the axolotls. I stayed watching them for an hour and left, unable to think of anything else.

In the library at Sainte-Geneviève, I consulted a dictionary and learned that axolotls are the larval stage (provided with gills) of a species of salamander of the genus Ambystoma. That they were Mexican I knew already by looking at them and their little pink Aztec faces and the placard at the top of the tank. I read that specimens of them had been found in Africa capable of living on dry land during the periods of drought, and continuing their life under water when the rainy season came. I found their Spanish name, *ajolote,* and the mention that they were edible, and that their oil was used (no longer used, it said) like cod-liver oil.

I didn't care to look up any of the specialized works, but the next day I went back to the Jardin des Plantes. I began to go every morning, morning and afternoon some days. The aquarium guard smiled perplexedly taking my ticket. I would lean up against the iron bar in front of the tanks and set to watching them. There's nothing strange in this, because after the first minute I knew that we were linked, that something infinitely lost and distant kept pulling us together. It had been enough to detain me that first morning in front of the sheet of glass where some bubbles rose through the water. The axolotls huddled on the wretched narrow (only I can know how narrow and wretched) floor of moss and stone in the tank. There were nine specimens, and the majority pressed their heads against the glass, looking with their eyes of gold at whoever came near them. Disconcerted, almost ashamed, I felt it a lewdness to be peering at these silent and immobile figures heaped at the bottom of the tank. Mentally I isolated one, situated on the right and somewhat apart from the others, to study it better. I saw a rosy little body, translucent (I thought of those Chinese figurines of milky glass), looking like a small lizard about six inches long, ending in a fish's tail of extraordinary delicacy, the most sensitive part of our body. Along the back ran a transparent fin which joined with the tail, but what obsessed me was the feet, of the slenderest nicety, ending in tiny fingers with minutely human nails. And then I discovered its eyes, its face. Inexpressive features, with no other trait save the eyes, two orifices, like brooches, wholly of transparent gold, lacking any life but looking, letting themselves be penetrated by my look, which seemed to travel past the golden level and lose itself in a diaphanous interior mystery. A very slender black halo ringed the eye and etched it onto the pink flesh, onto the rosy stone of the head, vaguely triangular, but with curved and irregular sides which gave it a total likeness to a statuette corroded by time. The mouth was masked by the triangular plane of the face, its considerable size would be guessed only in profile; in front a delicate crevice barely slit the lifeless stone. On both sides of the head where the ears should have been, there grew three tiny sprigs red as coral, a vegetal outgrowth, the gills, I suppose. And they were the only thing quick about it; every ten or fifteen seconds the sprigs pricked up stiffly and again subsided. Once in a while a foot would barely move, I saw the diminutive toes poise mildly on the moss. It's that we don't enjoy moving a lot and the tank is so cramped—we barely move in any direction and we're hitting one of the others with our tail or our head—difficulties arise, fights, tiredness. The time feels like it's less if we stay quietly.

It was their quietness that made me lean toward them fascinated the first time I saw the axolotls. Obscurely I seemed to understand their secret will, to abolish space and time with an indifferent immobility. I knew better later; the gill contraction, the tentative reckoning of the delicate feet on the stones, the abrupt swimming (some of them swim with a simple undulation of the body) proved to me that they were capable of escaping that mineral lethargy in which they spent whole hours. Above all else, their eyes obsessed me. In the standing tanks on either side of them, different fishes showed me the simple stupidity of their handsome eyes so similar to our own. The eyes of the axolotls spoke to me of the presence of a different life, of another way of seeing. Glueing my face to the glass (the guard would cough fussily once in a while), I tried to see better those diminutive golden points, that entrance to the infinitely slow and remote world of these rosy creatures. It was useless to tap with one finger on the glass directly in front of their faces; they never gave the least reaction. The golden eyes continued burning with their soft, terrible light; they continued looking at me from an unfathomable depth which made me dizzy.

And nevertheless they were close. I knew it before this, before being an axolotl. I learned it the day I came near them for the first time. The anthropomorphic features of a monkey reveal the reverse of what most people believe, the distance that is traveled from them to us. The absolute lack of similarity between axolotls and human beings proved to me that my recognition was valid, that I was not propping myself up with easy analogies. Only the little hands . . . But an eft, the common newt, has such hands also, and we are not at all alike. I think it was the axolotls' heads, that triangular pink shape with the tiny eyes of gold. That looked and knew. That laid the claim. They were not *animals*.

It would seem easy, almost obvious, to fall into mythology. I began seeing in the axolotls a metamorphosis which did not succeed in revoking a mysterious humanity. I imagined them aware, slaves of their bodies, condemned infinitely to the silence of the abyss, to a hopeless meditation. Their blind gaze, the diminutive gold disc without expression and nonetheless terribly shining, went through me like a message: "Save us, save us." I caught myself mumbling words of advice, conveying childish hopes. They continued to look at me, immobile; from time to time the rosy branches of the gills stiffened. In that instant I felt a muted pain; perhaps they were seeing me, attracting my strength to penetrate into the impenetrable thing of their lives. They were not human beings, but I had found in no animal such a profound relation with myself. The axolotls were like witnesses of something, and at times like horrible judges. I felt ignoble in front of them; there was such a terrifying purity in those transparent eyes. They were larvas, but larva means disguise and also phantom. Behind those Aztec faces, without expression but of an implacable cruelty, what semblance was awaiting its hour?

I was afraid of them. I think that had it not been for feeling the proximity of other visitors and the guard, I would not have been bold enough to remain alone with them. "You eat them alive with your eyes, hey," the guard said, laughing; he likely thought I was a little cracked. What he didn't notice was that it was they devouring me slowly with their eyes, in a cannibalism of gold. At any distance from the aquarium, I had only to think of them, it was as though I were being affected from a distance. It got to the point that I was going every day, and at night I thought of them immobile in the darkness, slowly putting a hand out which immediately encountered another. Perhaps their eyes could see in the dead of night, and for them the day continued indefinitely. The eyes of axolotls have no lids.

I know now that there was nothing strange, that that had to occur. Leaning over in front of the tank each morning, the recognition was greater. They were suffering, every fiber of my body reached toward that stifled pain, that stiff torment at the bottom of the tank. They were lying in wait for something, a remote dominion destroyed, an age of liberty when the world had been that of the axolotls. Not possible that such a terrible expression which was attaining the overthrow of that forced blankness on their stone faces should carry any message other than one of pain, proof of that eternal sentence, of that liquid hell they were undergoing. Hopelessly, I wanted to prove to myself that my own sensibility was projecting a nonexistent consciousness upon the axolotls. They and I knew. So there was nothing strange in what happened. My face was pressed against the glass of the aquarium, my eyes were attempting once more to penetrate the mystery of those eyes of gold without iris, without pupil. I saw from very close up the face of an axolotl immobile next to the glass. No transition and no surprise, I saw my face against the glass, I saw it on the outside of the tank, I saw it on the other side of the glass. Then my face drew back and I understood.

Only one thing was strange: to go on thinking as usual, to know. To realize that was, for the first moment, like the horror of a man buried alive awaking to his fate. Outside, my face came close to the glass again, I saw my mouth, the lips compressed with the effort of understanding the axolotls. I was an axolotl and now I knew instantly that no understanding was possible. He was outside the aquarium, his thinking was a thinking outside the tank. Recognizing him, being him himself, I was an axolotl and in my world. The horror began—I learned in the same moment—of believing myself prisoner in the body of an axolotl, metamorphosed into him with my human mind intact, buried alive in an axolotl, condemned to move lucidly among unconscious creatures. But that stopped when a foot just grazed my face, when I moved just a little to one side and saw an axolotl next to me who was looking at me, and understood that he knew also, no communication possible, but very clearly. Or I was also in him, or all of us were thinking humanlike, incapable of expression, limited to the golden splendor of our eyes looking at the face of the man pressed against the aquarium.

He returned many times, but he comes less often now. Weeks pass without his showing up. I saw him yesterday, he looked at me for a long time and left briskly. It seemed to me that he was not so much interested in us any more, that he was coming out of habit. Since the only thing I do is think, I could think about him a lot. It occurs to me that at the beginning we continued to communicate, that he felt more than ever one with the mystery which was claiming him. But the bridges were broken between him and me, because what was his obsession is now an axolotl, alien to his human life. I think that at the beginning I was capable of returning to him in a certain way—ah, only in a certain way—and of keeping awake his desire to know us better. I am an axolotl for good now, and if I think like a man it's only because every axolotl thinks like a man inside his rosy stone semblance. I believe that all this succeeded in communicating something to him in those first days, when I was still he. And in this final solitude to which he no longer comes, I console myself by thinking that perhaps he is going to write a story about us, that, believing he's making up a story, he's going to write all this about axolotls.

ROALD DAHL

THE WISH

Under the palm of one hand the child became aware of the scab of an old cut on his knee-cap. He bent forward to examine it closely. A scab was always a fascinating thing; it presented a special challenge he was never able to resist.

Yes, he thought, I will pick it off, even if it isn't ready, even if the middle of it sticks, even if it hurts like anything.

With a fingernail he began to explore cautiously around the edges of the scab. He got the nail underneath it, and when he raised it, but ever so slightly, it suddenly came off, the whole hard brown scab came off beautifully, leaving an interesting little circle of smooth red skin.

Nice. Very nice indeed. He rubbed the circle and it didn't hurt. He picked up the scab, put it on his thigh and flipped it with a finger so that it flew away and landed on the edge of the carpet, the enormous red and black and yellow carpet that stretched the whole length of the hall from the stairs on which he sat to the front door in the distance. A tremendous carpet. Bigger than the tennis lawn. Much bigger than that. He regarded it gravely, settling his eyes upon it with mild pleasure. He had never really noticed it before, but now, all of a sudden, the colours seemed to brighten mysteriously and spring out at him in a most dazzling way.

You see, he told himself, I know how it is. The red parts of the carpet are red-hot lumps of coal. What I must do is this: I must walk all the way along it to the front door without touching them. If I touch the red I will be burnt. As a matter of fact, I will be burnt up completely. And the black parts of the carpet . . . yes, the black parts are snakes, poisonous snakes, adders mostly, and cobras, thick like tree-trunks round the middle, and if I touch one of *them,* I'll be bitten and I'll die before tea time. And if I get across safely, without being burnt and without being bitten, I will be given a puppy for my birthday tomorrow.

He got to his feet and climbed higher up the stairs to obtain a better view of this vast tapestry of colour and death. Was it possible? Was there enough yellow? Yellow was the only colour he was allowed to walk on. Could it be done? This was not a journey to be undertaken lightly; the risks were too great for that. The child's face—a fringe of white-gold hair, two large blue eyes, a small pointed chin—peered down anxiously over the banisters. The yellow was a bit thin in places and there were one or two widish gaps, but it did seem to go all the way along to the other end. For someone who had only yesterday triumphantly travelled the whole length of the brick path from the stables to the summer-house without touching the cracks, this

carpet thing should not be too difficult. Except for the snakes. The mere
thought of snakes sent a fine electricity of fear running like pins down the
backs of his legs and under the soles of his feet.

He came slowly down the stairs and advanced to the edge of the carpet.
He extended one small sandaled foot and placed it cautiously upon a patch
of yellow. Then he brought the other foot up, and there was just enough
room for him to stand with the two feet together. There! He had started! His
bright oval face was curiously intent, a shade whiter perhaps than before,
and he was holding his arms out sideways to assist his balance. He took
another step, lifting his foot high over a patch of black, aiming carefully with
his toe for a narrow channel of yellow on the other side. When he had
completed the second step he paused to rest, standing very stiff and still. The
narrow channel of yellow ran forward unbroken for at least five yards and
he advanced gingerly along it, bit by bit, as though walking a tight-rope.
Where it finally curled off sideways, he had to take another long stride, this
time over a vicious looking mixture of black and red. Halfway across he
began to wobble. He waved his arms around wildly, windmill fashion, to
keep his balance, and he got across safely and rested again on the other side.
He was quite breathless now, and so tense he stood high on his toes all the
time, arms out sideways, fists clenched. He was on a big safe island of
yellow. There was lots of room on it, he couldn't possibly fall off, and he
stood there resting, hesitating, waiting, wishing he could stay for ever on this
big safe yellow island. But the fear of not getting the puppy compelled him
to go on.

Step by step, he edged further ahead, and between each one he paused to
decide exactly where next he should put his foot. Once, he had a choice of
ways, either to left or right, and he chose the left because although it seemed
the more difficult, there was not so much black in that direction. The black
was what made him nervous. He glanced quickly over his shoulder to see
how far he had come. Nearly halfway. There could be no turning back now.
He was in the middle and he couldn't turn back and he couldn't jump off
sideways either because it was too far, and when he looked at all the red and
all the black that lay ahead of him, he felt that old sudden sickening surge of
panic in his chest—like last Easter time, that afternoon when he got lost all
alone in the darkest part of Piper's Wood. 2081376

He took another step, placing his foot carefully upon the only little piece
of yellow within reach, and this time the point of the foot came within a
centimetre of some black. It wasn't touching the black, he could see it wasn't
touching, he could see the small line of yellow separating the toe of his
sandal from the black; but the snake stirred as though sensing the nearness,
and raised its head and gazed at the foot with bright beady eyes, watching to
see if it was going to touch.

*"I'm not touching you! You mustn't bite me! You know I'm not touching
you!"*

Another snake slid up noiselessly beside the first, raised its head, two
heads now, two pairs of eyes staring at the foot, gazing at a little naked place

just below the sandal strap where the skin showed through. The child went high up on his toes and stayed there, frozen stiff with terror. It was minutes before he dared to move again.

The next step would have to be a really long one. There was this deep curling river of black that ran clear across the width of the carpet, and he was forced by his position to cross it at its widest part. He thought first of trying to jump it, but decided he couldn't be sure of landing accurately on the narrow band of yellow the other side. He took a deep breath, lifted one foot, and inch by inch he pushed it out in front of him, far far out, then down and down until at last the tip of his sandal was across and resting safely on the edge of the yellow. He leaned forward, transferring his weight to this front foot. Then he tried to bring the back foot up as well. He strained and pulled and jerked his body, but the legs were too wide apart and he couldn't make it. He tried to get back again. He couldn't do that either. He was doing the splits and he was properly stuck. He glanced down and saw this deep curling river of black underneath him. Parts of it were stirring now, and uncoiling and sliding and beginning to shine with a dreadful oily glister. He wobbled, waved his arms frantically to keep his balance, but that seemed to make it worse. He was starting to go over. He was going over to the right, quite slowly he was going over, then faster and faster, and at the last moment, instinctively he put out a hand to break the fall and the next thing he saw was this bare hand of his going right into the middle of a great glistening mass of black and he gave one piercing cry of terror as it touched.

Outside in the sunshine, far away behind the house, the mother was looking for her son.

SHIRLEY JACKSON

THE LOTTERY

The morning of June 27th was clear and sunny, with the fresh warmth of a full-summer day; the flowers were blossoming profusely and the grass was richly green. The people of the village began to gather in the square, between the post office and the bank, around ten o'clock; in some towns there were so many people that the lottery took two days and had to be started on June 26th, but in this village, where there were only about three hundred people, the whole lottery took less than two hours, so it could begin at ten o'clock in the morning and still be through in time to allow the villagers to get home for noon dinner.

The children assembled first, of course. School was recently over for the summer, and the feeling of liberty sat uneasily on most of them; they tended to gather together quietly for a while before they broke into boisterous play, and their talk was still of the classroom and the teacher, of books and reprimands. Bobby Martin had already stuffed his pockets full of stones, and the other boys soon followed his example, selecting the smoothest and roundest stones; Bobby and Harry Jones and Dickie Delacroix—the villagers pronounced this name "Dellacroy"—eventually made a great pile of stones in one corner of the square and guarded it against the raids of the other boys. The girls stood aside, talking among themselves, looking over their shoulders at the boys, and the very small children rolled in the dust or clung to the hands of their older brothers or sisters.

Soon the men began to gather, surveying their own children, speaking of planting and rain, tractors and taxes. They stood together, away from the pile of stones in the corner, and their jokes were quiet and they smiled rather than laughed. The women, wearing faded house dresses and sweaters, came shortly after their menfolk. They greeted one another and exchanged bits of gossip as they went to join their husbands. Soon the women, standing by their husbands, began to call to their children, and the children came reluctantly, having to be called four or five times. Bobby Martin ducked under his mother's grasping hand and ran, laughing, back to the pile of stones. His father spoke up sharply, and Bobby came quickly and took his place between his father and his oldest brother.

The lottery was conducted—as were the square dances, the teenage club, the Halloween program—by Mr. Summers, who had time and energy to devote to civic activities. He was a round-faced, jovial man and he ran the coal business, and people were sorry for him, because he had no children and his wife was a scold. When he arrived in the square, carrying the black wooden box, there was a murmur of conversation among the villagers, and he waved and called, "Little late today, folks." The postmaster, Mr. Graves, followed him, carrying a three-legged stool, and the stool was put in the center of the square and Mr. Summers set the black box down on it. The villagers kept their distance, leaving a space between themselves and the stool, and when Mr. Summers said, "Some of you fellows want to give me a hand?" there was a hesitation before two men, Mr. Martin and his oldest son, Baxter, came forward to hold the box steady on the stool while Mr. Summers stirred up the papers inside it.

The original paraphernalia for the lottery had been lost long ago, and the black box now resting on the stool had been put to use even before Old Man Warner, the oldest man in town, was born. Mr. Summers spoke frequently to the villagers about making a new box, but no one liked to upset even as much tradition as was represented by the black box. There was a story that the present box had been made with some pieces of the box that had preceded it, the one that had been constructed when the first people settled down to make a village here. Every year, after the lottery, Mr. Summers began talking again about a new box, but every year the subject was allowed to fade off without anything's being done. The black box grew shabbier each year; by now it was no longer completely black but splintered badly along one side to show the original wood color, and in some places faded or stained.

Mr. Martin and his oldest son, Baxter, held the black box securely on the stool until Mr. Summers had stirred the papers thoroughly with his hand. Because so much of the ritual had been forgotten or discarded, Mr. Summers had been successful in having slips of paper substituted for the chips of wood that had been used for generations. Chips of wood, Mr. Summers had argued, had been all very well when the village was tiny, but now that the population was more than three hundred and likely to keep on growing, it was necessary to use something that would fit more easily into the black box. The night before the lottery, Mr. Summers and Mr. Graves made up the slips of paper and put them in the box, and it was then taken to the safe of Mr. Summers's coal company and locked up until Mr. Summers was ready to take it to the square next morning. The rest of the year, the box was put away, sometimes one place, sometimes another; it had spent one year in Mr. Graves's barn and another year underfoot in the post office, and sometimes it was set on a shelf in the Martin grocery and left there.

There was a great deal of fussing to be done before Mr. Summers declared the lottery open. There were the lists to make up—of heads of families, heads of households in each family, members of each household in each family. There was the proper swearing-in of Mr. Summers by the postmaster, as the official of the lottery; at one time, some people remembered, there had been a recital of some sort, performed by the official of the lottery, a perfunctory, tuneless chant that had been rattled off duly each year; some people believed that the official of the lottery used to stand just so when he said or sang it, others believed that he was supposed to walk among the people, but years and years ago this part of the ritual had been allowed to lapse. There had been, also, a ritual salute, which the official of the lottery had had to use in addressing each person who came up to draw from the box, but this also had changed with time, until now it was felt necessary only for the official to speak to each person approaching. Mr. Summers was very good at all this; in his clean white shirt and blue jeans, with one hand resting carelessly on the black box, he seemed very proper and important as he talked interminably to Mr. Graves and the Martins.

Just as Mr. Summers finally left off talking and turned to the assembled villagers, Mrs. Hutchinson came hurriedly along the path to the square, her sweater thrown over her shoulders, and slid into place in the back of the crowd. "Clean forgot what day it was," she said to Mrs. Delacroix, who stood next to her, and they both laughed softly. "Thought my old man was out back stacking wood," Mrs. Hutchinson went on, "and then I looked out the window and the kids was gone, and then I remembered it was the twenty-seventh and came a-running." She dried her hands on her apron, and Mrs. Delacroix said, "You're in time, though. They're still talking away up there."

Mrs. Hutchinson craned her neck to see through the crowd and found her husband and children standing near the front. She tapped Mrs. Delacroix on the arm as a farewell and began to make her way through the crowd. The people separated good-humoredly to let her through; two or three people said, in voices just loud enough to be heard across the crowd, "Here comes your Missus, Hutchinson," and "Bill, she made it after all." Mrs. Hutchinson reached her husband, and Mr. Summers, who had been waiting, said cheerfully, "Thought we were going to have to get on without you, Tessie." Mrs. Hutchinson said, grinning, "Wouldn't have me leave m'dishes in the sink, now, would you, Joe?" and soft laughter ran through the crowd as the people stirred back into position after Mrs. Hutchinson's arrival.

"Well, now," Mr. Summers said soberly, "guess we better get started, get this over with, so's we can go back to work. Anybody ain't here?"

"Dunbar," several people said, "Dunbar, Dunbar."

Mr. Summers consulted his list. "Clyde Dunbar," he said. "That's right. He's broke his leg, hasn't he? Who's drawing for him?"

"Me, I guess," a woman said, and Mr. Summers turned to look at her. "Wife draws for her husband," Mr. Summers said. "Don't you have a grown boy to do it for you, Janey?" Although Mr. Summers and everyone else in the village knew the answer perfectly well, it was the business of the official of the lottery to ask such questions formally. Mr. Summers waited with an expression of polite interest while Mrs. Dunbar answered.

"Horace's not but sixteen yet," Mrs. Dunbar said regretfully. "Guess I gotta fill in for the old man this year."

"Right," Mr. Summers said. He made a note on the list he was holding. Then he asked, "Watson boy drawing this year?"

A tall boy in the crowd raised his hand. "Here," he said. "I'm drawing for m'mother and me." He blinked his eyes nervously and ducked his head as several voices in the crowd said things like "Good fellow, Jack," and "Glad to see your mother's got a man to do it."

"Well," Mr. Summers said, "guess that's everyone. Old Man Warner make it?"

"Here," a voice said, and Mr. Summers nodded.

A sudden hush fell on the crowd as Mr. Summers cleared his throat and looked at the list. "All ready?" he called. "Now, I'll read the names—heads of families first—and the men come up and take a paper out of the box. Keep the paper folded in your hand without looking at it until everyone has had a turn. Everything clear?"

The people had done it so many times that they only half listened to the directions; most of them were quiet, wetting their lips, not looking around. Then Mr. Summers raised one hand high and said, "Adams." A man disengaged himself from the crowd and came forward. "Hi, Steve," Mr. Summers said, and Mr. Adams said, "Hi, Joe." They grinned at one another humorlessly and nervously. Then Mr. Adams reached into the black box and took out a folded paper. He held it firmly by one corner as he turned and went hastily back to his place in the crowd, where he stood a little apart from his family, not looking down at his hand.

"Allen," Mr. Summers said. "Anderson. . . . Bentham."

"Seems like there's not time at all between lotteries any more," Mrs. Delacroix said to Mrs. Graves in the back row. "Seems like we got through with the last one only last week."

"Time sure goes fast," Mrs. Graves said.

"Clark. . . . Delacroix."

"There goes my old man," Mrs. Delacroix said. She held her breath while her husband went forward.

"Dunbar," Mr. Summers said, and Mrs. Dunbar went steadily to the box while one of the women said, "Go on, Janey," and another said, "There she goes."

"We're next," Mrs. Graves said. She watched while Mr. Graves came around from the side of the box, greeted Mr. Summers gravely, and selected a slip of paper from the box. By now, all through the crowd there were men holding the small folded papers in their large hands, turning them over and over nervously. Mrs. Dunbar and her two sons stood together, Mrs. Dunbar holding the slip of paper.

"Harburt. . . . Hutchinson."

"Get up there, Bill," Mrs. Hutchinson said, and the people near her laughed.

"Jones."

"They do say," Mr. Adams said to Old Man Warner, who stood next to him, "that over in the north village they're talking of giving up the lottery."

Old Man Warner snorted. "Pack of crazy fools," he said. "Listening to the young folks, nothing's good enough for *them*. Next thing you know, they'll be wanting to go back to living in caves, nobody work any more, live *that* way for a while. Used to be a saying about 'Lottery in June, corn be heavy soon.' First thing you know, we'd all be eating stewed chickweed and acorns. There's *always* been a lottery," he added petulantly. "Bad enough to see young Joe Summers up there joking with everybody."

"Some places have already quit lotteries," Mrs. Adams said.

"Nothing but trouble in *that,*" Old Man Warner said stoutly. "Pack of young fools."

"Martin." And Bobby Martin watched his father go forward. "Overdyke.... Percy."

"I wish they'd hurry," Mrs. Dunbar said to her older son. "I wish they'd hurry."

"They're almost through," her son said.

"You get ready to run tell Dad," Mrs. Dunbar said.

Mr. Summers called his own name and then stepped forward precisely and selected a slip from the box. Then he called, "Warner."

"Seventy-seventh year I been in the lottery," Old Man Warner said as he went through the crowd. "Seventy-seventh time."

"Watson." The tall boy came awkwardly through the crowd. Someone said, "Don't be nervous, Jack," and Mr. Summers said, "Take your time, son."

"Zanini."

After that, there was a long pause, a breathless pause, until Mr. Summers, holding his slip of paper in the air, said, "All right, fellows." For a minute, no one moved, and then all the slips of paper were opened. Suddenly, all the women began to speak at once, saying, "Who is it?," "Who's got it?," "Is it the Dunbars?," "Is it the Watsons?" Then the voices began to say, "It's Hutchinson. It's Bill," "Bill Hutchinson's got it."

"Go tell your father," Mrs. Dunbar said to her older son.

People began to look around to see the Hutchinsons. Bill Hutchinson was standing quiet, staring down at the paper in his hand. Suddenly, Tessie Hutchinson shouted to Mr. Summers, "You didn't give him time enough to take any paper he wanted. I saw you. It wasn't fair!"

"Be a good sport, Tessie," Mrs. Delacroix called, and Mrs. Graves said, "All of us took the same chance."

"Shut up, Tessie," Bill Hutchinson said.

"Well, everyone," Mr. Summers said, "that was done pretty fast, and now we've got to be hurrying a little more to get done in time." He consulted his next list. "Bill," he said, "you draw for the Hutchinson family. You got any other households in the Hutchinsons?"

"There's Don and Eva," Mrs. Hutchinson yelled. "Make *them* take their chance!"

"Daughters draw with their husbands' families, Tessie," Mr. Summers said gently. "You know that as well as anyone else."

"It wasn't *fair,*" Tessie said.

"I guess not, Joe," Bill Hutchinson said regretfully. "My daughter draws with her husband's family, that's only fair. And I've got no other family except the kids."

"Then, as far as drawing for families is concerned, it's you," Mr. Summers said in explanation, "and as far as drawing for households is concerned, that's you, too. Right?"

"Right," Bill Hutchinson said.

"How many kids, Bill?" Mr. Summers asked formally.

"Three," Bill Hutchinson said. "There's Bill, Jr., and Nancy, and little Dave. And Tessie and me."

"All right, then," Mr. Summers said. "Harry, you got their tickets back?"

Mr. Graves nodded and held up the slips of paper. "Put them in the box, then," Mr. Summers directed. "Take Bill's and put it in."

"I think we ought to start over," Mrs. Hutchinson said, as quietly as she could. "I tell you it wasn't *fair.* You didn't give him time enough to choose. *Every*body saw that."

Mr. Graves had selected the five slips and put them in the box, and he dropped all the papers but those onto the ground, where the breeze caught them and lifted them off.

"Listen, everybody," Mrs. Hutchinson was saying to the people around her.

"Ready, Bill?" Mr. Summers asked, and Bill Hutchinson, with one quick glance around at his wife and children, nodded.

"Remember," Mr. Summers said, "take the slips and keep them folded until each person has taken one. Harry, you help little Dave." Mr. Graves took the hand of the little boy, who came willingly with him up to the box. "Take a paper out of the box, Davy," Mr. Summers said. Davy put his hand into the box and laughed. "Take just *one* paper," Mr. Summers said. "Harry, you hold it for him." Mr. Graves took the child's hand and removed the folded paper from the tight fist and held it while little Dave stood next to him and looked up at him wonderingly.

"Nancy next," Mr. Summers said. Nancy was twelve, and her school friends breathed heavily as she went forward, switching her skirt, and took a slip daintily from the box. "Bill, Jr.," Mr. Summers said, and Billy, his face red and his feet overlarge, nearly knocked the box over as he got a paper out. "Tessie," Mr. Summers said. She hesitated for a minute, looking around defiantly, and then set her lips and went up to the box. She snatched a paper out and held it behind her.

"Bill," Mr. Summers said, and Bill Hutchinson reached into the box and felt around, bringing his hand out at last with the slip of paper in it.

The crowd was quiet. A girl whispered, "I hope it's not Nancy," and the sound of the whisper reached the edges of the crowd.

"It's not the way it used to be," Old Man Warner said clearly. "People ain't the way they used to be."

"All right," Mr. Summers said. "Open the papers. Harry, you open little Dave's."

Mr. Graves opened the slip of paper and there was a general sigh through the crowd as he held it up and everyone could see that it was blank. Nancy and Bill, Jr., opened theirs at the same time, and both beamed and laughed, turning around to the crowd and holding their slips of paper above their heads.

"Tessie," Mr. Summers said. There was a pause, and then Mr. Summers looked at Bill Hutchinson, and Bill unfolded his paper and showed it. It was blank.

"It's Tessie," Mr. Summers said, and his voice was hushed. "Show us her paper, Bill."

Bill Hutchinson went over to his wife and forced the slip of paper out of her hand. It had a black spot on it, the black spot Mr. Summers had made the night before with the heavy pencil in the coal-company office. Bill Hutchinson held it up, and there was a stir in the crowd.

"All right, folks," Mr. Summers said. "Let's finish quickly."

Although the villagers had forgotten the ritual and lost the original black box, they still remembered to use stones. The pile of stones the boys had made earlier was ready; there were stones on the ground with the blowing scraps of paper that had come out of the box. Mrs. Delacroix selected a stone so large she had to pick it up with both hands and turned to Mrs. Dunbar. "Come on," she said. "Hurry up."

Mrs. Dunbar had small stones in both hands, and she said, gasping for breath, "I can't run at all. You'll have to go ahead and I'll catch up with you."

The children had stones already, and someone gave little Davy Hutchinson a few pebbles.

Tessie Hutchinson was in the center of a cleared space by now, and she held her hands out desperately as the villagers moved in on her. "It isn't fair," she said. A stone hit her on the side of the head.

Old Man Warner was saying, "Come on, come on, everyone." Steve Adams was in the front of the crowd of villagers, with Mrs. Graves beside him.

"It isn't fair, it isn't right," Mrs. Hutchinson screamed, and then they were upon her.

JEROME BIXBY

IT'S A GOOD LIFE

Aunt Amy was out on the front porch, rocking back and forth in the highbacked chair and fanning herself, when Bill Soames rode his bicycle up the road and stopped in front of the house.

Perspiring under the afternoon "sun," Bill lifted the box of groceries out of the big basket over the front wheel of the bike, and came up the front walk.

Little Anthony was sitting on the lawn, playing with a rat. He had caught the rat down in the basement—he had made it think that it smelled cheese, the most rich-smelling and crumbly-delicious cheese a rat had ever thought it smelled, and it had come out of its hole, and now Anthony had hold of it with his mind and was making it do tricks.

When the rat saw Bill Soames coming, it tried to run, but Anthony thought at it, and it turned a flip-flop on the grass, and lay trembling, its eyes gleaming in small black terror.

Bill Soames hurried past Anthony and reached the front steps, mumbling. He always mumbled when he came to the Fremont house, or passed by it, or even thought of it. Everybody did. They thought about silly things, things that didn't mean very much, like two-and-two-is-four-and-twice-is-eight and so on; they tried to jumble up their thoughts to keep them skipping back and forth, so Anthony couldn't read their minds. The mumbling helped. Because if Anthony got anything strong out of your thoughts, he might take a notion to do something about it—like curing your wife's sick headaches or your kid's mumps, or getting your old milk cow back on schedule, or fixing the privy. And while Anthony mightn't actually mean any harm, he couldn't be expected to have much notion of what was the right thing to do in such cases.

That was if he liked you. He might try to help you, in his way. And that could be pretty horrible.

If he didn't like you ... well, that could be worse.

Bill Soames set the box of groceries on the porch railing and stopped his mumbling long enough to say, "Everythin' you wanted, Miss Amy."

"Oh, fine, William," Amy Fremont said lightly. "My, ain't it terrible hot today?"

Bill Soames almost cringed. His eyes pleaded with her. He shook his head violently *no,* and then interrupted his mumbling again, though obviously he didn't want to: "Oh, don't say that, Miss Amy . . . it's fine, just fine. A real *good* day!"

Amy Fremont got up from the rocking chair, and came across the porch. She was a tall woman, thin, a smiling vacancy in her eyes. About a year ago, Anthony had gotten mad at her, because she'd told him he shouldn't have turned the cat into a cat-rug, and although he had always obeyed her more than anyone else, which was hardly at all, this time he'd snapped at her. With his mind. And that had been the end of Amy Fremont's bright eyes, and the end of Amy Fremont as everyone had known her. And that was when word got around in Peaksville (population: 46) that even the members of Anthony's own family weren't safe. After that, everyone was twice as careful.

Someday Anthony might undo what he'd done to Aunt Amy. Anthony's Mom and Pop hoped he would. When he was older, and maybe sorry. If it was possible, that is. Because Aunt Amy had changed a lot, and besides, now Anthony wouldn't obey anyone.

"Land alive, William," Aunt Amy said, "you don't have to mumble like that. Anthony wouldn't hurt you. My goodness, Anthony likes you!" She raised her voice and called to Anthony, who had tired of the rat and was making it eat itself. "Don't you, dear? Don't you like Mr. Soames?"

Anthony looked across the lawn at the grocery man—a bright, wet, purple gaze. He didn't say anything. Bill Soames tried to smile at him. After a second Anthony returned his attention to the rat. It had already devoured its tail, or at least chewed it off—for Anthony had made it bite faster than it could swallow, and little pink and red furry pieces lay around it on the green grass. Now the rat was having trouble reaching its hindquarters.

Mumbling silently, thinking of nothing in particular as hard as he could, Bill Soames went stiff-legged down the walk, mounted his bicycle and pedaled off.

"We'll see you tonight, William," Aunt Amy called after him.

As Bill Soames pumped the pedals, he was wishing deep down that he could pump twice as fast, to get away from Anthony all the faster, and away from Aunt Amy, who sometimes just forgot how *careful* you had to be. And he shouldn't have thought that. Because Anthony caught it. He caught the desire to get away from the Fremont house as if it was something *bad,* and his purple gaze blinked and he snapped a small, sulky thought after Bill Soames—just a small one, because he was in a good mood today, and besides, he liked Bill Soames, or at least didn't dislike him, at least today. Bill Soames wanted to go away—so, petulantly, Anthony helped him.

Pedaling with superhuman speed—or rather, appearing to, because in reality the bicycle was pedaling *him*—Bill Soames vanished down the road in a cloud of dust, his thin, terrified wail drifting back across the summerlike heat.

Anthony looked at the rat. It had devoured half its belly, and had died from pain. He thought it into a grave out deep in the cornfield—his father had once said, smiling, that he might do that with the things he killed—and went around the house, casting his odd shadow in the hot, brassy light from above.

In the kitchen, Aunt Amy was unpacking the groceries. She put the Mason-jarred goods on the shelves, and the meat and milk in the icebox, and the beet sugar and coarse flour in big cans under the sink. She put the cardboard box in the corner, by the door, for Mr. Soames to pick up next time he came. It was stained and battered and torn and worn fuzzy, but it was one of the few left in Peaksville. In faded red letters it said *Campbell's Soup.* The last cans of soup, or of anything else, had been eaten long ago, except for a small communal hoard which the villagers dipped into for special occasions—but the box lingered on, like a coffin, and when it and the other boxes were gone, the men would have to make some out of wood.

Aunt Amy went out in back, where Anthony's Mom—Aunt Amy's sister— sat in the shade of the house, shelling peas. The peas, every time Mom ran a finger along a pod, went *lollop-lollop-lollop* into the pan on her lap.

"William brought the groceries," Aunt Amy said. She sat down wearily in the straightbacked chair beside Mom, and began fanning herself again. She wasn't really old; but ever since Anthony had snapped at her with his mind, something had seemed to be wrong with her body as well as her mind, and she was tired all the time.

"Oh, good," said Mom. *Lollop* went the fat peas into the pan.

Everybody in Peaksville always said "Oh, fine," or "Good," or "Say, that's swell!" when almost anything happened or was mentioned—even unhappy things like accidents or even deaths. They'd always say "Good," because if they didn't try to cover up how they really felt, Anthony might overhear with his mind, and then nobody knew what might happen. Like the time Mrs. Kent's husband, Sam, had come walking back from the graveyard, because Anthony liked Mrs. Kent and had heard her mourning.

Lollop.

"Tonight's television night," said Aunt Amy. "I'm glad I look forward to it so much every week. I wonder what we'll see tonight?"

"Did Bill bring the meat?" asked Mom.

"Yes." Aunt Amy fanned herself, looking up at the featureless brassy glare of the sky. "Goodness, it's so hot. I wish Anthony would make it just a little cooler—"

"Amy!"

"Oh!" Mom's sharp tone had penetrated, where Bill Soames's agonized expression had failed. Aunt Amy put one thin hand to her mouth in exaggerated alarm. "Oh ... I'm sorry, dear." Her pale blue eyes shuttled around, right and left, to see if Anthony was in sight. Not that it would make any difference if he was or wasn't—he didn't have to be near you to know what you were thinking. Usually, though, unless he had his attention on somebody, he would be occupied with thoughts of his own.

But some things attracted his attention—you could never be sure just what.

"This weather's just *fine,*" Mom said.

Lollop.

"Oh, yes," Aunt Amy said. "It's a wonderful day. I wouldn't want it changed for the world!"

Lollop.

Lollop.

"What time is it?" Mom asked.

Aunt Amy was sitting where she could see through the kitchen window to the alarm clock on the shelf above the stove. "Four-thirty," she said.

Lollop.

"I want tonight to be something special," Mom said. "Did Bill bring a good lean roast?"

"Good and lean, dear. They butchered just today, you know, and sent us over the best piece."

"Dan Hollis will be so surprised when he finds out that tonight's television party is a birthday party for him too!"

"Oh *I* think he will! Are you sure nobody's told him?"

"Everybody swore they wouldn't."

"That'll be real nice," Aunt Amy nodded, looking off across the cornfield. "A birthday party."

"Well—" Mom put the pan of peas down beside her, stood up and brushed her apron. "I'd better get the roast on. Then we can set the table." She picked up the peas.

Anthony came around the corner of the house. He didn't look at them, but continued on down through the carefully kept garden—*all* the gardens in Peaksville were carefully kept, very carefully kept—and went past the rusting, useless hulk that had been the Fremont family car, and went smoothly over the fence and out into the cornfield.

"Isn't this a lovely day!" said Mom, a little loudly, as they went toward the back door.

Aunt Amy fanned herself. "A beautiful day, dear. Just *fine!*"

Out in the cornfield, Anthony walked between the tall, rustling rows of green stalks. He liked to smell the corn. The alive corn overhead, and the old dead corn underfoot. Rich Ohio earth, thick with weeds and brown, dry-rotting ears of corn, pressed between his bare toes with every step—he had made it rain last night so everything would smell and feel nice today.

He walked clear to the edge of the cornfield, and over to where a grove of shadowy green trees covered cool, moist, dark ground, and lots of leafy undergrowth, and jumbled moss-covered rocks, and a small spring that made a clear, clean pool. Here Anthony liked to rest and watch the birds and insects and small animals that rustled and scampered and chirped about. He liked to lie on the cool ground and look up through the moving greenness overhead, and watch the insects flit in the hazy soft sunbeams that stood like slanting, glowing bars between ground and treetops. Somehow, he liked the thoughts of the little creatures in this place better than the thoughts outside; and while the thoughts he picked up here weren't very strong or very clear, he could get enough out of them to know what the little creatures liked and wanted, and he spent a lot of time making the grove more like what they wanted it to be. The spring hadn't always been here; but one time he had found thirst in one small furry mind, and had brought subterranean water to the surface in a clear cold flow, and had watched blinking as the creature drank, feeling its pleasure. Later he had made the pool, when he found a small urge to swim.

He had made rocks and trees and bushes and caves, and sunlight here and shadows there, because he had felt in all the tiny minds around him the desire—or the instinctive want—for this kind of resting place, and that kind of mating place, and this kind of place to play, and that kind of home.

And somehow the creatures from all the fields and pastures around the grove had seemed to know that this was a good place, for there were always more of them coming in—every time Anthony came out here there were more creatures than the last time, and more desires and needs to be tended to. Every time there would be some kind of creature he had never seen before, and he would find its mind, and see what it wanted, and then give it to it.

He liked to help them. He liked to feel their simple gratification.

Today, he rested beneath a thick elm, and lifted his purple gaze to a red and black bird that had just come to the grove. It twittered on a branch over his head, and hopped back and forth, and thought its tiny thoughts, and Anthony made a big, soft nest for it, and pretty soon it hopped in.

A long, brown, sleek-furred animal was drinking at the pool. Anthony found its mind next. The animal was thinking about a smaller creature that was scurrying along the ground on the other side of the pool, grubbing for insects. The little creature didn't know that it was in danger. The long, brown animal finished drinking and tensed its legs to leap, and Anthony thought it into a grave in the cornfield.

He didn't like those kinds of thoughts. They reminded him of the thoughts outside the grove. A long time ago some of the people outside had thought that way about him, and one night they'd hidden and waited for him to come back from the grove—and he'd just thought them all into the cornfield. Since then, the rest of the people hadn't thought that way—at least, very clearly. Now their thoughts were all mixed up and confusing whenever they thought about him or near him, so he didn't pay much attention.

He liked to help them too, sometimes—but it wasn't simple, or very gratifying either. They never thought happy thoughts when he did—just the jumble. So he spent more time out here.

He watched all the birds and insects and furry creatures for a while, and played with a bird, making it soar and dip and streak madly around tree trunks until, accidentally, when another bird caught his attention for a moment, he ran it into a rock. Petulantly, he thought the rock into a grave in the cornfield; but he couldn't do anything more with the bird. Not because it was dead, though it was; but because it had a broken wing. So he went back to the house. He didn't feel like walking back through the cornfield, so he just *went* to the house, right down into the basement.

It was nice down here. Nice and dark and damp and sort of fragrant, because once Mom had been making preserves in a rack along the far wall, and then she'd stopped coming down ever since Anthony had started spending time here, and the preserves had spoiled and leaked down and spread over the dirt floor, and Anthony liked the smell.

He caught another rat, making it smell cheese, and after he played with it, he thought it into a grave right beside the long animal he'd killed in the grove. Aunt Amy hated rats, and so he killed a lot of them, because he liked Aunt Amy most of all and sometimes did things that Aunt Amy wanted. Her mind was more like the little furry minds out in the grove. She hadn't thought anything bad at all about him for a long time.

After the rat, he played with a big black spider in the corner under the stairs, making it run back and forth until its web shook and shimmered in the light from the cellar window like a reflection in silvery water. Then he drove fruit flies into the web until the spider was frantic trying to wind them all up. The spider liked flies, and its thoughts were stronger than theirs, so he did it. There was something bad in the way it liked flies, but it wasn't clear—and besides, Aunt Amy hated flies too.

He heard footsteps overhead—Mom moving around in the kitchen. He blinked his purple gaze, and almost decided to make her hold still—but instead he *went* up to the attic, and, after looking out the circular window at the front end of the long X-roofed room for a while at the front lawn and the dusty road and Henderson's tip-waving wheatfield beyond, he curled into an unlikely shape and went partly to sleep.

Soon people would be coming for television, he heard Mom think.

He went more to sleep. He liked television night. Aunt Amy had always liked television a lot, so one time he had thought some for her, and a few other people had been there at the time, and Aunt Amy had felt disappointed when they wanted to leave. He'd done something to them for that—and now everybody came to television.

He liked all the attention he got when they did.

Anthony's father came home around six-thirty, looking tired and dirty and bloody. He'd been over in Dunn's pasture with the other men, helping pick out the cow to be slaughtered this month and doing the job, and then butchering the meat and salting it away in Soames's icehouse. Not a job he cared for, but every man had his turn. Yesterday, he had helped scythe down old McIntyre's wheat. Tomorrow, they would start threshing. By hand. Everything in Peaksville had to be done by hand.

He kissed his wife on the cheek and sat down at the kitchen table. He smiled and said, "Where's Anthony?"

"Around someplace," Mom said.

Aunt Amy was over at the wood-burning stove, stirring the big pot of peas. Mom went back to the oven and opened it and basted the roast.

"Well, it's been a *good* day," Dad said. By rote. Then he looked at the mixing bowl and breadboard on the table. He sniffed at the dough. "M'm," he said. "I could eat a loaf all by myself, I'm so hungry."

"No one told Dan Hollis about its being a birthday party, did they?" his wife asked.

"Nope. We kept as quiet as mummies."

"We've fixed up such a lovely surprise!"

"Um, what?"

"Well . . . you know how much Dan likes music. Well, last week Thelma Dunn found a *record* in her attic!"

"No!"

"Yes! And we had Ethel sort of ask—you know, without really *asking*—if he had that one. And he said no. Isn't that a wonderful surprise?"

"Well, now, it sure is. A record, imagine! That's a real nice thing to find! What record is it?"

"Perry Como, singing *You Are My Sunshine.*"

"Well, I'll be darned. I always liked that tune." Some raw carrots were lying on the table. Dad picked up a small one, scrubbed it on his chest, and took a bite. "How did Thelma happen to find it?"

"Oh, you know—just looking around for new things."

"M'm." Dad chewed the carrot. "Say, who has that picture we found a while back? I kind of liked it—that old clipper sailing along—"

"The Smiths. Next week the Sipichs get it, and they give the Smiths old McIntyre's music-box, and we give the Sipichs—" and she went down the tentative order of things that would change hands among the women at church this Sunday.

He nodded. "Looks like we can't have the picture for a while, I guess. Look, honey, you might try to get that detective book back from the Reillys. I was so busy the week we had it, I never got to finish all the stories—"

"I'll try," his wife said doubtfully. "But I hear the van Husens have a stereoscope they found in the cellar." Her voice was just a little accusing. "They had it two whole months before they told anybody about it—"

"Say," Dad said, looking interested. "That'd be nice, too. Lots of pictures?"

"I suppose so. I'll see on Sunday. I'd like to have it—but we still owe the van Husens for their canary. I don't know why that bird had to pick *our* house to die . . . it must have been sick when we got it. Now there's just no satisfying Betty van Husen—she even hinted she'd like our *piano* for a while!"

"Well, honey, you try for the stereoscope—or just anything you think we'll like." At last he swallowed the carrot. It had been a little young and tough. Anthony's whims about the weather made it so that people never knew what crops would come up, or what shape they'd be in if they did. All they could do was plant a lot; and always enough of something came up any one season to live on. Just once there had been a grain surplus; tons of it had been hauled to the edge of Peaksville and dumped off into the nothingness. Otherwise, nobody could have breathed, when it started to spoil.

"You know," Dad went on. "It's nice to have the new things around. It's nice to think that there's probably still a lot of stuff nobody's found yet, in cellars and attics and barns and down behind things. They help, somehow. As much as anything can help—"

"Sh-h!" Mom glanced nervously around.

"Oh," Dad said, smiling hastily. "It's all right! The new things are *good!* It's *nice* to be able to have something around you've never seen before, and know that something you've given somebody else is making them happy . . . that's a real good thing."

"A good thing," his wife echoed.

"Pretty soon," Aunt Amy said, from the stove, "there won't be any more new things. We'll have found everything there is to find. Goodness, that'll be too bad—"

"*Amy!*"

"Well—" her pale eyes were shallow and fixed, a sign of her recurrent vagueness. "It will be kind of a shame—no new things—"

"Don't *talk* like that," Mom said, trembling. "Amy, be *quiet!*"

"It's *good,*" said Dad, in the loud, familiar, wanting-to-be-overheard tone of voice. "Such talk is *good.* It's okay, honey—don't you see? It's good for Amy to talk any way she wants. It's good for her to feel bad. Everything's good. Everything *has* to be good . . ."

Anthony's mother was pale. And so was Aunt Amy—the peril of the moment had suddenly penetrated the clouds surrounding her mind. Sometimes it was difficult to handle words so that they might not prove disastrous. You just never *knew.* There were so many things it was wise not to say, or even think—but remonstration for saying or thinking them might be just as bad, if Anthony heard and decided to do anything about it. You could just never tell what Anthony was liable to do.

Everything had to be good. Had to be fine just as it was, even if it wasn't. Always. Because any changes might be worse. So terribly much worse.

"Oh, my goodness, yes, of course it's good," Mom said. "You talk any way you want to, Amy, and it's just fine. Of course, you want to remember that some ways are *better* than others . . ."

Aunt Amy stirred the peas, fright in her pale eyes.

"Oh, yes," she said. "But I don't feel like talking right now. It . . . it's *good* that I don't feel like talking."

Dad said tiredly, smiling, "I'm going out and wash up."

They started arriving around eight o'clock. By that time, Mom and Aunt Amy had the big table in the dining room set, and two more tables off to the side. The candles were burning, and the chairs situated, and Dad had a big fire going in the fireplace.

The first to arrive were the Sipichs, John and Mary. John wore his best suit, and was well-scrubbed and pink-faced after his day in McIntyre's pasture. The suit was neatly pressed, but getting threadbare at elbows and cuffs. Old McIntyre was working on a loom, designing it out of schoolbooks, but so far it was slow going. McIntyre was a capable man with wood and tools, but a loom was a big order when you couldn't get metal parts. McIntyre had been one of the ones who, at first, had wanted to try to get Anthony to make things the villagers needed, like clothes and canned goods and medical supplies and gasoline. Since then, he felt that what had happened to the whole Terrance family and Joe Kinney was his fault, and he worked hard trying to make it up to the rest of them. And since then, no one had tried to get Anthony to do anything.

Mary Sipich was a small, cheerful woman in a simple dress. She immediately set about helping Mom and Aunt Amy put the finishing touches on the dinner.

The next arrivals were the Smiths and the Dunns, who lived right next to each other down the road, only a few yards from the nothingness. They drove up in the Smiths' wagon, drawn by their old horse.

Then the Reillys showed up, from across the darkened wheatfield, and the evening really began. Pat Reilly sat down at the big upright in the front room, and began to play from the popular sheet music on the rack. He played softly, as expressively as he could—and nobody sang. Anthony liked piano playing a whole lot, but not singing; often he would come up from the basement, or down from the attic, or just *come,* and sit on top of the piano, nodding his head as Pat played *Lover* or *Boulevard of Broken Dreams* or *Night and Day.* He seemed to prefer ballads, sweet-sounding songs—but the one time somebody had started to sing, Anthony had looked over from the top of the piano and done something that made everybody afraid of singing from then on. Later, they'd decided that the piano was what Anthony had heard first, before anybody had ever tried to sing, and now anything else added to it didn't sound right and distracted him from his pleasure.

So, every television night, Pat would play the piano, and that was the beginning of the evening. Wherever Anthony was, the music would make him happy, and put him in a good mood, and he would know that they were gathering for television and waiting for him.

By eight-thirty everybody had shown up, except for the seventeen children and Mrs. Soames, who was off watching them in the schoolhouse at the far end of town. The children of Peaksville were never, never allowed near the Fremont house—not since little Fred Smith had tried to play with Anthony on a dare. The younger children weren't even told about Anthony. The others had mostly forgotten about him, or were told that he was a nice, nice goblin but they must never go near him.

Dan and Ethel Hollis came late, and Dan walked in not suspecting a thing. Pat Reilly had played the piano until his hands ached—he'd worked pretty hard with them today—and now he got up, and everybody gathered around to wish Dan Hollis a happy birthday.

"Well, I'll be darned," Dan grinned. "This is swell. I wasn't expecting this at all ... gosh, this is *swell!*"

They gave him his presents—mostly things they had made by hand, though some were things that people had possessed as their own and now gave him as his. John Sipich gave him a watch charm, hand-carved out of a piece of hickory wood. Dan's watch had broken down a year or so ago, and there was nobody in the village who knew how to fix it, but he still carried it around because it had been his grandfather's and was a fine old heavy thing of gold and silver. He attached the charm to the chain, while everybody laughed and said John had done a nice job of carving. Then Mary Sipich gave him a knitted necktie, which he put on, removing the one he'd worn.

The Reillys gave him a little box they had made, to keep things in. They didn't say what things, but Dan said he'd keep his personal jewelry in it. The Reillys had made it out of a cigar box, carefully peeled of its paper and lined on the inside with velvet. The outside had been polished, and carefully if not expertly carved by Pat—but his carving got complimented too. Dan Hollis received many other gifts—a pipe, a pair of shoelaces, a tie pin, a knit pair of socks, some fudge, a pair of garters made from old suspenders.

He unwrapped each gift with vast pleasure, and wore as many of them as he could right there, even the garters. He lit up the pipe, and said he'd never had a better smoke; which wasn't quite true, because the pipe wasn't broken in yet. Pete Manners had had it lying around ever since he'd received it as a gift four years ago from an out-of-town relative who hadn't known he'd stopped smoking.

Dan put the tobacco into the bowl very carefully. Tobacco was precious. It was only pure luck that Pat Reilly had decided to try to grow some in his backyard just before what had happened to Peaksville had happened. It didn't grow very well, and then they had to cure it and shred it and all, and it was just precious stuff. Everybody in town used wooden holders old McIntyre had made, to save on butts.

Last of all, Thelma Dunn gave Dan Hollis the record she had found.

Dan's eyes misted even before he opened the package. He knew it was a record.

"Gosh," he said softly. "What one is it? I'm almost afraid to look . . ."

"You haven't got it, darling," Ethel Hollis smiled. "Don't you remember, I asked about *You Are My Sunshine?*"

"Oh, gosh," Dan said again. Carefully he removed the wrapping and stood there fondling the record, running his big hands over the worn grooves with their tiny, dulling crosswise scratches. He looked around the room, eyes shining, and they all smiled back, knowing how delighted he was.

"Happy birthday, darling!" Ethel said, throwing her arms around him and kissing him.

He clutched the record in both hands, holding it off to one side as she pressed against him. "Hey," he laughed, pulling back his head. "Be careful . . . I'm holding a priceless object!" He looked around again, over his wife's arms, which were still around his neck. His eyes were hungry. "Look . . . do you think we could play it? Lord, what I'd give to hear some new music . . . just the first part, the orchestra part, before Como sings?"

Faces sobered. After a minute, John Sipich said, "I don't think we'd better, Dan. After all, we don't know just where the singer comes in—it'd be taking too much of a chance. Better wait till you get home."

Dan Hollis reluctantly put the record on the buffet with all his other presents. "It's *good,*" he said automatically, but disappointedly, "that I can't play it here."

"Oh, yes," said Sipich. "It's good." To compensate for Dan's disappointed tone, he repeated, "It's *good.*"

They ate dinner, the candles lighting their smiling faces, and ate it all right down to the last delicious drop of gravy. They complimented Mom and Aunt Amy on the roast beef, and the peas and carrots, and the tender corn on the cob. The corn hadn't come from the Fremont's cornfield, naturally—everybody knew what was out there; and the field was going to weeds.

Then they polished off the dessert—homemade ice cream and cookies. And then they sat back, in the flickering light of the candles, and chatted, waiting for television.

There never was a lot of mumbling on television night—everybody came and had a good dinner at the Fremonts', and that was nice, and afterwards there was television and nobody really thought much about that—it just had to be put up with. So it was a pleasant enough get-together, aside from your having to watch what you said just as carefully as you always did everyplace. If a dangerous thought came into your mind, you just started mumbling, even right in the middle of a sentence. When you did that, the others just ignored you until you felt happier again and stopped.

Anthony liked television night. He had done only two or three awful things on television night in the whole past year.

Mom had put a bottle of brandy on the table, and they each had a tiny glass of it. Liquor was even more precious than tobacco. The villagers could make wine, but the grapes weren't right, and certainly the techniques weren't, and it wasn't very good wine. There were only a few bottles of real liquor left in the village—four rye, three Scotch, three brandy, nine real wine and half a bottle of Drambuie belonging to old McIntyre (only for marriages)—and when those were gone, that was it.

Afterward, everybody wished that the brandy hadn't been brought out. Because Dan Hollis drank more of it than he should have, and mixed it with a lot of the homemade wine. Nobody thought anything about it at first, because he didn't show it much outside, and it was his birthday party and a happy party, and Anthony liked these get-togethers and shouldn't see any reason to do anything even if he was listening.

But Dan Hollis got high, and did a fool thing. If they'd seen it coming, they'd have taken him outside and walked him around.

The first thing they knew, Dan stopped laughing right in the middle of the story about how Thelma Dunn had found the Perry Como record and dropped it and it hadn't broken because she'd moved faster than she ever had before in her life and caught it. He was fondling the record again, and looking longingly at the Fremonts' gramophone over in the corner, and suddenly he stopped laughing and his face got slack, and then it got ugly, and he said, "Oh, *Christ!*"

Immediately the room was still. So still they could hear the whirring movement of the grandfather's clock out in the hall. Pat Reilly had been playing the piano, softly. He stopped, his hands poised over the yellowed keys.

The candles on the dining-room table flickered in a cool breeze that blew through the lace curtains over the bay window.

"Keep playing, Pat," Anthony's father said softly.

Pat started again. He played *Night and Day,* but his eyes were sidewise on Dan Hollis, and he missed notes.

Dan stood in the middle of the room, holding the record. In his other hand he held a glass of brandy so hard his hand shook.

They were all looking at him.

"Christ," he said again, and he made it sound like a dirty word.

Reverend Younger, who had been talking with Mom and Aunt Amy by the dining-room door, said "Christ" too—but he was using it in a prayer. His hands were clasped, and his eyes were closed.

John Sipich moved forward. "Now, Dan . . . it's *good* for you to talk that way. But you don't want to talk too much, you know."

Dan shook off the hand Sipich put on his arm.

"Can't even play my record," he said loudly. He looked down at the record, and then around at their faces. "Oh, my *God . . .*"

He threw the glassful of brandy against the wall. It splattered and ran down the wallpaper in streaks.

Some of the women gasped.

"Dan," Sipich said in a whisper. "Dan, cut it out—"

Pat Reilly was playing *Night and Day* louder, to cover up the sounds of the talk. It wouldn't do any good, though, if Anthony was listening.

Dan Hollis went over to the piano and stood by Pat's shoulder, swaying a little.

"Pat," he said. "Don't play *that.* Play *this.*" And he began to sing. Softly, hoarsely, miserably: "Happy birthday to me . . . Happy birthday to me . . ."

"Dan!" Ethel Hollis screamed. She tried to run across the room to him. Mary Sipich grabbed her arm and held her back. "Dan," Ethel screamed again. "Stop—"

"My God, be quiet!" hissed Mary Sipich, and pushed her toward one of the men, who put his hand over her mouth and held her still.

"—Happy birthday, dear Danny," Dan sang. "Happy birthday to me!" He stopped and looked down at Pat Reilly. "Play it, Pat. Play it, so I can sing right . . . you know I can't carry a tune unless somebody plays it!"

Pat Reilly put his hand on the keys and began *Lover*—in a slow waltz tempo, the way Anthony liked it. Pat's face was white. His hands fumbled.

Dan Hollis stared over at the dining-room door. At Anthony's mother, and at Anthony's father, who had gone to join her.

"You had him," he said. Tears gleamed on his cheeks as the candlelight caught them. *"You* had to go and *have* him . . ."

He closed his eyes, and the tears squeezed out. He sang loudly, "You are my sunshine . . . my only sunshine . . . you make me happy . . . when I am blue . . ."

Anthony *came* into the room.

Pat stopped playing. He froze. Everybody froze. The breeze rippled the curtains. Ethel Hollis couldn't even try to scream—she had fainted.

"Please don't take my sunshine . . . away . . ." Dan's voice faltered into silence. His eyes widened. He put both hands out in front of him, the empty glass in one, the record in the other. He hiccupped and said, *"No—"*

"Bad man," Anthony said, and thought Dan Hollis into something like nothing anyone would have believed possible, and then he thought the thing into a grave deep, deep in the cornfield.

The glass and record thumped on the rug. Neither broke.

Anthony's purple gaze went around the room.

Some of the people began mumbling. They all tried to smile. The sound of mumbling filled the room like a far-off approval. Out of the murmuring came one or two clear voices:

"Oh, it's a very *good* thing," said John Sipich.

"A good thing," said Anthony's father, smiling. He'd had more practice in smiling than most of them. "A wonderful thing."

"It's swell . . . just swell," said Pat Reilly, tears leaking from eyes and nose, and he began to play the piano again, softly, his trembling hands feeling for *Night and Day.*

Anthony climbed up on top of the piano, and Pat played for two hours.

Afterward, they watched television. They all went into the front room, and lit just a few candles, and pulled up chairs around the set. It was a small-screen set, and they couldn't all sit close enough to it to see, but that didn't matter. They didn't even turn the set on. It wouldn't have worked anyway, there being no electricity in Peaksville.

They just sat silently, and watched the twisting, writhing shapes on the screen, and listened to the sounds that came out of the speaker, and none of them had any idea of what it was all about. They never did. It was always the same.

"It's real nice," Aunt Amy said once, her pale eyes on meaningless flickers and shadows. "But I liked it a little better when there were cities outside and we could get real—"

"Why, Amy!" said Mom. "It's good for you to say such a thing. Very good. But how can you mean it? Why, this television is *much* better than anything we ever used to get!"

"Yes," chimed in John Sipich. "It's fine. It's the best show we've ever seen!"

He sat on the couch, with two other men, holding Ethel Hollis flat against the cushions, holding her arms and legs and putting their hands over her mouth, so she couldn't start screaming again.

"It's really *good!*" he said again.

Mom looked out of the front window, across the darkened road, across Henderson's darkened wheatfield to the vast, endless, gray nothingness in which the little village of Peaksville floated like a soul—the huge nothingness that was evident at night, when Anthony's brassy day had gone.

It did no good to wonder where they were . . . no good at all. Peaksville was just someplace. Someplace away from the world. It was wherever it had been since that day three years ago when Anthony had crept from her womb and old Doc Bates—God rest him—had screamed and dropped him and tried to kill him, and Anthony had whined and done the thing. He had taken the village someplace. Or had destroyed the world and left only the village, nobody knew which.

It did no good to wonder about it. Nothing at all did any good—except to live as they must live. Must always, always live, if Anthony would let them.

These thoughts were dangerous, she thought.

She began to mumble. The others started mumbling too. They had all been thinking, evidently.

The men on the couch whispered and whispered to Ethel Hollis, and when they took their hands away, she mumbled too.

While Anthony sat on top of the set and made television, they sat around and mumbled and watched the meaningless, flickering shapes far into the night.

Next day it snowed, and killed off half the crops—but it was a *good* day.

ANTHONY BOUCHER

THEY BITE

There was no path, only the almost vertical ascent. Crumbled rock for a few yards, with the roots of sage finding their scanty life in the dry soil. Then jagged outcroppings of crude crags, sometimes with accidental footholds, sometimes with overhanging and untrustworthy branches of greasewood, sometimes with no aid to climbing but the leverage of your muscles and the ingenuity of your balance.

The sage was as drably green as the rock was drably brown. The only color was the occasional rosy spikes of a barrel cactus.

Hugh Tallant swung himself up onto the last pinnacle. It had a deliberate, shaped look about it—a petrified fortress of Lilliputians, a Gibraltar of pygmies. Tallant perched on its battlements and unslung his field glasses.

The desert valley spread below him. The tiny cluster of buildings that was Oasis, the exiguous cluster of palms that gave name to the town and shelter of his own tent and the shack he was building, the dead-ended highway leading straighforwardly to nothing, the oiled roads diagraming the vacant blocks of an optimistic subdivision.

Tallant saw none of these. His glasses were fixed beyond the oasis and the town of Oasis on the dry lake. The gliders were clear and vivid to him, and the uniformed men busy with them were as sharply and minutely visible as a nest of ants under glass. The training school was more than usually active. One glider in particular, strange to Tallant, seemed the focus of attention. Men would come and examine it and glance back at the older models in comparison.

Only the corner of Tallant's left eye was not preoccupied with the new glider. In that corner something moved, something little and thin and brown as the earth. Too large for a rabbit, much too small for a man. It darted across the corner of vision, and Tallant found gliders oddly hard to concentrate on.

He sat down the bifocals and deliberately looked about him. His pinnacle surveyed the narrow, flat area of the crest. Nothing stirred. Nothing stood out against the sage and rock but one barrel of rosy spikes. He took up the glasses again and resumed his observations. When he was done, he methodically entered the results in the little black notebook.

His hand was still white. The desert is cold and often sunless in winter. But it was a firm hand, and as well trained as his eyes, fully capable of recording faithfully the designs and dimensions which they had registered so accurately.

Once his hand slipped, and he had to erase and redraw, leaving a smudge

58

that displeased him. The lean, brown thing had slipped across the edge of his vision again. Going toward the east edge, he would swear, where that set of rocks jutted like the spines on the back of a stegosaur.

Only when his notes were completed did he yield to curiosity, and even then with cynical self-reproach. He was physically tired, for him an unusual state, from this daily climbing and from clearing the ground for his shack-to-be. The eye muscles play odd nervous tricks. There could be nothing behind the stegosaur's armor.

There was nothing. Nothing alive and moving. Only the torn and half-plucked carcass of a bird, which looked as though it had been gnawed by some small animal.

It was halfway down the hill—hill in Western terminology, though anywhere east of the Rockies it would have been considered a sizable mountain—that Tallant again had a glimpse of a moving figure.

But this was no trick of a nervous eye. It was not little nor thin nor brown. It was tall and broad and wore a loud red-and-black lumberjacket. It bellowed, "Tallant!" in a cheerful and lusty voice.

Tallant drew near the man and said, "Hello." He paused and added, "Your advantage, I think."

The man grinned broadly. "Don't know me? Well, I daresay ten years is a long time, and the California desert ain't exactly the Chinese rice fields. How's stuff? Still loaded down with Secrets for Sale?"

Tallant tried desperately not to react to that shot, but he stiffened a little. "Sorry. The prospector getup had me fooled. Good to see you again, Morgan."

The man's eyes narrowed. "Just having my little joke," he smiled. "Of course you wouldn't have no serious reason for mountain climbing around a glider school, now, would you? And you'd kind of need field glasses to keep an eye on the pretty birdies."

"I'm out here for my health." Tallant's voice sounded unnatural even to himself.

Sure, sure. You were always in it for your health. And come to think of it, my own health ain't been none too good lately. I've got me a little cabin way to hell-and-gone around here, and I do me a little prospecting now and then. And somehow it just strikes me, Tallant, like maybe I hit a pretty good lode today."

"Nonsense, old man. You can see—"

"I'd sure hate to tell any of them Army men out at the field some of the stories I know about China and the kind of men I used to know out there. Wouldn't cotton to them stories a bit, the Army wouldn't. But if I was to have a drink too many and get talkative-like—"

"Tell you what," Tallant suggested brusquely. "It's getting near sunset now, and my tent's chilly for evening visits. But drop around in the morning and we'll talk over old times. Is rum still your tipple?"

"Sure is. Kind of expensive now, you understand—"

"I'll lay some in. You can find the place easily–over by the oasis. And we
.. we might be able to talk about your prospecting, too."

Tallant's thin lips were set firm as he walked away.

The bartender opened a bottle of beer and plunked it on the damp-circled
counter. "That'll be twenty cents," he said, then added as an afterthought,
"Want a glass? Sometimes tourists do."

Tallant looked at the others sitting at the counter–the red-eyed and
unshaven old man, the flight sergeant unhappily drinking a Coke–it was
after Army hours for beer–the young man with the long, dirty trench coat
and the pipe and the new-looking brown beard–and saw no glasses. "I guess
I won't be a tourist," he decided.

This was the first time Tallant had had a chance to visit the Desert Sport
Spot. It was as well to be seen around in a community. Otherwise people
begin to wonder and say, "Who is that man out by the oasis? Why don't you
ever see him anyplace?"

The Sport Spot was quiet that night. The four of them at the counter, two
Army boys shooting pool, and a half-dozen of the local men gathered about
a round poker table, soberly and wordlessly cleaning a construction worker
whose mind seemed more on his beer than on his cards.

"You just passing through?" the bartender asked sociably.

Tallant shook his head. "I'm moving in. When the Army turned me down
for my lungs, I decided I better do something about it. Heard so much about
your climate here I thought I might as well try it."

"Sure thing," the bartender nodded. "You take up until they started this
glider school, just about every other guy you meet in the desert is here for
his health. Me, I had sinus, and look at me now. It's the air."

Tallant breathed the atmosphere of smoke and beer suds, but did not
smile. "I'm looking forward to miracles."

"You'll get 'em. Whereabouts you staying?"

"Over that way a bit. The agent called it 'the old Carker place.' "

Tallant felt the curious listening silence and frowned. The bartender had
started to speak and then thought better of it. The young man with the beard
looked at him oddly. The old man fixed him with red and watery eyes that
had a faded glint of pity in them. For a moment, Tallant felt a chill that had
nothing to do with the night air of the desert.

The old man drank his beer in quick gulps and frowned as though trying
to formulate a sentence. At last he wiped beer from his bristly lips and said,
"You wasn't aiming to stay in the adobe, was you?"

"No. It's pretty much gone to pieces. Easier to rig me up a little shack than
try to make the adobe livable. Meanwhile, I've got a tent."

"That's all right, then, mebbe. But mind you don't go poking around that
there adobe."

"I don't think I'm apt to. But why not? Want another beer?"

The old man shook his head reluctantly and slid from his stool to the ground. "No thanks. I don't rightly know as I—"

"Yes?"

"Nothing. Thanks all the same." He turned and shuffled to the door.

Tallant smiled. "But why should I stay clear of the adobe?" he called after him.

The old man mumbled.

"What?"

"They bite," said the old man, and went out shivering into the night.

The bartender was back at his post. "I'm glad he didn't take that beer you offered him," he said. "Along about this time in the evening I have to stop serving him. For once he had the sense to quit."

Tallant pushed his own empty bottle forward. "I hope I didn't frighten him away."

"Frighten? Well, mister, I think maybe that's just what you did do. He didn't want beer that sort of came, like you might say, from the old Carker place. Some of the old-timers here, they're funny that way."

Tallant grinned. "Is it haunted?"

"Not what you'd call hanted, no. No ghosts there that I ever heard of." He wiped the counter with a cloth and seemed to wipe the subject away with it.

The flight sergeant pushed his Coke bottle away, hunted in his pocket for nickels, and went over to the pinball machine. The young man with the beard slid onto his vacant stool. "Hope old Jake didn't worry you," he said.

Tallant laughed. "I suppose every town has its deserted homestead with a grisly tradition. But this sounds a litle different. No ghosts, and they bite. Do you know anything about it?"

"A little," the young man said seriously. "A little. Just enough to—"

Tallant was curious. "Have one on me and tell me about it."

The flight sergeant swore bitterly at the machine.

Beer gurgled through the beard. "You see," the young man began, "the desert's so big you can't be alone in it. Ever notice that? It's all empty and there's nothing in sight, but there's always somthing moving over there where you can't quite see it. It's something very dry and thin and brown, only when you look around it isn't there. Ever see it?"

"Optical fatigue—" Tallant began.

"Sure. I know. Every man to his own legend. There isn't a tribe of Indians hasn't got some way of accounting for it. You've heard of the Watchers? And the twentieth-century white man comes along, and it's optical fatigue. Only in the nineteenth century things weren't quite the same, and there were the Carkers."

"You've got a special localized legend?"

"Call it that. You glimpse things out of the corner of your mind, same like you glimpse lean, dry things out of the corner of your eye. You encase 'em in solid circumstance and they're not so bad. That is known as the Growth of Legend. The Folk Mind in Action. You take the Carkers and the things you don't quite see and you put 'em together. And they bite."

Tallant wondered how long that beard had been absorbing beer. "And what were the Carkers?" he prompted politely.

"Ever hear of Sawney Bean? Scotland—reign of James First, or maybe the Sixth, though I think Roughead's wrong on that for once. Or let's be more modern—ever hear of the Benders? Kansas in the 1870s? No? Ever hear of Procrustes? Or Polyphemus? Or Fee fi-fo-fum?

"There are ogres, you know. They're no legend. They're fact, they are. The inn where nine guests left for every ten that arrived, the mountain cabin that sheltered travelers from the snow, sheltered them all winter till the melting spring uncovered their bones, the lonely stretches of road that so many passengers traveled halfway—you'll find 'em everywhere. All over Europe and pretty much in this country too before communications became what they are. Profitable business. And it wasn't just the profit. The Benders made money, sure; but that wasn't why they killed all their victims as carefully as a kosher butcher. Sawney Bean got so he didn't give a damn about the profit; he just needed to lay in more meat for the winter.

"And think of the chances you'd have at an oasis."

"So these Carkers of yours were, as you call them, ogres?"

"Carkers, ogres—maybe they were Benders. The Benders were never seen alive, you know, after the townspeople found those curiously butchered bones. There's a rumor they got this far west. And the time checks pretty well. There wasn't any town here in the eighties. Just a couple of Indian families, last of a dying tribe living on at the oasis. They vanished after the Carkers moved in. That's not so surprising. The white race is a sort of super-ogre, anyway. Nobody worried about them. But they used to worry about why so many travelers never got across this stretch of desert. The travelers used to stop over at the Carkers', you see, and somehow they often never got any farther. Their wagons'd be found maybe fifteen miles beyond in the desert. Sometimes they found the bones, too, parched and white. Gnawed-looking, they said sometimes."

"And nobody ever did anything about these Carkers?"

"Oh, sure. We didn't have King James Sixth—only I still think it was First—to ride up on a great white horse for a gesture, but twice Army detachments came here and wiped them all out."

"Twice? One wiping-out would do for most families." Tallant smiled.

"Uh-uh. That was no slip. They wiped out the Carkers twice because, you see, once didn't do any good. They wiped 'em out and still travelers vanished and still there were gnawed bones. So they wiped 'em out again. After that they gave up, and people detoured the oasis. It made a longer, harder trip, but after all—"

Tallant laughed. "You mean to say these Carkers were immortal?"

"I don't know about immortal. They somehow just didn't die very easy. Maybe, if they were the Benders—and I sort of like to think they were—they learned a little more about what they were doing out here on the desert. Maybe they put together what the Indians knew and what they knew, and it worked. Maybe Whatever they made their sacrifices to understood them better out here than in Kansas."

"And what's become of them—aside from seeing them out of the corner of the eye?"

"There's forty years between the last of the Carker history and this new settlement at the oasis. And people won't talk much about what they learned here in the first year or so. Only that they stay away from that old Carker adobe. They tell some stories—The priest says he was sitting in the confessional one hot Saturday afternoon and thought he heard a penitent come in. He waited a long time and finally lifted the gauze to see was anybody there. Something was there, and it bit. He's got three fingers on his right hand now, which looks funny as hell when he gives a benediction."

Tallant pushed their two bottles toward the bartender. "That yarn, my young friend, has earned another beer. How about it, bartender? Is he always cheerful like this, or is this just something he's improvised for my benefit?"

The bartender set out the fresh bottles with great solemnity. "Me, I wouldn't've told you all that myself, but then, he's a stranger too and maybe don't feel the same way we do here. For him it's just a story."

"It's more comfortable that way," said the young man with the beard, and he took a firm hold on his beer bottle.

"But as long as you've heard that much," said the bartender, "you might as well—It was last winter, when we had that cold spell. You heard funny stories that winter. Wolves coming into prospectors' cabins just to warm up. Well, business wasn't so good. We don't have a license for hard liquor, and the boys don't drink much beer when it's that cold. But they used to come in anyway because we've got that big oil burner.

"So one night there's a bunch of 'em in here—old Jake was here, that you was talking to, and his dog Jigger—and I think I hear somebody else come in. The door creaks a little. But I don't see nobody, and the poker game's going, and we're talking just like we're talking now, and all of a sudden I hear a kind of a noise like crack! over there in that corner behind the juke box near the burner.

"I go over to see what goes and it gets away before I can see it very good. But it was little and thin and it didn't have no clothes on. It must've been damned cold that winter."

"And what was the cracking noise?" Tallant asked dutifully.

"That? That was a bone. It must've strangled Jigger without any noise. He was a little dog. It ate most of the flesh, and if it hadn't cracked the bone for the marrow it could've finished. You can still see the spots over there. The blood never did come out."

There had ben silence all through the story. Now suddenly all hell broke loose. The flight sergeant let out a splendid yell and began pointing excitedly at the pinball machine and yelling for his payoff. The construction worker dramatically deserted the poker game, knocking his chair over in the process, and announced lugubriously that these guys here had their own rules, see?

Any atmosphere of Carker-inspired horror was dissipated. Tallant whistled as he walked over to put a nickel in the jukebox. He glanced casually at the floor. Yes, there was a stain, for what that was worth.

He smiled cheerfully and felt rather grateful to the Carkers. They were going to solve his blackmail problem very neatly.

Tallant dreamed of power that night. It was a common dream with him. He was a ruler of the new American Corporate State that would follow the war; and he said to this man, "Come!" and he came, and to that man, "Go!" and he went, and to his servants, "Do this!" and they did it.

Then the young man with the beard was standing before him, and the dirty trench coat was like the robes of an ancient prophet. And the young man said, "You see youself riding high, don't you? Riding the crest of the wave—the Wave of the Future, you call it. But there's a deep, dark undertow that you don't see, and that's a part of the Past. And the Present and even your Future. There is evil in mankind that is blacker even than your evil, and infinitely more ancient."

And there was something in the shadows behind the young man, something little and lean and brown.

Tallant's dream did not disturb him the following morning. Nor did the thought of the approaching interview with Morgan. He fried his bacon and eggs and devoured them cheerfully. The wind had died down for a change, and the sun was warm enough so that he could strip to the waist while he cleared land for his shack. His machete glinted brilliantly as it swung through the air and struck at the roots of the brush.

When Morgan arrived his full face was red and sweating.

"It's cool over there in the shade of the adobe," Tallant suggested. "We'll be more comfortable." And in the comfortable shade of the adobe he swung the machete once and clove Morgan's full, red, sweating face in two.

It was so simple. It took less effort than uprooting a clump of sage. And it was so safe. Morgan lived in a cabin way to hell-and-gone and was often away on prospecting trips. No one would notice his absence for months, if then. No one had any reason to connect him with Tallant. And no one in Oasis would hunt for him in the Carker-haunted adobe.

The body was heavy, and the blood dripped warm on Tallant's bare skin. With relief he dumped what had been Morgan on the floor of the adobe. There were no boards, no flooring. Just the earth. Hard, but not too hard to dig a grave in. And no one was likely to come poking around in this taboo territory to notice the grave. Let a year or so go by, and the grave and the bones it contained would be attributed to the Carkers.

The corner of Tallant's eye bothered him again. Deliberately he looked about the interior of the adobe.

The little furniture was crude and heavy, with no attempt to smooth down the strokes of the ax. It was held together with wooden pegs or half-rotted thongs. There were age-old cinders in the fireplace, and the dusty shards of a cooking jar among them.

And there was a deeply hollowed stone, covered with stains that might have been rust, if stone rusted. Behind it was a tiny figure, clumsily fashioned of clay and sticks. It was something like a man and something like a lizard, and something like the things that flit across the corner of the eye.

Curious now, Tallant peered about further. He penetrated to the corner that the one unglassed window lighted but dimly. And there he let out a little choking gasp. For a moment he was rigid with horror. Then he smiled and all but laughed aloud.

This explained everything. Some curious individual had seen this, and from his accounts had burgeoned the whole legend. The Carkers had indeed learned something from the Indians, but that secret was the art of embalming.

It was a perfect mummy. Either the Indian art had shrunk bodies, or this was that of a ten-year-old boy. There was no flesh. Only skin and bone and taut, dry stretches of tendon between. The eyelids were closed; the sockets looked hollow under them. The nose was sunken and almost lost. The scant lips were tightly curled back from the long and very white teeth, which stood forth all the more brilliantly against the deep-brown skin.

It was a curious little trove, this mummy. Tallant was already calculating the chances for raising a decent sum of money from an interested anthropologist—murder can produce such delightfully profitable chance byproducts—when he noticed the infinitesimal rise and fall of the chest.

The Carker was not dead. It was sleeping.

Tallant did not dare stop to think beyond the instant. This was no time to pause to consider if such things were possible in a well-ordered world. It was no time to reflect on the disposal of the body of Morgan. It was a time to snatch up your machete and get out of there.

But in the doorway he halted. There, coming across the desert, heading for the adobe, clearly seen this time, was another—a female.

He made an involuntary gesture of indecision. The blade of the machete clanged ringingly against the adobe wall. He heard the dry shuffling of a roused sleeper behind him.

He turned fully now, the machete raised. Dispose of this nearer one first, then face the female. There was no room even for terror in his thoughts, only for action.

The lean brown shape darted at him avidly. He moved lightly away and stood poised for its second charge. It shot forward again. He took one step back, machete arm raised, and fell headlong over the corpse of Morgan. Before he could rise, the thin thing was upon him. Its sharp teeth had met through the palm of his left hand.

The machete moved swiftly. The thin dry body fell headless to the floor. There was no blood.

The grip of the teeth did not relax. Pain coursed up Tallant's left arm—

sharper, more bitter pain than you would expect from a bit. Almost as though venom—

He dropped the machete, and his strong white hand plucked and twisted at the dry brown lips. The teeth stayed clenched, unrelaxing. He sat bracing his back against the wall and gripped the head between his knees. He pulled. His flesh ripped, and blood formed dusty clots on the dirt floor. But the bite was firm.

His world had become reduced now to that hand and that head. Nothing outside mattered. He must free himself. He raised his aching arm to his face, and with his own teeth he tore at that unrelenting grip. The dry flesh crumbled away in desert dust, but the teeth were locked fast. He tore his lip against their white keenness, and tasted in his mouth the sweetness of blood and something else.

He staggered to his feet again. He knew what he must do. Later he could use cautery, a tourniquet, see a doctor with a story about a Gila monster—their heads grip too, don't they?—but he knew what he must do now.

He raised the machete and struck again.

His white hand lay on the brown floor, gripped by the white teeth in the brown face. He propped himself against the adobe wall, momentarily unable to move. His open wrist hung over the deeply hollowed stone. His blood and his strength and his life poured out before the little figure of sticks and clay.

The female stood in the doorway now, the sun bright on her thin brownness. She did not move. He knew that she was waiting for the hollow stone to fill.

RAY BRADBURY

THE LAST NIGHT OF THE WORLD

"What would you do if you knew that this was the last night of the world?"

"What would I do? You mean seriously?"

"Yes, seriously."

"I don't know. I hadn't thought."

He poured some coffee. In the background the two girls were playing blocks on the parlor rug in the light of the green hurricane lamps. There was an easy, clean aroma of the brewed coffee in the evening air.

"Well, better start thinking about it," he said.

"You don't mean it!"

He nodded.

"A war?"

He shook his head.

"Not the hydrogen or atom bomb?"

"No."

"Or germ warfare?"

"None of those at all," he said, stirring his coffee slowly. "But just, let's say, the closing of a book."

"I don't think I understand."

"No, nor do I, really; it's just a feeling. Sometimes it frightens me, sometimes I'm not frightened at all but at peace." He glanced in at the girls and their yellow hair shining in the lamplight. "I didn't say anything to you. It first happened about four nights ago."

"What?"

"A dream I had. I dreamed that it was all going to be over, and a voice said it was; not any kind of voice I can remember, but a voice anyway, and it said things would stop here on Earth. I didn't think too much about it the next day, but then I went to the office and caught Stan Willis looking out the window in the middle of the afternoon, and I said a penny for your thoughts, Stan, and he said, I had a dream last night, and before he even told me the dream I knew what it was. I could have told him, but he told me and I listened to him."

"It was the same dream?"

"The same. I told Stan I had dreamed it too. He didn't seem surprised. He relaxed, in fact. Then we started walking through the office, for the hell of it. It wasn't planned. We didn't say, 'Let's walk around.' We just walked on our own, and everywhere we saw people looking at their desks or their hands or out windows. I talked to a few. So did Stan."

"And they all had dreamed?"

"All of them. The same dream, with no difference."

"Do you believe in it?"

"Yes. I've never been more certain."

"And when will it stop? The world, I mean."

"Sometime during the night for us, and then as the night goes on around the world, that'll go too. It'll take twenty-four hours for it all to go."

They sat awhile not touching their coffee. Then they lifted it slowly and drank, looking at each other.

"Do we deserve this?" she said.

"It's not a matter of deserving; it's just that things didn't work out. I notice you didn't even argue about this. Why not?"

"I guess I've a reason," she said.

"The same one everyone at the office had?"

She nodded slowly. "I didn't want to say anything. It happened last night. And the women on the block talked about it, among themselves, today. They dreamed. I thought it was only a coincidence." She picked up the evening paper. "There's nothing in the paper about it."

"Everyone knows, so there's no need."

He sat back in his chair, watching her. "Are you afraid?"

"No. I always thought I would be, but I'm not."

"Where's that spirit called self-preservation they talk so much about?"

"I don't know. You don't get too excited when you feel things are logical. This is logical. Nothing else but this could have happened from the way we've lived."

"We haven't been too bad, have we?"

"No, nor enormously good. I suppose that's the trouble—we haven't been very much of anything except us, while a big part of the world was busy being lots of quite awful things."

The girls were laughing in the parlor.

"I always thought people would be screaming in the streets at a time like this."

"I guess not. You don't scream about the real thing."

"Do you know, I won't miss anything but you and the girls. I never liked cities or my work or anything except you three. I won't miss a thing except perhaps the change in the weather, and a glass of ice water when it's hot, and I might miss sleeping. How can we sit here and talk this way?"

"Because there's nothing else to do."

"That's it, of course; for if there were, we'd be doing it. I suppose this is the first time in the history of the world that everyone has known just what they were going to do during the night."

"I wonder what everyone else will do now, this evening, for the next few hours."

"Go to a show, listen to the radio, watch television, play cards, put the children to bed, go to bed themselves, like always."

"In a way that's something to be proud of—like always."

They sat a moment and then he poured himself another coffee. "Why do you suppose it's tonight?"

"Because."

"Why not some other night in the last century, or five centuries ago, or ten?"

"Maybe it's because it was never October 19, 1969, ever before in history, and now it is and that's it; because this date means more than any other date ever meant; because it's the year when things are as they are all over the world and that's why it's the end."

"There are bombers on their schedules both ways across the ocean tonight that'll never see land."

"That's part of the reason why."

"Well," he said, getting up, "what shall it be? Wash the dishes?"

They washed the dishes and stacked them away with special neatness. At eight-thirty the girls were put to bed and kissed good night and the little lights by their beds turned on and the door left open just a trifle.

"I wonder," said the husband, coming from the bedroom and glancing back, standing there with his pipe for a moment.

"What?"

"If the door will be shut all the way, or if it'll be left just a little ajar so some light comes in."

"I wonder if the children know."

"No, of course not."

They sat and read the papers and talked and listened to some radio music and then sat together by the fireplace watching the charcoal embers as the clock struck ten-thirty and eleven and eleven-thirty. They thought of all the other people in the world who had spent their evening, each in his own special way.

"Well," he said at last.

He kissed his wife for a long time.

"We've been good for each other, anyway."

"Do you want to cry?" he asked.

"I don't think so."

They moved through the house and turned out the lights and went into the bedroom and stood in the night cool darkness undressing and pushing back the covers. "The sheets are so clean and nice."

"I'm tired."

"We're all tired."

They got into bed and lay back.

"Just a moment," she said.

He heard her get out of bed and go into the kitchen. A moment later she returned. "I left the water running in the sink," she said.

Something about this was so very funny that he had to laugh.

She laughed with him, knowing what it was that she had done that was funny. They stopped laughing at last and lay in their cool night bed, their hands clasped, their heads together.

"Good night," he said, after a moment.

"Good night," she said.

RICHARD MATHESON

BORN OF MAN AND WOMAN

X—This day when it had light mother called me retch. You retch she said. I saw in her eyes the anger. I wonder what it is a retch.

This day it had water falling from upstairs. It fell all around. I saw that. The ground of the back I watched from the little window. The ground it sucked up the water like thirsty lips. It drank too much and it got sick and runny brown. I didn't like it.

Mother is a pretty I know. In my bed place with cold walls around I have a paper things that was behind the furnace. It says on it SCREENSTARS. I see in the pictures faces like of mother and father. Father says they are pretty. Once he said it.

And also mother he said. Mother so pretty and me decent enough. Look at you he said and didnt have the nice face. I touched his arm and said it is alright father. He shook and pulled away where I couldnt reach.

Today mother let me off the chain a little so I could look out the little window. Thats how I saw the water falling from upstairs.

XX—This day it had goldness in the upstairs. As I know when I looked at it my eyes hurt. After I look at it the cellar is red.

I think this was church. They leave the upstairs. The big machine swallows them and rolls out past and is gone. In the back part is the little mother. She is much smaller than me. I am I can see out the little window all I like.

In this day when it got dark I had eat my food and some bugs. I hear laughs upstairs. I like to know why there are laughs for. I took the chain from the wall and wrapped it around me. I walked squish to the stairs. They creak when I walk on them. My legs slip on them because I dont walk on stairs. My feet stick to the wood.

I went up and opened a door. It was a white place. White as white jewels that come from upstairs sometime. I went in and stood quiet. I hear the laughing some more. I walk to the sound and look through to the people. More people than I thought was. I thought I should laugh with them.

Mother came out and pushed the door in. It hit me and hurt. I fell back on the smooth floor and the chain made noise. I cried. She made a hissing noise into her and put her hand on her mouth. Her eyes got big.

She looked at me. I heard father call. What fell he called. She said a iron

71

board. Come help pick it up she said. He came and said now is *that* so heavy
you need. He saw me and grew big. The anger came in his eyes. He hit me. I
spilled some of the drip on the floor from one arm. It was not nice. It made
ugly green on the floor.

Father told me to go to the cellar. I had to go. The light it hurt some now
in my eyes. It is not so like that in the cellar.

Father tied my legs and arms up. He put me on my bed. Upstairs I heard
laughing while I was quiet there looking on a black spider that was swinging
down to me. I thought what father said. Ohgod he said. And only eight.

XXX—This day father hit in the chain before it had light. I have to try pull
it out again. He said I was bad to come upstairs. He said never do that again
or he would beat me hard. That hurts.

I hurt. I slept the day and rested my head against the cold wall. I thought
of the white place upstairs.

XXXX—I got the chain from the wall out. Mother was upstairs. I heard
little laughs very high. I looked out the window. I saw all little people like
the little mother and little fathers too. They are pretty.

They were making nice noise and jumping around the ground. Their legs
was moving hard. They are like mother and father. Mother says all right
people look like they do.

One of the little fathers saw me. He pointed at the window. I let go and
slid down the wall in the dark. I curled up as they would not see. I heard
their talks by the window and foots running. Upstairs there was a door
hitting. I heard the little mother call upstairs. I heard heavy steps and I
rushed in my bed place. I hit the chain in the wall and lay down on my front.

I heard mother come down. Have you been at the window she said. I
heard the anger. *Stay* away from the window. You have pulled the chain out
again.

She took the stick and hit me with it. I didnt cry. I cant do that. But the
drip ran all over the bed. She saw it and twisted away and made a noise. Oh
mygodmygod she said why have you *done* this to me? I heard the stick go
bounce on the stone floor. She ran upstairs. I slept the day.

XXXXX—This day it had water again. When mother was upstairs I heard
the little one come slow down the steps. I hidded myself in the coal bin for
mother would have anger if the little mother saw me.

She had a little live thing with her. It walked on the arms and had pointy
ears. She said things to it.

It was all right except the live thing smelled me. It ran up the coal and
looked down at me. The hairs stood up. In the throat it made an angry noise.
I hissed but it jumped on me.

I didnt want to hurt it. I got fear because it bit me harder than the rat
does. I hurt and the little mother screamed. I grabbed the live thing tight. It

made sounds I never heard. I pushed it all together. It was all lumpy and red on the black coal.

I hid there when mother called. I was afraid of the stick. She left. I crept over the coal with the thing. I hid it under my pillow and rested on it. I put the chain in the wall again.

X—This is another times. Father chained me tight. I hurt because he beat me. This time I hit the stick out of his hands and made noise. He went away and his face was white. He ran out of my bed place and locked the door.

I am not so glad. All day it is cold in here. The chain comes slow out of the wall. And I have a bad anger with mother and father. I will show them. I will do what I did that once.

I will screech and laugh loud. I will run on the walls. Last I will hang head down by all my legs and laugh and drip green all over until they are sorry they didnt be nice to me.

If they try to beat me again Ill hurt them. I will.

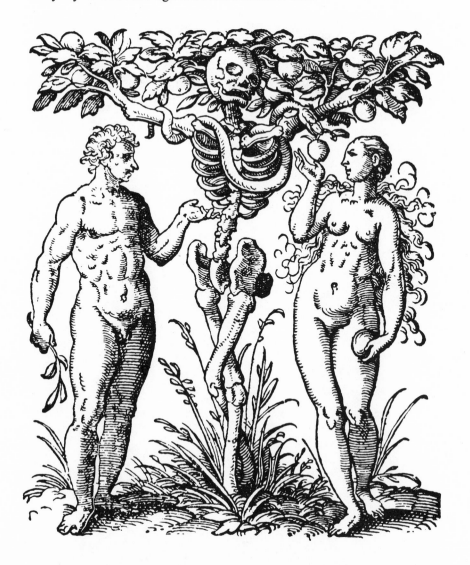

JOHN CROWE RANSOM

PIAZZA PIECE

—I am a gentleman in a dustcoat trying
To make you hear. Your ears are soft and small
And listen to an old man not at all,
They want the young men's whispering and sighing.
But see the roses on your trellis dying
And hear the spectral singing of the moon;
For I must have my lovely lady soon,
I am a gentleman in a dustcoat trying.

—I am a lady young in beauty waiting
Until my truelove comes, and then we kiss.
But what grey man among the vines is this
Whose words are dry and faint as in a dream?
Back from my trellis, Sir, before I scream!
I am a lady young in beauty waiting.

JORGE LUIS BORGES

THE SOUTH

The man who landed in Buenos Aires in 1871 bore the name of Johannes Dahlmann and he was a minister in the Evangelical Church. In 1939, one of his grandchildren, Juan Dahlmann, was secretary of a municipal library on Calle Córdoba, and he considered himself profoundly Argentinian. His maternal grandfather had been that Francisco Flores, of the Second Line-Infantry Division, who had died on the frontier of Buenos Aires, run through with a lance by Indians from Catriel; in the discord inherent between his two lines of descent, Juan Dahlmann (perhaps driven to it by his Germanic blood) chose the line represented by his romantic ancestor, his ancestor of the romantic death. An old sword, a leather frame containing the daguerreotype of a blank-faced man with a beard, the dash and grace of certain music, the familiar strophes of *Martín Fierro,* the passing years, boredom and solitude, all went to foster this voluntary, but never ostentatious nationalism. At the cost of numerous small privations, Dahlmann had managed to save the empty shell of a ranch in the South which had belonged to the Flores family; he continually recalled the image of the balsamic eucalyptus trees and the great rose-colored house which had once been crimson. His duties, perhaps even indolence, kept him in the city. Summer after summer he contented himself with the abstract idea of possession and with the certitude that his ranch was waiting for him on a precise site in the middle of the plain. Late in February, 1939, something happened to him.

Blind to all fault, destiny can be ruthless at one's slightest distraction. Dahlmann had succeeded in acquiring, on that very afternoon, an imperfect copy of Weil's edition of *The Thousand and One Nights.* Avid to examine this find, he did not wait for the elevator but hurried up the stairs. In the obscurity, something brushed by his forehead: a bat, a bird? On the face of the woman who opened the door to him he saw horror engraved, and the hand he wiped across his face came away red with blood. The edge of a recently painted door which someone had forgotten to close had caused this wound. Dahlmann was able to fall asleep, but from the moment he awoke at dawn the savor of all things was atrociously poignant. Fever wasted him and the pictures in *The Thousand and One Nights* served to illustrate nightmares. Friends and relatives paid him visits and, with exaggerated smiles, assured him that they thought he looked fine. Dahlmann listened to them with a kind of feeble stupor and he marveled at their not knowing that he was in hell. A week, eight days passed, and they were like eight centuries. One afternoon, the usual doctor appeared, accompanied by a new doctor, and they carried him off to a sanitarium on the Calle Ecuador, for it was necessary to X-ray him. Dahlmann, in the hackney coach which bore them away, thought that he would, at last, be able to sleep in a room different from his own. He felt happy and communicative. When he arrived at his destination, they undressed him, shaved his head, bound him with metal fastenings to a stretcher; they shone bright lights on him until he was blind and dizzy, auscultated him, and a masked man stuck a needle into his arm. He awoke with a feeling of nausea, covered with a bandage, in a cell with something of a well about it; in the days and nights which followed the operation he came to realize that he had merely been, up until then, in a suburb of hell. Ice in his mouth did not leave the least trace of freshness. During these days Dahlmann hated himself in minute detail: he hated his identity, his bodily necessities, his humiliation, the beard which bristled upon his face. He stoically endured the curative measures, which were painful, but when the surgeon told him he had been on the point of death from septicemia, Dahlmann dissolved in tears of self-pity for his fate. Physical wretchedness and the incessant anticipation of horrible nights had not allowed him time to think of anything so abstract as death. On another day, the surgeon told him he was healing and that, very soon, he would be able to go to his ranch for convalescence. Incredibly enough, the promised day arrived.

Reality favors symmetries and slight anachronisms: Dahlmann had arrived at the sanitarium in a hackney coach and now a hackney coach was to take him to the Constitución station. The first fresh tang of autumn, after the summer's oppressiveness, seemed like a symbol in nature of his rescue and release from fever and death. The city, at seven in the morning, had not lost that air of an old house lent it by the night; the streets seemed like long vestibules, the plazas were like patios. Dahlmann recognized the city with joy on the edge of vertigo: a second before his eyes registered the phenomena themselves, he recalled the corners, the billboards, the modest variety of Buenos Aires. In the yellow light of the new day, all things returned to him.

Every Argentine knows that the South begins at the other side of Rivadavia. Dahlmann was in the habit of saying that this was no mere convention, that whoever crosses this street enters a more ancient and sterner world. From inside the carriage he sought out, among the new buildings, the iron grille window, the brass knocker, the arched door, the entranceway, the intimate patio.

At the railroad station he noted that he still had thirty minutes. He quickly recalled that in a café on the Calle Brazil (a few dozen feet from Yrigoyen's house) there was an enormous cat which allowed itself to be caressed as if it were a disdainful divinity. He entered the café. There was the cat, asleep. He ordered a cup of coffee, slowly stirred the sugar, sipped it (this pleasure had been denied him in that clinic), and thought, as he smoothed the cat's black coat, that this contact was an illusion and that the two beings, man and cat, were as good as separated by a glass, for man lives in time, in succession, while the magical animal lives in the present, in the eternity of the instant.

Along the next to the last platform the train lay waiting. Dahlmann walked through the coaches until he found one almost empty. He arranged his baggage in the network rack. When the train started off, he took down his valise and extracted, after some hesitation, the first volume of *The Thousand and One Nights*. To travel with this book, which was so much a part of the history of his ill-fortune, was a kind of affirmation that his ill-fortune had been annulled; it was a joyous and secret defiance of the frustrated forces of evil.

Along both sides of the train the city dissipated into suburbs; this sight, and then a view of the gardens and villas, delayed the beginning of his reading. The truth was that Dahlmann read very little. The magnetized mountain and the genie who swore to kill his benefactor are—who would deny it?—marvelous, but not so much more than the morning itself and the mere fact of being. The joy of life distracted him from paying attention to Scheherazade and her superfluous miracles. Dahlmann closed his book and allowed himself to live.

Lunch—the bouillon served in shining metal bowls, as in the remote summers of childhood—was one more peaceful and rewarding delight.

Tomorrow I'll wake up at the ranch, he thought, and it was as if he was two men at a time: the man who traveled through the autumn day and across the geography of the fatherland, and the other one, locked up in a sanitarium and subject to methodical servitude. He saw unplastered brick houses, long and angled, timelessly watching the trains go by; he saw horsemen along the dirt roads; he saw gullies and lagoons and ranches; he saw great luminous clouds that resembled marble; and all these things were accidental, casual, like dreams of the plain. He also thought he recognized trees and crop fields; but he would not have been able to name them, for his actual knowledge of the countryside was quite inferior to his nostalgic and literary knowledge.

From time to time he slept, and his dreams were animated by the impetus of the train. The intolerable white sun of high noon had already become the yellow sun which precedes nightfall, and it would not be long before it would turn red. The railroad car was now also different; it was not the same as the one which had quit the station siding at Constitución; the plain and the hours had transfigured it. Outside, the moving shadow of the railroad car stretched toward the horizon. The elemental earth was not perturbed either by settlements or other signs of humanity. The country was vast but at the same time intimate and, in some measure, secret. The limitless country sometimes contained only a solitary bull. The solitude was perfect, perhaps hostile, and it might have occurred to Dahlmann that he was traveling into the past and not merely south. He was distracted from these considerations by the railroad inspector who, on reading his ticket, advised him that the train would not let him off at the regular station but at another: an earlier stop, one scarcely known to Dahlmann. (The man added an explanation which Dahlmann did not attempt to understand, and which he hardly heard, for the mechanism of events did not concern him.)

The train laboriously ground to a halt, practically in the middle of the plain. The station lay on the other side of the tracks; it was not much more than a siding and a shed. There was no means of conveyance to be seen, but the station chief supposed that the traveler might secure a vehicle from a general store and inn to be found some ten or twelve blocks away.

Dahlmann accepted the walk as a small adventure. The sun had already disappeared from view, but a final splendor exalted the vivid and silent plain, before the night erased its color. Less to avoid fatigue than to draw out his enjoyment of these sights, Dahlmann walked slowly, breathing in the odor of clover with sumptuous joy.

The general store at one time had been painted a deep scarlet, but the years had tempered this violent color for its own good. Something in its poor architecture recalled a steel engraving, perhaps one from an old edition of *Paul et Virginie.* A number of horses were hitched up to the paling. Once inside, Dahlmann thought he recognized the shopkeeper. Then he realized that he had been deceived by the man's resemblance to one of the male nurses in the sanitarium. When the shopkeeper heard Dahlmann's request, he said he would have the shay made up. In order to add one more event to that day and to kill time, Dahlmann decided to eat at the general store.

Some country louts, to whom Dahlmann did not at first pay any attention, were eating and drinking at one of the tables. On the floor, and hanging on to the bar, squatted an old man, immobile as an object. His years had reduced and polished him as water does a stone or the generations of men do a sentence. He was dark, dried up, diminutive, and seemed outside time, situated in eternity. Dahlmann noted with satisfaction the kerchief, the thick poncho, the long *chiripá,* and the colt boots, and told himself, as he recalled futile discussions with people from the Northern counties or from the province of Entre Rios, that gauchos like this no longer existed outside the South.

Dahlmann sat down next to the window. The darkness began overcoming the plain, but the odor and sound of the earth penetrated the iron bars of the window. The shop owner brought him sardines, followed by some roast meat. Dahlmann washed the meal down with several glasses of red wine. Idling, he relished the tart savor of the wine, and let his gaze, now grown somewhat drowsy, wander over the shop. A kerosene lamp hung from a beam. There were three customers at the other table: two of them appeared to be farm workers; the third man, whose features hinted at Chinese blood, was drinking with his hat on. Of a sudden Dahlmann felt something brush lightly against his face. Next to the heavy glass of turbid wine, upon one of the stripes in the tablecloth, lay a spit ball of breadcrumb. That was all: but someone had thrown it there.

The men at the other table seemed totally cut off from him. Perplexed, Dahlmann decided that nothing had happened, and he opened the volume of *The Thousand and One Nights,* by way of suppressing reality. After a few moments another little ball landed on his table, and now the *peones* laughed outright. Dahlmann said to himself that he was not frightened, but he reasoned that it would be a major blunder if he, a convalescent, were to allow himself to be dragged by strangers into some chaotic quarrel. He determined to leave, and had already gotten to his feet when the owner came up and exhorted him in an alarmed voice:

"*Señor* Dahlmann, don't pay any attention to those lads; they're half high."

Dahlmann was not surprised to learn that the other man, now, knew his name. But he felt that these conciliatory words served only to aggravate the situation. Previously to this moment, the *peones'* provocation was directed against an unknown face, against no one in particular, almost against no one at all. Now it was an attack against him, against his name, and his neighbors knew it. Dahlmann pushed the owner aside, confronted the *peones,* and demanded to know what they wanted of him.

The tough with the Chinese look staggered heavily to his feet. Almost in Juan Dahlmann's face he shouted insults, as if he had been a long way off. His game was to exaggerate his drunkenness, and this extravagance constituted a ferocious mockery. Between curses and obscenities, he threw a long knife into the air, followed it with his eyes, caught and juggled it, and challenged Dahlmann to a knife fight. The owner objected in a tremulous voice, pointing out that Dahlmann was unarmed. At this point, something unforeseeable occurred.

From a corner of the room, the old ecstatic gaucho—in whom Dahlmann saw a summary and cipher of the South (his South)—threw him a naked dagger, which landed at his feet, It was as if the South had resolved that Dahlmann should accept the duel. Dahlmann bent over to pick up the dagger, and felt two things. The first, that this almost instinctive act bound him to fight. The second, that the weapon, in his torpid hand, was no defense at all, but would merely serve to justify his murder. He had once played with a poniard, like all men, but his idea of fencing and knife-play did not go further than the notion that all strokes should be directed upward, with the cutting edge held inward. *They would not have allowed such things to happen to me in the sanitarium,* he thought.

"Let's get on our way," said the other man.

They went out and if Dahlmann was without hope, he was also without fear. As he crossed the threshold, he felt that to die in a knife fight, under the open sky, and going forward to the attack, would have been a liberation, a joy, and a festive occasion, on the first night in the sanitarium, when they stuck him with the needle. He felt that if he had been able to choose, then, or to dream his death, this would have been the death he would have chosen or dreamt.

Firmly clutching his knife, which he perhaps would not know how to wield, Dahlmann went out into the plain.

—Translated by Anthony Kerrigan

GEORGE LANGELAAN

THE FLY

Telephones and telephone bells have always made me uneasy. Years ago, when they were mostly wall fixtures, I disliked them, but nowadays, when they are planted in every nook and corner, they are a downright intrusion. We have a saying in France that a coalman is master in his own house; with the telephone that is no longer true, and I suspect that even the Englishman is no longer king in his own castle.

At the office, the sudden ringing of the telephone annoys me. It means that, no matter what I am doing, in spite of the switchboard operator, in spite of my secretary, in spite of doors and walls, some unknown person is coming into the room and onto my desk to talk right into my very ear, confidentially—and that whether I like it or not. At home, the feeling is still more disagreeable, but the worst is when the telephone rings in the dead of the night. If anyone could see me turn on the light and get up blinking to answer it, I suppose I would look like any other sleepy man annoyed at being disturbed. The truth in such a case, however, is that I am struggling against panic, fighting down a feeling that a stranger has broken into the house and is in my bedroom. By the time I manage to grab the receiver and say: *"Ici Monsieur Delambre. Je vous écoute,"* I am outwardly calm, but I only get back to a more normal state when I recognize the voice at the other end and when I know what is wanted of me.

This effort at dominating a purely animal reaction and fear had become so effective that when my sister-in-law called me at two in the morning, asking me to come over, but first to warn the police that she had just killed my brother, I quietly asked her how and why she had killed Andre.

"But, Francois! . . . I can't explain all that over the telephone. Please call the police and come quickly."

"Maybe I had better see you first, Helene?"

"No, you'd better call the police first; otherwise they will start asking you all sorts of awkward questions. They'll have enough trouble as it is to believe that I did it alone . . . And, by the way, I suppose you ought to tell them that Andre . . . Andre's body, is down at the factory. They may want to go there first."

"Did you say that Andre is at the factory?"

"Yes . . . under the steam-hammer."

"Under the what!"

"The steam-hammer! But don't ask so many questions. Please come quickly Francois! Please understand that I'm afraid . . . that my nerves won't stand it much longer!"

Have you ever tried to explain to a sleepy police officer that your sister-in-law has just phoned to say that she has killed your brother with a steam-hammer? I repeated my explanation, but he would not let me.

"*Oui, Monsieur, oui,* I hear . . . but who are you? What is your name? Where do you live? I said, where do you live!"

It was then that Commissaire Charas took over the line and the whole business. He at least seemed to understand everything. Would I wait for him? Yes, he would pick me up and take me over to my brother's house. When? In five or 10 minutes.

I had just managed to pull on my trousers, wriggle into a sweater and grab a hat and coat, when a black Citroen, headlights blazing, pulled up at the door.

"I assume you have a night watchman at your factory, Monsieur De-lambre. Has he called you?" asked Commissaire Charas, letting in the clutch as I sat down beside him and slammed the door of the car.

"No, he hasn't. Though of course my brother could have entered the factory through his laboratory where he often works late at night . . . all night sometimes."

"Is Professor Delambre's work connected with your business?"

"No, my brother is, or was, doing research work for the Ministère de l'Air. As he wanted to be away from Paris and yet within reach of where skilled workmen could fix up or make gadgets big and small for his experiments, I offered him one of the old workshops of the factory and he came to live in the first house built by our grandfather on the top of the hill at the back of the factory."

"Yes, I see. Did he talk about his work? What sort of research work?"

"He rarely talked about it, you know; I suppose the Air Ministry could tell you. I only know that he was about to carry out a number of experiments he had been preparing for some months, something to do with the disintegration of matter, he told me."

Barely slowing down, the Commissaire swung the car off the road, slid it through the open factory gate and pulled up sharp by a policeman apparently expecting him.

I did not need to hear the policeman's confirmation. I knew now that my brother was dead, it seemed that I had been told years ago. Shaking like a leaf, I scrambled out after the Commissaire.

Another policeman stepped out of a doorway and led us towards one of the shops where all the lights had been turned on. More policemen were standing by the hammer, watching two men setting up a camera. It was tilted downwards, and I made an effort to look.

It was far less horrid than I had expected. Though I had never seen my brother drunk, he looked just as if he were sleeping off a terrific binge, flat on his stomach across the narrow line on which the white-hot slabs of metal were rolled up to the hammer. I saw at a glance that his head and arm could only be a flattened mess, but that seemed quite impossible; it looked as if he had somehow pushed his head and arm right into the metallic mass of the hammer.

Having talked to his colleagues, the Commissaire turned towards me:

"How can we raise the hammer, Monsieur Delambre?"

"I'll raise it for you."

"Would you like us to get some of your men over?"

"No, I'll be all right. Look, here is the switchboard. It was originally a steam-hammer, but everything is worked electrically here now. Look Commissaire, the hammer has been set at 50 tons and its impact at zero."

"At zero . . . ?"

"Yes, level with the ground if you prefer. It is also set for single strokes, which means that it has to be raised after each blow. I don't know what Helene, my sister-in-law, will have to say about all this, but one thing I am sure of: she certainly did not know how to set and operate the hammer."

"Perhaps it was set that way last night when work stopped?"

"Certainly not. The drop is never set at zero, Monsieur le Commissaire."

"I see. Can it be raised gently?"

"No. The speed of the upstroke cannot be regulated. But in any case it is not very fast when the hammer is set for single strokes."

"Right. Will you show me what to do? It won't be very nice to watch, you know."

"No, no, Monsieur le Commissaire. I'll be all right."

"All set?" asked the Commissaire of the others. "All right then, Monsieur Delambre. Whenever you like."

Watching my brother's back, I slowly but firmly pushed the upstroke button.

The unusual silence of the factory was broken by the sigh of compressed air rushing into the cylinders, a sigh that always makes me think of a giant taking a deep breath before solemnly socking another giant, and the steel mass of the hammer shuddered and then rose swiftly. I also heard the sucking sound as it left the metal base and thought I was going to panic when I saw Andre's body heave forward as a sickly gush of blood poured all over the ghastly mess bared by the hammer.

"No danger of it coming down again, Monsieur Delambre?"

"No, none whatever," I mumbled as I threw the safety switch and, turning around, I was violently sick in front of a young green-faced policeman.

For weeks after, Commissaire Charas worked on the case, listening, questioning, running all over the place, making out reports, telegraphing and telephoning right and left. Later, we became quite friendly and he owned that he had for a long time considered me as suspect number one, but had finally given up that idea because, not only was there no clue of any sort, but not even a motive.

Helene, my sister-in-law, was so calm throughout the whole business that the doctors finally confirmed what I had long considered the only possible solution: that she was mad. That being the case, there was of course no trial.

My brother's wife never tried to defend herself in any way and even got quite annoyed when she realized that people thought her mad, and this of course was considered proof that she was indeed mad. She owned up to the murder of her husband and proved easily that she knew how to handle the hammer; but she would never say why, exactly how, or under what circumstances she had killed my brother. The great mystery was how and why had my brother so obligingly stuck his head under the hammer, the only possible explanation for his part in the drama.

The night watchman had heard the hammer all right; he had even heard it twice, he claimed. This was very strange, and the stroke-counter, which was always set back to nought after a job, seemed to prove him right, since it marked the figure two. Also, the foreman in charge of the hammer confirmed that after cleaning up the day before the murder, he had as usual turned the stroke-counter back to nought. In spite of this, Helene maintained that she had only used the hammer once, and this seemed just another proof of her insanity.

Commissaire Charas, who had been put in charge of the case, at first wondered if the victim were really my brother. But of that there was no possible doubt, if only because of the great scar running from his knee to his thigh, the result of a shell that had landed within a few feet of him during the retreat in 1940; and there were also the fingerprints of his left hand which corresponded to those found all over his laboratory and his personal belongings up at the house.

A guard had been put on his laboratory and the next day half-a-dozen officials came down from the Air Ministry. They went through all his papers and took away some of his instruments, but before leaving, they told the Commissaire that the most interesting documents and instruments had been destroyed.

The Lyons police laboratory, one of the most famous in the world, reported that Andre's head had been wrapped up in a piece of velvet when it was crushed by the hammer, and one day Commissaire Charas showed me a tattered drapery which I immediately recognized as the brown velvet cloth I had seen on a table in my brother's laboratory, the one on which his meals were served when he could not leave his work.

After only a very few days in prison, Helene had been transferred to a nearby asylum, one of the three in France where insane criminals are taken care of. My nephew Henri, a boy of six, the very image of his father, was entrusted to me, and eventually all legal arrangements were made for me to become his guardian and tutor.

Helene, one of the quietest patients of the asylum, was allowed visitors and I went to see her on Sundays. Once or twice the Commissaire had accompanied me and, later, I learned that he had also visited Helene alone. But we were never able to obtain any information from my sister-in-law, who seemed to have become utterly indifferent. She rarely answered my questions and hardly ever those of the Commissaire. She spent a lot of her time sewing, but her favorite pastime seemed to be catching flies which she invariably released unharmed after having examined them carefully.

Helene only had one fit of raving—more like a nervous breakdown than a fit, said the doctor who had administered morphia to quiet her—the day she saw a nurse swatting flies.

The day after Helene's one and only fit, Commissaire Charas came to see me.

"I have a strange feeling that there lies the key to the whole business, Monsieur Delambre," he said.

I did not ask him how it was that he already knew all about Helene's fit.

"I do not follow you, Commissaire. Poor Madame Delambre could have shown an exceptional interest for anything else, really. Don't you think that flies just happen to be the border-subject of her tendency to raving?"

"Do you believe she is really mad?" he asked.

"My dear Commissaire, I don't see how there can be any doubt. Do you doubt it?"

"I don't know. In spite of all the doctors say, I have the impression that Madame Delambre has a very clear brain . . . even when catching flies."

"Supposing you were right, how would you explain her attitude with regard to her little boy? She never seems to consider him as her own child."

"You know, Monsieur Delambre, I have thought about that also. She may be trying to protect him. Perhaps she fears the boy or, for all we know, hates him?"

"I'm afraid I don't understand, my dear Commissaire."

"Have you noticed, for instance, that she never catches flies when the boy is there?"

"No. But come to think of it, you are quite right. Yes, that is strange . . . Still, I fail to understand."

"So do I, Monsieur Delambre. And I'm very much afraid that we shall never understand, unless perhaps your sister-in-law should *get better*."

"The doctors seem to think that there is no hope of any sort you know."

"Yes. Do you know if your brother ever experimented with flies?"

"I really don't know, but I shouldn't think so. Have you asked the Air Ministry people? They knew all about the work."

"Yes, and they laughed at me."

"I can understand that."

"You are very fortunate to understand anything, Monsieur Delambre. I do not . . . but I hope to some day."

"Tell me, Uncle, do flies live a long time?"

We were just finishing our lunch and, following an established tradition between us, I was just pouring some wine into Henri's glass for him to dip a biscuit in.

Had Henri not been staring at his glass gradually being filled to the brim, something in my look might have frightened him.

This was the first time that he had ever mentioned flies, and I shuddered at the thought that Commissaire Charas might quite easily have been present. I could imagine the glint in his eye as he would have answered my nephew's question with another question. I could almost hear him saying:

"I don't know, Henri. Why do you ask?"

"Because I have again seen the fly that *Maman* was looking for."

And it was only after drinking off Henri's own glass of wine that I realized that he had answered my spoken thought.

"I did not know that your mother was looking for a fly."

"Yes, she was. It had grown quite a lot, but I recognized it all right."

"Where did you see this fly, Henri, and . . . how did you recognize it?"

"This morning on your desk, Uncle Francois. Its head is white instead of black, and it has a funny sort of leg."

Feeling more and more like Commissaire Charas, but trying to look unconcerned, I went on:

"And when did you see this fly for the first time?"

"The day that Papa went away. I had caught it, but *Maman* made me let it go. And then after, she wanted me to find it again. She'd changed her mind," and shrugging his shoulders just as my brother used to, he added, "You know what women are."

"I think that fly must have died long ago, and you must be mistaken, Henri," I said, getting up and walking to the door.

But as soon as I was out of the dining room, I ran up the stairs to my study. There was no fly anywhere to be seen.

I was bothered, far more than I cared to even think about. Henri had just proved that Charas was really closer to a clue than had seemed when he told me about his thoughts concerning Helene's pastime.

For the first time I wondered if Charas did not really know much more than he let on. For the first time also, I wondered about Helene. Was she really insane? A strange, horrid feeling was growing on me, and the more I thought about it, the more I felt that, somehow, Charas was right: Helene was *getting away with it!*

What could possibly have been the reason for such a monstrous crime? What had led up to it? Just what had happened?

I thought of all the hundreds of questions that Charas had put to Helene, sometimes gently like a nurse trying to soothe, sometimes stern and cold, sometimes barking them furiously. Helene had answered very few, always in a calm quiet voice and never seeming to pay any attention to the way in which the question had been put. Though dazed, she had seemed perfectly sane then.

Refined, well-bred and well-read, Charas was more than just an intelligent police official. He was a keen psychologist and had an amazing way of smelling out a fib or an erroneous statement even before it was uttered. I knew that he had accepted as true the few answers she had given him. But then there had been all those questions which she never answered: the most direct and important ones. From the very beginning, Helene had adopted a very simple system. "I cannot answer that question," she would say in her low quiet voice. And that was that! The repetition of the same question never seemed to annoy her. In all the hours of questioning that she underwent, Helene did not once point out to the Commissaire that he had already asked her this or that. She would simply say, "I cannot answer that question," as though it was the very first time that that particular question had been asked and the very first time she had made that answer.

This cliché had become the formidable barrier beyond which Commissaire Charas could not even get a glimpse, an idea of what Helene might be thinking. She had very willingly answered all questions about her life with my brother—which seemed a happy and uneventful one—up to the time of his end. About his death, however, all that she would say was that she had killed him with the steam-hammer, but she refused to say why, what had led up to the drama and how she got my brother to put his head under it. She never actually refused outright; she would just go blank and, with no apparent emotion, would switch over to, "I cannot answer that question."

Helene, as I have said, had shown the Commissaire that she knew how to set and operate the steam-hammer.

Charas could only find one single fact which did not coincide with Helene's declarations, the fact that the hammer had been used twice. Charas was no longer willing to attribute this to insanity. That evident flaw in Helene's stonewall defense seemed a crack which the Commissaire might possibly enlarge. But my sister-in-law finally cemented it by acknowledging:

"All right, I lied to you. I did use the hammer twice. But do not ask me why, because I cannot tell you."

"Is that your only . . . misstatement, Madame Delambre?" had asked the Commissaire, trying to follow up what looked at last like an advantage.

"It is . . . and you know it, Monsieur le Commissaire."

And, annoyed, Charas had seen that Helene could read him like an open book.

I had thought of calling on the Commissaire, but the knowledge that he would inevitably start questioning Henri made me hesitate. Another reason also made me hesitate, a vague sort of fear that he would look for and find the fly Henri had talked of. And that annoyed me a good deal because I could find no satisfactory explanation for that particular fear.

Andre was definitely not the absent-minded sort of professor who walks about in pouring rain with a rolled umbrella under his arm. He was human, had a keen sense of humor, loved children and animals and could not bear to see anyone suffer. I had often seen him drop his work to watch a parade of the local fire brigade, or see the *Tour de France* cyclists go by, or even follow a circus parade all around the village. He liked games of logic and precision, such as billiards and tennis, bridge and chess.

How was it then possible to explain his death? What could have made him put his head under that hammer? It could hardly have been the result of some stupid bet or a test of his courage. He hated betting and had no patience with those who indulged in it. Whenever he heard a bet proposed, he would invariably remind all present that, after all, a bet was but a contract between a fool and a swindler, even if it turned out to be a toss-up as to which was which.

It seemed there were only two possible explanations to Andre's death. Either he had gone mad, or else he had a reason for letting his wife kill him in such a strange and terrible way. And just what could have been his wife's role in all this? They surely could not have been both insane?

Having finally decided not to tell Charas about my nephew's innocent revelations, I thought I myself would try to question Helene.

She seemed to have been expecting my visit, for she came into the parlor almost as soon as I had made myself known to the matron and been allowed inside.

"I wanted to show you my garden," explained Helene as I looked at the coat slung over her shoulders.

As one of the "reasonable" inmates, she was allowed to go into the garden during certain hours of the day. She had asked for and obtained the right to a little patch of ground where she could grow flowers, and I had sent her seeds and some rosebushes out of my garden.

She took me straight to a rustic wooden bench which had been made in the men's workshop and only just set up under a tree close to her little patch of ground.

Searching for the right way to broach the subject of Andre's death, I sat for a while tracing vague designs on the ground with the end of my umbrella.

"Francois, I want to ask you something," said Helene after a while.

"Anything I can do for you, Helene?"

"No, just something I want to know. Do flies live very long?"

Staring at her, I was about to say that her boy had asked the very same question a few hours earlier when I suddenly realized that here was the opening I had been searching for and perhaps even the possibility of striking a great blow, a blow perhaps powerful enough to shatter her stonewall defense, be it sane or insane.

Watching her carefully, I replied:

"I don't really know, Helene; but the fly you were looking for was in my study this morning."

No doubt about it, I had struck a shattering blow. She swung her head round with such force that I heard the bones crack in her neck. She opened her mouth, but said not a word; only her eyes seemed to be screaming with fear.

Yes, it was evident that I had crashed through something, but what? Undoubtedly, the Commissaire would have known what to do with such an advantage; I did not. All I knew was that he would never have given her time to think, to recuperate, but all I could do, and even that was a strain, was to maintain my best poker-face, hoping against hope that Helene's defenses would go on crumbling.

She must have been quite a while without breathing, because she suddenly gasped and put both her hands over her still open mouth.

"Francois . . . Did you kill it?" she whispered, her eyes no longer fixed, but searching every inch of my face.

"No."

"You have it then . . . You have it on you! Give it to me!" she almost shouted, touching me with both her hands, and I knew that had she felt strong enough, she would have tried to search me.

"No, Helene, I haven't got it."

"But you know now . . . You have guessed, haven't you?"

"No, Helene. I only know one thing, and that is that you are not insane. But I mean to know all, Helene, and, somehow, I am going to find out. You can choose: either you tell me everything and I'll see what is to be done, or . . ."

"Or what? Say it!"

"I was going to say it, Helene . . . or I assure you that your friend the Commissaire will have that fly first thing tomorrow morning."

She remained quite still, looking down at the palms of her hands on her lap and, although it was getting chilly, her forehead and hands were moist.

Without even brushing aside a wisp of long brown hair blown across her mouth by the breeze, she murmured:

"If I tell you . . . will you promise to destroy that fly before doing anything else?"

"No, Helene. I can make no such promise before knowing."

"But Francois, you must understand. I promised Andre that fly would be destroyed. That promise must be kept and I can say nothing until it is."

I could sense the deadlock ahead. I was not yet losing ground, but I was losing the initiative. I tried a shot in the dark:

"Helene, of course you understand that as soon as the police examine that fly, they will know that you are not insane, and then . . ."

"Francois, no! For Henri's sake! Don't you see? I was expecting that fly; I was hoping it would find me here but it couldn't know what had become of me. What else could it do but go to others it loves, to Henri, to you . . . you who might know and understand what was to be done!"

Was she really mad, or was she simulating again? But mad or not, she was cornered. Wondering how to follow up and how to land the knockout blow without running the risk of seeing her slip away out of reach, I said very quietly:

"Tell me all, Helene. I can then protect your boy."

"Protect my boy from what? Don't you understand that if I am here, it is merely so that Henri won't be the son of a woman who was guillotined for having murdered his father? Don't you understand that I would by far prefer the guillotine to the living death of this lunatic asylum?"

"I understand Helene, and I'll do my best for the boy whether you tell me or not. If you refuse to tell me, I'll still do the best I can to protect Henri, but you must understand that the game will be out of my hands, because Commissaire Charas will have the fly."

"But why must you know?" said, rather than asked, my sister-in-law, struggling to control her temper.

"Because I must and will know how and why my brother died, Helene."

"All right. Take me back to the ... house. I'll give you what your Commissaire would call my 'Confession.' "

"Do you mean to say that you have written it!"

"Yes. It was not really meant for you, but more likely for *your friend,* the Commissaire. I had foreseen that, sooner or later, he would get too close to the truth."

"You then have no objection to his reading it?"

"You will act as you think fit, Francois. Wait for me a minute."

Leaving me at the door of the parlor, Helene ran upstairs to her room. In less than a minute she was back with a large brown envelope.

"Listen Francois; you are not nearly as bright as was your poor brother, but you are not unintelligent. All I ask is that you read this alone. After that, you may do as you wish."

"That I promise you, Helene," I said, taking the precious envelope. "I'll read it tonight and although tomorrow is not a visiting day, I'll come down to see you."

"Just as you like," said my sister-in-law without even saying good-bye as she went back upstairs.

It was only on reaching home, as I walked from the garage to the house, that I read the inscription on the envelope:

TO WHOM IT MAY CONCERN

(Probably Commissaire Charas)

Having told the servants that I would have only a light supper to be served immediately in my study and that I was not to be disturbed after, I ran upstairs, threw Helene's envelope on my desk and made another careful search of the room before closing the shutters and drawing the curtains. All I could find was a long since dead mosquito stuck to the wall near the ceiling.

Having motioned to the servant to put her tray down on a table by the fireplace, I poured myself a glass of wine and locked the door behind her. I then disconnected the telephone—I always did this now at night—and turned out all the lights but the lamp on my desk.

Slitting open Helene's fat envelope, I extracted a thick wad of closely written pages. I read the following lines neatly centered in the middle of the top page:

> *This is not a confession because, although I killed my husband, I am not a murderess. I simply and very faithfully carried out his last wish by crushing his head and right arm under the steam-hammer of his brother's factory.*

Without even touching the glass of wine by my elbow, I turned the page and started reading.

For very nearly a year before his death *(the manuscript began)*, my husband had told me of some of his experiments. He knew full well that his colleagues of the Air Ministry would have forbidden some of them as too dangerous, but he was keen on obtaining positive results before reporting his discovery.

Whereas only sound and pictures had been, so far, gransmitted through space by radio and television, Andre claimed to have discovered a way of transmitting matter. Matter, any solid objects placed in his "transmitter" was instantly disintegrated and reintegrated in a special receiving set.

Andre considered his discovery as perhaps the most important since that of the wheel sawn off the end of a tree trunk. He reckoned that the transmission of matter by instantaneous "disintegration-reintegration" would completely change life as we had known it so far. It would mean the end of all means of transport, not only of goods, including food, but also of human beings. Andre, the practical scientist who never allowed theories or daydreams to get the better of him, already foresaw the time when there would no longer be any airplanes, ships, trains or cars and, therefore, no longer any roads or railway lines, ports, airports or stations. All that would be replaced by matter-transmitting and receiving stations throughout the world. Travelers and goods would be placed in special cabins and, at a given signal, would simply disappear and reappear almost immediately at the chosen receiving station.

Andre's receiving set was only a few feet away from his transmitter, in an adjoining room of his laboratory, and he at first ran into all sorts of snags. His first successful experiment was carried out with an ash tray taken from his desk, a souvenir we had brought back from a trip to London.

That was the first time he told me about his experiments and I had no idea of what he was talking about the day he came dashing into the house and threw the ash tray in my lap.

"Helene, look! For a fraction of a second, a bare 10-millionth of a second, that ash tray has been completely disintegrated. For one little moment it no longer existed! Gone! Nothing left, absolutely nothing! Only atoms traveling through space at the speed of light! And the moment after, the atoms were once more gathered together in the shape of an ash tray!"

"Andre, please . . . please! What on earth are you raving about?"

He started sketching all over a letter I had been writing. He laughed at my wry face, swept all my letters off the table and said:

"You don't understand? Right. Let's start all over again. Helene, do you remember I once read you an article about the mysterious flying stones that seem to come from nowhere in particular, and which are said to occasionally fall in certain houses in India? They come flying in as though thrown from outside and that, in spite of closed doors and windows."

"Yes, I remember. I also remember that Professor Augier, your friend of the College de France, who had come down for a few days, remarked that if there was no trickery about it, the only possible explanation was that the stones had been disintegrated after having been thrown from outside, come through the walls, and then been integrated before hitting the floor or the opposite wall."

"That's right. And I added that there was, of course, one other possibility, namely the momentary and partial disintegration of the walls as the stone or stones came through."

"Yes, Andre. I remember all that, and I suppose you also remember that I failed to understand, and that you got quite annoyed. Well, I still do not understand why and how, even disintegrated, stones should be able to come through a wall or a closed door."

"But it is possible, Helene, because the atoms that go to make up matter are not close together like the bricks of a wall. They are separated by relative immensities of space."

"Do you mean to say that you have disintegrated that ash tray, and then put it together again after pushing it through something?"

"Precisely, Helene. I projected it through the wall that separates my transmitter from my receiving set."

"And would it be foolish to ask how humanity is to benefit from ash trays that can go through walls?"

Andre seemed quite offended, but he soon saw that I was only teasing, and again waxing enthusiastic, he told me of some of the possibilities of his discovery.

"Isn't it wonderful, Helene?" he finally gasped, out of breath.

"Yes, Andre. But I hope you won't ever transmit me; I'd be too much afraid of coming out at the other end like our ash tray."

"What do you mean?"

"Do you remember what was written under that ash tray?"

"Yes, of course: MADE IN JAPAN. That was the great joke of our typically British souvenir."

"The words are still there Andre; but . . . look!"

He took the ash tray out of my hands, frowned, and walked over to the window. Then he went quite pale, and I knew that he had seen what had proved to me that he had indeed carried out a strange experiment.

The three words were still there, but reversed and reading:

Made in Japan

Without a word, having completely forgotten me, Andre rushed off to his laboratory. I only saw him the next morning, tired and unshaven after a whole night's work.

A few days later, Andre had a new reverse which put him out of sorts and made him fussy and grumpy for several weeks. I stood it patiently enough for a while, but being myself bad tempered one evening, we had a silly row over some futile thing, and I reproached him for his moroseness.

"I'm sorry, *cherie.* I've been working my way through a maze of problems and have given you all a very rough time. You see, my very first experiment with a live animal proved a complete fiasco."

"Andre! You tried that experiment with Dandelo, didn't you?"

"Yes. How did you know?" he answered sheepishly. "He disintegrated perfectly, but he never reappeared in the receiving set."

"Oh, Andre! What became of him then?"

"Nothing . . . there is just no more Dandelo; only the dispersed atoms of a cat wandering, God knows where, in the universe."

Dandelo was a small white cat the cook had found one morning in the garden and which we had promptly adopted. Now I knew how it had disappeared and was quite angry about the whole thing, but my husband was so miserable over it all that I said nothing.

I saw little of my husband during the next few weeks. He had most of his meals sent down to the laboratory. I would often wake up in the morning and find his bed unslept in. Sometimes, if he had come in very late, I would find that storm-swept appearance which only a man can give a bedroom by getting up very early and fumbling around in the dark.

One evening he came home to dinner all smiles, and I knew that his troubles were over. His face dropped, however, when he saw I was dressed for going out.

"Oh. Were you going out, Helene?"

"Yes, the Drillons invited me for a game of bridge, but I can easily phone them and put it off."

"No, it's all right."

"It isn't all right. Out with it, dear!"

"Well, I've at last got everything perfect and I wanted you to be the first to see the miracle."

"*Magnifique,* Andre! Of course I'll be delighted."

Having telephoned our neighbors to say how sorry I was and so forth, I ran down to the kitchen and told the cook that she had exactly 10 minutes in which to prepare a "celebration dinner."

"An excellent idea, Helene," said my husband when the maid appeared with the champagne after our candlelight dinner. "We'll celebrate with reintegrated champagne!" and taking the tray from the maid's hands, he led the way down to the laboratory.

"Do you think it will be as good as before its disintegration?" I asked, holding the tray while he opened the door and switched on the lights.

"Have no fear. You'll see! Just bring it here, will you," he said, opening the door of a telephone call-box he had bought and which had been transformed into what he called a transmitter. "Put it down on that now," he added, putting a stool inside the box.

Having carefully closed the door, he took me to the other end of the room and handed me a pair of very dark sun glasses. He put on another pair and walked back to a switchboard by the transmitter.

"Ready Helene?" said my husband turning out all the lights. "Don't remove your glasses till I give the word."

"I won't budge Andre, go on," I told him, my eyes fixed on the tray which I could just see in a greenish shimmering light through the glass paneled door of the telephone booth.

"Right," said Andre, throwing a switch.

The whole room was brilliantly illuminated by an orange flash. Inside the cabin I had seen a crackling ball of fire and felt its heat on my face, neck and hands. The whole thing lasted but the fraction of a second, and I found myself blinking at green-edged black holes like those one sees after having stared at the sun.

"*Et voilà!* You can take off your glasses, Helene."

A little theatrically perhaps, my husband opened the door of the cabin. Though Andre had told me what to expect, I was astonished to find that the champagne, glasses, tray and stool were no longer there.

Andre ceremoniously led me by the hand into the next room, in a corner of which stood a second telephone booth. Opening the door wide, he triumphantly lifted the champagne tray off the stool.

Feeling somewhat like the good natured kind-member-of-the-audience that has been dragged onto the music hall stage by the magician, I repressed from saying, "All done with mirrors," which I knew would have annoyed my husband.

"Sure it's not dangerous to drink?" I asked as the cork popped.

"Absolutely sure, Helene," he said, handing me a glass. "But that was nothing. Drink this off and I'll show you something much more astounding."

We went back into the other room.

"Oh, Andre! Remember poor Dandelo!"

"This is only a guinea pig, Helene. But I'm positive it will go through all right."

He set the furry little beast down on the green enamelled floor of the booth and quickly closed the door. I again put on my dark glasses and saw and felt the vivid crackling flash.

Without waiting for Andre to open the door, I rushed into the next room where the lights were still on and looked into the receiving booth.

"Oh, Andre! *Cheri!* He's there all right!" I shouted excitedly, watching the little animal trotting round and round. "It's wonderful Andre. It works! You've succeeded!"

"I hope so, but I must be patient. I'll know for sure in a few weeks' time."

"What do you mean? Look! He's as full of life as when you put him in the other cabin."

"Yes, so he seems. But we'll have to see if all his organs are intact, and that will take some time. If that little beast is still full of life in a month's time, we then consider the experiment a success."

I begged Andre to let me take care of the guinea pig.

"All right, but don't kill it by overfeeding," he agreed with a grin for my enthusiasm.

"Though not allowed to take Hop-la—the name I had given the guinea pig—out of its box in the laboratory, I had tied a pink ribbon round its neck and was allowed to feed it twice a day.

Hop-la soon got used to its pink ribbon and became quite a tame little pet, but that month of waiting seemed a year.

And then one day, Andre put Miquette, our cocker spaniel, into his "transmitter." He had not told me beforehand, knowing full well that I would never have agreed to such an experiment with our dog. But when he did tell me, Miquette had been successfully transmitted half-a-dozen times and seemed to be enjoying the operation thoroughly; no sooner was she let out of the "reintegrator" than she dashed madly into the next room, scratching at the "transmitter" door to have "another go," as Andre called it.

I now expected that my husband would invite some of his colleagues and Air Ministry specialists to come down. He usually did this when he had finished a research job and, before handing them long detailed reports which he always typed himself, he would carry out an experiment or two before them. But this time, he just went on working. One morning I finally asked him when he intended throwing his usual "surprise party," as we called it.

"No, Helene; not for a long while yet. This discovery is much too important. I have an awful lot of work to do on it still. Do you realize that there are some parts of the transmission proper which I do not yet myself fully understand? It works all right, but you see, I can't just say to all these eminent professors that I do this and that and, poof, it works! I must be able to explain how and why it works. And what is even more important, I must be ready and able to refute every destructive argument they will not fail to trot out, as they usually do when faced with anything really good."

I was occasionally invited down to the laboratory to witness some new experiment, but I never went unless Andre invited me, and only talked about his work if he broached the subject first. Of course it never occurred to me that he would, at that stage at least, have tried an experiment with a human being; though, had I thought about it—knowing Andre—it would have been obvious that he would never have allowed anyone into the "transmitter" before he had been through to test it first. It was only after the accident that I discovered he had duplicated all his switches inside the disintegration booth, so that he could try it out by himself.

The morning Andre tried this terrible experiment, he did not show up for lunch. I sent the maid down with a tray, but she brought it back with a note she had found pinned outside the laboratory door: "Do not disturb me, I am working."

He did occasionally pin such notes on his door and, though I noticed it, I paid no particular attention to the unusually large handwriting of his note.

It was just after that, as I was drinking my coffee, that Henri came bouncing into the room to say that he had caught a funny fly, and would I like to see it. Refusing even to look at his closed fist, I ordered him to release it immediately.

"But, *Maman,* it has such a funny white head!"

Marching the boy over to the open window, I told him to release the fly immediately, which he did. I knew that Henri had caught the fly merely because he thought it looked curious or different from other flies, but I also knew that his father would never stand for any form of cruelty to animals, and that there would be a fuss should he discover that our son had put a fly in a box or a bottle.

At dinnertime that evening, Andre had still not shown up, and a little worried, I ran down to the laboratory and knocked at the door.

He did not answer my knock, but I heard him moving around and a moment later he slipped a note under the door. It was typewritten:

Helene, I am having trouble. Put the boy to bed and come back in an hour's time. A.

Frightened, I knocked and called, but Andre did not seem to pay any attention and, vaguely reassured by the familiar noise of his typewriter, I went back to the house.

Having put Henri to bed, I returned to the laboratory where I found another note slipped under the door. My hand shook as I picked it up because I knew by then that something must be radically wrong. I read:

Helene, first of all I count on you not to lose your nerve or do anything rash because you alone can help me. I have had a serious accident. I am not in any particular danger for the time being though it is a matter of life and death. It is useless calling to me or saying anything. I cannot answer, I cannot speak. I want you to do exactly and very carefully all that I ask. After having knocked three times to show that you understand and agree, fetch me a bowl of milk laced with rum. I have had nothing all day and can do with it.

Shaking with fear, not knowing what to think and repressing a furious desire to call Andre and bang away until he opened, I knocked three times as requested and ran all the way home to fetch what he wanted.

In less than five minutes I was back. Another note had been slipped under the door:

Helene, follow these instructions carefully. When you knock I'll open the door. You are to walk over to my desk and put down the bowl of milk. You will then go into the other room where the receiver is. Look carefully and try to find a fly which ought to be there but which I am unable to find. Unfortunately I cannot see small things very easily.

Before you come in you must promise to obey me implicitly. Do not look at me and remember that talking is quite useless. I cannot answer. Knock again three times and that will mean I have your promise. My life depends entirely on the help you can give me.

I had to wait a while to pull myself together, and then I knocked slowly three times.

I heard Andre shuffling behind the door, then his hand fumbling with the lock, and the door opened.

Out of the corner of my eye, I saw that he was standing behind the door, but without looking round, I carried the bowl of milk to his desk. He was evidently watching me and I felt I must at all cost appear calm and collected.

"Cheri, you can count on me," I said gently, and putting the bowl down under his desk lamp, the only one alight, I walked into the next room where all the lights were blazing.

My first impression was that some sort of hurricane must have blown out of the receiving booth. Papers were scattered in every direction, a whole row of test tubes lay smashed in a corner, chairs and stools were upset and one of the window curtains hung half torn from its bent rod. In a large enamel basin on the floor a heap of burned documents was still smoldering.

I knew that I would not find the fly Andre wanted me to look for. Women know things that men only suppose by reasoning and deduction; it is a form of knowledge very rarely accessible to them and which they disparagingly call intuition. I already knew that the fly Andre wanted was the one which Henri had caught and which I had made him release.

I heard Andre shuffling around in the next room and then a strange gurgling and sucking as though he had trouble in drinking his milk.

"Andre, there is no fly here. Can you give me any sort of indication that might help? If you can't speak, rap or something . . . you know: once for yes, twice for no."

I had tried to control my voice and speak as though perfectly calm, but I had to choke down a sob of desperation when he rapped twice for "no."

"May I come to you Andre? I don't know what can have happened, but whatever it is, I'll be courageous, dear."

After a moment of silent hesitation, he tapped once on his desk.

At the door I stopped aghast at the sight of Andre standing with his head and shoulders covered by the brown velvet cloth he had taken from a table by his desk, the table on which he usually ate when he did not want to leave his work. Suppressing a laugh that might easily have turned to sobbing, I said:

"Andre, we'll search thoroughly tomorrow, by daylight. Why don't you go to bed? I'll lead you to the guest room if you like, and won't let anyone else see you."

His left hand tapped the desk twice.

"Do you need a doctor, Andre?"

"No," he rapped.

"Would you like me to call up Professor Augier? He might be of more help . . ."

Twice he rapped "no" sharply. I did not know what to do or say. And then I told him:

"Henri caught a fly this morning which he wanted to show me, but I made him release it. Could it have been the one you are looking for? I didn't see it, but the boy said its head was white."

Andre emitted a strange metallic sigh, and I just had time to bite my fingers fiercely in order not to scream. He had let his right arm drop, and instead of his long-fingered muscular hand, a gray stick with little buds on it like the branch of a tree, hung out of his sleeve almost down to his knee.

"Andre, *mon cheri,* tell me what happened. I might be of more help to you if I knew. Andre . . . oh, it's terrible!" I sobbed, unable to control myself.

Having rapped once for yes, he pointed to the door with his left hand.

I stepped out and sank down crying as he locked the door behind me. He was typing again and I waited. At last he shuffled to the door and slid a sheet of paper under it.

Helene, come back in the morning. I must think and will have typed out an explanation for you. Take one of my sleeping tablets and go straight to bed. I need you fresh and strong tomorrow, *ma pauvre cherie.* A.

"Do you want anything for the night, Andre?" I shouted through the door.

He knocked twice for no, and a little later I heard the typewriter again.

The sun full on my face woke me up with a start. I had set the alarm-clock for five but had not heard it, probably because of the sleeping tablets. I had indeed slept like a log, without a dream. Now I was back in my living nightmare and crying like a child I sprang out of bed. It was just on seven!

Rushing into the kitchen, without a word for the startled servants, I rapidly prepared a trayload of coffee, bread and butter with which I ran down to the laboratory.

Andre opened the door as soon as I knocked and closed it again as I carried the tray to his desk. His head was still covered, but I saw from his crumpled suit and his open camp-bed that he must have at least tried to rest.

On his desk lay a typewritten sheet for me which I picked up. Andre opened the other door, and taking this to mean that he wanted to be left alone, I walked into the next room. He pushed the door to and I heard him pouring out the coffee and I read:

Do you remember the ash tray experiment? I have had a similar accident. I "transmitted" myself successfully the night before last. During a second experiment yesterday a fly which I did not see must have got into the "disintegrator." My only hope is to find that fly and go through again with it. Please search for it carefully since, if it is not found, I shall have to find a way of putting an end to all this.

If only Andre had been more explicit! I shuddered at the thought that he must be terribly disfigured and then cried softly as I imagined his face inside-out, or perhaps his eyes in place of his ears, or his mouth at the back of his neck, or worse!

Andre must be saved! For that, the fly must be found!

Pulling myself together, I said:

"Andre, may I come in?"

He opened the door.

"Andre, don't despair; I am going to find that fly. It is no longer in the laboratory, but it cannot be very far. I suppose you're disfigured, perhaps terribly so, but there can be no question of putting an end to all of this, as you say in your note; that I will never stand for. If necessary, if you do not wish to be seen, I'll make you a mask or a cowl so that you can go on with your work until you get well again. If you cannot work, I'll call Professor Augier, and he and all your other friends will save you, Andre."

Again I heard that curious metallic sigh as he rapped violently on his desk.

"Andre, don't be annoyed; please be calm. I won't do anything without first consulting you, but you must rely on me, have faith in me and let me help you as best I can. Are you terribly disfigured, dear? Can't you let me see your face? I won't be afraid . . . I am your wife you know."

But my husband again rapped a decisive "no" and pointed to the door.

"All right. I am going to search for the fly now, but promise me you won't do anything foolish; promise you won't do anything rash or dangerous without first letting me know all about it!"

He extended his left hand, and I knew I had his promise.

I will never forget that ceaseless day-long hunt for a fly. Back home, I turned the house inside-out and made all the servants join in the search. I told them that a fly had escaped from the Professor's laboratory and that it must be captured alive, but it was evident they already thought me crazy. They said so to the police later, and that day's hunt for a fly most probably saved me from the guillotine later.

I questioned Henri and as he failed to understand right away what I was talking about, I shook him and slapped him, and made him cry in front of the roundeyed maids. Realizing that I must not let myself go, I kissed and petted the poor boy and at last made him understand what I wanted of him. Yes, he remembered, he had found the fly just by the kitchen window; yes, he had released it immediately as told to.

Even in summer time we had very few flies because our house is on the top of a hill and the slightest breeze coming across the valley blows round it. In spite of that, I managed to catch dozens of flies that day. On all the window sills and all over the garden I had put saucers of milk, sugar, jam, meat—all the things likely to attract flies. Of all those we caught, and many others which we failed to catch but which I saw, none resembled the one Henri had caught the day before. One by one, with a magnifying glass, I examined every unusual fly, but none had anything like a white head.

At lunch time, I ran down to Andre with some milk and mashed potatoes. I also took some of the flies we had caught, but he gave me to understand that they could be of no possible use to him.

"If that fly has not been found tonight, Andre, we'll have to see what is to be done. And this is what I propose: I'll sit in the next room. When you can't answer by the yes-no method of rapping, you'll type out whatever you want to say and then slip it under the door. Agreed?"

"Yes," rapped Andre.

By nightfall we had still not found the fly. At dinner time, as I prepared Andre's tray, I broke down and sobbed in the kitchen in front of the silent servants. My maid thought that I had had a row with my husband, probably about the mislaid fly, but I learned later that the cook was already quite sure that I was out of my mind.

Without a word, I picked up the tray and then put it down again as I stopped by the telephone. That this was really a matter of life and death for Andre, I had no doubt. Neither did I doubt that he fully intended committing suicide, unless I could make him change his mind, or at least put off such a drastic decision. Would I be strong enough? He would never forgive me for not keeping a promise, but under the circumstances, did that really matter? To the devil with promises and honor! At all costs Andre must be saved! And having thus made up my mind, I looked up and dialed Professor Augier's number.

"The Professor is away and will not be back before the end of the week," said a polite neutral voice at the other end of the line.

That was that! I would have to fight alone and fight I would. I would save Andre come what may.

All my nervousness had disappeared as Andre let me in and, after putting the tray of food down on his desk, I went into the other room as agreed.

"The first thing I want to know," I said as he closed the door behind me, "is what happened exactly. Can you please tell me, Andre?"

I waited patiently while he typed an answer which he pushed under the door a little later.

Helene, I would rather not tell you. Since go I must, I would rather you remember me as I was before. I must destroy myself in such a way that none can possibly know what has happened to me. I have of course thought of simply disintegrating myself in my transmitter, but I had better not because, sooner or later, I might find myself reintegrated. Some day, somewhere, some scientist is sure to make the same discovery. I have therefore thought of a way which is neither simple nor easy, but you can and will help me.

For several minutes I wondered if Andre had not simply gone stark raving mad.

"Andre," I said at last, "whatever you may have chosen or thought of, I cannot and will never accept such a cowardly solution. No matter how awful the result of your experiment or accident, you are alive, you are a man, a brain . . . and you have a soul. You have no right to destroy yourself! You know that!"

The answer was soon typed and pushed under the door.

I am alive all right, but I am already no longer a man. As to my brain or intelligence, it may disappear at any moment. As it is, it is no longer intact. And there can be no soul without intelligence . . . and you know that!

"Then you must tell the other scientists about your discovery. They will help you and save you, Andre!"

I staggered back frightened as he angrily thumped the door twice.

"Andre . . . why? Why do you refuse the aid you know they would give you with all their hearts?"

A dozen furious knocks shook the door and made me understand that my husband would never accept such a solution. I had to find other arguments.

For hours, it seemed, I talked to him about our boy, about me, about his family, about his duty to us and to the rest of humanity. He made no reply of any sort. At last I cried:

"Andre . . . do you hear me?"

"Yes," he knocked very gently.

"Well, listen then. I have another idea. You remember your first experiment with the ash tray? . . . Well, do you think that if you had put it through again a second time, it might possibly have come out with the letters turned back the right way?"

Before I had finished speaking, Andre was busily typing and a moment later I read his answer:

> I have already thought of that. And that was why I needed the fly. It has got to go through with me. There is no hope otherwise.

"Try all the same, Andre. You never know!"

> I have tried seven times already.

was the typewritten reply I got to that.

"Andre! Try again, please!"

The answer this time gave me a flutter of hope, because no woman has ever understood, or will ever understand, how a man about to die can possibly consider anything funny.

> I deeply admire your delicious feminine logic. We could go on doing this experiment until doomsday. However, just to give you that pleasure, probably the very last I shall ever be able to give you, I will try once more. If you cannot find the dark glasses, turn your back to the machine and press your hands over your eyes. Let me know when you are ready.

"Ready Andre!" I shouted, without even looking for the glasses and following his instructions.

I heard him move around and then open and close the door of his "disintegrator." After what seemed a very long wait, but probably was not more than a minute or so, I heard a violent crackling noise and perceived a bright flash through my eyelids and fingers.

I turned around as the cabin door opened.

His head and shoulders still covered with the brown velvet carpet, Andre was gingerly stepping out of it.

"How do you feel Andre? Any difference?" I asked, touching his arm.

He tried to step away from me and caught his foot in one of the stools which I had not troubled to pick up. He made a violent effort to regain his balance, and the velvet carpet slowly slid off his shoulders and head as he fell heavily backwards.

The horror was too much for me, too unexpected. As a matter of fact, I am sure that, even had I known, the horror-impact could hardly have been less powerful. Trying to push both hands into my mouth to stifle my screams and although my fingers were bleeding, I screamed again and again. I could not take my eyes off him, I could not even close them, and yet I knew that if I looked at the horror much longer, I would go on screaming for the rest of my life.

Slowly, the monster, the thing that had been my husband, covered its head, got up and groped its way to the door and passed it. Though still screaming, I was able to close my eyes.

I who had ever been a true Catholic, who believed in God and another, better life hereafter, have today but one hope: that when I die, I really die, and that there may be no after-life of any sort because, if there is, then I shall never forget! Day and night, awake or asleep, I see it, and I know that I am condemned to see it forever, even perhaps into oblivion!

Until I am totally extinct, nothing can, nothing will ever make me forget that dreadful white hairy head with its low flat skull and its two pointed ears. Pink and moist, the nose was also that of a cat, a huge cat. But the eyes! Or rather, where the eyes should have been were two brown bumps the size of saucers. Instead of a mouth, animal or human, was a long hairy vertical slit from which hung a black quivering trunk that widened at the end, trumpet-like, and from which saliva kept dripping.

I must have fainted, because I found myself flat on my stomach on the cold cement floor of the laboratory, staring at the closed door behind which I could hear the noise of Andre's typewriter.

Numb, numb and empty. I must have looked as people do immediately after a terrible accident, before they fully understand what has happened. I could only think of a man I had once seen on the platform of a railway station, quite conscious, and looking stupidly at his leg still on the line where the train had just passed.

My throat was aching terribly, and that made me wonder if my vocal cords had not perhaps been torn, and whether I would ever be able to speak again.

The noise of the typewriter suddenly stopped and I felt I was going to scream again as something touched the door and a sheet of paper slid from under it.

Shivering with fear and disgust, I crawled over to where I could read it without touching it:

Now you understand. That last experiment was a new disaster my poor Helene. I suppose you recognized part of Dandelo's head. When I went into the disintegrator just now, my head was only that of a fly. I now only have its eyes and mouth left. The rest has been replaced by parts of the cat's head. Poor Dandelo whose atoms had never come together. You see now that there can only be one possible solution, don't you? I must disappear. Knock on the door when you are ready and I shall explain what you have to do.

Of course he was right, and it had been wrong and cruel of me to insist on a new experiment. And I knew that there was now no possible hope, that any further experiments could only bring about worse results.

Getting up dazed, I went to the door and tried to speak, but no sound came out of my throat ... so I knocked once!

You can of course guess the rest. He explained his plan in short typewritten notes, and I agreed, I agreed to everything!

My head on fire, but shivering with cold, like an automaton, I followed him into the silent factory. In my hand was a full page of explanations: what I had to know about the steam-hammer.

Without stopping or looking back, he pointed to the switchboard that controlled the steam-hammer as he passed it. I went no further and watched him come to a halt before the terrible instrument.

He knelt down, carefully wrapped the carpet round his head, and then stretched out flat on the ground.

It was not difficult. I was not killing my husband. Andre, poor Andre, had gone long ago, years ago it seemed. I was merely carrying out his last wish ... and mine.

Without hesitating, my eyes on the long still body, I firmly pushed the "stroke" button right in. The great metallic mass seemed to drop slowly. It was not so much the resounding clang of the hammer that made me jump as the sharp cracking which I had distinctly heard at the same time. My hus ... the thing's body shook a second and then lay still.

It was then I noticed that he had forgotten to put his right arm, his fly-leg, under the hammer. The police would never understand but the scientists would, and they must not! That had been Andre's last wish, also!

I had to do it and quickly, too; the night watchman must have heard the hammer and would be round any moment. I pushed the other button and the hammer slowly rose. Seeing but trying not to look, I ran up, leaned down, lifted and moved forward the right arm which seemed terribly light. Back at the switchboard, again I pushed the red button, and down came the hammer a second time. Then I ran all the way home.

You know the rest and can now do whatever you think right.

So ended Helene's manuscript.

The following day I telephoned Commissaire Charas to invite him to dinner.

"With pleasure, Monsieur Delambre. Allow me, however, to ask: is it the Commissaire you are inviting, or just Monsieur Charas?"

"Have you any preference?"

"No, not at the present moment."

"Well then, make it whichever you like. Will eight o'clock suit you?"

Although it was raining, the Commissaire arrived on foot that evening.

"Since you did not come tearing up to the door in your black Citroen, I take it you have opted for Monsieur Charas, off duty?"

"I left the car up a side-street," mumbled the Commissaire with a grin as the maid staggered under the weight of his raincoat.

"Merci," he said a minute later as I handed him a glass of Pernod into which he tipped a few drops of water, watching it turn the golden amber .iquid to pale blue milk.

"You heard about my poor sister-in-law?"

"Yes, shortly after you telephoned me this morning, I am sorry, but perhaps it was all for the best. Being already in charge of your brother's case, the inquiry automatically comes to me."

"I suppose it was suicide."

"Without a doubt. Cyanide, the doctors say quite rightly; I found a second tablet in the unstitched hem of her dress."

"Monsieur est servi," announced the maid.

"I would like to show you a very curious document afterwards, Charas."

"Ah, yes. I heard that Madame Delambre had been writing a lot, but we could find nothing beyond the short note informing us that she was committing suicide."

During our tête-à-tête dinner, we talked politics, books and films, and the local football club of which the Commissaire was a keen supporter.

After dinner, I took him up to my study where a bright fire—a habit I had picked up in England during the war—was burning.

Without even asking him, I handed him his brandy and mixed myself what he called "crushed-bug juice in soda water"—his appreciation of whiskey.

"I would like you to read this, Charas; first because it was partly intended for you and, secondly, because it will interest you. If you think Commissaire Charas has no objection, I would like to burn it after."

Without a word, he took the wad of sheets Helene had given me the day before and settled down to read them.

"What do you think of it all?" I asked some 20 minutes later as he carefully folded Helene's manuscript, slipped it into the brown envelope, and put it into the fire.

Charas watched the flames licking the envelope from which wisps of gray smoke were escaping, and it was only when it burst into flames that he said, slowly raising his eyes to mine:

"I think it proves very definitely that Madame Delambre was quite insane."

For a long while we watched the fire eating up Helene's "confession."

"A funny thing happened to me this morning, Charas. I went to the cemetery, where my brother is buried. It was quite empty and I was alone."

"Not quite, Monsieur Delambre. I was there, but I did not want to disturb you."

"Then you saw me . . ."

"Yes. I saw you bury a matchbox."

"Do you know what was in it?"

"A fly, I suppose."

"Yes. I had found it early this morning, caught in a spider's web in the garden."

"Was it dead?"

"No, not quite. I . . . crushed it . . . between two stones. Its head was . . . white . . . all white."

ALGERNON BLACKWOOD

THE DOLL

Some nights are merely dark, others are dark in a suggestive way as though something ominous, mysterious, is going to happen. In certain remote outlying suburbs, at any rate, this seems true, where great spaces between the lamps go dead at night, where little happens, where a ring at the door is a summons almost, and people cry "Let's go to town!" In the villa gardens the mangy cedars sigh in the wind, but the hedges stiffen, there is a muffling of spontaneous activity.

On this particular November night a moist breeze barely stirred the silver pine in the narrow drive leading to the "Laurels" where Colonel Masters lived, Colonel Hymber Masters, late of an Indian regiment, with many distinguished letters after his name. The housemaid in the limited staff being out, it was the cook who answered the bell when it rang with a sudden, sharp clang soon after ten o'clock—and gave an audible gasp half of surprise, half of fear. The bell's sudden clangour was an unpleasant and unwelcome sound. Monica, the Colonel's adored yet rather neglected child, was asleep upstairs, but the cook was not frightened lest Monica be disturbed, nor because it seemed a bit late for the bell to ring so violently; she was frightened because when she opened the door to let the fine rain drive in she saw a black man standing on the steps. There, in the wind and the rain, stood a tall, slim nigger holding a parcel.

Dark-skinned, at any rate, he was, she reflected afterwards, whether negro, hindu or arab; the word "nigger" describing any man not really white. Wearing a stained yellow mackintosh and dirty slouch hat, and "looking like a devil, so help me, God," he shoved the little parcel at her out of the gloom, the light from the hall flaring red into his gleaming eyes. "For Colonel Masters," he whispered rapidly, "and very special into his own personal touch and no one else." And he melted away into the night with his "strange foreign accent, his eyes of fire, and his nasty hissing voice."

He was gone, swallowed up in the wind and rain.

"But I saw his eyes," swore the cook the next morning to the housemaid, "his fiery eyes, and his nasty look, and his black hands and long thin fingers, and his nails all shiny pink, and he looked to me—if you know wot I mean—he looked like—death. . . ."

Thus the cook, so far as she was intelligently articulate next day, but standing now against the closed door with the small brown paper parcel in her hands, impressed by the orders that it was to be given into his personal touch, she was relieved by the fact that Colonel Masters never returned till after midnight and that she need not act at once. The reflection brought a certain comfort that restored her equanimity a little, though she still stood there, holding the parcel gingerly in her grimy hands, reluctant, hesitating, uneasy. A parcel, even brought by a mysterious dark stranger, was not in itself frightening, yet frightened she certainly felt. Instinct and superstition worked perhaps; the wind, the rain, the fact of being alone in the house, the unexpected black man, these also contributed to her discomfort. A vague sense of horror touched her, her Irish blood stirred ancient dreams, so that she began to shake a little, as though the parcel contained something alive, explosive, poisonous, unholy almost as though it moved, and, her fingers loosening their hold, the parcel–dropped. It fell on the tiled floor with a queer, sharp clack, but it lay motionless. She eyed it closely, cautiously, but, thank God, it did not move, an inert, brown-paper parcel. Brought by an errand boy in daylight, it might have been groceries, tobacco, even a mended shirt. She peeped and tinkered, that sharp clack puzzled her. Then, after a few minutes, remembering her duty, she picked it up gingerly even while she shivered. It was to be handed into the Colonel's "personal touch." She compromised, deciding to place it on his desk and to tell him about it in the morning; only Colonel Masters, with those mysterious years in the East behind him, his temper and his tyrannical orders, was not easy of direct approach at the best of times, in the morning least of all.

The cook left it at that—that is, she left it on the desk in his study, but left out all explanations about its arrival. She had decided to be vague about such unimportant details, for Mrs. O'Reilly was afraid of Colonel Masters, and only his professed love of Monica made her believe that he was quite human. He paid her well, oh yes, and sometimes he smiled, and he was a handsome man, if a bit too dark for her fancy, yet he also paid her an occasional compliment about her curry, and that soothed her for the moment. They suited one another, at any rate, and she stayed, robbing him comfortably, if cautiously.

"It ain't no good," she assured the housemaid next day, "wot with that 'personal touch into his hands, and no one else,' and that black man's eyes and that crack when it came away in my hands and fell on the floor. It ain't no good, not to us nor anybody. No man as black as he was means lucky stars to anybody. A parcel indeed—with those devil's eyes—"

"What did you do with it?" enquired the housemaid.

The cook looked her up and down. "Put it in the fire o'course," she replied. "On the stove if you want to know exact."

It was the housemaid's turn to look the cook up and down.

"I don't think," she remarked.

The cook reflected, probably because she found no immediate answer.

"Well," she puffed out presently, "d'you know wot *I* think? You don't. So I'll tell you. It was something the master's afraid of, that's wot it was. He's afraid of something—ever since I been here I've known that. And that's wot it was. He done somebody wrong in India long ago and that lanky nigger brought wot's coming to him, and that's why I says I put it on the stove—see?" She dropped her voice. "It was a bloody idol," she whispered, "that's wot it was, that parcel, and he—why, he's a bloody secret worshipper." And she crossed herself. "That's why I said I put it on the stove—see?"

The housemaid stared and gasped.

"And you mark my words, young Jane!" added the cook, turning to her dough.

And there the matter rested for a period, for the cook, being Irish, had more laughter in her than tears, and beyond admitting to the scared housemaid that she had not really burnt the parcel but had left it on the study table, she almost forgot the incident. It was not her job, in any case, to answer the front door. She had "delivered" the parcel. Her conscience was quite clear.

Thus, nobody "marked her words" apparently, for nothing untoward happened, as the way is in remote Suburbia, and Monica in her lonely play was happy, and Colonel Masters as tyrannical and grim as ever. The moist wintry wind blew through the silver pine, the rain beat against the bow window, and no one called. For a week this lasted, a longish time in uneventful Suburbia.

But suddenly one morning Colonel Masters rang his study bell and, the housemaid being upstairs, it was the cook who answered. He held a brown paper parcel in his hands, half opened, the string dangling.

"I found this on my desk. I haven't been in my room for a week. Who brought it? And when did it come?" His face, yellow as usual, held a fiery tinge.

Mrs. O'Reilly replied, post-dating the arrival vaguely.

"I asked *who* brought it?" he insisted sharply.

"A stranger," she fumbled. "Not any one," she added nervously, "from hereabouts. No one I ever seen before. It was a man."

"What did he look like?" The question came like a bullet.

Mrs. O'Reilly was rather taken by surprise. "D-darkish," she stumbled. "Very darkish," she added, "if I saw him right. Only he came and went so quick I didn't get his face proper like, and . . ."

"Any message?" the Colonel cut her short.

She hesitated. "There was no answer," she began, remembering former occasions.

"Any *message*, I asked you?" he thundered.

"No message, sir, none at all. And he was gone before I could get his name and address, sir, but I think it was a sort of black man, or it may have been the darkness of the night—I couldn't reely say, sir . . ."

In another minute she would have burst into tears or dropped to the floor in a faint, such was her terror of her employer especially when she was lying blind. The Colonel, however, saved her both disasters by abruptly holding out the half opened parcel towards her. He neither cross-examined nor cursed her as she had expected. He spoke with the curtness that betrayed anger and anxiety, almost, it occurred to her, distress.

"Take it away and burn it," he ordered in his army voice, passing it into her outstretched hands. "Burn it," he repeated it, "or chuck the damned thing away." He almost flung it at her as though he did not want to touch it. "If the man comes back," he ordered in a voice of steel, "tell him it's been destroyed—and say it *didn't reach me*," laying tremendous emphasis on the final words. "You understand?" He almost chucked it at her.

"Yes, sir. Exactly, sir," and she turned and stumbled out, holding the parcel gingerly in her arms rather than in her hands and fingers, as though it contained something that might bite or sting.

Yet her fear had somehow lessened, for if he, Colonel Masters, could treat the parcel so contemptuously, why should she feel afraid of it. And, once alone in her kitchen among her household gods, she opened it. Turning back the thick paper wrappings, she started, and to her rather disappointed amazement, she found herself staring at nothing but a fair, waxen faced doll that could be bought in any toy-shop for one shilling and sixpence. A commonplace little cheap doll! Its face was pallid, white, expressionless, its flaxen hair was dirty, its tiny ill-shaped hands and fingers lay motionless by its side, its mouth was closed, though somehow grinning, no teeth visible, its eyelashes ridiculously like a worn tooth brush, its entire presentment in its flimsy skirt, contemptible, harmless, even ugly.

A doll! She giggled to herself, all fear evaporated.

"Gawd!" she thought. "The master must have a conscience like the floor of a parrot's cage! And worse than that!" She was too afraid of him to despise him, her feeling was probably more like pity. "At any rate," she reflected, "he had the wind up pretty bad. It was something else he expected—not a two-penny halfpenny doll!" Her warm heart felt almost sorry for him.

Instead of "chucking the damned thing away or burning it," however,—for it was quite a nice looking doll, she presented it to Monica, and Monica, having few new toys, instantly adored it, promising faithfully, as gravely warned by Mrs. O'Reilly, that she would never *never* let her father know she had it.

Her father, Colonel Hymber Masters, was, it seems, what's called a "disappointed" man, a man whose fate forced him to live in surroundings he detested, disappointed in his career probably, possibly in love as well, Monica a love-child doubtless, and limited by his pension to face daily conditions that he loathed.

He was a silent, bitter sort of fellow, no more than that, and not so much disliked in the neighbourhood, as misunderstood. A sombre man they reckoned him, with his dark, furrowed face and silent ways. Yet "dark" in the suburbs meant mysterious, and "silent" invited female fantasy to fill the vacuum. It's the frank, corn-haired man who invites sympathy and generous comment. He enjoyed his Bridge, however, and was accepted as a first-class player. Thus, he went out nightly, and rarely came back before midnight. He was welcome among the gamblers evidently, while the fact that he had an adored child at home softened the picture of this "mysterious" man.

Monica, though rarely seen, appealed to the women of the neighbourhood, and "whatever her origin" said the gossips, "he loves her."

To Monica, meanwhile, in her rather play-less, toy-less life, the doll, her new treasure, was a spot of gold. The fact that it was a "secret" present from her father, added to its value. Many other presents had come to her like that; she thought nothing of it; only, he had never given her a doll before, and it spelt rapture. Never, never, would she betray her pleasure and delight; it should remain her secret and his; and that made her love it all the more. She loved her father too, his taciturn silence was something she vaguely respected and adored. "That's just like father," she always said, when a strange new present came, and she knew instinctively that she must never say *Thank you* for it, for that was part of the lovely game between them. But this doll was exceptionally marvellous.

"It's much more real and alive than my teddy bear," she told the cook, after examining it critically. "What ever made him think of it? Why, it even talks to me!" and she cuddled and fondled the half misshapened toy. "It's my baby," she cried taking it against her cheek.

For no teddy-bear could really be a child; cuddly bears were not offspring, whereas a doll was a potential baby. It brought sweetness, as both cook and governess realized, into a rather grim house, hope and tenderness, a maternal flavour almost, something anyhow that no young bear could possibly bring. A child, a human baby! And yet both cook and governess— for both were present at the actual delivery—recalled later that Monica opened the parcel and recognised the doll with a yell of wild delight that seemed almost a scream of pain. There was this too high note of delirious exultation as though some instinctive horror of revulsion were instantly smothered and obliterated in a whirl of overmastering joy. It was Madame Jodzka who recalled—long afterwards—this singular contradiction.

"I did think she shrieked at it a bit, now you ask me," admitted Mrs. O'Reilly later, though at the actual moment all she said was "Oh, lovely, darling, ain't it a pet!" While all Madame Jodzka said was a cautionary "If you squash its mouth like that, Monica, it won't be able to breathe!"

While Monica, paying no attention to either of them, fell to cuddling the doll with ecstasy.

A cheap little flaxen-haired, waxen-faced doll.

That so strange a case should come to us at second hand is, admittedly, a pity; that so much of the information should reach us largely through a cook and housemaid and through a foreigner of questionable validity, is equally unfortunate. Where precisely the reported facts creep across the feathery frontier into the incredible and thence into the fantastic would need the spider's thread of the big telescopes to define. With the eye to the telescope, the thread of that New Zealand spider seems thick as a rope; but with the eye examining second-hand reports the thread becomes elusive gossamer.

The Polish governess, Madame Jodzka, left the house rather abruptly. Though adored by Monica and accepted by Colonel Masters, she left not long after the arrival of the doll. She was a comely, youngish widow of birth and breeding, tactful, discreet, understanding. She adored Monica, and Monica was happy with her; she feared her employer, yet perhaps secretly admired him as the strong, silent, dominating Englishman. He gave her great freedom, she never took liberties, everything went smoothly. The pay was good and she needed it. Then suddenly, she left. In the suddenness of her departure, as in the odd reason she gave for leaving, lie doubtless the first hints of this remarkable affair, creeping across that "feathery frontier" into the incredible and fantastic. An understandable reason she gave for leaving was that she was too frightened to stay in the house another night. She left at twenty-four hours' notice. Her reason was absurd, even if understandable, because any woman might find herself so frightened in a certain building that it has become intolerable to her nerves. Foolish or otherwise, this is understandable. An *idée fixe,* an obsession, once lodged in the mind of a superstitious, therefore hysterically-favoured woman, cannot be dislodged by argument. It may be absurd, yet it is "understandable."

The story behind the reason for Madame Jodzka's sudden terror is another matter, and it is best given quite simply. It relates to the doll. She swears by all her gods that she saw the doll "walking by itself." It was walking in a disjointed, hoppity, hideous fashion across the bed in which Monica lay sleeping

In the gleam of the night-light, Madame Jodzka swears she saw this happen. She was half inside the opened door, peeping in, as her habit and duty decreed, to see if all was well with the child before going up to bed herself. The light, if faint, was clear. A jerky movement on the counterpane first caught her attention, for a smallish object seemed blundering awk-wardly across its slippery silken surface. Something rolling, possibly, some object Monica had left outside on falling asleep rolling mechanically as the child shifted or turned over.

After staring for some seconds, she then saw that it was not merely an "object," since it had a living outline, nor was it rolling mechanically, or sliding, as she had first imagined. It was horribly taking steps, small but quite deliberate steps as though alive. It had a tiny, dreadful face, it had an expressionless tiny face, and the face had eyes—small, brightly shining eyes, and the eyes looked straight at Madame Jodzka.

She watched for a few seconds thunderstruck, and then suddenly realised with a shock of utter horror that this small, purposive monster was the doll, Monica's doll! And this doll was moving towards her across the tumbled surface of the counterpane. It was coming in her direction—straight at her.

Madame Jodzka gripped herself, physically and mentally, making a great effort, it seems, to deny the abnormal, the incredible. She denied the ice in her veins and down her spine. She prayed. She thought frantically of her priest in Warsaw. Making no audible sound, she screamed in her mind. But the doll, quickening its pace, came hobbling straight towards her, its glassy eyes fixed hard upon her own.

Then Madame Jodzka fainted.

That she was, in some ways, a remarkable woman, with a sense of values, is clear from the fact that she realised this story "wouldn't wash," for she confided it only to the cook in cautious whispers, while giving her employer some more "washable" tale about a family death that obliged her to hurry home to Warsaw. Nor was there the slightest attempt at embroidery, for on recovering consciousness she had recovered her courage, too—and done a remarkable thing: she had compelled herself to investigate. Aided and fortified by her religion, she compelled herself to make an examination. She had tiptoed further into the room, had made sure that Monica was sleeping peacefully, and that the doll lay motionless—half way down the counterpane. She gave it a long, concentrated look. Its lidless eyes, fringed by hideously ridiculous black lashes, were fixed on space. Its expression was not so much innocent, as blankly stupid, idiotic, a mask of death that aped cheaply a pretence of life, where life could never be. Not ugly merely, it was revolting.

Madame Jodzka, however, did more than study this visage with concentration, for with admirable pluck she forced herself to touch the little horror. She actually picked it up. Her faith, her deep religious conviction denied the former evidence of her senses. She had *not* seen movement. It was incredible, impossible. The fault lay somewhere in herself. This persuasion, at any rate, lasted long enough to enable her to touch the repulsive little toy, to pick it up, to lift it. She placed it steadily on the table near the bed between the bowls of flowers and the night-light, where it lay on its back helpless, innocent, yet horrible, and only then on shaking legs did she leave the room and go up to her own bed. That her fingers remained ice-cold until eventually she fell asleep can be explained, of course, too easily and naturally to claim examination.

Whether imagined or actual, it must have been, none the less, a horrifying spectacle—a mechanical outline from a commercial factory walking like a living thing with a purpose. It holds the nightmare touch. To Madame Jodzka, protected since youth within cast-iron tenets, it came as a shock. And a shock dislocates. The sight smashed everything she knew as possible and real. The flow of her blood was interrupted, it froze, there came icy terror into her heart, her normal mechanism failed for a moment, she fainted. And fainting seemed a natural result. Yet it was the shock of the incredible masquerade that gave her the courage to act. She loved Monica, apart from any consideration of paid duty. The sight of this tiny monstrosity strutting across the counterpane not far from the child's sleeping face and folded hands—it was this that enabled her to pick it up with naked fingers and set it out of reach. . . .

For hours, before falling asleep, she reviewed the incredible thing, alternately denying the facts, then accepting them, yet taking into sleep finally the assured conviction that her senses had not deceived her. There seems little, indeed, that in a court of law could have been advanced against her character for reliability, for sincerity, for the logic of her detailed account.

"I'm sorry," said Colonel Masters quietly, referring to her bereavement. He looked searchingly at her. "And Monica will miss you," he added with one of his rare smiles. "She needs you." Then just as she turned away, he suddenly extended his hand. "If perhaps later you can come back—do let me know. Your influence is—so helpful—and good."

She mumbled some phrase with a promise in it, yet she left with a queer, deep impression that it was not merely, not chiefly perhaps Monica who needed her. She wished he had not used quite those words. A sense of shame lay in her, almost as though she were running away from duty, or at least from a chance to help God had put in her way. "Your influence is—so good."

Already in the train and on the boat conscience attacked her, biting, scratching, gnawing. She had deserted a child she loved, a child who needed her, because she was scared out of her wits. No, that was a one-sided statement. She had left a house because the Devil had come into it. No, that was only partially true. When a hysterical temperament, engrained since early childhood in fixed dogmas, begins to sift facts and analyse reactions, logic and common sense themselves become confused. Thought led one way, emotion another, and no honest conclusion dawned on her mind.

She hurried on to Warsaw, to a stepfather, a retired General whose gay life had no place for her and who would not welcome her return. It was a derogatory prospect for this youngish widow who had taken a job in order to escape from his vulgar activities to return now empty-handed. Yet it was easier, perhaps, to face a stepfather's selfish anger than to go and tell Colonel Masters her real reason for leaving his service. Her conscience, too, troubled her on another score as thoughts and memories travelled backwards and half-forgotten details emerged.

Those spots of blood, for instance, mentioned by Mrs. O'Reilly, the superstitious Irish cook. She had made it a rule to ignore Mrs. O'Reilly's silly fairy tales, yet now she recalled suddenly those ridiculous discussions about the laundry list and the foolish remarks that the cook and housemaid had let fall.

"But there ain't no paint in a doll, I tell you. It's all sawdust and wax and muck," from the housemaid. "I know red paint when I sees it, and that ain't paint, it's blood." And from Mrs. O'Reilly later: "Mother o' God! Another red blob! She's biting her finger-nails—and that's not *my* job. . .!"

The red stains on sheets and pillow cases were puzzling certainly, but Madame Jodzka, hearing these remarks by chance as it were, had paid no particular attention to them at the moment. The laundry lists were hardly her affair. These ridiculous servants anyhow. . . ! And yet, now in the train, those spots of red, be they paint or blood, crept back to trouble her.

Another thing, oddly enough, also troubled her—the ill-defined feeling that she was deserting a man who needed help, help that she could give. It was too vague to put into words. Was it based on his remark that her influence was "good" perhaps? She could not say. It was an intuition, and few intuitions bear analysis. Supporting it, however, was a conviction she had felt since first she entered the service of Colonel Masters, the conviction, namely, that he had a Past that frightened him. There was something he had done, something he regretted and was probably ashamed of, something at any rate, for which he feared retribution. A retribution, moreover, he expected; a punishment that would come like a thief in the night and seize him by the throat.

It was against this dreaded vengeance that her influence was "good," a protective influence possibly that her religion supplied, something on the side of the angels, in any case, that her personality provided.

Her mind worked thus, it seems; and whether a concealed admiration for this sombre and mysterious man, an admiration and protective instinct never admitted even to her inmost self, existed below the surface, hidden yet urgent, remains the secret of her own heart.

It was naturally and according to human nature, at any rate, that after a few weeks of her stepfather's outrageous behaviour in the house, his cruelty too, she decided to return. She prayed to her gods incessantly, also she found oppressive her sense of neglected duty and failure of self-respect. She returned to the soulless suburban villa. It was understandable; the welcome from Monica was also understandable, the relief and pleasure of Colonel Masters still more so. It was expressed, this latter, in a courteous message only, tactfully worded, as though she had merely left for brief necessity, for it was some days before she actually saw him to speak to. From cook and housemaid the welcome was voluble and—disquieting. There were no more inexplicable "spots of red," but there were other unaccountable happenings even more distressing.

"She's missed you something terrible," said Mrs. O'Reilly, "though she's found something else to keep her quiet—if you like to put it that way." And she made the sign of the cross.

"The doll?" asked Madame Jodzka with a start of shocked horror, forcing herself to come straight to the point and forcing herself also to speak lightly, casually.

"That's it, Madame. The bleeding doll."

The governess had heard the strange adjective many times already, but did not know whether to take it figuratively or not. She chose the latter.

"Blood?" she asked in a lowered voice.

The cook's body gave an odd jerk. "Well," she explained, "I meant more the way it goes on. Like a thing of flesh and blood, if you get me. And the way *she* treats it and plays with it," and her voice, while loud, had a hush of fear in it somewhere. She held her arms before her in a protective, shielding way, as though to ward off aggression.

"Scratches ain't proof of nothing," interjected the housemaid scornfully.

"You mean," asked Madame Jodzka gravely, "there's a question of—of injury—to someone?" She suppressed an involuntary gasp, but paid no attention to the maid's interruption otherwise.

Mrs. O'Reilly seemed to mis-manage her breath for a moment.

"It ain't Miss Monica it's after," she announced in a defiant whisper as soon as she recovered herself, "it's someone else. *That's* what I mean. And no man as black as *he* was," she let herself go, "ever brought no good into a house, not since I was born."

"Someone else—?" repeated Madame Jodzka almost to herself, seizing the vital words.

"You and yer black man!" interjected the housemaid. "Get along with yer! Thank God I ain't a Christian or anything like that! But I did 'ear them sort of jerky shuffling footsteps one night, I admit, and the doll did look bigger—swollen like—when I peeked in and looked—"

"Stop it!" cried Mrs. O'Reilly, "for you ain't saying what's true or what you reely know."

She turned to the governess.

"There's more talk what means nothing about this doll," she said by way of apology, "than all the fairy tales I was brought up with as a child in Mayo, and I—I wouldn't be believing anything of it."

Turning her back contemptuously on the chattering housemaid, she came close to Madame Jodzka.

"There's no harm coming to Miss Monica, Madame," she whispered vehemently, "you can be quite sure about *her*. Any trouble there may be is for someone else." And again she crossed herself.

Madame Jodzka, in the privacy of her room, reflected between her prayers. She felt a deep, a dreadful uneasiness.

A doll! A cheap, tawdry little toy made in factories by the hundred, by the thousand, a manufactured article of commerce for children to play with . . . But . . .

"The way she treats it and plays with it . . ." rang on in her disturbed mind.

A doll! But for the maternal suggestion, a doll was a pathetic, even horrible plaything, yet to watch a child busy with it involved deep reflections, since here the future mother prophesied. The child fondles and caresses her doll with passionate love, cares for it, seeks its welfare, yet stuffs it down into the perambulator, its head and neck twisted, its limbs broken and contorted, leaving it atrociously upside down so that blood and breathing cannot possibly function, while she runs to the window to see if the rain has stopped or the sun has come out. A blind and hideous automatism dictated by the Race, provided nothing of more immediate interest interferes, yet a herd-instinct that overcomes all obstacles, its vitality insuperable. The maternity instinct defies, even denies death. The doll, whether left upside down on the floor with broken teeth and ruined eyes, or lovingly arranged to be overlaid in the night, squashed, tortured, mutilated, survives all cruelties and disasters, and asserts finally its immortal qualities. It is unkillable. It is beyond death.

A child with her doll, reflected Madame Jodzka, is an epitome of nature's remorseless and unconquerable passion, of her dominant purpose—the survival of the race. . . .

Such thoughts, influenced perhaps by her bitter subconscious grievance against nature for depriving her of a child of her own, were unable to hold that level for long; they soon dropped back to the concrete case that perplexed and frightened her—Monica and her flaxen haired, sightless, idiotic doll. In the middle of her prayers, falling asleep incontinently, she did not even dream of it, and she woke refreshed and vigorous, facing the fact that sooner or later, sooner probably, she would have to speak to her employer.

She watched and listened. She watched Monica; she watched the doll. All seemed as normal as in a thousand other homes. Her mind reviewed the position, and where mind and superstition clashed, the former held its own easily. During her evening off she enjoyed the local cinema, leaving the heated building with the conviction that coloured fantasy benumbed the faculties, and that ordinary life was in itself prosaic. Yet before she had covered the half-mile to the house, her deep, unaccountable uneasiness returned with overmastering power.

Mrs. O'Reilly had seen Monica to bed for her, and it was Mrs. O'Reilly who let her in. Her face was like the dead.

"It's been talking," whispered the cook, even before she closed the door. She was white about the gills.

"Talking! *Who's* been talking? What do you mean?"

Mrs. O'Reilly closed the door softly. "Both," she stated with dramatic emphasis, then sat down and wiped her face. She looked distraught with fear.

Madame took command, if only a command based on dreadful insecurity.

"Both?" she repeated, in a voice deliberately loud so as to counteract the other's whisper. "What are you talking about?"

"They've *both* been talking—talking together," stated the cook.

The governess kept silent for a moment, fighting to deny a shrinking heart.

"You've heard them talking together, you mean?" she asked presently in a shaking voice that tried to be ordinary.

Mrs. O'Reilly nodded, looking over her shoulder as she did so. Her nerves were, obviously, in rags. "I thought you'd *never* come back," she whimpered. "I could hardly stay in the house."

Madame looked intently into her frightened eyes.

"You *heard* . . . ?" she asked quietly.

"I listened at the door. There were two voices. Different voices."

Madame Jodzka did not insist or cross-examine, as though acute fear helped her to a greater wisdom.

"You mean, Mrs. O'Reilly," she said in flat, quiet tones, "that you heard Miss Monica talking to her doll as she always does, and herself inventing the doll's answers in a changed voice? Isn't that what you mean you heard?"

But Mrs. O'Reilly was not to be shaken. By way of answer she crossed herself and shook her head.

She spoke in a low whisper. "Come up now and listen with me, Madame, and judge for yourself."

Thus, soon after midnight, and Monica long since asleep, these two, the cook and governess in a suburban villa, took up their places in the dark corridor outside a child's bedroom door. It was a quiet windless night; Colonel Masters, whom they both feared, doubtless long since gone to his room in another corner of the ungainly villa. It must have been a long dreary wait before sounds in the child's bedroom first became audible—the low quiet sound of voices talking audibly—two voices. A hushed, secretive, unpleasant sound in the room where Monica slept peacefully with her beloved doll beside her. Yet two voices assuredly, it was.

Both women sat erect, both crossed themselves involuntarily, exchanging glances. Both were bewildered, terrified. Both sat aghast.

What lay in Mrs. O'Reilly's superstitious mind, only the gods of "ould Oireland" can tell, but what the Polish woman's contained was clear as a bell; it was not two voices talking, it was only one. Her ear was pressed against the crack in the door. She listened intently; shaking to the bone, she listened. Voices in sleep-talking, she remembered, changed oddly.

"The child's talking to herself in sleep," she whispered firmly, "and that's all it is, Mrs. O'Reilly. She's just talking in her sleep," she repeated with emphasis to the woman crowding against her shoulder as though in need of support. "Can't you hear it," she added loudly, half angrily, "isn't it the same voice always? Listen carefully and you'll see I'm right."

She listened herself more closely than before.

"Listen! Hark . . .!" she repeated in a breathless whisper, concentrating her mind upon the curious sound, "isn't that the same voice—answering itself?"

Yet, as she listened, another sound disturbed her concentration, and this time it seemed a sound behind her—a faint, rustling, shuffling sound rather like footsteps hurrying away on tiptoe. She turned her head sharply and found that she had been whispering to no one. There was no one beside her. She was alone in the darkened corridor. Mrs. O'Reilly was gone. From the well of the house below a voice came up in a smothered cry beneath the darkened stairs: "Mother o'God and all the Saints . . ." and more besides.

A gasp of surprise and alarm escaped her doubtless at finding herself deserted and alone but in the same instant, exactly as in the story books, came another sound that caught her breath still more aghast—the rattle of a key in the front door below. Colonel Masters, after all, had not yet come in and gone to bed as expected: he was coming in now. Would Mrs. O'Reilly have time to slip across the hall before he caught her? More—and worse—would he come up and peep into Monica's bedroom on his way up to bed, as he rarely did? Madame Jodzka listened, her nerves in rags. She heard him fling down his coat. He was a man quick in such actions. The stick or umbrella was banged down noisily, hastily. The same instant his step sounded on the stairs. He was coming up. Another minute and he would start into the passage where she crouched against Monica's door.

He was mounting rapidly, two stairs at a time.

She, too, was quick in action and decision. She thought in a flash. To be caught crouching outside the door was ludicrous, but to be caught inside the door would be natural and explicable. She acted at once.

With a palpitating heart, she opened the bedroom door and stepped inside. A second later she heard Colonel Masters' tread, as he stumped along the corridor up to bed. He passed the door. He went on. She heard this with intense relief.

Now, inside the room, the door closed behind her, she saw the picture clearly.

Monica, sound asleep, was playing with her beloved doll, but in her sleep. She was indubitably in deep slumber. Her fingers, however, were roughing the doll this way and that, as though some dream perplexed her. The child was mumbling in her sleep, though no words were distinguishable. Muffled sighs and groans issued from her lips. Yet another sound there certainly was, though it could not have issued from the child's mouth. Whence, then, did it come?

Madame Jodzka paused, holding her breath, her heart panting. She watched and listened intently. She heard squeaks and grunts, but a moment's examination convinced her whence these noises came. They did not come from Monica's lips. They issued indubitably from the doll she clutched and twisted in her dream. The joints, as Monica twisted them, emitted these odd sounds, as though the sawdust in knees and elbows wheezed and squeaked against the unnatural rubbing. Monica obviously was wholly unconscious of these noises. As the doll's neck screwed round, the material— wax, thread, sawdust—produced this curious grating sound that was almost like syllables of a word or words.

Madame Jodzka stared and listened. She felt icy cold. Seeking for a natural explanation she found none. Prayer and terror raced in her helter-skelter. Her skin began to sweat.

Then suddenly Monica, her expression peaceful and composed, turned over in her sleep, and the dreadful doll, released from the dream-clutch, fell to one side on the bed and lay apparently lifeless and inert. In which moment, to Madame Jodzka's unbelieving yet horrified ears, it continued to squeak and utter. It went on mouthing by itself. Worse than that, the next instant it stood abruptly upright, rising on its twisted legs. It started moving. It began to move, walking crookedly, across the counterpane. Its glassy, sightless eyes seemed to look straight at her. It presented an inhuman and appalling picture, a picture of the utterly incredible. With a queer, hoppity motion of its broken legs and joints, it came fumbling and tumbling across the rough unevenness of the slippery counterpane towards her. Its appearance was deliberate and aggressive. The sounds, as of syllables, came with it—strange, meaningless syllables that yet managed to convey anger. It stumbled towards her like a living thing. Its whole presentment conveyed attack.

Once again, this effect of a mere child's toy, aping the life of some awful monstrosity with purpose and passion in its hideous tiny outline, brought collapse to the plucky Polish governess. The rush of blood without control drained her heart, and a moment of unconsciousness supervened so that everything, as it were, turned black.

This time, however, the moment of dark unconsciousness passed instantly: it came and went, almost like a moment of forgetfulness in passion. Passionate it certainly was, for the reaction came upon her like a storm. With recovered consciousness a sudden rage rushed into her woman heart—perhaps a coward's rage, an exaggerated fury against her own weakness? It rushed, in any case, to help her. She staggered, caught her breath, clutched violently at the cupboard next her, and—recovered her self-control. A fury of resentment blazed through her, fury against this utterly incredible exhibition of a wax doll walking and squawking as though it were something intelligently alive that could utter syllables. Syllables, she felt convinced, in a language she did not know.

If the monstrous can paralyse, it also can affront. The sight and sound of this cheap factory toy behaving with a will and heart of its own stung her into an act of violence that became imperative. For it was more than she could stand. Irresistibly, she rushed forward. She hurled herself against it, her only available weapon the high-heeled shoe her foot kicked loose on the instant, determined to smash down the frightful apparition into fragments and annihilate it. Hysterical, no doubt, she was at the moment, and yet logical: the godless horror must be blotted out of visible existence. This one thing obsessed her—to destroy beyond all possibility of survival. It must be smashed into fragments, into dust.

They stood close, face to face, the glassy eyes staring into her own, her hand held high for the destruction she craved—but the hand did not fall. A stinging pain, sharp as a serpent's bite, darted suddenly through her fingers, wrist and arm, her grip was broken, the shoe spun sideways across the room, and in the flickering light of the candle, it seemed to her, the whole room quivered. Paralysed and helpless, she stood utterly aghast. What gods or saints could come to aid her? None. Her own will alone could help her. Some effort, at any rate, she made, trembling, on the edge of collapse: "My God!" she heard her half whispering, strangled voice cry out. "It is not true! You are a lie! My God denies you! I call upon my God. . . !"

Whereupon, to her added horror, the dreadful little doll, waving a broken arm, squawked back at her, as though in definite answer, the strange disjointed syllables she could not understand, syllables as though in another tongue. The same instant it collapsed abruptly on the counterpane like a toy balloon that had been pricked. It shrank down in a mutilated mess before her eyes, while Monica—added touch of horror—stirred uneasily in her sleep, turning over and stretching out her hands as though feeling blindly for something that she missed. And this sight of the innocently sleeping child fumbling instinctively towards an incomprehensibly evil and dangerous something that attracted her proved again too strong for the Polish woman to control.

The blackness intervened a second time.

It was undoubtedly a blur in memory that followed, emotion and superstition proving too much for common-sense to deal with. She just remembers violent, unreasoned action on her part before she came back to clearer consciousness in her own room, praying volubly on her knees against her own bed. The interval of transit down the corridor and upstairs remained a blank. Yet her shoe was with her, clutched tightly in her hand. And she remembered also having clutched an inert, waxen doll with frantic fingers, clutched and crushed and crumpled its awful little frame till the sawdust came spurting from its broken joints and its tiny body was mutilated beyond recognition, if not annihilated . . . then stuffing it down ruthlessly on a table far out of Monica's reach, Monica lying peacefully in deepest sleep. She remembered that. She also saw the clear picture of the small monster lying upside down, grossly untidy, an obscene attitude in the disorder of its flimsy dress and exposed limbs, lying motionless, its eyes crookedly aglint, motionless, yet alive still, alive moreover with intense and malignant purpose.

No duration or intensity of prayer could obliterate the picture.

She knew now that a plain, face to face talk with her employer was essential; her conscience, her peace of mind, her sanity, her sense of duty all demanded this. Deliberately, and she was sure, rightly, she had never once risked a word with the child herself. Danger lay that way, the danger of emphasizing something in the child's mind that was best left ignored. But with Colonel Masters, who paid her for her services, believed in her integrity, trusted her, with him there must be an immediate explanation.

An interview was absurdly difficult; in the first place because he loathed and avoided such occasions; secondly because he was so exceedingly impervious to approach, being so rarely even visible at all. At night he came home late, in the mornings no one dared go near him. He expected the little household, once its routine established, to run itself. The only inmate who dared beard him was Mrs. O'Reilly, who periodically, once every six months, walked straight into his study, gave notice, received an addition to her wages, and then left him alone for another six months.

Madame Jodzka, knowing his habits, waylaid him in the hall next morning while Monica was lying down before lunch, as usual. He was on his way out and she had been watching from the upper landing. She had hardly set eyes on him since her return from Warsaw. His lean, upright figure, his dark, emotionless face, she thought magnificent. He was the perfect expression of the soldier. Her heart fluttered as she raced downstairs. Her carefully prepared sentences, however, evaporated when he stopped and looked at her, a jumble of wild words pouring from her in confused English instead. He cut her rigmarole short, though he listened politely enough at first.

"I'm so glad you were able to come back to us, as I told you. Monica missed you very much—"

"She has something now she plays with—"

"The very thing," he interrupted. "No doubt the kind of toy she needs . . . Your excellent judgment . . . Please tell me if there's anything else you think . . ." and he half turned as though to move away.

"But I didn't get it. It's a horrible—*horrible*—"

Colonel Masters uttered one of his rare laughs. "Of course, all children's toys are horrible, but if she's pleased with . . . I haven't seen it, I'm no judge . . . If you can buy something better—" and he shrugged his shoulders.

"I didn't buy it," she cried desperately. "It was brought. It makes sounds by itself—syllables. I've seen it move—move by itself. It's a doll."

He turned from the front door which he had just reached as though he had been shot; the skin held a sudden pallor beneath the flush and something contradicted the blazing eyes, something that seemed to shrink.

"A doll," he repeated in a very quiet voice. "You said—a doll?"

But his eyes and face disconcerted her, so that she merely gave a fumbling account of a parcel that had been brought. His question about a parcel he had ordered strictly to be destroyed added to her confusion.

"Wasn't it?" he asked in a rasping whisper, as though a disobeyed order seemed incredible.

"It was thrown away, I believe," she prevaricated, unable to meet his eyes, anxious to protect the cook as well. "I think Monica—perhaps found it." She despised her lack of courage, but his intensity scattered her wits; she was conscious, moreover, of a strange desire not to give him pain, as though his safety and happiness, not Monica's, were at stake. "It—talks!—as well as *moves*," she cried desperately, forcing herself at last to look at him.

Colonel Masters seemed to stiffen; his breath caught oddly.

"You say Monica has it? Plays with it? You've seen movement and heard sounds like syllables?" He asked the question in a low voice, almost as though talking to himself. "You've—listened?" he whispered.

Unable to find convincing words, she bowed her head, while some terror in him came across to her like a blast of icy wind. The man was afraid in his heart. Instead, however, of some explosive reply by way of blame or criticism, he spoke quietly, even calmly: "You did right to come and tell me this—quite right," adding then in so low a tone that she barely caught the ominous words, "for I have been expecting something of the sort . . . sooner or later . . . it was bound to come . . ." the voice dying away into the handkerchief he put to his face.

And abruptly then, as though aware of an appeal for sympathy, an emotional reaction swept her fear away. Stepping closer, she looked her employer straight in the eyes.

"See the child for yourself," she said with sudden firmness. "Come and listen with me. Come into the bedroom."

She saw him stagger. For a moment he said nothing.

"Who," he then asked, the low voice unsteady, "who brought the parcel?"

"A man, I believe."

There was a pause that seemed like minutes before his next question.

"White," he asked, "or—black?"

"Dark," she told him, "very dark."

He was shaking like a leaf, the skin of his face blanched; he leaned against the door, wilted, limp; unless she somehow took command there threatened a collapse she did not wish to witness.

"You shall come with me tonight," she said firmly, "and we shall listen together. Wait till I return now. I go for brandy," and a minute later as she came back breathless and watched him gulp down half a tumbler full, she knew that she had done right in telling him. His obedience proved it, though it seemed strange that cowardice should borrow from its like to produce courage.

"Tonight," she repeated, "tonight after your Bridge. We meet in the corridor outside the bedroom. I shall be there. At half-past twelve."

He pulled himself into an upright position, staring at her fixedly, making a movement of his head, half bow, half nod.

"Twelve thirty," he muttered, "in the passage outside the bedroom door," and using his stick heavily rather, he opened the door and passed out into the drive. She watched him go, aware that her fear had changed to pity, aware also that she watched the stumbling gait of a man too conscience-stricken to know a moment's peace, too frightened even to think of God.

Madame Jodzka kept the appointment; she had eaten no supper, but had stayed in her room—praying. She had first put Monica to bed.

"My doll," the child pleaded, good as gold, after being tucked up. "I must have my doll or else I'll never get to sleep," and Madame Jodzka had brought it with reluctant fingers, placing it on the night-table beside the bed.

"She'll sleep quite comfortably here, Monica, darling. Why not leave her outside the sheets?" It had been carefully mended, she noticed, patched together with pins and stitches.

The child grabbed at it. "I want her in bed beside me, close against me," she said with a happy smile. "We tell each other stories. If she's too far away I can't hear what she says." And she seized it with a cuddling pleasure that made the woman's heart turn cold.

"Of course, darling—if it helps you to fall asleep quickly, you shall have it," and Monica did not see the trembling fingers, not notice the horror in the face and voice. Indeed, hardly was the doll against her cheek on the pillow, her fingers half stroking the flaxen hair and pink wax cheeks, than her eyes closed, a sigh of deep content breathed out, and Monica was asleep.

Madame Jodzka, fearful of looking behind her, tiptoed to the door, and left the room. In the passage she wiped a cold sweat from her forehead. "God bless her and protect her," her heart murmured, "and may God forgive me if I've sinned."

She kept the appointment; she knew Colonel Masters would keep it, too.

It had been a long wait from eight o'clock till after midnight. With great determination she had kept away from the bedroom door, fearful lest she might hear a sound that would necessitate action on her part: she went to her room and stayed there. But praying exhausted itself, for it both excited and betrayed her. If her God could help, a brief request alone was needed. To go on praying for help hour by hour was not only an insult to her deity, but it also wore her out physically. She stopped, therefore, and read some pages of a Polish saint which she did not understand. Later she fell into a state of horrified nervous drowse. In due course, she slept . . .

A noise awoke her—steps going softly past her door. A glance at her watch showed eleven o'clock. The steps, though stealthy, were familiar. Mrs. O'Reilly was waddling up to bed. The sounds died away. Madame Jodzka, a trifle ashamed, though she hardly knew why, returned to her Polish saint, yet determined to keep her ears open. Then slept again . . .

What woke her a second time she could not tell. She was startled. She listened. The night was unpleasantly still, the house quiet as the grave. No casual traffic passed. No wind stirred the gloomy evergreens in the drive. The world outside was silent. And then, as she saw by her watch that it was some minutes after midnight, a sharp click became audible that acted like a pistol shot to her keyed-up nerves. It was the front door closing softly. Steps followed across the hall below, then up the stairs, unsteadily a little. Colonel Masters had come in. He was coming up slowly, unwillingly she felt, to keep the appointment. Madame Jodzka started from her chair, looked in the glass, mumbled a quick confused prayer, and opened her door into the dark passage.

She stiffened, physically and mentally. "Now, he'll hear and perhaps see— for himself," she thought. "And God help him!"

She marched along the passage and reached the door of Monica's bedroom, listening with such intentness that she seemed to hear only the confused running murmur of her own blood. Having reached the appointed spot, she stood stock still and waited while his steps approached. A moment later his bulk blocked the passage, shown up as a dark shadow by the light in the hall below. This bulk came nearer, came right up to her. She believed she said "Good evening," and that he mumbled something about "I said I'd come . . . damned nonsense . . ." or words to that effect, whereupon the couple stood side by side in the darkened silence of the corridor, remote from the rest of the house, and waited without further words. They stood shoulder to shoulder outside the door of Monica's bedroom. Her heart was knocking against her side.

She heard his breathing, there came a whiff of spirits, of stale tobacco smoke, his outline seemed to shift against the wall unsteadily, he moved his feet; and a sudden, extraordinary wave of emotion swept over her, half of protective maternal yearning, half almost of sexual desire, so that for a passing instant she burned to take him in her arms and kiss him savagely, and at the same time shield him from some appalling danger his blunt ignorance laid him open to. With revulsion, pity, and a sense of sin and passion, she acknowledged this odd sudden weakness in herself, but the face of the Warsaw priest flashed across her fuddled mind the next instant. There was evil in the air. This meant the Devil. She felt herself trembling dreadfully, shaking in her shoes, losing her balance, her whole body leaning over, but leaning in his direction. A moment more and she must have fallen towards him, dropped into his arms.

A sound broke the silence, and she drew up just in time. It came from beyond the door, from inside the bedroom.

"Hark!" she whispered, her hand upon his arm, and while he made no movement, spoke no word, she saw his head and shoulders bend down toward the panel of the closed door. There was a noise, upon the other side, there were noises, Monica's voice distinctly recognizable, another slighter, shriller sound accompanying it, breaking in upon it, answering it. Two voices.

"Listen," she repeated in a whisper scarcely audible, and felt his warm hand grip her own so fiercely that it hurt her.

No words were distinguishable at first, just these odd broken sounds of two separate voices in that dark corridor of the silent house—the voice of a child, and the other a strange faint, hardly a human sound, while yet a voice.

"Que le bon Dieu—" she began, then faltered, breath failing her, for she saw Colonel Masters stoop down suddenly and do the last thing that would have occurred to her as likely: he put his eye to the key-hole and kept it there steadily, for the best part of a minute, his hand still gripping her own firmly. He knelt on one knee to keep his balance.

The sounds had ceased, no movement now stirred inside the room. The night-light, she knew, would show him clearly the pillows of the bed, Monica's head, the doll in her arms. Colonel Masters must see clearly anything there was to see, and he yet gave no sign that he saw anything. She experienced a queer sensation for a few seconds—almost as though she had perhaps imagined everything and proved herself a consummate, idiotic, hysterical fool. For a few seconds this ghastly thought flashed over her, the odd silence emphasizing it. Had she been after all, just a crazy lunatic? Had her senses all deceived her? Why should he see nothing, make no sign? Why had the voice, the voices, ceased? Not a murmur of any sort was audible in the room.

Then Colonel Masters, suddenly releasing his grip of her hand, shuffled on to both feet and stood up straight, while in the same instant she herself stiffened, trying to prepare for the angry scorn, the contemptuous abuse he was about to pour upon her. Protecting herself against this attack, expecting it, she was the more amazed at what she did hear:

"I saw it," came in a strangled whisper. "I saw it walk!"

She stood paralysed.

"It's watching me," he added, scarcely audible. "Me!"

The revulsion of feeling at first left her speechless; it was the sheer terror in his strangled whisper that restored a measure of self possession to her. Yet it was he who found words first, awful whispered words, words spoken to himself, it seemed, more than to her.

"It's what I've always feared—I knew it must come some day—yet not like this. Not this way."

Then immediately the voice in the room became audible, and it was a sweet and gentle voice, sincere and natural, with feeling in it—Monica's childish voice, pleading:

"Don't go, don't leave me! Come back into bed—please."

An incomprehensible sound followed, as though by way of answer. There were syllables in that faint, creaky tone Madame Jodzka recognised, but syllables she could not comprehend. They seemed to enter her like point of ice. She froze. And facing her stood the motionless, inanimate bulk of him, his outline, then leaned over towards her, his lips so close to her own face that, as he spoke, she felt the breath upon her cheek.

"Buth laga . . ." she heard him repeat the syllables to himself again and again. *"Revenge . . .* in Hindustani . . .!" He drew a long, anguished breath. The sounds sank into her like drops of poison, the syllables she had heard several times already but had not understood. At last she understood their meaning. Revenge!

"I must go in, go in," he was mumbling to himself. "I must go in and face it." Her intuition was justified: the danger was not for Monica but for himself. Her sudden protective maternal instinct found its explanation too. The lethal power concentrated in that hideous puppet was aimed at *him.* He began to edge impetuously past her.

"No!" she cried. "I'll go! Let me go in!" pushing him aside with all her strength. But his hand was already on the knob and the next instant the door was open and he was inside the room. On the threshold they stood still a second side by side, though she was slightly behind, struggling to shove past him and stand protectively in front.

She stared across his shoulder, her eyes so wide open that the intense strain to note everything at once threatened to defeat its own end. Sight, none the less, worked normally; she saw all there was to see, and that was—nothing; nothing unusual, that is, nothing abnormal, nothing terrifying, so that this second time the threat of anti-climax rose to her mind. Had she worked herself up to this peak of horror merely to behold Monica lying sound asleep in a safe and quiet room? The flickering night-light revealed no more than a child in natural slumber without a toy of any sort against her pillow. There stood the glass of water beside the flowers in their saucer, the picture-book on the sill of the window within reach, the window opened a little at the bottom, and there also lay the calm face of Monica with eyes tight shut upon the pillow. Her breathing was deep and regular, no sign of disquiet anywhere, no hint of disturbance that might have accompanied that pleading sentence of two minutes ago, except that the bedclothes were perhaps somewhat tumbled. The counterpane humped itself in folds towards the foot of the bed, she noticed, as though Monica, finding it too warm, had tossed it away in sleep. No more than that.

In that first moment Colonel Masters and the governess took in this whole pretty picture complete. The room was so still that the child's breathing was distinctly audible. Their eyes roved all over. Nothing was anywhere in movement. Yet the same instant Madame Jodzka became aware that there *was* movement. Something stirred. The report came, perhaps, through her skin, for no sense announced it. It was undeniable; in that still, silent room there was movement somewhere, and with that unreported movement there was danger.

Certain, rightly or wrongly, that she herself was safe, also that the quietly sleeping child was safe, she was equally certain that Colonel Masters was the one in danger. She knew that in her very bones.

"Wait here by the door," she said almost peremptorily, as she felt him pushing past her further into the quiet room. "You saw it watching you. It's somewhere—Take care!"

She clutched at him, but he was already beyond her.

"Damned nonsense," he muttered and strode forward.

Never before in her whole life had she admired a man more than in this instant when she saw him moving towards what she knew to be physical and spiritual danger—never before, and never again, was such a hideous and dreadful sight to be repeatable in a woman's life. Pity and horror drowned her in a sea of passionate, futile longing. A man going to meet his fate, it flashed over her, was something none, without power to help, should witness. No human power can stay the course of the stars.

Her eye rested, as it were by chance, on the crumpled ridges and hollows of the discarded counterpane. These lay by the foot of the bed in shadow, confused a little in their contours and their masses. Had Monica not moved, they must have lain thus till morning. But Monica did move. At this particular moment she turned over in her sleep. She stretched her little legs before settling down in the new position, and this stretching squeezed and twisted the contours of the heavy counterpane at the foot of the bed. The tiny landscape altered thus a fraction, its immediate detail shifted. And an outline—a very small outline—emerged. Hitherto, it had lain concealed among the shadows. It emerged now with disconcerting rapidity. As though a spring released it. Out of its nest of darkness it seemed almost to leap forward. Fast it came, supernaturally fast, its velocity actually shocking, for a shock came with it. It was exceedingly small, it was exceedingly dreadful, its head erect and venomous and the movement of its legs and arms, as of its bitter, glittering eyes, aping humanity. Malignant evil, personified and aggressive, shaped itself in this otherwise ridiculous outline.

It was the doll.

Racing with incredible security across the slippery surface of the crumpled silk counterpane, it dived and climbed and shot forward with an appearance of complete control and deliberate purpose. That it had a definite aim was overwhelmingly obvious. Its fixed, glassy eyes were concentrated upon a point beyond and behind the terrified governess, the point precisely where Colonel Masters, her employer, stood against her shoulder.

A frantic, half protective movement on her part, seemed lost in the air. . . .

She turned instinctively, putting an arm about his shoulders, which he instantly flung off.

"Let the bloody thing come," he cried. "I'll deal with it . . .!" He thrust her violently aside.

The doll came at him. The hinges of its diminutive broken arms and its jointed legs emitted a thin, creaking sound as it came darting—the syllables Madame Jodzka had already heard more than once. Syllables she had heard without understanding—*"buth laga"*—but syllables now packed with awful meaning: *Revenge.*

The sounds hissed and squeaked, yet clear as a bell as the beast advanced at this miraculous speed.

Before Colonel Masters could move an inch backwards or forwards in self protection, before he could command himself to any sort of action, or contrive the smallest measure of self defence, it was off the bed and at him. It settled. Savagely, its little jaws of tiny make-believe were bitten deep into Colonel Masters' throat, fastened tightly.

In a flash this happened, in a flash it was over. In Madame Jodzka's memory it remained like the impression of a lightning flash, simultaneously etched in black and white. It had happened in the present as though it had no past. It came and was gone again. Her faculties, as after a vivid lightning flash, were momentarily paralysed, without past or present. She had witnessed these awful things, but had not realized them. It was this lack of realization that struck her motionless and dumb.

Colonel Masters, on the other hand, stood beside her quietly as though nothing unusual had happened, wholly master of himself, calm, collected. At the moment of attack no sound had left his lips, there had been no gesture even of defence. Whatever had come, he had apparently accepted. The words that now fell from his lips were, thus, all the more dreadful in their appalling commonplaceness.

"Hadn't you better put that counterpane straight a bit. . . . Perhaps?"

Common sense, as always, enables the gas of hysteria to escape. Madame Jodzka gasped, but she obeyed. Automatically she moved across to do his bidding, yet aware, even as she thus moved, that he flicked something from his neck, as though a wasp, a mosquito, or some poisonous insect, had tried to sting him. She remembered no more than that, for he, in his calmness, had contributed nothing else.

Fumbling with the folds of slippery counterpane she tried to straighten out, she was startled to find that Monica was sitting up in bed, awake.

"Oh, Doska—you here!" the child exclaimed innocently, straight out of sleep and using the affectionate nickname. "And Daddy, too! Oh, my goodness. . . !"

"Sm-moothing your bed, darling," she stammered, hardly aware of what she said. "You ought to be asleep. I just looked in to see . . ." She mumbled a few other automatic words.

"And Daddy with you!" repeated the child excitedly, sleep still about her, wondering what it all meant. "Ooh! Ooh!" holding out her arms.

This brief exchange of spoken words, though it takes a minute to describe, occurred simultaneously with the action—perhaps ten seconds all told, for while the governess fumbled with the counterpane, Colonel Masters was in the act of brushing something from his neck. Nothing else was audible, nothing but his quick gasp and sudden intake of breath: but something else—she swears it on her Warsaw priest—was visible. Madame Jodzka maintains by all her gods she saw this other thing.

In moments of paralysing stress it is not the senses that act less speedily nor with less precision; their action, on the contrary, is intensified and speeded up: what takes longer is the registration of their reports. The numbed brain causes the apparent delay; realization is slowed down.

Madame Jodzka thus only realized a fraction of a second later what her eyes had indubitably witnessed; a dark-skinned arm slanting in through the open window by the bed and snatching at a small object that lay on the floor after dropping from Colonel Masters' throat, then withdrawing again at lightning speed into the darkness of the night outside.

No one but herself, apparently, had seen this—it was almost super-naturally swift.

"And now you'll be asleep again in two minutes, lucky Monica," Colonel Masters was whispering over by the bed. "I just peeped in to see that you were all right . . ." His voice was thin, dreadfully soundless.

Madame Jodzka, against the door, frozen, terrified, looked on and listened.

"Are you quite well, Daddy? Sure? I had a dream, but it's gone now."

"Splendid. Never better in my life. But better still if I saw you sound asleep. Come now, I'll blow out this silly night-light, for that's what woke you up, I'll be bound."

He blew it out, he and the child blew it out together, the latter with sleepy laughter that then hushed. And Colonel Masters tiptoed to join Madame Jodzka at the door. "A lot of damned fuss about nothing," she heard him muttering in that same thin dreadful voice, and then, as they closed the door and stood a moment in the darkened passage, he did suddenly an unex-pected thing. He took the Polish woman in his arms, held her fiercely to him for a second, kissed her vehemently, and flung her away.

"Bless you and thank you," he said in a low, angry voice. "You did your best. You made a great fight. But I got what I deserved. I've been waiting years for it." And he was off down the stairs to his own quarters. Half way down he stopped and looked up to where she stood against the rails. "Tell the doctor," he whispered hoarsely, "that I took a sleeping draught—an overdose." And he was gone.

And this was, roughly, what she did tell the doctor next morning when a hurried telephone summons brought him to the bed whereon a dead man lay with a swollen, blackened tongue. She told the same tale at the inquest too and an emptied bottle of a powerful sleeping-draught supported her . . .

And Monica, too young to realize grief beyond its trumpery meaning of a selfishly felt loss, never once—oddly enough—referred to the absence of her lovely doll that had comforted so many hours, proved such an intimate companion day and night in a life that held no other playmates. It seemed forgotten, expunged utterly from her memory, as though it had never existed at all. She stared blankly, stupidly, when a doll was mentioned: she preferred her worn-out teddy bears. The slate of memory in this particular, was wiped clean.

"They're so warm and comfy," she described her bears, "and they cuddle without tickling. Besides," she added innocently, "they don't squeak and try to slip away . . ."

Thus in the suburbs, where great spaces between the lamps go dead at night, where the moist wind comes whispering through the mournful branches of the silver-pines, where nothing happens and people cry "Let's go to town!" there are occasional stirrings among the dead dry bones that hide behind respectable villa walls. . . .

RICHARD HUGHES

THE GHOST

He killed me quite easily by bumping my head on the cobbles. *Bang!* Lord, what a fool I was! All my hate went out with that first bang: a fool to have kicked up that fuss just because I had found him with another woman. And now he was doing this to me—*bang!* That was the second one, and with it *everything* went out.

My sleek young soul must have glistened somewhat in the moonlight, for I saw him look up from the body in a fixed sort of way. That gave me an idea: I would haunt him. All my life I had been scared of ghosts: now I was one myself I would get a bit of my own back. *He* never was; he said there weren't such things as ghosts. Oh weren't there! I'd soon teach him. John stood up, still staring in front of him: I could see him plainly: gradually all my hate came back. I thrust my face close up against his: but he didn't seem to see it, he just stared. Then he began to walk forward, as if to walk through me and I was afeard. Silly, for me—a spirit—to be afeard of his solid flesh; but there you are, fear doesn't act as you would expect, ever: and I gave back before him, then slipped aside to let him pass. Almost he was lost in the street-shadows before I recovered myself and followed him.

And yet I don't think he could have given me the slip: there was still something between us that drew me to him—willy-nilly, you might say, I followed him up High Street, and down Lily Lane.

Lily Lane was all shadows; but yet I could still see him as clear as if it was daylight. Then my courage came back to me: I quickened my pace till I was ahead of him—turned round, flapping my hands and making a moaning sort of noise like the ghosts did I'd read of. He began to smile a little, in a sort of satisfied way: but yet he didn't seem properly to see me. Could it be that his hard disbelief in ghosts made him so that he *couldn't see me? "Hoo!"* I whistled through my small teeth. *"Hoo! Murderer! Murderer!"*—Someone flung up a top window. "Who's that?" she called. "What's the matter?" So other people could hear, at any rate. But I kept silent; I wouldn't give him away—not yet. And all the time he walked straight forward, smiling to himself. He never had any conscience, I said to myself. There he is with new murder on his mind, smiling as easy as if it was nothing. But there was a sort of hard look about him, *all* the same.

It was odd, my being a ghost so suddenly, when ten minutes ago I was a living woman: and now, walking on air, with the wind clear and wet between my shoulder-blades. Ha-ha! I gave a regular shriek and a screech of laughter, it all felt so funny . . . surely John must have heard *that:* but no, he just turned the corner into Pole Street.

All along Pole Street the plane-trees were shedding their leaves, and then I knew what I would do. I made those dead leaves rise up on their thin edges, as if the wind was doing it. All along Pole Street they followed him, pattering on the roadway with their five dry fingers. But John just stirred among them with his feet, and went on, and I followed him: for, as I said, there was still some tie between us that drew me.

Once only he turned and seemed to see me; there was a sort of recognition in his face: but no fear, only triumph. "You're glad you've killed me," thought I, "but I'll make you sorry!"

And then all at once the fit left me. A nice sort of Christian, I, scarcely fifteen minutes dead and still thinking of revenge, instead of preparing to meet my Lord! Some sort of voice in me seemed to say: "Leave him, Millie, leave him alone *before it is too late!*" Too late? Surely I could leave him when I wanted to? Ghosts haunt as they like, don't they? I'd make just one more attempt at terrifying him, then I'd give it up and think about going to heaven.

He stopped and turned, and faced me full.

I pointed at him with both my hands.

"John!" I cried. "John! It's all very well for you to stand there and smile, and stare with your great fish-eyes and think you've won, but you haven't! I'll do you, I'll finish you! I'll—"

I stopped and laughed a little. Windows shot up. "Who's that? What's the row?"—and so on. They had all heard: but he only turned and walked on.

"Leave him, Millie, before it is too late," the voice said.

So that's what the voice meant: leave him before I betrayed his secret and had the crime of revenge on my soul. Very well, I would: I'd leave him. I'd go straight to heaven before any accident happened. So I stretched up two arms, and tried to float into the air, but at once some force seized me like a great gust, and I was swept away after him down the street. There was something stirring in me that still bound me to him.

Strange that I should be so real to all those people that they thought me still a living woman, but he—who had most reason to fear me—why, it seemed doubtful whether he even saw me. And where was he going to, right up the desolate long length of Pole Street? He turned into Rope Street. I saw a blue lamp: that was the police station.

"Oh, Lord," I thought, "I've done it! Oh, Lord, he's going to give himself up."

"You drove him to it," the voice said. "You fool, did you think he didn't see you? What did you expect? Did you think he'd shriek, and gibber with fear at you? Did you think your John was a coward? Now his death is on your head!"

"I didn't do it, I didn't!" I cried. "I never wished him any harm, never, not *really!* I wouldn't hurt him, not for anything, I wouldn't. Oh, John, don't stare like that! There's still time . . . time!"

And all this while he stood in the door, looking at me, while the policemen came out and stood round in a ring. He couldn't escape now.

"Oh, John," I sobbed, "forgive me! I didn't mean to do it! It was jealousy, John, that did it . . . because I loved you."

Still the police took no notice of him.

"That's her," said one of them in a husky voice. "Done it with a hammer, she done it . . . brained him. But, Lord, isn't her face ghastly. Haunted, like."

"Look at her 'ead, poor girl. Looks as if she tried to do herself in with the hammer after."

Then the sergeant stepped forward.

"Anything you say will be taken down as evidence against you."

"John!" I cried softly, and held out my arms—for at last his face had softened.

"Holy Mary!" said the one policeman, crossing himself. "She's seeing him!"

"They'll not hang her," another whispered. "Did you notice her condition, poor girl?"

T. F. POWYS

THE HUNTED
BEAST

Mr Walter Gidden, the vicar of East Dodder, climbed the stile slowly. He rested upon it as if he had a long hour in which to do nothing before he went home. Then he looked back. Something had happened, something horrible. Something that he could not bring his mind to think of. . . .

Nature sometimes looks with a curious pity at a man upon whom has fallen, from who knows where, an awful event. But the pity of nature is dumb: it is also unthinking. It pities the victim and the torturer. It pities the dead by the look it gives them—and the living it pities by their fears.

Mr Gidden climbed softly over the stile, he leant against it and tried to think.

He was in the lane that led to the village and to his house. Upon either side of the lane the hedges were covered with honeysuckle. The sweet and odorous scent of new-mown hay filled the air. Everywhere there were flowers, and a little way down the lane a tiny rabbit sat and busily scratched itself. Suddenly, coming from nowhere, rich colour went by—a peacock butterfly. . . .

Unthinking nature can deceive as well as pity. All seemed the same as it ever had been in this quiet country lane. Evidently nature wished to blot out, for a moment at least, in Mr Gidden's mind, what had happened, but only that the horrid wave should gather force to break.

A great many times had Mr Gidden, happy with the contentment that belongs to a good man, strayed to that very spot to loiter.

An evil dream might have overtaken him. Perhaps he had lain down beside the stile—he might never have gone into the field. Then nothing had happened—the lane was the same. He knew the blackbird that sang from the ash tree—he knew him by one white feather. Mr Gidden looked down at his boots. . . .

Mr Gidden had lived at East Dodder for twenty-five years. He had been married for thirty years. During all that time he had loved his wife and she had loved him. The two living children—there had been a girl, Mary, who had died—were both dutiful and good. The family were united lovingly and their thoughts were for one another. . . .

There was no one in sight. Away towards the village a herd of cows was feeding peacefully. No one interrupted them: they might have been feeding there for ever. No crash came, the heavens did not fall, no earthquake happened, the sky was just the same.

But Mr Gidden trembled. Had he the ague? His teeth chattered. Suddenly he seized his own throat: he held tight for a moment, gasped, and let go. Why did not the green summer fields gape and pour out hell-fire? How could all the sweetness of summer be there still—with him standing there?

He now walked along the lane uneasily. He thought he staggered, but he was wrong, for he walked with his usual stride as if nothing had happened.

Before he knew where he was he opened his own gate, and he was careful to close it after him. His wife was sitting upon a garden-seat, sewing. Mr Gidden wondered what she was sewing.

He had returned a little earlier than usual from his afternoon walk; there was nothing untoward in that. It was kind of him, that was all, for he was often late. Mrs Gidden spoke to him and went on with her sewing—she was darning a table-cloth. He might have felt the sun in the lane a little too warm. Or the downs a little fatiguing? She had seen him there, and a little before he reached the summit, she had also noticed the children.

When she saw the children she found a new rent in the table-cloth. Village washerwomen are very careless!

Mrs Gidden had watched before she began to repair the rent she had found. She wished well to those children, employing her kindest thoughts about them. She even knew them at that distance away—the two Budden boys and Nellie Webber. Her husband was upon the down and those children in the fields below.

As she had watched him there, there rose in her heart a wonderful feeling of gratitude to God for giving her such a happy life. She hoped to do more good yet, to help others more. She ought to say something to Nellie Webber, who was a trifle too merry with her young limbs, but young girls soon grow. . . .

Mr Gidden had gone quietly into the house. She heard the study door shut; he would be still there when tea was ready. . . .

Mr Gidden sat at his study table, the round inkpot was in front of him and his favourite pen. He took up the sermon that he had been writing before he went out. He had begun and ended his sermon with the word 'God'—that was curious.

He rose from his chair and took the clock—a heavy one—from the mantelpiece, and placed it upon the table in front of him.

He carefully calculated the movement of time.

Those two Budden boys, when they ran off and left Nellie alone, could not have run far. They must have watched what he had done to Nellie, from some hiding-place near.

As soon as he was out of sight they would have gone to her again. He had probably reached home when they had found her all bloody in the ditch.

Mr Gidden knew a little about boys. Boys like to look at anything strange: they stand and stare for five minutes and then they run away. They would wait and see if she moved. They they would run home to tell Mrs Webber—ten minutes!

Mrs Webber, a stout talkative woman, who bore an ill character in the village, wouldn't hurry to the policeman's cottage; she would talk to people on her way. No one ever hurried in Dodder. It would be fully half an hour, from the time Mrs Webber set off to tell the policeman, to the moment when Constable Burr would call at the Rectory.

Mr Gidden looked at the clock. What had he done? He must try to think; he must remember what it was.

But his thoughts wandered. It was hard to hold them to the point. Something seemed to be pulling at his coat-tails. That was his past life. His past life pleaded with him and tried to pull him back.

There had been many joys in it—harmless, peaceful joys. 'That may be continued,' said the past, 'for many more years.'

But what had he decided to do?—to die. And for what? He must remember what it was that he had to die for.

He had been walking along the top of the downs when the rabbit screamed. He knew the sound at once and he knew what it was—a rabbit caught in a snare but not killed. He had come upon a rabbit before, caught in a gin, and had killed the poor beast at once with a blow of his stick. He would put this one out of its pain in the same manner. Perhaps if it were only wired he would release it and let it go.

But, this time, Mr Gidden wasn't the first to find the rabbit. No, nor yet the first to hear its scream, for the children had heard it. Mr Gidden watched the children going to the rabbit, and he followed them.

For some reason or other he felt nervous. It occurred to him that the children might think if they saw him that he had come not to save the rabbit but to steal it.

Mr Gidden was not ignorant of the behaviour of village minds. A country child thinks that the wrong he does is only the wrong that another would do if he had the same chance. When once, by mistake, Mr Gidden had surprised two persons lying together in a lane, whom he supposed to be fighting, he had heard a voice say over the hedge, ' 'E do wish old Peter were 'e.'

The children, in their eagerness to get to the rabbit, had not seen the clergyman coming after them, and Mr Gidden was able to conceal himself behind a bush only a little way from the snared rabbit. He watched what went on.

The boys had taken the rabbit out of the snare and had given it to Nellie to hold. Nellie was fourteen years old, a plump, coarse, sturdy girl.

She held the rabbit firmly while the boys examined every part of it. They all laughed to see how the fleas from the rabbit hopped about.

Presently Jack Budden took out from his pocket a blunt knife, and Nellie said jokingly, ' 'Tis they eyes stoats do first bite at.' To the horror of Mr Gidden, Jack, in imitation of the stoats' behaviour, gouged out the rabbit's eyes with the blunt knife.

For a moment while he watched, Mr Gidden could not move. The children placed the rabbit upon the grass to see what it did.

Then a terrible rage overcame Mr Gidden. He rushed out of his hiding-place and beat the blind rabbit to death with his stick. He turned upon the children, meaning to beat them too.

The boys escaped his hands and ran off. But the girl wasn't so fortunate; she did not run so quickly as the boys; perhaps she wanted to know what the clergyman would do to her.

Mr Gidden threw himself upon her. He tore at her clothes. She struggled and fell into the ditch. He struck her, lay upon her in his fury, and held to her throat. His stick was broken; he took up a great bone that lay near and struck her with that. There was blood upon the bone, and Nellie now lay very still.

During the struggle Mr Gidden had wished to do the very worst a man could do. He had wished to violate her—to give her cruelty for cruelty, pain for pain. But her clothes conquered him. He did not know what to do, he did not understand young girls. He looked down at her—she did not move. He was satisfied, he had avenged the rabbit. Though the world delivered no justice, he had delivered it. He had toppled over the world. . . .

The Reverend Walter Gidden looked at the clock, he calculated the minutes that must elapse before the policeman would come for him.

Mr Gidden hadn't lived in the country for twenty-five years for nothing, he knew the people a little, he had read the local paper, he had listened to the village news. He might not have quite killed Nellie, but he knew what they would say he had done to her. He also remembered that his wife had said sadly—though a moment after she had remarked more gaily that young girls soon grow—that a cripple had been a little too kind to Nellie a few days before. . . .

Mr Gidden rose hurriedly. Some one had opened and shut the front gate, cautiously, sedately, gently.

Mr Gidden looked out of the side window. It was, as he expected, the constable—Mr William Burr. Mr Gidden crossed the room to the larger window that led into the back garden. He leaped out of it.

He climbed some railings, he was in a little field beyond the garden. Two calves were in the field; these galloped away. Mr Gidden lay down in a small pit.

They would not search for him at once. Mr Burr would only enquire after him. Mr. Burr would not wish to shock the lady, he would ask about him as if he were merely enquiring about his health. If Mr Gidden was out, Burr would go to the inspector at Stonebridge to ask what he ought to do.

Mr Burr would say, 'Is Mr Gidden at home?' and Mrs Gidden would reply, 'He was sitting in the study a moment ago, but perhaps he has gone out for another little walk.'

But Mr Gidden couldn't stay where he was; even though the hounds were not actually after him he knew himself to be a hunted beast. He left the pit and crept on with his back bent, hiding and running. He came to a hedge that he could not remember ever having noticed before. Everything looked different. The earth and sky were not the same now; the green grass mocked at him.

He clambered through the hedge and found himself in a field of corn. He crept into the corn, treading carefully. He began to crawl, he crawled on and on, and then he lay down.

He had now time to think. He lay upon his back and looked up at the corn. A little mouse, moving amongst the corn, came to have a look at him. How high the corn was! It touched the sky. Every reed of corn appeared to have a distinct life. Each stalk was wonderful. They grew up high to heaven and to God. Could he but become a stalk of corn or a little mouse!

Mr Gidden endeavoured to calm his mind and to look philosophically at the event that had befallen him and at what must come of it. That morning he had received a letter from his son John, who was a curate in Bloomsbury. His daughter, too, had written from Bedford College. He had read their letters happily, in his study before breakfast. He had felt comfortable and contented; the warm weather, the letters, had pleased him.

He remembered his age—fifty-four. He was in good health except for a little chest weakness, and that always made him take the greater care of himself. He might have lived, in all comfort and happiness, until he was very old. But the bolt had fallen, and he was not going to be taken alive.

That thought twisted and bent him, and yet he held firmly to it. It struggled in him, changing into different forms, trying to escape. He held it firm; he would not let it go. He would never live to make sport for the mob. Let the evil ones toss him to and fro—when he was dead—what would he care?

When his name was cried round the streets of Weyminster by the newsboys he wouldn't know of it. It was his wish now—to die.

Shouts came from the village. He was being called for. Every one, he was sure, must know by this time what he had done. He must go farther, he must fly. He said the last words aloud, and so they reminded him of the prayer for the sick—'We fly to Thee for succour in behalf of this Thy servant.'

Mr Gidden crept on all fours out of the corn. He came to another hedge; a gap in it was guarded by a broken hurdle, round which nettles grew. Mr Gidden crawled through the nettles. He ran, taking an uncertain course, running by this hedge and by that, crushing the pretty flowers with his feet, breaking through the tall weeds. Sometimes he would creep so that he might more conveniently hide himself.

Once he stopped, peered through some bushes, and looked at the village. The village appeared to be quiet, he even thought he saw Nellie walking over the green with something white round her head—a bandage. But he couldn't believe his own eyes when he remembered what he had done to her. He did not know how hardy children are.

At last, after crossing the road that led to Shelton, he crept into a little spinney where there were pools of water and thick tufts and tussocks of grass. Mr Gidden threw himself down amongst them. His hands and his face burned and tingled; he had both stung and scratched himself. His clothes, that had that morning been so sleek and black, were now all spotted and torn. He leaned over a pool of clear water and saw his face reflected. He was become horrible; the face he saw was distorted with anguish; he looked pale and ghastly. He had never seen even a dying man look as he did. The dying, for the most part, were carefully tended in Dodder. And though they might gasp and their breath rattle—yet they lay upon soft pillows. He was far more awful to look at than the worst of them.

From the place in which Mr Gidden had concealed himself, he could see the downs and the field, too, where the children had been. He saw two men there, and now and again one of them would kneel down as though to examine the ground.

'Of course,' thought Mr Gidden, 'they must have carried her away,' but they were still looking for anything that he might have left to prove his guilt. Perhaps he had left his hat. He fancied now that it had fallen into the ditch. He couldn't remember having his hat upon his head when he reached home. Was he wearing it now?—no—then he must have left it behind him somewhere.

As he lay in the marsh his past life crept up to him, as a little dog might come who feared a whipping.

Mr Gidden had entered the world upon a Christmas Day—the longed-for and prayed-for child of gentle and pious parents. He was born in a comfortable parsonage home in Wiltshire. There was a brook in front of the house, where there used to be kingfishers. Upon the south wall of the house there grew a wonderful magnolia. He had adored, with a vast adoration, the great white flowers. His mother had told him that they were beautiful because they had committed no sin. His mother used to lift him up to touch them. He remembered his own little hands, his clean shirt cuffs, and the stainless flowers. Nothing harmed him then.

There was the great Bible—and the first words that he learned to read— 'And the Lord called Samuel again the third time.'

He read easily.

He had been delicate, and he could never bear to witness the least cruelty. Once he found another little boy cutting off the whiskers of a cat—a common practice in the country. Walter had rushed upon him, brandishing a wooden sword in his hand. The boy fled.

After those magic days of childhood were over, Mr Gidden's life had passed on evenly, nothing surprising ever happened. There was, he had ever believed, a loving God who, when it was for their eternal good, healed the sick and gave to those He healed a new chance to do better and to ask for pardon for their sins.

Those gentle thoughts were now all gone—a brutal thief had stolen them away; they were with him no more. Why was he a man? Had he been but one of those tussocks of grass, all might have been well. Strange hummocks they were, whose roots, after many years of growth, had built up a pedestal for the living grass above—a yard or two above the ground some of them were! Here was Nature's mournful plan, the living built up upon the dead. Only the summit of all the bones was green.

Mr Gidden shut his eyes. Perhaps when he opened them he would be in his study. Or else, was it a dream? Had he laid him down to sleep near to a bunch of thyme upon the down? Then he had dreamed a rather strange dream. Did he use to walk about in his dreams—perhaps to kill? A girl had been found dead upon the heath a year before. Some one must have killed her, too. Perhaps it was he—Walter Gidden. Thus moves the devil's cruelty in the earth. The worlds shudder, the skies weep. The deed is done.

Mr Gidden raised his head: he heard voices. Two men were walking toward him from the direction of the Shelton road. They were two rabbit-catchers, the very two who had been under the hill, setting their snares. They were accompanied by a little black dog. Mr Gidden did not recognize them.

Mr Gidden crept to the farther side of the copse. His hands were torn by thorns, his knees sank into the mud, but he was going away from the men.

He crept into a ditch and under a low railing. He was in the meadow. He raised himself and ran, hoping to reach the hedge across the meadow before he was seen. But he had not run far before he knew that he could not escape. The men must see him before he reached safety. What was he to do?

The field he was crossing was a water meadow, in which there were ditches. He cast himself into a ditch in which was half a foot of water. The water ran into a tunnel that burrowed under a grassy roadway where the haycarts rumbled in summer and the cows plodded in winter.

Mr Gidden peeped out of the ditch through the meadow-sweet and mint. The two men were coming directly to the place where he lay. He crept into the tunnel to hide. He could not crawl in, the place was too low for that. He moved along like a snake or a worm.

He lay still in the middle of the tunnel. The water trickled over his clothes and soaked him through. He heard voices: the men had evidently come to that very place and were resting beside the little ditch, talking and laughing. They were speaking of some one who had disgraced himself. Mr Gidden supposed they were speaking about him. Presently something dashed into the opening, and a dog barked.

Mr Gidden was filled with horror. They would have him yet, he thought.

The dog spluttered and splashed. Mr Gidden was wary. The little dog came on inquisitively, barking with short, sharp barks. It came near; Mr Gidden clutched at it and held it by the throat. He strangled the dog slowly. When one hand grew tired, he used the other. At length he moved so that he could clasp the dog's throat with both his hands.

After he had strangled the dog, he held its head under the water.

The men did not seem to be aware that the dog had crept into the tunnel; they had moved away and were now calling their dog out of the spinney. They supposed it had run in there. Mr Gidden let the dead dog go.

He buried his own face in the water. He gasped and spluttered like the dog. But he could not drown there, he must take stronger means than that.

He had avenged the cruelty done to the rabbit, and now he had killed this dog. Who could prevent the cruelty of the world? No one. But he could end himself, and that would be something done.

For some hours he lay there, and then crept out of the tunnel.

The evening was very still. A few dim stars were in the sky, looking faint, weary, and sad.

Mr Gidden lay on the grass, his limbs were cramped, he could hardly stir. Below him in the ditch was the dead body of the little dog.

Mr Gidden tried to get up; he succeeded at the third attempt. His limbs were heavy, as though Death had already touched him with his clammy hands. He limped out of the field, and cautiously crossed the road, taking nearly the same way that he had come. He went along in the same cornfield that he had hid himself in.

He was near his home, and he heard the supper-bell ring. The sound called him. He listened. He thought he heard his wife calling him by name. His legs, without his command, moved towards his home. In a few moments he would be there.

He stopped suddenly. Some one in the village laughed—a horrible laugh. It was the hunchback. The cripple didn't trouble about Nellie now. He could laugh as he chose.

Mr Gidden turned to go to the sea. He was very careful of himself. He did not wish to faint by the way.

Mr Gidden had always been careful not to take cold. But he had done queer things that day. He had lain in a swamp—in a ditch. He had always been careful about other things too. He was very cleanly, he shaved every morning. If he had the smallest pimple upon his face he would look at it askance and shave the more carefully. The remainder of his body was always as smooth and white as a child's. How would he look after a few days in the sea?—God's Judgment.

Mr Gidden climbed down the cliff slowly; he did not wish to fall. He looked to his steps.

At the bottom of the cliff he picked up a child's boat. He walked, with the boat in his hand, into the sea.

He knew he could not swim far. His clothes hung heavy, but still he swam out and the tide helped him. He let himself sink, but rose in a moment gasping, and hitting the water with his hands, letting the little boat go.

The little boat floated away. Mr Gidden began to fight horribly for his life.

He heard the hunchback laugh. The water closed over his head. He thought he was on the top of it, in the child's boat, but he sank deeper.

LANGSTON HUGHES

END

There are
No clocks on the wall
And no time,
No shadows that move
From dawn to dusk
Across the floor.

There is neither light
Nor dark
Outside the door.

There is no door!

BEN HECHT

THE RIVAL DUMMY

I was dining in a place where vaudeville "artists" congregate to gossip and boast, when my friend Joe Ferris, the booking agent, pointed to a stocky little man with a gray toupée, alone at a table and said:

"There is, I think, the strangest, weirdest, craziest man in New York."

I looked a second time, and noted, despite this identification, nothing more unusual than the aforesaid gray toupée, a certain bewildered and shifty manner about the eyes, and a pair of nervous sensitive hands. He reminded me—this solitary diner—of some second-rate Hungarian fiddler worn out with poverty, alcohol, and egotism.

"That," said Joe Ferris, "is the man who ten years ago used to be known as Gabbo the Great—the world's most famous ventriloquist. I guess he heard me"—the booking agent lowered his voice—"but it doesn't matter. He'll pretend he didn't. We're not supposed to know who he is, you know. That's what the toupée is for. Disguise. Mad—madder than a cuckoo. It gives me the shivers just to look at him.

"I'll tell you his story," continued Ferris, "and maybe you can figure it out. That's more than I can. Being a newspaperman, you won't call me a liar. I hate to tell stories to people who are always certain that anything they never heard of before is a lie.

"This particular yarn"—Ferris smiled—"began way back before the war. He came over from Belgium, Gabbo. That's where a good percentage of the best performers come from. God knows why. Jugglers, contortionists, trapeze acts, strong men, and all that kind of stuff. Belgium and Lithuania, sometimes.

"I booked Gabbo when he first landed. The best all-around ventriloquist that ever played the big time—if I do say so. And nuts, of course. But you got to expect that from the talent. I never see a first-rate act that wasn't at least half nutty.

"The first time I met him I ask what his name is.

" 'Gabbo what?' I ask.

" 'Gabbo the Great,' is the answer. And then he adds very seriously, 'I was born great.'

"I thought at first this was the foreign equivalent for a gag. But there was less humor about Gabbo than a dead mackerel. He used to sign his letters G. G. Imagine. And—to give you a rough idea of what kind of a loon this baby was—he always opened his act with the *Marseillaise*.

141

"He used to come out in the middle of it, stand at attention till it was finished, and then, in a low, embarrassed voice, announce: 'Ladies and Gentlemen: I have the honor to present to you tonight the world's most gifted ventriloquist—Gabbo the Great.'

"And he would take a bow. That's pretty cuckoo, ain't it? But it always went big. You'd be surprised at what an audience will swallow and applaud.

"Well, the first time I came to the conclusion that there was something definitely cockeyed about Gabbo was when I called on him one night after his performance at the Palace. It was up in his room at the hotel. He'd just got in and was taking his dummy out of its black case. It had velvet lining in it, this case, and was trimmed in black and gold like a magician's layout.

"Let me tell you about this dummy—if I can. You've seen them. One of those red-cheeked, round-headed marionettes with popping, glassy eyes and a wide mouth that opens and shuts.

"Well, Jimmy—that was the name of this wooden-headed thing—was no different than the rest of them. That is, you wouldn't think so to look at it. That thing haunts me, honest to God. I can still see its dangling legs with the shoes painted on its feet and—let's forget about it. Where was I?

"Oh, yes. I go up to his room and stand there talking to him, and just as I'm making some remark or other, he sits Jimmy up on the bed, and all of a sudden turns to him—or it or whatever you want to call the thing—and starts holding a conversation.

" 'I suppose,' says Gabbo, angry as blazes and glaring at this nutty dummy, 'I suppose you're proud of yourself, eh? After the way you acted tonight?'

"And Jimmy, the dummy, so help me, answers back in a squeaky voice, 'Aw, go soak your head. Listen to who's talkin'.'

"Then this nutty ventriloquist speaks up kind of heatedly. 'I'm talkin',' he says. 'And I'll ask you to listen to what I have to say. You forgot your jokes tonight, and if it happens again you get no milk.'

"Well, I thought it was a gag. You know, a bit of clowning for my benefit. So I stand by, grinning like an ape, although it don't look funny at all, while Gabbo pours a glass of milk and, opening Jimmy's mouth, feeds it to him. Then he turns to me, like I was a friend of the family, and says coolly: 'This Jimmy is getting worse and worse. What I wanted to see you about, Mr. Ferris, is taking his picture off the billing. I want to teach him a lesson.'

"I've had them before—cuckoos, I mean—and it didn't surprise me. Much. They come pretty queer in vaudeville.

"Remind me to tell you sometime about the prima donna I had who used to come on with a dagger and throw it on the stage. If it stuck, landed on its point, she'd go on with the act and sing. If it didn't she wouldn't. Walk right off.

"She was pretty expert at tossing the old dagger, so it usually landed right—they ain't ever too crazy. And on that account of the dagger always landing right, I never find out what it's all about for weeks. Until one night she up cold and walks out on herself. On an opening night at the Palace, too, where she's being featured. And when I come galloping back, red in the face, to ask her what the hell, she answers me very naughty: 'Go ask the dagger. He tell you.'

"Well, that's another story, and not so good, either. About this night in Gabbo's room, as I was saying. I took in Gabbo's little act with the dummy, and said nothing.

"But I started making a few inquiries the next day, and I find out plenty. I find out that this nutty give-and-take with the dummy is just a regular routine for Gabbo. That he keeps up a more or less steady conversation with the dummy like he was a kid brother. And not only that, but that this idiotic dummy is the only human being—or whatever you call him—that Gabbo ever says more than hello to. Barring me, of course.

"Look"—and Ferris snorted—"can you imagine him sitting at that table now and looking at me and pretending he don't know me? And, what's more, that I don't know him? On account he's got a nine-dollar toupée on. Well, that's part of the story, and I'll come to it.

"The way I figured it at the time—and I may be wrong—was that Gabbo was such an egotist that he could only talk to himself. You know, there's lots of hoofers, for instance, who won't watch anybody but themselves dance. They stand in front of a mirror—for diversion, mind you—and do their stuff. And applaud it. That's vaudeville for you.

"So I figured Gabbo that way. That he was so stuck on himself he got a big kick out of talking to himself. That's what he was doing, of course, when he held these pow-wows with Jimmy.

"As you can imagine, it kind of interested me. I got so I'd always try to drop around Gabbo's dressing room whenever I had time, just to catch this loony business with the dummy. I didn't think it exactly funny, you know, and it never made me laugh. I guess it was just morbid curiosity on my part. Anyway, I sort of become part of the family.

"The fights they used to have—Gabbo and this crazy dummy; fighting all the time. Usually about the act. Gabbo sore as the devil at Jimmy if anything went wrong with the turn—if one of the gags missed fire, for instance, he'd accuse him of stalling, laying down on the job, and honest to God, once he sailed into the damn thing because he was sure it wasn't getting enough sleep. Believe me or not, they were as quarrelsome as a team of hoofers.

"And after I got used to these spats—you know you can get used to anything—I got to thinking of Jimmy almost the way Gabbo did. I got to imagining it was him answering back—squealing, kidding, and swearing. And not Gabbo talking with his stomach—or whatever it is ventriloquists talk with.

"But with all this fighting between them, you could see that Gabbo had a soft spot for Jimmy. He fed him milk. There was a can or something fitted up inside. That's where the milk went.

"For instance, just to show you the pretty side of the picture, about three months after I change the billing and take Jimmy's name off the one-sheets, Gabbo arrives in my office with a demand that I put the picture back and the name too, in twice as big lettering as before.

"And one other time he comes to me, Gabbo does, and says Jimmy isn't getting enough money. Well, as you can imagine, this sounds a bit phony. There's such a thing as carrying a gag too far, is my first reaction. But so help me, he meant it. And he won't go on with the act unless I come through.

"Well, I learned long before that it don't pay to win arguments with the talent. It's worse than winning an argument with your own wife. Costs you more.

"So I finally control my temper and asks, 'How much of a raise does Jimmy want?'

"'Five dollars a week more,' says Gabbo. And Gabbo was pulling down four hundred dollars for the act; so you can see the whole thing was on the square—asking a raise for Jimmy, I mean. Then he explains to me he has been paying Jimmy ninety-five dollars per week right along, and he wants to make it an even hundred because Jimmy has been working very hard and so on.

"So much for that. Here's where the plot thickens. About three weeks or so after this conference, I get wind of the fact that Gabbo has fallen for a dame; and that the thing has become quite a joke among the talent.

"I can hardly believe my ears. Gabbo never looked at a dame ever since he was on the circuit. The loneliest, stuck-up professor I'd ever known. He used to walk around like Kaiser Wilhelm. Grand, gloomy, and peculiar. And with a mustache. Don't look now—he's shaved it off. Part of the disguise. But those days it was his pride and joy.

"Well, the next thing I heard about his love's young dream is from Gabbo himself in person. He comes back to New York, and comes walking into the office with the information that he is adding a woman to his act; Mlle. Rubina. I look at him and say, 'What for, for the love of Pete? What do you need a jane in the act for, and why Rubina?'

"'For the water,' he answers. 'To bring on the glass of water which I drink. And take it off.' And he scowls at me as if to say, 'Do you want to make anything out of it?' And when I nod sort of dumbly, he goes on: 'She is willing to join me for a hundred dollars a week.'

"Well, this is pretty nuts. Rubina was a bowlegged wench working in a juggling act. Fetched plates and Indian clubs for Allen and Allen. And worth all of fifty cents a year as talent. Not even a looker. But go argue with Gabbo. I tried a little taffy about his going over so much better alone—that is, with his pal Jimmy to help him out. But he waves his hand at me, pulls his mustache, and begins to jump up and down with excitement.

"So I agree, and he then becomes the gentleman. He'll stand for a fifty dollar cut in his salary—that is twenty-five dollars out of his take and twenty-five out of Jimmy's. That's the way he puts it. And I should kick in with the other fifty for Rubina's graft.

"That's how this Rubina joined the act.

"I went over to catch it three nights later and see what was going on. I came right in the middle of Gabbo's turn. There he stood, with Jimmy sitting on the table, and this peroxide Rubina all dressed up in red plush knickerbockers with green bows on the sides of the knees, hovering around and 'acting'—registering surprise and delight every time the dummy made a wise crack. It almost ruined the turn.

"But what I noticed most was that Gabbo was a changed man. His whole attitude was different. He wasn't making his usual goo-goo eyes at the audience or shooting over personality—which had been his long suit.

"He was all wrapped up in Rubina, staring at her like a sick puppy with the heaves. And calling her over every half-minute, between gags, and demanding another glass of water. And bowing like an idiot whenever she handed it to him. He must have drank fourteen glasses of water during the act.

"And that, my friend, was just the beginning. The circuit thought it a big joke—Gabbo's crush on Rubina.

"And what everybody considered the funniest part of the racket was that Rubina was as fond of Gabbo as if he had been a rattlesnake. She never had anything but a sneer and a wise crack for him, and, when he got too fancy with his bow, just a low-down scowl. She would have none of him. Why, God only knows. Except perhaps that he was a little too nutty even for her. And she was no picker, believe me.

"In about two months things begin to grow serious. It seems, according to reports which come in from every town on the circuit, that Gabbo has carried his anger against Jimmy to such lengths that he'll hardly talk to him on the stage, mind you. Keeps sneering at his jokes and trying to trip him up, and bawling him out in front of the audience.

"And then, after the act, he sits him up on the table in his dressing room and starts in hurling curses at the dummy and screaming. It scares people out of their wits. The actors back-stage, I mean. You know, it's kind of woozy to pass a room where you know a man is alone and hear him yelling at the top of his voice. And, what's more, answering himself.

"And all this excitement, it seems, is due to jealousy. That was the whole point. It seems that this Rubina valentine had tumbled to the fact that Gabbo treated Jimmy like a living person. So, out of sheer cussedness, she had taken to patting Jimmy's wooden cheeks on the stage. Or winking at him during the turn. And the blow-off came, I learned, when she slipped Jimmy a caramel as he was sitting on Gabbo's lap in the dressing room. This was just downright morbid viciousness on Rubina's part.

"After that there was nothing could straighten the thing out. As soon as

Gabbo lands in town, I go back-stage with him. He's in his dressing room, and he stands there—the turn being over—just motioning me away and raging at this maniac dummy of his.

" 'That is the kind of a one you are,' he screams. 'That is the way you show your gratitude. After all I've done for you. Trying to steal the woman I love from me. The woman I love above everything.' And then I listen to Jimmy answer, and, so help me, for a minute I thought it was that damned wooden image speaking.

" 'My life is my own,' says Jimmy, squealing wilder than usual. 'I can do what I want. And I'll ask you to mind your own business, you big tub of lard.'

"At these words Gabbo jumped into the air and pulled his hair out in handfuls.

" 'Viper,' he howled at the dummy.

" 'Idiot,' Jimmy squeals back at him.

"What could I do? I just sneaked off and left them calling each other names like a pair of fishwives. I crossed my fingers and hoped that the act wouldn't split up—that's where I was chiefly concerned, you understand.

"Then came the second stage. I don't know whatever got into this Rubina dame. She'd never pulled down more than thirty dollars a week in her life. And here she was getting a hundred. For doing nothing. And yet she writes me a long misspelled letter, that she's quitting the act on Saturday and for me to find someone to take her place.

"I was of course tickled silly. Fifty dollars is fifty dollars. And, besides, I sort of liked Gabbo and I felt this Rubina was dangerous to him. It's best for lunatics to steer clear of women—or for anybody for that matter.

"But my satisfaction didn't last long. I get a telephone call the following Monday to hurry over to the Bronx where Gabbo is opening—being starred, mind you. My great ventriloquist, it seems, has gone out of his head.

"I get there just as the bill has started. Gabbo has just told the manager he won't go on. He won't act. He knows what he owes to his art and his public, but would rather be torn by wild horses than to step out on the stage alongside of that black imp of hell—Jimmy.

"And as he says these things he walks up and down in his dressing room, cursing Jimmy and glowering at him like a maniac. They're having an out-and-out bust-up, like a team. Calling each other hams, among other less repeatable things.

"The house manager and all the actors were frightened silly at the noise. But I was used to Gabbo by this time, and began trying to calm him down. But I got no chance to get in a word edgewise—what with the way these two were going after each other. Gabbo thundering in his baritone and that damned dummy squealing back at him in his falsetto.

"I saw at once that Gabbo had really sort of gone over the edge. This time there was a murderous rage in his voice. And in Jimmy's, too.

"I got so mixed up I began to worry—for Gabbo. Dummy or no dummy, I began to think that . . .

"Well, anyway, it appears that Rubina, his adored, the light of his life, has flown. And Gabbo's idea, nutty as it sounds, is that Jimmy knows where she is. That she and Jimmy have framed against him. That Jimmy, the dirty hound, has stolen her love. Can you beat it?

"There's no use trying to reason under such circumstances. Any more than getting logical with a man who has the D. T.'s. Gabbo won't go on with the act. And he don't. He's through. And I stand still, and say nothing, and watch him hurl Jimmy into his black case, grab it under his arm, and start out with it.

"And I follow him out of the theater. He starts walking peculiarly, like a man half stewed. Then I see that he's doubling on his tracks, trying to elude somebody. Me, I figured. But I kept on. Finally he goes into a store, and I watch him through the window. It's a hardware store, and he stays in there for five minutes, and then comes out and makes a beeline for the hotel.

"I got to his room almost as soon as he did. But the door was locked. I stood there listening, and all of a sudden I hear screaming. In English, French, and several other languages. I swear to you, it scared me silly.

"I started banging on the door. But it's no use. Finally I beat it down after the manager. We're back in five minutes. And we open the door.

"Well, the room is silent and empty.

"I stood staring for a minute. Then I saw something. The floor is covered with pieces of wood. Splinters, sticks. It's Jimmy. Chopped to pieces, cut to smithereens. He'd murdered Jimmy, honest to God.

"We looked all around the room, and found the ax he'd bought in the hardware store. And then found that he'd lit out through the window. Made his getaway down the fire-escape.

"And that's the last trace we could pick up of him. We hunted high and low. I had two men scouring the town. But he was gone, leaving everything behind him. Fled—like a murderer, a murderer fleeing from justice, so help me.

"I'd gathered Jimmy up and put him in a piece of wrapping paper. That's how confused I was. And I carried him to the office and finally threw him in the wastebasket. And then I went home, and was unable to sleep for six nights.

"That's almost the end of the story. Except that two years ago I come in here one night after the show, and I see somebody familiar sitting at a table. I can't place him for a few minutes, and then all of a sudden I see it's Gabbo—Gabbo the Great—with a gray toupée and the mustache shaved.

"I rush over to him and begin talking. And he stared at me—highty-tighty like.

" 'My name,' he says, "is Mr. Lawrence. I am sorry you make a mistake.'

"Well, I'm not unusually dense, and as I stood there it dawned on me that Gabbo didn't want to be known. That he'd come back after fleeing from justice for eight years—come back disguised and with a different name, so that the police wouldn't pick him up for his great crime.

"And here he sits." Ferris looked at me with a mirthless smile. "Everybody knows his story in this place, and we all kid him along, calling him Mr. Lawrence and keeping his secret. Yeah, and when we get funny we call him the Ax Murderer. You know, just a gag among ourselves.

"Wait till he leaves"—Ferris picked up his glass—"and I'll take you over to the table where he's sitting."

This struck me as a rather empty offer.

"What for?" I inquired.

"So you can see what Jimmy looked like."

Ferris suddenly laughed. "He always draws a picture of that damned idiotic dummy on the tablecloth—every night."

E. F. BENSON

CATERPILLARS

I saw a month ago in an Italian paper that the Villa Casana, in which I once stayed, had been pulled down, and that a manufactory of some sort was in process of erection on its site. There is therefore no longer any reason for refraining from writing of those things which I myself saw (or imagined I saw) in a certain room and on a certain landing of the villa in question, nor from mentioning the circumstances which followed, which may or may not (according to the opinion of the reader) throw some light on, or be somehow connected with this experience.

The Villa Casana was in all ways but one a perfectly delightful house, yet, if it were standing now, nothing in the world—I use the phrase in its literal sense—would induce me to set foot in it again, for I believe it to have been haunted in a very terrible and practical manner. Most ghosts, when all is said and done, do not do much harm; they may perhaps terrify, but the person whom they visit usually gets over their visitation. They may on the other hand be entirely friendly and beneficent. But the appearances in the Villa Casana were not beneficent, and had they made their "visit" in a very slightly different manner, I do not suppose I should have got over it any more than Arthur Inglis did.

The house stood on an ilex-clad hill not far from Sestri di Levante on the Italian Riviera, looking out over the iridescent blues of that enchanted sea, while behind it rose the pale green chestnut woods that climb up the hillsides till they give place to the pines that, black in contrast with them, crown the slopes. All round it the garden in the luxuriance of mid-spring bloomed and was fragrant, and the scent of magnolia and rose, borne on the salt freshness of the winds from the sea, flowed like a stream through the cool, vaulted rooms.

On the ground floor a broad pillared *loggia* ran round three sides of the house, the top of which formed a balcony for certain rooms on the first floor. The main staircase, broad and of grey marble steps, led up from the hall to the landing outside these rooms, which were three in number, namely, two big sitting rooms and a bedroom arranged *en suite*. The latter was unoccupied, the sitting rooms were in use. From here the main staircase continued up to the second floor, where were situated certain bedrooms, one of which I occupied, while on the other side of the first-floor landing some half-dozen steps led to another suite of rooms, where, at the time I am speaking of, Arthur Inglis, the artist, had his bedroom and studio. Thus the landing outside my bedroom, at the top of the house, commanded both the landing of the first floor, and also the steps that led to Inglis' rooms. Jim Stanley and his wife, finally (whose guest I was), occupied rooms in another wing of the house, where also were the servants' quarters.

I arrived just in time for lunch on a brilliant noon of mid-May. The garden was shouting with colour and fragrance, and not less delightful, after my broiling walk up from the *marina,* should have been the coming from the reverberating heat and blaze of the day into the marble coolness of the villa. Only (the reader has my bare word for this, and nothing more), the moment I set foot in the house I felt that something was wrong. This feeling, I may say, was quite vague though very strong, and I remember that when I saw letters waiting for me on the table in the hall I felt certain that the explanation was here: I was convinced that there was bad news of some sort for me. Yet when I opened them I found no such explanation of my premonition: my correspondents all reeked of prosperity. Yet this clear miscarriage of a presentiment did not dissipate my uneasiness. In that cool fragrant house there was something wrong.

I am at pains to mention this because it may explain why it was that, though I am as a rule so excellent a sleeper that the extinction of a light on getting into bed is apparently contemporaneous with being called on the following morning, I slept very badly on my first night in the Villa Casana. It may also explain the fact that when I did sleep (if it was indeed in sleep that I saw what I thought I saw) I dreamed in a very vivid and original manner, original, that is to say, in the sense that something which, as far as I knew, had never previously entered into my consciousness, usurped it then. But since, in addition to this evil premonition, certain words and events occurring during the rest of the day, might have suggested something of what I thought happened that night, it will be well to relate them.

After lunch, then, I went round the house with Mrs. Stanley, and during our tour she referred, it is true, to the unoccupied bedroom on the first floor, which opened out of the room where we had lunched.

"We left that unoccupied," she said, "because Jim and I have a charming bedroom and dressing room, as you saw, in the wing, and if we used it ourselves we should have to turn the dining room into a dressing room and have our meals downstairs. As it is, however, we have our little flat there, Arthur Inglis has his little flat in the other passage; and I remembered (aren't I extraordinary?) that you once said that the higher up you were in a house the better you were pleased. So I put you at the top of the house, instead of giving you that room."

It is true that a doubt, vague as my uneasy premonition, crossed my mind at this. I did not see why Mrs. Stanley should have explained all this, if there had not been more to explain. I allow, therefore, that the thought that there was something to explain about the unoccupied bedroom was momentarily present to my mind.

The second thing that may have borne on my dream was this.

At dinner the conversation turned for a moment on ghosts. Inglis, with the certainty of conviction, expressed his belief that anybody who could possibly believe in the existence of supernatural phenomena was unworthy of the name of an ass. The subject instantly dropped. As far as I can recollect, nothing else occurred or was said that could bear on what follows.

We all went to bed rather early, and personally I yawned my way upstairs, feeling hideously sleepy. My room was rather hot, and I threw all the windows wide, and from without poured in the white light of the moon, and the love song of many nightingales. I undressed quickly, and got into bed, but though I had felt so sleepy before, I now felt extremely wide-awake. But I was quite content to be awake: I did not toss or turn, I felt perfectly happy listening to the song and seeing the light. Then, it is possible, I may have gone to sleep, and what follows may have been a dream. I thought anyhow that after a time the nightingales ceased singing and the moon sank. I thought also that if, for some unexplained reason, I was going to lie awake all night, I might as well read, and I remembered that I had left a book in which I was interested in the dining room on the first floor. So I got out of bed, lit a candle, and went downstairs. I entered the room, saw on a side table the book I had come to look for, and then, simultaneously, saw that the door into the unoccupied bedroom was open. A curious grey light, not of dawn nor of moonshine, came out of it, and I looked in. The bed stood just opposite the door, a big four-poster, hung with tapestry at the head. Then I saw that the greyish light of the bedroom came from the bed, or rather from what was on the bed. For it was covered with great caterpillars, a foot or more in length, which crawled over it. They were faintly luminous, and it was the light from them that showed me the room. Instead of the sucker-feet of ordinary caterpillars they had rows of pincers like crabs and they moved by grasping what they lay on with their pincers, and then sliding their bodies forward. In colour these dreadful insects were yellowish grey, and they were covered with irregular lumps and swellings. There must have been hundreds of them, for they formed a sort of writhing, crawling pyramid on the bed. Occasionally one fell off onto the floor, with a soft fleshy thud, and though the floor was of hard concrete, it yielded to the pincer-feet as if it had been putty, and crawling back, the caterpillar would mount on to the bed again, to rejoin its fearful companions. They appeared to have no faces, so to speak, but at one end of them there was a mouth that opened sideways in respiration.

Then, as I looked, it seemed to me as if they all suddenly became conscious of my presence. All the mouths at any rate were turned in my direction, and the next moment they began dropping off the bed with those soft fleshy thuds onto the floor, and wriggling towards me. For one second the paralysis of nightmare was on me, but the next I was running upstairs again to my room, and I remember feeling the cold of the marble steps on my bare feet. I rushed into my bedroom, and slammed the door behind me, and then—I was certainly wide awake now—I found myself standing by my bed with the sweat of terror pouring from me. The noise of the banged door still rang in my ears. But, as would have been more usual, if this had been mere nightmare, the terror that had been mine when I saw those foul beasts crawling about the bed or dropping softly onto the floor did not cease then.

Awake now, if dreaming before, I did not at all recover from the horror of dream: it did not seem to me that I had dreamed. And until dawn, I sat or stood, not daring to lie down, thinking that every rustle or movement that I heard was the approach of the caterpillars. To them and the claws that bit into the cement the wood of the door was child's play: steel would not keep them out.

But with the sweet and noble return of day the horror vanished: the whisper of wind became benignant again: the nameless fear, whatever it was, was smoothed out and terrified me no longer. Dawn broke, hueless at first; then it grew dove-coloured, then the flaming pageant of light spread over the sky.

The admirable rule of the house was that everybody had breakfast where and when he pleased, and in consequence it was not till lunchtime that I met any of the other members of our party, since I had breakfast on my balcony, and wrote letters and other things till lunch. In fact, I got down to that meal rather late, after the other three had begun. Between my knife and fork there was a small pillbox of cardboard, and as I sat down Inglis spoke.

"Do look at that," he said, "since you are interested in natural history. I found it crawling on my counterpane last night, and I don't know what it is."

I think that before I opened the pillbox I expected something of the sort which I found in it. Inside it, anyhow, was a small caterpillar, greyish-yellow in colour, with curious bumps and excrescences on its wings. It was extremely active, and hurried round the box, this way and that. Its feet were unlike the feet of any caterpillar I ever saw: they were like the pincers of a crab. I looked, and shut the lid down again.

"No, I don't know it," I said, "but it looks rather unwholesome. What are you going to do with it?"

"Oh, I shall keep it," said Inglis. "It has begun to spin: I want to see what sort of a moth it turns into."

I opened the box again, and saw that these hurrying movements were indeed the beginning of the spinning of the web of its cocoon. Then Inglis spoke again.

"It has got funny feet, too," he said. "They are like crabs' pincers. What's the Latin for crab? Oh, yes, Cancer. So in case it is unique, let's christen it: 'Cancer Inglisensis.' "

Then something happened in my brain, some momentary piecing together of all that I had seen or dreamed. Something in his words seemed to me to throw light on it all, and my own intense horror at the experience of the night before linked itself onto what he had just said. In effect, I took the box and threw it, caterpillar and all, out of the window. There was a gravel path just outside, and beyond it a fountain playing into a basin. The box fell onto the middle of this.

Inglis laughed.

"So the students of the occult don't like solid facts," he said. "My poor caterpillar!"

The talk went off again at once on to other subjects, and I have only given in detail, as they happened, these trivialities in order to be sure myself that I have recorded everything that could have borne on occult subjects or on the subject of caterpillars. But at the moment when I threw the pillbox into the fountain, I lost my head: my only excuse is that, as is probably plain, the tenant of it was, in miniature, exactly what I had seen crowded onto the bed in the unoccupied room. And though this translation of those phantoms into flesh and blood—or whatever it is that caterpillars are made of—ought perhaps to have relieved the horror of the night, as a matter of fact it did nothing of the kind. It only made the crawling pyramid that covered the bed in the unoccupied room more hideously real.

After lunch we spent a lazy hour or two strolling about the garden or sitting in the *loggia,* and it must have been about four o'clock when Stanley and I started off to bathe, down the path that led by the fountain into which I had thrown the pillbox. The water was shallow and clear, and at the bottom of it I saw its white remains. The soaking had disintegrated the cardboard, and it had become no more than a few strips and shreds of sodden paper. The centre of the fountain was a marble Italian Cupid which squirted the water out of a wineskin held under its arm. And crawling up its leg was the caterpillar. Strange and scarcely credible as it seemed, it must have survived the falling-to-bits of its prison, and made its way to shore, and there it was, out of arm's reach, weaving and waving this way and that as it evolved its cocoon.

Then, as I looked at it, it seemed to me again that, like the caterpillars I had seen last night, it saw me, and breaking out of the threads that surrounded it, it crawled down the marble leg of the Cupid and began swimming like a snake across the water of the fountain towards me. It came with extraordinary speed (the fact of a caterpillar being able to swim was new to me), and in another moment was crawling up the marble lip of the basin. Just then Inglis joined us.

"Why, if it isn't old 'Cancer Inglisensis' again," he said, catching sight of the beast. "What a tearing hurry it is in."

We were standing side by side on the path, and when the caterpillar had advanced to within about a yard of us, it stopped, and began waving again, as if in doubt as to the direction in which it should go. Then it appeared to make up its mind, and crawled onto Inglis' shoe.

"It likes me best," he said, "but I don't really know that I like it. And as it won't drown I think perhaps—"

He shook it off his shoe onto the gravel path and trod on it.

All the afternoon the air got heavier and heavier with the sirocco that was without doubt coming up from the south, and that night again I went up to bed feeling very sleepy, but below my drowsiness, so to speak, there was the consciousness, stronger than before, that there was something wrong in the house, that something dangerous was close at hand. But I fell asleep at once, and—how long after I do not know—either woke or dreamed I awoke, feeling that I must get up at once, *or I should be too late.* Then (dreaming or awake) I lay and fought this fear, telling myself that I was but the prey of my own nerves disordered by sirocco or what not, and at the same time quite clearly knowing in another part of my mind, so to speak, that every moment's delay added to the danger. At last this second feeling became irresistible, and I put on coat and trousers and went out of my room onto the landing. And then I saw that I had already delayed too long, and that I was now too late.

The whole of the landing of the first floor below was invisible under the swarm of caterpillars that crawled there. The folding doors into the sitting room from which opened the bedroom where I had seen them last night were shut, but they were squeezing through the cracks of it, and dropping one by one through the keyhole, elongating themselves into mere string as they passed, and growing fat and lumpy again on emerging. Some, as if exploring, were nosing about the steps into the passage at the end of which were Inglis' rooms, others were crawling on the lowest steps of the staircase that led up to where I stood. The landing, however, was completely covered with them: I was cut off. And of the frozen horror that seized me when I saw that, I can give no idea in words.

Then at last a general movement began to take place, and they grew thicker on the steps that led to Inglis' room. Gradually, like some hideous tide of flesh, they advanced along the passage, and I saw the foremost, visible by the pale grey luminousness that came from them, reach his door. Again and again I tried to shout and warn him, in terror all the time that they should turn at the sound of my voice and mount my stair instead, but for all my efforts I felt that no sound came from my throat. They crawled along the hinge-crack of his door, passing through as they had done before, and still I stood there making impotent efforts to shout to him, to bid him escape while there was time.

At last the passage was completely empty: they had all gone, and at that moment I was conscious for the first time of the cold of the marble landing on which I stood barefooted. The dawn was just beginning to break in the eastern sky.

Six months later I met Mrs. Stanley in a country house in England. We talked on many subjects, and at last she said:

"I don't think I have seen you since I got the dreadful news about Arthur Inglis a month ago."

"I haven't heard," said I.

"No? He has got cancer. They don't even advise an operation, for there is no hope of a cure: he is riddled with it, the doctors say."

Now during all these six months I do not think a day had passed on which I had not had in my mind the dreams (or whatever you like to call them) which I had seen in the Villa Casana.

"It is awful, is it not?" she continued, "and I feel, I can't help feeling, that he may have—"

"Caught it at the Villa?" I asked.

She looked at me in blank surprise.

"Why did you say that?" she asked. "How did you know?"

Then she told me. In the unoccupied bedroom a year before there had been a fatal case of cancer. She had, of course, taken the best advice and had been told that the utmost dictates of prudence would be obeyed so long as she did not put anybody to sleep in the room, which had also been thoroughly disinfected and newly whitewashed and painted. But—

EDWARD LUCAS WHITE

LUKUNDOO

"It stands to reason," said Twombly, "that a man must accept the evidence of his own eyes, and when eyes and ears agree, there can be no doubt. He has to believe what he has both seen and heard."

"Not always," put in Singleton, softly.

Every man turned toward Singleton. Twombly was standing on the hearthrug, his back to the grate, his legs spread out, with his habitual air of dominating the room. Singleton, as usual, was as much as possible effaced in a corner. But when Singleton spoke he said something. We faced him in that flattering spontaneity of expectant silence which invites utterance.

"I was thinking," he said, after an interval, "of something I both saw and heard in Africa."

Now, if there was one thing we had found impossible, it had been to elicit from Singleton anything definite about his African experiences. As with the Alpinist in the story, who could tell only that he went up and came down, the sum of Singleton's revelations had been that he went there and came away. His words now riveted our attention at once. Twombly faded from the hearthrug, but not one of us could ever recall having seen him go. The room readjusted itself, focused on Singleton, and there was some hasty and furtive lighting of fresh cigars. Singleton lit one also, but it went out immediately, and he never relit it.

I

We were in the Great Forest, exploring for pigmies. Van Rieten had a theory that the dwarfs found by Stanley and others were a mere cross-breed between ordinary negroes and the real pigmies. He hoped to discover a race of men three feet tall at most, or shorter. We had found no trace of any such beings.

Natives were few, game scarce; food, except game, there was none; and the deepest, dankest, drippingest forest all about. We were the only novelty in the country, no native we met had ever seen a white man before, most had never heard of white men. All of a sudden, late one afternoon, there came into our camp an Englishman, and pretty well used up he was, too. We had heard no rumor of him; he had not only heard of us but had made an amazing five-day march to reach us. His guide and two bearers were nearly as done up as he. Even though he was in tatters and had five days' beard on, you could see he was naturally dapper and neat and the sort of man to shave daily. He was small, but wiry. His face was the sort of British face from which emotion has been so carefully banished that a foreigner is apt to think the wearer of the face incapable of any sort of feeling; the kind of face which, if it has any expression at all, expresses principally the resolution to go through the world decorously, without intruding upon or annoying anyone.

His name was Etcham. He introduced himself modestly, and ate with us so deliberately that we should never have suspected, if our bearers had not had it from his bearers, that he had had but three meals in the five days, and those small. After we had lit up he told us why he had come.

"My chief is ve'y seedy," he said between puffs. "He is bound to go out if he keeps this way. I thought perhaps . . ."

He spoke quietly in a soft, even tone, but I could see little beads of sweat oozing out on his upper lip under his stubby mustache, and there was a tingle of repressed emotion in his tone, a veiled eagerness in his eye, a palpitating inward solicitude in his demeanor that moved me at once. Van Rieten had no sentiment in him; if he was moved he did not show it. But he listened. I was surprised at that. He was just the man to refuse at once. But he listened to Etcham's halting, difficult hints. He even asked questions.

"Who is your chief?"

"Stone," Etcham lisped.

That electrified both of us.

"Ralph Stone?" we ejaculated together.

Etcham nodded.

For some minutes Van Rieten and I were silent. Van Rieten had never seen him, but I had been a classmate of Stone's, and Van Rieten and I had discussed him over many a campfire. We had heard of him two years before, south of Luebo in the Balunda country, which had been ringing with his theatrical strife against a Balunda witch-doctor, ending in the sorcerer's complete discomfiture and the abasement of his tribe before Stone. They had even broken the fetish-man's whistle and given Stone the pieces. It had been like the triumph of Elijah over the prophets of Baal, only more real to the Balunda.

We had thought of Stone as far off, if still in Africa at all, and here he turned up ahead of us and probably forestalling our quest.

II

Etcham's naming of Stone brought back to us all his tantalizing story, his fascinating parents, their tragic death; the brilliance of his college days; the dazzle of his millions; the promise of his young manhood; his wide notoriety, so nearly real fame; his romantic elopement with the meteoric authoress whose sudden cascade of fiction had made her so great a name so young, whose beauty and charm were so much heralded; the frightful scandal of the breach-of-promise suit that followed; his bride's devotion through it all; their sudden quarrel after it was all over; their divorce; the too much advertised announcement of his approaching marriage to the plaintiff in the breach-of-promise suit; his precipitate remarriage to his divorced bride; their second quarrel and second divorce; his departure from his native land; his advent in the dark continent. The sense of all this rushed over me and I believe Van Rieten felt it, too, as he sat silent.

Then he asked:

"Where is Werner?"

"Dead," said Etcham. "He died before I joined Stone."

"You were not with Stone above Luebo?"

"No," said Etcham, "I joined him at Stanley Falls."

"Who is with him?" Van Rieten asked.

"Only his Zanzibar servants and the bearers," Etcham replied.

"What sort of bearers?" Van Rieten demanded.

"Mang-Battu men," Etcham responded simply.

Now that impressed both Van Rieten and myself greatly. It bore out Stone's reputation as a notable leader of men. For up to that time no one had been able to use Mang-Battu as bearers outside of their own country, or to hold them for long or difficult expeditions.

"Were you long among the Mang-Battu?" was Van Rieten's next question.

"Some weeks," said Etcham. "Stone was interested in them and made up a fair-sized vocabulary of their words and phrases. He had a theory that they are an offshoot of the Balunda and he found much confirmation in their customs."

"What do you live on?" Van Rieten enquired.

"Game, mostly," Etcham lisped.

"How long has Stone been laid up?" Van Rieten next asked.

"More than a month," Etcham answered.

"And you have been hunting for the camp?" Van Rieten exclaimed.

Etcham's face, burnt and flayed as it was, showed a flush.

"I missed some easy shots," he admitted ruefully. "I've not felt ve'y fit myself."

"What's the matter with your chief?" Van Rieten enquired.

"Something like carbuncles," Etcham replied.

"He ought to get over a carbuncle or two," Van Rieten declared.

"They are not carbuncles," Etcham explained. "Nor one or two. He has had dozens, sometimes five at once. If they had been carbuncles he would have been dead long ago. But in some ways they are not so bad, though in others they are worse."

"How do you mean?" Van Rieten queried.

"Well," Etcham hesitated, "they do not seem to inflame so deep nor so wide as carbuncles, nor to be so painful, nor to cause so much fever. But then they seem to be part of a disease that affects his mind. He let me help him dress the first, but the others he has hidden most carefully, from me and from the men. He keeps his tent when they puff up, and will not let me change the dressings or be with him at all."

"Have you plenty of dressings?" Van Rieten asked.

"We have some," said Etcham doubtfully. "But he won't use them; he washes out the dressings and uses them over and over."

"How is he treating the swellings?" Van Rieten enquired.

"He slices them off clean down to flesh level, with his razor."

"What?" Van Rieten shouted.

Etcham made no answer but looked him steadily in the eyes.

"I beg pardon," Van Rieten hastened to say. "You startled me. They can't be carbuncles. He'd have been dead long ago."

"I thought I had said they are not carbuncles," Etcham lisped.

"But the man must be crazy!" Van Rieten exclaimed.

"Just so," said Etcham. "He is beyond my advice or control."

"How many has he treated that way?" Van Rieten demanded.

"Two, to my knowledge," Etcham said.

"Two?" Van Rieten queried.

Etcham flushed again.

"I saw him," he confessed, "through a crack in the hut. I felt impelled to keep a watch on him, as if he was not responsible."

"I should think not," Van Rieten agreed. "And you saw him do that twice?"

"I conjecture," said Etcham, "that he did the like with all the rest."

"How many has he had?" Van Rieten asked.

"Dozens," Etcham lisped.

"Does he eat?" Van Rieten enquired.

"Like a wolf," said Etcham. "More than any two bearers."

"Can he walk?" Van Rieten asked.

"He crawls a bit, groaning," said Etcham simply.

"Little fever, you say," Van Rieten ruminated.

"Enough and too much," Etcham declared.

"Has he been delirious?" Van Rieten asked.

"Only twice," Etcham replied; "once when the first swelling broke, and once later. He would not let anyone come near him then. But we could hear him talking, talking steadily, and it scared the natives.

"Was he talking their patter in delirium?" Van Rieten demanded.

"No," said Etcham, "but he was talking some similar lingo. Hamed Burghash said he was talking Balunda. I know too little Balunda. I do not learn languages readily. Stone learned more Mang-Battu in a week than I could have learned in a year. But I seemed to hear words like Mang-Battu words. Anyhow, the Mang-Battu bearers were scared."

"Scared?" Van Rieten repeated, questioningly.

"So were the Zanzibar men, even Hamed Burghash, and so was I," said Etcham, "only for a different reason. He talked in two voices."

"In two voices," Van Rieten reflected.

"Yes," said Etcham, more excitedly than he had yet spoken. "In two voices, like a conversation. One was his own, one a small, thin, bleaty voice like nothing I ever heard. I seemed to make out, among the sounds the deep voice made, something like Mang-Battu words I knew, as *nedru, metababa,* and *nedo,* their terms for 'head,' 'shoulder,' 'thigh,' and perhaps *kudra* and *nekere* ('speak' and 'whistle'); and among the noises of the shrill voice *matomipa, angunzi,* and *kamomami* ('kill,' 'death,' and 'hate'). Hamed Burghash said he also heard those words. He knew Mang-Battu far better than I."

"What did the bearers say?" Van Rieten asked.

"They said, *'Lukundoo, Lukundoo!'* " Etcham replied. "I did not know the word; Hamed Burghash said it was Mang-Battu for 'leopard.' "

"It's Mang-Battu for 'witchcraft,' " said Van Rieten.

"I don't wonder they thought so," said Etcham. "It was enough to make one believe in sorcery to listen to those two voices."

"One voice answering the other?" Van Rieten asked perfunctorily.

Etcham's face went gray under his tan.

"Sometimes both at once," he answered huskily.

"Both at once!" Van Rieten ejaculated.

"It sounded that way to the men, too," said Etcham. "And that was not all."

He stopped and looked helplessly at us for a moment.

"Could a man talk and whistle at the same time?" he asked.

"How do you mean?" Van Rieten queried.

"We could hear Stone talking away, his big, deep-chested baritone rumbling along, and through it all we could hear a high, shrill whistle, the oddest, wheezy sound. You know, no matter how shrilly a grown man may whistle, the note has a different quality from the whistle of a boy or a woman or a little girl. They sound more treble, somehow. Well, if you can imagine the smallest girl who could whistle keeping it up tunelessly right along, that whistle was like that, only even more piercing, and it sounded right through Stone's bass tones."

"And you didn't go to him?" Van Rieten cried.

"He is not given to threats," Etcham disclaimed. "But he had threatened, not volubly, nor like a sick man, but quietly and firmly, that if any man of us (he lumped me in with the men) came near him while he was in his trouble, that man should die. And it was not so much his words as his manner. It was like a monarch commanding respected privacy for a deathbed. One simply could not transgress."

"I see," said Van Rieten shortly.

"He's ve'y seedy," Etcham repeated helplessly. "I thought perhaps...."

His absorbing affection for Stone, his real love for him, shone out through his envelope of conventional training. Worship of Stone was plainly his master passion.

Like many competent men, Van Rieten had a streak of hard selfishness in him. It came to the surface then. He said we carried our lives in our hands from day to day just as genuinely as Stone; that he did not forget the ties of blood and calling between any two explorers, but that there was no sense in imperiling one party for a very problematical benefit to a man probably beyond any help; that it was enough of a task to hunt for one party; that if two were united, providing food would be more than doubly difficult; that the risk of starvation was too great. Deflecting our march seven full days' journey (he complimented Etcham on his marching powers) might ruin our expedition entirely.

III

Van Rieten had logic on his side and he had a way with him. Etcham sat there apologetic and deferential, like a fourth-form schoolboy before a head master. Van Rieten wound up.

"I am after pigmies, at the risk of my life. After pigmies I go."

"Perhaps, then, these will interest you," said Etcham, very quietly.

He took two objects out of the sidepocket of his blouse, and handed them to Van Rieten. They were round, bigger than big plums, and smaller than small peaches, about the right size to enclose in an average hand. They were black, and at first I did not see what they were.

"Pigmies!" Van Rieten exclaimed. "Pigmies, indeed! Why, they wouldn't be two feet high! Do you mean to claim that these are adult heads?"

"I claim nothing," Etcham answered evenly. "You can see for yourself."

Van Rieten passed one of the heads to me. The sun was just setting and I examined it closely. A dried head it was, perfectly preserved, and the flesh as hard as Argentine jerked beef. A bit of a vertebra stuck out where the muscles of the vanished neck had shriveled into folds. The puny chin was sharp on a projecting jaw, the minute teeth white and even between the retracted lips, the tiny nose was flat, the little forehead retreating, there were inconsiderable clumps of stunted wool on the Lilliputian cranium. There was nothing babyish, childish or youthful about the head; rather it was mature to senility.

"Where did these come from?" Van Rieten enquired.

"I do not know," Etcham replied precisely. "I found them among Stone's effects while rummaging for medicines or drugs or anything that could help me to help him. I do not know where he got them. But I'll swear he did not have them when we entered this district."

"Are you sure?" Van Rieten queried, his eyes big and fixed on Etcham's.

"Ve'y sure," lisped Etcham.

"But how could he have come by them without your knowledge?" Van Rieten demurred.

"Sometimes we were apart ten days at a time hunting," said Etcham. "Stone is not a talking man. He gave me no account of his doings, and Hamed Burghash keeps a still tongue and a tight hold on the men."

"You have examined these heads?" Van Rieten asked.

"Minutely," said Etcham.

Van Rieten took out his notebook. He was a methodical chap. He tore out a leaf, folded it and divided it equally into three pieces. He gave one to me and one to Etcham.

"Just for a test of my impressions," he said, "I want each of us to write separately just what he is most reminded of by these heads. Then I want to compare the writings."

I handed Etcham a pencil and he wrote. Then he handed the pencil back to me and I wrote.

"Read the three," said Van Rieten, handing me his piece.

Van Rieten had written:

"An old Balunda witch-doctor."

Etcham had written:

"An old Mang-Battu fetish-man."

I had written:

"An old Katongo magician."

"There!" Van Rieten exclaimed. "Look at that! There is nothing Wagabi or Batwa or Wambuttu or Wabotu about these heads. Nor anything pigmy either."

"I thought as much," said Etcham.

"And you say he did not have them before?"

"To a certainty he did not," Etcham asserted.

"It is worth following up," said Van Rieten. "I'll go with you. And first of all, I'll do my best to save Stone."

He put out his hand and Etcham clasped it silently. He was grateful all over.

IV

Nothing but Etcham's fever of solicitude could have taken him in five days over the track. It took him eight days to retrace with full knowledge of it and our party to help. We could not have done it in seven, and Etcham urged us on, in a repressed fury of anxiety, no mere fever of duty to his chief, but a real ardor of devotion, a glow of personal adoration for Stone which blazed under his dry conventional exterior and showed in spite of him.

We found Stone well cared for. Etcham had seen to a good, high thorn *zareeba* round the camp, the huts were well built, and thatched and Stone's was as good as their resources would permit. Hamed Burghash was not named after two Seyyids for nothing. He had in him the making of a sultan. He had kept the Mang-Battu together, not a man had slipped off, and he had kept them in order. Also he was a deft nurse and a faithful servant.

The two other Zanzibaris had done some creditable hunting. Though all were hungry, the camp was far from starvation.

Stone was on a canvas cot and there was a sort of collapsible camp-stool-table, like a Turkish tabouret, by the cot. It had a water-bottle and some vials on it and Stone's watch, also his razor in its case.

Stone was clean and not emaciated, but he was far gone; not unconscious, but in a daze; past commanding or resisting anyone. He did not seem to see us enter or to know we were there. I should have recognized him anywhere. His boyish dash and grace had vanished utterly, of course. But his head was even more leonine; his hair was still abundant, yellow and wavy; the close, crisped blond beard he had grown during his illness did not alter him. He was big and big-chested yet. His eyes were dull and he mumbled and babbled mere meaningless syllables, not words.

Etcham helped Van Rieten to uncover him and look him over. He was in good muscle for a man so long bedridden. There were no scars on him except about his knees, shoulders and chest. On each knee and above it he had a full score of roundish cicatrices, and a dozen or more on each shoulder, all in front. Two or three were open wounds and four or five barely healed. He had no fresh swellings, except two, one on each side, on his pectoral muscles, the one on the left being higher up and farther out than the other. They did not look like boils or carbuncles, but as if something blunt and hard were being pushed up through the fairly healthy flesh and skin, not much inflamed.

"I should not lance those," said Van Rieten, and Etcham assented.

They made Stone as comfortable as they could, and just before sunset we looked in at him again. He was lying on his back, and his chest showed big and massive yet, but he lay as if in a stupor. We left Etcham with him and went into the next hut, which Etcham had resigned to us. The jungle noises were no different than anywhere else for months past, and I was soon fast asleep.

v

Sometime in the pitch dark I found myself awake and listening. I could hear two voices, one Stone's, the other sibilant and wheezy. I knew Stone's voice after all the years that had passed since I heard it last. The other was like nothing I remembered. It had less volume than the wail of a new-born baby, yet there was an insistent carrying power to it, like the shrilling of an insect. As I listened I heard Van Rieten breathing near me in the dark; then he heard me and realized that I was listening, too. Like Etcham I knew little Balunda, but I could make out a word or two. The voices alternated, with intervals of silence between.

Then suddenly both sounded at once and fast. Stone's baritone basso, full as if he were in perfect health, and that incredibly stridulous falsetto, both jabbering at once like the voices of two people quarreling and trying to talk each other down.

"I can't stand this," said Van Rieten. "Let's have a look at him."

He had one of those cylindrical electric night-candles. He fumbled about for it, touched the button and beckoned me to come with him. Outside the hut he motioned me to stand still, and instinctively turned off the light, as if seeing made listening difficult.

Except for a faint glow from the embers of the bearers' fire we were in complete darkness, little starlight struggled through the trees, the river made but a faint murmur. We could hear the two voices together and then suddenly the creaking voice changed into a razor-edged, slicing whistle, indescribably cutting, continuing right through Stone's grumbling torrent of croaking words.

"Good God!" exclaimed Van Rieten.

Abruptly he turned on the light.

We found Etcham utterly asleep, exhausted by his long anxiety and the exertions of his phenomenal march, and relaxed completely now that the load was in a sense shifted from his shoulders to Van Rieten's. Even the light on his face did not wake him.

The whistle had ceased and the two voices now sounded together. Both came from Stone's cot, where the concentrated white ray showed him lying just as we had left him, except that he had tossed his arms above his head and had torn the coverings and bandages from his chest.

The swelling on his right breast had broken. Van Rieten aimed the center line of the light at it and we saw it plainly. From his flesh, grown out of it, there protruded a head, such a head as the dried specimens Etcham had shown us, as if it were a miniature of the head of a Balunda fetish-man. It was black, shining black as the blackest African skin; it rolled the whites of its wicked, wee eyes and showed its microscopic teeth between lips repulsively negroid in their red fullness, even in so diminutive a face. It had crisp, fuzzy wool on its minikin skull, it turned malignantly from side to side and chittered incessantly in that inconceivable falsetto. Stone babbled brokenly against its patter.

Van Rieten turned from Stone and waked Etcham, with some difficulty. When he was awake and saw it all, Etcham stared and said not one word.

"You saw him slice off two swellings?" Van Rieten asked.

Etcham nodded, chokingly.

"Did he bleed much?" Van Rieten demanded.

"Ve'y little," Etcham replied.

"You hold his arms," said Van Rieten to Etcham.

He took up Stone's razor and handed me the light. Stone showed no sign of seeing the light or of knowing we were there. But the little head mewled and screeched at us.

Van Rieten's hand was steady, and the sweep of the razor even and true. Stone bled amazingly little and Van Rieten dressed the wound as if it had been a bruise or scrape.

Stone had stopped talking the instant the excrescent head was severed. Van Rieten did all that could be done for Stone and then fairly grabbed the light from me. Snatching up a gun he scanned the ground by the cot and brought the butt down once and twice, viciously.

We went back to our hut, but I doubt if I slept.

VI

Next day, near noon, in broad daylight, we heard the two voices from Stone's hut. We found Etcham dropped asleep by his charge. The swelling on the left had broken, and just such another head was there miauling and spluttering. Etcham woke up and the three of us stood there and glared. Stone interjected hoarse vocables into the tinkling gurgle of the portent's utterance.

Van Rieten stepped forward, took up Stone's razor and knelt down by the cot. The atomy of a head squealed a wheezy snarl at him.

Then suddenly Stone spoke English.

"Who are you with my razor?"

Van Rieten started back and stood up.

Stone's eyes were clear now and bright, they roved about the hut.

"The end," he said; "I recognize the end. I seem to see Etcham, as if in life. But Singleton! Ah, Singleton! Ghosts of my boyhood come to watch me pass! And you, strange specter with the black beard and my razor! Aroint ye all!"

"I'm no ghost, Stone," I managed to say. "I'm alive. So are Etcham and Van Rieten. We are here to help you."

"Van Rieten!" he exclaimed. "My work passes on to a better man. Luck go with you, Van Rieten."

Van Rieten went nearer to him.

"Just hold still a moment, old man," he said soothingly. "It will be only one twinge."

"I've held still for many such twinges," Stone answered quite distinctly. "Let me be. Let me die in my own way. The hydra was nothing to this. You can cut off ten, a hundred, a thousand heads, but the curse you can not cut off, or take off. What's soaked into the bone won't come out of the flesh, any more than what's bred there. Don't hack me any more. Promise!"

His voice had all the old commanding tone of his boyhood and it swayed Van Rieten as it always had swayed everybody.

"I promise," said Van Rieten.

Almost as he said the word Stone's eyes filmed again.

Then we three sat about Stone and watched that hideous, gibbering prodigy grow up out of Stone's flesh, till two horrid, spindling little black arms disengaged themselves. The infinitesimal nails were perfect to the barely perceptible moon at the quick, the pink spot on the palm was horridly natural. These arms gesticulated and the right plucked toward Stone's blond beard.

"I can't stand this," Van Rieten exclaimed and took up the razor again.

Instantly Stone's eyes opened, hard and glittering.

"Van Rieten break his word?" he enunciated slowly. "Never!"

"But we must help you," Van Rieten gasped.

"I am past all help and all hurting," said Stone. "This is my hour. This curse is not put on me; it grew out of me, like this horror here. Even now I go."

His eyes closed and we stood helpless, the adherent figure spouting shrill sentences.

In a moment Stone spoke again.

"You speak all tongues?" he asked quickly.

And the mergent minikin replied in sudden English:

"Yea, verily, all that you speak," putting out its microscopic tongue, writhing its lips and wagging its head from side to side. We could see the thready ribs on its exiguous flanks heave as if the thing breathed.

"Has she forgiven me?" Stone asked in a muffled strangle.

"Not while the moss hangs from the cypresses," the head squeaked. "Not while the stars shine on Lake Pontchartrain will she forgive."

And then Stone, all with one motion, wrenched himself over on his side. The next instant he was dead.

When Singleton's voice ceased the room was hushed for a space. We could hear each other breathing. Twombly, the tactless, broke the silence.

"I presume," he said, "you cut off the little minikin and brought it home in alcohol."

Singleton turned on him a stern countenance.

"We buried Stone," he said, "unmutilated as he died."

"But," said the unconscionable Twombly, "the whole thing is incredible."

Singleton stiffened.

"I did not expect you to believe it," he said; "I began by saying that although I heard and saw it, when I look back on it I cannot credit it myself."

SAKI (H. H. MUNRO)

SREDNI VASHTAR

Conradin was ten years old, and the doctor had pronounced his professional opinion that the boy would not live another five years. The doctor was silky and effete, and counted for little, but his opinion was endorsed by Mrs. De Ropp, who counted for nearly everything. Mrs. De Ropp was Conradin's cousin and guardian, and in his eyes she represented those three-fifths of the world that are necessary and disagreeable and real; the other two-fifths, in perpetual antagonism to the foregoing, were summed up in himself and his imagination. One of these days Conradin supposed he would succumb to the mastering pressure of wearisome necessary things—such as illnesses and coddling restrictions and drawn-out dulness. Without his imagination, which was rampant under the spur of loneliness, he would have succumbed long ago.

Mrs. De Ropp would never, in her honestest moments, have confessed to herself that she disliked Conradin, though she might have been dimly aware that thwarting him "for his good" was a duty which she did not find particularly irksome. Conradin hated her with a desperate sincerity which he was perfectly able to mask. Such few pleasures as he could contrive for himself gained an added relish from the likelihood that they would be displeasing to his guardian, and from the realm of his imagination she was locked out—an unclean thing, which should find no entrance.

In the dull, cheerless garden, overlooked by so many windows that were ready to open with a message not to do this or that, or a reminder that medicines were due, he found little attraction. The few fruit-trees that it contained were set jealously apart from his plucking, as though they were rare specimens of their kind blooming in an arid waste; it would probably have been difficult to find a market-gardener who would have offered ten shillings for their entire yearly produce. In a forgotten corner, however, almost hidden behind a dismal shrubbery, was a disused tool-shed of respectable proportions, and within its walls Conradin found a haven, something that took on the varying aspects of a playroom and a cathedral. He had peopled it with a legion of familiar phantoms, evoked partly from fragments of history and partly from his own brain, but it also boasted two inmates of flesh and blood. In one corner lived a ragged-plumaged Houdan hen, on which the boy lavished an affection that had scarcely another outlet. Further back in the gloom stood a large hutch, divided into two compartments, one of which was fronted with close iron bars. This was the abode of a large polecat-ferret, which a friendly butcher-boy had once smuggled, cage and all, into its present quarters, in exchange for a long-secreted hoard of small silver. Conradin was dreadfully afraid of the lithe, sharp-fanged beast, but it was his most treasured possession. Its very presence in the tool-shed was a secret and fearful joy, to be kept scrupulously from the knowledge of the Woman, as he privately dubbed his cousin. And one day, out of Heaven knows what material, he spun the beast a wonderful name, and from that moment it grew into a god and a religion. The Woman indulged in religion once a week at a church near by, and took Conradin with her, but to him the church service was an alien rite in the House of Rimmon. Every Thursday, in the dim and musty silence of the tool-shed, he worshipped with mystic and elaborate ceremonial before the wooden hutch where dwelt Sredni Vashtar, the great ferret. Red flowers in their season and scarlet berries in the winter-time were offered at his shrine, for he was a god who laid some special stress on the fierce impatient side of things, as opposed to the Woman's religion, which, as far as Conradin could observe, went to great lengths in the contrary direction. And on great festivals powdered nutmeg was strewn in front of his hutch, an important feature of the offering being that the nutmeg had to be stolen. These festivals were of irregular occurrence, and were chiefly appointed to celebrate some passing event. On one occasion, when Mrs. De Ropp suffered from acute toothache for three days, Conradin kept up the festival during the entire three days, and almost succeeded in persuading himself that Sredni Vashtar was personally responsible for the toothache. If the malady had lasted for another day the supply of nutmeg would have given out.

The Houdan hen was never drawn into the cult of Sredni Vashtar. Conradin had long ago settled that she was Anabaptist. He did not pretend to have the remotest knowledge as to what an Anabaptist was, but he privately hoped that it was dashing and not very respectable. Mrs. De Ropp was the ground plan on which he based and detested all respectability.

After a while Conradin's absorption in the tool-shed began to attract the notice of his guardian. "It is not good for him to be pottering down there in all weathers," she promptly decided, and at breakfast one morning she announced that the Houdan hen had been sold and taken away overnight. With her short-sighted eyes she peered at Conradin, waiting for an outbreak of rage and sorrow, which she was ready to rebuke with a flow of excellent precepts and reasoning. But Conradin said nothing; there was nothing to be said. Something perhaps in his white set face gave her a momentary qualm, for at tea that afternoon there was toast on the table, a delicacy which she usually banned on the ground that it was bad for him; also because the making of it "gave trouble," a deadly offence in the middle-class feminine eye.

"I thought you liked toast," she exclaimed, with an injured air, observing that he did not touch it.

"Sometimes," said Conradin.

In the shed that evening there was an innovation in the worship of the hutch-god. Conradin had been wont to chant his praises; tonight he asked a boon.

"Do one thing for me, Sredni Vashtar."

The thing was not specified. As Sredni Vashtar was a god he must be supposed to know. And choking back a sob as he looked at that other empty corner, Conradin went back to the world he so hated.

And every night, in the welcome darkness of his bedroom, and every evening in the dusk of the tool-shed, Conradin's bitter litany went up: "Do one thing for me, Sredni Vashtar."

Mrs. De Ropp noticed that the visits to the shed did not cease, and one day she made a further journey of inspection.

"What are you keeping in that locked hutch?" she asked. "I believe it's guinea-pigs. I'll have them all cleared away."

Conradin shut his lips tight, but the Woman ransacked his bedroom till she found the carefully hidden key, and forthwith marched down to the shed to complete her discovery. It was a cold afternoon, and Conradin had been bidden to keep to the house. From the furthest window of the dining-room the door of the shed could just be seen beyond the corner of the shrubbery, and there Conradin stationed himself. He saw the Woman enter, and then he imagined her opening the door of the sacred hutch and peering down with her short-sighted eyes into the thick straw bed where his god lay hidden. Perhaps she would prod at the straw in her clumsy impatience. And Conradin fervently breathed his prayer for the last time. But he knew as he prayed that he did not believe. He knew that the Woman would come out presently with the pursed smile he loathed so well on her face, and that in an hour or two the gardener would carry away his wonderful god, a god no longer, but a simple brown ferret in a hutch. And he knew that the Woman would triumph always as she triumphed now, and that he would grow ever more sickly under her pestering and domineering and superior wisdom, till one day nothing would matter much more with him, and the doctor would be proved right. And in the sting and misery of his defeat, he began to chant loudly and defiantly the hymn of his threatened idol:

> Sredni Vashtar went forth,
> His thoughts were red thoughts and his teeth were white.
> His enemies called for peace, but he brought them death.
> Sredni Vashtar the Beautiful.

And then of a sudden he stopped his chanting and drew closer to the window-pane. The door of the shed still stood ajar as it had been left, and the minutes were slipping by. They were long minutes, but they slipped by nevertheless. He watched the starlings running and flying in little parties across the lawn; he counted them over and over again, with one eye always on that swinging door. A sour-faced maid came in to lay the table for tea, and still Conradin stood and waited and watched. Hope had crept by inches into his heart, and now a look of triumph began to blaze in his eyes that had only known the wistful patience of defeat. Under his breath, with a furtive exultation, he began once again the paean of victory and devastation. And presently his eyes were rewarded: out through that doorway came a long, low, yellow-and-brown beast, with eyes a-blink at the waning daylight, and dark wet stains around the fur of jaws and throat. Conradin dropped on his knees. The great polecat-ferret made its way down to a small brook at the foot of the garden, drank for a moment, then crossed a little plank bridge and was lost to sight in the bushes. Such was the passing of Sredni Vashtar.

"Tea is ready," said the sour-faced maid; "where is the mistress?"

"She went down to the shed some time ago," said Conradin.

And while the maid went to summon her mistress to tea, Conradin fished a toasting-fork out of the sideboard drawer and proceeded to toast himself a piece of bread. And during the toasting of it and the buttering of it with much butter and the slow enjoyment of eating it, Conradin listened to the noises and silences which fell in quick spasms beyond the dining-room door. The loud foolish screaming of the maid, the answering chorus of wondering ejaculations from the kitchen region, the scuttering footsteps and hurried embassies for outside help, and then, after a lull, the scared sobbings and the shuffling tread of those who bore a heavy burden into the house.

"Whoever will break it to the poor child? I couldn't for the life of me!" exclaimed a shrill voice. And while they debated the matter among themselves, Conradin made himself another piece of toast.

H. P. LOVECRAFT

THE PICTURE
IN THE HOUSE

Searchers after horror haunt strange, far places. For them are the catacombs of Ptolemais, and the carven mausolea of the nightmare countries. They climb to the moonlit towers of ruined Rhine castles, and falter down black cobwebbed steps beneath the scattered stones of forgotten cities in Asia. The haunted wood and the desolate mountain are their shrines, and they linger around the sinister monoliths on uninhabited islands. But the true epicure in the terrible, to whom a new thrill of unutterable ghastliness is the chief end and justification of existence, esteems most of all the ancient, lonely farmhouses of backwoods New England; for there the dark elements of strength, solitude, grotesqueness and ignorance combine to form the perfection of the hideous.

Most horrible of all sights are the little unpainted wooden houses remote from travelled ways, usually squatted upon some damp, grassy slope or leaning against some gigantic outcropping of rock. Two hundred years and more they have leaned or squatted there, while the vines have crawled and the trees have swelled and spread. They are almost hidden now in lawless luxuriances of green and guardian shrouds of shadow; but the small-paned windows still stare shockingly, as if blinking through a lethal stupor which wards off madness by dulling the memory of unutterable things.

In such houses have dwelt generations of strange people, whose like the world has never seen. Seized with a gloomy and fanatical belief which exiled them from their kind, their ancestors sought the wilderness for freedom. There the scions of a conquering race indeed flourished free from the restrictions of their fellows, but cowered in an appalling slavery to the dismal phantasms of their own minds. Divorced from the enlightenment of civilization, the strength of these Puritans turned into singular channels; and in their isolation, morbid self-repression, and struggle for life with relentless Nature, there came to them dark furtive traits from the prehistoric depths of their cold Northern heritage. By necessity practical and by philosophy stern, these folks were not beautiful in their sins. Erring as all mortals must, they were forced by their rigid code to seek concealment above all else; so that they came to use less and less taste in what they concealed. Only the silent, sleepy, staring houses in the backwoods can tell all that has lain hidden since the early days, and they are not communicative, being loath to shake off the drowsiness which helps them forget. Sometimes one feels that it would be merciful to tear down these houses, for they must often dream.

It was to a time-battered edifice of this description that I was driven one afternoon in November, 1896, by a rain of such chilling copiousness that any shelter was preferable to exposure. I had been travelling for some time amongst the people of the Miskatonic Valley in quest of certain genealogical data; and from the remote, devious, and problematical nature of my course, had deemed it convenient to employ a bicycle despite the lateness of the season. Now I found myself upon an apparently abandoned road which I had chosen as the shortest cut to Arkham, overtaken by the storm at a point far from any town, and confronted with no refuge save the antique and repellent wooden building which blinked with bleared windows from between two huge leafless elms near the foot of a rocky hill. Distant though it is from the remnant of a road, this house none the less impressed me unfavourably the very moment I espied it. Honest, wholesome structures do not stare at travellers so slyly and hauntingly, and in my genealogical researches I had encountered legends of a century before which biased me against places of this kind. Yet the force of the elements was such as to overcome my scruples, and I did not hesitate to wheel my machine up the weedy rise to the closed door which seemed at once so suggestive and secretive.

I had somehow taken it for granted that the house was abandoned, yet as I approached it I was not so sure, for though the walks were indeed overgrown with weeds, they seemed to retain their nature a little too well to argue complete desertion. Therefore instead of trying the door I knocked, feeling as I did so a trepidation I could scarcely explain. As I waited on the rough, mossy rock which served as a door-step, I glanced at the neighbouring windows and the panes of the transom above me, and noticed that although old, rattling, and almost opaque with dirt, they were not broken. The building, then, must still be inhabited, despite its isolation and general neglect. However, my rapping evoked no response, so after repeating the summons I tried the rusty latch and found the door unfastened. Inside was a little vestibule with walls from which the plaster was falling, and through the doorway came a faint but peculiarly hateful odour. I entered, carrying my bicycle, and closed the door behind me. Ahead rose a narrow staircase, flanked by a small door probably leading to the cellar, while to the left and right were closed doors leading to rooms on the ground floor.

Leaning my cycle against the wall I opened the door at the left, and crossed into a small low-ceilinged chamber but dimly lighted by its two dusty windows and furnished in the barest and most primitive possible way. It appeared to be a kind of sitting-room, for it had a table and several chairs, and an immense fireplace above which ticked an antique clock on a mantel. Books and papers were very few, and in the prevailing gloom I could not readily discern the titles. What interested me was the uniform air of archaism as displayed in every visible detail. Most of the houses in this region I had found rich in relics of the past, but here the antiquity was curiously complete; for in all the room I could not discover a single article of definitely post-Revolutionary date. Had the furnishings been less humble, the place would have been a collector's paradise.

As I surveyed this quaint apartment, I felt an increase in that aversion first excited by the bleak exterior of the house. Just what it was that I feared or loathed, I could by no means define; but something in the whole atmosphere seemed redolent of unhallowed age, of unpleasant crudeness, and of secrets which should be forgotten. I felt disinclined to sit down, and wandered about examining the various articles which I had noticed. The first object of my curiosity was a book of medium size lying upon the table and presenting such an antediluvian aspect that I marvelled at beholding it outside a museum or library. It was bound in leather with metal fittings, and was in an excellent state of preservation; being altogether an unusual sort of volume to encounter in an abode so lowly. When I opened it to the title page my wonder grew even greater, for it proved to be nothing less rare than Pigafetta's account of the Congo region, written in Latin from the notes of the sailor Lopez and printed at Frankfurt in 1598. I had often heard of this work, with its curious illustrations by the brothers De Bry, hence for a moment forgot my uneasiness in my desire to turn the pages before me. The engravings were indeed interesting, drawn wholly from imagination and careless descriptions, and represented Negroes with white skins and Caucasian features; nor would I soon have closed the book had not an exceedingly trivial circumstance upset my tired nerves and revived my sensation of disquiet. What annoyed me was merely the persistent way in which the volume tended to fall open of itself at Plate XII, which represented in gruesome detail a butcher's shop of the cannibal Anziques. I experienced some shame at my susceptibility to so slight a thing, but the drawing nevertheless disturbed me, especially in connection with some adjacent passages descriptive of Anzique gastronomy.

I had turned to a neighbouring shelf and was examining its meagre literary contents—an eighteenth-century Bible, a *Pilgrim's Progress* of like period, illustrated with grotesque woodcuts and printed by the almanack-maker Isaiah Thomas, the rotting bulk of Cotton Mather's *Magnalia Christi Americana,* and a few other books of evidently equal age—when my attention was aroused by the unmistakable sound of walking in the room overhead. At first astonished and startled, considering the lack of response to my recent knocking at the door, I immediately afterwards concluded that the walker had just awakened from a sound sleep, and listened with less surprise as the footsteps sounded on the creaking stairs. The tread was heavy, yet seemed to contain a curious quality of cautiousness; a quality which I disliked the more because the tread was heavy. When I entered the room I had shut the door behind me. Now, after a moment of silence during which the walker may have been inspecting my bicycle in the hall, I heard a fumbling at the latch and saw the panelled portal swing open again.

In the doorway stood a person of such singular appearance that I should have exclaimed aloud but for the restraints of good breeding. Old, white-bearded, and ragged, my host possessed a countenance and physique which inspired equal wonder and respect. His height could not have been less than six feet, and despite a general air of age and poverty he was stout and powerful in proportion. His face, almost hidden by a long beard which grew high on the cheeks, seemed abnormally ruddy and less wrinkled than one might expect; while over a high forehead fell a shock of white hair little thinned by the years. His blue eyes, though a trifle bloodshot, seemed inexplicably keen and burning. But for his horrible unkemptness the man would have been as distinguished-looking as he was impressive. This un-kemptness, however, made him offensive despite his face and figure. Of what his clothing consisted I could hardly tell, for it seemed to me no more than a mass of tatters surmounting a pair of high, heavy boots; and his lack of cleanliness surpassed description.

The appearance of this man, and the instinctive fear he inspired, prepared me for something like enmity; so that I almost shuddered through surprise and a sense of uncanny incongruity when he motioned me to a chair and addressed me in a thin, weak voice full of fawning respect and ingratiating hospitality. His speech was very curious, an extreme form of Yankee dialect I had thought long extinct; and I studied it closely as he sat down opposite me for conversation.

"Ketched in the rain, be ye?" he greeted. "Glad ye was nigh the haouse en' hed the sense ta come right in. I calc'late I was asleep, else I'd a heered ye—I ain't as young as I uster be, an' I need a paowerful sight o' naps naowadays. Trav'lin' fur? I hain't seed many folks 'long this rud sence they tuk off the Arkham stage."

I replied that I was going to Arkham, and apologized for my rude entry into his domicile, whereupon he continued.

"Glad to see ye, young Sir—new faces is scurce araount here, an' I hain't got much ta cheer me up these days. Guess yew hail from Bosting, don't ye? I never ben thar, but I kin tell a taown man when I see 'im—we hed one fer deestrick schoolmaster in 'eighty-four, but he quit suddent an' no one never heerd on 'im sence—" here the old man lapsed into a kind of chuckle, and made no explanation when I questioned him. He seemed to be in an aboundingly good humour, yet to possess those eccentricities which one might guess from his grooming. For some time he rambled on with an almost feverish geniality, when it struck me to ask him how he came by so rare a book as Pigafetta's *Regnum Congo*. The effect of this volume had not left me, and I felt a certain hesitancy in speaking of it, but curiosity overmastered all the vague fears which had steadily accumulated since my first glimpse of the house. To my relief the question did not seem an awkward one, for the old man answered freely and volubly.

"Oh, that Afriky book? Cap'n Ebenezer Holt traded me thet in 'sixty-eight—him as was kilt in the war." Something about the name of Ebenezer Holt caused me to look up sharply. I had encountered it in my genealogical work, but not in any record since the Revolution. I wondered if my host could help me in the task at which I was labouring, and resolved to ask hĭm about it later on. He continued.

"Ebenezer was on a Salem merchantman for years, an' picked up a sight o' queer stuff in every port. He got this in London, I guess—he uster like ter buy things at the shops. I was up ta his haouse onct, on the hill, tradin' hosses, when I see this book. I relished the picters, so he give it in on a swap. 'Tis a queer book—here, leave me git on my spectacles—" The old man fumbled among his rags, producing a pair of dirty and amazingly antique glasses with small octagonal lenses and steel bows. Donning these, he reached for the volume on the table and turned the pages lovingly.

"Ebenezer cud read a leetle o' this—'tis Latin—but I can't. I had two er three schoolmasters read me a bit, and Passon Clark, him they say got draownded in the pond—kin yew make anything outen it?" I told him that I could, and translated for his benefit a paragraph near the beginning. If I erred, he was not scholar enough to correct me; for he seemed childishly pleased at my English version. His proximity was becoming rather obnoxious, yet I saw no way to escape without offending him. I was amused at the childish fondness of this ignorant old man for the pictures in a book he could not read, and wondered how much better he could read the few books in English which adorned the room. This revelation of simplicity removed much of the ill-defined apprehension I had felt, and I smiled as my host rambled on:

"Queer haow picters kin set a body thinkin'. Take this un here near the front. Hev yew ever seed trees like thet, with big leaves a-floppin' over an' daown? And them men—them can't be niggers—they dew beat all. Kinder like Injuns, I guess, even ef they be in Afriky. Some o' these here critters looks like monkeys, or half monkeys an' half men, but I never heerd o' nothin' like this un." Here he pointed to a fabulous creature of the artist, which one might describe as a sort of dragon with the head of an alligator.

"But naow I'll show ye the best un—over here nigh the middle—" The old man's speech grew a trifle thicker and his eyes assumed a brighter glow; but his fumbling hands, though seemingly clumsier than before, were entirely adequate to their mission. The book fell open, almost of its own accord and as if from frequent consultation at this place, to the repellent twelfth plate showing a butcher's shop amongst the Anzique cannibals. My sense of restlessness returned, though I did not exhibit it. The especially bizarre thing was that the artist had made his Africans look like white men—the limbs and quarters hanging about the walls of the shop were ghastly, while the butcher with his axe was hideously incongruous. But my host seemed to relish the view as much as I disliked it.

"What d'ye think o' this—ain't never see the like hereabouts, eh? When I see this I told Eb Holt, 'That's suthin' ta stir ye up an' make yer blood tickle.' When I read in Scripter about slayin'—like them Midianites was slew—I kinder think things, but I ain't got no picter of it. Here a body kin see all they is to it—I s'pose 'tis sinful, but ain't we all born an' livin' in sin?—

Thet feller bein' chopped up gives me a tickle every time I look at 'im—I hev ta keep lookin' at 'im—see whar the butcher cut off his feet? Thar's his head on thet bench, with one arm side of it, an' t'other arm's on the other side o' the meat block."

As the man mumbled on in his shocking ecstasy the expression on his hairy, spectacled face became indescribable, but his voice sank rather than mounted. My own sensations can scarcely be recorded. All the terror I had dimly felt before rushed upon me actively and vividly, and I knew that I loathed the ancient and abhorrent creature so near me with an infinite intensity. His madness, or at least his partial perversion, seemed beyond dispute. He was almost whispering now, with a huskiness more terrible than a scream, and I trembled as I listened.

"As I says, 'tis queer haow picters sets ye thinkin'. D'ye know, young Sir, I'm right sot on this un here. Arter I got the book off Eb I uster look at it a lot, especial when I'd heerd Passon Clark rant o' Sundays in his big wig. Onct I tried suthin' funny—here, young Sir, don't git skeert—all I done was ter look at the picter afore I kilt the sheep for market—killin' sheep was kinder more fun arter lookin' at it—" The tone of the old man now sank very low, sometimes becoming so faint that his words were hardly audible. I listened to the rain, and to the rattling of the bleared, small-paned windows, and marked a rumbling of approaching thunder quite unusual for the season. Once a terrific flash and peal shook the frail house to its foundations, but the whisperer seemed not to notice it.

"Killin' sheep was kinder more fun—but d'ye know, 'twan't quite *satisfyin'*. Queer haow a cravin' gits a holt on ye—As ye love the Almighty, young man, don't tell nobody, but I swar ter Gawd thet picter begun ta make me *hungry fer victuals I couldn't raise nor buy*—here, set still, what's ailin' ye?—I didn't do nothin', only I wondered haow 'twud be if I *did*—They say meat makes blood an' flesh, an' gives ye a new life, so I wondered ef 'twudn't make a man live longer an' longer ef 'twas *more the same*—" But the whisperer never continued. The interruption was not produced by my fright, nor by the rapidly increasing storm amidst whose fury I was presently to open my eyes on a smoky solitude of blackened ruins. It was produced by a very simple though somewhat unusual happening.

The open book lay flat between us, with the picture staring repulsively upwards. As the old man whispered the words *"more the same"* a tiny splattering impact was heard, and something showed on the yellowed paper of the upturned volume. I thought of the rain and of a leaky roof, but rain is not red. On the butcher's shop of the Anzique cannibals a small red spattering glistened picturesquely, lending vividness to the horror of the engraving. The old man saw it, and stopped whispering even before my expression of horror made it necessary; saw it and glanced quickly towards the floor of the room he had left an hour before. I followed his glance, and beheld just above us on the loose plaster of the ancient ceiling a large irregular spot of wet crimson which seemed to spread even as I viewed it. I did not shriek nor move, but merely shut my eyes. A moment later came the titanic thunderbolt of thunderbolts; blasting that accursed house of unutterable secrets and bringing the oblivion which alone saved my mind.

H. G. WELLS

POLLOCK AND THE PORROH MAN

It was in a swampy village on the lagoon river behind the Turner Peninsula that Pollock's first encounter with the Porroh man occurred. The women of that country are famous for their good looks—they are Gallinas with a dash of European blood that dates from the days of Vasco da Gama and the English slave-traders, and the Porroh man, too, was possibly inspired by a faint Caucasian taint in his composition. (It's a curious thing to think that some of us may have distant cousins eating men on Sherboro Island or raiding with the Sofas.) At any rate, the Porroh man stabbed the woman to the heart as though he had been a mere low-class Italian, and very narrowly missed Pollock. But Pollock, using his revolver to parry the lightning stab which was aimed at his deltoid muscle, sent the iron dagger flying, and, firing, hit the man in the hand.

He fired again and missed, knocking a sudden window out of the wall of the hut. The Porroh man stooped in the doorway, glancing under his arm at Pollock. Pollock caught a glimpse of his inverted face in the sunlight, and then the Englishman was alone, sick and trembling with the excitement of the affair, in the twilight of the place. It had all happened in less time than it takes to read about it.

The woman was quite dead, and having ascertained this, Pollock went to the entrance of the hut and looked out. Things outside were dazzling bright. Half-a-dozen of the porters of the expedition were standing up in a group near the green huts they occupied, and staring towards him, wondering what the shots might signify. Behind the little group of men was the broad stretch of black fetid mud by the river, a green carpet of rafts of papyrus and water-grass, and then the leaden water. The mangroves beyond the stream loomed indistinctly through the blue haze. There were no signs of excitement in the squat village, whose fence was just visible above the cane-grass.

Pollock came out of the hut cautiously and walked towards the river, looking over his shoulder at intervals. But the Porroh man had vanished. Pollock clutched his revolver nervously in his hand.

One of his men came to meet him, and as he came, pointed to the bushes behind the hut in which the Porroh man had disappeared. Pollock had an irritating persuasion of having made an absolute fool of himself; he felt bitter, savage, at the turn things had taken. At the same time, he would have to tell Waterhouse—the moral, exemplary, cautious Waterhouse—who would inevitably take the matter seriously. Pollock cursed bitterly at his luck, at

Waterhouse, and especially at the West Coast of Africa. He felt consummately sick of the expedition. And in the back of his mind all the time was a speculative doubt where precisely within the visible horizon the Porroh man might be.

It is perhaps rather shocking, but he was not at all upset by the murder that had just happened. He had seen so much brutality during the last three months, so many dead women, burnt huts, drying skeletons, up the Kittam River in the wake of the Sofa cavalry, that his senses were blunted. What disturbed him was the persuasion that this business was only beginning.

He swore savagely at the black, who ventured to ask a question, and went on into the tent under the orange-trees where Waterhouse was lying, feeling exasperatingly like a boy going into the headmaster's study.

Waterhouse was still sleeping off the effects of his last dose of chlorodyne, and Pollock sat down on a packing-case beside him, and, lighting his pipe, waited for him to awake. About him were scattered the pots and weapons Waterhouse had collected from the Mendi people, and which he had been repacking for the canoe voyage to Sulyma.

Presently Waterhouse woke up, and after judicial stretching, decided he was all right again. Pollock got him some tea. Over the tea the incidents of the afternoon were described by Pollock, after some preliminary beating about the bush. Waterhouse took the matter even more seriously than Pollock had anticipated. He did not simply disapprove, he scolded, he insulted.

"You're one of those infernal fools who think a black man isn't a human being," he said. "I can't be ill a day without you must get into some dirty scrape or other. This is the third time in a month that you have come crossways-on with a native, and this time you're in for it with a vengeance. Porroh, too! They're down upon you enough as it is, about that idol you wrote your silly name on. And they're the most vindictive devils on earth! You make a man ashamed of civilization. To think you come of a decent family! If ever I cumber myself up with a vicious, stupid young lout like you again—"

"Steady on, now," snarled Pollock, in the tone that always exasperated Waterhouse; "steady on."

At that Waterhouse became speechless. He jumped to his feet.

"Look here, Pollock," he said, after a struggle to control his breath. "You must go home. I won't have you any longer. I'm ill enough as it is through you—"

"Keep your hair on," said Pollock, staring in front of him. "I'm ready enough to go."

Waterhouse became calmer again. He sat down on the campstool. "Very well," he said. "I don't want a row, Pollock, you know, but it's confoundedly annoying to have one's plans put out by this kind of thing. I'll come to Sulyma with you, and see you safe aboard—"

"You needn't," said Pollock. "I can go alone. From here."

"Not far," said Waterhouse. "You don't understand this Porroh business."

"How should *I* know she belonged to a Porroh man?" said Pollock bitterly.

"Well, she did," said Waterhouse; "and you can't undo the thing. Go alone, indeed! I wonder what they'd do to you. You don't seem to understand that this Porroh hokey-pokey rules this country, is its law, religion, constitution, medicine, magic. . . . They appoint the chiefs. The Inquisition, at its best, couldn't hold a candle to these chaps. He will probably set Awajale, the chief here, on to us. It's lucky our porters are Mendis. We shall have to shift this little settlement of ours . . . Confound you, Pollock! And, of course, you must go and miss him."

He thought, and his thoughts seemed disagreeable. Presently he stood up and took his rifle. "I'd keep close for a bit, if I were you," he said, over his shoulder, as he went out. "I'm going out to see what I can find out about it."

Pollock remained sitting in the tent, meditating. "I was meant for a civilized life," he said to himself, regretfully, as he filled his pipe. "The sooner I get back to London or Paris the better for me."

His eye fell on the sealed case in which Waterhouse had put the feather-less poisoned arrows they had bought in the Mendi country. "I wish I had hit the beggar somewhere vital," said Pollock viciously.

Waterhouse came back after a long interval. He was not communicative, though Pollock asked him questions enough. The Porroh man, it seems, was a prominent member of that mystical society. The village was interested, but not threatening. No doubt the witch-doctor had gone into the bush. He was a great witch-doctor. "Of course, he's up to something," said Waterhouse, and became silent.

"But what can he do?" asked Pollock, unheeded.

"I must get you out of this. There's something brewing, or things would not be so quiet," said Waterhouse, after a gap of silence. Pollock wanted to know what the brew might be. "Dancing in a circle of skulls," said Waterhouse; "brewing a stink in a copper pot." Pollock wanted particulars. Waterhouse was vague, Pollock pressing. At last Waterhouse lost his temper.

"How the devil should *I* know?" he said to Pollock's twentieth inquiry what the Porroh man would do. "He tried to kill you off-hand in the hut. *Now,* I fancy he will try something more elaborate. But you'll see fast enough. I don't want to help unnerve you. It's probably all nonsense."

That night, as they were sitting at their fire, Pollock again tried to draw Waterhouse out on the subject of Porroh methods. "Better get to sleep," said Waterhouse, when Pollock's bent became apparent; "we start early to-morrow. You may want all your nerve about you."

"But what line will he take?"

"Can't say. They're versatile people. They know a lot of rum dodges. You'd better get that copper-devil, Shakespeare, to talk."

There was a flash and a heavy bang out of the darkness behind the huts, and a clay bullet came whistling close to Pollock's head. This, at least, was crude enough. The blacks and half-breeds sitting and yarning round their own fire jumped up, and someone fired into the dark.

"Better go into one of the huts," said Waterhouse quietly, still sitting unmoved.

Pollock stood up by the fire and drew his revolver. Fighting, at least, he was not afraid of. But a man in the dark is in the best of armour. Realizing the wisdom of Waterhouse's advice, Pollock went into the tent and lay down there.

What little sleep he had was disturbed by dreams, variegated dreams, but chiefly of the Porroh man's face, upside down, as he went out of the hut, and looked up under his arm. It was odd that this transitory impression should have stuck so firmly in Pollock's memory. Moreover, he was troubled by queer pains in his limbs.

In the white haze of the early morning, as they were loading the canoes, a barbed arrow suddenly appeared quivering in the ground close to Pollock's foot. The boys made a perfunctory effort to clear out the thicket, but it led to no capture.

After these two occurrences, there was a disposition on the part of the expedition to leave Pollock to himself, and Pollock became, for the first time in his life, anxious to mingle with blacks. Waterhouse took one canoe, and Pollock, in spite of a friendly desire to chat with Waterhouse, had to take the other. He was left all alone in the front part of the canoe, and he had the greatest trouble to make the men—who did not love him—keep to the middle of the river, a clear hundred yards or more from either shore. However, he made Shakespeare, the Freetown half-breed, come up to his own end of the canoe and tell him about Porroh, which Shakespeare, failing in his attempts to leave Pollock alone, presently did with considerable freedom and gusto.

The day passed. The canoe glided swiftly along the ribbon of lagoon water, between the drift of water-figs, fallen trees, papyrus, and palm-wine palms, and with the dark mangrove swamp to the left, through which one could hear now and then the roar of the Atlantic surf. Shakespeare told in his soft, blurred English of how the Porroh could cast spells; how men withered up under their malice; how they could send dreams and devils; how they tormented and killed the sons of Ijibu; how they kidnapped a white trader from Sulyma who had maltreated one of the sect, and how his body looked when it was found. And Pollock after each narrative cursed under his breath at the want of missionary enterprise that allowed such things to be, and at the inert British Government that ruled over this dark heathendom of Sierra Leone. In the evening they came to the Kasi Lake, and sent a score of crocodiles lumbering off the island on which the expedition camped for the night.

The next day they reached Sulyma, and smelt the sea breeze, but Pollock had to put up there for five days before he could get on to Freetown. Waterhouse, considering him to be comparatively safe here, and within the pale of Freetown influence, left him and went back with the expedition to Gbemma, and Pollock became very friendly with Perea, the only resident white trader at Sulyma—so friendly, indeed, that he went about with him everywhere. Perea was a little Portuguese Jew, who had lived in England,

and he appreciated the Englishman's friendship as a great compliment.

For two days nothing happened out of the ordinary; for the most part Pollock and Perea played Nap—the only game they had in common—and Pollock got into debt. Then, on the second evening, Pollock had a disagreeable intimation of the arrival of the Porroh man in Sulyma by getting a flesh-wound in the shoulder from a lump of filed iron. It was a long shot, and the missile had nearly spent its force when it hit him. Still it conveyed its message plainly enough. Pollock sat up in his hammock, revolver in hand, all that night, and next morning confided, to some extent, in the Anglo-Portuguese.

Perea took the matter seriously. He knew the local customs pretty thoroughly. "It is a personal question, you must know. It is revenge. And of course he is hurried by your leaving de country. None of de natives or half-breeds will interfere wid him very much—unless you make it wort deir while. If you come upon him suddenly, you might shoot him. But den he might shoot you.

"Den dere's dis—infernal magic," said Perea. "Of course, I don't believe in it—superstition—but still it's not nice to tink dat wherever you are, dere is a black man, who spends a moonlight night now and den a-dancing about a fire to send you bad dreams. . . . Had any bad dreams?"

"Rather," said Pollock. "I keep on seeing the beggar's head upside down grinning at me and showing all his teeth as he did in the hut, and coming close up to me, and then going ever so far off, and coming back. It's nothing to be afraid of, but somehow it simply paralyses me with terror in my sleep. Queer things—dreams. I know it's a dream all the time, and I can't wake up from it."

"It's probably only fancy," said Perea. "Den my niggers say Porroh men can send snakes. Seen any snakes lately?"

"Only one. I killed him this morning, on the floor near my hammock. Almost trod on him as I got up."

"*Ah!*" said Perea, and then reassuringly, "Of course it is a—coincidence. Still I would keep my eyes open. Den dere's pains in de bones."

"I thought they were due to miasma," said Pollock.

"Probably dey are. When did dey begin?"

Then Pollock remembered that he first noticed them the night after the fight in the hut. "It's my opinion he don't want to kill you," said Perea—"at least not yet. I've heard deir idea is to scare and worry a man wid deir spells, and narrow misses, and rheumatic pains, and bad dreams, and all dat, until he's sick of life. Of course, it's all talk, you know. You mustn't worry about it. . . . But I wonder what he'll be up to next."

"*I* shall have to be up to something first," said Pollock, staring gloomily at the greasy cards that Perea was putting on the table. "It don't suit my dignity to be followed about, and shot at, and blighted in this way. I wonder if Porroh hokey-pokey upsets your luck at cards."

He looked at Perea suspiciously.

"Very likely it does," said Perea warmly, shuffling. "Dey are wonderful people."

That afternoon Pollock killed two snakes in his hammock, and there was also an extraordinary increase in the number of red ants that swarmed over the place; and these annoyances put him in a fit temper to talk over business with a certain Mendi rough he had interviewed before. The Mendi rough showed Pollock a little iron dagger, and demonstrated where one struck in the neck, in a way that made Pollock shiver, and in return for certain considerations Pollock promised him a double-barrelled gun with an ornamental lock.

In the evening, as Pollock and Perea were playing cards, the Mendi rough came in through the doorway, carrying something in a blood-soaked piece of native cloth.

"Not here!" said Pollock very hurriedly. "Not here!"

But he was not quick enough to prevent the man, who was anxious to get to Pollock's side of the bargain, from opening the cloth and throwing the head of the Porroh man upon the table. It bounded from there on to the floor, leaving a red trail on the cards, and rolled into a corner, where it came to rest upside down, but glaring hard at Pollock.

Perea jumped up as the thing fell among the cards, and began in his excitement to gabble in Portuguese. The Mendi was bowing, with the red cloth in his hand. "De gun!" he cried. Pollock stared back at the head in the corner. It bore exactly the expression it had in his dreams. Something seemed to snap in his own brain as he looked at it.

Then Perea found his English again.

"You got him killed?" he said. "You did not kill him yourself?"

"Why should I?" said Pollock.

"But he will not be able to take it off now!"

"Take *what* off?" said Pollock.

"And all dese cards are spoiled!"

"*What* do you mean by taking off?" said Pollock.

"You must send me a new pack from Freetown. You can buy dem dere."

"But—'take it off'?"

"It is only superstition. I forgot. De niggers say dat if de witches—he was a witch—But it is rubbish. . . . You must make de Porroh man take it off, or kill him yourself. . . . It is very silly."

Pollock swore under his breath, still staring hard at the head in the corner.

"I can't stand that glare," he said. Then suddenly he rushed at the thing and kicked it. It rolled some yards or so, and came to rest in the same position as before, upside down, and looking at him.

"He is ugly," said the Anglo-Portuguese. "Very ugly. Dey do it on deir faces with little knives."

Pollock would have kicked the head again, but the Mendi man touched him on the arm. "De gun?" he said, looking nervously at the head.

"Two—if you will take that beastly thing away," said Pollock.

The Mendi shook his head, and intimated that he only wanted one gun now due to him, and for which he would be obliged. Pollock found neither cajolery nor bullying any good with him. Perea had a gun to sell (at a profit of three hundred per cent), and with that the man presently departed. Then Pollock's eyes, against his will, were recalled to the thing on the floor.

"It is funny dat his head keeps upside down," said Perea, with an uneasy laugh. "His brains must be heavy, like de weight in de little images one sees dat keep always upright wid lead in dem. You will take him wiv you when you go presently. You might take him now. De cards are all spoilt. Dere is a man sell dem in Freetown. De room is in a filthy mess as it is. You should have killed him yourself."

Pollock pulled himself together, and went and picked up the head. He would hang it up by the lamp-hook in the middle of the ceiling of his room, and dig a grave for it at once. He was under the impression that he hung it up by the hair, but that must have been wrong, for when he returned for it, it was hanging by the neck upside down.

He buried it before sunset on the north side of the shed he occupied, so that he should not have to pass the grave after dark when he was returning from Perea's. He killed two snakes before he went to sleep. In the darkest part of the night he awoke with a start, and heard a pattering sound and something scraping on the floor. He sat up noiselessly and felt under his pillow for his revolver. A mumbling growl followed, and Pollock fired at the sound. There was a yelp, and something dark passed for a moment across the hazy blue of the doorway. "A dog!" said Pollock, lying down again.

In the early dawn he awoke again with a peculiar sense of unrest. The vague pain in his bones had returned. For some time he lay watching the red ants that were swarming over the ceiling, and then, as the light grew brighter, he looked over the edge of his hammock and saw something dark on the floor. He gave such a violent start that the hammock overset and flung him out.

He found himself lying, perhaps, a yard away from the head of the Porroh man. It had been disinterred by the dog, and the nose was grievously battered. Ants and flies swarmed over it. By an odd coincidence, it was still upside down, and with the same diabolical expression in the inverted eyes.

Pollock sat paralysed, and stared at the horror for some time. Then he got up and walked round it—giving it a wide berth—and out of the shed. The clear light of the sunrise, the living stir of vegetation before the breath of the dying land breeze and the empty grave with the marks of the dog's paws, lightened the weight upon his mind a little.

He told Perea of the business as though it was a jest—a jest to be told with white lips. "You should not have frighten de dog," said Perea, with poorly simulated hilarity.

The next two days, until the steamer came, were spent by Pollock in making a more effectual disposition of his possession. Overcoming his aversion to handling the thing, he went down to the river mouth and threw it into the sea-water, but by some miracle it escaped the crocodiles, and was cast up by the tide on the mud a little way up the river, to be found by an intelligent Arab half-breed, and offered for sale to Pollock and Perea as a curiosity, just on the edge of night. The native hung about in the brief twilight, making lower and lower offers, and at last, getting scared in some way by the evident dread these wise white men had for the thing, went off, and, passing Pollock's shed, threw his burden in there for Pollock to discover in the morning.

At this Pollock got into a kind of frenzy. He would burn the thing. He went out straightway into the dawn, and had constructed a big pyre of brushwood before the heat of the day. He was interrupted by the hooter of the little paddle steamer from Monrovia to Bathurst, which was coming through the gap in the bar. "Thank Heaven!" said Pollock, with infinite piety, when the meaning of the sound dawned upon him. With trembling hands he lit his pile of wood hastily, threw the head upon it, and went away to pack his portmanteau and make his adieux to Perea.

That afternoon, with a sense of infinite relief, Pollock watched the flat swampy foreshore of Sulyma grow small in the distance. The gap in the long line of white surge became narrower and narrower. It seemed to be closing in and cutting him off from his trouble. The feeling of dread and worry began to slip from him bit by bit. At Sulyma belief in Porroh malignity and Porroh magic had been in the air, his sense of Porroh had been vast, pervading, threatening, dreadful. Now manifestly the domain of Porroh was only a little place, a little black band between the sea and the blue cloudy Mendi uplands.

"Good-bye, Porroh!" said Pollock. "Good-bye—certainly not *au revoir*."

The captain of the steamer came and leant over the rail beside him, and wished him good-evening, and spat at the froth of the wake in token of friendly ease.

"I picked up a rummy curio on the beach this go," said the captain. "It's a thing I never saw done this side of Indy before."

"What might that be?" said Pollock.

"Pickled 'ed," said the captain.

"*What!*" said Pollock.

" 'Ed—smoked. 'Ed of one of these Porroh chaps, all ornamented with knife-cuts. Why! What's up? Nothing? I shouldn't have took you for a nervous chap. Green in the face. By gosh! you're a bad sailor. All right, eh? Lord, how funny you went! . . . Well, this 'ed I was telling you of is a bit rum in a way. I've got it, along with some snakes, in a jar of spirit in my cabin what I keeps for such curios, and I'm hanged if it don't float upsy down. Hullo!"

Pollock had given an incoherent cry, and had his hands in his hair. He ran towards the paddle-boxes with a half-formed idea of jumping into the sea, and then he realised his position and turned back towards the captain.

"Here!" said the captain. "Jack Philips, just keep him off me! Stand off! No nearer, mister! What's the matter with you? Are you mad?"

Pollock put his hand to his head. It was no good explaining. "I believe I

am pretty nearly mad at times," he said. "It's a pain I have here. Comes
suddenly. You'll excuse me, I hope."

He was white and in a perspiration. He saw suddenly very clearly all the
danger he ran of having his sanity doubted. He forced himself to restore the
captain's confidence, by answering his sympathetic inquiries, noting his
suggestions, even trying a spoonful of neat brandy in his cheek, and, that
matter settled, asking a number of questions about the captain's private
trade in curiosities. The captain described the head in detail. All the while
Pollock was struggling to keep under a preposterous persuasion that the ship
was as transparent as glass, and that he could distinctly see the inverted face
looking at him from the cabin beneath his feet.

Pollock had a worse time almost on the steamer than he had at Sulyma.
All day he had to control himself in spite of his intense perception of the
imminent presence of that horrible head that was overshadowing his mind.
At night his old nightmare returned, until, with a violent effort, he would
force himself awake, rigid with the horror of it, and with the ghost of a
hoarse scream in his throat.

He left the actual head behind at Bathurst, where he changed ship for
Teneriffe, but not his dreams nor the dull ache in his bones. At Teneriffe
Pollock transferred to a Cape liner, but the head followed him. He gambled,
he tried chess, he even read books, but he knew the danger of drink. Yet
whenever a round black shadow, a round black object came into his range,
there he looked for the head, and—saw it. He knew clearly enough that his
imagination was growing traitor to him, and yet at times it seemed the ship
he sailed in, his fellow-passengers, the sailors, the wide sea were all part of a
filmy phantasmagoria that hung, scarcely veiling it, between him and a
horrible real world. Then the Porroh man, thrusting his diabolical face
through that curtain, was the one real and undeniable thing. At that he
would get up and touch things, taste something, gnaw something, burn his
hand with a match, or run a needle into himself.

So, struggling grimly and silently with his excited imagination, Pollock
reached England. He landed at Southampton, and went on straight from
Waterloo to his banker's in Cornhill in a cab. There he transacted some
business with the manager in a private room, and all the while the head
hung like an ornament under the black marble mantel and dripped upon the
fender. He could hear the drops fall, and see the red on the fender.

"A pretty fern," said the manager, following his eyes. "But it makes the
fender rusty."

"Very," said Pollock; "a *very* pretty fern. And that reminds me. Can you
recommend me a physician for mind troubles? I've got a little—what is it?—
hallucination."

The head laughed savagely, wildly. Pollock was surprised the manager did
not notice it. But the manager only stared at his face.

With the address of a doctor, Pollock presently emerged in Cornhill.
There was no cab in sight, and so he went on down to the western end of the
street, and essayed the crossing opposite the Mansion House. The crossing is

hardly easy even for the expert Londoner; cabs, vans, carriages, mail-carts, omnibuses go by in one incessant stream; to anyone fresh from the malarious solitudes of Sierra Leone it is a boiling, maddening confusion. But when an inverted head suddenly comes bouncing, like an India-rubber ball, between your legs, leaving distinct smears of blood every time it touches the ground, you can scarcely hope to avoid an accident. Pollock lifted his feet convulsively to avoid it, and then kicked at the thing furiously. Then something hit him violently in the back, and a hot pain ran up his arm.

He had been hit by the pole of an omnibus, and three of the fingers of his left hand smashed by the hoof of one of the horses—the very fingers, as it happened, that he shot from the Porroh man. They pulled him out from between the horses' legs, and found the address of the physician in his crushed hand.

For a couple of days Pollock's sensations were full of the sweet, pungent smell of chloroform, of painful operations that caused him no pain, of lying still and being given food and drink. Then he had a slight fever, and was very thirsty, and his old nightmare came back. It was only when it returned that he noticed it had left him for a day.

"If my skull had been smashed instead of my fingers, it might have gone altogether," said Pollock, staring thoughtfully at the dark cushion that had taken on for the time the shape of the head.

Pollock at the first opportunity told the physician of his mind trouble. He knew clearly that he must go mad unless something should intervene to save him. He explained that he had witnessed a decapitation in Dahomey, and was haunted by one of the heads. Naturally, he did not care to state the actual facts. The physician looked grave.

Presently he spoke hesitatingly. "As a child, did you get very much religious training?"

"Very little," said Pollock.

A shade passed over the physician's face. "I don't know if you have heard of the miraculous cures—it may be, of course, they are not miraculous—at Lourdes."

"Faith-healing will hardly suit me, I am afraid," said Pollock, with his eye on the dark cushion.

The head distorted its scarred features in an abominable grimace. The physician went upon a new track. "It's all imagination," he said, speaking with sudden briskness. "A fair case for faith-healing, anyhow. Your nervous system has run down, you're in that twilight state of health when the bogles come easiest. The strong impression was too much for you. I must make you up a little mixture that will strengthen your nervous system—especially your brain. And you must take exercise."

"I'm not good for faith-healing," said Pollock.

"And therefore we must restore tone. Go in search of stimulating air—Scotland, Norway, the Alps—"

"Jericho, if you like," said Pollock—"where Naaman went."

However, so soon as his fingers would let him, Pollock made a gallant attempt to follow out the doctor's suggestion. It was now November. He tried football, but to Pollock the game consisted in kicking a furious inverted head about a field. He was no good at the game. He kicked blindly, with a kind of horror, and when they put him back into goal, and the ball came swooping down upon him, he suddenly yelled and got out of its way. The discreditable stories that had driven him from England to wander in the tropics shut him off from any but men's society, and now his increasingly strange behaviour made even his man friends avoid him. The thing was no longer a thing of the eye merely; it gibbered at him, spoke to him. A horrible fear came upon him that presently, when he took hold of the apparition, it would no longer become some mere article of furniture, but would *feel* like a real dissevered head. Alone, he would curse at the thing, defy it, entreat it; once or twice, in spite of his grim self-control, he addressed it in the presence of others. He felt the growing suspicion in the eyes of the people that watched him—his landlady, the servant, his man.

One day early in December his cousin Arnold—his next of kin—came to see him and draw him out, and watch his sunken yellow face with narrow eager eyes. And it seemed to Pollock that the hat his cousin carried in his hand was no hat at all, but a Gorgon head that glared at him upside down, and fought with its eyes against his reason. However, he was still resolute to see the matter out. He got a bicycle, and, riding over the frosty road from Wandsworth to Kingston, found the thing rolling along at his side, and leaving a dark trail behind it. He set his teeth and rode faster. Then suddenly, as he came down the hill towards Richmond Park, the apparition rolled in front of him and under his wheel, so quickly that he had no time for thought, and, turning quickly to avoid it, was flung violently against a heap of stones and broke his left wrist.

The end came on Christmas morning. All night he had been in a fever, the bandages encircling his wrist like a band of fire, his dreams more vivid and terrible than ever. In the cold, colourless, uncertain light that came before the sunrise, he sat up in his bed, and saw the head upon the bracket in the place of the bronze jar that had stood there overnight.

"I know that is a bronze jar," he said, with a chill doubt at his heart. Presently the doubt was irresistible. He got out of bed slowly, shivering, and advanced to the jar with his hand raised. Surely he would see now his imagination had deceived him, recognise the distinctive sheen of bronze. At last, after an age of hesitation, his fingers came down on the patterned cheek of the head. He withdrew them spasmodically. The last stage was reached. His sense of touch had betrayed him.

Trembling, stumbling against the bed, kicking against his shoes with his bare feet, a dark confusion eddying round him, he groped his way to the dressing-table, took his razor from the drawer, and sat down on the bed with this in his hand. In the looking-glass he saw his own face, colourless, haggard, full of the ultimate bitterness of despair.

He beheld in swift succession the incidents in the brief tale of his experience. His wretched home, his still more wretched school-days, the years of vicious life he had led since then, one act of selfish dishonour leading to another; it was all clear and pitiless now, all its squalid folly, in the cold light of the dawn. He came to the hut, to the fight with the Porroh man, to the retreat down the river to Sulyma, to the Mendi assassin and his red parcel, to his frantic endeavours to destroy the head, to the growth of his hallucination. It was a hallucination! He *knew* it was. A hallucination merely. For a moment he snatched at hope. He looked away from the glass, and on the bracket, the inverted head grinned and grimaced at him. . . . With the stiff fingers of his bandaged hand he felt at his neck for the throb of his arteries. The morning was very cold, the steel blade felt like ice.

HANS HEINZ EWERS

THE SPIDER

When the student of medicine, Richard Bracquemont, decided to move into room #7 of the small Hotel Stevens, Rue Alfred Stevens (Paris 6), three persons had already hanged themselves from the cross-bar of the window in that room on three successive Fridays.

The first was a Swiss traveling salesman. They found his corpse on Saturday evening. The doctor determined that the death must have occurred between five and six o'clock on Friday afternoon. The corpse hung on a strong hook that had been driven into the window's cross-bar to serve as a hanger for articles of clothing. The window was closed, and the dead man had used the curtain cord as a noose. Since the window was very low, he hung with his knees practically touching the floor—a sign of the great discipline the suicide must have exercised in carrying out his design. Later, it was learned that he was a married man, a father. He had been a man of a continually happy disposition; a man who had achieved a secure place in life. There was not one written word to be found that would have shed light on his suicide . . . not even a will. Furthermore, none of his acquaintances could recall hearing anything at all from him that would have permitted anyone to predict his end.

The second case was not much different. The artist, Karl Krause, a high wire cyclist in the nearby Medrano Circus, moved into room #7 two days later. When he did not show up at Friday's performance, the director sent an employee to the hotel. There, he found Krause in the unlocked room hanging from the window cross-bar in circumstances exactly like those of the previous suicide. This death was as perplexing as the first. Krause was popular. He earned a very high salary, and had appeared to enjoy life at its fullest. Once again, there was no suicide note; no sinister hints. Krause's sole survivor was his mother to whom the son had regularly sent 300 marks on the first of the month.

For Madame Dubonnet, the owner of the small, cheap guesthouse whose clientele was composed almost completely of employees in a nearby Montmartre vaudeville theater, this second curious death in the same room had very unpleasant consequences. Already several of her guests had moved out, and other regular clients had not come back. She appealed for help to her personal friend, the inspector of police of the ninth precinct, who assured her that he would do everything in his power to help her. He pushed zealously ahead not only with the investigation into the grounds for the suicides of the two guests, but he also placed an officer in the mysterious room.

This man, Charles-Maria Chaumié, actually volunteered for the task. Chaumié was an old "Marsouin," a marine sergeant with eleven years of service, who had lain so many nights at posts in Tonkin and Annam, and had greeted so many stealthily creeping river pirates with a shot from his rifle that he seemed ideally suited to encounter the "ghost" that everyone on Rue Alfred Stevens was talking about.

From then on, each morning and each evening, Chaumié paid a brief visit to the police station to make his report, which, for the first few days, consisted only of his statement that he had not noticed anything unusual. On Wednesday evening, however, he hinted that he had found a clue. Pressed to say more, he asked to be allowed more time before making any comment, since he was not sure that what he had discovered had any relationship to the two deaths, and he was afraid he might say something that would make him look foolish.

On Thursday, his behavior seemed a bit uncertain, but his mood was noticeably more serious. Still, he had nothing to report. On Friday morning, he came in very excited and spoke, half humorously, half seriously, of the strangely attractive power that his window had. He would not elaborate this notion and said that, in any case, it had nothing to do with the suicides; and that it would be ridiculous of him to say any more. When, on that same Friday, he failed to make his regular evening report, someone went to his room and found him hanging from the cross-bar of the window.

All the circumstances, down to the minutest detail, were the same here as in the previous cases. Chaumié's legs dragged along the ground. The curtain cord had been used for a noose. The window was closed, the door to the room had not been locked and death had occurred at six o'clock. The dead man's mouth was wide open, and his tongue protruded from it.

Chaumié's death, the third in as many weeks in room #7, had the following consequences: all the guests, with the exception of a German high-school teacher in room #16, moved out. The teacher took advantage of the occasion to have his rent reduced by a third. The next day, Mary Garden, the famous Opéra Comique singer, drove up to the Hotel Stevens and paid two hundred francs for the red curtain cord, saying it would bring her luck. The story, small consolation for Madame Dubonnet, got into the papers.

If these events had occurred in summer, in July or August, Madame Dubonnet would have secured three times that price for her cord, but as it was in the middle of a troubled year, with elections, disorders in the Balkans, bank crashes in New York, the visit of the King and Queen of England, the result was that the *affaire Rue Alfred Stevens* was talked of less than it deserved to be. As for the newspaper accounts, they were brief, being essentially the police reports word for word.

These reports were all that Richard Bracquemont, the medical student, knew of the matter. There was one detail about which he knew nothing because neither the police inspector nor any of the eyewitnesses had mentioned it to the press. It was only later, after what happened to the medical student, that anyone remembered that when the police removed Sergeant Charles-Maria Chaumié's body from the window cross-bar a large black spider crawled from the dead man's open mouth. A hotel porter flicked it away, exclaiming, "Ugh, another of those damned creatures." When in later investigations which concerned themselves mostly with Bracquemont the servant was interrogated, he said that he had seen a similar spider crawling on the Swiss traveling salesman's shoulder when his body was removed from the window cross-bar. But Richard Bracquemont knew nothing of all this.

It was more than two weeks after the last suicide that Bracquemont moved into the room. It was a Sunday. Bracquemont conscientiously recorded everything that happened to him in his journal. That journal now follows.

Monday, February 28

I moved in yesterday evening. I unpacked my two wicker suitcases and straightened the room a little. Then I went to bed. I slept so soundly that it was nine o'clock the next morning before a knock at my door woke me. It was my hostess, bringing me breakfast herself. One could read her concern for me in the eggs, the bacon and the superb *café au lait* she brought me. I washed and dressed, then smoked a pipe as I watched the servant make up the room.

So, here I am. I know well that the situation may prove dangerous, but I think I may just be the one to solve the problem. If, once upon a time, Paris was worth a mass (conquest comes at a dearer rate these days), it is well worth risking my life *pour un si bel enjeu*. I have at least one chance to win, and I mean to risk it.

As it is, I'm not the only one who has had this notion. Twenty-seven people have tried for access to the room. Some went to the police, some went directly to the hotel owner. There were even three women among the candidates. There was plenty of competition. No doubt the others are poor devils like me.

And yet, it was I who was chosen. Why? Because I was the only one who hinted that I had some plan—or the semblance of a plan. Naturally, I was bluffing.

These journal entries are intended for the police. I must say that it amuses me to tell those gentlemen how neatly I fooled them. If the Inspector has any sense, he'll say, "Hm. This Bracquemont is just the man we need." In any case, it doesn't matter what he'll say. The point is I'm here now, and I take it as a good sign that I've begun my task by bamboozling the police.

I had gone first to Madame Dubonnet, and it was she who sent me to the police. They put me off for a whole week—as they put off my rivals as well. Most of them gave up in disgust, having something better to do than hang around the musty squad room. The Inspector was beginning to get irritated at my tenacity. At last, he told me I was wasting my time. That the police had no use for bungling amateurs. "Ah, if only you had a plan. Then . . . "

On the spot, I announced that I had such a plan, though naturally I had no such thing. Still, I hinted that my plan was brilliant, but dangerous, that it might lead to the same end as that which had overtaken the police officer, Chaumié. Still, I promised to describe it to him if he would give me his word that he would personally put it into effect. He made excuses, claiming he was too busy but when he asked me to give him at least a hint of my plan, I saw that I had picqued his interest.

I rattled off some nonsense made up of whole cloth. God alone knows where it all came from. I told him that six o'clock of a Friday is an occult hour. It is the last hour of the Jewish week; the hour when Christ disappeared from his tomb and descended into hell. That he would do well to remember that the three suicides had taken place at approximately that hour. That was all I could tell him just then, I said, but I pointed him to *The Revelations of St. John.*

The Inspector assumed the look of a man who understood all that I had been saying, then he asked me to come back that evening.

I returned, precisely on time, and noted a copy of the *New Testament* on the Inspector's desk. I had, in the meantime, been at the *Revelations* myself, without however having understood a syllable. Perhaps the Inspector was cleverer than I. Very politely—nay—deferentially, he let me know that, despite my extremely vague intimations, he believed he grasped my line of thought and was ready to expedite my plan in every way.

And here, I must acknowledge that he has indeed been tremendously helpful. It was he who made the arrangement with the owner that I was to have anything I needed so long as I stayed in the room. The Inspector gave me a pistol and a police whistle, and he ordered the officers on the beat to pass through the Rue Alfred Stevens as often as possible, and to watch my window for any signal. Most important of all, he had a desk telephone installed which connects directly with the police station. Since the station is only four minutes away, I see no reason to be afraid.

Wednesday, March 1

Nothing has happened. Not yesterday. Not today.

Madame Dubonnet brought a new curtain cord from another room—the rooms are mostly empty, of course. Madame Dubonnet takes every opportunity to visit me, and each time she brings something with her. I have asked her to tell me again everything that happened here, but I have learned nothing new. She has her own opinion of the suicides. Her view is that the music hall artist, Krause, killed himself because of an unhappy love affair. During the last year that Krause lived in the hotel, a young woman had made frequent visits to him. These visits had stopped, just before his death. As for the Swiss gentleman, Madame Dubonnet confessed herself baffled. On the other hand, the death of the policeman was easy to explain. He had killed himself just to annoy her.

These are sad enough explanations, to be sure, but I let her babble on to take the edge off my boredom.

Thursday, March 3

Still nothing. The Inspector calls twice a day. Each time, I tell him that all is well. Apparently, these words do not reassure him.

I have taken out my medical books and I study, so that my self-imposed confinement will have some purpose.

Friday, March 4

I ate uncommonly well at noon. The landlady brought me half a bottle of champagne. It seemed a meal for a condemned man. Madame Dubonnet looked at me as if I were already three-quarters dead. As she was leaving, she begged me tearfully to come with her, fearing no doubt that I would hang myself "just to annoy her."

I studied the curtain cord once again. Would I hang myself with it? Certainly, I felt little desire to do so. The cord is stiff and rough—not the sort of cord one makes a noose of. One would need to be truly determined before one could imitate the others.

I am seated now at my table. At my left, the telephone. At my right, the revolver. I'm not frightened; but I am curious.

Six o'clock, the same evening

Nothing has happened. I was about to add, "Unfortunately." The fatal hour has come—and has gone, like any six o'clock on any evening. I won't hide the fact that I occasionally felt a certain impulse to go to the window, but for a quite different reason than one might imagine.

The Inspector called me at least ten times between five and six o'clock. He was as impatient as I was. Madame Dubonnet, on the other hand, is happy. A week has passed without someone in #7 hanging himself. Marvelous.

Monday, March 7

I have a growing conviction that I will learn nothing; that the previous suicides are related to the circumstances surrounding the lives of the three men. I have asked the Inspector to investigate the cases further, convinced that someone will find their motivations. As for me, I hope to stay here as long as possible. I may not conquer Paris here, but I live very well and I'm fattening up nicely. I'm also studying hard, and I am making real progress. There is another reason, too, that keeps me here.

Wednesday, March 9

So! I have taken one step more. Clarimonda.

I haven't yet said anything about Clarimonda. It is she who is my "third" reason for staying here. She is also the reason I was tempted to go to the window during the "fateful" hour last Friday. But of course, not to hang myself.

Clarimonda. Why do I call her that? I have no idea what her name is, but it ought to be Clarimonda. When finally I ask her name, I'm sure it will turn out to be Clarimonda.

I noticed her almost at once . . . in the very first days. She lives across the narrow street; and her window looks right into mine. She sits there, behind her curtains.

I ought to say that she noticed me before I saw her; and that she was obviously interested in me. And no wonder. The whole neighborhood knows I am here, and why. Madame Dubonnet has seen to that.

I am not of a particularly amorous disposition. In fact, my relations with women have been rather meager. When one comes from Verdun to Paris to study medicine, and has hardly money enough for three meals a day, one has something else to think about besides love. I am then not very experienced with women, and I may have begun my adventure with her stupidly. Never mind. It's exciting just the same.

At first, the idea of establishing some relationship with her simply did not occur to me. It was only that, since I was here to make observations, and, since there was nothing in the room to observe, I thought I might as well observe my neighbor—openly, professionally. Anyhow, one can't sit all day long just reading.

Clarimonda, I have concluded, lives alone in the small flat across the way. The flat has three windows, but she sits only before the window that looks into mine. She sits there, spinning on an old-fashioned spindle, such as my grandmother inherited from a great aunt. I had no idea anyone still used such spindles. Clarimonda's spindle is a lovely object. It appears to be made of ivory; and the thread she spins is of an exceptional fineness. She works all day behind her curtains, and stops spinning only as the sun goes down. Since darkness comes abruptly here in this narrow street and in this season of fogs, Clarimonda disappears from her place at five o'clock each evening.

I have never seen a light in her flat.

What does Clarimonda look like? I'm not quite sure. Her hair is black and wavy; her face pale. Her nose is short and finely shaped with delicate nostrils that seem to quiver. Her lips, too, are pale; and when she smiles, it seems that her small teeth are as keen as those of some beast of prey. Her eyelashes are long and dark; and her huge dark eyes have an intense glow. I guess all these details more than I know them. It is hard to see clearly through the curtains.

Something else: she always wears a black dress embroidered with a lilac motif; and black gloves, no doubt to protect her hands from the effects of her work. It is a curious sight: her delicate hands moving perpetually, swiftly grasping the thread, pulling it, releasing it, taking it up again; as if one were watching the indefatigable motions of an insect.

Our relationship? For the moment, still very superficial, though it *feels* deeper. It began with a sudden exchange of glances in which each of us noted the other. I must have pleased her, because one day she studied me a while longer, then smiled tentatively. Naturally, I smiled back. In this fashion, two days went by, each of us smiling more frequently with the passage of time. Yet something kept me from greeting her directly.

Until today. This afternoon, I did it. And Clarimonda returned my greeting. It was done subtly enough, to be sure, but I saw her nod.

Thursday, March 10

Yesterday, I sat for a long time over my books, though I can't truthfully say that I studied much. I built castles in the air and dreamed of Clarimonda.

I slept fitfully.

This morning, when I approached my window, Clarimonda was already in her place. I waved, and she nodded back. She laughed and studied me for a long time.

I tried to read, but I felt much too uneasy. Instead, I sat down at my window and gazed at Clarimonda. She too had laid her work aside. Her hands were folded in her lap. I drew my curtain wider with the window cord, so that I might see better. At the same moment, Clarimonda did the same with the curtains at her window. We exchanged smiles.

We must have spent a full hour gazing at each other.

Finally, she took up her spinning.

Saturday, March 12

The days pass. I eat and drink. I sit at the desk. I light my pipe; I look down at my book but I don't read a word, though I try again and again. Then I go to the window where I wave to Clarimonda. She nods. We smile. We stare at each other for hours.

Yesterday afternoon, at six o'clock, I grew anxious. The twilight came early, bringing with it something like anguish. I sat at my desk. I waited until I was invaded by an irresistible need to go to the window—not to hang myself; but just to see Clarimondà. I sprang up and stood beside the curtain where it seemed to me I had never been able to see so clearly, though it was already dark. Clarimonda was spinning, but her eyes looked into mine. I felt myself strangely contented even as I experienced a light sensation of fear.

The telephone rang. It was the Inspector tearing me out of my trance with his idiotic questions. I was furious.

This morning, the Inspector and Madame Dubonnet visited me. She is enchanted with how things are going. I have now lived for two weeks in room #7. The Inspector, however, does not feel he is getting results. I hinted mysteriously that I was on the trail of something most unusual. The jackass took me at my word and fulfilled my dearest wish. I've been allowed to stay in the room for another week. God knows it isn't Madame Dubonnet's cooking or wine-cellar that keeps me here. How quickly one can be sated with such things. No. I want to stay because of the window Madame Dubonnet fears and hates. That beloved window that shows me Clarimonda.

I have stared out of my window, trying to discover whether she ever leaves her room, but I've never seen her set foot on the street.

As for me, I have a large, comfortable armchair and a green shade over the lamp whose glow envelopes me in warmth. The Inspector has left me with a huge packet of fine tobacco—and yet I cannot work. I read two or three pages only to discover that I haven't understood a word. My eyes see the letters, but my brain refuses to make any sense of them. Absurd. As if my brain were posted: "No Trespassing." It is as if there were no room in my head for any other thought than the one: Clarimonda. I push my books away; I lean back deeply into my chair. I dream.

Sunday, March 13

This morning I watched a tiny drama while the servant was tidying my room. I was strolling in the corridor when I paused before a small window in which a large garden spider had her web. Madame Dubonnet will not have it removed because she believes spiders bring luck, and she's had enough misfortunes in her house lately. Today, I saw a much smaller spider, a male, moving across the strong threads towards the middle of the web, but when his movements alerted the female, he drew back shyly to the edge of the web from which he made a second attempt to cross it. Finally, the female in the middle appeared attentive to his wooing, and stopped moving. The male tugged at a strand gently, then more strongly till the whole web shook. The female stayed motionless. The male moved quickly forward and the female received him quietly, calmly, giving herself over completely to his embraces. For a long minute, they hung together motionless at the center of the huge web.

Then I saw the male slowly extricating himself, one leg over the other. It was as if he wanted tactfully to leave his companion alone in the dream of love, but as he started away, the female, overwhelmed by a wild life, was after him, hunting him ruthlessly. The male let himself drop from a thread; the female followed, and for a while the lovers hung there, imitating a piece of art. Then they fell to the window-sill where the male, summoning all his strength, tried again to escape. Too late. The female already had him in her powerful grip, and was carrying him back to the center of the web. There, the place that had just served as the couch for their lascivious embraces took on quite another aspect. The lover wriggled, trying to escape from the female's wild embrace, but she was too much for him. It was not long before she had wrapped him completely in her thread, and he was helpless. Then she dug her sharp pincers into his body, and sucked full draughts of her young lover's blood. Finally, she detached herself from the pitiful and unrecognizable shell of his body and threw it out of her web.

So that is what love is like among these creatures. Well for me that I am not a spider.

Monday, March 14

I don't look at my books any longer. I spend my days at the window.

When it is dark, Clarimonda is no longer there, but if I close my eyes, I continue to see her.

This journal has become something other than I intended. I've spoken about Madame Dubonnet, about the Inspector; about spiders and about Clarimonda. But I've said nothing about the discoveries I undertook to make. It can't be helped.

Tuesday, March 15

We have invented a strange game, Clarimonda and I. We play it all day long. I greet her; then she greets me. Then I tap my fingers on the windowpanes. The moment she sees me doing that, she too begins tapping. I wave to her; she waves back. I move my lips as if speaking to her; she does the same. I run my hand through my sleep-disheveled hair and instantly her hand is at her forehead. It is a child's game, and we both laugh over it. Actually, she doesn't laugh. She only smiles a gently contained smile. And I smile back in the same way.

The game is not as trivial as it seems. It's not as if we were grossly imitating each other—that would weary us both. Rather, we are communicating with each other. Sometimes, telepathically, it would seem, since Clarimonda follows my movements instantaneously almost before she has had time to see them. I find myself inventing new movements, or new combinations of movements, but each time she repeats them with disconcerting speed. Sometimes, I change the order of the movements to surprise her, making whole series of gestures as rapidly as possible; or I leave out some motions and weave in others, the way children play "Simon Says." What is amazing is that Clarimonda never once makes a mistake, no matter how quickly I change gestures.

That's how I spend my days . . . but never for a moment do I feel that I'm killing time. It seems, on the contrary, that never in my life have I been better occupied.

Wednesday, March 16

Isn't it strange that it hasn't occurred to me to put my relationship with Clarimonda on a more serious basis than these endless games. Last night, I thought about this . . . I can, of course, put on my hat and coat, walk down two flights of stairs, take five steps across the street and mount two flights to her door which is marked with a small sign that says "Clarimonda." Clarimonda what? I don't know. Something. Then I can knock and . . .

Up to this point I imagine everything very clearly, but I cannot see what should happen next. I know that the door opens. But then I stand before it, looking into a dark void. Clarimonda doesn't come. Nothing comes. Nothing is there, only the black, impenetrable dark.

Sometimes, it seems to me that there can be no other Clarimonda but the one I see in the window; the one who plays gesture-games with me. I cannot imagine a Clarimonda wearing a hat, or a dress other than her black dress with the lilac motif. Nor can I imagine a Clarimonda without black gloves.

The very notion that I might encounter Clarimonda somewhere in the streets or in a restaurant eating, drinking or chatting is so improbable that it makes me laugh.

Sometimes I ask myself whether I love her. It's impossible to say, since I have never loved before. However, if the feeling that I have for Clarimonda is really—love, then love is something entirely different from anything I have seen among my friends or read about in novels.

It is hard for me to be sure of my feelings and harder still to think of anything that doesn't relate to Clarimonda or, what is more important, to our game. Undeniably, it is our game that concerns me. Nothing else—and this is what I understand least of all.

There is no doubt that I am drawn to Clarimonda, but with this attraction there is mingled another feeling, fear. No. That's not it either. Say rather a vague apprehension in the presence of the unknown. And this anxiety has a strangely voluptuous quality so that I am at the same time drawn to her even as I am repelled by her. It is as if I were moving in giant circles around her, sometimes coming close, sometimes retreating . . . back and forth, back and forth.

Once, I am sure of it, it will happen, and I will join her.

Clarimonda sits at her window and spins her slender, eternally fine thread, making a strange cloth whose purpose I do not understand. I am amazed that she is able to keep from tangling her delicate thread. Hers is surely a remarkable design, containing mythical beasts and strange masks.

Thursday, March 17

I am curiously excited. I don't talk to people any more. I barely say "hello" to Madame Dubonnet or to the servant. I hardly give myself time to eat. All I can do is sit at the window and play the game with Clarimonda. It is an enthralling game. Overwhelming.

I have the feeling something will happen tomorrow.

Friday, March 18

Yes. Yes. Something will happen today. I tell myself—as loudly as I can— that that's why I am here. And yet, horribly enough, I am afraid. And in the fear that the same thing is going to happen to me as happened to my predecessors, there is strangely mingled another fear: a terror of Clarimonda. And I cannot separate the two fears.

I am frightened. I want to scream.

Six o'clock, evening

I have my hat and coat on. Just a couple of words.

At five o'clock, I was at the end of my strength. I'm perfectly aware now that there is a relationship between my despair and the "sixth hour" that was so significant in the previous weeks. I no longer laugh at the trick I played the Inspector.

I was sitting at the window, trying with all my might to stay in my chair, but the window kept drawing me. I had to resume the game with Clarimonda. And yet, the window horrified me. I saw the others hanging there: the Swiss traveling salesman, fat, with a thick neck and a grey stubbly beard; the thin artist; and the powerful police sergeant. I saw them, one after the other, hanging from the same hook, their mouths open, their tongues sticking out. And then, I saw myself among them.

Oh, this unspeakable fear. It was clear to me that it was provoked as much by Clarimonda as by the cross-bar and the horrible hook. May she pardon me ... but it is the truth. In my terror, I keep seeing the three men hanging there, their legs dragging on the floor.

And yet, the fact is I had not felt the slightest desire to hang myself; nor was I afraid that I would want to do so. No, it was the window I feared; and Clarimonda. I was sure that something horrid was going to happen. Then I was overwhelmed by the need to go to the window—to stand before it. I had to ...

The telephone rang. I picked up the receiver and before I could hear a word, I screamed, "Come. Come at once."

It was as if my shrill cry had in that instant dissipated the shadows from my soul. I grew calm. I wiped the sweat from my forehead. I drank a glass of water. Then I considered what I should say to the Inspector when he arrived. Finally, I went to the window. I waved and smiled. And Clarimonda too waved and smiled.

Five minutes later, the Inspector was here. I told him that I was getting to the bottom of the matter, but I begged him not to question me just then. That very soon I would be in a position to make important revelations. Strangely enough, though I was lying to him, I myself had the feeling that I was telling the truth. Even now, against my will, I have that same conviction.

The Inspector could not help noticing my agitated state of mind, especially since I apologized for my anguished cry over the telephone. Naturally, I tried to explain it to him, and yet I could not find a single reason to give for it. He said affectionately that there was no need ever to apologize to him; that he was always at my disposal; that that was his duty. It was better that he should come a dozen times to no effect rather than fail to be here when he was needed. He invited me to go out with him for the evening. It would be a distraction for me. It would do me good not to be alone for a while. I accepted the invitation though I was very reluctant to leave the room.

Saturday, March 19

We went to the *Gaieté Rochechouart, La Cigale,* and *La Lune Rousse.* The Inspector was right: It was good for me to get out and breathe the fresh air. At first, I had an uncomfortable feeling, as if I were doing something wrong; as if I were a deserter who had turned his back on the flag. But that soon went away. We drank a lot, laughed and chatted. This morning, when I went to my window, Clarimonda gave me what I thought was a look of reproach, though I may only have imagined it. How could she have known that I had gone out last night? In any case, the look lasted only for an instant, then she smiled again.

We played the game all day long.

Sunday, March 20
Only one thing to record: we played the game.

Monday, March 21
We played the game—all day long.

Tuesday, March 22
Yes, the game. We played it again. And nothing else. Nothing at all.

Sometimes I wonder what is happening to me? What is it I want? Where is all this leading? I know the answer: there is nothing else I want except what is happening. *It* is what I want . . . what I long for. This only.

Clarimonda and I have spoken with each other in the course of the last few days, but very briefly; scarcely a word. Sometimes we moved our lips, but more often we just looked at each other with deep understanding.

I was right about Clarimonda's reproachful look because I went out with the Inspector last Friday. I asked her to forgive me. I said it was stupid of me, and spiteful to have gone. She forgave me, and I promised never to leave the window again. We kissed, pressing our lips against each of our windowpanes.

Wednesday, March 23
I know now that I love Clarimonda. That she has entered into the very fiber of my being. It may be that the loves of other men are different. But does there exist one head, one ear, one hand that is exactly like hundreds of millions of others? There are always differences, and it must be so with love. My love is strange, I know that, but is it any the less lovely because of that? Besides, my love makes me happy.

If only I were not so frightened. Sometimes my terror slumbers and I forget it for a few moments, then it wakes and does not leave me. The fear is like a poor mouse trying to escape the grip of a powerful serpent. Just wait a bit, poor sad terror. Very soon, the serpent love will devour you.

Thursday, March 24
I have made a discovery: I don't play with Clarimonda. She plays with me.

Last night, thinking as always about our game, I wrote down five new and intricate gesture patterns with which I intended to surprise Clarimonda today. I gave each gesture a number. Then I practiced the series, so I could do the motions as quickly as possible, forwards or backwards. Or sometimes only the even-numbered ones, sometimes the odd. Or the first and the last of the five patterns. It was tiring work, but it made me happy and seemed to bring Clarimonda closer to me. I practiced for hours until I got all the motions down pat, like clockwork.

This morning, I went to the window. Clarimonda and I greeted each other, then our game began. Back and forth! It was incredible how quickly she understood what was to be done; how she kept pace with me.

There was a knock at the door. It was the servant bringing me my shoes. I took them. On my way back to the window, my eye chanced to fall on the slip of paper on which I had noted my gesture patterns. It was then that I understood: in the game just finished, *I had not made use of a single one of my patterns.*

I reeled back and had to hold on to the chair to keep from falling. It was unbelievable. I read the paper again—and again. It was still true: I had gone through a long series of gestures at the window, and not one of the patterns had been mine.

I had the feeling, once more, that I was standing before Clarimonda's wide open door, through which, though I stared, I could see nothing but a dark void. I knew, too, that if I chose to turn from that door now, I might be saved; and that I still had the power to leave. And yet, I did not leave— because I felt myself at the very edge of the mystery: as if I were holding the secret in my hands. "Paris! You will conquer Paris," I thought. And in that instant, Paris was more powerful than Clarimonda.

I don't think about that any more. Now, I feel only love. Love, and a delicious terror.

Still, the moment itself endowed me with strength. I read my notes again, engraving the gestures on my mind. Then I went back to the window only to become aware that *there was not one of my patterns that I wanted to use.* Standing there, it occurred to me to rub the side of my nose; instead I found myself pressing my lips to the windowpane. I tried to drum with my fingers on the window sill; instead, I brushed my fingers through my hair. And so I understood that it was not that Clarimonda did what I did. Rather, my gestures followed her lead and with such lightning rapidity that we seemed to be moving simultaneously. I, who had been so proud because I thought I had been influencing her, I was in fact being influenced by her. Her influence . . . so gentle . . . so delightful.

I have tried another experiment. I clenched my hands and put them in my pockets firmly intending not to move them one bit. Clarimonda raised her hand and, smiling at me, made a scolding gesture with her finger. I did not budge, and yet I could feel how my right hand *wished* to leave my pocket. I shoved my fingers against the lining, but against my will, my hand left the pocket; my arm rose into the air. In my turn, I made a scolding gesture with my finger and smiled. It seemed to me that it was not I who was doing all this. It was a stranger whom I was watching. But, of course, I was mistaken. It was I making the gesture, and the person watching me was the stranger; that very same stranger who, not long ago, was so sure that he was on the edge of a great discovery. In any case, it was not I.

Of what use to me is this discovery? I am here to do Clarimonda's will. Clarimonda, whom I love with an anguished heart.

Friday, March 25

I have cut the telephone cord. I have no wish to be continually disturbed by the idiotic inspector just as the mysterious hour arrives.

God. Why did I write that? Not a word of it is true. It is as if someone else were directing my pen.

But I want to . . . want to . . . to write the truth here . . . though it is costing me great effort. But I want to . . . once more . . . do what *I* want.

I have cut the telephone cord . . . ah . . .

Because I had to . . . there it is. Had to . . .

We stood at our windows this morning and played the game, which is now different from what it was yesterday. Clarimonda makes a movement and I resist it for as long as I can. Then I give in and do what she wants without further struggle. I can hardly express what a joy it is to be so conquered; to surrender entirely to her will.

We played. All at once, she stood up and walked back into her room, where I could not see her; she was so engulfed by the dark. Then she came back with a desk telephone, like mine, in her hands. She smiled and set the telephone on the window sill, after which she took a knife and cut the cord. Then I carried my telephone to the window where I cut the cord. After that, I returned my phone to its place.

That's how it happened . . .

I sit at my desk where I have been drinking tea the servant brought me. He has come for the empty teapot, and I ask him for the time, since my watch isn't running properly. He says it is five fifteen. Five fifteen . . .

I know that if I look out of my window, Clarimonda will be there making a gesture that I will have to imitate. I will look just the same. Clarimonda is there, smiling. If only I could turn my eyes away from hers.

Now she parts the curtain. She takes the cord. It is red, just like the cord in my window. She ties a noose and hangs the cord on the hook in the window cross-bar.

She sits down and smiles.

No. Fear is no longer what I feel. Rather, it is a sort of oppressive terror which I would not want to avoid for anything in the world. Its grip is irresistible, profoundly cruel, and voluptuous in its attraction.

I could go to the window, and do what she wants me to do, but I wait. I struggle, I resist though I feel a mounting fascination that becomes more intense each minute.

Here I am once more. Rashly, I went to the window where I did what Clarimonda wanted. I took the cord, tied a noose, and hung it on the hook . . .

Now, I want to see nothing else—except to stare at this paper. Because if I look, I know what she will do . . . now . . . at the sixth hour of the last day of the week. If I see her, I will have to do what she wants. Have to . . .

I won't see her ...

I laugh. Loudly. No. I'm not laughing. Something is laughing in me, and I know why. It is because of my "I won't ..."

I won't, and yet I know very well that I have to ... have to look at her. I must ... must ... and then ... all that follows.

If I still wait, it is only to prolong this exquisite torture. Yes, that's it. This breathless anguish is my supreme delight. I write quickly, quickly ... just so I can continue to sit here; so I can attenuate these seconds of pain.

Again, terror. Again. I know that I will look toward her. That I will stand up. That I will hang myself.

That doesn't frighten me. That is beautiful ... even precious.

There is something else. *What will happen afterwards?* I don't know, but since my torment is so delicious, I feel ... feel that something horrible must follow.

Think ... think ... Write something. Anything at all ... to keep from looking toward her ...

My name ... Richard Bracquemont. Richard Bracquemont ... Richard Bracquemont ... Richard ...

I can't ... go on. I must ... no ... no ... must look at her ... Richard Bracquemont ... no ... no more ... Richard ... Richard Bracque— ...

The inspector of the ninth precinct, after repeated and vain efforts to telephone Richard, arrived at the Hotel Stevens at 6:05. He found the body of the student Richard Bracquemont hanging from the cross-bar of the window in room #7, in the same position as each of his three predecessors.

The expression on the student's face, however, was different, reflecting an appalling fear. Bracquemont's eyes were wide open and bulging from their sockets. His lips were drawn into a *rictus,* and his jaws were clamped together. A huge black spider whose body was dotted with purple spots lay crushed and nearly bitten in two between his teeth.

On the table, there lay the student's journal. The inspector read it and went immediately to investigate the house across the street. What he learned was that the second floor of that building had not been lived in for many months.

Paris 1908

FREDERICK MARRYAT

THE WHITE WOLF OF THE HARTZ MOUNTAINS

I

Before noon Philip and Krantz had embarked, and made sail in the peroqua.

They had no difficulty in steering their course; the islands by day, and the clear stars by night, were their compass. It is true that they did not follow the more direct track, but they followed the more secure, working up the smooth waters, and gaining to the northward more than to the west. Many times they were chased by the Malay proas, which infested the islands, but the swiftness of their little peroqua was their security; indeed, the chase was, generally speaking, abandoned as soon as the smallness of the vessel was made out by the pirates, who expected that little or no booty was to be gained.

One morning, as they were sailing between the isles, with less wind than usual, Philip observed—

"Krantz, you said that there were events in your own life, or connected with it, which would corroborate the mysterious tale I confided to you. Will you now tell me to what you referred?"

"Certainly," replied Krantz; "I have often thought of doing so, but one circumstance or another has hitherto prevented me; this is, however, a fitting opportunity. Prepare therefore to listen to a strange story, quite as strange, perhaps, as your own.

"I take it for granted that you have heard people speak of the Hartz Mountains," observed Krantz.

"I have never heard people speak of them, that I can recollect," replied Philip; "but I have read of them in some book, and of the strange things which have occurred there."

"It is indeed a wild region," rejoined Krantz, "and many strange tales are told of it; but strange as they are, I have good reason for believing them to be true.

"My father was not born, or originally a resident, in the Hartz Mountains; he was a serf of an Hungarian nobleman, of great possessions, in Transylvania; but although a serf, he was not by any means a poor or illiterate man. In fact, he was rich, and his intelligence and respectability were such, that he had been raised by his lord to the stewardship; but whoever may

205

happen to be born a serf, a serf must he remain, even though he become a wealthy man: such was the condition of my father. My father had been married for about five years; and by his marriage had three children—my eldest brother Caesar, myself (Hermann), and a sister named Marcella. You know, Philip, that Latin is still the language spoken in that country; and that will account for our high-sounding names. My mother was a very beautiful woman, unfortunately more beautiful than virtuous: she was seen and admired by the lord of the soil; my father was sent away upon some mission; and during his absence, my mother, flattered by the attentions, and won by the assiduities, of this nobleman, yielded to his wishes. It so happened that my father returned very unexpectedly, and discovered the intrigue. The evidence of my mother's shame was positive: he surprised her in the company of her seducer! Carried away by the impetuosity of his feelings, he watched the opportunity of a meeting taking place between them, and murdered both his wife and her seducer. Conscious that, as a serf, not even the provocation which he had received would be allowed as a justification of his conduct, he hastily collected together what money he could lay his hands upon, and, as we were then in the depth of winter, he put his horses to the sleigh, and taking his children with him, he set off in the middle of the night, and was far away before the tragical circumstance had transpired. Aware that he would be pursued, and that he had no chance of escape if he remained in any portion of his native country (in which the authorities could lay hold of him), he continued his flight without intermission until he had buried himself in the intricacies and seclusions of the Hartz Mountains. Of course, all that I have now told you I learned afterwards. My oldest recollections are knit to a rude, yet comfortable cottage, in which I lived with my father, brother, and sister. It was on the confines of one of those vast forests which cover the northern part of Germany; around it were a few acres of ground, which, during the summer months, my father cultivated, and which, though they yielded a doubtful harvest, were sufficient for our support. In the winter we remained much indoors, for, as my father followed the chase, we were left alone, and the wolves during that season incessantly prowled about. My father had purchased the cottage, and land about it, of one of the rude foresters, who gain their livelihood partly by hunting, and partly by burning charcoal, for the purpose of smelting the ore from the neighbouring mines; it was distant about two miles from any other habitation. I can call to mind the whole landscape now; the tall pines which rose up on the mountain above us, and the wide expanse of the forest beneath, on the topmost boughs and heads of whose trees we looked down from our cottage, as the mountain below us rapidly descended into the distant valley. In summer time the prospect was beautiful: but during the severe winter a more desolate scene could not well be imagined.

"I said that, in the winter, my father occupied himself with the chase; every day he left us, and often would he lock the door, that we might not leave the cottage. He had no one to assist him, or to take care of us—indeed, it was not easy to find a female servant who would live in such a solitude;

but, could he have found one, my father would not have received her, for he had imbibed a horror of the sex, as the difference of his conduct towards us, his two boys, and my poor little sister Marcella evidently proved. You may suppose we were sadly neglected; indeed, we suffered much, for my father, fearful that we might come to some harm, would not allow us fuel when he left the cottage; and we were obliged, therefore, to creep under the heaps of bears' skins, and there to keep ourselves as warm as we could until he returned in the evening, when a blazing fire was our delight. That my father chose this restless sort of life may appear strange, but the fact was, that he could not remain quiet; whether from the remorse for having committed murder, or from the misery consequent on his change of situation, or from both combined, he was never happy unless he was in a state of activity. Children, however, when left so much to themselves, acquire a thoughtfulness not common to their age. So it was with us; and during the short cold days of winter, we would sit silent, longing for the happy hours when the snow would melt and the leaves burst out, and the birds begin their songs, and when we should again be set at liberty.

"Such was our peculiar and savage sort of life until my brother Caesar was nine, myself seven, and my sister five years old, when the circumstances occurred on which is based the extraordinary narrative which I am about to relate.

"One evening my father returned home rather later than usual; he had been unsuccessful, and as the weather was very severe, and many feet of snow were upon the ground, he was not only very cold, but in a very bad humour. He had brought in wood, and we were all three gladly assisting each other in blowing on the embers to create a blaze, when he caught poor little Marcella by the arm and threw her aside; the child fell, struck her mouth, and bled very much. My brother ran to raise her up. Accustomed to ill-usage, and afraid of my father, she did not dare to cry, but looked up in his face very piteously. My father drew his stool nearer to the hearth, muttered something in abuse of women, and busied himself with the fire, which both my brother and I had deserted when our sister was so unkindly treated. A cheerful blaze was soon the result of his exertions; but we did not, as usual, crowd round it. Marcella, still bleeding, retired to a corner, and my brother and I took our seats beside her, while my father hung over the fire gloomily and alone. Such had been our position for about half an hour, when the howl of a wolf, close under the window of the cottage fell on our ears. My father started up, and seized his gun; the howl was repeated; he examined the priming, and then hastily left the cottage, shutting the door after him. We all waited (anxiously listening), for we thought that if he succeeded in shooting the wolf, he would return in a better humour; and, although he was harsh to all of us, and particularly so to our little sister, still we loved our father, and loved to see him cheerful and happy, for what else had we to look up to? And I may here observe, that perhaps there never were three children who were fonder of each other; we did not, like other children, fight and dispute together; and if, by chance, any disagreement did arise, between my elder brother and me, little Marcella would run to us, and kissing us both, seal, through her entreaties, the peace between us. Marcella was a lovely, amiable child; I can recall her beautiful features even now. Alas! poor little Marcella."

"She is dead, then?" observed Philip.

"Dead! yes, dead! but how did she die?—But I must not anticipate, Philip; let me tell my story.

"We waited for some time, but the report of the gun did not reach us, and my elder brother then said, 'Our father has followed the wolf, and will not be back for some time. Marcella, let us wash the blood from your mouth, and then we will leave this corner and go to the fire to warm ourselves.'

"We did so, and remained there until near midnight, every minute wondering, as it grew later, why our father did not return. We had no idea that he was in any danger, but we thought that he must have chased the wolf for a very long time. 'I will look out and see if father is coming,' said my brother Caesar, going to the door. 'Take care,' said Marcella, 'the wolves must be about now, and we cannot kill them, brother.' My brother opened the door very cautiously, and but a few inches; he peeped out. 'I see nothing,' said he, after a time, and once more he joined us at the fire. 'We have had no supper,' said I, for my father usually cooked the meat as soon as he came home; and during his absence we had nothing but the fragments of the preceding day.

" 'And if our father comes home, after his hunt, Caesar,' said Marcella, 'he will be pleased to have some supper; let us cook it for him and for ourselves.' Caesar climbed upon the stool, and reached down some meat—I forget now whether it was venison or bear's meat, but we cut off the usual quantity, and proceeded to dress it, as we used to do under our father's superintendence. We were all busy putting it into the platters before the fire, to await his coming, when we heard the sound of a horn. We listened —there was a noise outside, and a minute afterwards my father entered, ushered in a young female and a large dark man in a hunter's dress.

"Perhaps I had better now relate what was only known to me many years afterwards. When my father had left the cottage, he perceived a large white wolf about thirty yards from him; as soon as the animal saw my father, it retreated slowly, growling and snarling. My father followed; the animal did not run, but always kept at some distance; and my father did not like to fire until he was pretty certain that his ball would take effect; thus they went on for some time, the wolf now leaving my father far behind, and then stopping and snarling defiance at him, and then, again, on his approach, setting off at speed.

"Anxious to shoot the animal (for the white wolf is very rare), my father continued the pursuit for several hours, during which he continually ascended the mountain.

"You must know, Philip, that there are peculiar spots on those mountains which are supposed, and, as my story will prove, truly supposed, to be inhabited by the evil influences: they are well known to the huntsmen, who invariably avoid them. Now, one of these spots, an open space in the pine forest above us, had been pointed out to my father as dangerous on that account. But whether he disbelieved these wild stories, or whether, in his eager pursuit of the case, he disregarded them, I know not; certain, however, it is, that he was decoyed by the white wolf to this open space, when the animal appeared to slacken her speed. My father approached, came close up to her, raised his gun to his shoulder and was about to fire, when the wolf suddenly disappeared. He thought that the snow on the ground must have dazzled his sight, and he let down his gun to look for the beast—but she was gone; how she could have escaped over the clearance, without his seeing her, was beyond his comprehension. Mortified at the ill-success of his chase, he was about to retrace his steps, when he heard the distant sound of a horn. Astonishment at such a sound—at such an hour—in such a wilderness, made him forget for the moment his disappointment, and he remained riveted to the spot. In a minute the horn was blown a second time, and at no great distance; my father stood still, and listened; a third time it was blown. I forget the term used to express it, but it was the signal which, my father well knew, implied that the party was lost in the woods. In a few minutes more my father beheld a man on horseback, with a female seated on the crupper, enter the cleared space, and ride up to him. At first, my father called to mind the strange stories which he had heard of the supernatural beings who were said to frequent these mountains; but the nearer approach of the parties satisfied him that they were mortals like himself. As soon as they came up to him, the man who guided the horse accosted him. 'Friend hunter, you are out late, the better fortune for us; we have ridden far, and are in fear of our lives, which are eagerly sought after. These mountains have enabled us to elude our pursuers; but if we find not shelter and refreshment, that will avail us little, as we must perish from hunger and the inclemency of the night. My daughter, who rides behind me, is now more dead than alive—say, can you assist us in our difficulty?'

" 'My cottage is some few miles distant,' replied my father, 'but I have little to offer you besides a shelter from the weather; to the little I have you are welcome. May I ask whence you come?'

" 'Yes, friend, it is no secret now; we have escaped from Transylvania, where my daughter's honour and my life were equally in jeopardy!'

"This information was quite enough to raise an interest in my father's heart. He remembered his own escape: he remembered the loss of his wife's honour, and the tragedy by which it was wound up. He immediately, and warmly, offered all the assistance which he could afford them.

" 'There is no time to be lost, then, good sir,' observed the horseman; 'my daughter is chilled with the frost, and cannot hold out much longer against the severity of the weather.'

" 'Follow me,' replied my father, leading the way towards his home.

" 'I was lured away in pursuit of a large white wolf,' observed my father; 'it came to the very window of my hut, or I should not have been out at this time of night.'

" 'The creature passed by us just as we came out of the wood,' said the female, in a silvery tone.

" 'I was nearly discharging my piece at it,' observed the hunter; 'but since it did us such good service, I am glad that I allowed it to escape.'

"In about an hour and a half, during which my father walked at a rapid pace, the party arrived at the cottage, and, as I said before, came in.

" 'We are in good time, apparently,' observed the dark hunter, catching the smell of the roasted meat, as he walked to the fire and surveyed my brother and sister and myself. 'You have young cooks here, Meinheer.' 'I am glad that we shall not have to wait,' replied my father. 'Come, mistress, seat yourself by the fire; you require warmth after your cold ride.' 'And where can I put up my horse, Meinheer?' observed the huntsman. 'I will take care of him,' replied my father, going out of the cottage door.

"The female must, however, be particularly described. She was young, and apparently twenty years of age. She was dressed in a travelling dress, deeply bordered with white fur, and wore a cap of white ermine on her head. Her features were very beautiful, at least I thought so, and so my father has since declared. Her hair was flaxen, glossy, and shining, and bright as a mirror; and her mouth, although somewhat large when it was open, showed the most brilliant teeth I have ever beheld. But there was something about her eyes, bright as they were, which made us children afraid; they were so restless, so furtive; I could not at that time tell why, but I felt as if there was cruelty in her eye; and when she beckoned us to come to her, we approached her with fear and trembling. Still she was beautiful, very beautiful. She spoke kindly to my brother and myself, patted our heads and caressed us; but Marcella would not come near her; on the contrary, she slunk away, and hid herself in the bed, and would not wait for the supper, which half an hour before she had been so anxious for.

"My father, having put the horse into a close shed, soon returned, and supper was placed on the table. When it was over, my father requested the young lady would take possession of the bed, and he would remain at the fire, and sit up with her father. After some hesitation on her part, this arrangement was agreed to, and I and my brother crept into the other bed with Marcella, for we had as yet always slept together.

"But we could not sleep; there was something so unusual, not only in seeing strange people, but in having those people sleep at the cottage, that we were bewildered. As for poor little Marcella, she was quiet, but I perceived that she trembled during the whole night, and sometimes I thought that she was checking a sob. My father had brought out some spirits, which he rarely used, and he and the strange hunter remained drinking and talking before the fire. Our ears were ready to catch the slightest whisper—so much was our curiosity excited.

" 'You said you came from Transylvania?' observed my father.

" 'Even so, Meinheer,' replied the hunter. 'I was a serf to the noble house of———; my master would insist upon my surrendering up my fair girl to his wishes; it ended in my giving him a few inches of my hunting-knife.'

" 'We are countrymen and brothers in misfortune,' replied my father, taking the huntsman's hand and pressing it warmly.

" 'Indeed! Are you then from that country?'

" 'Yes; and I too have fled for my life. But mine is a melancholy tale.'

" 'Your name?' inquired the hunter.

" 'Krantz.'

" 'What! Krantz of———? I have heard your tale; you need not renew your grief by repeating it now. Welcome, most welcome, Meinheer, and, I may say, my worthy kinsman. I am your second cousin, Wilfred of Barnsdorf,' cried the hunter, rising up and embracing my father.

"They filled their horn-mugs to the brim, and drank to one another after the German fashion. The conversation was then carried on in a low tone; all that we could collect from it was that our new relative and his daughter were to take up their abode in our cottage, at least for the present. In about an hour they both fell back in their chairs and appeared to sleep.

" 'Marcella, dear, did you hear?' said my brother, in a low tone.

" 'Yes,' replied Marcella, in a whisper, 'I heard all. Oh! brother, I cannot bear to look upon that woman—I feel so frightened.'

"My brother made no reply, and shortly afterwards we were all three fast asleep.

"When we awoke the next morning, we found that the hunter's daughter had risen before us. I thought she looked more beautiful than ever. She came up to little Marcella and caressed her; the child burst into tears, and sobbed as if her heart would break.

"But not to detain you with too long a story, the huntsman and his daughter were accommodated in the cottage. My father and he went out hunting daily, leaving Christina with us. She performed all the household duties; was very kind to us children; and gradually the dislike even of little Marcella wore away. But a great change took place in my father; he appeared to have conquered his aversion to the sex, and was most attentive to Christina. Often, after her father and we were in bed, would he sit up with her, conversing in a low tone by the fire. I ought to have mentioned that my father and the huntsman Wilfred slept in another portion of the cottage, and that the bed which he formerly occupied, and which was in the same room as ours, had been given up to the use of Christina. These visitors had been about three weeks at the cottage, when, one night, after we children had been sent to bed, a consultation was held. My father had asked Christina in marriage, and had obtained both her own consent and that of Wilfred; after this, a conversation took place, which was, as nearly as I can recollect, as follows:—

" 'You may take my child, Meinheer Krantz, and my blessing with her, and I shall then leave you and seek some other habitation—it matters little where.'

" 'Why not remain here, Wilfred?'

" 'No, no, I am called elsewhere; let that suffice, and ask no more questions. You have my child.'

" 'I thank you for her, and will duly value her; but there is one difficulty.'

" 'I know what you would say; there is no priest here in this wild country; true; neither is there any law to bind. Still must some ceremony pass between you, to satisfy a father. Will you consent to marry her after my fashion? if so, I will marry you directly.'

" 'I will,' replied my father.

" 'Then take her by the hand. Now, Meinheer, swear.'

" 'I swear,' repeated my father.

" 'By all the spirits of the Hartz Mountains—'

" 'Nay, why not by Heaven?' interrupted my father.

" 'Because it is not my humour,' rejoined Wilfred. 'If I prefer that oath, less binding, perhaps, than another, surely you will not thwart me.'

" 'Well, be it so, then; have your humour. Will you make me swear by that in which I do not believe?'

" 'Yet many do so, who in outward appearance are Christians,' rejoined Wilfred; 'say, will you be married, or shall I take my daughter away with me?'

" 'Proceed,' replied my father impatiently.

" 'I swear by all the spirits of the Hartz Mountains, by all their power for good or for evil, that I take Christina for my wedded wife; that I will ever protect her, cherish her, and love her; that my hand shall never be raised against her to harm her.'

"My father repeated the words after Wilfred.

" 'And if I fail in this my vow, may all the vengeance of the spirits fall upon me and upon my children; may they perish by the vulture, by the wolf, or other beasts of the forest; may their flesh be torn from their limbs, and their bones blanch in the wilderness: all this I swear.'

"My father hesitated, as he repeated the last words; little Marcella could not restrain herself, and as my father repeated the last sentence, she burst into tears. This sudden interruption appeared to discompose the party, particularly my father; he spoke harshly to the child, who controlled her sobs, burying her face under the bedclothes.

"Such was the second marriage of my father. The next morning, the hunter Wilfred mounted his horse and rode away.

"My father resumed his bed, which was in the same room as ours; and things went on much as before the marriage, except that our new mother-in-law did not show any kindness towards us; indeed, during my father's absence, she would often beat us, particularly little Marcella, and her eyes would flash fire, as she looked eagerly upon the fair and lovely child.

"One night my sister awoke me and my brother.

" 'What is the matter?' said Caesar.

" 'She has gone out,' whispered Marcella.

" 'Gone out!'

" 'Yes, gone out at the door, in her night-clothes,' replied the child; 'I saw her get out of bed, look at my father to see if he slept, and then she went out at the door.'

"What could induce her to leave her bed, and all undressed to go out, in such bitter wintry weather, with the snow deep on the ground, was to us incomprehensible; we lay awake, and in about an hour we heard the growl of a wolf close under the window.

" 'There is a wolf,' said Caesar. 'She will be torn to pieces.'

" 'Oh, no!' cried Marcella.

"In a few minutes afterwards our mother-in-law* appeared; she was in her night-dress, as Marcella had stated. She let down the latch of the door, so as to make no noise, went to a pail of water, and washed her face and hands, and then slipped into the bed where my father lay.

"We all three trembled—we hardly knew why; but we resolved to watch the next night. We did so; and not only on the ensuing night, but on many others, and always at about the same hour, would our mother-in-law rise from her bed and leave the cottage; and after she was gone we invariably heard the growl of a wolf under our window, and always saw her on her return wash herself before she retired to bed. We observed also that she seldom sat down to meals, and that when she did she appeared to eat with dislike; but when the meat was taken down to be prepared for dinner, she would often furtively put a raw piece into her mouth.

"My brother Caesar was a courageous boy; he did not like to speak to my father until he knew more. He resolved that he would follow her out, and ascertain what she did. Marcella and I endeavoured to dissuade him from the project; but he would not be controlled; and the very next night he lay down in his clothes, and as soon as our mother-in-law had left the cottage he jumped up, took down my father's gun, and followed her.

"You may imagine in what a state of suspense Marcella and I remained during his absence. After a few minutes we heard the report of a gun. It did not awaken my father; and we lay trembling with anxiety. In a minute afterwards we saw our mother-in-law enter the cottage—her dress was bloody. I put my hand to Marcella's mouth to prevent her crying out, although I was myself in great alarm. Our mother-in-law approached my father's bed, looked to see if he was asleep, and then went to the chimney and blew up the embers into a blaze.

" 'Who is there?' said my father, waking up.

" 'Lie still, dearest,' replied my mother-in-law; "it is only me; I have lighted the fire to warm some water; I am not quite well.'

"My father turned round, and was soon asleep; but we watched our mother-in-law. She changed her linen, and threw the garments she had worn into the fire; and we then perceived that her right leg was bleeding profusely, as if from a gun-shot wound. She bandaged it up, and then dressing herself, remained before the fire until the break of day.

"Poor little Marcella, her heart beat quick as she pressed me to her side—so indeed did mine. Where was our brother Caesar? How did my mother-in-law receive the wound unless from his gun? At last my father rose, and then

* stepmother

for the first time I spoke, saying, 'Father, where is my brother Caesar?'

" 'Your brother?' exclaimed he; 'why, where can he be?'

" 'Merciful Heaven! I thought as I lay very restless last night,' observed our mother-in-law, 'that I heard somebody open the latch of the door; and, dear me, husband, what has become of your gun?'

"My father cast his eyes above the chimney, and perceived that his gun was missing. For a moment he looked perplexed; then, seizing a broad axe, he went out of the cottage without saying another word.

"He did not remain away from us long; in a few minutes he returned, bearing in his arms the mangled body of my poor brother; he laid it down, and covered up his face.

"My mother-in-law rose up, and looked at the body, while Marcella and I threw ourselves by its side, wailing and sobbing bitterly.

" 'Go to bed again, children,' said she sharply. 'Husband,' continued she, 'your boy must have taken the gun down to shoot a wolf, and the animal has been too powerful for him. Poor boy! he has paid dearly for his rashness.'

"My father made no reply. I wished to speak—to tell all—but Marcella, who perceived my intention, held me by the arm, and looked at me so imploringly, that I desisted.

"My father, therefore, was left in his error; but Marcella and I, although we could not comprehend it, were conscious that our mother-in-law was in some way connected with my brother's death.

"That day my father went out and dug a grave; and when he laid the body in the earth he piled up stones over it, so that the wolves should not be able to dig it up. The shock of this catastrophe was to my poor father very severe; for several days he never went to the chase, although at times he would utter bitter anathemas and vengeance against the wolves.

"But during this time of mourning on his part, my mother-in-law's nocturnal wanderings continued with the same regularity as before.

"At last my father took down his gun to repair to the forest; but he soon returned, and appeared much annoyed.

" 'Would you believe it, Christina, that the wolves—perdition to the whole race!—have actually contrived to dig up the body of my poor boy, and now there is nothing left of him but his bones.'

" 'Indeed!' replied my mother-in-law. Marcella looked at me, and I saw in her intelligent eye all she would have uttered.

" 'A wolf growls under our window every night, father,' said I.

" 'Ay, indeed! Why did you not tell me, boy? Wake me the next time you hear it.'

"I saw my mother-in-law turn away; her eyes flashed fire, and she gnashed her teeth.

"My father went out again, and covered up with a larger pile of stones the little remains of my poor brother which the wolves had spared. Such was the first act of the tragedy.

"The spring now came on; the snow disappeared, and we were permitted to leave the cottage; but never would I quit for one moment my dear little sister, to whom, since the death of my brother, I was more ardently attached than ever; indeed, I was afraid to leave her alone with my mother-in-law, who appeared to have a particular pleasure in ill-treating the child. My father was now employed upon his little farm, and I was able to render him some assistance.

"Marcella used to sit by us while we were at work, leaving my mother-in-law alone in the cottage. I ought to observe that, as the spring advanced, so did my mother-in-law decrease her nocturnal rambles, and that we never heard the growl of the wolf under the window after I had spoken of it to my father.

"One day, when my father and I were in the field, Marcella being with us, my mother-in-law came out, saying that she was going into the forest to collect some herbs my father wanted, and that Marcella must go to the cottage and watch the dinner. Marcella went; and my mother-in-law disappeared in the forest, taking a direction quite contrary to that in which the cottage stood, and leaving my father and me, as it were, between her and Marcella.

"About an hour afterwards we were startled by shrieks from the cottage—evidently the shrieks of little Marcella. 'Marcella has burnt herself, father,' said I, throwing down my spade. My father threw down his, and we both hastened to the cottage. Before we could gain the door, out darted a large white wolf, which fled with the utmost celerity. My father had no weapon; he rushed into the cottage, and there saw poor little Marcella expiring. Her body was dreadfully mangled and the blood pouring from it had formed a large pool on the cottage floor. My father's first intention had been to seize his gun and pursue; but he was checked by this horrid spectacle; he knelt down by his dying child, and burst into tears. Marcella could just look kindly on us for a few seconds, and then her eyes were closed in death.

"My father and I were still hanging over my poor sister's body when my mother-in-law came in. At the dreadful sight she expressed much concern; but she did not appear to recoil from the sight of blood, as most women do.

" 'Poor child!' said she, 'it must have been that great white wolf which passed me just now, and frightened me so. She's quite dead, Krantz.'

" 'I know it!—I know it!' cried my father, in agony.

"I thought my father would never recover from the effects of this second tragedy; he mourned bitterly over the body of his sweet child, and for several days would not consign it to its grave, although frequently requested by my mother-in-law to do so. At last he yielded, and dug a grave for her close by that of my poor brother, and took every precaution that the wolves should not violate her remains.

"I was now really miserable as I lay alone in the bed which I had formerly shared with my brother and sister. I could not help thinking that my mother-in-law was implicated in both their deaths, although I could not account for the manner; but I no longer felt afraid of her; my little heart was full of hatred and revenge.

"The night after my sister had been buried, as I lay awake, I perceived my mother-in-law get up and go out of the cottage. I waited some time, then dressed myself, and looked out through the door, which I half opened. The moon shone bright, and I could see the spot where my brother and sister had been buried; and what was my horror when I perceived my mother-in-law busily removing the stones from Marcella's grave!

"She was in her white night-dress, and the moon shone full upon her. She was digging with her hands, and throwing away the stones behind her with all the ferocity of a wild beast. It was some time before I could collect my senses and decide what I should do. At last I perceived that she had arrived at the body, and raised it up to the side of the grave. I could bear it no longer: I ran to my father and awoke him.

" 'Father, father!' cried I, 'dress yourself, and get your gun.'

" 'What!' cried my father, 'the wolves are there, are they?'

"He jumped out of bed, threw on his clothes, and in his anxiety did not appear to perceive the absence of his wife. As soon as he was ready I opened the door, he went out, and I followed him.

"Imagine his horror, when (unprepared as he was for such a sight) he beheld, as he advanced towards the grave, not a wolf, but his wife, in her night-dress, on her hands and knees, crouching by the body of my sister, and tearing off large pieces of the flesh, and devouring them with all the avidity of a wolf. She was too busy to be aware of our approach. My father dropped his gun; his hair stood on end, so did mine; he breathed heavily, and then his breath for a time stopped. I picked up the gun and put it into his hand. Suddenly he appeared as if concentrated rage had restored him to double vigour; he levelled his piece, fired, and with a loud shriek down fell the wretch whom he had fostered in his bosom.

" 'God of heaven!' cried my father, sinking down upon the earth in a swoon, as soon as he had discharged his gun.

"I remained some time by his side before he recovered. 'Where am I?' said he, 'what has happened? Oh!—yes, yes! I recollect now. Heaven forgive me!'

"He rose and we walked up to the grave; what again was our astonishment and horror to find that, instead of the dead body of my mother-in-law, as we expected, there was lying over the remains of my poor sister a large white she-wolf.

" 'The white wolf,' exclaimed my father, 'the white wolf which decoyed me into the forest—I see it all now—I have dealt with the spirits of the Hartz Mountains.'

"For some time my father remained in silence and deep thought. He then carefully lifted up the body of my sister, replaced it in the grave, and covered it over as before, having struck the head of the dead animal with the heel of his boot, and raving like a madman. He walked back to the cottage, shut the door, and threw himself on the bed; I did the same, for I was in a stupor of amazement.

"Early in the morning we were both roused by a loud knocking at the door, and in rushed the hunter Wilfred.

" 'My daughter—man—my daughter!—where is my daughter?' cried he in a rage.

" 'Where the wretch, the fiend should be, I trust,' replied my father, starting up, and displaying equal choler: 'where she should be—in hell! Leave this cottage, or you may fare worse.'

" 'Ha—ha!' replied the hunter, 'would you harm a potent spirit of the Hartz Mountains? Poor mortal, who must needs wed a werewolf.'

" 'Out, demon! I defy thee and thy power.'

" 'Yet shall you feel it; remember your oath—your solemn oath—never to raise your hand against her to harm her.'

" 'I made no compact with evil spirits.'

" 'You did, and if you failed in your vow, you were to meet the vengeance of the spirits. Your children were to perish by the vulture, the wolf—'

" 'Out, out, demon!'

" 'And their bones blanch in the wilderness. Ha—ha!'

"My father, frantic with rage, seized his axe and raised it over Wilfred's head to strike.

" 'All this I swear,' continued the huntsman mockingly.

"The axe descended; but it passed through the form of the hunter, and my father lost his balance, and fell heavily on the floor.

" 'Mortal!' said the hunter, striding over my father's body, 'we have power over those only who have committed murder. You have been guilty of a double murder: you shall pay the penalty attached to your marriage vow. Two of your children are gone, the third is yet to follow—and follow them he will, for your oath is registered. Go—it were kindness to kill thee—your punishment is, that you live!'

"With these words the spirit disappeared. My father rose from the floor, embraced me tenderly, and knelt down in prayer.

"The next morning he quitted the cottage for ever. He took me with him, and bent his steps to Holland, where we safely arrived. He had some little money with him; but he had not been many days in Amsterdam before he was seized with a brain fever, and died raving mad. I was put into the asylum, and afterwards was sent to sea before the mast. You now know all my history. The question is, whether I am to pay the penalty of my father's oath? I am myself perfectly convinced that, in some way or another, I shall."

II

On the twenty-second day the high land of the south of Sumatra was in view: as there were no vessels in sight, they resolved to keep their course through the Straits, and run for Pulo Penang, which they expected, as their vessel lay so close to the wind, to reach in seven or eight days. By constant exposure Philip and Krantz were now so bronzed, that with their long beards and Mussulman dresses, they might easily have passed off for natives. They had steered during the whole of the days exposed to a burning sun; they had lain down and slept in the dew of the night; but their health had not suffered. But for several days, since he had confided the history of his family to Philip, Krantz had become silent and melancholy; his usual flow of spirits had vanished, and Philip had often questioned him as to the cause. As they entered the Straits, Philip talked of what they should do upon their arrival at Goa; when Krantz gravely replied, "For some days, Philip, I have had a presentiment that I shall never see that city."

"You are out of health, Krantz," replied Philip.

"No, I am in sound health, body and mind. I have endeavoured to shake off the presentiment, but in vain; there is a warning voice that continually tells me that I shall not be long with you. Philip, will you oblige me by making me content on one point? I have gold about my person which may be useful to you; oblige me by taking it, and securing it on your own."

"What nonsense, Krantz."

"It is no nonsense, Philip. Have you not had your warnings? Why should I not have mine? You know that I have little fear in my composition, and that I care not about death; but I feel the presentiment which I speak of more strongly every hour. . . ."

"These are the imaginings of a disturbed brain, Krantz; why you, young, in full health and vigour, should not pass your days in peace, and live to a good old age, there is no cause for believing. You will be better to-morrow."

"Perhaps so," replied Krantz; "but you still must yield to my whim, and take the gold. If I am wrong, and we do arrive safe, you know, Philip, you can let me have it back," observed Krantz, with a faint smile—"but you forget, our water is nearly out, and we must look out for a rill on the coast to obtain a fresh supply."

"I was thinking of that when you commenced this unwelcome topic. We had better look out for the water before dark, and as soon as we have replenished our jars, we will make sail again."

At the time that this conversation took place, they were on the eastern side of the Strait, about forty miles to the northward. The interior of the coast was rocky and mountainous, but it slowly descended to low land of alternate forest and jungles, which continued to the beach; the country appeared to be uninhabited. Keeping close in to the shore, they discovered, after two hours' run, a fresh stream which burst in a cascade from the mountains, and swept its devious course through the jungle, until it poured its tribute into the waters of the Strait.

They ran close into the mouth of the stream, lowered the sails, and pulled the peroqua against the current, until they had advanced far enough to assure them that the water was quite fresh. The jars were soon filled, and they were again thinking of pushing off, when enticed by the beauty of the spot, the coolness of the fresh water, and wearied with their long confinement on board of the peroqua, they proposed to bathe—a luxury hardly to be appreciated by those who have not been in a similar situation. They threw off their Mussulman dresses, and plunged into the stream, where they remained for some time. Krantz was the first to get out; he complained of feeling chilled, and he walked on to the banks where their clothes had been laid. Philip also approached nearer to the beach, intending to follow him.

"And now, Philip," said Krantz, "this will be a good opportunity for me to give you the money. I will open my sash and pour it out, and you can put it into your own before you put it on."

Philip was standing in the water, which was about level with his waist.

"Well, Krantz," said he, "I suppose if it must be so, it must; but it appears to me an idea so ridiculous—however, you shall have your own way."

Philip quitted the run, and sat down by Krantz, who was already busy in shaking the doubloons out of the folds of his sash; at last he said—

"I believe, Philip, you have got them all, now?—I feel satisfied."

"What danger there can be to you, which I am not equally exposed to, I cannot conceive," replied Philip; "however—"

Hardly had he said these words, when there was a tremendous roar—a rush like a mighty wind through the air—a blow which threw him on his back—a loud cry—and a contention. Philip recovered himself, and perceived the naked form of Krantz carried off with the speed of an arrow by an enormous tiger through the jungle. He watched with distended eyeballs; in a few seconds the animal and Krantz had disappeared.

"God of heaven! would that Thou hadst spared me this," cried Philip, throwing himself down in agony on his face. "O Krantz! my friend—my brother—too sure was your presentiment. Merciful God! have pity—but Thy will be done." And Philip burst into a flood of tears.

For more than an hour did he remain fixed upon the spot, careless and indifferent to the danger by which he was surrounded. At last, somewhat recovered, he rose, dressed himself, and then again sat down—his eyes fixed upon the clothes of Krantz, and the gold which still lay on the sand.

"He would give me that gold. He foretold his doom. Yes! yes! it was his destiny, and it has been fulfilled. *His bones will bleach in the wilderness,* and the spirit-hunter and his wolfish daughter are avenged."

SAX ROHMER

TCHÉRIAPIN

I

The Rose

"Examine it closely," said the man in the unusual caped overcoat. "It will repay examination."

I held the little object in the palm of my hand, bending forward over the marble-topped table and looking down at it with deep curiosity. The babel of tongues so characteristic of Malay Jack's, and that mingled odour of stale spirits, greasy humanity, tobacco, cheap perfume, and opium, which distinguishes the establishment, faded from my ken. A sense of loneliness came to me.

Perhaps I should say that it became complete. I had grown conscious of its approach at the very moment that the cadaverous white-haired man had addressed me. There was a quality in his steadfast gaze and in his oddly pitched deep voice which from the first had wrapped me about—as though he were cloaking me in his queer personality and withdrawing me from the common plane.

Having stared for some moments at the object in my palm, I touched it gingerly; whereupon my acquaintance laughed—a short bass laugh.

"It looks fragile," he said. "But have no fear. It is nearly as hard as a diamond."

Thus encouraged, I took the thing up between finger and thumb, and held it before my eyes. For long enough I looked at it, and looking, my wonder grew. I thought that here was the most wonderful example of the lapidary's art which I had ever met with, East or West.

It was a tiny pink rose, no larger than the nail of my little finger. Stalk and leaves were there, and golden pollen lay in its delicate heart. Each fairy-petal blushed with June fire; the frail leaves were exquisitely green. Withal it was as hard and unbendable as a thing of steel.

"Allow me," said the masterful voice.

A powerful lens was passed by my acquaintance. I regarded the rose through the glass, and thereupon I knew, beyond doubt, that there was something phenomenal about the gem—if gem it were. I could plainly trace the veins and texture of every petal.

I suppose I looked somewhat startled. Although, baldly stated, the fact may not seem calculated to affrighten, in reality there was something so weird about this unnatural bloom that I dropped it on the table. As I did so I

220

uttered an exclamation; for in spite of the stranger's assurances on the point, I had by no means overcome my idea of the thing's fragility.

"Don't be alarmed," he said, meeting my startled gaze. "It would need a steam-hammer to do any serious damage."

He replaced the jewel in his pocket, and when I returned the lens to him he acknowledged it with a grave inclination of the head. As I looked into his sunken eyes, in which I thought lay a sort of sardonic merriment, the fantastic idea flashed through my mind that I had fallen into the clutches of an expert hypnotist who was amusing himself at my expense; that the miniature rose was a mere hallucination produced by the same means as the notorious Indian rope trick.

Then, looking around me at the cosmopolitan groups surrounding the many tables, and catching snatches of conversations dealing with subjects so diverse as the quality of whisky in Singapore, the frail beauty of Chinese maidens, and the ways of "bloody greasers," common sense reasserted itself.

I looked into the grey face of my acquaintance.

"I cannot believe," I said slowly, "that human ingenuity could so closely duplicate the handiwork of nature. Surely the gem is unique?—possibly one of those magical talismans of which we read in eastern stories?"

My companion smiled.

"It is not a gem," he replied, "and whilst in a sense it is a product of human ingenuity, it is also the handiwork of nature."

I was badly puzzled, and doubtless revealed the fact, for the stranger laughed in his short fashion, and:

"I am not trying to mystify you," he assured me. "But the truth is so hard to believe sometimes that in the present case I hesitate to divulge it. Did you ever meet Tchériapin?"

This abrupt change of topic somewhat startled me, but nevertheless:

"I once heard him play," I replied. "Why do you ask the question?"

"For this reason: Tchériapin possessed the only other example of this art which so far as I am aware ever left the laboratory of the inventor. He occasionally wore it in his buttonhole."

"It is then a manufactured product of some sort?"

"As I have said, in a sense it is; but"—he drew the tiny exquisite ornament from his pocket again and held it up before me—"it is a natural bloom."

"What?"

"It is a natural bloom," replied my acquaintance, fixing his penetrating gaze upon me. "By a perfectly simple process invented by the cleverest chemist of his age it has been reduced to this gem-like state whilst retaining unimpaired every one of its natural beauties, every shade of its natural colour. You are incredulous?"

"On the contrary," I replied, "having examined it through a magnifying glass I had already assured myself that no human hand had fashioned it. You arouse my curiosity intensely. Such a process, with its endless possibilities, should be worth a fortune to the inventor."

The stranger nodded grimly and again concealed the rose in his pocket.

"You are right," he said, "and the secret died with the man who discovered it—in the great explosion at the Vortex Works in 1917. You recall it? The T.N.T. factory? It shook all London, and fragments were cast into three counties."

"I recall it perfectly well."

"You remember also the death of Dr. Kreener, the chief chemist? He died in an endeavor to save some of the work-people."

"I remember."

"He was the inventor of the process, but it was never put upon the market. He was a singular man, sir; as was once said of him: 'A Don Juan of science.' Dame Nature gave him her heart unwooed. He trifled with science as some men trifle with love, tossing aside with a smile discoveries which would have made another famous. This"—tapping his breast pocket—"was one of them."

"You astound me. Do I understand you to mean that Dr. Kreener had invented a process for reducing any form of plant life to this condition?"

"Almost any form," was the guarded reply. "And some forms of animal life."

"What!"

"If you like"—the stranger leaned forward and grasped my arm—"I will tell you the story of Dr. Kreener's last experiment."

I was now intensely interested. I had not forgotten the heroic death of the man concerning whose work this chance acquaintance of mine seemed to know so much. And in the cadaverous face of the stranger as he sat there regarding me fixedly there was a promise and an allurement. I stood on the verge of strange things; so that, looking into the deep-set eyes, once again I felt the cloak being drawn about me, and I resigned myself willingly to the illusion.

From the moment when he began to speak again until that when I rose and followed him from Malay Jack's, as I shall presently relate, I became oblivious of my surroundings. I lived and moved through those last fevered hours in the lives of Dr. Kreener, Tchériapin, the violinist, and that other tragic figure around whom the story centered. I append:

The Stranger's Story

I asked you (said the man in the caped coat) if you had ever seen Tchériapin, and you replied that you had once heard him play. Having once heard him play you will not have forgotten him. At that time, although war still raged, all musical London was asking where he had come from, and to what nation he belonged. Then when he disappeared it was variously reported, you will recall, that he had been shot as a spy and that he had escaped from England and was serving with the Austrian army. As to his parentage I can enlighten you in a measure. He was an Eurasian. His father was an aristocratic Chinaman, and his mother a Polish ballet-dancer—that was his parentage; but I would scarcely hesitate to affirm that he came from Hell; and I shall presently show you that he has certainly returned there.

You remember the strange stories current about him. The cunning ones said that he had a clever press agent. This was true enough. One of the most prominent agents in London discovered him playing in a Paris cabaret. Two months later he was playing at the Queen's Hall, and musical London lay at his feet.

He had something of the personality of Paganini, as you remember, except that he was a smaller man; long, gaunt, yellowish hands and the face of a haggard Mephistopheles. The critics quarrelled about him, as critics only quarrel about real genius, and whilst one school proclaimed that Tchériapin had discovered an entirely new technique, a revolutionary system of violin playing, another school was equally positive in declaring that he could not play at all, that he was a mountebank, a trickster, whose proper place was in a variety theatre.

There were stories, too, that were never published—not only about Tchériapin, but concerning the Strad upon which he played. If all this atmosphere of mystery which surrounded the man had truly been the work of a press agent, then the agent must have been as great a genius as his client. But I can assure you that the stories concerning Tchériapin, true and absurd alike, were not inspired for business purposes; they grew up around him like fungi.

I can see him now, a lean, almost emaciated figure, with slow, sinuous movements, and a trick of glancing sideways with those dark, unfathomable, slightly oblique eyes. He could take up his bow in such a way as to create an atmosphere of electrical suspense. He was loathsome, yet fascinating. One's mental attitude towards him was one of defence, of being tensely on guard. Then he would play.

You have heard him play, and it is therefore unnecessary for me to attempt to describe the effect of that music. The only composition which ever bore his name—I refer to "The Black Mass"—affected me on every occasion when I heard it, as no other composition has ever done.

Perhaps it was Tchériapin's playing rather than the music itself which reached down into hitherto unplumbed depths within me, and awakened dark things which, unsuspected, lay there sleeping. I never heard "The Black Mass" played by anyone else; indeed, I am not aware that it was ever published. But had it been we should rarely hear it. Like Locke's music to *Macbeth* it bears an unpleasant reputation; to include it in any concert programme would be to court disaster. An idle superstition, perhaps, but there is much naïveté in the artistic temperament.

Men detested Tchériapin, yet when he chose he could win over his bitterest enemies. Women followed him as children followed the Pied Piper; he courted none, but was courted by all. He would glance aside with those black, slanting eyes, shrug in his insolent fashion, and turn away. And they would follow. God knows how many of them followed—whether through the dens of Limehouse or the more fashionable salons of vice in the West End—they followed—perhaps down to Hell. So much for Tchériapin.

At the time when the episode occurred to which I have referred, Dr. Kreener occupied a house in Regent's Park, to which, when his duties at the munition works allowed, he would sometimes retire at week-ends. He was a man of complex personality. I think no one ever knew him thoroughly; indeed, I doubt if he knew himself.

He was hail-fellow-well-met with the painters, sculptors, poets and social reformers who have made of Soho a new Mecca. No movement in art was so modern that Dr. Kreener was not conversant with it; no development in Bolshevism so violent or so secret that Dr. Kreener could not speak of it complacently and with inside knowledge.

These were his Bohemian friends, these dreamers and schemers. Of this side of his life his scientific colleagues knew little or nothing, but in his hours of leisure at Regent's Park it was with these dreamers that he loved to surround himself rather than with his brethren of the laboratory. I think if Dr. Kreener had not been a great chemist he would have been a great painter, or perhaps a politician, or even a poet. Triumph was his birthright, and the fruits for which lesser men reached out in vain fell ripe into his hands.

The favourite meeting-place for these oddly assorted boon companions was the doctor's laboratory, which was divided from the house by a moderately large garden. Here on a Sunday evening one might meet the very "latest" composer, the sculptor bringing a new "message," or the man destined to supplant with the ballet the time-worn operatic tradition.

But whilst some of these would come and go, so that one could never count with certainty upon meeting them, there was one who never failed to be present when such an informal reception was held. Of him I must speak at greater length, for a reason which will shortly appear.

Andrews was the name by which he was known to the circles in which he moved. No one, from Sir John Tennier, the fashionable portrait painter, to Kruski, of the Russian ballet, disputed Andrews's right to be counted one of the elect. Yet it was known, nor did he trouble to hide the fact, that Andrews was employed at a large printing works in South London, designing advertisements. He was a great, red-bearded, unkempt Scotsman, and only once can I remember to have seen him strictly sober; but to hear him talk about painters and painting in his thick Caledonian accent was to look into the soul of an artist.

He was as sour as an unripe grape-fruit, cynical, embittered, a man savagely disappointed with life and the world; and tragedy was written all over him. If anyone knew the secret of his wasted life it was Dr. Kreener, and Dr. Kreener was a reliquary of so many secrets that this one was safe as if the grave had swallowed it.

One Sunday Tchériapin joined the party. That he would gravitate there sooner or later was inevitable, for the laboratory in the garden was a *kaaba* to which all such spirits made at least one pilgrimage. He had just set musical London on fire with his barbaric playing, and already those stories to which I have referred were creeping into circulation.

Although Dr. Kreener never expected anything of his guests beyond an interchange of ideas, it was a fact that the laboratory contained an almost unique collection of pencil and charcoal studies by famous artists, done upon the spot; of statuettes in wax, putty, soap, and other extemporized materials, by the newest sculptors. Whilst often enough from the drawing-room which opened upon the other end of the garden had issued the strains of masterly piano-playing, and it was no uncommon thing for little groups to gather in the neighbouring road to listen, gratis, to the voice of some great vocalist.

From the first moment of their meeting an intense antagonism sprang up between Tchériapin and Andrews. Neither troubled very much to veil it. In Tchériapin it found expression in covert sneers and sidelong glances, whilst the big, lion-maned Scotsman snorted open contempt of the Eurasian violinist. However, what I was about to say was that Tchériapin on the occasion of his first visit brought his violin.

It was there, amid those incongruous surroundings, that I first had my spirit tortured by the strains of "The Black Mass."

There were five of us present, including Tchériapin, and not one of the four listeners was unaffected by the music. But the influence which it exercised upon Andrews was so extraordinary as almost to reach the phenomenal. He literally writhed in his chair, and finally interrupted the performance by staggering rather than walking out of the laboratory.

I remember that he upset a jar of acid in his stumbling exit. It flowed across the floor almost to the feet of Tchériapin, and the way in which the little black-haired man skipped, squealing, out of the path of the corroding fluid was curiously like that of a startled rabbit. Order was restored in due course, but we could not induce Tchériapin to play again, nor did Andrews return until the violinist had taken his departure. We found him in the dining-room, a nearly empty whisky-bottle beside him, and:

"I had to gang awa'," he explained thickly; "he was temptin' me to murder him. I should ha' had to do it if I had stayed. Damn his hell-music."

Tchériapin revisited Dr. Kreener on many occasions afterwards, although for a long time he did not bring his violin again. The doctor had prevailed upon Andrews to tolerate the Eurasian's company, and I could not help noticing how Tchériapin skilfully and deliberately goaded the Scotsman, seeming to take a fiendish delight in disagreeing with his pet theories, and in discussing any topic which he had found to be distasteful to Andrews.

Chief among these was that sort of irreverent criticism of women in which male parties so often indulge. Bitter cynic though he was, women were sacred to Andrews. To speak disrespectfully of a woman in his presence was like uttering blasphemy in the study of a cardinal. Tchériapin very quickly detected the Scotsman's weakness, and one night he launched out into a series of amorous adventures which set Andrews writhing as he had writhed under the torture of "The Black Mass."

On this occasion the party was only a small one, comprising myself, Dr. Kreener, Andrews, and Tchériapin. I could feel the storm brewing, but was powerless to check it. How presently it was to break in tragic violence I could not foresee. Fate had not meant that I should foresee it.

Allowing for the free play of an extravagant artistic mind, Tchériapin's career on his own showing had been that of a callous blackguard. I began by being disgusted and ended by being fascinated, not by the man's scandalous adventures, but by the scarcely human psychology of the narrator.

From Warsaw to Budapesth, Shanghai to Paris, and Cairo to London, he passed, leaving ruin behind him with a smile—airily flicking cigarette ash upon the floor to indicate the termination of each "episode."

Andrews watched him in a lowering way which I did not like at all. He had ceased to snort his scorn; indeed, for ten minutes or so he had uttered no word or sound; but there was something in the pose of his ungainly body which strangely suggested that of a great dog preparing to spring. Presently the violinist recalled what he termed a "charming idyll of Normandy."

"There is one poor fool in the world," he said, shrugging his slight shoulders, "who never knew how badly he should hate me. Ha! ha! of him I shall tell you. Do you remember, my friends, some few years ago, a picture that was published in Paris and London? Everybody bought it; everyone said: 'He is a made man, this fellow who can paint so fine.' "

"To what picture do you refer?" asked Dr. Kreener.

"It was called 'A Dream at Dawn.' "

As he spoke the words I saw Andrews start forward, and Dr. Kreener exchanged a swift glance with him. But the Scotsman, unseen by the vainglorious half-caste, shook his head fiercely.

The picture to which Tchériapin referred will, of course, be perfectly familiar to you. It had phenomenal popularity some eight years ago. Nothing was known of the painter—whose name was Colquhoun—and nothing has been seen of his work since. The original painting was never sold, and after a time this promising new artist was, of course, forgotten.

Presently Tchériapin continued:

"It is the figure of a slender girl—ah! angels of grace!—what a girl!" He kissed his hand rapturously. "She is posed bending gracefully forward, and looking down at her own lovely reflection in the water. It is a seashore, you remember, and the little ripples play about her ankles. The first blush of the dawn robes her white body in a transparent mantle of light. Ah! God's mercy! it was as she stood so, in a little cove of Normandy, that I saw her!"

He paused, rolling his dark eyes; and I could hear Andrews's heavy breathing; then:

"It was the 'new art'—the posing of the model not in a lighted studio, but in the scene to be depicted. And the fellow who painted her!—the man with the barbarous name! Bah! he was big—as big as our Mr. Andrews—and ugly—pooh! uglier than he! A moon-face, with cropped skull like a prize-fighter and no soul. But yes, he could paint. 'A Dream at Dawn' was genius—yes, some soul he must have had.

"He could paint, dear friends, but he could not love. Him I counted as—puff!"

He blew imaginary down into space.

"Her I sought out, and presently found. She told me, in those sweet stolen rambles along the shore, when the moonlight made her look like a Madonna, that she was his inspiration—his art—his life. And she wept; she wept, and I kissed her tears away.

"To please her I waited until 'A Dream at Dawn' was finished. With the finish of the picture, finished also *his* dream of dawn—the moon-faced one's."

Tchériapin laughed, and lighted a fresh cigarette.

"Can you believe that a man could be so stupid? He never knew of my existence, this big, red booby. He never knew that I existed until—until 'his dream' had fled—with me! In a week we were in Paris, that dream-girl and I—in a month we had quarrelled. I always end these matters with a quarrel; it makes the complete finish. She struck me in the face—and I laughed. She turned and went away. We were tired of one another.

"Ah!" Again he airily kissed his hand. "There were others after I had gone. I heard for a time. But her memory is like a rose, fresh and fair and sweet. I am glad I can remember her so, and not as she afterwards became. That is the art of love. She killed herself with absinthe, my friends. She died in Marseilles in the first year of the great war."

Thus far Tchériapin had proceeded, and was in the act of airily flicking ash upon the floor, when, uttering a sound which I can only describe as a roar, Andrews hurled himself upon the smiling violinist.

His great red hands clutching Tchériapin's throat, the insane Scotsman, for insane he was at that moment, forced the other back upon the settee from which he had half arisen. In vain I sought to drag him away from the writhing body, but I doubt if any man could have relaxed that deadly grip. Tchériapin's eyes protruded hideously and his tongue lolled forth from his mouth. One could hear the breath whistling through his nostrils as Andrews silently, deliberately, squeezed the life out of him.

It all occupied only a few minutes, and then Andrews, slowly opening his rigidly crooked fingers, stood panting and looking down at the distorted face of the dead man.

For once in his life the Scotsman was sober, and turning to Dr. Kreener:

"I have waited seven long years for this," he said, "and I'll hang wi' contentment."

I can never forget the ensuing moments, in which, amid a horrible silence only broken by the ticking of a clock, and the heavy breathing of Colquhoun (so long known to us as Andrews) we stood watching the contorted body on the settee.

And as we watched, slowly the rigid limbs began to relax, and Tchériapin slid gently on to the floor, collapsing there with a soft thud, where he squatted like some hideous Buddha, resting back against the cushions, one spectral yellow hand upraised, the fingers still clutching a big gold tassel.

Andrews (for so I always think of him) was seized with a violent fit of trembling, and he dropped into the chair from which he had made that dreadful spring, muttering to himself and looking down wild-eyed at his twitching fingers. Then he began to laugh, high-pitched laughter, in little short peals.

"Here!" cried the doctor sharply. "Drop that!"

Crossing to Andrews he grasped him by the shoulders and shook him roughly.

The laughter ceased, and—

"Send for the police," said Andrews in a queer, shaky voice. "Dinna fear but I'm ready. I'm only sorry it happened here."

"You ought to be glad," said Dr. Kreener.

There was a covert meaning in the words—a fact which penetrated even to the dulled intelligence of the Scotsman, for he glanced up haggardly at his friend.

"You ought to be glad," repeated Dr. Kreener.

Turning, he walked to the laboratory door and locked it. He next lowered all the blinds.

"I pray that we have not been overlooked," he said, "but we must chance it."

He mixed a drink for Andrews and himself. His quiet decisive manner had had its effect, and Andrews was now more composed. Indeed, he seemed to be in a half-dazed condition; but he persistently kept his back turned to the crouching figure propped up against the settee.

"If you think you can follow me," said Dr. Kreener abruptly, "I will show you the result of a recent experiment."

Unlocking a cupboard he took out a tiny figure some two inches long by one inch high, mounted upon a polished wooden pedestal. It was that of a guinea-pig. The flaky fur gleamed like the finest silk, and one felt that the coat of the minute creature would be as floss to the touch; whereas in reality it possessed the rigidity of steel. Literally one could have done it little damage with a hammer. Its weight was extraordinary.

"I am learning new things about this process every day," continued Dr. Kreener, placing the little figure upon a table. "For instance, whilst it seems to operate uniformly upon vegetable matter, there are curious modifications where one applies it to animal and mineral substances. I have now definitely decided that the result of this particular enquiry must never be published. You, Colquhoun, I believe, possess an example of the process, a tiger lily, I think? I must ask you to return it to me. Our late friend, Tchériapin, wears a pink rose in his coat which I have treated in the same way. I am going to take the liberty of removing it."

He spoke in the hard, incisive manner which I had heard him use in the lecture theatre, and it was evident enough that his design was to prepare

Andrews for something which he contemplated. Facing the Scotsman where he sat hunched up in the big armchair, dully watching the speaker:

"There is one experiment," said Dr. Kreener, speaking very deliberately, "which I have never before had a suitable opportunity of attempting. Of its result I am personally confident, but science always demands proof."

His voice rang now with a note of repressed excitement. He paused for a moment, and then:

"If you were to examine this little specimen very closely," he said, and rested his finger upon the tiny figure of the guinea-pig, "you would find that in one particular it is imperfect. Although a diamond drill would have to be employed to demonstrate the fact, the animal's organs, despite their having undergone a chemical change quite new to science, are intact, perfect down to the smallest detail. One part of the creature's structure alone defied my process. In short, *dental enamel* is impervious to it. This little animal, otherwise as complete as when it lived and breathed, has no teeth. I found it necessary to extract them before submitting the body to the reductionary process."

He paused.

"Shall I go on?" he asked.

Andrews, to whose mind, I think, no conception of the doctor's project had yet penetrated, shuddered, but slowly nodded his head.

Dr. Kreener glanced across the laboratory at the crouching figure of Tchériapin, then, resting his hands upon Andrews's shoulders, he pushed him back in the chair and stared into his dull eyes.

"Brace yourself, Colquhoun," he said tersely.

Turning, he crossed to a small mahogany cabinet at the farther end of the room. Pulling out a glass tray he judicially selected a pair of dental forceps.

II

"The Black Mass"

Thus far the stranger's appalling story had progressed when that singular cloak in which hypnotically he had enwrapped me seemed to drop, and I found myself clutching the edge of the table and staring into the grey face of the speaker.

I became suddenly aware of the babel of voices about me, of the noisome smell of Malay Jack's, and of the presence of Jack in person, who was enquiring if there were any further orders. I was conscious of nausea.

"Excuse me," I said, rising unsteadily, "but I fear the oppressive atmosphere is affecting me."

"If you prefer to go out," said my acquaintance, in that deep voice which throughout the dreadful story had rendered me oblivious of my surroundings, "I should be much favoured if you would accompany me to a spot not five hundred yards from here."

Seeing me hesitate:

"I have a particular reason for asking," he added.

"Very well," I replied, inclining my head, "if you wish it. But certainly I must seek the fresh air."

Going up the steps and out through the door above which the blue lantern burned, we came to the street, turned to the left, to the left again, and soon were threading that maze of narrow ways which complicates the map of Pennyfields.

I felt somewhat recovered. Here, in the narrow but familiar highways the spell of my singular acquaintance lost much of its potency, and I already found myself doubting the story of Dr. Kreener and Tchériapin. Indeed, I began to laugh at myself, conceiving that I had fallen into the hands of some comedian who was making sport of me; although why such a person should visit Malay Jack's was not apparent.

I was about to give expression to these new and saner ideas when my companion paused before a door half hidden in a little alley which divided the back of a Chinese restaurant from the tawdry-looking establishment of a cigar merchant. He apparently held the key, for although I did not actually hear the turning of the lock I saw that he had opened the door.

"May I request you to follow me?" came his deep voice out of the darkness. "I will show you something which will repay your trouble."

Again the cloak touched me, but it was without entirely resigning myself to the compelling influence that I followed my mysterious acquaintance up an uncarpeted and nearly dark stair. On the landing above a gas lamp was burning, and opening a door immediately facing the stair the stranger conducted me into a barely furnished and untidy room.

The atmosphere smelled like that of a pot-house, the odours of stale spirits and of tobacco mingling unpleasantly. As my guide removed his hat and stood there, a square, gaunt figure in his queer, caped overcoat, I secured for the first time a view of his face in profile; and found it to be startlingly unfamiliar. Seen thus, my acquaintance was another man. I realized that there was something unnatural about the long, white hair, the grey face; that the sharp outline of brow, nose and chin was that of a much younger man than I had supposed him to be.

All this came to me in a momentary flash of perception, for immediately my attention was riveted upon a figure hunched up on a dilapidated sofa on the opposite side of the room. It was that of a big man, bearded and very heavily built, but whose face was scarred as by years of suffering, and whose eyes confirmed the story indicated by the smell of stale spirits with which the air of the room was laden. A nearly empty bottle stood on a table at his elbow, a glass beside it, and a pipe lay in a saucer full of ashes near the glass.

As we entered, the glazed eyes of the man opened widely and he clutched at the table with big red hands, leaning forward and staring horribly.

Saving this derelict figure and some few dirty utensils and scattered garments which indicated that the apartment was used both as a sleeping and living room, there was so little of interest in the place that automatically my wandering gaze strayed from the figure on the sofa to a large oil painting, unframed, which rested upon the mantelpiece above the dirty grate, in which the fire had become extinguished.

I uttered a stifled exclamation. It was "A Dream at Dawn"—evidently the original painting!

On the left of it, from a nail in the wall, hung a violin and bow, and on the right stood a sort of cylindrical glass case or closed jar upon a wooden base.

From the moment that I perceived the contents of this glass case a sense of fantasy claimed me, and I ceased to know where reality ended and mirage began.

It contained a tiny and perfect figure of a man. He was arrayed in a beautifully fitting dress-suit such as a doll might have worn, and he was posed as if in the act of playing a violin, although no violin was present. At the elfin black hair and Mephistophelian face of this horrible, wonderful image, I stared fascinatedly.

I looked and looked at the dwarfed figure of . . . *Tchériapin!*

All these impressions came to me in the space of a few hectic moments, when in upon my mental tumult intruded a husky whisper from the man on the sofa.

"Kreener!" he said. *"Kreener!"*

At the sound of that name, and because of the way in which it was pronounced, I felt my blood running cold. The speaker was staring straight at my companion.

I clutched at the open door. I felt that there was still some crowning horror to come. I wanted to escape from that reeking room, but my muscles refused to obey me, and there I stood whilst:

"Kreener!" repeated the husky voice, and I saw that the speaker was rising unsteadily to his feet. "You have brought him again. Why have you brought him again? He will play. He will play me a step nearer to Hell!"

"Brace yourself, Colquhoun," said the voice of my companion. "Brace yourself."

"Take him awa'!" came in a sudden frenzied shriek. "Take him awa'! He's there at your elbow, Kreener, mockin' me, and pointing to that damned violin."

"Here!" said the stranger, a high note of command in his voice. "Drop that! Sit down at once."

Even as the other obeyed him, the cloaked stranger, stepping to the mantelpiece, opened a small box which lay there beside the glass case. He turned to me; and I tried to shrink away from him. For I knew—I knew—yet I loathed to look upon—what was in the box. Muffled as though reaching me through fog, I heard the words:

"A perfect human body . . . in miniature . . . every organ intact by means of . . . process . . . rendered indestructible. Tchériapin as he was in life may be seen by the curious, ten thousand years hence. Incomplete . . . one respect . . . here in this box . . ."

The spell was broken by a horrifying shriek from the man whom my companion had addressed as Colquhoun, and whom I could only suppose to be the painter of the celebrated picture which rested upon the mantel shelf.

"Take him awa,' Kreener! He is reaching for the violin!"

Animation returned to me, and I fell rather than ran down the darkened stair. How I opened the street door I know not, but even as I stepped out into the squalid alleys of Pennyfields the cloaked figure was beside me. A hand was laid upon my shoulder.

"Listen!" commanded a deep voice.

Clearly, with an eerie sweetness, an evil, hellish beauty indescribable, the wailing of a Stradivarius violin crept to my ears from the room above. Slowly—slowly the music began, and my soul rose up in revolt.

"Listen!" repeated the voice. "Listen! It is 'The Black Mass'!"

LOLA RIDGE

A SELECTION FROM
SUN-UP AND OTHER POEMS

My doll Janie has no waist
and her body is like a tub with feet on it.
Sometimes I beat her
but I always kiss her afterwards.
When I have kissed all the paint off her body
I shall tie a ribbon about it
so she shan't look shabby.
But it must be blue—
it mustn't be pink—
pink shows the dirt on her face
that won't wash off.

I beat Janie
and beat her . . .
but still she smiled . . .
so I scratched her between the eyes with a pin.
Now she doesn't love me any more . . .
she scowls . . . and scowls . . .
though I've begged her to forgive me
and poured sugar in the hole at the back of her head.

W. W. JACOBS

THE MONKEY'S PAW

I

Without, the night was cold and wet, but in the small parlour of Laburnum Villa the blinds were drawn and the fire burned brightly. Father and son were at chess; the former, who possessed ideas about the game involving radical changes, putting his king into such sharp and unnecessary perils that it even provoked comment from the white-haired old lady knitting placidly by the fire.

"Hark at the wind," said Mr. White, who, having seen a fatal mistake after it was too late, was amiably desirous of preventing his son from seeing it.

"I'm listening," said the latter, grimly surveying the board as he stretched out his hand. "Check."

"I should hardly think that he'd come to-night," said his father, with his hand poised over the board.

"Mate," replied the son.

"That's the worst of living so far out," bawled Mr. White, with sudden and unlooked-for violence; "of all the beastly, slushy, out-of-the-way places to live in, this is the worst. Path's a bog, and the road's a torrent. I don't know what people are thinking about. I suppose because only two houses in the road are let, they think it doesn't matter."

"Never mind, dear," said his wife soothingly; "perhaps you'll win the next one."

Mr. White looked up sharply, just in time to intercept a knowing glance between mother and son. The words died away on his lips, and he hid a guilty grin in his thin gray beard.

"There he is," said Herbert White, as the gate banged to loudly and heavy footsteps came toward the door.

The old man rose with hospitable haste, and opening the door, was heard condoling with the new arrival. The new arrival also condoled with himself, so that Mrs. White said, "Tut tut!" and coughed gently as her husband entered the room, followed by a tall, burly man, beady of eye and rubicund of visage.

"Sergeant-Major Morris," he said, introducing him.

The sergeant-major shook hands, and taking the proffered seat by the fire, watched contentedly while his host got out whisky and tumblers and stood a small copper kettle on the fire.

At the third glass his eyes got brighter, and he began to talk, the little family circle regarding with eager interest this visitor from distant parts, as he squared his broad shoulders in the chair, and spoke of wild scenes and doughty deeds; of wars and plagues, and strange peoples.

"Twenty-one years of it," said Mr. White, nodding at his wife and son. "When he went away he was a slip of a youth in the warehouse. Now look at him."

"He don't look to have taken much harm," said Mrs. White politely.

"I'd like to go to India myself," said the old man, "just to look around a bit, you know."

"Better where you are," said the sergeant-major, shaking his head. He put down the empty glass, and sighing softly, shook it again.

"I should like to see those old temples and fakirs and jugglers," said the old man. "What was that you started telling me the other day about a monkey's paw or something, Morris?"

"Nothing," said the soldier hastily. "Leastways nothing worth hearing."

"Monkey's paw?" said Mrs. White curiously.

"Well, it's just a bit of what you might call magic, perhaps," said the sergeant-major off-handedly.

His three listeners leaned forward eagerly. The visitor absent-mindedly put his empty glass to his lips and then set it down again. His host filled it for him.

"To look at," said the sergeant-major, fumbling in his pocket, "it's just an ordinary little paw, dried to a mummy."

He took something out of his pocket and proffered it. Mrs. White drew back with a grimace, but her son, taking it, examined it curiously.

"And what is there special about it?" inquired Mr. White as he took it from his son, and having examined it, placed it upon the table.

"It had a spell put on it by an old fakir," said the sergeant-major, "a very holy man. He wanted to show that fate ruled people's lives, and that those who interfered with it did so to their sorrow. He put a spell on it so that three separate men could each have three wishes from it."

His manner was so impressive that his hearers were conscious that their light laughter jarred somewhat.

"Well, why don't you have three, sir?" said Herbert White cleverly.

The soldier regarded him in the way that middle age is wont to regard presumptuous youth. "I have," he said quietly, and his blotchy face whitened.

"And did you really have the three wishes granted?" asked Mrs. White.

"I did," said the sergeant-major, and his glass tapped against his strong teeth.

"And has anybody else wished?" persisted the old lady.

"The first man had his three wishes. Yes," was the reply; "I don't know what the first two were, but the third was for death. That's how I got the paw."

His tones were so grave that a hush fell upon the group.

"If you've had your three wishes, it's no good to you now then, Morris," said the old man at last. "What do you keep it for?"

The soldier shook his head. "Fancy, I suppose," he said slowly. "I did have some idea of selling it, but I don't think I will. It has caused enough mischief already. Besides, people won't buy. They think it's a fairy tale, some of them; and those who do think anything of it want to try it first and pay me afterward."

"If you could have another three wishes," said the old man, eyeing him keenly, "would you have them?"

"I don't know," said the other. "I don't know."

He took the paw, and dangling it between his forefinger and thumb, suddenly threw it upon the fire. White, with a slight cry, stooped down and snatched it off.

"Better let it burn," said the soldier solemnly.

"If you don't want it, Morris," said the other, "give it to me."

"I won't," said his friend doggedly. "I threw it on the fire. If you keep it, don't blame me for what happens. Pitch it on the fire again like a sensible man."

The other shook his head and examined his new possession closely. "How do you do it?" he inquired.

"Hold it up in your right hand and wish aloud," said the sergeant-major, "but I warn you of the consequences."

"Sounds like the *Arabian Nights*," said Mrs. White, as she rose and began to set the supper. "Don't you think you might wish for four pairs of hands for me?"

Her husband drew the talisman from his pocket, and then all three burst into laughter as the sergeant-major, with a look of alarm on his face, caught him by the arm.

"If you must wish," he said gruffly, "wish for something sensible."

Mr. White dropped it back in his pocket, and placing chairs, motioned his friend to the table. In the business of supper the talisman was partly forgotten, and afterward the three sat listening in an enthralled fashion to a second installment of the soldier's adventures in India.

"If the tale about the monkey's paw is not more truthful than those he has been telling us," said Herbert, as the door closed behind their guest, just in time to catch the last train, "we shan't make much out of it."

"Did you give him anything for it, father?" inquired Mrs. White, regarding her husband closely.

"A trifle," said he, colouring slightly. "He didn't want it, but I made him take it. And he pressed me again to throw it away."

"Likely," said Herbert, with pretended horror. "Why, we're going to be rich, and famous, and happy. Wish to be an emperor, father, to begin with; then you can't be henpecked."

He darted round the table, pursued by the maligned Mrs. White armed with an antimacassar.

Mr. White took the paw from his pocket and eyed it dubiously. "I don't know what to wish for, and that's a fact," he said slowly. "It seems to me I've got all I want."

"If you only cleared the house, you'd be quite happy, wouldn't you!" said Herbert, with his hand on his shoulder. "Well, wish for two hundred pounds, then; that'll just do it."

His father, smiling shamefacedly at his own credulity, held up the talisman, as his son, with a solemn face, somewhat marred by a wink at his mother, sat down at the piano and struck a few impressive chords.

"I wish for two hundred pounds," said the old man distinctly.

A fine crash from the piano greeted the words, interrupted by a shuddering cry from the old man. His wife and son ran toward him.

"It moved," he cried, with a glance of disgust at the object as it lay on the floor. "As I wished, it twisted in my hand like a snake."

"Well, I don't see the money," said his son, as he picked it up and placed it on the table, "and I bet I never shall."

"It must have been your fancy, father," said his wife, regarding him anxiously.

He shook his head. "Never mind, though; there's no harm done, but it gave me a shock all the same."

They sat down by the fire again while the two men finished their pipes. Outside, the wind was higher than ever, and the old man started nervously at the sound of a door banging upstairs. A silence unusual and depressing settled upon all three, which lasted until the old couple rose to retire for the night.

"I expect you'll find the cash tied up in a big bag in the middle of your bed," said Herbert, as he bade them good night, "and something horrible squatting up on top of the wardrobe watching you pocket your ill-gotten gains."

He sat alone in the darkness, gazing at the dying fire, and seeing faces in it. The last face was so horrible and so simian that he gazed at it with amazement. It got so vivid that, with a little uneasy laugh, he felt on the table for a glass containing a little water to throw over it. His hand grasped the monkey's paw, and with a little shiver he wiped his hand on his coat and went up to bed.

II

In the brightness of the wintery sun next morning as it streamed over the breakfast table he laughed at his fears. There was an air of prosaic wholesomeness about the room which it had lacked on the previous night, and the dirty, shrivelled little paw was pitched on the side-board with a carelessness which betokened no great belief in its virtues.

"I suppose all old soldiers are the same," said Mrs. White. "The idea of our listening to such nonsense! How could wishes be granted in these days? And if they could, how could two hundred pounds hurt you, father?"

"Might drop on his head from the sky," said the frivolous Herbert.

"Morris said the things happened so naturally," said his father, "that you might if you so wished attribute it to coincidence."

"Well, don't break into the money before I come back," said Herbert as he rose from the table. "I'm afraid it'll turn you into a mean, avaricious man, and we will have to disown you."

His mother laughed, and following him to the door, watched him down the road; and returning to the breakfast table, was very happy at the expense of her husband's credulity. All of which did not prevent her from scurrying to the door at the postman's knock, nor prevent her from referring somewhat shortly to retired sergeant-majors of bibulous habits when she found that the post brought a tailor's bill.

"Herbert will have some more of his funny remarks, I expect, when he comes home," she said, as they sat at dinner.

"I dare say," said Mr. White, pouring himself out some beer; "but for all that, the thing moved in my hand; that I'll swear to."

"You thought it did," said the old lady soothingly.

"I say it did," replied the other. "There was no thought about it; I had just—What's the matter?"

His wife made no reply. She was watching the mysterious movements of a man outside, who, peering in an undecided fashion at the house, appeared to be trying to make up his mind to enter. In mental connection with the two hundred pounds, she noticed that the stranger was well dressed, and wore a silk hat of glossy newness. Three times he paused at the gate, and then walked on again. The fourth time he stood with his hand upon it, and then with a sudden resolution flung it open and walked up the path. Mrs. White at the same moment placed her hands behind her, and hurriedly unfastening the strings on her apron, put that useful article of apparel beneath the cushion of her chair.

She brought the stranger, who seemed ill at ease, into the room. He gazed at her furtively, and listened in a preoccupied fashion as the old lady apologized for the appearance of the room, and her husband's coat, a garment he usually reserved for the garden. She then waited as patiently as her sex would permit, for him to broach his business, but he was at first strangely silent.

"I—was asked to call," he said at last, and stooped and picked a piece of cotton from his trousers. "I come from 'Maw and Meggins.'"

The old lady started. "Is anything the matter?" she asked breathlessly. "Has anything happened to Herbert? What is it? What is it?"

Her husband interposed. "There, there, mother," he said hastily. "Sit down, and don't jump to conclusions. You've not brought bad news, I'm sure, sir"; and he eyed the other wistfully.

"I'm sorry—" began the visitor.

"Is he hurt?" demanded the mother wildly.

The visitor bowed in assent. "Badly hurt," he said quietly, "but he is not in any pain."

"Oh, thank God!" said the old woman, clasping her hands. "Thank God for that! Thank—"

She broke off suddenly as the sinister meaning of the assurance dawned upon her, and she saw the awful confirmation of her fears in the other's averted face. She caught her breath, and turning to her slower-witted husband, laid her trembling old hand upon his. There was a long silence.

"He was caught in the machinery," said the visitor at length in a low voice.

"Caught in the machinery," repeated Mr. White, in a dazed fashion, "yes."

He sat staring blankly out at the window, and taking his wife's hand between his own, pressed it as he had been wont to do in their old courting days nearly forty years before.

"He was the only one left to us," he said, turning gently to the visitor. "It is hard."

The other coughed, and rising, walked slowly to the window.

"The firm wished me to convey their sincere sympathy with you in your great loss," he said, without looking round. "I beg that you will understand I am only their servant and merely obeying orders."

There was no reply; the old woman's face was white, her eyes staring, and her breath inaudible; on the husband's face was a look such as his friend the sergeant might have carried into his first action.

"I was to say that Maw and Meggins disclaim all responsibility," continued the other. "They admit no liability at all, but in consideration of your son's services, they wish to present you with a certain sum as compensation."

Mr. White dropped his wife's hand, and rising to his feet, gazed with a look of horror at his visitor. His dry lips shaped the words, "How much?"

"Two hundred pounds," was the answer.

Unconscious of his wife's shriek, the old man smiled faintly, put out his hands like a sightless man, and dropped, a senseless heap, to the floor.

III

In the huge new cemetery, some two miles distant, the old people buried their dead, and came back to the house steeped in shadow and silence. It was all over so quickly that at first they could hardly realise it, and remained in a state of expectation as though of something else to happen—something else which was to lighten this load, too heavy for old hearts to bear.

But the days passed, and expectation gave place to resignation—the hopeless resignation of the old, sometimes miscalled apathy. Sometimes they hardly exchanged a word, for now they had nothing to talk about, and their days were long to weariness.

It was about a week after, that the old man, waking suddenly in the night, stretched out his hand and found himself alone. The room was in darkness, and the sound of subdued weeping came from the window. He raised himself in bed and listened.

"Come back," he said tenderly. "You will be cold."

"It is colder for my son," said the old woman, and wept afresh.

The sound of her sobs died away on his ears. The bed was warm, and his eyes heavy with sleep. He dozed fitfully, and then slept until a sudden wild cry from his wife awoke him with a start.

"The paw!" she cried wildly. "The monkey's paw!"

He started up in alarm. "Where? Where is it? What's the matter?"

She came stumbling across the room toward him. "I want it," she said quietly. "You've not destroyed it?"

"It's in the parlour, on the bracket," he replied, marvelling. "Why?"

She cried and laughed together, and bending over, kissed his cheek.

"I only just thought of it," she said hysterically. "Why didn't I think of it before? Why didn't *you* think of it?"

"Think of what?" he questioned.

"The other two wishes," she replied rapidly. "We've only had one."

"Was not that enough?" he demanded fiercely.

"No," she cried triumphantly; "we'll have one more. Go down and get it quickly, and wish our boy alive again."

The man sat up in bed and flung the bedclothes from his quaking limbs. "Good God, you are mad!" he cried, aghast.

"Get it," she panted; "get it quickly, and wish— Oh, my boy, my boy!"

Her husband struck a match and lit the candle. "Get back to bed," he said unsteadily. "You don't know what you are saying."

"We had the first wish granted," said the old woman feverishly; "why not the second?"

"A coincidence," stammered the old man.

"Go and get it and wish," cried his wife, quivering with excitement.

The old man turned and regarded her, and his voice shook. "He has been dead ten days, and besides he—I would not tell you else, but—I could only recognize him by his clothing. If he was too terrible for you to see then, how now?"

"Bring him back," cried the old woman, and dragged him toward the door. "Do you think I fear the child I have nursed?"

He went down in the darkness, and felt his way to the parlour, and then to the mantelpiece. The talisman was in its place, and a horrible fear that the unspoken wish might bring his mutilated son before him ere he could escape from the room seized upon him, and he caught his breath as he found that he had lost the direction of the door. His brow cold with sweat, he felt his way round the table, and groped along the wall until he found himself in the small passage with the unwholesome thing in his hand.

Even his wife's face seemed changed as he entered the room. It was white and expectant, and to his fears seemed to have an unnatural look upon it. He was afraid of her.

"Wish!" she cried, in a strong voice.

"It is foolish and wicked," he faltered.

"Wish!" repeated his wife.

He raised his hand. "I wish my son alive again."

The talisman fell to the floor, and he regarded it fearfully. Then he sank trembling into a chair as the old woman, with burning eyes, walked to the window and raised the blind.

He sat until he was chilled with the cold, glancing occasionally at the figure of the old woman peering through the window. The candle-end, which had burned below the rim of the china candlestick, was throwing pulsating shadows on the ceiling and walls, until, with a flicker larger than the rest it expired. The old man, with an unspeakable sense of relief at the failure of the talisman, crept back to his bed, and a minute or two afterward the old woman came silently and apathetically beside him.

Neither spoke, but lay silently listening to the ticking of the clock. A stair creaked, and a squeaky mouse scurried noisily through the wall. The darkness was oppressive, and after lying for some time screwing up his courage, he took the box of matches, and striking one, went downstairs for a candle.

At the foot of the stairs the match went out, and he paused to strike another; and at the same moment a knock, so quiet and stealthy as to be scarcely audible, sounded on the front door.

The matches fell from his hand and spilled in the passage. He stood motionless, his breath suspended until the knock was repeated. Then he turned and fled swiftly back to his room, and closed the door behind him. A third knock sounded through the house.

"What's that?" cried the old woman, starting up.

"A rat," said the old man in shaking tones—"a rat. It passed me on the stairs."

His wife sat up in bed listening. A loud knock resounded through the house.

"It's Herbert!" she screamed. "It's Herbert!"

She ran to the door, but her husband was before her, and catching her by the arm, held her tightly.

"What are you going to do?" he whispered hoarsely.

"It's my boy; it's Herbert!" she cried, struggling mechanically. "I forgot it was two miles away. What are you holding me for? Let go. I must open the door."

"For God's sake don't let it in," cried the old man, trembling.

"You're afraid of your own son," she cried, struggling. "Let me go. I'm coming, Herbert; I'm coming."

There was another knock, and another. The old woman with a sudden wrench broke free and ran from the room. Her husband followed to the landing, and called after her appealingly as she hurried downstairs. He heard the chain rattle back and the bottom bolt drawn slowly and stiffly from the socket. Then the old woman's voice strained and panting.

"The bolt," she cried loudly. "Come down. I can't reach it."

But her husband was on his hands and knees groping wildly on the floor in search of the paw. If he could only find it before the thing outside got in.

A perfect fusillade of knocks reverberated through the house, and he heard the scraping of a chair as his wife put it down in the passage against the door. He heard the creaking of the bolt as it came slowly back, and at the same moment he found the monkey's paw, and frantically breathed his third and last wish.

The knocking ceased suddenly, although the echoes of it were still in the house. He heard the chair drawn back, and the door opened. A cold wind rushed up the staircase, and a long loud wail of disappointment and misery from his wife gave him courage to run down to her side, and then to the gate beyond. The street lamp flickering opposite shone on a quiet and deserted road.

RUDYARD KIPLING

THE MARK OF
THE BEAST

Your Gods and my Gods—do you or I know which are the stronger?

Native Proverb

East of Suez, some hold, the direct control of Providence ceases; Man being there handed over to the power of the Gods and Devils of Asia, and the Church of England Providence only exercising occasional and modified supervision in the case of Englishmen.

This theory accounts for some of the more unnecessary horrors of life in India: it may be stretched to explain my story.

My friend Strickland of the Police, who knows as much of natives of India as is good for any man, can bear witness to the facts of the case. Dumoise, our doctor, also saw what Strickland and I saw. The inference which he drew from the evidence was entirely incorrect. He is dead now; he died in a rather curious manner, which has been elsewhere described.

When Fleete came to India he owned a little money and some land in the Himalayas near a place called Dharmsala. Both properties had been left him by an uncle, and he came out to finance them. He was a big, heavy, genial, and inoffensive man. His knowledge of natives was, of course, limited, and he complained of the difficulties of the language.

He rode in from his place in the hills to spend New Year in the station, and he stayed with Strickland. On New Year's Eve there was a big dinner at the club, and the night was excusably wet. When men foregather from the uttermost ends of the Empire, they have a right to be riotous. The Frontier had sent down a contingent o' Catch-'em-Alive-O's who had not seen twenty white faces for a year, and were used to ride fifteen miles to dinner at the next Fort at the risk of a Khyberee bullet where their drinks should lie. They profited by their new security, for they tried to play pool with a curled-up hedgehog found in the garden, and one of them carried the marker round the room in his teeth. Half a dozen planters had come in from the south and were talking "horse" to the Biggest Liar in Asia, who was trying to cap all their stories at once. Everybody was there, and there was a general closing up of ranks and taking stock of our losses in dead or disabled that had fallen during the past year. It was a very wet night, and I remember that we sang "Auld Lang Syne" with our feet in the Polo Championship Cup, and our heads among the stars, and swore that we were all dear friends. Then some of us went away and annexed Burma, and some tried to open up the Soudan and were opened up by Fuzzies in that cruel scrub outside Suakim, and

243

some found stars and medals, and some were married, which was bad, and some did other things which were worse, and the others of us stayed in our chains and strove to make money on insufficient experiences.

Fleete began the night with sherry and bitters, drank champagne steadily up to dessert, then raw, rasping Capri with all the strength of whiskey, took Benedictine with his coffee, four or five whiskies and sodas to improve his pool strokes, beer and bones at half-past two, winding up with old brandy. Consequently, when he came out, at half-past three in the morning, into fourteen degrees of frost, he was very angry with his horse for coughing, and tried to leapfrog into the saddle. The horse broke away and went to his stables; so Strickland and I formed a Guard of Dishonour to take Fleete home.

Our road lay through the bazar, close to a little temple of Hanuman, the Monkey-god, who is a leading divinity worthy of respect. All gods have good points, just as have all priests. Personally, I attach much importance to Hanuman, and am kind to his people—the great gray apes of the hills. One never knows when one may want a friend.

There was a light in the temple, and as we passed we could hear voices of men chanting hymns. In a native temple the priests rise at all hours of the night to do honour to their god. Before we could stop him, Fleete dashed up the steps, patted two priests on the back, and was gravely grinding the ashes of his cigar-butt into the forehead of the red stone image of Hanuman. Strickland tried to drag him out, but he sat down and said solemnly:

"Shee that? 'Mark of the B-beasht! I made it. Ishn't it fine?"

In half a minute the temple was alive and noisy, and Strickland, who knew what came of polluting gods, said that things might occur. He, by virtue of his official position, long residence in the country, and weakness for going among the natives, was known to the priests, and he felt unhappy. Fleete sat on the ground and refused to move. He said that "good old Hanuman" made a very soft pillow.

Then, without any warning, a Silver Man came out of a recess behind the image of the god. He was perfectly naked in that bitter, bitter cold, and his body shone like frosted silver, for he was what the Bible calls "a leper as white as snow." Also he had no face, because he was a leper of some years' standing, and his disease was heavy upon him. We two stooped to haul Fleete up, and the temple was filling and filling with folk who seemed to spring from the earth, when the Silver Man ran in under our arms, making a noise exactly like the mewing of an otter, caught Fleete round the body and dropped his head on Fleete's breast before we could wrench him away. Then he retired to a corner and sat mewing while the crowd blocked all the doors.

The priests were very angry until the Silver Man touched Fleete. That nuzzling seemed to sober them.

At the end of a few minutes' silence one of the priests came to Strickland and said, in perfect English, "Take your friend away. He has done with

Hanuman, but Hanuman has not done with him." The crowd gave room and we carried Fleete into the road.

Strickland was very angry. He said that we might all three have been knifed, and that Fleete should thank his stars that he had escaped without injury.

Fleete thanked no one. He said that he wanted to go to bed. He was gorgeously drunk.

We moved on, Strickland silent and wrathful, until Fleete was taken with violent shivering fits and sweating. He said that the smells of the bazar were overpowering, and he wondered why slaughterhouses were permitted so near English residences.

"Can't you smell the blood?" said Fleete.

We put him to bed at last, just as the dawn was breaking, and Strickland invited me to have another whiskey and soda. While we were drinking he talked of the trouble in the temple, and admitted that it baffled him completely. Strickland hates being mystified by natives, because his business in life is to overmatch them with their own weapons. He has not yet succeeded in doing this, but in fifteen or twenty years he will have made some small progress.

"They should have mauled us," he said, "instead of mewing at us. I wonder what they meant. I don't like it one little bit."

I said that the Managing Committee of the temple would in all probability bring a criminal action against us for insulting their religion. There was a section of the Indian Penal Code which exactly met Fleete's offence. Strickland said he only hoped and prayed that they would do this. Before I left I looked into Fleete's room, and saw him lying on his right side, scratching his left breast. Then I went to bed, cold, depressed, and unhappy at seven o'clock in the morning.

At one o'clock I rode over to Strickland's house to inquire after Fleete's head. I imagined that it would be a sore one. Fleete was breakfasting and seemed unwell. His temper was gone, for he was abusing the cook for not supplying him with an underdone chop. A man who can eat raw meat and after a wet night is a curiosity. I told Fleete this, and he laughed.

"You breed queer mosquitoes in these parts," he said. "I've been bitten to pieces, but only in one place."

"Let have a look at the bite," said Strickland. "It may have gone down since this morning."

While the chops were being cooked, Fleete opened his shirt and showed us, just over his left breast, a mark, the perfect double of the black rosettes—the five or six irregular blotches arranged in a circle—on a leopard's hide. Strickland looked and said, "It was only pink this morning. It's grown black now."

Fleete ran to a glass.

"By Jove!" he said, "this is nasty. What is it?"

We could not answer. Here the chops came in, all red and juicy, and

Fleete bolted three in a most offensive manner. He ate on his right grinders only, and threw his head over his right shoulder as he snapped the meat. When he had finished, it struck him that he had been behaving strangely, for he said apologetically, "I don't think I ever felt so hungry in my life. I've bolted like an ostrich."

After breakfast Strickland said to me, "Don't go. Stay here, and stay for the night."

Seeing that my house was not three miles from Strickland's, this request was absurd. But Strickland insisted, and was going to say something when Fleete interrupted by declaring in a shamefaced way that he felt hungry again. Strickland sent a man to my house to fetch over my bedding and a horse, and we three went down to Strickland's stables to pass the hours until it was time to go for a ride. The man who has a weakness for horses never wearies of inspecting them; and when two men are killing time in this way they gather knowledge and lies the one from the other.

There were five horses in the stables, and I shall never forget the scene as we tried to look them over.They seemed to have gone mad. They reared and screamed and nearly tore up their pickets; they sweated and shivered and lathered and were distraught with fear. Strickland's horses used to know him as well as his dogs; which made the matter more curious. We left the stable for fear of the brutes throwing themselves in their panic. Then Strickland turned back and called me. The horses were still frightened, but they let us "gentle" and make much of them, and put their heads in our bosoms.

"They aren't afraid of *us*," said Strickland. "D'you know, I'd give three months' pay if Outrage here could talk."

But Outrage was dumb, and could only cuddle up to his master and blow out his nostrils, as is the custom of horses when they wish to explain things but can't. Fleete came up when we were in the stalls, and as soon as the horses saw him their fright broke out afresh. It was all that we could do to escape from the place unkicked. Strickland said, "They don't seem to love you, Fleete."

"Nonsense," said Fleete; "my mare will follow me like a dog." He went to her; she was in a loose-box; but as he slipped the bars she plunged, knocked him down, and broke away into the garden. I laughed, but Strickland was not amused. He took his moustache in both fists and pulled at it till it nearly came out. Fleete, instead of going off to chase his property, yawned, saying that he felt sleepy. He went to the house to lie down, which was a foolish way of spending New Year's Day.

Strickland sat with me in the stables and asked if I had noticed anything peculiar in Fleete's manner. I said that he ate his food like a beast; but that this might have been the result of living alone in the hills out of the reach of society as refined and elevating as ours, for instance. Strickland was not amused. I do not think that he listened to me, for his next sentence referred to the mark on Fleete's breast, and I said that it might have been caused by blister-flies, or that it was possibly a birth-mark newly born and now visible for the first time. We both agreed that it was unpleasant to look at, and Strickland found occasion to say that I was a fool.

"I çan't tell you what I think now," said he, "because you would call me a madman; but you must stay with me for the next few days, if you can. I want you to watch Fleete, but don't tell me what you think till I have made up my mind."

"But I am dining out to-night," I said.

"So am I," said Strickland, "and so is Fleete. At least if he doesn't change his mind."

We walked about the garden smoking, but saying nothing—because we were friends, and talking spoils good tobacco—till our pipes were out. Then we went to wake up Fleete. He was wide awake and fidgeting about his room.

"I say, I want some more chops," he said. "Can I get them?"

We laughed and said, "Go and change. The ponies will be round in a minute."

"All right," said Fleete. "I'll go when I got the chops—underdone ones, mind."

He seemed to be quite in earnest. It was four o'clock, and we had had breakfast at one; still, for a long time, he demanded those underdone chops. Then he changed into riding clothes and went out into the verandah. His pony—the mare had not been caught—would not let him come near. All three horses were unmanageable—and with fear—and finally Fleete said that he would stay at home and get something to eat. Strickland and I rode out wondering. As we passed the temple of Hanuman, the Silver Man came out and mewed at us.

"He is not one of the regular priests of the temple," said Strickland. "I think I should peculiarly like to lay my hands on him."

There was no spring in our gallop on the racecourse that evening. The horses were stale, and moved as though they had been ridden out.

"The fright after breakfast has been too much for them," said Strickland.

That was the only remark he made through the remainder of the ride. Once or twice I think he swore to himself; but that did not count.

We came back in the dark at seven o'clock, and saw that there were no lights in the bungalow.

"Careless ruffians my servants are!" said Strickland.

My horse reared at something on the carriage-drive, and Fleete stood up under its nose.

"What are you doing, grovelling about the garden?" said Strickland.

But both horses bolted and nearly threw us. We dismounted by the stables and returned to Fleete, who was on his hands and knees under the orange-bushes.

"What the devil's wrong with you?" said Strickland.

"Nothing, nothing in the world," said Fleete, speaking very quickly and thickly. "I've been gardening—botanising, you know. The smell of the earth is delightful. I think I'm going for a walk—a long walk—all night."

Then I saw that there was something excessively out of order somewhere, and I said to Strickland, "I am not dining out."

"Bless you!" said Strickland. "Here, Fleete, get up. You'll catch fever there. Come in to dinner and let's have the lamps lit. We'll all dine at home."

Fleete stood up unwillingly, and said, "No lamps—no lamps. It's much nicer here. Let's dine outside and have some more chops—lots of 'em and underdone—bloody ones with gristle."

Now a December evening in Northern India is bitterly cold, and Fleete's suggestion was that of a maniac.

"Come in," said Strickland sternly. "Come in at once."

Fleete came, and when the lamps were brought, we saw that he was literally plastered with dirt from head to foot. He must have been rolling in the garden. He shrank from the light and went to his room. His eyes were horrible to look at. There was a green light behind them, not in them, if you understand, and the man's lower lip hung down.

Strickland said, "There is going to be trouble—big trouble—to-night. Don't you change your riding-things."

We waited and waited for Fleete's reappearance, and ordered dinner in the meantime. We could hear him moving about his own room, but there was no light there. Presently from the room came the long-drawn howl of a wolf.

People write and talk lightly of blood running cold and hair standing up and things of that kind. Both sensations are too horrible to be trifled with. My heart stopped as though a knife had been driven through it, and Strickland turned as white as the tablecloth.

The howl was repeated, and was answered by another howl far across the fields.

That set the gilded roof on the horror. Strickland dashed into Fleete's room. I followed, and we saw Fleete getting out of the window. He made beast-noises in the back of his throat. He could not answer us when we shouted at him. He spat.

I don't quite remember what followed, but I think that Strickland must have stunned him with the long boot-jack or else I should never have been able to sit on his chest. Fleete could not speak, he could only snarl, and his snarls were those of a wolf, not of a man. The human spirit must have been giving way all day and have died out with the twilight. We were dealing with a beast that had once been Fleete.

The affair was beyond any human and rational experience. I tried to say "Hydrophobia," but the word wouldn't come, because I knew that I was lying.

We bound this beast with leather thongs of the punkah-rope, and tied its thumbs and big toes together, and gagged it with a shoe-horn, which makes a very efficient gag if you know how to arrange it. Then we carried it into the dining-room, and sent a man to Dumoise, the doctor, telling him to come over at once. After we had despatched the messenger and were drawing breath, Strickland said, "It's no good. This isn't any doctor's work." I, also, knew that he spoke the truth.

The beast's head was free, and it threw it about from side to side. Any one entering the room would have believed that we were curing a wolf's pelt. That was the most loathsome accessory of all.

Strickland sat with his chin in the heel of his fist, watching the beast as it wriggled on the ground, but saying nothing. The shirt had been torn open in the scuffle and showed the black rosette mark on the left breast. It stood out like a blister.

In the silence of the watching we heard something without mewing like a she-otter. We both rose to our feet, and, I answer for myself, not Strickland, felt sick—actually and physically sick. We told each other, as did the men in "Pinafore," that it was the cat.

Dumoise arrived, and I never saw a little man so unprofessionally shocked. He said that it was a heart-rending case of hydrophobia, and that nothing could be done. At least any palliative measures would only prolong the agony. The beast was foaming at the mouth. Fleete, as we told Dumoise, had been bitten by dogs once or twice. Any man who keeps half a dozen terriers must expect a nip now and again. Dumoise could offer no help. He could only certify that Fleete was dying of hydrophobia. The beast was then howling, for it had managed to spit out the shoe-horn. Dumoise said that he would be ready to certify to the cause of death, and that the end was certain. He was a good little man, and he offered to remain with us; but Strickland refused the kindness. He did not wish to poison Dumoise's New Year. He would only ask him not to give the real cause of Fleete's death to the public.

So Dumoise left, deeply agitated; and as soon as the noise of the cart-wheels had died away, Strickland told me, in a whisper, his suspicions. They were so wildly improbable that he dared not say them out aloud; and I, who entertained all Strickland's beliefs, was so ashamed of owning to them that I pretended to disbelieve.

"Even if the Silver Man had bewitched Fleete for polluting the image of Hanuman, the punishment could not have fallen so quickly."

As I was whispering this the cry outside the house rose again, and the beast fell into a fresh paroxysm of struggling till we were afraid that the thongs that held it would give way.

"Watch!" said Strickland. "If this happens six times I shall take the law into my own hands. I order you to help me."

He went into his room and came out in a few minutes with the barrels of an old shot-gun, a piece of fishing-line, some thick cord, and his heavy wooden bedstead. I reported that the convulsions had followed the cry by two seconds in each case, and the beast seemed perceptibly weaker.

Strickland muttered, "But he can't take away the life! He can't take away the life!"

I said, though I knew that I was arguing against myself, "It may be a cat. It must be a cat. If the Silver Man is responsible, why does he dare to come here?"

Strickland arranged the wood on the hearth, put the gun-barrels into the glow of the fire, spread the twine on the table, and broke a walking-stick in two. There was one yard of fishing-line, gut, lapped with wire, such as is used for *mabseer*-fishing, and he tied the two ends together in a loop.

Then he said, "How can we catch him? He must be taken alive and unhurt."

I said that we must trust in Providence, and go out softly with polo-sticks into the shrubbery at the front of the house. The man or animal that made the cry was evidently moving round the house as regularly as a night-watchman. We could wait in the bushes till he came by, and knock him over.

Strickland accepted this suggestion, and we slipped out from a bath-room window into the front verandah and then across the carriage-drive into the bushes.

In the moonlight we could see the leper coming round the corner of the house. He was perfectly naked and from time to time he mewed and stopped to dance with his shadow. It was an unattractive sight and thinking of poor Fleete, brought to such degradation by so foul a creature, I put away all my doubts and resolved to help Strickland from the heated gun-barrels to the loop of twine—from the loins to the head and back again—with all tortures that might be needful.

The leper halted in the front porch for a moment and we jumped out on him with the sticks. He was wonderfully strong, and we were afraid that he might escape or be fatally injured before we caught him. We had an idea that lepers were frail creatures, but this proved to be incorrect. Strickland knocked his legs from under him, and I put my foot on his neck. He mewed hideously and even through my riding-boots I could feel that his flesh was not the flesh of a clean man.

He struck at us with his hand and feet-stumps. We looped the lash of a dog-whip round him, under the arm-pits, and dragged him backwards into the hall and so into the dining-room where the beast lay. There we tied him with trunk-straps. He made no attempt to escape, but mewed.

When we confronted him with the beast the scene was beyond description. The beast doubled backwards into a bow, as though he had been poisoned with strychnine, and moaned in the most pitiable fashion. Several other things happened also, but they cannot be put down here.

"I think I was right," said Strickland. "Now we will ask him to cure this case."

But the leper only mewed. Strickland wrapped a towel round his hand and took the gun-barrels out of the fire. I put the half of the broken walkingstick through the loop of fishing-line and buckled the leper comfortably to Strickland's bedstead. I understood then how men and women and little children can endure to see a witch burnt alive; for the beast was moaning on the floor, and though the Silver Man had no face, you could see horrible feelings passing through the slab that took its place, exactly as waves of heat play across red-hot iron—gun-barrels for instance.

Strickland shaded his eyes with his hands for a moment, and we got to work. This part is not to be printed.

*　　　　*　　　　*　　　　*　　　　*　　　　*

The dawn was beginning to break when the leper spoke. His mewings had not been satisfactory up to that point. The beast had fainted from exhaustion, and the house was very still. We unstrapped the leper and told him to take away the evil spirit. He crawled to the beast and laid his hand upon the left breast. That was all. Then he fell face down and whined, drawing in his breath as he did so.

We watched the face of the beast, and saw the soul of Fleete coming back into the eyes. Then a sweat broke out on the forehead, and the eyes—they were human eyes—closed. We waited for an hour, but Fleete still slept. We carried him to his room and bade the leper go, giving him the bedstead, and the sheet on the bedstead to cover his nakedness, the gloves and the towels with which we had touched him, and the whip that had been hooked round his body. He put the sheet about him and went out into the early morning without speaking or mewing.

Strickland wiped his face and sat down. A nightgong, far away in the city, made seven o'clock.

"Exactly four-and-twenty hours!" said Strickland. "And I've done enough to ensure my dismissal from the service, besides permanent quarters in a lunatic asylum. Do you believe that we are awake?"

The red-hot gun-barrel had fallen on the floor and was singeing the carpet. The smell was entirely real.

That morning at eleven we two together went to wake up Fleete. We looked and saw that the black leopard-rosette on his chest had disappeared. He was very drowsy and tired, but as soon as he saw us, he said, "Oh! Confound you fellows. Happy New Year to you. Never mix your liquors. I'm nearly dead."

"Thanks for your kindness, but you're over time," said Strickland. "To-day is the morning of the second. You've slept the clock round with a vengeance."

The door opened, and little Dumoise put his head in. He had come on foot, and fancied that we were laying out Fleete.

"I've brought a nurse," said Dumoise. "I suppose that she can come in for . . . what is necessary."

"By all means," said Fleete cheerily, sitting up in bed. "Bring on your nurses."

Dumoise was dumb. Strickland led him out and explained that there must have been a mistake in the diagnosis. Dumoise remained dumb and left the house hastily. He considered that his professional reputation had been injured, and was inclined to make a personal matter of the recovery. Strickland went out too. When he came back, he said that he had been to call on the temple of Hanuman to offer redress for the pollution of the god, and had been solemnly assured that no white man had ever touched the idol, and that he was an incarnation of all the virtues laboring under a delusion. "What do you think?" said Strickland.

I said, "There are more things . . . "

But Strickland hates that quotation. He says that I have worn it threadbare.

One other curious thing happened which frightened me as much as anything in all the night's work. When Fleete was dressed he came into the dining-room and sniffed. He had a quaint trick of moving his nose when he sniffed. "Horrid doggy smell, here," said he, "You should really keep those terriers of yours in better order. Try sulphur, Strick."

But Strickland did not answer. He caught hold of the back of a chair, and, without warning, went into an amazing fit of hysterics. It is terrible to see a strong man overtaken with hysteria. Then it struck me that we had fought for Fleete's soul with the Silver Man in that room, and had disgraced ourselves as Englishmen forever, and I laughed and gasped and gurgled just as shamefully as Strickland, while Fleete thought that we had both gone mad. We never told him what we had done.

Some years later, when Strickland had married and was a church-going member of society for his wife's sake, we reviewed the incident dispassionately, and Strickland suggested that I should put it before the public.

I cannot myself see that this step is likely to clear up the mystery; because, in the first place, no one will believe a rather unpleasant story, and, in the second, it is well known to every right-minded man that the gods of the heathen are stone and brass, and any attempt to deal with them otherwise is justly condemned.

STEPHEN CRANE

MANACLED

In the First Act there had been a farm scene, wherein real horses had drunk real water out of real buckets, afterward dragging a real wagon off stage L. The audience was consumed with admiration of this play, and the great Theater Nouveau rang to its roof with the crowd's plaudits.

The Second Act was now well advanced. The hero, cruelly victimized by his enemies, stood in prison garb, panting with rage, while two brutal warders fastened real handcuffs on his wrists and real anklets on his ankles. And the hovering villain sneered.

" 'Tis well, Aubrey Pettingill," said the prisoner. "You have so far succeeded; but, mark you, there will come a time—"

The villain retorted with a cutting allusion to the young lady whom the hero loved.

"Curse you," cried the hero, and he made as if to spring upon his demon; but, as the pitying audience saw, he could only take steps four inches long.

Drowning the mocking laughter of the villain came cries from both the audience and the people in back of the wings. "Fire! Fire! Fire!" Throughout the great house resounded the roaring crashes of a throng of human beings moving in terror, and even above this noise could be heard the screams of women more shrill than whistles. The building hummed and shook; it was like a glade which holds some bellowing cataract of the mountains. Most of the people who were killed on the stairs still clutched their playbills in their hands as if they had resolved to save them at all costs.

The Theater Nouveau fronted upon a street which was not of the first importance, especially at night, when it only aroused when the people came to the theater, and aroused again when they came out to go home. On the night of the fire, at the time of the scene between the enchained hero and his tormentor, the thoroughfare echoed with only the scraping shovels of some streetcleaners, who were loading carts with blackened snow and mud. The gleam of lights made the shadowed pavement deeply blue, save where lay some yellow plum-like reflection.

Suddenly a policeman came running frantically along the street. He charged upon the firebox on the corner. Its red light touched with flame each of his brass buttons and the municipal shield. He pressed a lever. He had been standing in the entrance of the theater chatting to the lonely man in the box office. To send an alarm was a matter of seconds.

Out of the theater poured the first hundreds of fortunate ones, and some were not altogether fortunate. Women, their bonnets flying, cried out tender names; men, white as death, scratched and bleeding, looked wildly from face to face. There were displays of horrible blind brutality by the strong. Weaker men clutched and clawed like cats. From the theater itself came the howl of a gale.

The policeman's fingers had flashed into instant life and action the most perfect counterattack to the fire. He listened for some seconds, and presently he heard the thunder of a charging engine. She swept around a corner, her three shining enthrilled horses leaping. Her consort, the hosecart, roared behind her. There were the loud clicks of the steel-shod hoofs, hoarse shouts, men running, the flash of lights, while the crevice-like streets resounded with the charges of other engines.

At the first cry of fire, the two brutal warders had dropped the arms of the hero and run off the stage with the villain. The hero cried after them angrily: "Where are you going? Here, Pete—Tom—you've left me chained up, damn you!"

The body of the theater now resembled a mad surf amid rocks, but the hero did not look at it. He was filled with fury at the stupidity of the two brutal warders, in forgetting that they were leaving him manacled. Calling loudly, he hobbled off stage L., taking steps four inches long.

Behind the scenes he heard the hum of flames. Smoke, filled with sparks sweeping on spiral courses, rolled thickly upon him. Suddenly his face turned chalk-color beneath his skin of manly bronze for the stage. His voice shrieked: "Pete—Tom—damn you—come back—you've left me chained up."

He had played in this theater for seven years, and he could find his way without light through the intricate passages which mazed out behind the stage. He knew that it was a long way to the street door.

The heat was intense. From time to time masses of flaming wood sung down from above him. He began to jump. Each jump advanced him about three feet, but the effort soon became heartbreaking. Once he fell, it took time to get upon his feet again.

There were stairs to descend. From the top of this flight he tried to fall feet first. He precipitated himself in a way that would have broken his hip under common conditions. But every step seemed covered with glue, and on almost every one he stuck for a moment. He could not even succeed in falling downstairs. Ultimately he reached the bottom, windless from the struggle.

There were stairs to climb. At the foot of the flight he lay for an instant with his mouth close to the floor, trying to breathe. Then he tried to scale this frightful precipice up the face of which many an actress had gone at a canter.

Each succeeding step arose eight inches from its fellow. The hero dropped to a seat on the third step, and pulled his feet to the second step. From this position he lifted himself to a seat on the fourth step. He had not gone far in this manner before his frenzy caused him to lose his balance, and he rolled to the foot of the flight. After all, he could fall downstairs.

He lay there whispering. "They all got out but I. All but I." Beautiful flames flashed above him; some were crimson, some were orange, and here and there were tongues of purple, blue, green.

A curiously calm thought came into his head. "What a fool I was not to foresee this! I shall have Rogers furnish manacles of papier-mâché tomorrow."

The thunder of the fire-lions made the theater have a palsy.

Suddenly the hero beat his handcuffs against the wall, cursing them in a loud wail. Blood started from under his fingernails. Soon he began to bite the hot steel, and blood fell from his blistered mouth. He raved like a wolf.

Peace came to him again. There were charming effects amid the flames. . . . He felt very cool, delightfully cool. . . . "They've left me chained up."

LAFCADIO HEARN

YUKI-ONNA

In a village of Musashi Province, there lived two woodcutters: Mosaku and Minokichi. At the time of which I am speaking, Mosaku was an old man; and Minokichi, his apprentice, was a lad of eighteen years. Every day they went together to a forest situated about five miles from their village. On the way to that forest there is a wide river to cross; and there is a ferryboat. Several times a bridge was built where the ferry is; but the bridge was each time carried away by a flood. No common bridge can resist the current there when the river rises.

Mosaku and Minokichi were on their way home, one very cold evening, when a great snowstorm overtook them. They reached the ferry; and they found that the boatman had gone away, leaving his boat on the other side of the river. It was no day for swimming; and the woodcutters took shelter in the ferryman's hut—thinking themselves lucky to find any shelter at all. There was no brazier in the hut, nor any place in which to make a fire: it was only a two-mat hut, with a single door, but no window. Mosaku and Minokichi fastened the door, and lay down to rest, with their straw raincoats over them. At first they did not feel very cold; and they thought that the storm would soon be over.

The old man almost immediately fell asleep; but the boy, Minokichi, lay awake a long time, listening to the awful wind, and the continual slashing of the snow against the door. The river was roaring; and the hut swayed and creaked like a junk at sea. It was a terrible storm; and the air was every moment becoming colder; and Minokichi shivered under his raincoat. But at last, in spite of the cold, he too fell asleep.

He was awakened by a showering of snow in his face. The door of the hut had been forced open; and, by the snow-light *(yuki-akari)*, he saw a woman in the room—a woman all in white. She was bending above Mosaku, and blowing her breath upon him—and her breath was like a bright white smoke. Almost in the same moment she turned to Minokichi, and stooped over him. He tried to cry out, but found that he could not utter any sound. The white woman bent down over him, lower and lower, until her face almost touched him; and he saw that she was very beautiful,—though her eyes made him afraid. For a little time she continued to look at him; then she smiled, and she whispered: "I intended to treat you like the other man. But I cannot help feeling some pity for you, because you are so young. . . . You are a pretty boy, Minokichi; and I will not hurt you now. But, if you ever tell anybody—

even your own mother—about what you have seen this night, I shall know it; and then I will kill you. . . . Remember what I say!"

With these words, she turned from him and passed through the doorway. Then he found himself able to move; and he sprang up, and looked out. But the woman was nowhere to be seen; and the snow was driving furiously into the hut. Minokichi closed the door, and secured it by fixing several billets of wood against it. He wondered if the wind had blown it open; he thought that he might have been only dreaming, and might have mistaken the gleam of the snow-light in the doorway for the figure of a white woman: but he could not be sure. He called to Mosaku, and was frightened because the old man did not answer. He put out his hand in the dark, and touched Mosaku's face, and found that it was ice! Mosaku was stark and dead. . . .

By dawn the storm was over; and when the ferryman returned to his station, a little after sunrise, he found Minokichi lying senseless beside the frozen body of Mosaku. Minokichi was promptly cared for, and soon came to himself; but he remained a long time ill from the effects of the cold of that terrible night. He had been greatly frightened also by the old man's death; but he said nothing about the vision of the woman in white. As soon as he got well again, he returned to his calling—going alone every morning to the forest, and coming back at nightfall with his bundles of wood, which his mother helped him to sell.

One evening, in the winter of the following year, as he was on his way home, he overtook a girl who happened to be traveling by the same road. She was a tall, slim girl, very good-looking; and she answered Minokichi's greeting in a voice as pleasant to the ear as the voice of a song-bird. Then he walked beside her; and they began to talk. The girl said that her name was O-Yuki; that she had lately lost both of her parents; and that she was going to Yedo, where she happened to have some poor relations, who might help her to find a situation as servant. Minokichi soon felt charmed by this strange girl; and the more that he looked at her, the handsomer she appeared to be. He asked her whether she was yet betrothed; and she answered, laughingly, that she was free. Then, in her turn, she asked Minokichi whether he was married, or pledged to marry; and he told her that, although he had only a widowed mother to support, the question of an "honorable daughter-in-law" had not yet been considered, as he was very young. . . . After these confidences, they walked on for a long while without speaking; but, as the proverb declares, *Ki ga aréba, mé mo kuchi hodo ni mono wo iu:* "When the wish is there, the eyes can say as much as the mouth." By the time they reached the village, they had become very much pleased with each other; and then Minokichi asked O-Yuki to rest awhile at his house. After some shy hesitations, she went there with him; and his mother made her welcome, and prepared a warm meal for her. O-Yuki behaved so nicely that Minokichi's mother took a sudden fancy to her, and persuaded her to delay her journey to Yedo. And the natural end of the matter was that Yuki never went to Yedo at all. She remained in the house, as an "honorable daughter-in-law."

O-Yuki proved a very good daughter-in-law. When Minokichi's mother came to die,—some five years later—her last words were words of affection and praise for the wife of her son. And O-Yuki bore Minokichi ten children, boys and girls—handsome children all of them, and very fair of skin.

The country-folk thought O-Yuki a wonderful person, by nature different from themselves. Most of the peasant-women age early; but O-Yuki, even after having become the mother of ten children, looked as young and fresh as on the day when she had first come to the village.

One night, after the children had gone to sleep, O-Yuki was sewing by the light of a paper lamp; and Minokichi, watching her, said:—

"To see you sewing there, with the light on your face, makes me think of a strange thing that happened when I was a lad of eighteen. I then saw somebody as beautiful and white as you are now—indeed, she was very like you."

Without lifting her eyes from her work, O-Yuki responded:—

"Tell me about her. . . . Where did you see her?"

Then Minokichi told her about the terrible night in the ferryman's hut— and about the White Woman that had stooped above him, smiling and whispering—and about the silent death of old Mosaku. And he said:

"Asleep or awake, that was the only time that I saw a being as beautiful as you. Of course, she was not a human being; and I was afraid of her—very much afraid—but she was so white! . . . Indeed, I have never been sure whether it was a dream that I saw, or the Woman of the Snow."

O-Yuki flung down her sewing, and arose, and bowed above Minokichi where he sat, and shrieked into his face:

"It was I—I—I! Yuki it was! And I told you then that I would kill you if you ever said one word about it! . . . But for those children asleep there, I would kill you this moment! And now you had better take very, very good care of them; for if ever they have reason to complain of you, I will treat you as you deserve!"

Even as she screamed, her voice came thin, like a crying of wind; then she melted into a bright white mist that spired to the roof-beams, and shuddered away through the smoke-hole. . . . Never again was she seen.

LAFCADIO HEARN

MUJINA

On the Akasaka Road, in Tōkyō, there is a slope called Kii-no-kuni-zaka—which means the Slope of the Province of Kii. I do not know why it is called the Slope of the Province of Kii. On one side of this slope you see an ancient moat, deep and very wide, with high green banks rising up to some palace gardens;—and on the other side of the road extend the long and lofty walls of an imperial palace. Before the era of street-lamps and jinrikishas, this neighborhood was very lonesome after dark; and belated pedestrians would go miles out of their way rather than mount the Kii-no-kuni-zaka, alone, after sunset.

All because of a Mujina that used to walk there.

The last man who saw the Mujina was an old merchant of the Kyōbashi quarter, who died about thirty years ago. This is the story, as he told it:

One night, at a late hour, he was hurrying up the Kii-no-kuni-zaka, when he perceived a woman crouching by the moat, all alone, and weeping bitterly. Fearing that she intended to drown herself, he stopped to offer her any assistance or consolation in his power. She appeared to be a slight and graceful person, handsomely dressed; and her hair was arranged like that of a young girl of good family. "O-jochū," [1] he exclaimed, approaching her—"O-jochū, do not cry like that! . . . Tell me what the trouble is; and if there be any way to help you, I shall be glad to help you." (He really meant what he said, for he was a very kind man.) But she continued to weep—hiding her face from him with one of her long sleeves. "O-jochū," he said again, as gently as he could,—"please, please listen to me! . . . This is no place for a young lady at night! Do not cry, I implore you!—only tell me how I may be of some help to you!" Slowly she rose up, but turned her back to him, and continued to moan and sob behind her sleeve. He laid his hand lightly upon her shoulder, and pleaded:—"O-jochū!—O-jochū!—O-jochū! Listen to me, just for one little moment! . . . O-jochū!—O-jochū!" Then that O-jochū turned round, and dropped her sleeve, and stroked her face with her hand;—and the man saw that she had no eyes or nose or mouth,—and he screamed and ran away.

Up Kii-no-kuni-zaka he ran and ran; and all was black and empty before him. On and on he ran, never daring to look back; and at last he saw a lantern, so far away that it looked like the gleam of a firefly; and he made

---

[1] O-jochū ("honorable damsel") is a polite form of address used in speaking to a young lady whom one does not know.

259

for it. It proved to be only the lantern of an itinerant *soba*-seller,[1] who had set down his stand by the roadside; but any light and any human companionship were good after that experience; and he flung himself down at the feet of the *soba*-seller, crying out, "Aa!—*aa!*—aa!!!"

Koré! koré!" roughly exclaimed the *soba*-man. "Here! what is the matter with you? Anybody hurt you?"

"No—nobody hurt me," panted the other—"only . . . *Aa!—aa!"* . . .

"—Only scared you?" queried the peddler, unsympathetically. "Robbers?"

"Not robbers—not robbers," gasped the terrified man. . . "I saw . . . I saw a woman—by the moat—and she showed me . . . *Aa!* I cannot tell you what she showed me!" . . .

"*Hé!* Was it anything like *this* that she showed you?" cried the *soba*-man, stroking his own face—which therewith became like unto an Egg. . . . And, simultaneously, the light went out.

<hr />

[1] *Soba* is a preparation of buckwheat, somewhat resembling vermicelli.

BRAM STOKER

THE SQUAW

Nurnberg at the time was not so much exploited as it has been since then. Irving had not been playing *Faust,* and the very name of the old town was hardly known to the great bulk of the traveling public. My wife and I being in the second week of our honeymoon, naturally wanted someone else to join our party, so that when the cheery stranger, Elias P. Hutcheson, hailing from Isthmian City, Bleeding Gulch, Maple Tree County, Neb. turned up at the station at Frankfort and casually remarked that he was going on to see the most all-fired old Methuselah of a town in Yurrup, and that he guessed that so much travelling alone was enough to send an intelligent, active citizen into the melancholy ward of a daft house, we took the pretty broad hint and suggested that we should join forces. We found, on comparing notes afterwards, that we had each intended to speak with some diffidence or hesitation so as not to appear too eager, such not being a good compliment to the success of our married life; but the effect was entirely marred by our both beginning to speak at the same instant—stopping simultaneously and then going on together again. Anyhow, no matter how, it was done; and Elias P. Hutcheson became one of our party. Straightway Amelia and I found the pleasant benefit; instead of quarrelling, as we had been doing, we found that the restraining influence of a third party was such that we now took every opportunity of spooning in odd corners. Amelia declares that ever since she has, as the result of that experience, advised all her friends to take a friend on the honeymoon. Well, we 'did' Nurnberg together, and much enjoyed the racy remarks of our Transatlantic friend, who, from his quaint speech and his wonderful stock of adventures, might have stepped out of a novel. We kept for the last object of interest in the city to be visited the Burg. and on the day appointed for the visit strolled round the outer wall of the city by the eastern side.

The Burg is seated on a rock dominating the town and an immensely deep fosse guards it on the northern side. Nurnberg has been happy in that it was never sacked; had it been it would certainly not be so spick and span perfect as it is at present. The ditch has not been used for centuries, and now its base is spread with tea-gardens and orchards, of which some of the trees are of quite respectable growth. As we wandered round the wall, dawdling in the hot July sunshine, we often paused to admire the views spread before us, and in especial the great plain covered with towns and villages and bounded with a blue line of hills, like a landscape of Claude Lorraine. From this we always turned with new delight to the city itself, with its myriad of quaint old gables and acre-wide red roofs dotted with dormer windows, tier upon tier. A little to our right rose the towers of the Burg, and nearer still, standing grim, the Torture Tower, which was, and is, perhaps, the most interesting place in the city. For centuries the tradition of the Iron Virgin of Nurnberg has been handed down as an instance of the horrors of cruelty of which man is capable; we had long looked forward to seeing it; and here at last was its home.

In one of our pauses we leaned over the wall of the moat and looked down. The garden seemed quite fifty or sixty feet below us, and the sun pouring into it with an intense, moveless heat like that of an oven. Beyond rose the grey, grim wall seemingly of endless height, and losing itself right and left in the angles of bastion and counterscarp. Trees and bushes crowned the wall, and above again towered the lofty houses on whose massive beauty Time has only set the hand of approval. The sun was hot and we were lazy; time was our own, and we lingered, leaning on the wall. Just below us was a pretty sight—a great black cat lying stretched in the sun, whilst round her gambolled prettily a tiny black kitten. The mother would wave her tail for the kitten to play with, or would raise her feet and push away the little one as an encouragement to further play. They were just at the foot of the wall, and Elias P. Hutcheson, in order to help the play, stooped and took from the walk a moderate sized pebble.

'See!' he said, 'I will drop it near the kitten, and they will both wonder where it came from.'

'Oh, be careful,' said my wife; 'you might hit the dear little thing!'

'Not me, ma'am,' said Elias P. 'Why, I'm as tender as a Maine cherry-tree. Lor, bless ye, I wouldn't hurt the poor pooty little critter more'n I'd scalp a baby. An' you may bet your variegated socks on that! See, I'll drop it fur away on the outside so's not to go near her!' Thus saying, he leaned over and held his arm out at full length and dropped the stone. It may be that there is some attractive force which draws lesser matters to greater; or more proba- bly that the wall was not plump but sloped to its base—we not noticing the inclination from above; but the stone fell with a sickening thud that came up to us through the hot air, right on the kitten's head, and shattered out its little brains then and there. The black cat cast a swift upward glance, and we saw her eyes like green fire fixed an instant on Elias P. Hutcheson; and then her attention was given to the kitten, which lay still with just a quiver of her tiny limbs, whilst a thin red stream trickled from a gaping wound. With a muffled cry, such as a human being might give, she bent over the kitten licking its wounds and moaning. Suddenly she seemed to realise that it was dead, and again threw her eyes up at us. I shall never forget the sight, for she looked the perfect incarnation of hate. Her green eyes blazed with lurid fire, and the white, sharp teeth seemed to almost shine through the blood which dabbled her mouth and whiskers. She gnashed her teeth, and her claws stood out stark and at full length on every paw. Then she made a wild rush up the wall as if to reach us, but when the momentum ended fell back, and further added to her horrible appearance for she fell on the kitten, and rose with her black fur smeared with its brains and blood. Amelia turned quite faint, and I had to lift her back from the wall. There was a seat close by in shade of a spreading plane-tree, and here I placed her whilst she composed herself. Then I went back to Hutcheson, who stood without moving, looking down on the angry cat below.

'Wall, I guess that air the savagest beast I ever see—'cept once when an Apache squaw had an edge on a half-breed what they nicknamed "Splinters" 'cos of the way he fixed up her papoose which he stole on a raid just to show that he appreciated the way they had given his mother the fire torture. She got that kinder look so set on her face that it jest seemed to grow there. She followed Splinters mor'n three year till at last the braves got him and handed him over to her. They did say that no man, white or Injun, had ever been so long a-dying under the tortures of the Apaches. The only time I ever see her smile was when I wiped her out. I kem on the camp just in time to see Splinters pass in his checks, and he wasn't sorry to go either. He was a hard citizen, and though I never could shake with him after that papoose business—for it was bitter bad, and he should have been a white man, for he looked like one—I see he had got paid out in full. Durn me, but I took a piece of his hide from one of his skinnin' posts an' had it made into a pocket-book. It's here now!' and he slapped the breast pocket of his coat.

Whilst he was speaking the cat was continuing her frantic efforts to get up the wall. She would take a run back and then charge up, sometimes reaching an incredible height. She did not seem to mind the heavy fall which she got each time but started with renewed vigour; and at every tumble her appearance became more horrible. Hutcheson was a kind hearted man—my wife and I had both noticed little acts of kindness to animals as well as to persons—and he seemed concerned at the state of fury to which the cat had wrought herself.

'Wall, now!' he said, 'I du declare that that poor critter seems quite desperate. There! there! poor thing, it was all an accident—though that won't bring back your little one to you. Say! I wouldn't have had such a thing happen for a thousand! Just shows what a clumsy fool of a man can do when he tries to play! Seems I'm too darned slipperhanded to even play with a cat. Say Colonel!' it was a pleasant way he had to bestow titles freely—'I hope your wife don't hold no grudge against me on account of this unpleasantness? Why, I wouldn't have had it occur on no account.'

He came over to Amelia and apologised profusely, and she with her usual kindness of heart hastened to assure him that she quite understood that it was an accident. Then we all went again to the wall and looked over.

The cat missing Hutcheson's face had drawn back across the moat, and was sitting on her haunches as though ready to spring. Indeed the very instant she saw him she did spring, and with a blind unreasoning fury, which would have been grotesque, only that it was so frightfully real. She did not try to run up the wall, but simply launched herself at him as though hate and fury could lend her wings to pass straight through the great distance between them. Amelia, womanlike, got quite concerned, and said to Elias P. in a warning voice:

'Oh! you must be very careful. That animal would try to kill you if she were here; her eyes look like positive murder.'

He laughed out jovially. 'Excuse me, ma'am,' he said, 'but I can't help laughin'. Fancy a man that has fought grizzlies an' Injuns bein' careful of bein' murdered by a cat!'

When the cat heard him laugh, her whole demeanour seemed to change. She no longer tried to jump or run up the wall, but went quietly over, and sitting again beside the dead kitten began to lick and fondle it as though it were alive.

'See!' said I, 'the effect of a really strong man. Even the animal in the midst of her fury recognises the voice of a master, and bows to him!'

'Like a squaw!' was the only comment of Elias P. Hutcheson, as we moved on our way round the city fosse. Every now and then we looked over the wall and each time saw the cat following us. At first she had kept going back to the dead kitten, and then as the distance grew greater took it in her mouth and so followed. After a while, however, she abandoned this, for we saw her following all alone; she had evidently hidden the body somewhere. Amelia's alarm grew at the cat's persistence, and more than once she repeated her warning; but the American always laughed with amusement, till finally, seeing that she was beginning to be worried, he said:

'I say, ma'am, you needn't be skeered over that cat. I go heeled, I du!' Here he slapped his pistol pocket at the back of his lumbar region. 'Why sooner'n have you worried, I'll shoot the critter, right here, an' risk the police interferin' with a citizen of the United States for carryin' arms contrairy to reg'lations!' As he spoke he looked over the wall, but the cat on seeing him, retreated, with a growl, into a bed of tall flowers, and was hidden. He went on: 'Blest if that ar critter ain't got more sense of what's good for her than most Christians. I guess we've seen the last of her! You bet, she'll go back now to that busted kitten and have a private funeral of it, all to herself!'

Amelia did not like to say more, lest he might, in mistaken kindness to her, fulfil his threat of shooting the cat: and so we went on and crossed the little wooden bridge leading to the gateway whence ran the steep paved roadway between the Burg and the pentagonal Torture Tower. As we crossed the bridge we saw the cat again down below us. When she saw us her fury seemed to return, and she made frantic efforts to get up the steep wall. Hutcheson laughed as he looked down at her, and said:

"Goodbye, old girl. Sorry I injured your feelin's, but you'll get over it in time! So long!' And then we passed through the long, dim archway and came to the gate of the Burg.

When we came out again after our survey of this most beautiful old place which not even the well-intentioned efforts of the Gothic restorers of forty years ago have been able to spoil—though their restoration was then glaring white—we seemed to have quite forgotten the unpleasant episode of the morning. The old lime tree with its great trunk gnarled with the passing of nearly nine centuries, the deep well cut through the heart of the rock by those captives of old, and the lovely view from the city wall whence we heard, spread over almost a full quarter of an hour, the multitudinous chimes of the city, had all helped to wipe out from our minds the incident of the slain kitten.

We were the only visitors who had entered the Torture Tower that morning—so at least said the old custodian—and as we had the place all to ourselves were able to make a minute and more satisfactory survey than would have otherwise been possible. The custodian, looking to us as the sole source of his gains for the day, was willing to meet our wishes in any way. The Torture Tower is truly a grim place, even now when many thousands of visitors have sent a stream of life, and the joy that follows life, into the place; but at the time I mention it wore its grimmest and most gruesome aspect. The dust of ages seemed to have settled on it, and the darkness and the horror of its memories seem to have become sentient in a way that would have satisfied the Pantheistic souls of Philo or Spinoza. The lower chamber where we entered was seemingly, in its normal state, filled with incarnate darkness; even the hot sunlight streaming in through the door seemed to be lost in the vast thickness of the walls, and only showed the masonry rough as when the builder's scaffolding had come down, but coated with dust and marked here and there with patches of dark stain which, if walls could speak, could have given their own dread memories of fear and pain. We were glad to pass up the dusty wooden staircase, the custodian leaving the outer door open to light us somewhat on our way; for to our eyes the one long-wick'd, evil-smelling candle stuck in a sconce on the wall gave an inadequate light. When we came up through the open trap in the corner of the chamber overhead, Amelia held on to me so tightly that I could actually feel her heart beat. I must say for my own part that I was not surprised at her fear, for this room was even more gruesome than that below. Here there was certainly more light, but only just sufficient to realise the horrible surroundings of the place. The builders of the tower had evidently intended that only they who should gain the top should have any of the joys of light and prospect. There, as we had noticed from below, were ranges of windows, albeit of mediaeval smallness, but elsewhere in the tower were only a very few narrow slits such as were habitual in places of mediaeval defence. A few of these only lit the chamber, and these so high up in the wall that from no part could the sky be seen through the thickness of the walls. In racks, and leaning in disorder against the walls, were a number of headsmen's swords, great double-handed weapons with broad blade and keen edge. Hard by were several blocks whereon the necks of the victims had lain, with here and there deep notches where the steel had bitten through the guard of flesh and shored into the wood. Round the chamber, placed in all sorts of irregular ways, were many implements of torture which made one's heart ache to see—chairs full of spikes which gave instant and excruciating pain; chairs and couches with dull knobs whose torture was seemingly less, but which, though slower, were equally efficacious; racks, belts, boots, gloves, collars, all made for compressing at will; steel baskets in which the head could be slowly crushed into a pulp if necessary; watchmen's hooks with long handle and knife that cut at resistance—this a speciality of the old Nurnberg police system; and many, many other devices for man's injury to man. Amelia grew quite pale with the horror of the things, but fortunately did not faint, for being a little overcome she sat down on a torture chair, but jumped up again with a shriek, all tendency to faint gone. We both pretended that it was the injury done to her dress by the dust of the chair, and the rusty spikes which had upset her, and Mr. Hutcheson acquiesced in accepting the explanation with a kind-hearted laugh.

But the central object in the whole of this chamber of horrors was the engine known as the Iron Virgin, which stood near the centre of the room. It was a rudely-shaped figure of a woman, something of the bell order, or, to make a closer comparison, of the figure of Mrs. Noah in the children's Ark, but without that slimness of waist and perfect *rondeur* of hip which marks the aesthetic type of the Noah family. One would hardly have recognised it as intended for a human figure at all had not the founder shaped on the forehead a rude semblance of a woman's face. This machine was coated with rust without, and covered with dust; a rope was fastened to a ring in the front of the figure, about where the waist should have been, and was drawn through a pulley, fastened on the wooden pillar which sustained the flooring above. The custodian pulling this rope showed that a section of the front was hinged like a door at one side, we then saw that the engine was of considerable thickness, leaving just room enough inside for a man to be placed. The door was of equal thickness and of great weight, for it took the custodian all his strength, aided though he was by the contrivance of the pulley, to open it. This weight was partly due to the fact that the door was of manifest purpose hung so as to throw its weight downwards, so that it might shut of its own accord when the strain was released. The inside was honey-combed with rust—nay more, the rust alone that comes through time would hardly have eaten so deep into the iron walls; the rust of the cruel stains was deep indeed! It was only, however, when we came to look at the inside of the door that the diabolical intention was manifest to the full. Here were several long spikes, square and massive, broad at the base and sharp at the point, placed in such a position that when the door should close the upper ones would pierce the eyes of the victim, and the lower ones his heart and vitals. The sight was too much for poor Amelia, and this time she fainted dead off, and I had to carry her down the stairs, and place her on bench outside till she recovered. That she felt it to the quick was afterwards shown by the fact that my eldest son bears to this day a rude birthmark on his breast, which has, by family consent, been accepted as representing the Nurnberg Virgin.

When we got back to the chamber we found Hutcheson still opposite the Iron Virgin; he had been evidently philosophising, and now gave us the benefit of his thought in the shape of a sort of exordium.

'Wall, I guess I've been learnin' somethin' here while madam has been gettin' over her faint. 'Pears to me that we're a long way behind the times on our side of the big drink. We uster think out on the plains that the Injun could give us points in tryin' to make a man uncomfortable; but I guess your old mediaeval law-and-order party could raise him every time. Splinters was pretty good in his bluff on the squaw, but this here young miss held a straight flush all high on him. The points of them spikes air sharp enough still, though even the edges air eaten out by what uster be on them. It'd be a good thing for our Indian section to get some specimens of this here play-toy to send round to the Reservations jest to knock the stuffin' out of the bucks, and the squaws too, by showing them as how old civilisation lays over them at their best. Guess but I'll get in that box a minute jest to see how it feels.'

'Oh no! no!' said Amelia. 'It is too terrible!'

'Guess, ma'am, nothin's too terrible to the explorin' mind. I've been in some queer places in my time. Spent a night inside a dead horse while a prairie fire swept over me in Montana Territory—an' another time slept inside a dead buffler when the Comanches was on the war path an' I didn't keer to leave my kyard on them. I've been two days in a caved-in tunnel in the Billy Broncho gold mine in New Mexico, an' was one of the four shut up for three parts of a day in the caisson what slid over on her side when we were settin' the foundations of the Buffalo Bridge. I've not funked an odd experience yet, an' I don't propose to begin now!'

We saw that he was set on the experiment, so I said: 'Well, hurry up, old man, and get through it quick!'

'All right, General,' said he, 'but I calculate we ain't quite ready yet. The gentlemen, my predecessors, what stood in that thar canister, didn't volunteer for the office—not much! And I guess there was some ornamental tyin' up before the big stroke was made. I want to go into this thing fair and square, so I must get fixed up proper first. I dare say this old galoot can rise some string and tie me up accordin' to sample?'

This was said interrogatively to the old custodian, but the latter, who understood the drift of his speech, though perhaps not appreciating to the full the niceties of dialect and imagery, shook his head. His protest was, however, only formal and made to be overcome. The American thrust a gold piece into his hand, saying: 'Take it, pard! it's your pot; and don't be skeer'd. This ain't no necktie party that you're asked to assist in!' He produced some thin frayed rope and proceeded to bind our companion with sufficient strictness for the purpose. When the upper part of his body was bound, Hutcheson said:

'Hold on a moment, Judge. Guess I'm too heavy for you to tote into the canister. You just let me walk in, and then you can wash up regardin' my legs!'

Whilst speaking he had backed himself into the opening which was just enough to hold him. It was a close fit and no mistake. Amelia looked on with fear in her eyes, but she evidently did not like to say anything. Then the custodian completed his task by tying the American's feet together so that he was now absolutely helpless and fixed in his voluntary prison. He seemed to really enjoy it, and the incipient smile which was habitual to his face blossomed into actuality as he said:

'Guess this here Eve was made out of the rib of a dwarf! There ain't much room for a full-grown citizen of the United States to hustle. We uster make our coffins more roomier in Idaho territory. Now, Judge, you jest begin to let this door down, slow, on to me. I want to feel the same pleasure as the other jays had when those spikes began to move toward their eyes!'

'Oh no! no! no!' broke in Amelia hysterically. 'It is too terrible! I can't bear to see it!—I can't! I can't!' But the American was obdurate. 'Say, Colonel,' said he, 'why not take Madame for a little promenade? I wouldn't hurt her feelin's for the world; but now that I am here, havin' kem eight thousand miles, wouldn't it be too hard to give up the very experience I've been pinin' an' pantin' fur? A man can't get to feel like canned goods every time! Me and the Judge here'll fix up this thing in no time, an' then you'll come back, an' we'll all laugh together!'

Once more the resolution that is born of curiosity triumphed, and Amelia stayed holding tight to my arm and shivering whilst the custodian began to slacken slowly inch by inch the rope that held back the iron door. Hutcheson's face was positively radiant as his eyes followed the first movement of the spikes.

'Wall!' he said, 'I guess I've not had enjoyment like this since I left Noo York. Bar a scrap with a French sailor at Wapping—an' that warn't much of a picnic neither—I've not had a show fur real pleasure in this dod-rotted Continent, where there ain't no b'ars nor no Injuns, an' wheer nary man goes heeled. Slow there, Judge! Don't you rush this business! I want a show for my money this game—I du!'

The custodian must have had in him some of the blood of his predecessors in that ghastly tower, for he worked the engine with a deliberate and excruciating slowness which after five minutes, in which the outer edge of the door had not moved half as many inches, began to overcome Amelia. I saw her lips whiten, and felt her hold upon my arm relax. I looked around an instant for a place whereon to lay her, and when I looked at her again found that her eyes had become fixed on the side of the Virgin. Following its direction I saw the black cat crouching out of sight. Her green eyes shone like danger lamps in the gloom of the place, and their colour was heightened by the blood which still smeared her coat and reddened her mouth. I cried out:

'The cat! look out for the cat!' for even then she sprang out before the engine. At this moment she looked like a triumphant demon. Her eyes blazed with ferocity, her hair bristled out till she seemed twice her normal size, and her tail lashed about as does a tiger's when the quarry is before it. Elias P. Hutcheson when he saw her was amused, and his eyes positively sparkled with fun as he said:

'Darned if the squaw hain't got on all her war paint! Jest give her a shove off if she comes any of her tricks on me, for I'm so fixed everlastingly by the boss, that durn my skin if I can keep my eyes from her if she wants them! Easy there, Judge! Don't you slack that ar rope or I'm euchered!'

At this moment Amelia completed her faint, and I had to clutch hold of her round the waist or she would have fallen to the floor. Whilst attending to her I saw the black cat crouching for a spring, and jumped up to turn the creature out.

But at that instant, with a sort of hellish scream, she hurled herself, not as we expected at Hutcheson, but straight at the face of the custodian. Her claws seemed to be tearing wildly as one sees in the Chinese drawings of the dragon rampant, and as I looked I saw one of them light on the poor man's eye, and actually tear through it and down his cheek, leaving a wide band of red where the blood seemed to spurt from every vein.

With a yell of sheer terror which came quicker than even his sense of pain, the man leaped back, dropping as he did so the rope which held back the iron door. I jumped for it, but was too late, for the cord ran like lightning through the pulley-block, and the heavy mass fell forward from its own weight.

As the door closed I caught a glimpse of our poor companion's face. He seemed frozen with terror. His eyes stared with a horrible anguish as if dazed, and no sound came from his lips.

And then the spikes did their work. Happily the end was quick, for when I wrenched open the door they had pierced so deep that they had locked in the bones of the skull through which they had crushed, and actually tore him—it—out of his iron prison till, bound as he was, he fell at full length with a sickly thud upon the floor, the face turning upward as he fell.

I rushed to my wife, lifted her up and carried her out, for I feared for her very reason if she should wake from her faint to such a scene. I laid her on the bench outside and ran back. Leaning against the wooden column was the custodian moaning in pain whilst he held his reddening handkerchief to his eyes. And sitting on the head of the poor American was the cat, purring loudly as she licked the blood which trickled through the gashed socket of his eyes.

I think no one will call me cruel because I seized one of the old executioner's swords and shore her in two as she sat.

CHARLOTTE PERKINS GILMAN

THE YELLOW WALLPAPER

It is very seldom that mere ordinary people like John and myself secure ancestral halls for the summer.

A colonial mansion. a hereditary estate, I would say a haunted house, and reach the height of romantic felicity—but that would be asking too much of fate!

Still I will proudly declare that there is something queer about it.

Else, why should it be let so cheaply? And why have stood so long untenanted?

John laughs at me, of course, but one expects that in marriage.

John is practical in the extreme. He has no patience with faith, an intense horror of superstition, and he scoffs openly at any talk of things not to be felt and seen and put down in figures.

John is a physician, and *perhaps*—(I would not say it to a living soul, of course, but this is dead paper and a great relief to my mind)—*perhaps* that is one reason I do not get well faster.

You see he does not believe I am sick!

And what can one do?

If a physician of high standing, and one's own husband, assures friends and relatives that there is really nothing the matter with one but temporary nervous depression—a slight hysterical tendency—what is one to do?

My brother is also a physician, and also of high standing, and he says the same thing.

So I take phosphates or phosphites—whichever it is, and tonics, and journeys, and air, and exercise, and am absolutely forbidden to "work" until I am well again.

Personally, I disagree with their idea.

Personally, I believe that congenial work, with excitement and change, would do me good.

But what is one to do?

I did write for a while in spite of them; but it *does* exhaust me a good deal—having to be so sly about it, or else meet with heavy opposition.

I sometimes fancy that in my condition if I had less opposition and more society and stimulus—but John says the very worst thing I can do is to think about my condition, and I confess it always makes me feel bad.

So I will let it alone and talk about the house.

The most beautiful place! It is quite alone, standing well back from the

270

road, quite three miles from the village. It makes me think of English places that you read about, for there are hedges and walls and gates that lock, and lots of separate little houses for the gardeners and people.

There is a *delicious* garden! I never saw such a garden—large and shady, full of box-bordered paths, and lined with long grape-covered arbors with seats under them.

There were greenhouses, too, but they are all broken now.

There was some legal trouble, I believe, something about the heirs and coheirs; anyhow, the place has been empty for years.

That spoils my ghostliness, I am afraid, but I don't care—there is something strange about the house—I can feel it.

I even said so to John one moonlight evening but he said what I felt was a *draught,* and shut the window.

I get unreasonably angry with John sometimes. I'm sure I never used to be so sensitive. I think it is due to this nervous condition.

But John says if I feel so, I shall neglect proper self-control; so I take pains to control myself—before him, at least, and that makes me very tired.

I don't like our room a bit. I wanted one downstairs that opened on the piazza and had roses all over the window, and such pretty old-fashioned chintz hangings! but John would not hear of it.

He said there was only one window and not room for two beds, and no near room for him if he took another.

He is very careful and loving, and hardly lets me stir without special direction.

I have a schedule prescription for each hour in the day; he takes all care from me, and so I feel basely ungrateful not to value it more.

He said we came here solely on my account, that I was to have perfect rest and all the air I could get. "Your exercise depends on your strength, my dear," said he, "and your food somewhat on your appetite; but air you can absorb all the time." So we took the nursery at the top of the house.

It is a big, airy room, the whole floor nearly, with windows that look all ways, and air and sunshine galore. It was nursery first and then playroom and gymnasium, I should judge; for the windows are barred for little children, and there are rings and things in the walls.

The paint and paper look as if a boys' school had used it. It is stripped off—the paper—in great patches all around the head of my bed, about as far as I can reach, and in a great place on the other side of the room low down. I never saw a worse paper in my life.

One of those sprawling flamboyant patterns committing every artistic sin.

It is dull enough to confuse the eye in following, pronounced enough to constantly irritate and provoke study, and when you follow the lame uncertain curves for a little distance they suddenly commit suicide—plunge off at outrageous angles, destroy themselves in unheard of contradictions.

The color is repellent, almost revolting; a smouldering unclean yellow, strangely faded by the slow-turning sunlight.

It is a dull yet lurid orange in some places, a sickly sulphur tint in others.

No wonder the children hated it! I should hate it myself if I had to live in this room long.

There comes John, and I must put this away,—he hates to have me write a word.

We have been here two weeks, and I haven't felt like writing before, since that first day.

I am sitting by the window now, up in this atrocious nursery, and there is nothing to hinder my writing as much as I please, save lack of strength.

John is away all day, and even some nights when his cases are serious.

I am glad my case is not serious!

But these nervous troubles are dreadfully depressing.

John does not know how much I really suffer. He knows there is no *reason* to suffer, and that satisfies him.

Of course it is only nervousness. It does weigh on me so not to do my duty in any way!

I meant to be such a help to John, such a real rest and comfort, and here I am a comparative burden already!

Nobody would believe what an effort it is to do what little I am able—to dress and entertain, and order things.

It is fortunate Mary is so good with the baby. Such a dear baby!

And yet I *cannot* be with him, it makes me so nervous.

I suppose John never was nervous in his life. He laughs at me so about this wall-paper!

At first he meant to repaper the room, but afterwards he said that I was letting it get the better of me, and that nothing was worse for a nervous patient than to give way to such fancies.

He said that after the wall-paper was changed it would be the heavy bedstead, and then the barred windows, and then that gate at the head of the stairs, and so on.

"You know the place is doing you good," he said, "and really, dear, I don't care to renovate the house just for a three months' rental."

"Then do let us go downstairs," I said, "there are such pretty rooms there."

Then he took me in his arms and called me a blessed little goose, and said he would go down to the cellar, if I wished, and have it whitewashed into the bargain.

But he is right enough about the beds and windows and things.

It is an airy and comfortable room as any one need wish, and, of course, I would not be so silly as to make him uncomfortable just for a whim.

I'm really getting quite fond of the big room, all but that horrid paper.

Out of one window I can see the garden, those mysterious deepshaded arbors, the riotous old-fashioned flowers, and bushes and gnarly trees.

Out of another I get a lovely view of the bay and a little private wharf belonging to the estate. There is a beautiful shaded lane that runs down there from the house. I always fancy I see people walking in these numerous paths and arbors, but John has cautioned me not to give way to fancy in the least. He says that with my imaginative power and habit of story-making, a nervous weakness like mine is sure to lead to all manner of excited fancies, and that I ought to use my will and good sense to check the tendency. So I try.

I think sometimes that if I were only well enough to write a little it would relieve the press of ideas and rest me.

But I find I get pretty tired when I try.

It is so discouraging not to have any advice and companionship about my work. When I get really well, John says we will ask Cousin Henry and Julia down for a long visit; but he says he would as soon put fireworks in my pillow-case as to let me have those stimulating people about now.

I wish I could get well faster.

But I must not think about that. This paper looks to me as if it *knew* what a vicious influence it had!

There is a recurrent spot where the patter lolls like a broken neck and two bulbous eyes stare at you upside down.

I get positively angry with the impertinence of it and the everlastingness. Up and down and sideways they crawl, and those absurd, unblinking eyes are everywhere. There is one place where two breadths didn't match, and the eyes go all up and down the line, one a little higher than the other.

I never saw so much expression in an inanimate thing before, and we all know how much expression they have! I used to lie awake as a child and get more entertainment and terror out of blank walls and plain furniture than most children could find in a toy-store.

I remember what a kindly wink the knobs of our big, old bureau used to have, and there was one chair that always seemed like a strong friend.

I used to feel that if any of the other things looked too fierce I could always hop into that chair and be safe.

The furniture in this room is no worse than inharmonious, however, for we had to bring it all from downstairs. I suppose when this was used as a playroom they had to take the nursery things out, and no wonder! I never saw such ravages as the children have made here.

The wall-paper, as I said before, is torn off in spots, and it sticketh closer than a brother—they must have had perseverance as well as hatred.

Then the floor is scratched and gouged and splintered, the plaster itself is dug out here and there, and this great heavy bed which is all we found in the room, looks as if it had been through the wars.

But I don't mind it a bit—only the paper.

There comes John's sister. Such a dear girl as she is, and so careful of me! I must not let her find me writing.

She is a perfect and enthusiastic housekeeper, and hopes for no better profession. I verily believe she thinks it is the writing which made me sick!

But I can write when she is out, and see her a long way off from these windows.

There is one that commands the road, a lovely shaded winding road, and one that just looks off over the country. A lovely country, too, full of great elms and velvet meadows.

This wall-paper has a kind of sub-pattern in a different shade, a particularly irritating one, for you can only see it in certain lights, and not clearly then.

But in the places where it isn't faded and where the sun is just so—I can see a strange, provoking, formless sort of figure, that seems to skulk about behind that silly and conspicuous front design.

There's sister on the stairs!

Well, the Fourth of July is over! The people are all gone and I am tired out. John thought it might do me good to see a little company, so we just had mother and Nellie and the children down for a week.

Of course I didn't do a thing. Jennie sees to everything now.

But it tired me all the same.

John says if I don't pick up faster he shall send me to Weir Mitchell in the fall.

But I don't want to go there at all. I had a friend who was in his hands once, and she says he is just like John and my brother, only more so!

Besides, it is such an undertaking to go so far.

I don't feel as if it was worth while to turn my hand over for anything, and I'm getting dreadfully fretful and querulous.

I cry at nothing, and cry most of the time.

Of course I don't when John is here, or anybody else, but when I am alone.

And I am alone a good deal just now. John is kept in town very often by serious cases, and Jennie is good and lets me alone when I want her to.

So I walk a little in the garden or down that lovely lane, sit on the porch under the roses, and lie down up here a good deal.

I'm getting really fond of the room in spite of the wall-paper. Perhaps *because* of the wall-paper.

It dwells in my mind so!

I lie here on this great immovable bed—it is nailed down, I believe—and follow that pattern about by the hour. It is as good as gymnastics, I assure you. I start, we'll say, at the bottom, down in the corner over there where it has not been touched, and I determine for the thousandth time that I *will* follow that pointless pattern to some sort of a conclusion.

I know a little of the principle of design, and I know this thing was not arranged on any laws of radiation, or alternation, or repetition, or symmetry, or anything else that I ever heard of.

It is repeated, of course, by the breadths, but not otherwise.

Looked at in one way each breadth stands alone, the bloated curves and flourishes—a kind of "debased Romanesque" with *delirium tremens*—go waddling up and down in isolated columns of fatuity.

But, on the other hand, they connect diagonally, and the sprawling outlines run off in great slanting waves of optic horror, like a lot of wallowing seaweeds in full chase.

The whole thing goes horizontally, too, at least it seems so, and I exhaust myself in trying to distinguish the order of its going in that direction.

They have used a horizontal breadth for a frieze, and that adds wonderfully to the confusion.

There is one end of the room where it is almost intact, and there, when the crosslights fade and the low sun shines directly upon it, I can almost fancy radiation after all,—the interminable grotesques seem to form around a common centre and rush off in headlong plunges of equal distraction.

It makes me tired to follow it. I will take a nap I guess.

I don't know why I should write this.

I don't want to.

I don't feel able.

And I know John would think it absurd. But I *must* say what I feel and think in some way—it is such a relief!

But the effort is getting to be greater than the relief.

Half the time now I am awfully lazy and lie down ever so much.

John says I mustn't lose my strength, and has me take cod liver oil and lots of tonics and things, to say nothing of ale and wine and rare meat.

Dear John! He loves me very dearly, and hates to have me sick. I tried to have a real earnest reasonable talk with him the other day, and tell him how I wish he would let me go and make a visit to Cousin Henry and Julia.

But he said I wasn't able to go, nor able to stand it after I got there; and I did not make out a very good case for myself, for I was crying before I had finished.

It is getting to be a great effort for me to think straight. Just this nervous weakness I suppose.

And dear John gathered me up in his arms, and just carried me upstairs and laid me on the bed, and sat by me and read to me till it tired my head.

He said I was his darling and his comfort and all he had, and that I must take care of myself for his sake, and keep well.

He says no one but myself can help me out of it, that I must use my will and self-control and not let any silly fancies run away with me.

There's one comfort, the baby is well and happy, and does not have to occupy this nursery with the horrid wall-paper.

If we had not used it, that blessed child would have! What a fortunate escape! Why, I wouldn't have a child of mine, an impressionable little thing live in such a room for worlds.

I never thought of it before, but it is lucky that John kept me here after all, I can stand it so much easier than a baby, you see.

Of course I never mention it to them any more—I am too wise,—but I keep watch of it all the same.

There are things in that paper that nobody knows but me, or ever will.

Behind that outside pattern the dim shapes get clearer every day.

It is always the same shape, only very numerous.

And it is like a woman stooping down and creeping about behind that pattern. I don't like it a bit. I wonder—I begin to think—I wish John would take me away from here!

It is so hard to talk with John about my case, because he is so wise, and because he loves me so.

But I tried it last night.

It was moonlight. The moon shines in all around just as the sun does.

I hate to see it sometimes, it creeps so slowly, and always comes in by one window or another.

John was asleep and I hated to waken him, so I kept still and watched the moonlight on the undulating wall-paper till I felt creepy.

The faint figure behind seemed to shake the pattern, just as if she wanted to get out.

I got up softly and went to feel and see if the paper *did* move, and when I came back John was awake.

"What is it, little girl?" he said. "Don't go walking about like that—you'll get cold."

I thought it was a good time to talk, so I told him that I really was not gaining here, and that I wished he would take me away.

"Why darling!" said he, "our lease will be up in three weeks, and I can't see how to leave before.

"The repairs are not done at home, and I cannot possibly leave town just now. Of course if you were in any danger, I could and would, but you really are better, dear, whether you can see it or not. I am a doctor, dear, and I know. You are gaining flesh and color, your appetite is better, I feel really much easier about you."

"I don't weigh a bit more," said I, "nor as much; and my appetite may be better in the evening when you are here, but it is worse in the morning when you are away!"

"Bless her little heart!" said he with a big hug, "she shall be as sick as she pleases! But now let's improve the shining hours by going to sleep, and talk about it in the morning!"

"And you won't go away?" I asked gloomily.

"Why, how can I, dear? It is only three weeks more and then we will take a nice little trip of a few days while Jennie is getting the house ready. Really dear you are better!"

"Better in body perhaps—" I began, and stopped short, for he sat up straight and looked at me with such a stern, reproachful look that I could not say another word.

"My darling," said he, "I beg of you, for my sake and for our child's sake, as well as for your own, that you will never for one instant let that idea enter your mind! There is nothing so dangerous, so fascinating, to a temperament like yours. It is a false and foolish fancy. Can you not trust me as a physician when I tell you so?"

So of course I said no more on that score, and we went to sleep before long. He thought I was asleep first, but I wasn't and lay there for hours trying to decide whether that front pattern and the back pattern really did move together or separately.

On a pattern like this, by daylight, there is a lack of sequence, a defiance of law, that is a constant irritant to a normal mind.

The color is hideous enough, and unreliable enough, and infuriating enough, but the pattern is torturing.

You think you have mastered it, but just as you get well underway in following, it turns a back-somersault and there you are. It slaps you in the face, knocks you down, and tramples upon you. It is like a bad dream.

The outside pattern is a florid arabesque, reminding one of a fungus. If you can imagine a toadstool in joints, an interminable string of toadstools, budding and sprouting in endless convolutions—why, that is something like it.

That is, sometimes!

There is one marked peculiarity about this paper, a thing nobody seems to notice but myself, and that is that it changes as the light changes.

When the sun shoots in through the east window—I always watch for that first long, straight ray—it changes so quickly that I never can quite believe it.

That is why I watch it always.

By moonlight—the moon shines in all night when there is a moon—I wouldn't know it was the same paper.

At night in any kind of light, in twilight, candle light, lamplight, and worst of all by moonlight, it becomes bars! The outside pattern I mean, and the woman behind it is as plain as can be.

I didn't realize for a long time what the thing was that showed behind, that dim sub-pattern, but now I am quite sure it is a woman.

By daylight she is subdued, quiet. I fancy it is the pattern that keeps her so still. It is so puzzling. It keeps me quiet by the hour.

I lie down so much now. John says it is good for me, and to sleep all I can.

Indeed he started the habit by making me lie down for an hour after each meal.

It is a very bad habit I am convinced, for you see I don't sleep.

And that cultivates deceit, for I don't tell them I'm awake—O no!

The fact is I am getting a little afraid of John.

He seems very queer sometimes, and even Jennie has an inexplicable look.

It strikes me occasionally, just as a scientific hypothesis,—that perhaps it is the paper!

I have watched John when he did not know I was looking, and come into the room suddenly on the most innocent excuses, and I've caught him several times *looking at the paper!* And Jennie too. I caught Jennie with her hand on it once.

She didn't know I was in the room, and when I asked her in a quiet, a very quiet voice, with the most restrained manner possible, what she was doing with the paper—she turned around as if she had been caught stealing, and looked quite angry—asked me why I should frighten her so!

Then she said that the paper stained everything it touched, that she had found yellow smooches on all my clothes and John's, and she wished we would be more careful!

Did not that sound innocent? But I know she was studying that pattern, and I am determined that nobody shall find it out but myself!

Life is very much more exciting now than it used to be. You see I have something more to expect, to look forward to, to watch. I really do eat better, and am more quiet than I was.

John is so pleased to see me improve! He laughed a little the other day, and said I seemed to be flourishing in spite of my wall-paper.

I turned it off with a laugh. I had no intention of telling him it was *because* of the wall-paper—he would make fun of me. He might even want to take me away.

I don't want to leave now until I have found it out. There is a week more, and I think that will be enough.

I'm feeling ever so much better! I don't sleep much at night, for it is so interesting to watch developments; but I sleep a good deal in the daytime.

In the daytime it is tiresome and perplexing.

There are always new shoots on the fungus, and new shades of yellow all over it. I cannot keep count of them, though I have tried conscientiously.

It is the strangest yellow, that wall-paper! It makes me think of all the yellow things I ever saw—not beautiful ones like buttercups, but old foul, bad yellow things.

But there is something else about that paper—the smell! I noticed it the moment we came into the room, but with so much air and sun it was not bad. Now we have had a week of fog and rain, and whether the windows are open or not, the smell is here.

It creeps all over the house.

I find it hovering in the dining-room, skulking in the parlor, hiding in the hall, lying in wait for me on the stairs.

It gets into my hair.

Even when I go to ride, if I turn my head suddenly and surprise it—there is that smell!

Such a peculiar odor, too! I have spent hours in trying to analyze it, to find what it smelled like.

It is not bad—at first, and very gentle, but quite the subtlest, most enduring odor I ever met.

In this damp weather it is awful, I wake up in the night and find it hanging over me.

It used to disturb me at first. I thought seriously of burning the house—to reach the smell.

But now I am used to it. The only thing I can think of that it is like is the *color* of the paper! A yellow smell.

There is a very funny mark on this wall, low down, near the mopboard. A streak that runs round the room. It goes behind every piece of furniture, except the bed, a long, straight, even *smooch*, as if it had been rubbed over and over.

I wonder how it was done and who did it, and what they did it for. Round and round and round—round and round and round—it makes me dizzy!

I really have discovered something at last.

Through watching so much at night, when it changes so, I have finally found out.

The front pattern *does* move—and no wonder! The woman behind shakes it!

Sometimes I think there are a great many women behind, and sometimes only one, and she crawls around fast, and her crawling shakes it all over.

Then in the very bright spots she keeps still, and in the very shady spots she just takes hold of the bars and shakes them hard.

And she is all the time trying to climb through. But nobody could climb through that pattern—it strangles so; I think that is why it has so many heads.

They get through, and then the pattern strangles them off and turns them upside down, and makes their eyes white!

If those heads were covered or taken off it would not be half so bad.

I think that woman gets out in the daytime!

And I'll tell you why—privately—I've seen her!

I can see her out of every one of my windows!

It is the same woman, I know, for she is always creeping, and most women do not creep by daylight.

I see her on the long road under the trees, creeping along, and when a carriage comes she hides under the blackberry vines.

I don't blame her a bit. It must be very humiliating to be caught creeping by daylight!

I always lock the door when I creep by daylight. I can't do it at night, for I know John would suspect something at once.

And John is so queer now, that I don't want to irritate him. I wish he would take another room! Besides, I don't want anybody to get that woman out at night but myself.

I often wonder if I could see her out of all the windows at once.

But, turn as fast as I can, I can only see out of one at one time.

And though I always see her, she *may* be able to creep faster than I can turn!

I have watched her sometimes away off in the open country, creeping as fast as a cloud shadow in a high wind.

If only that top pattern could be gotten off from the under one! I mean to try it, little by little.

I have found out another funny thing, but I shan't tell it this time! It does not do to trust people too much.

There are only two more days to get this paper off, and I believe John is beginning to notice. I don't like the look in his eyes.

And I heard him ask Jennie a lot of professional questions about me. She had a very good report to give.

She said I slept a good deal in the daytime.

John knows I don't sleep very well at night, for all I'm so quiet!

He asked me all sorts of questions, too, and pretended to be very loving and kind.

As if I couldn't see through him!

Still, I don't wonder he acts so, sleeping under this paper for three months.

It only interests me, but I feel sure John and Jennie are secretly affected by it.

Hurrah! This is the last day, but it is enough. John to stay in town over night, and won't be out until this evening.

Jennie wanted to sleep with me—the sly thing! but I told her I should undoubtedly rest better for a night all alone.

That was clever, for really I wasn't alone a bit! As soon as it was moonlight and that poor thing began to crawl and shake the pattern, I got up and ran to help her.

I pulled and she shook, I shook and she pulled, and before morning we had peeled off yards of that paper.

A strip about as high as my head and half around the room.

And then when the sun came and that awful pattern began to laugh at me, I declared I would finish it to-day!

We go away to-morrow, and they are moving all my furniture down again to leave things as they were before.

Jennie looked at the wall in amazement but I told her merrily that I did it out of pure spite at the vicious thing.

She laughed and said she wouldn't mind doing it herself, but I must not get tired.

How she betrayed herself that time!

But I am here, and no person touches this paper but me,—not *alive!*

She tried to get me out of the room—it was too patent! But I said it was so quiet and empty and clean now that I believed I would lie down again and sleep all I could; and not to wake me even for dinner—I would call when I woke.

So now she is gone, and the servants are gone, and the things are gone, and there is nothing left but that great bedstead nailed down, with the canvas mattress we found on it.

We shall sleep downstairs to-night, and take the boat home to-morrow.

I quite enjoy the room, now it is bare again.

How those children did tear about there!

This bedstead is fairly gnawed!

But I must get to work.

I have locked the door and thrown the key down into the front path.

I don't want to go out, and I don't want to have anybody come in, till John comes.

I want to astonish him.

I've got a rope up here that even Jennie did not find. If that woman does get out, and tries to get away, I can tie her!

But I forgot I could not reach far without anything to stand on!

This bed will *not* move!

I tried to lift and push it until I was lame, and then I got so angry I bit off a little piece at one corner—but it hurt my teeth.

Then I peeled off all the paper I could reach standing on the floor. It sticks horribly and the pattern just enjoys it! All those strangled heads and bulbous eyes and waddling fungus growths just shriek with derision!

I am getting angry enough to do something desperate. To jump out of the window would be admirable exercise, but the bars are too strong even to try.

Besides I wouldn't do it. Of course not. I know well enough that a step like that is improper and might be misconstrued.

I don't like to *look* out of the windows even—there are so many of those creeping women and they creep so fast.

I wonder if they all come out of that wall-paper as I did?

But I am securely fastened now by my well-hidden rope—you don't get *me* out in the road there!

I suppose I shall have to get back behind the pattern when it comes night, and that is hard!

It is so pleasant to be out in this great room and creep around as I please!

I don't want to go outside. I won't, even if Jennie asks me to.

For outside you have to creep on the ground, and everything is green instead of yellow.

But here I can creep smoothly on the floor, and my shoulder just fits in that long smooch around the wall, so I cannot lose my way.

Why there's John at the door!

It is no use, young man, you can't open it!

How he does call and pound!

Now he's crying for an axe.

It would be a shame to break down that beautiful door!

"John dear!" said I in the gentlest voice, "the key is down by the front steps, under a plantain leaf!"

That silenced him for a few moments.

Then he said—very quietly indeed, "Open the door, my darling!"

"I can't," said I. "The key is down by the front door under a plantain leaf!"

And then I said it again, several times, very gently and slowly, and said it so often that he had to go and see, and he got it of course, and came in. He stopped short by the door.

"What is the matter?" he cried. "For God's sake, what are you doing!"

I kept on creeping just the same, but I looked at him over my shoulder.

"I've got out at last," said I, "in spite of you and Jane. And I've pulled off most of the paper, so you can't put me back!"

Now why should that man have fainted? But he did, and right across my path by the wall, so that I had to creep over him every time!

J. K. HUYSMANS

THE BLACK MASS

Episode from *Là-bas* (Down There)

Chapter XIX

. . . .
. . . .
. . . .

"This is the place," said Mme. Chantelouve.

She rang. The grating opened. She raised her veil. A shaft of lantern light struck her full in the face, the door opened noiselessly, and they penetrated into a garden.

"Good evening, madame."

"Good evening, Marie. In the chapel?"

"Yes. Does madame wish me to guide her?"

"No, thanks."

The woman with the lantern scrutinized Durtal. He perceived, beneath a hood, wisps of grey hair falling in disorder over a wrinkled old face, but she did not give him time to examine her and returned to a tent beside the wall serving her as a lodge.

He followed Hyacinthe, who traversed the dark lanes, between rows of palms, to the entrance of a building. She opened the doors as if she were quite at home, and her heels clicked resolutely on the flagstones.

"Be careful," she said, going through a vestibule. "There are three steps."

They came out into a court and stopped before an old house. She rang. A little man advanced, hiding his features, and greeted her in an affected, sing-song voice. She passed, saluting him, and Durtal brushed a fly-blown face, the eyes liquid, gummy, the cheeks plastered with cosmetics, the lips painted.

"I have stumbled into a lair of sodomists.—You didn't tell me that I was to be thrown into such company," he said to Hyacinthe, overtaking her at the turning of a corridor lighted by a lamp.

"Did you expect to meet saints here?"

She shrugged her shoulders and opened a door. They were in a chapel with a low ceiling crossed by beams gaudily painted with coal-tar pigment. The windows were hidden by great curtains. The walls were cracked and dingy. Durtal recoiled after a few steps. Gusts of humid, mouldy air and of that indescribable new-stove acridity poured out of the registers to mingle with an irritating odour of alkali, resin, and burnt herbs. He was choking, his temples throbbing.

He advanced groping, attempting to accustom his eyes to the half-darkness. The chapel was vaguely lighted by sanctuary lamps suspended from chandeliers of gilded bronze with pink glass pendants. Hyacinthe made him a sign to sit down, then she went over to a group of people sitting on divans in a dark corner. Rather vexed at being left here, away from the centre of activity, Durtal noticed that there were many women and few men present, but his efforts to discover their features were unavailing. As here and there a lamp swayed, he occasionally caught sight of a Junonian brunette, then of a smooth-shaven, melancholy man. He observed that the women were not chattering to each other. Their conversation seemed awed and grave. Not a laugh, not a raised voice, was heard, but an irresolute, furtive whispering, unaccompanied by gesture.

"Hmm," he said to himself. "It doesn't look as if Satan made his faithful happy."

A choir boy, clad in red, advanced to the end of the chapel and lighted a stand of candles. Then the altar became visible. It was an ordinary church altar on a tabernacle above which stood an infamous, derisive Christ. The head had been raised and the neck lengthened, and wrinkles, painted in the cheeks, transformed the grieving face to a bestial one twisted into a mean laugh. He was naked, and where the loincloth should have been, there was a viril member projecting from a bush of horsehair. In front of the tabernacle the chalice, covered with a pall, was placed. The choir boy folded the altar cloth, wiggled his haunches, stood tiptoe on one foot and flipped his arms as if to fly away like a cherub, on pretext of reaching up to light the black tapers whose odour of coal tar and pitch was now added to the pestilential smell of the stuffy room.

Durtal recognized beneath the red robe the "fairy" who had guarded the chapel entrance, and he understood the rôle reserved for this man, whose sacrilegious nastiness was substituted for the purity of childhood acceptable to the Church.

Then another choir boy, more hideous yet, exhibited himself. Hollow chested, racked by coughs, withered, made up with white grease paint and vivid carmine, he hobbled about humming. He approached the tripods flanking the altar, stirred the smouldering incense pots and threw in leaves and chunks of resin.

Durtal was beginning to feel uncomfortable when Hyacinthe rejoined him. She excused herself for having left him by himself so long, invited him to change his place, and conducted him to a seat far in the rear, behind all the rows of chairs.

"This is a real chapel, isn't it?" he asked.

"Yes. This house, this church, the garden that we crossed, are the remains of an old Ursuline convent. For a long time this chapel was used to store hay. The house belonged to a livery-stable keeper, who sold it to that woman," and she pointed out a stout brunette of whom Durtal before had caught a fleeting glimpse.

"Is she married?"

"No. She is a former nun who was debauched long ago by Docre."

"Ah. And those gentlemen who seem to be hiding in the darkest places?"

"They are Satanists. There is one of them who was a professor in the School of Medicine. In his home he has an oratorium where he prays to a statue of Venus Astarte mounted on an altar."

"No!"

"I mean it. He is getting old, and his demoniac orisons increase tenfold his forces, which he is using up with creatures of that sort," and with a gesture she indicated the choir boys.

"You guarantee the truth of this story?"

"You will find it narrated at great length in a religious journal. *Les annales de la sainteté*. And though his identity was made pretty patent in the article, the man did not dare prosecute the editors.—What's the matter with you?" she asked, looking at him closely.

"I'm strangling. The odour from those incense burners is unbearable."

"You will get used to it in a few seconds."

"But what do they burn that smells like that?"

"Asphalt from the street, leaves of henbane, datura, dried nightshade, and myrrh. These are perfumes delightful to Satan, our master." She spoke in that changed, guttural voice which had been hers at times when in bed with him. He looked her squarely in the face. She was pale, the lips pressed tight, the pluvious eye blinking rapidly.

"Here he comes!" she murmured suddenly, while women in front of them scurried about or knelt in front of the chairs.

Preceded by the two choir boys the canon entered, wearing a scarlet bonnet from which two buffalo horns of red cloth protruded. Durtal examined him as he marched toward the altar. He was tall, but not well built, his bulging chest being out of proportion to the rest of his body. His peeled forehead made one continuous line with his straight nose. The lips and cheeks bristled with that kind of hard, clumpy beard which old priests have who have always shaved themselves. The features were round and insinuating, the eyes, like apple pips, close together, phosphorescent. As a whole his face was evil and sly, but energetic, and the hard, fixed eyes were not the furtive, shifty orbs that Durtal had imagined.

The canon solemnly knelt before the altar, then mounted the steps and began to say mass. Durtal saw then that he had nothing on beneath his sacrificial habit. His black socks and his flesh bulging over the garters, attached high up on his legs, were plainly visible. The chasuble had the shape of an ordinary chasuble but was of the dark red colour of dried blood, and in the middle, in a triangle around which was an embroidered border of colchicum, savin, sorrel, and spurge, was the figure of a black billy-goat presenting his horns.

Docre made the genuflexions, the full- or half-length inclinations specified by the ritual. The kneeling choir boys sang the Latin responses in a crystalline voice which trilled on the ultimate syllables of the words.

"But it's a simple low mass," said Durtal to Mme. Chantelouve.

She shook her head. Indeed, at that moment the choir boys passed behind the altar and one of them brought back copper chafing-dishes, the other, censers, which they distributed to the congregation. All the women enveloped themselves in the smoke. Some held their heads right over the chafing-dishes and inhaled deeply, then, fainting, unlaced themselves, heaving raucous sighs.

The sacrifice ceased. The priest descended the steps backward, knelt on the last one, and in a sharp, tripidant voice cried:

"Master of Slanders, Dispenser of the benefits of crime, Administrator of sumptuous sins and great vices, Satan, thee we adore, reasonable God, just God!

"Superadmirable legate of false trances, thou receivest our beseeching tears; thou savest the honour of families by aborting wombs impregnated in the forgetfulness of the good orgasm; thou dost suggest to the mother the hastening of untimely birth, and thine obstetrics spares the still-born children the anguish of maturity, the contamination of original sin.

"Mainstay of the despairing Poor, Cordial of the Vanquished, it is thou who endowest them with hypocrisy, ingratitude, and stiff-neckedness, that they may defend themselves against the children of God, the Rich.

"Suzerain of Resentment, Accountant of Humiliations, Treasurer of old Hatreds, thou alone dost fertilize the brain of man whom injustice has crushed; thou breathest into him the idea of meditated vengeance, sure misdeeds; thou incitest him to murder; thou givest him the abundant joy of accomplished reprisals and permittest him to taste the intoxicating draught of the tears of which he is the cause.

"Hope of Virility, Anguish of the Empty Womb, thou dost not demand the bootless offering of chaste loins, thou dost not sing the praises of Lenten follies; thou alone receivest the carnal supplications and petitions of poor and avaricious families. Thou determinest the mother to sell her daughter, to give her son; thou aidest sterile and reprobate loves; Guardian of strident Neuroses, Leaden Tower of Hysteria, bloody Vase of Rape!

"Master, thy faithful servants, on their knees, implore thee and supplicate thee to satisfy them when they wish the torture of all those who love them and aid them; they supplicate thee to assure them the joy of delectable misdeeds unknown to justice, spells whose unknown origin baffles the reason of man; they ask, finally, glory, riches, power, of thee, King of the Disinherited, Son who art to overthrow the inexorable Father!"

Then Docre rose, and erect, with arms outstretched, vociferated in a ringing voice of hate:

"And thou, thou whom, in my quality of priest, I force, whether thou wilt or no, to descend into this host, to incarnate thyself in this bread, Jesus, Artisan of Hoaxes, Bandit of Homage, Robber of Affection, hear! Since the day when thou didst issue from the complaisant bowels of a Virgin, thou hast failed all thine engagements, belied all thy promises. Centuries have wept, awaiting thee, fugitive God, mute God! Thou wast to redeem man and thou hast not, thou wast to appear in thy glory, and thou sleepest. Go, lie, say to the wretch who appeals to thee, 'Hope, be patient, suffer; the hospital of souls will receive thee; the angels will assist thee; Heaven opens to thee.' Impostor! thou knowest well that the angels, disgusted at thine inertness, abandon thee! Thou wast to be the Interpreter of our plaints, the Chamberlain of our tears; thou wast to convey them to the Father and thou hast not done so, for this intercession would disturb thine eternal sleep of happy satiety.

"Thou hast forgotten the poverty thou didst preach, enamoured vassal of Banks! Thou hast seen the weak crushed beneath the press of profit; thou hast heard the death rattle of the timid, paralyzed by famine, of women disembowelled for a bit of bread, and thou hast caused the Chancery of thy Simoniacs, thy commercial representatives, thy Popes, to answer by dilatory excuses and evasive promises, sacristy Shyster, huckster God!

"Master, whose inconceivable ferocity engenders life and inflicts it on the innocent whom thou darest damn—in the name of *what* original sin?—whom thou darest punish—by the virtue of *what* covenants?—we would have thee confess thine impudent cheats, thine inexpiable crimes! We would drive deeper the nails into thy hands, press down the crown of thorns upon thy brow, bring blood and water from the dry wounds of thy sides.

"And that we can and will do by violating the quietude of thy body, Profaner of ample vices, Abstractor of stupid purities, cursed Nazarene, do-nothing King, coward God!"

"Amen!" trilled the soprano voices of the choir boys.

Durtal listened in amazement to this torrent of blasphemies and insults. The foulness of the priest stupefied him. A silence succeeded the litany. The chapel was foggy with the smoke of the censers. The women, hitherto taciturn, flustered now, as, remounting the altar, the canon turned toward them and blessed them with his left hand in a sweeping gesture. And suddenly the choir boys tinkled the prayer bells.

It was a signal. The women fell to the carpet and writhed. One of them seemed to be worked by a spring. She threw herself prone and waved her legs in the air. Another, suddenly struck by a hideous strabism, clucked, then becoming tongue-tied stood with her mouth open, the tongue turned back, the tip cleaving to the palate. Another, inflated, livid, her pupils dilated, lolled her head back over her shoulders, then jerked it brusquely erect and belaboured herself, tearing her breast with her nails. Another, sprawling on her back, undid her skirts, drew forth a rag, enormous, meteorized; then her face twisted into a horrible grimace, and her tongue, which she could not control, stuck out, bitten at the edges, harrowed by red teeth, from a bloody mouth.

Suddenly Durtal rose, and now he heard and saw Docre distinctly.

Docre contemplated the Christ surmounting the tabernacle, and with arms spread wide apart he spewed forth frightful insults, and, at the end of his forces, muttered the billingsgate of a drunken cabman. One of the choir boys knelt before him with his back toward the altar. A shudder ran around the priest's spine. In a solemn but jerky voice he said, *"Hoc est enim corpus meum,"* then, instead of kneeling, after the consecration, before the precious Body, he faced the congregation, and appeared tumefied, haggard, dripping with sweat. He staggered between the two choir boys, who, raising the chasuble, displayed his naked belly. Docre made a few passes and the host sailed, tainted and sailed, over the steps.

Durtal felt himself shudder. A whirlwind of hysteria shook the room. While the choir boys sprinkled holy water on the pontiff's nakedness, women rushed upon the Eucharist and, grovelling in front of the altar, clawed from the bread humid particles and drank and ate divine ordure.

Another woman, curled up over a crucifix, emitted a rending laugh, then cried to Docre, "Father, father!" A crone tore her hair, leapt, whirled around and around as on a pivot and fell over beside a young girl who, huddled to the wall, was writhing in convulsions, frothing at the mouth, weeping, and spitting out frightful blasphemies. And Durtal, terrified, saw through the fog the red horns of Docre, who, seated now, frothing with rage, was chewing up sacramental wafers, taking them out of his mouth, wiping himself with them, and distributing them to the women, who ground them underfoot, howling, or fell over each other struggling to get hold of them and violate them.

The place was simply a madhouse, a monstrous pandemonium of prostitutes and maniacs. Now, while the choir boys gave themselves to the men, and while the woman who owned the chapel, mounted the altar caught hold of the phallus of the Christ with one hand and with the other held a chalice between "His" naked legs, a little girl, who hitherto had not budged, suddenly bent over forward and howled, howled like a dog. Overcome with disgust, nearly asphyxiated, Durtal wanted to flee. He looked for Hyacinthe. She was no longer at his side. He finally caught sight of her close to the canon and, stepping over the writhing bodies on the floor, he went to her. With quivering nostrils she was inhaling the effluvia of the perfumes and of the couples.

"The sabbatic odour!" she said to him between clenched teeth, in a strangled voice.

"Here, let's get out of this!"

She seemed to wake, hesitated a moment, then without answering she followed him. He elbowed his way through the crowd, jostling women whose protruding teeth were ready to bite. He pushed Mme. Chantelouve to the door, crossed the court, traversed the vestibule, and, finding the portress' lodge empty, he drew the cord and found himself in the street.

There he stopped and drew the fresh air deep into his lungs. Hyacinthe, motionless, dizzy, huddled to the wall away from him.

He looked at her. "Confess that you would like to go in there again."

"No," she said with an effort. "These scenes shatter me. I am in a daze. I must have a glass of water."

And she went up the street, leaning on him, straight to the wine shop, which was open. It was an ignoble lair, a little room with tables and wooden benches, a zinc counter, cheap bar fixtures, and blue-stained wooden pitchers; in the ceiling a U-shaped gas bracket. Two pick-and shovel labourers were playing cards. They turned around and laughed. The proprietor took the excessively short-stemmed pipe from his mouth and spat into the sawdust. He seemed not at all surprised to see this fashionably gowned woman in his dive. Durtal, who was watching him, thought he surprised an understanding look exchanged by the proprietor and the woman.

The proprietor lighted a candle and mumbled into Durtal's ear, "Monsieur, you can't drink here with these people watching. I'll take you to a room where you can be alone."

"Hmmm," said Durtal to Hyacinthe, who was penetrating the mysteries of a spiral staircase, "a lot of fuss for a glass of water!"

But she had already entered a musty room. The paper was peeling from the walls, which were nearly covered with pictures torn out of illustrated weeklies and tacked up with hairpins. The floor was all in pieces. There were a wooden bed without any curtains, a chamber pot with a piece broken out of the side, a wash bowl and two chairs.

The man brought a decanter of gin, a large one of water, some sugar, and glasses, then went downstairs.

Her eyes were sombre, mad. She enlaced Durtal.

"No!" he shouted, furious at having fallen into this trap. "I've had enough of that. It's late. Your husband is waiting for you. It's time for you to go back to him——"

She did not even hear him.

"I want you," she said, and she took him treacherously and obliged him to desire her. She disrobed, threw her skirts on the floor, opened wide the abominable couch, and raising her chemise in the back she rubbed her spine up and down over the coarse grain of the sheets. A look of swooning ecstasy was in her eyes and a smile of joy on her lips.

She seized him, and, with ghoulish fury, dragged him into obscenities of whose existence he had never dreamed. Suddenly, when he was able to escape, he shuddered, for he perceived that the bed was strewn with fragments of hosts.

"Oh, you fill me with horror! Dress, and let's get out of here."

While, with a faraway look in her eyes, she was silently putting on her clothes, he sat down on a chair. The fetidness of the room nauseated him. Then, too—he was not absolutely convinced of Transubstantiation—he did not believe very firmly that the Saviour resided in that soiled bread—but—In spite of himself, the sacrilege he had involuntarily participated in saddened him.

"Suppose it were true," he said to himself, "that the Presence were real, as

Hyacinthe and that miserable priest attest— No, decidedly, I have had enough. I am through. The occasion is timely for me to break with this creature whom from our very first interview I have only tolerated, and I'm going to seize the opportunity."

THE MAGIC SHIRT

'There was a king and a knight, as there was and will be, and as grows the fir-tree, some of it crooked and some of it straight; and he was a king of Eirinn,' said the old tinker, and then came a wicked stepmother, who was incited to evil by a wicked hen-wife. The son of the first queen was at school with twelve comrades, and they used to play at shinny every day with silver shinnies and a golden ball. The hen-wife, for certain curious rewards, gave the step-dame a magic shirt, and she sent it to her stepson, 'Sheen Billy,' and persuaded him to put it on. He refused at first, but complied at last, and the shirt was a great snake about his neck. Then he was enchanted and under spells, and all manner of adventures happened; but at last he came to the house of a wise woman who had a beautiful daughter, who fell in love with the enchanted prince, and said she must and would have him.

'It will cost thee much sorrow,' said the mother.

'I care not,' said the girl, 'I must have him.'

'It will cost thee thy hair.'

'I care not.'

'It will cost thee thy right breast.'

I care not if it should cost me my life,' said the girl.

And the old woman agreed to help her to her will. A caldron was prepared and filled with plants; and the king's son was put into it and stripped to the magic shirt, and the girl was stripped to the waist. And the mother stood by with a great knife, which she gave to her daughter. Then the king's son was put down in the caldron; and the great serpent, which appeared to be a shirt about his neck, changed into its own form, and sprang on the girl and fastened on her; and she cut away the hold, and the king's son was freed from the spells. Then they were married, and a golden breast was made for the lady.

JOSEPH SHERIDAN LE FANU

CARMILLA

Prologue

Upon a paper attached to the Narrative which follows, Doctor Hesselius has written a rather elaborate note, which he accompanies with a reference to his Essay on the strange subject which the MS. illuminates.

This mysterious subject, he treats, in that Essay, with his usual learning and acumen, and with remarkable directness and condensation. It will form but one volume of the series of that extraordinary man's collected papers.

As I publish the case, in these volumes, simply to interest the "laity," I shall forestall the intelligent lady, who relates it, in nothing; and, after due consideration. I have determined, therefore, to abstain from presenting any *précis* of the learned Doctor's reasoning, or extract from his statement on a subject which he describes as "involving, not improbably, some of the profoundest arcana of our dual existence, and its intermediates."

I was anxious, on discovering this paper, to re-open the correspondence commenced by Doctor Hesselius, so many years before, with a person so clever and careful as his informant seems to have been. Much to my regret, however, I found that she had died in the interval.

She, probably, could have added little to the Narrative which she communicates in the following pages, with, so far as I can pronounce, such conscientious particularity.

Chapter I

In Styria, we, though by no means magnificent people, inhabit a castle, or schloss. A small income, in that part of the world, goes a great way. Eight or nine hundred a year does wonders. Scantily enough ours would have answered among wealthy people at home. My father is English, and I bear an English name, although I never saw England. But here, in this lonely and primitive place, where everything is so marvellously cheap, I really don't see how ever so much more money would at all materially add to our comforts, or even luxuries.

My father was in the Austrian service, and retired upon a pension and his patrimony, and purchased this feudal residence, and the small estate on which it stands, a bargain.

Nothing can be more picturesque or solitary. It stands on a slight eminence in a forest. The road, very old and narrow, passes in front of its drawbridge, never raised in my time, and its moat, stocked with perch, and sailed over by many swans, and floating on its surface white fleets of water-lilies.

Over all this the schloss shows its many-windowed front; its towers, and its Gothic chapel.

The forest opens in an irregular and very picturesque glade before its gate, and at the right a steep Gothic bridge carries the road over a stream that winds in deep shadow through the wood.

I have said that this is a very lonely place. Judge whether I say truth. Looking from the hall door towards the road, the forest in which our castle stands extends fifteen miles to the right, and twelve to the left. The nearest inhabited village is about seven of your English miles to the left. The nearest inhabited schloss of any historic associations, is that of old General Spielsdorf nearly twenty miles away to the right.

I have said "the nearest *inhabited* village," because there is, only three miles westward, that is to say in the direction of General Spielsdorf's schloss, a ruined village, with its quaint little church, now roofless, in the aisle of which are the mouldering tombs of the proud family of Karnstein, now extinct, who once owned the equally desolate château which, in the thick of the forest, overlooks the silent ruins of the town.

Respecting the cause of the desertion of this striking and melancholy spot, there is a legend which I shall relate to you another time.

I must tell you now, how very small is the party who constitute the inhabitants of our castle. I don't include servants, or those dependents who occupy rooms in the buildings attached to the schloss. Listen, and wonder! My father, who is the kindest man on earth, but growing old; and I, at the date of my story, only nineteen. Eight years have passed since then. I and my father constituted the family at the schloss. My mother, a Styrian lady, died in my infancy, but I had a good-natured governess, who had been with me from, I might almost say, my infancy. I could not remember the time when her fat, benignant face was not a familiar picture in my memory. This was Madame Perrodon, a native of Berne, whose care and good nature in part supplied to me the loss of my mother, whom I do not even remember, so early I lost her. She made a third at our little dinner party. There was a fourth, Mademoiselle De Lafontaine, a lady such as you term, I believe, "finishing governess." She spoke French and German, Madame Perrodon French and broken English, to which my father and I added English, which, partly to prevent its becoming a lost language among us, and partly from patriotic motives, we spoke every day. The consequence was a Babel, at which strangers used to laugh, and which I shall make no attempt to reproduce in this narrative. And there were two or three young lady friends besides, pretty nearly of my own age, who were occasional visitors, for longer or shorter terms; and these visits I sometimes returned.

These were our regular social resources; but of course there were chance visits from " neighbours" of only five or six leagues distance. My life was, notwithstanding, rather a solitary one, I can assure you.

The first occurrence in my existence, which produced a terrible impression upon my mind, which, in fact, never has been effaced, was one of the very earliest incidents of my life which I can recollect. Some people will think it so trifling that it should not be recorded here. You will see, however, by-and-by why I mention it. The nursery, as it was called, though I had it all to myself, was a large room in the upper story of the castle, with a steep oak roof. I can't have been more than six years old, when one night I awoke, and looking round the room from my bed, failed to see the nursery-maid. Neither was my nurse there; and I thought myself alone. I was not frightened, for I was one of those happy children who are studiously kept in ignorance of ghost stories, of fairy tales, and of all such lore as makes us cover up our heads when the door creaks suddenly, or the flicker of an expiring candle makes the shadow of a bed-post dance upon the wall, nearer to our faces. I was vexed and insulted at finding myself, as I conceived, neglected, and I began to whimper, preparatory to a hearty bout of roaring; when to my surprise, I saw a solemn, but very pretty face looking at me from the side of the bed. It was that of a young lady who was kneeling, with her hands under the coverlet. I looked at her with a kind of pleased wonder, and ceased whimpering. She caressed me with her hands, and lay down beside me on the bed, and drew me towards her, smiling; I felt immediately delightfully soothed, and fell asleep again. I was wakened by a sensation as if two needles ran into my breast very deep at the same moment, and I cried loudly. The lady started back, with her eyes fixed on me, and then slipped down upon the floor, and, as I thought, hid herself under the bed.

I was now for the first time frightened, and I yelled with all my might and main. Nurse, nursery-maid, housekeeper, all came running in, and hearing my story, they made light of it, soothing me all they could meanwhile. But, child as I was, I could perceive that their faces were pale with an unwonted look of anxiety, and I saw them look under the bed, and about the room, and peep under tables and pluck open cupboards; and the housekeeper whispered to the nurse: "Lay your hand along that hollow in the bed; some one *did* lie there, so sure as you did not; the place is still warm."

I remember the nursery-maid petting me, and all three examining my chest, where I told them I felt the puncture, and pronouncing that there was no sign visible that any such thing had happened to me.

The housekeeper and the two other servants who were in charge of the nursery, remained sitting up all night; and from that time a servant always sat up in the nursery until I was about fourteen.

I was very nervous for a long time after this. A doctor was called in, he was pallid and elderly. How well I remember his long saturnine face, slightly pitted with smallpox, and his chestnut wig. For a good while, every second day, he came and gave me medicine, which of course I hated.

The morning after I saw this apparition I was in a state of terror, and could not bear to be left alone, daylight though it was, of a moment.

I remember my father coming up and standing at the bedside, and talking cheerfully, and asking the nurse a number of questions, and laughing very heartily at one of the answers; and patting me on the shoulder, and kissing me, and telling me not be frightened, that it was nothing but a dream and could not hurt me.

But I was not comforted, for I knew the visit of the strange woman was *not* a dream; and I was *awfully* frightened.

Chapter II

I am now going to tell you something so strange that it will require all your faith in my veracity to believe my story. It is not only true, nevertheless, but truth of which I have been an eye-witness.

It was a sweet summer evening, and my father asked me, as he sometimes did, to take a little ramble with him along that beautiful forest vista which I have mentioned as lying in front of the schloss.

"General Spielsdorf cannot come to us so soon as I had hoped," said my father, as we pursued our walk.

He was to have paid us a visit of some weeks, and we had expected his arrival next day. He was to have brought with him a young lady, his niece and ward, Mademoiselle Rheinfeldt, whom I had never seen, but whom I had heard described as a very charming girl, and in whose society I had promised myself many happy days. I was more disappointed than a young lady living in a town, or a bustling neighbourhood can possibly imagine. This visit, and the new acquaintance it promised, had furnished my day dream for many weeks.

"And how soon does he come? I asked.

"Not till autumn. Not for two months, I dare say," he answered. "And I am very glad now, dear, that you never knew Mademoiselle Rheinfeldt."

"And why?" I asked, both mortified and curious.

"Because the poor young lady is dead," he replied. "I quite forgot I had not told you, but you were not in the room when I received the General's letter this evening."

I was very much shocked. General Spielsdorf had mentioned in his first letter, six or seven weeks before, that she was not so well as he would wish her, but there was nothing to suggest the remotest suspicion of danger.

"Here is the General's letter," he said handing it to me. "I am afraid he is in great affliction; the letter appears to me to have been written very nearly in distraction.

It said "I have lost my darling daughter, for as such I loved her. During the last days of dear Bertha's illness I was not able to write to you. Before then I had no idea of her danger. I have lost her, and now learn *all*, too late. She died in the peace of innocence, and in the glorious hope of a blessed futurity. The fiend who betrayed our infatuated hospitality has done it all. I thought I was receiving into my house innocence, gaiety, a charming companion for my lost Bertha. Heavens! what a fool have I been! I thank God my child died without a suspicion of the cause of her sufferings. She is gone without so much as conjecturing the nature of her illness, and the accursed passion of the agent of all this misery. I devote my remaining days to tracking and extinguishing a monster. I am told I may hope to accomplish my righteous and merciful purpose. At present there is scarcely a gleam of light to guide me. I curse my conceited incredulity, my despicable affectation of superiority, my blindness, my obstinacy-all-too-late. I cannot write or talk collectedly now. I am distracted. So soon as I shall have a little recovered, I mean to devote myself for a time to enquiry, which may possibly lead me as far as Vienna. Some time in the autumn, two months hence, or earlier if I live, I will see you—that is, if you permit me; I will then tell you all that I scarce dare put upon paper now. Farewell. Pray for me, dear friend."

In these terms ended this strange letter. Though I had never seen Bertha Rheinfeldt my eyes filled with tears at the sudden intelligence; I was startled, as well as profoundly disappointed.

The sun had now set, and it was twilight by the time I had returned the General's letter to my father.

It was a soft clear evening, and we loitered, speculating upon the possible meanings of the violent and incoherent sentences which I had just been reading. We had nearly a mile to walk before reaching the road that passes the schloss in front, and by that time the moon was shining brilliantly. At the drawbridge we met Madame Perrodon and Mademoiselle De Lafontaine, who had come out, without their bonnets, to enjoy the exquisite moonlight.

At this moment the unwonted sound of carriage wheels and many hoofs upon the road, arrested our attention.

They seemed to be approaching from the high ground overlooking the bridge, and very soon the equipage emerged from that point. Two horsemen first crossed the bridge, then came a carriage drawn by four horses, and two men rode behind.

It seemed to be the travelling carriage of a person of rank; and we were all immediately absorbed in watching that very unusual spectacle. It became, in a few moments, greatly more interesting, for just as the carriage had passed the summit of the steep bridge, one of the leaders, taking fright, communicated his panic to the rest, and after a plunge or two, the whole team broke into a wild gallop together, and dashing between the horsemen who rode in front, came thundering along the road towards us with the speed of a hurricane.

The excitement of the scene was made more painful by the clear, long-drawn screams of a female voice from the carriage window.

We all advanced in curiosity and horror; my father in silence, the rest with various ejaculations of terror.

Our suspense did not last long. Just before you reach the castle draw-bridge, on the route they were coming, there stands by the roadside a magnificent lime-tree, on the other stands an ancient stone cross, at sight of which the horses, now going at a pace that was perfectly frightful, swerved so as to bring the wheel over the projecting roots of the tree.

I knew what was coming. I covered my eyes, unable to see it out, and turned my head away; at the same moment I heard a cry from my lady-friends, who had gone on a little.

Curiosity opened my eyes, and I saw a scene of utter confusion. Two of the horses were on the ground, the carriage lay upon its side with two wheels in the air; the men were busy removing the traces, and a lady, with a commanding air and figure had got out, and stood with clasped hands, raising the handkerchief that was in them every now and then to her eyes. Through the carriage door was now lifted a young lady, who appeared to be lifeless. My dear old father was already beside the elder lady, with his hat in his hand, evidently tendering his aid and the resources of his schloss. The lady did not appear to hear him, or to have eyes for anything but the slender girl who was being placed against the slope of the bank.

I approached; the young lady was apparently stunned, but she was certainly not dead. My father, who piqued himself on being something of a physician, had just had his fingers on her wrist and assured the lady, who declared herself her mother, that her pulse, though faint and irregular, was undoubtedly still distinguishable. The lady clasped her hands and looked upward, as if in a momentary transport of gratitude; but immediately she broke out again in that theatrical way which is, I believe, natural to some people.

She was what is called a fine looking woman for her time of life, and must have been handsome; she was tall, but not thin, and dressed in black velvet, and looked rather pale, but with a proud and commanding countenance, though now agitated strangely.

"Was ever being so born to calamity?" I heard her say, with clasped hands, as I came up. "Here am I, on a journey of life and death, in prosecuting which to lose an hour is possibly to lose all. My child will not have recovered sufficiently to resume her route for who can say how long. I must leave her; I cannot, dare not, delay. How far on, sir, can you tell, is the nearest village? I must leave her there; and shall not see my darling, or even hear of her till my return, three months hence."

I plucked my father by the coat, and whispered earnestly in his ear: "Oh! papa, pray ask her to let her stay with us—it would be so delightful. Do, pray."

"If Madame will entrust her child to the care of my daughter, and of her good gouvernante, Madame Perrodon, and permit her to remain as our guest, under my charge, until her return, it will confer a distinction and an obligation upon us, and we shall treat her with all the care and devotion which so sacred a trust deserves."

"I cannot do that, sir, it would be to task your kindness and chivalry too cruelly," said the lady, distractedly.

"It would, on the contrary, be to confer on us a very great kindness at the moment when we most need it. My daughter has just been disappointed by a cruel misfortune, in a visit from which she had long anticipated a great deal of happiness. If you confide this young lady to our care it will be her best consolation. The nearest village on your route is distant, and affords no such inn as you could think of placing you daughter at; you cannot allow her to continue her journey for any considerable distance without danger. If, as you say, you cannot suspend your journey, you must part with her to-night, and nowhere could you do so with more honest assurances of care and tenderness than here."

The lady threw on her daughter a glance which I fancied was not quite so affectionate as one might have anticipated from the beginning of the scene; then she beckoned slightly to my father, and withdrew two or three steps with him out of hearing; and talked to him with a fixed and stern countenance, not at all like that with which she had hitherto spoken.

I was filled with wonder that my father did not seem to perceive the change, and also unspeakably curious to learn what it could be that she was speaking, almost in his ear, with so much earnestness and rapidity.

Two or three minutes at most I think she remained thus employed, then she turned, and a few steps brought her to where her daughter lay, supported by Madame Perrodon. She kneeled beside her for a moment and whispered, as Madame supposed, a little benediction in her ear; then hastily kissing her she stepped into her carriage, the door was closed, the footmen in stately liveries jumped up behind, the outriders spurred on, the postillions cracked their whips, the horses plunged and broke suddenly into a furious canter that threatened soon again to become a gallop, and the carriage whirled away, followed at the same rapid pace by the two horsemen in the rear.

Chapter III

We followed the *cortège* with our eyes until it was swiftly lost to sight in the misty wood; and the very sound of the hoofs and the wheels died away in the silent night air.

Nothing remained to assure us that the adventure had not been an illusion of a moment but the young lady, who just at that moment opened her eyes. I could not see, for her face was turned from me, but she raised her head, evidently looking about her, and I heard a very sweet voice ask complainingly, "Where is mamma?"

My father in the meantime had sent a servant on horseback for the physician, who lived about two leagues away; and a bedroom was being prepared for the young lady's reception.

The stranger now rose, and leaning on Madame's arm, walked slowly over the drawbridge and into the castle gate.

In the hall, servants waited to receive her, and she was conducted forthwith to her room.

The room we usually sat in as our drawing-room is long, having four windows, that looked over the moat and drawbridge, upon the forest scene I have just described.

"Did you remark a woman in the carriage, after it was set up again, who did not get out," inquired Mademoiselle, "but only looked from the window?"

"No, we had not seen her."

Then she described a hideous black woman, with a sort of coloured turban on her head, and who was gazing all the time from the carriage window, nodding and grinning derisively towards the ladies, with gleaming eyes and large white eye-balls, and her teeth set as if in fury.

"Did you remark what an ill-looking pack of men the servants were?" asked Madame.

"Yes," said my father, who had just come in, "ugly, hang-dog looking fellows, as ever I beheld in my life. I hope they mayn't rob the poor lady in the forest. They are clever rogues, however; they got everything to rights in a minute."

"I dare say they are worn out with too long travelling," said Madame. "Besides looking wicked, their faces were so strangely lean, and dark, and sullen. I am very curious, I own; but I dare say the young lady will tell us all about it to-morrow, if she is sufficiently recovered."

"I don't think she will," said my father, with a mysterious smile, and a little nod of his head, as if he knew more about it than he cared to tell us.

This made us all the more inquisitive as to what had passed between him and the lady in the black velvet, in the brief but earnest interview that had immediately preceded her departure.

We were scarcely alone, when I entreated him to tell me. He did not need much pressing.

"There is no particular reason why I should not tell you. She expressed a reluctance to trouble us with the care of her daughter, saying she was in delicate health, and nervous, but not subject to any kind of seizure—she volunteered that—nor to any illusion; being, in fact, perfectly sane."

"How very odd to say all that!" I interpolated. "It was so unnecessary."

"At all events it *was* said," he laughed, "and as you wish to know all that passed, which was indeed very little, I tell you. She then said, 'I am making a long journey of *vital* importance—she emphasised the word—rapid and secret; I shall return for my child in three months; in the meantime, she will be silent as to who we are, whence we come, and whither we are travelling. That is all she said. She spoke very pure French. When she said the word 'secret,' she paused for a few seconds, looking sternly, her eyes fixed on mine. I fancy she makes a great point of that. You saw how quickly she was gone. I hope I have not done a very foolish thing, in taking charge of the young lady."

When the physician came down to the drawing-room, it was to report very favourably upon his patient. She was now sitting up, her pulse quite regular, apparently perfectly well. She had sustained no injury, and the little shock to her nerves had passed away quite harmlessly. There could be no harm certainly in my seeing her, if we both wished it; and, with this permission, I sent, forthwith, to know whether she would allow me to visit her for a few minutes in her room.

There were candles at the bed-side. She was sitting up; her slender pretty figure enveloped in the soft silk dressing-gown, embroidered with flowers, and lined with thick quilted silk, which her mother had thrown over her feet as she lay upon the ground.

What was it that, as I reached the bed-side and had just begun my little greeting, struck me dumb in a moment, and made me recoil a step or two from before her? I will tell you.

I saw the very face which had visited me in my childhood at night, which remained so fixed in my memory, and on which I had for so many years so often ruminated with horror, when no one suspected of what I was thinking.

It was pretty, even beautiful; and when I first beheld it, wore the same melancholy expression.

But this almost instantly lighted into a strange fixed smile of recognition.

There was a silence of fully a minute, and then at length *she* spoke; I could not.

"How wonderful!" she exclaimed. "Twelve years ago, I saw your face in a dream, and it has haunted me ever since."

"Wonderful indeed!" I repeated, overcoming with an effort the horror that had for a time suspended my utterances. "Twelve years ago, in vision or reality, I certainly saw you. I could not forget your face. It has remained before my eyes ever since."

Her smile had softened. Whatever I had fancied strange in it, was gone, and it and her dimpling cheeks were now delightfully pretty and intelligent.

She answered my welcome very prettily. I sat down beside her, still wondering; and she said:

"I must tell you my vision about you; it is so very strange that you and I should have had, each of the other so vivid a dream, that each should have seen, I you and you me, looking as we do now, when of course we both were mere children. I was a child, about six years old, and I awoke from a confused and troubled dream, and found myself in a room, unlike my nursery, wainscoted clumsily in some dark wood, and with cupboards and bedsteads, and chairs, and benches placed about it. The beds were, I thought, all empty, and the room itself without anyone but myself in it; and I, after looking about me for some time, and admiring especially an iron candlestick, with two branches, which I should certainly know again, crept under one of the beds to reach the window; but as I got from under the bed, I heard someone crying; and looking up, while I was still upon my knees, I saw *you*—most assuredly you—as I see you now; a beautiful young lady, with golden hair and large blue eyes, and lips—your lips—you, as you are here. Your looks won me; I climbed on the bed and put my arms about you, and I think we both fell asleep. I was aroused by a scream; you were sitting up screaming. I was frightened, and slipped down upon the ground, and, it seemed to me, lost consciousness for a moment; and when I came to myself, I was again in my nursery at home. Your face I have never forgotten since. I could not be misled by mere resemblance. You *are* the lady whom I saw then."

It was now my turn to relate my corresponding vision, which I did, to the undisguised wonder of my new acquaintance.

"I don't know which should be most afraid of the other," she said, again smiling—"If you were less pretty I think I should be very much afraid of you, but being as you are, and you and I both so young, I feel only that I have made your acquaintance twelve years ago, and have already a right to your intimacy; at all events it does seem as if we were destined, from our earliest childhood, to be friends. I wonder whether you feel as strangely drawn towards me as I do to you; I have never had a friend—shall I find one now?" She sighed, and her fine dark eyes gazed passionately on me.

I perceived now something of languor and exhaustion stealing over her, and hastened to bid her good night.

Next day came and we met again. I was delighted with my companion; that is to say, in many respects.

Her looks lost nothing in daylight—she was certainly the most beautiful creature I had ever seen, and the unpleasant remembrance of the face presented in my early dream, had lost the effect of the first unexpected recognition.

She confessed that she had experienced a similar shock on seeing me, and precisely the same faint antipathy that had mingled with my admiration of her. We now laughed together over our momentary horrors.

Chapter IV

I told you that I was charmed with her in most particulars.

There were some that did not please me so well.

She was above the middle height of women. I shall begin by describing her. She was slender, and wonderfully graceful. Except that her movements were languid—*very* languid—indeed, there was nothing in her appearance to indicate an invalid. Her complexion was rich and brilliant; her features were small and beautifully formed; her eyes large, dark, and lustrous; her hair was quite wonderful, I never saw hair so magnificently thick and long when it was down about her shoulders; I have often placed my hands under it, and laughed with wonder at its weight. It was exquisitely fine and soft, and in colour a rich very dark brown, with something of gold. I loved to let it down, tumbling with its own weight, as, in her room, she lay back in her chair talking in her sweet low voice, I used to fold and braid it, and spread it out and play with it. Heavens! If I had but known all!

I said there were particulars which did not please me. I have told you that her confidence won me the first night I saw her; but I found that she exercised with respect to herself, her mother, her history, everything in fact connected with her life, plans, and people, an ever wakeful reserve.

There was a coldnes, it seemed to me, beyond her years, in her smiling melancholy persistent refusal to afford me the least ray of light.

She used to place her pretty arms about my neck, draw me to her, and laying her cheek to mine, murmur with her lips near my ear, "Dearest, your little heart is wounded; think me not cruel because I obey the irresistible law of my strength and weakness; if your dear heart is wounded, my wild heart bleeds with yours. In the rapture of my enormous humiliation I live in your warm life, and you shall die—die, sweetly die—into mine. I cannot help it; as I draw near to you, you, in your turn, will draw near to others, and learn the rapture of that cruelty, which yet is love; so, for a while, seek to know no more of me and mine, but trust me with all your loving spirit."

And when she had spoken such a rhapsody, she would press me more closely in her trembling embrace, and her lips in soft kisses gently glow upon my cheek.

Her agitations and her language were unintelligible to me.

From these foolish embraces, which were not of very frequent occurrence, I must allow, I used to wish to extricate myself; but my energies seemed to fail me. Her murmured words sounded like a lullaby in my ear, and soothed my resistance into a trance, from which I only seemed to recover myself when she withdrew her arms.

In some respects her habits were odd. Perhaps not so singular in the opinion of a town lady like you, as they appeared to us rustic people. She used to come down very late, generally not till one o'clock, she would then take a cup of chocolate, but eat nothing; we then went out for a walk, which was a mere saunter, and she seemed, almost immediately, exhausted, and either returned to the schloss or sat on one of the benches that were placed, here and there, among the trees. This was a bodily languor in which her mind did not sympathise. She was always an animated talker, and very intelligent.

As we sat thus one afternoon under the trees a funeral passed us by. It was that of a pretty young girl, whom I had often seen, the daughter of one of the rangers of the forest. The poor man was walking behind the coffin of his darling; she was his only child, and he looked quite heartbroken. Peasants walking two-and-two came behind, they were singing a funeral hymn.

I rose to mark my respects as they passed, and joined in the hymn they were very sweetly singing.

My companion shook me a little roughly, and I turned surprised.

She said brusquely. "Don't you perceive how discordant that is?"

"I think it very sweet, on the contrary," I answered, vexed at the interruption, and very uncomfortable, lest the people who composed the little procession should observe and resent what was passing.

I resumed, therefore, instantly, and was again interrupted. "You pierce my ears," said Carmilla, almost angrily, and stopping her ears with her tiny fingers. "Besides, how can you tell that your religion and mine are the same; your forms wound me, and I hate funerals. What a fuss! Why *you* must die— *everyone* must die; and all are happier when they do. Come home."

"My father has gone on with the clergyman to the churchyard. I thought you knew she was to be buried to-day."

"*She?* I don't trouble my head about peasants. I don't know who she is," answered Carmilla, with a flash from her fine eyes.

"She is the poor girl who fancied she saw a ghost a fortnight ago, and has been dying ever since, till yesterday, when she expired,"

"Tell me nothing about ghosts. I shan't sleep to-night if you do."

We had moved a little back, and had come to another seat.

This was the first time I had seen her exhibit any definable symptoms of that delicacy of health which her mother had spoken of. It was the first time, also, I had seen her exhibit anything like temper.

Both passed away like a summer cloud; and never but once afterwards did I witness on her part a momentary sign of anger. I will tell you how it happened.

She and I were looking out of one of the long drawing-room windows, when there entered the courtyard, over the drawbridge, a figure of a wanderer whom I knew very well. He used to visit the schloss generally twice a year.

Then he advanced to the window with many smiles and salutations, and his hat in his left hand, his fiddle under his arm, and with a fluency that never took breath, he gabbled a long advertisement of all his accomplishments, and the resources of the various arts which he placed at our service, and the curiosities and entertainments which it was in his power, at our bidding, to display.

He was looking up, and we were smiling down upon him, amused; at least, I can answer for myself. His piercing black eyes, as he looked up in our faces, seemed to detect something that fixed for a moment his curiosity.

In an instant he unrolled a leather case, full of all manner of odd little steel instruments.

"See here, my lady," he said, displaying it, and addressing me, "I profess, among other things less useful, the art of dentistry. Plague take the dog!" he interpolated, "Silence, beast! He howls so that your ladyships can scarcely hear a word. Your noble friend, the young lady at your right, has the sharpest tooth,—long, thin, pointed, like an awl, like a needle; ha ha! With my sharp and long sight, as I look up, I have seen it distinctly; now if it happens to hurt the young lady, and I think it must, here am I, here are my file, my punch, and nippers; I will make it round and blunt, if her ladyship pleases; no longer the tooth of a fish, but of a beautiful young lady as she is. Hey? Is the young lady displeased? Have I been too bold? Have I offended her?"

The young lady, indeed, looked very angry as she drew back from the window.

"How dares that mountebank insult us so? Where is your father? I shall demand redress from him. My father would have had the wretch tied up to the pump, and flogged with a cartwhip, and burnt to the bones with the castle brand!"

She retired from the window a step or two, and sat down, and had hardly lost sight of the offender, when her wrath subsided as suddenly as it had risen, and she gradually recovered her usual tone, and seemed to forget the little hunchback and his follies.

My father was out of spirits that evening. On coming in he told us that there had been another case very similar to the two fatal ones which had lately occurred. The sister of a young peasant on his estate, only a mile away, was very ill, had been, as she described it, attacked very nearly in the same way, and was now slowly but steadily sinking.

"The doctor said he would come here to-day," said my father, after a silence. "I want to know what he thinks about it, and what he thinks we had better do."

"Doctors never did me any good," said Carmilla.

"Then you have been ill?" I asked.

"More ill than ever you were," she answered.

"Long ago?"

"Yes, a long time. I suffered from this very illness; but I forget all but my pain and weakness, and they were not so bad as are suffered in other diseases."

"You were very young then?"

"I dare say; let us talk no more of it. You would not wound a friend?" She looked languidly in my eyes, and passed her arm round my waist lovingly, and led me out of the room. My father was busy over some papers near the window.

Chapter v

This evening there arrived from Gratz the grave, dark-faced son of the picture cleaner, with a horse and cart laden with two large packing cases, having many pictures in each. It was a journey of ten leagues, and whenever a messenger arrived at the schloss from our little capital of Gratz, we used to crowd about him in the hall, to hear the news.

My father had a list in his hand, from which he read, as the artist rummaged out the corresponding numbers. I don't know that the pictures were very good, but they were, undoubtedly, very old, and some of them very curious also. They had, for the most part, the merit of being now seen by me, I may say, for the first time; for the smoke and dust of time had all but obliterated them.

"There is a picture that I have not seen yet," said my father. "In one corner, at the top of it, is the name, as well as I could read, 'Marcia Karnstein,' and the date '1698'; and I am curious to see how it has turned out."

I remembered it; it was a small picture, about a foot and a half high, and nearly square, without a frame; but it was so blackened by age that I could not make it out.

The artist now produced it, with evident pride. It was quite beautiful; it was startling; it seemed to live. It was the effigy of Carmilla!

"Carmilla, dear, here is an absolute miracle. Here you are, living, smiling, ready to speak, in this picture. Isn't it beautiful, papa? And see, even the little mole on her throat."

The young lady did not acknowledge this pretty speech, did not seem to hear it. She was leaning back in her seat, her fine eyes under their long lashes gazing on me in contemplation, and she smiled in a kind of rapture.

"And now you can read quite plainly the name that is written in the corner. It is not Marcia; it looks as if it was done in gold. The name is Mircalla, Countess Karnstein, and this is a little coronet over it, and underneath A.D. 1698. I am descended from the Karnsteins; that is, mamma was."

"Ah!" said the lady, languidly, "So am I, I think, a very long descent, very ancient. Are there any Karnsteins living now?"

"None who bear the name, I believe. The family were ruined, I believe, in some civil wars, long ago, but the ruins of the castle are only about three miles away."

She was gazing on me with eyes from which all fire, all meaning had flown, and a face colourless and apathetic.

"You look ill, Carmilla; a little faint. You certainly must take some wine," I said.

Chapter VI

When we got into the drawing-room, and had sat down to our coffee and chocolate, although Carmilla did not take any, she seemed quite herself again, and Madame, and Mademoiselle De Lafontaine, joined us, and made a little card party, in the course of which papa came in for what he called his "dish of tea."

When the game was over he sat down beside Carmilla on the sofa, and asked her, a little anxiously, whether she had heard from her mother since her arrival.

She answered, "No."

He then asked whether she knew where a letter would reach her at present.

"I cannot tell," she answered ambiguously, "but I have been thinking of leaving you; you have been already too hospitable and too kind to me. I have given you an infinity of trouble, and I should wish to take a carriage to-morrow, and post in pursuit of her; I know where I shall ultimately find her, although I dare not yet tell you."

"But you must not dream of any such thing," exclaimed my father, to my great relief.

I accompanied Carmilla as usual to her room, and sat and chatted with her while she was preparing for bed.

I bid her good night, and crept from the room with an uncomfortable sensation.

The precautions of nervous people are infectious, and persons of a like temperament are pretty sure, after a time, to imitate them. I had adopted Carmilla's habit of locking her bedroom door, having taken into my head all her whimsical alarms about midnight invaders and prowling assassins. I had also adopted her precaution of making a brief search through her room, to satisfy herself that no lurking assassin or robber was "ensconced."

These wise measures taken, I got into my bed and fell asleep. A light was burning in my room. This was an old habit, of very early date, and which nothing could have tempted me to dispense with.

Thus fortified I might take my rest in peace. But dreams come through stone walls, light up dark rooms, or darken light ones, and their persons make their exits and their entrances as they please, and laugh at locksmiths.

I had a dream that night that was the beginning of a very strange agony.

I cannot call it a nightmare, for I was quite conscious of being asleep. But I was equally conscious of being in my room, and lying in bed, precisely as I actually was. I saw, or fancied I saw, the room and its furniture just as I had seen it last, except that it was very dark, and I saw something moving round the foot of the bed, which at first I could not accurately distinguish. But I soon saw that it was a sooty-black animal that resembled a monstrous cat. It appeared to me about four or five feet long, for it measured fully the length of the hearthrug as it passed over it; and it continued to-ing and fro-ing with the lithe, sinister restlessness of a beast in a cage. I could not cry out, although as you may suppose, I was terrified. Its pace was growing faster, and the room rapidly darker and darker, and at length so dark that I could no longer see anything of it but its eyes. I felt it spring lightly on the bed. The two broad eyes approached my face, and suddenly I felt a stinging pain as if two large needles darted, an inch or two apart, deep into my breast. I waked with a scream. The room was lighted by the candle that burnt there all through the night, and I saw a female figure standing at the foot of the bed, a little at the right side. It was in a dark loose dress, and its hair was down and covered its shoulders. A block of stone could not have been more still. There was not the slightest stir of respiration. As I stared at it, the figure appeared to have changed its place, and was now nearer the door; then, close to it, the door opened, and it passed out.

I was now relieved, and able to breathe and move. My first thought was that Carmilla had been playing me a trick, and that I had forgotten to secure my door. I hastened to it, and found it locked as usual on the inside. I was afraid to open it—I was horrified. I sprang into my bed and covered my head up in the bedclothes, and lay more dead than alive till morning.

Chapter VII

It would be vain my attempting to tell you the horror with which, even now, I recall the occurrence of that night. It was no such transitory terror as a dream leaves behind it. It seemed to deepen by time, and communicated itself to the room and the very furniture that had encompassed the apparition.

I could not bear next day to be alone for a moment. I should have told papa, but for two opposite reasons. At one time I thought he would laugh at my story, and I could not bear its being treated as a jest; and at another, I thought he might fancy that I had been attacked by the mysterious complaint which had invaded our neighbourhood. I had myself no misgivings of the kind, and as he had been rather an invalid for some time, I was afraid of alarming him.

I was comfortable enough with my good-natured companions, Madame Perrodon, and the vivacious Mademoiselle Lafontaine. They both perceived that I was out of spirits and nervous, and at length I told them what lay so heavy at my heart.

Carmilla came down rather later than usual that day.

"I was so frightened last night," she said, so soon as we were together, "and I am sure I should have seen something dreadful if it had not been for that charm I bought from the poor little hunchback whom I called such hard names. I had a dream of something black coming round my bed, and I awoke in a perfect horror, and I really thought, for some seconds, I saw a dark figure near the chimney-piece, but I felt under my pillow for my charm, and the moment my fingers touched it, the figure disappeared, and I felt quite certain, only that I had it by me, that something frightful would have made its appearance, and, perhaps, throttled me, as it did those poor people we heard of."

"Well, listen to me," I began, and recounted my adventure, at the recital of which she appeared horrified.

For some nights I slept profoundly; but still every morning I felt the same lassitude, and a languor weighed upon me all day. I felt myself a changed girl. A strange melancholy was stealing over me, a melancholy that I would have interrupted. Dim thoughts of death began to open, and an idea that I was slowly sinking took gentle, and, somehow, not unwelcome, possession of me. If it was sad, the tone of mind which this induced was also sweet. Whatever it might be, my soul acquiesced in it.

I would not admit that I was ill. I would not consent to tell my papa, or to have the doctor sent for.

Carmilla became more devoted to me than ever, and her strange paroxysms of languid adoration more frequent. She used to gloat on me with increasing ardour the more my strength and spirits waned. This always shocked me like a momentary glare of insanity.

Certain vague and strange sensations visited me in my sleep. The prevailing one was of that pleasant, peculiar cold thrill which we feel in bathing, when we move against the current of a river. This was soon accompanied by dreams that seemed interminable; and were so vague that I could never recollect their scenery and persons, or any one connected portion of their action. But they left an awful impression, and a sense of exhaustion, as if I had passed through a long period of great mental exertion and danger. After all these dreams there remained on waking a remembrance of having been in a place very nearly dark, and of having spoken to people whom I could not see; and especially of one clear voice, of a female's very deep, that spoke as if at a distance, slowly, and producing always the same sensation of indescribable solemnity and fear. Sometimes there came a sensation as if a hand was drawn softly along my cheek and neck. Sometimes it was as if warm lips kissed me, and longer and more lovingly as they reached my throat, but there the caress fixed itself. My heart beat faster, my breathing rose and fell rapidly and full drawn; a sobbing, that rose into a sense of strangulation, supervened, and turned into a dreadful convulsion, in which my senses left me and I became unconscious.

It was now three weeks since the commencement of this unaccountable state. My sufferings had, during the last week, told upon my appearance. I had grown pale, my eyes were dilated and darkened underneath and the languor which I had long felt began to display itself in my countenance.

My father asked me often whether I was ill; but, with an obstinacy which now seems to me unaccountable, I persisted in assuring him that I was quite well.

I am going to tell you now of a dream that led immediately to an odd discovery.

One night, instead of the voice I was accustomed to hear in the dark, I heard one, sweet and tender, and at the same time terrible, which said, "Your mother warns you to beware of the assassin." At the same time a light unexpectedly sprang up, and I saw Carmilla, standing, near the foot of my bed, in her white nightdress, bathed, from her chin to her feet, in one great stain of blood.

I wakened with a shriek, possessed with the one idea that Carmilla was being murdered. I remember springing from my bed, and my next recollection is that of standing on the lobby, crying for help.

Madame and Mademoiselle came scurrying out of their rooms in alarm; a lamp burned always in the lobby, and seeing me, they soon learned the cause of my terror.

I insisted on our knocking at Carmilla's door. Our knocking was unanswered. It soon became a pounding and an uproar. We shrieked her name, but all was vain.

We all grew frightened, for the door was locked. We hurried back, in panic, to my room. There we rang the bell long and furiously. If my father's room had been at the side of the house, we would have called him up at once to our aid. But, alas! he was quite out of hearing, and to reach him involved an excursion for which we none of us had courage.

Servants, however, soon came running up the stairs; I had got on my dressing-gown and slippers meanwhile, and my companions were already similarly furnished. Recognising the voices of the servants on the lobby, we sallied out together; and having renewed, as fruitlessly, our summons at Carmilla's door, I ordered the men to force the lock. They did so, and we stood, holding our lights aloft, in the doorway, and so stared into the room.

We called her by name; but there was still no reply. We looked round the room. Everything was undisturbed. It was exactly in the state in which I had left it on bidding her good night. But Carmilla was gone.

Chapter VIII

At sight of the room, perfectly undisturbed except for our violent entrance, we began to cool a little, and soon recovered our senses sufficiently to dismiss the men. It had struck Mademoiselle that possibly Carmilla had been wakened by the uproar at her door, and in her first panic had jumped from her bed, and hid herself in a press, or behind a curtain, from which she could not, of course, emerge until the majordomo and his myrmidons had withdrawn. We now recommenced our search, and began to call her by name again.

It was all to no purpose. Our perplexity and agitation increased. We examined the windows. But they were secured. I implored of Carmilla, if she had concealed herself, to play this cruel trick no longer—to come out, and to end our anxieties. It was all useless. I was by this time convinced that she was not in the room, nor in the dressing-room, the door of which was still locked on this side.

It was past four o'clock, and I preferred passing the remaining hours of darkness in Madame's room. Daylight brought no solution of the difficulty.

The whole household, with my father at its head, was in a state of agitation next morning. Every part of the château was searched.

The morning was passed in alarm and excitement. It was now one o'clock, and still no tidings. I ran up to Carmilla's room, and found her standing at her dressing-table. I was astounded. I could not believe my eyes. She beckoned me to her with her pretty finger, in silence. Her face expressed extreme fear.

I ran to her in an ecstasy of joy; I kissed and embraced her again and again. I ran to the bell and rang it vehemently, to bring others to the spot, who might at once relieve my father's anxiety.

"Dear Carmilla, what has become of you all this time? We have been in agonies of anxiety about you," I exclaimed. "Where have you been? How did you come back?"

"Last night has been a night of wonders," she said.

"For mercy's sake, explain all you can."

"It was past two last night," she said, "when I went to sleep as usual in my bed, with my doors locked, that of the dressing-room, and that opening upon the gallery. My sleep was uninterrupted, and, so far as I know, dreamless; but I woke just now on the sofa in the dressing-room there, and I found the door between the rooms open, and the other door forced. How could all this have happened without my being wakened? It must have been accompanied with a great deal of noise, and I am particularly easily wakened; and how could I have been carried out of my bed without my sleep having been interrupted, I whom the slightest stir startles?"

By this time, Madame, Mademoiselle, my father, and a number of the servants were in the room. Carmilla was, of course, overwhelmed with inquiries, congratulations, and welcomes. She had but one story to tell, and seemed the least able of all the party to suggest any way of accounting for what had happened.

My father took a turn up and down the room, thinking. I saw Carmilla's eye follow him for a moment with a sly, dark glance.

"Will you forgive me, my dear, if I risk a conjecture, and ask a question?"

Carmilla was leaning on her hand dejectedly; Madame and I were listening breathlessly.

"Now, my question is this. Have you ever been suspected of walking in your sleep?"

"Never, since I was very young indeed."

"But you did walk in your sleep when you were young?"

"Yes, I know I did. I have been told so often by my old nurse."

My father smiled and nodded.

Chapter IX

As Carmilla would not hear of an attendant sleeping in her room, my father arranged that a servant should sleep outside her door, so that she could not attempt to make another such excursion without being arrested at her own door.

That night passed quietly; and next morning early, the doctor, whom my father had sent for without telling me a word about it, arrived to see me.

I told him my story, and as I proceeded he grew graver and graver.

We were standing, he and I, in the recess of one of the windows, facing one another. When my statement was over, he leaned with his shoulders against the wall, and with his eyes fixed on me earnestly, with an interest in which was a dash of horror.

After a minute's reflection, he asked Madame if he could see my father.

He and the doctor talked for some time in the same recess where I had just conferred with the physician. It seemed an earnest and argumentative conversation. The room is very large and I and Madame stood together, burning with curiosity, at the farther end. Not a word could we hear, however, for they spoke in a very low tone, and the deep recess of the window quite concealed the doctor from view, and very nearly my father, whose foot, arm, and shoulder only could we see; and the voices were, I suppose, all the less audible for the sort of closet which the thick wall and window formed.

After a time my father's face looked into the room; it was pale, thoughtful, and, I fancied, agitated.

"Laura, dear, come here for a moment. Madame, we shan't trouble you, the doctor says, at present."

Accordingly I approached, for the first time a little alarmed; for, although I felt very weak, I did not feel ill; and strength, one always fancies, is a thing that may be picked up when we please.

My father held out his hand to me, as I drew near, but he was looking at the doctor, and he said:

"You mentioned a sensation like that of two needles piercing the skin, somewhere about your neck, on the night you experienced your first horrible dream. Is there still any soreness?"

"None at all," I answered.

"Can you indicate with your finger about the point at which you think this occurred?"

"Very little below, my throat—*here,*" I answered.

"You see it now with your own eyes," said the doctor, with a gloomy triumph.

"What is it?" I exclaimed, beginning to be frightened.

"Nothing, my dear young lady, but a small blue spot, about the size of the tip of your little finger; and now," he continued, turning to papa, "the question is what is best to be done?"

And then they repeated their directions to me and to Madame, and with this parting charge my father left us, and walked out with the doctor; and I saw them pacing together up and down between the road and the moat, on the grassy platform in front of the castle, evidently absorbed in earnest conversation.

About half an hour after my father came in—he had a letter in his hand—and said:

"This letter had been delayed; it is from General Spielsdorf. He might have been here yesterday, he may not come till to-morrow or he may be here to-day."

He turned and left the room, but came back before I had done wondering and puzzling over the oddity of all this; it was merely to say that he was going to Karnstein, and had ordered the carriage to be ready at twelve, and that I and Madame should accompany him; he was going to see the priest who lived near those picturesque grounds, upon business, and as Carmilla had never seen them, she could follow, when she came down, with Mademoiselle, who would bring materials for what you call a picnic, which might be laid for us in the ruined castle.

At twelve o'clock, accordingly, I was ready, and not long after, my father, Madame and I set out upon our projected drive.

Passing the drawbridge we turn to the right, and follow the road over the steep Gothic bridge, westward, to reach the deserted village and ruined castle of Karnstein.

The irregularities of the ground often lead the road out of its course, and cause it to wind beautifully round the sides of broken hollows and the steeper sides of the hills, among varieties of ground almost inexhaustible.

Turning one of these points, we suddenly encountered our old friend, the General, riding towards us attended by a mounted servant. His portmanteaus were following in a hired wagon, such as we term a cart.

The General dismounted as we pulled up, and, after the usual greetings, was easily persuaded to accept the vacant seat in the carriage and send his horse on with his servant to the schloss.

Chapter x

It was about ten months since we had last seen him; but that time had sufficed to make an alteration of years in his appearance. He had grown thinner; something of gloom and anxiety had taken the place of that cordial serenity which used to characterise his features.

You are going to the Ruins of Karnstein?" he said. "Yes, it is a lucky coincidence; do you know I was going to ask you to bring me there to inspect them. I have a special object in exploring. There is a ruined chapel, ain't there, with a great many tombs of that extinct family?"

"So there are—highly interesting," said my father. "I hope you are thinking of claiming the title and estates?"

My father said this gaily, but the General did not recollect the laugh, or even the smile, which courtesy exacts for a friend's joke; on the contrary, he looked grave and even fierce, ruminating on a matter that stirred his anger and horror.

"Something very different," he said, gruffly, "I mean to unearth some of those fine people. I hope, by God's blessing, to accomplish a pious sacrilege here, which will relieve our earth of certain monsters, and enable honest people to sleep in their beds without being assailed by murderers. I have strange things to tell you, my dear friend, such as I myself would have scouted as incredible a few months since."

My father looked at him again, but this time not with a glance of suspicion—with an eye, rather, of keen intelligence and alarm.

"The house of Karnstein," he said, "has been long extinct: a hundred years at least. My dear wife was maternally descended from the Karnsteins. But the name and title have long ceased to exist. The castle is a ruin; the very village is deserted; it is fifty years since the smoke of a chimney was seen there; not a roof left."

"Quite true. I have heard a great deal about that since I last saw you; a great deal that will astonish you. But I had better relate everything in the order in which it occurred," said the General, "You saw my dear ward—my child, I may call her. No creature could have been more beautiful, and only three months ago none more blooming.

"We have been very old friends; I knew you would feel for me, childless as I am. She had become an object of very near interest to me, and repaid my care by an affection that cheered my home and made my life happy. That is all gone. The years that remain to me on earth may not be very long; but by God's mercy I hope to accomplish a service to mankind before I die, and to subserve the vengeance of Heaven upon the fiends who have murdered my poor child in the spring of her hopes and beauty!"

"You said, just now, that you intended relating everything as it occurred," said my father. "Pray do; I assure you that it is not mere curiosity that prompts me."

Chapter XI

"With all my heart," said the General, with an effort; and after a short pause in which to arrange his subject he commenced one of the strangest narratives I ever heard.

"My dear child was looking forward with great pleasure to the visit you had been so good as to arrange for her to your charming daughter." Here he made me a gallant but melancholy bow. "In the meantime we had an invitation to my old friend the Count Carlsfeld, whose schloss is about six leagues to the other side of Karnstein. It was to attend the series of fêtes which, you remember, were given by him in honour of his illustrious visitor, the Grand Duke Charles."

"Yes; and very splendid, I believe, they were," said my father.

"Princely! But then his hospitalities are quite regal. He has Aladdin's lamp. The night from which my sorrow dates was devoted to a magnificent masquerade. The grounds were thrown open, the trees hung with coloured lamps. There was such a display of fireworks as Paris itself had never witnessed.

"My dear child was looking quite beautiful. She wore no mask. Her excitement and delight added an unspeakable charm to her features, always lovely. I remarked a young lady, dressed magnificently, but wearing a mask, who appeared to me to be observing my ward with extraordinary interest. I had seen her, earlier in the evening, in the great hall, and again, for a few minutes, walking near us, on the terrace under the castle windows, similarly employed. A lady, also masked, richly and gravely dressed, and with a stately air, like a person of rank, accompanied her as a chaperon. Had the young lady not worn a mask, I could, of course, have been much more certain upon the question whether she was really watching my poor darling. I am now well assured that she was.

"We were now in one of the *salons*. My poor dear child had been dancing, and was resting a little in one of the chairs near the door; I was standing near. The two ladies I have mentioned had approached and the younger took the chair next my ward; while her companion stood beside me and for a little time addressed herself, in a low tone, to her charge.

"Availing herself of the privilege of her mask, she turned to me, and in the tone of an old friend, and calling me by my name, opened a conversation with me, which piqued my curiosity a good deal. She referred to many scenes where she had met me at Court, and at distinguished houses. She alluded to little incidents which I had long ceased to think of, but which, I found, had only lain in abeyance in my memory, for they instantly started into life at her touch.

"In the meantime the young lady, whom her mother called by the odd name of Millarca, when she once or twice addressed her, had, with the same ease and grace, got into conversation with my ward.

"In the meantime, availing myself of the licence of a masquerade, I put not a few questions to the elder lady.

" 'You have puzzled me utterly,' I said, laughing. 'Is that not enough? Won't you, now, consent to stand on equal terms, and do me the kindness to remove your mask?'

" 'Can any request be more unreasonable?" she replied. 'Ask a lady to yield an advantage! Beside, how do you know you should recognise me? Years make changes.'

" 'At all events, you won't deny this,' I said, 'that being honoured by your permission to converse, I ought to know how to address you. Shall I say Madame la Comtesse?'

" 'As to that,' she began; but she was interrupted, almost as she opened her lips, by a gentleman, dressed in black, who looked particularly elegant and distinguished, with this drawback, that his face was the most deadly pale I ever saw, except in death. He was in no masquerade—in the plain evening dress of a gentleman; and he said, without a smile, but with a courtly and unusually low bow:—

" 'Will Madame la Comtesse permit me to say a very few words which may interest her?'

"The lady turned quickly to him, and touched her lip in token of silence; she then said to me, 'Keep my place for me, General; I shall return when I have said a few words.'

"I spent the interval in cudgelling my brains for a conjecture as to the indentity of the lady who seemed to remember me so kindly, and I was thinking of turning about and joining in the conversation between my pretty ward and the Countess's daughter, and trying whether, by the time she returned, I might not have a surprise in store for her, by having her name, title, château, and estates at my fingers' ends, But at this moment she returned, accompanied by the pale man in black, who said:

" 'I shall return and inform Madame la Comtesse when her carriage is at the door.'

"He withdrew with a bow."

Chapter XII

" 'Then we are to lose Madame La Comtesse, but I hope only for a few hours,' I said, with a low bow.

" 'It may be that only, or it may be a few weeks. It was very unlucky his speaking to me just now as he did. Do you not know me?'

"I assured her I did not.

" 'You shall know me,' she said, 'but not at present. We are older and better friends than, perhaps, you suspect. I cannot yet declare myself. I shall in three weeks pass your beautiful schloss, about which I have been making enquiries. I shall then look in upon you for an hour or two, and renew a friendship which I never think of without a thousand pleasant recollections. This moment a piece of news has reached me like a thunderbolt. I must set out now, and travel by a devious route, nearly a hundred miles, with all the dispatch I can possibly make.'

"She went on to make her petition, and it was in the tone of a person from whom such a request amounted to conferring, rather than seeking a favour. This was only in manner, and, as it seemed, quite unconsciously. Than the terms in which it was expressed, nothing could be more deprecatory. It was simply that I would consent to take charge of her daughter during her absence.

"At another time I should have told her to wait a little, until, at least, we knew who they were. But I had not a moment to think in. The two ladies assailed me together, and I must confess the refined and beautiful face of the young lady, about which there was something extremely engaging, as well as the elegance and fire of high birth, determined me; and quite overpowered, I submitted, and undertook, too easily, the care of the young lady, whom her mother called Millarca.

"The Countess beckoned to her daughter, who listened with grave attention while she told her, in general terms, how suddenly and peremptorily she had been summoned, and also of the arrangement she had made for her under my care, adding that I was one of her earliest and most valued friends.

"I made, of course, such speeches as the case seemed to call for, and found myself, on reflection, in a position which I did not half like.

"The gentleman in black returned, and very ceremoniously conducted the lady from the room.

"That day Millarca came home with us. I was only too happy, after all, to have secured so charming a companion for my dear girl."

Chapter XIII

"There soon, however, appeared some drawbacks. In the first place, Millarca complained of extreme languor—the weakness that remained after her late illness—and she never emerged from her room till the afternoon was pretty far advanced. In the next place, it was accidentally discovered, although she always locked her door on the inside, and never disturbed the key from its place till she admitted the maid to assist at her toilet, that she was undoubtedly sometimes absent from her room in the very early morning, and at various times later in the day, before she wished it to be understood that she was stirring. She was repeatedly seen from the windows of the schloss, in the first faint grey of the morning, walking through the trees, in an easterly direction, and looking like a person in a trance. This convinced me that she walked in her sleep. But this hypothesis did not solve the puzzle. How did she pass out from her room, leaving the door locked on the inside? How did she escape from the house without unbarring door or window?

"In the midst of my perplexities, an anxiety of a far more urgent kind presented itself.

"My dear child began to lose her looks and health, and that in a manner so mysterious, and even horrible, that I became thoroughly frightened.

"She was at first visited by appalling dreams; then, as she fancied, by a spectre, sometimes resembling Millarca, sometimes in the shape of a beast, indistinctly seen, walking round the foot of her bed, from side to side. Lastly came sensations. One, not unpleasant, but very peculiar, she said, resembled the flow of an icy stream against her breast. At a later time, she felt something like a pair of large needles pierce her a little below the throat, with a very sharp pain. A few nights after, followed a gradual and convulsive sense of strangulation; then came unconsciousness."

A vista opened in the forest; we were on a sudden under the chimneys and gables of the ruined village, and the towers and battlements of the dismantled castle, round which gigantic trees are grouped, overhung us from a slight eminence.

In a frightened dream I got down from the carriage, and in silence, for we had each abundant matter for thinking; we soon mounted the ascent, and were among the spacious chambers, winding stairs, and dark corridors of the castle.

"And this was once the palatial residence of the Karnsteins!" said the old General at length, as from a great window he looked out across the village, and saw the wide, undulating expanse of forest. "It was a bad family, and here its blood-stained annals were written," he continued. "It is hard that they should, after death, continue to plague the human race with their atrocious lusts. That is the chapel of the Karnsteins, down there."

The old General, though not I fear given to the praying mood, raised his hands and eyes to heaven, in mute thanksgiving for some moments.

"To-morrow," I heard him say; "the commissioner will be here, and the Inquisition will be held according to law."

The next day the formal proceedings took place in the Chapel of Karnstein. The grave of the Countess Mircalla was opened; and the General and my father recognised each his perfidious and beautiful guest, in the face now disclosed to view. The features, though a hundred and fifty years had passed since her funeral, were tinted with the warmth of life. Her eyes were open; no cadaverous smell exhaled from the coffin. The two medical men, one officially present, the other on the part of the promoter of the inquiry, attested the marvellous fact that there was a faint but appreciable respiration, and a corresponding action of the heart. The limbs were perfectly flexible, the flesh elastic; and the leaden coffin floated with blood, in which to a depth of seven inches, the body lay immersed. Here then, were all the admitted signs and proofs of vampirism. The body, therefore, in accordance with the ancient practice, was raised, and a sharp stake driven through the heart of the vampire, who uttered a piercing shriek at the moment, in all respects such as might escape from a living person in the last agony. Then the head was struck off, and a torrent of blood flowed from the severed neck. The body and head was next placed on a pile of wood, and reduced to ashes, which were thrown upon the river and borne away, and that territory has never since been plagued by the visits of a vampire.

ROSA MULHOLLAND

NOT TO BE TAKEN
AT BED-TIME

This is the legend of a house called the Devil's Inn, standing in the heather on the top of the Connemara mountains, in a shallow valley hollowed between five peaks. Tourists sometimes come in sight of it on September evenings; a crazy and weather-stained apparition, with the sun glaring at it angrily between the hills, and striking its shattered window-panes. Guides are known to shun it, however.

The house was built by a stranger, who came no one knew whence, and whom the people nicknamed Coll Dhu (Black Coll), because of his sullen bearing and solitary habits. His dwelling they called the Devil's Inn, because no tired traveller had ever been asked to rest under its roof, nor friend known to cross its threshold. No one bore him company in his retreat but a wizen-faced old man, who shunned the good-morrow of the trudging peasant when he made occasional excursions to the nearest village for provisions for himself and master, and who was as secret as a stone concerning all the antecedents of both.

For the first year of their residence in the country, there had been much speculation as to who they were, and what they did with themselves up there among the clouds and eagles. Some said that Coll Dhu was a scion of the old family from whose hands the surrounding lands had passed; and that, embittered by poverty and pride, he had come to bury himself in solitude, and brood over his misfortunes. Others hinted of crime, and flight from another country; others again whispered of those who were cursed from their birth, and could never smile, nor yet make friends with a fellow-creature till the day of their death. But when two years had passed, the wonder had somewhat died out, and Coll Dhu was little thought of, except when a herd looking for sheep crossed the track of a big dark man walking the mountains gun in hand, to whom he did not dare say "Lord save you!" or when a housewife rocking her cradle of a winter's night, crossed herself as a gust of storm thundered over her cabin-roof, with the exclamation, "Oh, then, it's Coll Dhu that has enough o' the fresh air about his head up there this night, the crature!"

Coll Dhu had lived thus in his solitude for some years, when it became known that Colonel Blake, the new lord of the soil, was coming to visit the country. By climbing one of the peaks encircling his eyrie, Coll could look sheer down a mountain-side, and see in miniature beneath him, a grey old

317

dwelling with ivied chimneys and weather-slated walls, standing amongst straggling trees and grim warlike rocks, that gave it the look of a fortress, gazing out to the Atlantic for ever with the eager eyes of all its windows, as if demanding perpetually, "What tidings from the New World?"

He could see now masons and carpenters crawling about below, like ants in the sun, over-running the old house from base to chimney, daubing here and knocking there, tumbling down walls that looked to Coll, up among the clouds, like a handful of jack-stones, and building up others that looked like the toy fences in a child's Farm. Throughout several months he must have watched the busy ants at their task of breaking and mending again, disfiguring and beautifying; but when all was done he had not the curiosity to stride down and admire the handsome panelling of the new billiard-room, nor yet the fine view which the enlarged bay-window in the drawing-room commanded of the watery highway to Newfoundland.

Deep summer was melting into autumn, and the amber streaks of decay were beginning to creep out and trail over the ripe purple of moor and mountain, when Colonel Blake, his only daughter, and a party of friends, arrived in the country. The grey house below was alive with gaiety, but Coll Dhu no longer found an interest in observing it from his eyrie. When he watched the sun rise or set, he chose to ascend some crag that looked on no human habitation. When he sallied forth on his excursion, gun in hand, he set his face towards the most isolated wastes, dipping into the loneliest valleys, and scaling the nakedest ridges. When he came by chance within call of other excursionists, gun in hand he plunged into the shade of some hollow, and avoided an encounter. Yet it was fated, for all that, that he and Colonel Black should meet.

Toward the evening of one bright September day, the wind changed, and in half an hour the mountains were wrapped in a thick blinding mist. Coll Dhu was far from his den, but so well had he searched these mountains, and inured himself to their climate, that neither storm, rain, nor fog, had power to disturb him. But while he stalked on his way, a faint and agonised cry from a human voice reached him through the smothering mist. He quickly tracked the sound, and gained the side of a man who was stumbling along in danger of death at every step.

"Follow me!" said Coll Dhu to this man, and, in an hour's time, brought him safely to the lowlands, and up to the walls of the eager-eyed mansion.

"I am Colonel Blake," said the frank soldier, when, having left the fog behind him, they stood in the starlight under the lighted windows. "Pray tell me quickly to whom I owe my life."

As he spoke, he glanced up at his benefactor, a large man with a sombre sun-burned face.

"Colonel Blake," said Coll Dhu, after a strange pause, "your father suggested to my father to stake his estates at the gaming table. They were staked, and the tempter won. Both are dead; but you and I live, and I have sworn to injure you."

The colonel laughed good humouredly at the uneasy face above him.

"And you began to keep your oath to-night by saving my life?" said he. "Come! I am a soldier, and know how to meet an enemy; but I had far rather meet a friend. I shall not be happy till you have eaten my salt. We have merrymaking to-night in honour of my daughter's birthday. Come in and join us?"

Coll Dhu looked at the earth doggedly.

"I have told you," he said, "who and what I am, and I will not cross your threshold."

But at this moment (so runs my story) a French window opened among the flower-beds by which they were standing, and a vision appeared which stayed the words on Coll's tongue. A stately girl, clad in white satin, stood framed in the ivied window, with the warm light from within streaming around her richly-moulded figure into the night. Her face was as pale as her gown, her eyes were swimming in tears, but a firm smile sat on her lips as she held out both hands to her father. The light behind her, touched the glistening folds of her dress—the lustrous pearls round her throat—the coronet of blood-red roses which encircled the knotted braids at the back of her head. Satin, pearls, and roses—had Coll Dhu, of the Devil's Inn, never set eyes upon such things before?

Evleen Blake was no nervous tearful miss. A few quick words—"Thank God! you're safe; the rest have been home an hour"—and a tight pressure of her father's fingers between her own jewelled hands, were all that betrayed the uneasiness she had suffered.

"Faith, my love, I owe my life to this brave gentleman!" said the blithe colonel. "Press him to come in and be our guest, Evleen. He wants to retreat to his mountains, and lose himself again in the fog where I found him; or, rather where he found me! Come, sir" (to Coll), "you must surrender to this fair besieger."

An introduction followed. "Coll Dhu!" murmured Evleen Blake, for she had heard the common tales of him; but with a frank welcome she invited her father's preserver to taste the hospitality of that father's house.

"I beg you to come in, sir," she said; "but for you our gaiety must have been turned into mourning. A shadow will be upon our mirth if our benefactor disdains to join in it."

With a sweet grace, mingled with a certain hauteur from which she was never free, she extended her white hand to the tall looming figure outside the window; to have it grasped and wrung in a way that made the proud girl's eyes flash their amazement, and the same little hand clench itself in displeasure, when it had hid itself like an outraged thing among the shining folds of her gown. Was this Coll Dhu mad, or rude?

The guest no longer refused to enter, but followed the white figure into a little study where a lamp burned; and the gloomy stranger, the bluff colonel, and the young mistress of the house, were fully discovered to each other's eyes. Evleen glanced at the newcomer's dark face, and shuddered with a feeling of indescribable dread and dislike; then, to her father, accounted for the shudder after a popular fashion, saying lightly: "There is someone walking over my grave."

So Coll Dhu was present at Evleen Blake's birthday ball. Here he was, under a roof which ought to have been his own, a stranger, known only by a nickname, shunned and solitary. Here he was, who had lived among the eagles and foxes, lying in wait with a fell purpose, to be revenged on the son of his father's foe for poverty and disgrace, for the broken heart of a dead mother, for the loss of a self-slaughtered father, for the dreary scattering of brothers and sisters. Here he stood, a Samson shorn of his strength; and all because a haughty girl had melting eyes, a winning mouth, and looked radiant in satin and roses.

Peerless where many were lovely, she moved among her friends, trying to be unconscious of the gloomy fire of those strange eyes which followed her unweariedly wherever she went. And when her father begged her to be gracious to the unsocial guest whom he would fain conciliate, she courteously conducted him to see the new picture-gallery adjoining the drawing-rooms; explained under what odd circumstances the colonel had picked up this little painting or that; using every delicate art her pride would allow to achieve her father's purpose, whilst maintaining at the same time her own personal reserve; trying to divert the guest's oppressive attention from herself to the objects for which she claimed her notice. Coll Dhu followed his conductress and listened to her voice, but what she said mattered nothing; nor did she wring many words of comment or reply from his lips, until they paused in a retired corner where the light was dim, before a window from which the curtain was withdrawn. The sashes were open, and nothing was visible but water; the night Atlantic, with the full moon riding high above a bank of clouds, making silvery tracks outward towards the distance of infinite mystery dividing two worlds. Here the following little scene is said to have been enacted.

"This window of my father's own planning, is it not creditable to his taste?" said the young hostess, as she stood, herself glittering like a dream of beauty, looking on the moonlight.

Coll Dhu made no answer; but suddenly, it is said, asked her for a rose from a cluster of flowers that nestled in the lace on her bosom.

For the second time that night Evleen Blake's eyes flashed with no gentle light. But this man was the saviour of her father. She broke off a blossom, and with such good grace, and also with such queen-like dignity as she might assume, presented it to him. Whereupon, not only was the rose seized, but also the hand that gave it, which was hastily covered with kisses.

Then her anger burst upon him.

"Sir," she cried, "if you are a gentleman you must be mad! If you are not mad, then you are not a gentleman!"

"Be merciful" said Coll Dhu; "I love you. My God, I never loved a woman before! Ah!" he cried, as a look of disgust crept over her face, "You hate me. You shuddered the first time your eyes met mine. I love you, and you hate me!"

"I do," cried Evleen, vehemently, forgetting everything but her indignation. "Your presence is like something evil to me. Love me?—your looks poison me. Pray, sir, talk no more to me in this strain."

"I will trouble you no longer," said Coll Dhu. And, stalking to the window, he placed one powerful hand upon the sash, and vaulted from it out of her sight.

Bare-headed as he was, Coll Dhu strode off to the mountains, but not towards his own home. All the remaining dark hours of that night he is believed to have walked the labyrinths of the hills, until dawn began to scatter the clouds with a high wind. Fasting, and on foot from sunrise the morning before, he was then glad enough to see a cabin right in his way. Walking in, he asked for water to drink, and a corner where he might throw himself to rest.

There was a wake in the house, and the kitchen was full of people, all wearied out with the night's watch; old men were dozing over their pipes in the chimney-corner, and here and there a woman was fast asleep with her head on a neighbour's knee. All who were awake crossed themselves when Coll Dhu's figure darkened the door, because of his evil name; but an old man of the house invited him in, and offering him milk, and promising him a roasted potato by-and-by, conducted him to a small room off the kitchen, one end of which was strewed with heather, and where there were only two women sitting gossiping over a fire.

"A thraveller," said the old man, nodding his head at the women, who nodded back, as if to say "he has the traveller's right." And Coll Dhu flung himself on the heather, in the furthest corner of the narrow room.

The women suspended their talk for a while; but presently, guessing the intruder to be asleep, resumed it in voices above a whisper. There was but a patch of window with the grey dawn behind it, but Coll could see the figures by the firelight over which they bent: an old woman sitting forward with her withered hands extended to the embers, and a girl reclining against the hearth wall, with her healthy face, bright eyes, and crimson draperies, glowing by turns in the flickering blaze.

"I do' know," said the girl, "but it's the quarest marriage iver I h'ard of. Sure it's not three weeks since he tould right an' left that he hated her like poison!"

"Whist, asthoreen!" said the colliagh, bending forward confidentially; "throth an' we all known that o' him. But what could he do, the crature! When she put the burragh-bos on him!"

"The *what?*" asked the girl.

"Then the burragh-bos machree-o? That's the spanchel o' death, avourneen; an' well she has him tethered to her now, bad luck to her!"

The old woman rocked herself and stilled the Irish cry breaking from her wrinkled lips by burying her face in her cloak.

"But what is it?" asked the girl, eagerly. "What's the burragh-bos, anyways, an' where did she get it?"

"Och, och! it's not fit for comin' over to young ears, but cuggir (whisper), acushla! It's a sthrip o' the skin o' a corpse, peeled from the crown o' the head to the heel, without crack or split, or the charm's broke; an' that, rowled up, an' put on a sthring roun' the neck o' the wan that's cowld by the wan that wants to be loved. An' sure enough it puts the fire in their hearts, hot an' sthrong, afore twenty-four hours is gone."

The girl had started from her lazy attitude, and gazed at her companion with eyes dilated by horror.

"Marciful Saviour!" she cried. "Not a sowl on airth would bring the curse out o' heaven by sich a black doin'!"

"Aisy, Biddeen alanna! an' there's wan that does it, an' isn't the divil. Arrah, asthoreen, did ye niver hear tell o' Pexie na Pishrogie, that lives betune two hills o' Maam Turk?"

"I h'ard o' her," said the girl, breathlessly.

"Well, sorra bit lie, but it's hersel' that does it. She'll do it for money any day. Sure they hunted her from the graveyard o' Salruck, where she had the dead raised; an' glory be to God! they would ha' murthered her, only they missed her thracks, an' couldn't bring it home to her afther."

"Whist, a-wauher" (my mother), said the girl; "here's the thraveller gettin' up to set off on his road again! Och, then, it's the short rest he tuk, the sowl!"

It was enough for Coll, however. He had got up, and now went back to the kitchen, where the old man had caused a dish of potatoes to be roasted, and earnestly pressed his visitor to sit down and eat of them. This Coll did readily; having recruited his strength by a meal, he betook himself to the mountains again, just as the rising sun was flashing among the waterfalls, and sending the night mists drifting down the glens. By sundown the same evening he was striding over the hills of Maam Turk, asking of herds his way to the cabin of one Pexie na Pishrogie.

In a hovel on a brown desolate heath, with scared-looking hills flying off into the distance on every side, he found Pexie: a yellow-faced hag, dressed in a dark-red blanket, with elf-locks of coarse black hair protruding from under an orange kerchief swathed round her wrinkled jaws. She was bending over a pot upon her fire, where herbs were simmering, and she looked up with an evil glance when Col Dhu darkened her door.

"The burragh-bos is it her honour wants?" she asked, when he had made known his errand. "Ay, ay; but the arighad, the arighad (money) for Pexie. The burragh-bos is ill to get."

"I will pay," said Coll Dhu, laying a sovereign on the bench before her.

The witch sprang upon it, and chuckling, bestowed on her visitor a glance which made even Coll Dhu shudder.

"Her honour is a fine king," she said, "an' her is fit to get the burragh-bos.

Ha! ha! her sall get the burragh-bos from Pexie. But the arighad is not enough. More, more!"

She stretched out her claw-like hand, and Coll dropped another sovereign into it. Whereupon she fell into more horrible convulsions of delight.

"Hark ye!" cried Coll. "I have paid you well, but if your infernal charm does not work, I will have you hunted for a witch!"

"Work!" cried Pexie, rolling up her eyes. "If Pexie's charrm not work, then her honour come back here an' carry these bits o' mountain away on her back. Ay, her will work. If the colleen hate her honour like the old diaoul hersel', still an' withal her love will love her honour like her own white sowl afore the sun sets or rises. That, (with a furtive leer,) or the colleen dhas go wild mad afore wan hour."

"Hag!" returned Coll Dhu; "the last part is a hellish invention of your own. I heard nothing of madness. If you want more money, speak out, but play none of your hideous tricks on me."

The witch fixed her cunning eyes on him, and took her cue at once from his passion.

"Her honour guess thrue," she simpered; "it is only the little bit more arighad poor Pexie want."

Again the skinny hand was extended. Coll Dhu shrank from touching it, and threw his gold upon the table.

"King, king!" chuckled Pexie. "Her honour is a grand king. Her honour is fit to get the buragh-bos. The colleen dhas sall love her like her own white sowl. Ha, ha!"

"When shall I get it?" asked Coll Dhu, impatiently.

"Her honour sall come back to Pexie in so many days, do-deag (twelve), so many days, fur that the burragh-bos is hard to get. The lonely graveyard is far away, an' dead man is hard to raise—"

"Silence!" cried Coll Dhu; "not a word more. I will have your hideous charm, but what it is, or where you get it, I will not know."

Then, promising to come back in twelve days, he took his departure. Turning to look back when a little way across the heath, he saw Pexie gazing after him, standing on her black hill in relief against the lurid flames of the dawn, seeming to his dark imagination like a fury with all hell at her back.

At the appointed time Coll Dhu got the promised charm. He sewed it with perfumes into a cover of cloth of gold, and slung it to a fine-wrought chain. Lying in a casket which had once held the jewels of Coll's broken-hearted mother, it looked a glittering bauble enough. Meantime the people of the mountains were cursing over their cabin fires, because there had been another unholy raid upon their graveyard, and were banding themselves to hunt the criminal down.

A fortnight passed. How or where could Coll Dhu find an opportunity to put the charm round the neck of the colonel's proud daughter? More gold was dropped into Pexie's greedy claw, and then she promised to assist him in his dilemma.

Next morning the witch dressed herself in decent garb, smoothed her elf-locks under a snowy cap, smoothed the evil wrinkles out of her face, and with a basket on her arm locked the door of the hovel, and took her way to the lowlands. Pexie seemed to have given up her disreputable calling for that of a simple mushroom-gatherer. The housekeeper at the grey house bought poor Muireade's mushrooms of her every morning. Every morning she left unfailingly a nosegay of wild flowers for Miss Evleen Blake, "God bless her! She had never seen the darling young lady with her own two longing eyes, but sure hadn't she heard tell of her sweet purty face, miles away!" And at last, one morning, whom should she meet but Miss Evleen herself returning along from a ramble. Whereupon poor Muireade "made bold" to present her flowers in person.

"Ah," said Evleen, "it is you who leave me the flowers every morning? They are very sweet."

Muireade had sought her only for a look at her beautiful face. And now that she had seen it, as bright as the sun, and as fair as the lily, she would take up her basket and go away contented. Yet she lingered a little longer.

"My lady never walk up big mountain?" said Pexie.

"No," said Evleen, laughing; she feared she could not walk up a mountain.

"Ah yes; my lady ought to go, with more gran' ladies an' gentlemen, ridin' on purty little donkeys, up the big mountains. Oh, gran' things up big mountains for my lady to see!"

Thus she set to work, and kept her listener enchained for an hour, while she related wonderful stories of those upper regions. And as Evleen looked up to the burly crowns of the hills, perhaps she thought there might be sense in this wild old woman's suggestion. It ought to be a grand world up yonder.

Be that as it may, it was not long after this when Coll Dhu got notice that a party from the grey house would explore the mountains next day; that Evleen Blake would be one of the number; and that he, Coll, must prepare to house and refresh a crowd of weary people, who in the evening should be brought, hungry and faint, to his door. The simple mushroom gatherer should be discovered laying in her humble stock among the green places between the hills, should volunteer to act as guide to the party, should lead them far out of their way through the mountains and up and down the most toilsome ascents and across dangerous places; to escape safely from which, the servants should be told to throw away the baskets of provision which they carried.

Coll Dhu was not idle. Such a feast was set forth, as had never been spread so near the clouds before. We are told of wonderful dishes furnished by unwholesome agency, and from a place believed much hotter than is necessary for purposes of cookery. We are told also how Coll Dhu's barren chambers were suddenly hung with curtains of velvet, and with fringes of gold; how the blank white walls glowed with delicate colours and gilding; how gems of pictures sprang into sight between the panels; how the tables blazed with plate and gold, and glittered with the rarest glass; how such wines flowed, as the guests had never tasted; how servants in the richest livery, amongst whom the wizen-faced old man was a mere nonentity, appeared, and stood ready to carry in the wonderful dishes, at whose extraordinary fragrance the eagles came pecking to the windows, and the foxes drew near the walls, snuffing. Sure enough, in all good time, the weary party came within sight of the Devil's Inn, and Coll Dhu sallied forth to invite them across his lonely threshold. Colonel Blake (to whom Evleen, in her delicacy, had said no word of the solitary's strange behaviour to herself) hailed his appearance with delight, and the whole party sat down to Coll's banquet in high good humour. Also, it is said, in much amazement at the magnificence of the mountain recluse.

All went in to Coll's feast, save Evleen Blake, who remained standing on the threshold of the outer door; weary, but unwilling to rest there; hungry, but unwilling to eat there. Her white cambric dress was gathered on her arms, crushed and sullied with the toils of the day; her bright cheek was a little sunburned; her small dark head with its braids a little tossed, was bared to the mountain air and the glory of the sinking sun; her hands were loosely tangled in the strings of her hat; and her foot sometimes tapped the threshold-stone. So she was seen.

The peasants tell that Coll Dhu and her father came praying her to enter, and that the magnificent servants brought viands to the threshold; but no step would she move inward, no morsel would she taste.

"Poison, poison!" she murmured, and threw the food in handfuls to the foxes, who were snuffing on the heath.

But it was different when Muireade, the kindly old woman, the simple mushroom-gatherer, with all the wicked wrinkles smoothed out of her face, came to the side of the hungry girl, and coaxingly presented a savoury mess of her own sweet mushrooms, served on a common earthen platter.

"An' darlin', my lady, poor Muireade her cook them hersel', an' no thing o' this house touch them or look at poor Muireade's mushrooms."

Then Evleen took the platter and ate a delicious meal. Scarcely was it finished when a heavy drowsiness fell upon her, and, unable to sustain herself on her feet, she presently sat down upon the door-stone. Leaning her head against the framework of the door, she was soon in a deep sleep, or trance. So she was found.

"Whimsical, obstinate little girl!" said the colonel, putting his hand on the beautiful slumbering head. And taking her in his arms, he carried her into a chamber which had been (say the story-tellers) nothing but a bare and sorry closet in the morning but which was now fitted up with Oriental splendour. And here on a luxurious couch she was laid, with a crimson coverlet wrapping her feet. And here in the tempered light coming through jewelled glass, where yesterday had been a coarse rough-hung window, her father looked his last upon her lovely face.

The colonel returned to his host and friends, and by-and-by the whole party sallied forth to see the after-glow of a fierce sunset swathing the hills in flames. It was not until they had gone some distance that Coll Dhu remembered to go back and fetch his telescope. He was not long absent. But he was absent long enough to enter that glowing chamber with a stealthy step, to throw a light chain around the neck of the sleeping girl, and to slip among the folds of her dress the hideous glittering burragh-bos.

After he had gone away again, Pexie came stealing to the door, and, opening it a little, sat down on the mat outside, with her cloak wrapped round her. An hour passed, and Evleen Blake still slept, her breathing scarcely stirring the deadly bauble on her breast. After that, she began to murmur and moan, and Pexie pricked up her ears. Presently a sound in the room told that the victim was awake and had risen. Then Pexie put her face to the aperture of the door and looked in, gave a howl of dismay, and fled from the house, to be seen in that country no more.

The light was fading among the hills, and the ramblers were returning towards the Devil's Inn, when a group of ladies who were considerably in advance of the rest, met Evleen Blake advancing towards them on the heath, with her hair disordered as by sleep, and no covering on her head. They noticed something bright, like gold, shifting and glancing with the motion of her figure. There had been some jesting among them about Evleen's fancy for falling asleep on the door-step instead of coming in to dinner, and they advanced laughing, to rally her on the subject. But she stared at them in a strange way, as if she did not know them, and passed on. Her friends were rather offended, and commented on her fantastic humour; only one looked after her, and got laughed at by her companions for expressing uneasiness on the wilful young lady's account.

So they kept their way, and the solitary figure went fluttering on, the white robe blushing, and the fatal burragh-bos glittering in the reflexion from the sky. A hare crossed her path, and she laughed out loudly, and clapping her hands, sprang after it. Then she stopped and asked questions of the stones, striking them with her open palm because they would not answer. (An amazed little herd sitting behind a rock, witnessed these strange proceedings.) By-and-by she began to call after the birds, in a wild shrill way startling the echoes of the hills as she went along. A party of gentlemen returning by a dangerous path, heard the unusual sound and stopped to listen.

"What is that?" asked one.

"A young eagle," said Coll Dhu, whose face had become livid; "they often give such cries."

"It was uncommonly like a woman's voice!" was the reply; and immediately another wild note rang towards them from the rocks above: a bare saw-like ridge, shelving away to some distance ahead, and projecting one hungry tooth over an abyss. A few more moments and they saw Evleen Blake's light figure fluttering out towards this dizzy point.

"My Evleen!" cried the colonel, recognising his daughter, "she is mad to venture on such a spot!"

"Mad!" repeated Coll Dhu. And then dashed off to the rescue with all the might and swiftness of his powerful limbs.

When he drew near her, Evleen had almost reached the verge of the terrible rock. Very cautiously he approached her, his object being to seize her in his strong arms before she was aware of his presence, and carry her many yards away from the spot of danger. But in a fatal moment Evleen turned her head and saw him. One wild ringing cry of hate and horror, which startled the very eagles and scattered a flight of curlews above her head, broke from her lips. A step backward brought her within a foot of death.

One desperate though wary stride, and she was struggling in Coll's embrace. One glance in her eyes, and he saw that he was striving with a mad woman. Back, back, she dragged him, and he had nothing to grasp by. The rock was slippery and his shod feet would not cling to it. Back, back! A hoarse panting, a dire swinging to and fro; and then the rock was standing naked against the sky, no one was there, and Coll Dhu and Evleen Blake lay shattered far below.

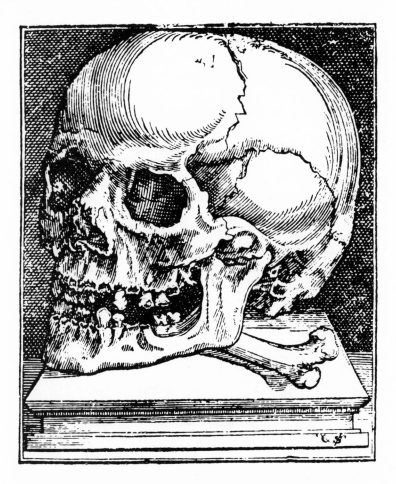

HEINRICH HOFFMANN

THE VERY SAD TALE
OF THE MATCHES

One day Paulinchen was alone
(Her parents from the house were gone)
And as she wandered here and there
She danced and sang a pretty air
When all at once, what did she spy
A box of matches, not too high.
It was a sight that gave her joy:
"Matches," the forbidden toy.
"I'll light them, that's just what I'll do
The way I've seen my mother do."

But Puss and Kitty, watching her
Set up a warning miaow and purr,
They rubbed around her legs and miaowed
"Your father says that's not allowed.
No, No, Miaow, Miaow and no!
Don't touch, it's dangerous you know."

Paulinchen would not listen. Oh,
Those matches burned and glittered so,
The fire crackled prettily
As, in the picture, you can see.
She lighted matches everywhere—
Not Puss nor Kitty would she hear.

But Puss and Kitty warning her
Set up such a miaow and purr,
They rubbed around her legs and miaowed
"Your mother says that's not allowed
No, No, Miaow, Miaow and no!
Please stop, it's dangerous you know."

Too bad. The fire seized the child,
Roared in her skirt and apron wild.
It burned her hands and pretty hair
And all Paulinchen, then and there.

Then Puss and Kitty miaowed and cried
"Help, oh help!" on every side,
"Won't someone help, Paulinchen's turning
In a blaze that's raging, burning."
Won't someone help, won't someone stop,
Our Paulinchen's burning up."

The child was burnt completely there
Her feet, her skin, her eyes, her hair
Nothing left but a pile of ashes
Two pretty shoes, some burnt out matches.

Then Puss and Kitty, for a while,
Wept beside the smouldering pile,
"Woe and miaow, miaow and woe,
Now where did her poor parents go?"
Those cats wept brooks. Oh what a pity
Poor Paulinchen was so naughty.

INDIAN FOLKTALE

THE MAN-TIGER

There was once a young man who when a boy had learnt witchcraft from some girl friends; he was married but his wife knew nothing about this. They lived happily together and were in the habit of paying frequent visits to the wife's parents. One day they were on their way together to pay such a visit and in passing through some jungle they saw, grazing with a herd of cattle, a very fine and fat bull calf. The man stopped and stripped himself to his waist cloth and told his wife to hold his clothes for him while he went and ate the calf that had stirred his appetite. His wife in astonishment asked him how he was going to eat a living animal; he answered that he was going to turn into a tiger and kill the animal and he impressed on her that she must on no account be frightened or run away and he handed her a piece of root and told her that she must give it him to smell when he came back and he would at once regain his human shape.

So saying he retired into a thicket and took off his waist cloth and at once became a tiger; then he swallowed the waist cloth and thereby grew a fine long tail. Then he sprang upon the calf and knocked it over and began to suck its blood. At this sight his wife was overwhelmed with terror and forgetting everything in her fear ran right off to her father's house taking with her her husband's clothes and the magic root. She arrived breathless and told her parents all that had happened. Meanwhile her husband had been deprived of the means of regaining his own form and was forced to spend the day hiding in the jungle as a tiger; when night fell he made his way to the village where his father-in-law lived. But when he got there all the dogs began to bark and when the villagers saw that there was a tiger they barricaded themselves in their houses.

The man-tiger went prowling round his father-in-law's house and at last his father-in-law plucked up courage and went out and threw the root which the wife had brought under the tiger's nose and he at once became a man again. Then they brought him into the house and washed his feet; and gave him hot rice-water to drink; and on drinking this he vomited up lumps of clotted blood. The next morning the father-in-law called the villagers and showed them this blood and told them all that had happened; then he turned to his son-in-law and told him to take himself off and vowed that his daughter should never go near him again. The man-tiger had no answer to make but went back silently and alone to his own home.

NOTE:—The following is a prescription for making an *Ulat bag* or were-tiger.

"The fibre of a plant (Bauhinia vahli) beaten out and cooked in mustard oil in a human skull."

COMTE DE LAUTRÉAMONT

THE HOURS IN THE LIFE OF A LOUSY-HAIRED MAN

Episode from *Maldoror*

There are certain hours in the life of a lousy-haired man when he fixes his staring eyes upon the green membranes of space; for he seems to hear before him the ironic mockery of a phantom. He staggers and bends his head; what he hears is the voice of his conscience. Then he rushes from the house with the speed of a madman and tears through the rugged plains of the countryside. But the yellow phantom does not lose sight of him and pursues him with an equal speed.

Sometimes on a stormy night while legions of winged octopi, in the distance resembling crows, hover above the clouds and fly stiffly towards the cities of men on a mission to warn them to alter their conduct, the gloomy-eyed pebble sees two beings pass by beneath the flashes of lightning, one behind the other; and, wiping away a furtive tear of compassion flowing from his frozen eye he cries out: "Certainly he deserves this; it is only justice." Having spoken thus he resumes his ferocious attitude and continues to watch the man-hunt, trembling nervously, and the wide lips of the vagina of darkness whence flow unceasingly like a river immense shadowy spermatozoa which take flight into the lugubrious ether concealing, with the vast manipulation of their bat's wings, the whole of nature and the solitary legions of octopi, grown dejected at the aspect of these obscure and inexplicable fulgurations.

But meanwhile the steeplechase continues between the two indefatigable runners, and the phantom belches forth torrents of flame upon the scorched back of the human antelope. If during the accomplishment of this duty he meets Pity trying to block his path, he accedes with repugnance to her pleas and lets the man escape. The phantom clicks his tongue as if to tell himself that he is about to give up to pursuit and retires to his kennel to await further orders. His voice, the voice of the damned, reaches to the uttermost limits of space; and when his appalling cries penetrate the heart of man, the latter would rather have, they say, death for his mother than remorse for his son. He buries his head up to the shoulders in the earthy complications of a hole; but conscience dissipates the ostrich's trick. The excavation evaporates like a drop of ether; light appears with its train of rays like a flock of curlews

331

descending upon lavender bushes and the man finds that he is again confronting himself with ghastly, staring eyes.

I have seen him making for the seashore, climbing a jagged sea-begirt promontory, and precipitating himself like an arrow into the waves. Now comes the miracle: the cadaver reappears the next day floating on the surface of the ocean which bears the fragment of flesh back to the shore. The man releases himself from the mould hollowed out by his body in the sand, and resumes the journey of life, his head muted and bowed.

Conscience judges our thoughts and our most secret actions severely and makes no mistakes. As she is often incapable of preventing evil, she persists in trailing man like a fox, especially after dark. From her vengeful eyes, that ignorant science calls *meteors,* livid flames are diffused, revolve upon one another, and articulate mysterious words.... that he understands! Then his bed is crushed beneath the tremors of his body, overwhelmed by the weight of insomnia, and he hears the sinister breathing of vague night noises. The angel of sleep himself, mortally wounded in the brow by a mysterious stone, abandons his task and returns to heaven.

Very well, this time I present myself to defend Man; I, the scorner of all the virtues; I, who have not been able to forget the Creator since the glorious day when, upsetting the stand upon which rested the annals of heaven whereby I know not what infamous chicanery were consigned *His* powers and *His* eternity, I applied my four hundred suckers to his armpits, making him cry out horribly. The cries changed into serpents as they left his mouth and went to lie in ambush in the brushwood and in ruined walls by day and by night. Those cries now cringe and writhe in countless coils with small flat heads and treacherous eyes; and they have sworn to lie in wait for human innocence; and when innocence goes walking in the tangled woodlands or over the hills or among the sand dunes, she soon changes her ideas. If, that is, there be still time; for sometimes man becomes aware of the poison introduced into the veins of his leg through an almost imperceptible bite before he has had time to retrace his steps and take to his heels. It is thus that the Creator, preserving an admirable sangfroid even in the face of the most atrocious sufferings, is able to extract harmful germs from the bosoms of earth's inhabitants.

How astounded he was when he saw Maldoror, changed into an octopus, bear down upon his body with eight enormous arms, any one of which solid lashes could easily have reached around the circumference of a planet! Taken unawares he struggled for a few moments against that viscous embrace, which contracted and contracted....

I feared some dirty trick on his part. After having abundantly nourished myself upon the globules of that holy blood, I detached myself abruptly from his majestic body and hid myself in a cave, which subsequently became my home. Here, after a fruitless search, he could not find me. This was all long ago; but I think he knows where I am now. He avoids my place and we both live like two neighboring monarchs who are aware of one another's respective powers, cannot overcome one another, and are weary of the useless battles of the past. He fears me and I fear him. Each, while unconquered, has sustained some severe injuries from his adversary, and we let it go at that. However, I am ready to resume the struggle whenever he so desires. But he had better not await some favorable moment for his secret plans. I shall always be on the look-out and keeping my eye on him. Let him never again inflict the earth with conscience and its tortures. I have taught mankind what weapons they may use to combat it advantageously. They are not as yet familiar with it, but you know that as far as I am concerned it is no more than a straw driven by the wind. That is as much as I make of it. If I wished to profit by the occasion that presents itself here of elaborating these poetic discussions, I might add that I would attach more importance to the straw than to conscience; for straw is useful to the cow chewing her cud, while conscience knows nothing beyond showing her steel talons.

These claws sustained a severe setback the day they came up against me. As conscience was sent by the Creator I thought it proper not to permit my passage to be obstructed by it. If it has approached me with the modesty and humility proper to its rank, and from which it should never have departed, I would have listened to it. I did not like its pride. I held out my hand and crushed the talons between my fingers. They fell into dust beneath the increasing pressure of this new kind of mortar. I stretched out my other hand and tore off its head. Then I chased that female conscience out of my house at the end of a whip and I have not seen her since. I kept her head as a souvenir of my victory. . . .

With a head in my hand, gnawing the skull, I stood on one foot like a heron at the edge of a precipice slashed into the flanks of a moutain. I was seen descending into the valley while the flesh of my bosom was still as calm as the lid of a tomb!

With a head in my hand, gnawing the skull, I swam down to the most dangerous depths of the ocean, among deadly reefs, and plunged deeper than the currents to assist like a foreigner at the battles between marine monsters. I swam from the shore farther than my piercing gaze could see, and hideous stingrays with their paralysing magnetism prowled around my limbs as they cut through the waves with robust movements, not daring to approach me. I was seen to return safe and sound to the beach, and the flesh of my bosom was still and calm as the lid of a tomb!

With a head in my hand, gnawing the skull, I climbed the steps of a high tower. Weary-limbed, I reached the dizzy summit. I gazed upon the countryside and the sea; I gazed upon the sun and the firmament; thrusting with my foot at the granite, which remained immovable, I defied death and divine punishment with a supreme howl and flung myself like a paving-stone into the jaws of space. Men heard the painful and reverberating crash that resulted from the encounter of the earth with the head of conscience, which I had dropped in my flight. I was seen to descend with the leisure of a bird, borne upon an invisible cloud, and pick up the head in order to force it to be witness of a triple crime that I was to commit that same day, while the flesh of my bosom was still and calm as the lid of a tomb!

With a head in my hand, gnawing the skull, I betook myself to the place where stand the posts that support the guillotine. I placed the smooth grace of the necks of three young girls beneath the blade. As executioner, I pulled the string with the apparent experience of an entire lifetime and the triangular steel, falling slantwise, sliced off three heads that regarded me meekly. Next I placed my own head beneath the heavy razor and the executioner prepared to accomplish his duty. Three times the blade descended between its grooves with a new vigor; three times my material body, especially at the base of the neck, was shaken to its foundations as when one dreams of being crushed by a falling building. The stupefied populace let me pass as I removed myself from that grisly spot. They saw me elbow my way through the undulating waves of the crowd, and bestir myself, full of life, head held erect, while the flesh of my bosom was still and calm as the lid of a tomb!

I did say that I would defend mankind this time. But I fear my apologia would not be the expression of truth, and consequently I prefer to be silent. Humanity will applaud this measure with gratitude!

It is time to apply the brakes to my inspiration and to pause for a while by the wayside, as when one looks upon the vagina of a woman. It is good to look back over the course already traveled, and then, the limbs rested, to rush on again with an impetuous bound. To accomplish a journey in one single breath is not easy, and the wings weary much during a high flight without hope and without remorse. No, let us lead no deeper into the explosives mines of this impious lay the haggard pack of swots and busybodies! The crocodile will not change one word of the vomit that issued from within his skull! Too bad if some furtive shadow, inspired with the praiseworthy ambition of revenging a humanity unjustly attacked by me, surreptitiously should open the door of my room, brushing against the wall like a sea-gull's wing, and plunge a dagger into the side of the plunderer of celestial flotsam and jetsam! Clay might as well dissolve its atoms in that manner as in another.

JAMES MALCOLM RYMER

VARNEY, THE VAMPYRE; OR, "THE FEAST OF BLOOD"

CHAPTER I

—"How graves give up their dead.
And how the night air hideous grows
With shrieks!"

Midnight.—The Hail-Storm.—The Dreadful Visitor.—The Vampyre

The solemn tones of an old cathedral clock have announced midnight—the air is thick and heavy—a strange, death like stillness pervades all nature. Like the ominous calm which precedes some more than usually terrific outbreak of the elements, they seem to have paused even in their ordinary fluctuations, to gather a terrific strength for the great effort. A faint peal of thunder now comes from far off. Like a signal gun for the battle of the winds to begin, it appeared to awaken them from their lethargy, and one awful, warring hurricane swept over a whole city, producing more devastation in the four or five minutes it lasted, than would a half century of ordinary phenomena.

It was as if some giant had blown upon some toy town, and scattered many of the buildings before the hot blast of his terrific breath; for as suddenly as that blast of wind had come did it cease, and all was as still and calm as before.

Sleepers awakened, and thought that what they had heard must be the confused chimera of a dream. They trembled and turned to sleep again.

All is still—still as the very grave. Not a sound breaks the magic of repose. What is that—a strange, pattering noise, as of a million of fairy feet? It is hail—yes, a hail-storm has burst over the city. Leaves are dashed from the trees, mingled with small boughs; windows that lie most opposed to the direct fury of the pelting particles of ice are broken, and the rapt repose that before was so remarkable in its intensity, is exchanged for a noise which, in its accumulation, drowns every cry of surprise or consternation which here and there arose from persons who found their houses invaded by the storm.

Now and then, too, there would come a sudden gust of wind that in its strength, as it blew laterally, would, for a moment, hold millions of the hailstones suspended in mid air, but it was only to dash them with redoubled force in some new direction, where more mischief was to be done.

335

Oh, how the storm raged! Hail—rain—wind. It was, in truth, an awful night.

There is an antique chamber in an ancient house. Curious and quaint carvings adorn the walls, and the large chimney-piece is a curiosity of itself. The ceiling is low, and a large bay window, from roof to floor, looks to the west. The window is latticed, and filled with curiously painted glass and rich stained pieces, which send in a strange, yet beautiful light, when sun or moon shines into the apartment. There is but one portrait in that room, although the walls seem panelled for the express purpose of containing a series of pictures. That portrait is of a young man, with a pale face, a stately brow, and a strange expression about the eyes, which no one cared to look on twice.

There is a stately bed in that chamber, of carved walnut-wood is it made, rich in design and elaborate in execution; one of those works of art which owe their existence to the Elizabethan era. It is hung with heavy silken and damask furnishing; nodding feathers are at its corners—covered with dust are they, and they lend a funereal aspect to the room. The floor is of polished oak.

God! how the hail dashes on the old bay window! Like an occasional discharge of mimic musketry, it comes clashing, beating, and cracking upon the small panes; but they resist it—their small size saves them; the wind, the hail, the rain, expend their fury in vain.

The bed in that old chamber is occupied. A creature formed in all fashions of loveliness lies in a half sleep upon that ancient couch—a girl young and beautiful as a spring morning. Her long hair has escaped from its confinement and streams over the blackened coverings of the bedstead; she has been restless in her sleep, for the clothing of the bed is in much confusion. One arm is over her head, the other hangs nearly off the side of the bed near to which she lies. A neck and bosom that would have formed a study for the rarest sculptor that ever Providence gave genius to, were half disclosed. She moaned slightly in her sleep, and once or twice the lips moved as if in prayer—at least one might judge so, for the name of Him who suffered for all came once faintly from them.

She has endured much fatigue, and the storm does not awaken her; but it can disturb the slumbers it does not possess the power to destroy entirely. The turmoil of the elements wakes the senses, although it cannot entirely break the repose they have lapsed into.

Oh, what a world of witchery was in that mouth, slightly parted, and exhibiting within the pearly teeth that glistened even in the faint light that came from that bay window. How sweetly the long silken eyelashes lay upon the cheek. Now she moves, and one shoulder is entirely visible—whiter, fairer than the spotless clothing of the bed on which she lies, is the smooth skin of that fair creature, just budding into womanhood, and in that transition state which presents to us all the charms of the girl—almost of the child, with the more matured beauty and gentleness of advancing years.

Was that lightning? Yes—an awful, vivid, terrifying flash—then a roaring peal of thunder, as if a thousand mountains were rolling one over the other in the blue vault of Heaven! Who sleeps now in that ancient city? Not one living soul. The dread trumpet of eternity could not more effectually have awakened any one.

The hail continues. The wind continues. The uproar of the elements seems at its height. Now she awakens—that beautiful girl on the antique bed; she opens those eyes of celestial blue, and a faint cry of alarm bursts from her lips. At least it is a cry which, amid the noise and turmoil without, sounds but faint and weak. She sits upon the bed and presses her hands upon her eyes. Heavens! what a wild torrent of wind, and rain, and hail! The thunder likewise seems intent upon awakening sufficient echoes to last until the next flash of forked lightning should again produce the wild concussion of the air. She murmurs a prayer—a prayer for those she loves best; the names of those dear to her gentle heart come from her lips; she weeps and prays; she thinks then of what devastation the storm must surely produce, and to the great God of Heaven she prays for all living things. Another flash—a wild, blue, bewildering flash of lightning streams across that bay window, for an instant bringing out every colour in it with terrible distinctness. A shriek bursts from the lips of the young girl, and then, with eyes fixed upon that window, which, in another moment, is all darkness, and with such an expression of terror upon her face as it had never before known, she trembled, and the perspiration of intense fear stood upon her brow.

"What—what was it?" she gasped; "real, or a delusion? Oh, God, what was it? A figure tall and gaunt, endeavouring from the outside to unclasp the window. I saw it. That flash of lightning revealed it to me. It stood the whole length of the window."

There was a lull of the wind. The hail was not falling so thickly—moreover, it now fell, what there was of it, straight, and yet a strange clattering sound came upon the glass of that long window. It could not be a delusion—she is awake, and she hears it. What can produce it? Another flash of lightning—another shriek—there could be now no delusion.

A tall figure is standing on the ledge immediately outside the long window. It is its finger-nails upon the glass that produces the sound so like the hail, now that the hail has ceased. Intense fear paralysed the limbs of that beautiful girl. That one shriek is all she can utter—with hands clasped, a face of marble, a heart beating so wildly in her bosom, that each moment it seems as if it would break its confines, eyes distended and fixed upon the window, she waits, froze with horror. The pattering and clattering of the nails continue. No word is spoken, and now she fancies she can trace the darker form of that figure against the window, and she can see the long arms moving to and fro, feeling for some mode of entrance. What strange light is that which now gradually creeps up into the air? red and terrible—brighter and brighter it grows. The lightning has set fire to a mill, and the reflection of the rapidly consuming building falls upon that long window. There can be no mistake. The figure is there, still feeling for an entrance, and clattering against the glass with its long nails, that appear as if the growth of many years had been untouched. She tries to scream again but a choking sensation comes over her, and she cannot. It is too dreadful—she tries to move—each limb seems weighed down by tons of lead—she can but in a hoarse faint whisper cry,—

"Help—help—help—help!"

And that one word she repeats like a person in a dream. The red glare of the fire continues. It throws up the tall gaunt figure in hideous relief against the long window. It shows, too, upon the one portrait that is in the chamber, and that portrait appears to fix its eyes upon the attempting intruder, while the flickering light from the fire makes it look fearfully life-like. A small pane of glass is broken, and the form from without introduces a long gaunt hand, which seems utterly destitute of flesh. The fastening is removed, and one-half of the window, which opens like folding doors, is swung wide open upon its hinges.

And yet now she could not scream—she could not move. "Help!—help!—help!" was all she could say. But, oh, that look of terror that sat upon her face, it was dreadful—a look to haunt the memory for a life-time—a look to obtrude itself upon the happiest moments, and turn them to bitterness.

The figure turns half round, and the light falls upon the face. It is perfectly white—perfectly bloodless. The eyes look like polished tin; the lips are drawn back, and the principal feature next to those dreadful eyes is the teeth—the fearful looking teeth—projecting like those of some wild animal, hideously, glaringly white, and fang-like. It approaches the bed with a strange, gliding movement. It clashes together the long nails that literally appear to hang from the finger ends. No sound comes from its lips. Is she going mad—that young and beautiful girl exposed to so much terror? she has drawn up all her limbs; she cannot even now say help. The power of articulation is gone, but the power of movement has returned to her; she can draw herself slowly along to the other side of the bed from that towards which the hideous appearance is coming.

But her eyes are fascinated. The glance of a serpent could not have produced a greater effect upon her than did the fixed gaze of those awful, metallic-looking eyes that were bent on her face. Crouching down so that the gigantic height was lost, and the horrible, protruding, white face was the most prominent object, came on the figure. What was it?—what did it want there? what made it look so hideous—so unlike an inhabitant of the earth, and yet to be on it?

Now she has got to the verge of the bed, and the figure pauses. It seemed as if when it paused she lost the power to proceed. The clothing of the bed was now clutched in her hands with unconscious power. She drew her breath short and thick. Her bosom heaves, and her limbs tremble, yet she cannot withdraw her eyes from that marble-looking face. He holds her with his glittering eye.

The storm has ceased—all is still. The winds are hushed; the church clock proclaims the hour of one: a hissing sound comes from the throat of the hideous being, and he raises his long, gaunt arms—the lips move. He advances. The girl places one small foot from the bed on to the floor. She is unconsciously dragging the clothing with her. The door of the room is in that direction—can she reach it? Has she power to walk?—can she withdraw her eyes from the face of the intruder, and so break the hideous charm? God of Heaven! is it real, or some dream so like reality as to nearly overturn the judgment for ever?

The figure has paused again, and half on the bed and half out of it that young girl lies trembling. Her long hair streams across the entire width of the bed. As she has slowly moved along she has left it streaming across the pillows. The pause lasted about a minute—oh, what an age of agony. That minute was, indeed, enough for madness to do its full work in.

With a sudden rush that could not be foreseen—with a strange howling cry that was enough to awaken terror in every breast, the figure seized the long tresses of her hair, and twining them round his bony hands he held her to the bed. Then she screamed—Heaven granted her then power to scream. Shriek followed shriek in rapid succession. The bed-clothes fell in a heap by the side of the bed—she was dragged by her long silken hair completely on to it again. Her beautifully rounded limbs quivered with the agony of her soul. The glassy, horrible eyes of the figure ran over that angelic form with a hideous satisfaction—horrible profanation. He drags her head to the bed's edge. He forces it back by the long hair still entwined in his grasp. With a plunge he seizes her neck in his fang-like teeth—a gush of blood, and a hideous sucking noise follows. *The girl has swooned, and the vampyre is at his hideous repast!*

GUY DE MAUPASSANT

THE HORLA OR MODERN GHOSTS

May 8. What a lovely day! I have spent all the morning lying in the grass in front of my house, under the enormous plane tree that shades the whole of it. I like this part of the country and I like to live here because I am attached to it by old associations, by those deep and delicate roots which attach a man to the soil on which his ancestors were born and died, which attach him to the ideas and usages of the place as well as to the food, to local expressions, to the peculiar twang of the peasants, to the smell of the soil, of the villages and of the atmosphere itself.

I love my house in which I grew up. From my windows I can see the Seine which flows alongside my garden, on the other side of the high road, almost through my grounds, the great and wide Seine, which goes to Rouen and Havre, and is covered with boats passing to and fro.

On the left, down yonder, lies Rouen, that large town, with its blue roofs, under its pointed Gothic towers. These are innumerable, slender or broad, dominated by the spire of the cathedral, and full of bells which sound through the blue air on fine mornings, sending their sweet and distant iron clang even as far as my home; that song of the metal, which the breeze wafts in my direction, now stronger and now weaker, according as the wind is stronger or lighter.

What a delicious morning it was!

About eleven o'clock, a long line of boats drawn by a steam tug as big as a fly, and which scarcely puffed while emitting its thick smoke, passed my gate.

After two English schooners, whose red flags fluttered in space, there came a magnificent Brazilian three-master; she was perfectly white, and wonderfully clean and shining. I saluted her, I hardly knew why, except that the sight of the vessel gave me great pleasure.

May 12. I have had a slight feverish attack for the last few days, and I feel ill, or rather I feel low-spirited.

Whence come those mysterious influences which change our happiness into discouragement, and our self-confidence into diffidence? One might almost say that the air, the invisible air, is full of unknowable Powers whose mysterious presence we have to endure. I wake up in the best spirits, with an inclination to sing. Why? I go down to the edge of the water, and suddenly, after walking a short distance, I return home wretched, as if some misfortune were awaiting me there. Why? Is it a cold shiver which, passing over my skin, has upset my nerves and given me low spirits? Is it the form of the clouds, the color of the sky, or the color of the surrounding objects, which is so changeable, that has troubled my thoughts as they passed before my eyes? Who can tell? Everything that surrounds us, everything that we see, without looking at it, everything that we touch, without knowing it, everything that we handle, without feeling it, all that we meet, without clearly distinguishing it, has a rapid, surprising and inexplicable effect upon us and upon our senses, and, through them, on our ideas and on our heart itself.

How profound that mystery of the Invisible is! We cannot fathom it with our miserable senses, with our eyes which are unable to perceive what is either too small or too great, too near to us, or too far from us—neither the inhabitants of a star nor of a drop of water; nor with our ears that deceive us, for they transmit to us the vibrations of the air in sonorous notes. They are fairies who work the miracle of changing these vibrations into sound, and by that metamorphosis give birth to music, which makes the silent motion of nature musical . . . with our sense of smell which is less keen than that of a dog, . . . with our sense of taste which can scarcely distinguish the age of a wine!

Oh! If we only had other organs which would work other miracles in our favor, what a number of fresh things we might discover around us!

May 16. I am ill, decidedly! I was so well last month! I am feverish, horribly feverish, or rather I am in a state of feverish enervation, which makes my mind suffer as much as my body. I have, continually, that horrible sensation of some impending danger, that apprehension of some coming misfortune, or of approaching death; that presentiment which is, no doubt, an attack of some illness which is still unknown, which germinates in the flesh and in the blood.

May 17. I have just come from consulting my physician, for I could no longer get any sleep. He said my pulse was rapid, my eyes dilated, my nerves highly strung, but there were no alarming symptoms. I must take a course of shower baths and of bromide of potassium.

May 25. No change! My condition is really very peculiar. As the evening comes on, an incomprehensible feeling of disquietude seizes me, just as if night concealed some threatening disaster. I dine hurriedly, and then try to read, but I do not understand the words, and can scarcely distinguish the letters. Then I walk up and down my drawing-room, oppressed by a feeling of confused and irresistible fear, the fear of sleep and fear of my bed.

About ten o'clock I go up to my room. As soon as I enter it I double-lock and bolt the door; I am afraid . . . of what? Up to the present time I have been afraid of nothing . . . I open my cupboards, and look under my bed; I listen . . . to what? How strange it is that a simple feeling of discomfort, impeded or heightened circulation, perhaps the irritation of a nerve fila-ment, a slight congestion, a small disturbance in the imperfect delicate functioning of our living machinery, may turn the most light-hearted of men into a melancholy one, and make a coward of the bravest? Then I go to bed, and wait for sleep as a man might wait for the executioner. I wait for its coming with dread, and my heart beats and my legs tremble, while my whole body shivers beneath the warmth of the bedclothes, until all at once I fall asleep, as though one should plunge into a pool of stagnant water in order to drown. I do not feel it coming on as I did formerly, this perfidious sleep which is close to me and watching me, which is going to seize me by the head, to close my eyes and annihilate me.

I sleep—a long time—two or three hours perhaps—then a dream—no—a nightmare lays hold on me. I feel that I am in bed and asleep . . . I feel it and I know it . . . and I feel also that somebody is coming close to me, is looking at me, touching me, is getting on to my bed, is kneeling on my chest, is taking my neck between his hands and squeezing it . . . squeezing it with all his might in order to strangle me.

I struggle, bound by that terrible sense of powerlessness which paralyzes us in our dreams; I try to cry out—but I cannot; I want to move—I cannot do so; I try, with the most violent efforts and breathing hard, to turn over and throw off this being who is crushing and suffocating me—I cannot!

And then, suddenly, I wake up, trembling and bathed in perspiration; I light a candle and find that I am alone, and after that crisis, which occurs every night, I at length fall asleep and slumber tranquilly till morning.

June 2. My condition has grown worse. What is the matter with me? The bromide does me no good, and the shower baths have no effect. Sometimes, in order to tire myself thoroughly, though I am fatigued enough already, I go for a walk in the forest of Roumare. I used to think at first that the fresh light and soft air, impregnated with the odor of herbs and leaves, would instill new blood into my veins and impart fresh energy to my heart. I turned into a broad hunting road, and then turned toward La Beauille, through a narrow path, between two rows of exceedingly tall trees, which placed a thick green, almost black, roof between the sky and me.

A sudden shiver ran through me, not a cold shiver, but a strange shiver of agony, and I hastened my steps, uneasy at being alone in the forest, afraid, stupidly and without reason, of the profound solitude. Suddenly it seemed to me as I were being followed, as if somebody were walking at my heels, close, quite close to me, near enough to touch me.

I turned round suddenly, but I was alone. I saw nothing behind me except the straight, broad path, empty and bordered by high trees, horribly empty; before me it also extended until it was lost in the distance, and looked just the same—terrible.

I closed my eyes. Why? And then I began to turn round on one heel very quickly, just like a top. I nearly fell down, and opened my eyes; the trees were dancing round me and the earth heaved; I was obliged to sit down. Then, ah! I no longer remembered how I had come! What a strange idea! What a strange, strange idea! I did not in the least know. I started off to the right, and got back into the avenue which had led me into the middle of the forest.

June 3. I have had a terrible night. I shall go away for a few weeks, for no doubt a journey will set me up again.

July 2. I have come back, quite cured, and have had a most delightful trip into the bargain. I have been to Mont Saint-Michel, which I had not seen before.

What a sight, when one arrives as I did, at Avranches toward the end of the day! The town stands on a hill, and I was taken into the public garden at the extremity of the town. I uttered a cry of astonishment. An extraordinarily large bay lay extended before me, as far as my eyes could reach, between two hills which were lost to sight in the mist; and in the middle of this immense yellow bay, under a clear, golden sky, a peculiar hill rose up, sombre and pointed in the midst of the sand. The sun had just disappeared, and under the still flaming sky appeared the outline of that fantastic rock which bears on its summit a fantastic monument.

At daybreak I went out to it. The tide was low, as it had been the night before, and I saw that wonderful abbey rise up before me as I approached it. After several hours' walking, I reached the enormous mass of rocks which supports the little town, dominated by the great church. Having climbed the steep and narrow street, I entered the most wonderful Gothic building that has ever been built to God on earth, as large as a town, full of low rooms which seem buried beneath vaulted roofs, and lofty galleries supported by delicate columns.

I entered this gigantic granite gem, which is as light as a bit of lace, covered with towers, with slender belfries with spiral staircases, which raise their strange heads that bristle with chimeras, with devils, with fantastic animals, with monstrous flowers, to the blue sky by day, and to the black sky at night, and are connected by finely carved arches.

When I had reached the summit I said to the monk who accompanied me: "Father, how happy you must be here!" And he replied: "It is very windy here, monsieur"; and so we began to talk while watching the rising tide, which ran over the sand and covered it as with a steel cuirass.

And then the monk told me stories, all the old stories belonging to the place, legends, nothing but legends.

One of them struck me forcibly. The country people, those belonging to the Mount, declare that at night one can hear voices talking on the sands, and that one then hears two goats bleating, one with a strong, the other with a weak voice. Incredulous people declare that it is nothing but the cry of the sea birds, which occasionally resembles bleatings, and occasionally, human lamentations; but belated fishermen swear that they have met an old shepherd wandering between tides on the sands around the little town. His head is completely concealed by his cloak and he is followed by a billy goat with a man's face, and a nanny goat with a woman's face, both having long, white hair and talking incessantly and quarreling in an unknown tongue. then suddenly they cease and begin to bleat with all their might.

"Do you believe it?" I asked the monk. "I scarcely know," he replied, and I continued: "If there are other beings besides ourselves on this earth, how comes it that we have not known it long since, or why have *you* not seen them? How is it that *I* have not seen them?" He replied: "Do you see the hundred-thousandth part of what exists? Look here; there is the wind, which is the strongest force in nature which knocks down men, and blows down buildings, uproots trees, raised the sea into mountains of water, destroys cliffs and casts great ships on the rocks; the wind which kills, which whistles, which sighs, which roars—have you ever seen it, and can you see it? It exists for all that, however."

I was silent before this simple reasoning. That man was a philosopher, or perhaps a fool; I could not say which exactly, so I held my tongue. What he had said had often been in my own thoughts.

July 3. I have slept badly; certainly there is some feverish influence here, for my coachman is suffering in the same way as I am. When I went back home yesterday, I noticed his singular paleness, and I asked him: "What is the matter with you, Jean?" "The matter is that I never get any rest, and my nights devour my days. Since your departure, monsieur, there has been a spell over me."

However, the other servants are all well, but I am very much afraid of having another attack myself.

July 4. I am decidedly ill again; for my old nightmares have returned. Last night I felt somebody leaning on me and sucking my life from between my lips. Yes, he was sucking it out of my throat, like a leech. Then he got up, satiated, and I woke up, so exhausted, crushed and weak that I could not move. If this continues for a few days, I shall certainly go away again.

July 5. Have I lost my reason? What happened last night is so strange that my head wanders when I think of it!

I had locked my door, as I do now every evening, and then, being thirsty, I drank half a glass of water, and accidentally noticed that the water bottle was full up to the cut-glass stopper.

Then I went to bed and fell into one of my terrible sleeps, from which I was aroused in about two hours by a still more frightful shock.

Picture to yourself a sleeping man who is being murdered and who wakes up with a knife in his lung, and whose breath rattles, who is covered with blood, and who can no longer breathe and is about to die, and does not understand—there you have it.

Having recovered my senses, I was thirsty again, so I lit a candle and went to the table on which stood my water bottle. I lifted it up and tilted it over my glass, but nothing came out. It was empty! It was completely empty! At first I could not understand it at all, and then suddenly I was seized by such a terrible feeling that I had to sit down, or rather I fell into a chair! Then I sprang up suddenly to look about me; then I sat down again, overcome by astonishment and fear, in front of the transparent glass bottle! I looked at it with fixed eyes, trying to conjecture, and my hands trembled! Somebody had drunk the water, but who? I? I, without any doubt. It could surely only be I. In that case I was a somnambulist; I lived, without knowing it, that mysterious double life which makes us doubt whether there are not two beings in us, or whether a strange, unknowable and invisible being does not at such moments, when our soul is in a state of torpor, animate our captive body, which obeys this other being, as it obeys us, and more than it obeys ourselves.

Oh! Who will understand my horrible agony? Who will understand the emotion of a man who is sound in mind, wide awake, full of common sense, who looks in horror through the glass of a water bottle for a little water that disappeared while he was asleep? I remained thus until it was daylight, without venturing to go to bed again.

July 6. I am going mad. Again all the contents of my water bottle have been drunk during the night—or rather, I have drunk it!

But is it I? Is it I? Who could it be? Who? Oh, God! Am I going mad? Who will save me?

July 10. I have just been through some surprising ordeals. Decidedly I am mad! And yet! . . .

On July 6, before going to bed, I put some wine, milk, water, bread and strawberries on my table. Somebody drank—I drank—all the water and a little of the milk, but neither the wine, bread, nor the strawberries were touched.

On the seventh of July I renewed the same experiment, with the same results, and on July 8, I left out the water and the milk, and nothing was touched.

Lastly, on July 9, I put only water and milk on my table, taking care to wrap up the bottles in white muslin and to tie down the stoppers. Then I rubbed my lips, my beard and my hands with pencil lead, and went to bed.

Irresistible sleep seized me, which was soon followed by a terrible awakening. I had not moved, and there was no mark of lead on the sheets. I rushed to the table. The muslin round the bottles remained intact; I undid the string, trembling with fear. All the water had been drunk, and so had the milk! Ah! Great God! . . .

I must start for Paris immediately.

July 12. Paris. I must have lost my head during the last few days! I must be the plaything of my enervated imagination, unless I am really a somnambulist, or perhaps I have been under the power of one of those hitherto unexplained influences which are called suggestions. In any case, my mental state bordered on madness, and twenty-four hours of Paris sufficed to restore my equilibrium.

Yesterday, after doing some business and paying some visits which instilled fresh and invigorating air into my soul, I wound up the evening at the *Théâtre-Français*. A play by Alexandre Dumas the younger was being acted, and his active and powerful imagination completed my cure. Certainly solitude is dangerous for active minds. We require around us men who can think and talk. When we are alone for a long time, we people space with phantoms.

I returned along the boulevards to my hotel in excellent spirits. Amid the jostling of the crowd I thought, not without irony, of my terrors and surmises of the previous week, because I had believed—yes, I had believed—that an invisible being lived beneath my roof. How weak our brains are, and how quickly they are terrified and led into error by a small incomprehensible fact.

Instead of saying simply: "I do not understand because I do not know the cause," we immediately imagine terrible mysteries and supernatural powers.

July 14. Fête of the Republic. I walked through the streets, amused as a child at the firecrackers and flags. Still it is very foolish to be merry on a fixed date, by Government decree. The populace is an imbecile flock of sheep, now stupidly patient, and now in ferocious revolt. Say to it: "Amuse yourself," and it amuses itself. Say to it: "Vote for the Emperor," and it votes for the Emperor, and then say to it: "Vote for the Republic," and it votes for the Republic.

Those who direct it are also stupid; only, instead of obeying men, they obey principles which can only be stupid, sterile, and false, for the very reason that they are principles, that is to say, ideas which are considered as certain and unchangeable, in this world where one is certain of nothing, since light is an illusion and noise is an illusion.

July 16. I saw some things yesterday that troubled me very much.

I was dining at the house of my cousin, Madame Sablé, whose husband is colonel of the 76th Chasseurs at Limoges. There were two young women there, one of whom had married a medical man, Dr. Parent, who devotes much attention to nervous diseases and to the remarkable manifestations taking place at this moment under the influence of hypnotism and suggestion.

He related to us at some length the wonderful results obtained by English scientists and by the doctors of the Nancy school; and the facts which he adduced appeared to me so strange that I declared that I was altogether incredulous.

"We are," he declared, "on the point of discovering one of the most important secrets of nature; I mean to say, one of its most important secrets on this earth, for there are certainly others of a different kind of importance up in the stars, yonder. Ever since man has thought, ever since he has been able to express and write down his thoughts, he has felt himself close to a mystery which is impenetrable to his gross and imperfect senses, and he endeavors to supplement through his intellect the inefficiency of his senses. As long as that intellect remained in its elementary stage, these apparitions of invisible spirits assumed forms that were commonplace, though terrifying. Thence sprang the popular belief in the supernatural, the legends of wandering spirits, of fairies, of gnomes, ghosts, I might even say the legend of God; for our conceptions of the workman-creator, from whatever religion they may have come down to us, are certainly the most mediocre, the most stupid and the most incredible inventions that ever sprang from the terrified brain of any human beings. Nothing is truer than what Voltaire says: 'God made man in His own image, but man has certainly paid Him back in his own coin.'

"However, for rather more than a century men seem to have had a presentiment of something new. Mesmer and some others have put us on an unexpected track, and, especially within the last two or three years, we have arrived at really surprising results."

My cousin, who is also very incredulous, smiled, and Dr. Parent said to her: "Would you like me to try and send you to sleep, madame?" "Yes, certainly."

She sat down in an easy chair, and he began to look at her fixedly, so as to fascinate her. I suddenly felt myself growing uncomfortable, my heart beating rapidly and a choking sensation in my throat. I saw Madame Sablé's eyes becoming heavy, her mouth twitching and her bosom heaving, and at the end of ten minutes she was asleep.

"Go behind her," the doctor said to me, and I took a seat behind her. He put a visiting card into her hands, and said to her: "This is a looking glass; what do you see in it?" And she replied: "I see my cousin." "What is he doing?" "He is twisting his mustache." "And now?" "He is taking a photograph out of his pocket." "Whose photograph is it?" "His own."

That was true, and the photograph had been given me that same evening at the hotel.

"What is his attitude in this portrait?" "He is standing up with his hat in his hand."

She saw, therefore, on that card, on that piece of white paste board, as if she had seen it in a mirror.

The young women were frightened, and exclaimed: "That is enough! Quite, quite enough!"

But the doctor said to Madame Sablé authoritatively: "You will rise at eight o'clock to-morrow morning; then you will go and call on your cousin at his hotel and ask him to lend you five thousand francs which your husband demands of you, and which he will ask for when he sets out on his coming journey."

Then he woke her up.

On returning to my hotel, I thought over this curious séance, and I was assailed by doubts, not as to my cousin's absolute and undoubted good faith, for I had known her as well as if she were my own sister ever since she was a child, but as to a possible trick on the doctor's part. Had he not, perhaps, kept a glass hidden in his hand, which he showed to the young woman in her sleep, at the same time as he did the card? Professional conjurors do things that are just as singular.

So I went home and to bed, and this morning at about half-past eight, I was awakened by my valet, who said to me: "Madame Sablé has asked to see you immediately, monsieur." I dressed hastily and went to her.

She sat down in some agitation, with her eyes on the floor, and without raising her veil she said to me: "My dear cousin, I am going to ask a great favor of you." "What is it, cousin?" "I do not like to tell you, and yet I must. I am in absolute need of five thousand francs." "What, you?" "Yes, I, or rather my husband, who has asked me to procure them for him."

I was so thunderstruck that I stammered out my answers. I asked myself whether she had not really been making fun of me with Dr. Parent, if it was not merely a well-acted farce which had been rehearsed beforehand. On looking at her attentively, however, all my doubts disappeared. She was trembling with grief, so painful was this step to her, and I was convinced that her throat was full of sobs.

I knew that she was very rich and I continued: "What! Has not your husband five thousand francs at his disposal? Come, think. Are you sure that he commissioned you to ask me for them?"

She hesitated for a few seconds, as if she were making a great effort to search her memory, and then she replied: "Yes ... yes, I am quite sure of it." "He has written to you?"

She hesitated again and reflected, and I guessed the torture of her thoughts. She did not know. She only knew that she was to borrow five thousand francs of me for her husband. So she told a lie. "Yes, he has written to me." "When, pray? You did not mention it to me yesterday." "I received his letter this morning." "Can you show it me?" "No ... no ... no ... it contains private matters ... things too personal to ourselves ... I burned it." "So your husband runs into debt?"

She hesitated again, and then murmured: "I do not know." Thereupon I said bluntly: "I have not five thousand francs at my disposal at this moment, my dear cousin."

She uttered a kind of cry as if she were in pain and said: "Oh! oh! I beseech you, I beseech you to get them for me. ..."

She got excited and clasped her hands as if she were praying to me! I heard her voice change its tone; she wept and stammered, harassed and dominated by the irresistible order that she had received.

"Oh! oh! I beg you to ... if you knew what I am suffering ... I want them to-day."

I had pity on her: "You shall have them by and by, I swear to you." "Oh! thank you! thank you! How kind you are."

I continued: "Do you remember what took place at your house last night?" "Yes." "Do you remember that Dr. Parent sent you to sleep?" "Yes." "Oh! Very well, then; he ordered you to come to me this morning to borrow five thousand francs, and at this moment you are obeying that suggestion."

She considered for a few moments, and then replied: "But as it is my husband who wants them—"

For a whole hour I tried to convince her, but could not succeed, and when she had gone I went to the doctor. He was just going out, and he listened to me with a smile, and said: "Do you believe now?" "Yes, I cannot help it." "Let us go to your cousin's."

She was already half asleep on a reclining chair, overcome with fatigue. The doctor felt her pulse, looked at her for some time with one hand raised toward her eyes, which she closed by degrees under the irresistible power of this magnetic influence, and when she was asleep, he said:

"Your husband does not require the five thousand francs any longer! You must, therefore, forget that you asked your cousin to lend them to you, and, if he speaks to you about it, you will not understand him."

Then he woke her up, and I took out a pocketbook and said: "Here is what you asked me for this morning, my dear cousin." But she was so surprised that I did not venture to persist; nevertheless, I tried to recall the circumstance to her, but she denied it vigorously, thought I was making fun of her, and, in the end, very nearly lost her temper.

There! I have just come back, and I have not been able to eat any lunch, for this experiment has altogether upset me.

July 19. Many people to whom I told the adventure laughed at me. I no longer know what to think. the wise man says: "It may be!"

July 21. I dined at Bougival, and then I spent the evening at a boatmen's ball. Decidedly everything depends on place and surroundings. It would be the height of folly to believe in the supernatural on the Ile de la Grenouillière . . . but on the top of Mont Saint-Michel? . . . and in India? We are terribly influenced by our surroundings. I shall return home next week.

July 30. I came back to my own house yesterday. Everything is going on well.

August 2. Nothing new; it is splendid weather, and I spent my days in watching the Seine flowing past.

August 4. Quarrels among my servants. They declare that the glasses are broken in the cupboards at night. The footman accuses the cook, who accuses the seamstress, who accuses the other two. Who is the culprit? It is a clever person who can tell.

August 6. This time I am not mad. I have seen . . . I have seen . . . I have seen! . . . I can doubt no longer . . . I have seen it! . . .

I was walking at two o'clock among my rose trees, in the full sunlight . . . in the walk bordered by autumn roses which are beginning to fall. As I stopped to look at a Géant de Bataille, which had three splendid blossoms, I distinctly saw the stalk of one of the roses near me bend, as if an invisible hand had bent it, and then break, as if that hand had picked it! Then the flower raised itself, following the curve which a hand would have described in carrying it toward a mouth, and it remained suspended in the transparent air, all alone and motionless, a terrible red spot, three yards from my eyes. In desperation I rushed at it to take it! I found nothing; it had disappeared. then I was seized with furious rage against myself, for a reasonable and serious man should not have such hallucinations.

But was it an hallucination? I turned round to look for the stalk, and I found it at once, on the bush, freshly broken, between two other roses which remained on the branch. I returned home then, my mind greatly disturbed; for I am certain now, as certain as I am of the alternation of day and night, that there exists close to me an invisible being that lives on milk and water, that can touch objects, take them and change their places; that is, consequently, endowed with a material nature, although it is imperceptible to our senses, and that lives as I do, under my roof—

August 7. I slept tranquilly. He drank the water out of my decanter, but did not disturb my sleep.

I wonder if I am mad. As I was walking just now in the sun by the riverside, doubts as to my sanity arose in me; not vague doubts such as I have had hitherto, but definite, absolute doubts. I have seen mad people, and I have known some who have been quite intelligent, lucid, even clear-sighted at every concern of life, except on one point. They spoke clearly, readily, profoundly on everything, when suddenly their mind struck upon the shoals of their madness and broke to pieces there, and scattered and foundered in that furious and terrible sea, full of rolling waves, fogs and squalls, which is called *madness.*

I certainly should think that I was mad, absolutely mad, if I were not conscious, did not perfectly know my condition, did not fathom it by analyzing it with the most complete lucidity. I should, in fact, be only a rational man who was laboring under an hallucination. Some unknown disturbance must have arisen in my brain, one of those disturbances which physiologists of the present day try to note and to verify; and that disturbance must have caused a deep gap in my mind and in the sequence and logic of my ideas. Similar phenomena occur in dreams which lead us among the most unlikely phantasmagoria, without causing us any surprise, because our verifying apparatus and our organ of control are asleep, while our imaginative faculty is awake and active. Is it not possible that one of the imperceptible notes of the cerebral keyboard has been paralyzed in me? Some men lose the recollection of proper names, of verbs, or of numbers, or merely of dates, in consequence of an accident. The localization of all the variations of thought has been established nowadays; why, then, should it be surprising if my faculty of controlling the unreality of certain hallucinations were dormant in me for the time being?

I thought of all this as I walked by the side of the water. The sun shone brightly on the river and made earth delightful, while it filled me with a love for life, for the swallows, whose agility always delights my eye, for the plants by the riverside, the rustle of whose leaves is a pleasure to my ears.

By degrees, however, an inexplicable feeling of discomfort seized me. It seemed as if some unknown force were numbing and stopping me, were preventing me from going further, and were calling me back. I felt that painful wish to return which oppresses you when you have left a beloved invalid at home, and when you are seized with a presentiment that he is worse.

I, therefore, returned in spite of myself, feeling certain that I should find some bad news awaiting me, a letter or a telegram. There was nothing, however, and I was more surprised and uneasy than if I had had another fantastic vision.

August 8. I spent a terrible evening yesterday. He does not show himself any more, but I feel that he is near me, watching me, looking at me, penetrating me, dominating me, and more redoubtable when he hides himself thus than if he were to manifest his constant and invisible presence by supernatural phenomena. However, I slept.

August 9. Nothing, but I am afraid.

August 10. Nothing; what will happen to-morrow?

August 11. Still nothing; I cannot stop at home with this fear hanging over me and these thoughts in my mind; I shall go away.

August 12. Ten o'clock at night. All day long I have been trying to get away, and have not been able. I wished to accomplish this simple and easy act of freedom—to go out—to get into my carriage in order to go to Rouen— and I have not been able to do it. What is the reason?

August 13. When we are attacked by certain maladies, all the springs of our physical being appear to be broken, all our energies destroyed, all our muscles relaxed; our bones, too, have become as soft as flesh, and our blood as liquid as water. I am experiencing these sensations in my moral being in a strange and distressing manner. I have no longer any strength, any courage, any self-control, not even any power to set my own will in motion. I have no power left to will anything; but someone does it for me and I obey.

August 14. I am lost! Somebody possesses my soul and dominates it. Somebody orders all my acts, all my movements, all my thoughts. I am no longer anything in myself, nothing except an enslaved and terrified spectator of all the things I do. I wish to go out; I cannot. He does not wish to, and so I remain, trembling and distracted, in the armchair in which he keeps me sitting. I merely wish to get up and to rouse myself; I cannot! I am riveted to my chair, and my chair adheres to the ground in such a manner that no power could move us.

Then, suddenly, I must, I must go to the bottom of my garden to pick some strawberries and eat them, and I go there. I pick the strawberries and eat them! oh, my God! my God! Is there a God? If there be one, deliver me! Save me! Succor me! Pardon! Pity! Mercy! Save me! Oh, what sufferings! What torture! What horror!

August 15. This is certainly the way in which my poor cousin was possessed and controlled when she came to borrow five thousand francs of me. She was under the power of a strange will which had entered into her, like another soul, like another parasitic and dominating soul. Is the world coming to an end?

But who is he, this invisible being that rules me? This unknowable being, this rover of a supernatural race?

Invisible beings exist, then! How is it, then, that since the beginning of the world they have never manifested themselves precisely as they do to me? I have never read of anything that resembles what goes on in my house. Oh, if I could only leave it, if I could only go away, escape, and never return! I should be saved, but I cannot.

August 16. I managed to escape to-day for two hours, like a prisoner who finds the door of his dungeon accidentally open. I suddenly felt that I was free and that he was far away, and so I gave orders to harness the horses as quickly as possible, and I drove to Rouen. Oh, how delightful to be able to say to a man who obeys you: "Go to Rouen!"

I made him pull up before the library, and I begged them to lend me Dr. Herrmann Herestauss' treaties on the unknown inhabitants of the ancient and modern world.

Then, as I was getting into my carriage, I intended to say: "To the railway station!" but instead of this I shouted—I did not say, but I shouted—in such a loud voice that all the passers-by turned round: "Home!" and I fell back on the cushion of my carriage, overcome by mental agony. He had found me again and regained possession of me.

August 17. Oh, what a night! What a night! And yet it seems to me that I ought to rejoice. I read until one o'clock in the morning! Herestauss, doctor of philosophy and theogony, wrote the history of the manifestation of all those invisible beings which hover around man, or of whom he dreams. He describes their origin, their domain, their power; but none of them resembles the one which haunts me. One might say that man, ever since he began to think, has had a foreboding fear of a new being, stronger than himself, his successor in this world, and that, feeling his presence, and not being able to foresee the nature of that master, he has, in his terror, created the whole race of occult beings, of vague phantoms born of fear.

Having, therefore, read until one o'clock in the morning, I went and sat down at the open window, in order to cool my forehead and my thoughts, in the calm night air. It was very pleasant and warm! How I should have enjoyed such a night formerly!

There was no moon, but the stars darted out their rays in the dark heavens. Who inhabits those worlds? What forms, what living beings, what animals are there yonder? What do the thinkers in those distant worlds know more than we do? What can they do more than we can? What do they see which we do not know? Will not one of them, some day or other, traversing space, appear on our earth to conquer it, just as the Norsemen formerly crossed the sea in order to subjugate nations more feeble than themselves?

We are so weak, so defenseless, so ignorant, so small, we who live on this particle of mud which revolves in a drop of water.

I fell asleep, dreaming thus in the cool night air, and when I had slept for about three-quarters of an hour, I opened my eyes without moving, awakened by I know not what confused and strange sensation. At first I saw nothing, and then suddenly it appeared to me as if a page of a book which had remained open on my table turned over of its own accord. Not a breath of air had come in at my window, and I was surprised, and waited. In about four minutes, I saw, I saw, yes, I saw with my own eyes, another page lift itself up and fall down on the others, as if a finger had turned it over. My armchair was empty, appeared empty, but I knew that he was there, he, and sitting in my place, and that he was reading. With a furious bound, the bound of an enraged wild beast that springs at its tamer, I crossed my room to seize him, to strangle him, to kill him! But before I could reach it, the chair fell over as if somebody had run away from me—my table rocked, my lamp fell and went out, and my window closed as if some thief had been surprised and had fled out into the night, shutting it behind him.

So he had run away; he had been afraid; he, afraid of me!

But—but—to-morrow—or later—some day or other—I should be able to hold him in my clutches and crush him against the ground! Do not dogs occasionally bite and strangle their masters?

August 18. I have been thinking the whole day long. Oh, yes I will obey him, follow his impulses, fulfill all his wishes, show myself humble, submissive, a coward. He is the stronger; but the hour will come—

August 19. I know—I know—I know all! I have just read the following in the *Revue du Monde Scientifique:* "A curious piece of news comes to us from Rio de Janeiro. Madness, an epidemic of madness, which may be compared to that contagious madness which attacked the people of Europe in the Middle Ages, is at this moment raging in the Province of San-Paolo. The terrified inhabitants are leaving their houses, saying that they are pursued, possessed, dominated like human cattle by invisible, though tangible, beings, a species of vampires, which feed on their life while they are asleep, and which, besides, drink water and milk without appearing to touch any other nourishment.

Professor Don Pedro Henriques, accompanied by several medical savants, has gone to the Province of San-Paolo, in order to study the origin and the manifestations of this surprising madness on the spot, and to propose such measures to the Emperor as may appear to him to be most fitted to restore the mad population to reason."

Ah! Ah! I remember now that fine Brazilian three-master which passed in front of my windows as she was going up the Seine, on the 8th day of last May! I thought she looked so pretty, so white and bright! That Being was on board of her, coming from there, where its race originated. And it saw me! It saw my house which was also white, and it sprang from the ship onto the land. Oh, merciful heaven!

Now I know, I can divine. The reign of man is over, and he has come. He who was feared by primitive man; whom disquieted priests exorcised; whom sorcerers evoked on dark nights, without having seen him appear, to whom the imagination of the transient masters of the world lent all the monstrous or graceful forms of gnomes, spirits, genii, fairies and familiar spirits. After the coarse conceptions of primitive fear, more clear-sighted men foresaw it more clearly. Mesmer divined it, and ten years ago physicians accurately discovered the nature of his power, even before he exercised it himself. They played with this new weapon of the Lord, the sway of a mysterious will over the human soul, which had become a slave. They called it magnetism, hypnotism, suggestion—what do I know? I have seen them amusing them-

selves like rash children with this horrible power! Woe to us! Woe to man!
He has come, the—the—what does he call himself—the—I fancy that he is
shouting out his name to me and I do not hear him—the—yes——he is
shouting it out—I am listening—I cannot—he repeats it—the—Horla—I hear—
the Horla—it is he—the Horla—he has come!

Ah! the vulture has eaten the pigeon; the wolf has eaten the lamb; the
lion has devoured the sharp-horned buffalo; man has killed the lion with an
arrow, with a sword, with gunpowder; but the Horla will make of man what
we have made of the horse and of the ox; his chattel, his slave and his food,
by the mere power of his will. Woe to us!

But, nevertheless, the animal sometimes revolts and kills the man who has
subjugated it. I should also like—I shall be able to—but I must know him,
touch him, see him! Scientists say that animals' eyes, being different from
ours, do not distinguish objects as ours do. And my eye cannot distinguish
this newcomer who is oppressing me.

Why? Oh, now I remember the words of the monk at Mont Saint-Michel:
"Can we see the hundred-thousandth part of what exists? See here; there is
the wind, which is the strongest force in nature, which knocks men down,
and wrecks buildings, uproots trees, raises the sea into mountains of water,
destroys cliffs and casts great ships on the breakers; the wind which kills,
which whistles, which sighs, which roars—have you ever seen it, and can you
see it? It exists for all that, however!"

And I went on thinking: my eyes are so weak, so imperfect, that they do
not even distinguish hard bodies, if they are as transparent as glass! If a glass
without tinfoil behind it were to bar my way, I should run into it, just as a
bird which has flown into a room breaks its head against the windowpanes.
A thousand things, moreover, deceive man and lead him astray. Why should
it then be surprising that he cannot perceive an unknown body through
which the light passes?

A new being! Why not? It was assuredly bound to come! Why should we
be the last? We do not distinguish it any more than all the others created
before us! The reason is, that its nature is more perfect, its body finer and
more finished than ours, that ours is so weak, so awkwardly constructed,
encumbered with organs that are always tired, always on the strain like
machinery that is too complicated, which lives like a plant and like a beast,
nourishing itself with difficulty on air, herbs and flesh, an animal machine
which is a prey to maladies, to malformations, to decay; broken-winded,
badly regulated, simple and eccentric, ingeniously badly made, at once a
coarse and a delicate piece of workmanship, the rough sketch of a being that
might become intelligent and grand.

We are only a few, so few in this world, from the oyster up to man. Why
should there not be one more, once that period is passed which separates the
successive apparitions from all the different species?

Why not one more? Why not, also, other trees with immense, splendid
flowers, perfuming whole regions? Why not other elements besides fire, air,
earth and water? There are four, only four, those nursing fathers of various

beings! What a pity! Why are there not forty, four hundred, four thousand? How poor everything is, how mean and wretched! grudgingly produced, roughly constructed, clumsily made! Ah, the elephant and the hippopotamus, what grace! And the camel, what elegance!

But the butterfly, you will say, a flying flower! I dream of one that should be as large as a hundred worlds, with wings whose shape, beauty, colors and motion I cannot even express. But I see it—it flutters from star to star, refreshing them and perfuming them with the light and harmonious breath of its flight! And the people up there look at it as it passes in an ecstasy of delight!

What is the matter with me? It is he, the Horla, who haunts me, and who makes me think of these foolish things! He is within me, he is becoming my soul; I shall kill him!

August 29. I shall kill him. I have seen him! Yesterday I sat down at my table and pretended to write very assiduously. I knew quite well that he would come prowling round me, quite close to me, so close that I might perhaps be able to touch him, to seize him. And then—then I should have the strength of desperation; I should have my hands, my knees, my chest, my forehead, my teeth to strangle him, to crush him, to bite him, to tear him to pieces. And I watched for him with all my overexcited senses.

I had lighted my two lamps and the eight wax candles on my mantelpiece, as if with this light I could discover him.

My bedstead, my old oak post bedstead, stood opposite to me; on my right was the fireplace; on my left, the door which was carefully closed, after I had left it open for some time in order to attract him; behind me was a very high wardrobe with a looking glass in it, before which I stood to shave and dress every day, and in which I was in the habit of glancing at myself from head to foot every time I passed it.

I pretended to be writing in order to deceive him, for he also was watching me, and suddenly I felt—I was certain that he was reading over my shoulder, that he was there, touching my ear.

I got up, my hands extended, and turned around so quickly that I almost fell. Eh! well? It was as bright as at midday, but I did not see my reflection in the mirror! It was empty, clear, profound, full of light! But my figure was not reflected in it—and I, I was opposite to it! I saw the large clear glass from top to bottom, and I looked at it with unsteady eyes; and I did not dare to advance; I did not venture to make a movement, feeling that he was there, but that he would escape me again, he whose imperceptible body had absorbed my reflection.

How frightened I was! And then, suddenly, I began to see myself in a mist in the depths of the looking glass, in a mist as it were a sheet of water; and it seemed to me as if this water were flowing clearer every moment. It was like the end of an eclipse. Whatever it was that hid me did not appear to possess any clearly defined outlines, but a sort of opaque transparency which gradually grew clearer.

At last I was able to distinguish myself completely, as I do every day when I look at myself.

I had seen it! And the horror of it remained with me, and makes me shudder even now.

August 30. How could I kill it, as I could not get hold of it? Poison? But it would see me mix it with the water; and then, would our poisons have any effect on its impalpable body? No—no—no doubt about the matter—Then—then?—

August 31. I sent for a blacksmith from Rouen, and ordered iron shutters for my room, such as some private hotels in Paris have on the ground floor, for fear of burglars, and he is going to make me an iron door as well. I have made myself out a coward, but I do not care about that!

September 10.—Rouen, Hotel Continental. It is done—it is done—but is he dead? My mind is thoroughly upset by what I have seen.

Well then, yesterday, the locksmith having put on the iron shutters and door, I left everything open until midnight, although it was getting cold.

Suddenly I felt that he was there, and joy, mad joy, took possession of me. I got up softly, and walked up and down for some time, so that he might not suspect anything; then I took off my boots and put on my slippers carelessly; then I fastened the iron shutters, and, going back to the door, quickly double-locked it with a padlock, putting the key into my pocket.

Suddenly I noticed that he was moving restlessly round me, that in his turn he was frightened and was ordering me to let him out. I nearly yielded; I did not, however, but, putting my back to the door, I half opened it, just enough to allow me to go out backward, and as I am very tall my head touched the casing. I was sure that he had not been able to escape, and I shut him up quite alone, quite alone. What happiness! I had him fast. Then I ran downstairs; in the drawing-room, which was under my bedroom, I took the two lamps and I poured all the oil on the carpet, the furniture, everywhere; then I set fire to it and made my escape, after having carefully double-locked the door.

I went and hid myself at the bottom of the garden, in a clump of laurel bushes. How long it seemed! How long it seemed! Everything was dark, silent, motionless, not a breath of air and not a star, but heavy banks of clouds which one could not see, but which weighed, oh, so heavily on my soul.

I looked at my house and waited. How long it was! I already began to think that the fire had gone out of its own accord, or that he had ex-tinguished it, when one of the lower windows gave way under the violence of the flames, and a long, soft, caressing sheet of red flame mounted up the white wall, and enveloped it as far as the roof. The light fell on the trees, the branches, and the leaves, and a shiver of fear pervaded them also! The birds awoke, a dog began to howl, and it seemed to me as if the day were breaking! Almost immediately two other windows flew into fragments, and I saw that the whole of the lower part of my house was nothing but a terrible furnace. But a cry, a horrible, shrill, heartrending cry, a woman's cry, sounded through the night, and two garret windows were opened! I had forgotten the servants! I saw their terror-stricken faces, and their arms waving frantically.

Then, overwhelmed with horror, I set off to run to the village, shouting: "Help! help! fire! fire!" I met some people who were already coming to the scene, and I returned with them.

By this time the house was nothing but a horrible and magnificent funeral pile, a monstrous funeral pile which lit up the whole country, a funeral pile where men were burning, and where he was burning also. He, He, my prisoner, that new Being, the new master, the Horla!

Suddenly the whole roof fell in between the walls, and a volcano of flames darted up to the sky. Through all the windows which opened on that furnace, I saw the flames darting, and I thought that he was there, in that kiln, dead.

Dead? Perhaps.—His body? Was not his body, which was transparent, indestructible by such means as would kill ours?

If he were not dead?—Perhaps time alone has power over that Invisible and Redoubtable Being. Why this transparent, unrecognizable body, this body belonging to a spirit, if it also has to fear ills, infirmities and premature destruction?

Premature destruction? All human terror springs from that! After man, the Horla. After him who can die every day, at any hour, at any moment, by any accident, comes the one who will die only at his own proper hour, day, and minute, because he has touched the limits of his existence!

No—no—without any doubt—he is not dead—Then—then—I suppose I must kill *myself!* . . .

CHARLES BAUDELAIRE

A CARRION

Do you remember the thing we saw,
    Oh my soul,
That morning, that lovely summer morning?

At the turn of a path, an unspeakable
    Carrion sprawled
On a bed strewn with pebbles.

Its legs in the air, like those
    Of a woman in heat
Feverish and sweating poisons

Spread nonchalantly, cynically
    Wide
Its belly-gases sighing.

The sun shone on that rot as if to roast
    It to a turn.
As if it meant to give back

To almighty nature
    All that it had
Joined together.

And the sky looked down on that
    Splendid carcass,
On that flowering flesh.

And the stink was so great
    That you believed
You would faint on the grass.

The flies buzzed above
    The putrescent belly
From which battalions of larvae coursed

Like a thick fluid moving
    Beside
Those living rags.

The whole thing ebbed and flowed
    Like a wave,
Or streamed forth glistening.

One might have thought that the body
    Swollen
By a vague breath lived

    By multiplying itself.

And the world it was, gave off
    A strange music
Like flowing water or the wind.

Or the rhythmic sound
    The winnower makes
Turning and moving the winnow.

Shapes disappear and are no more
    Than a dream.
A sketch slow to appear

On the forgotten canvas the artist
    Completes
With the help of memory only.

From behind rocks we were watched
    By an uneasy
Mean-eyed bitch

Biding her time when she might
    Snatch from the bones
The bit of meat she had dropped.

—For all that . . . you will resemble
    Such filth,
Such loathesome infection . . .

Light of my eyes. Oh bright sun
    Of my being,
You, my angel; my passion!

Yes, you will be like that,
    O queen of all graces.
After the final sacraments,

When you lie under the green
    And the flowering
Grasses and moulder among bones,

Then, my beauty, say to the
    Worms
Devouring you with kisses,

That I have kept intact
    The divine essence
And form of my decayed love.

EDGAR ALLAN POE

THE PIT AND THE PENDULUM

Impia tortorum longas hic turba furores
Sanguinis innocui, non satiata, aluit.
Sospite nunc patria, fracto nunc funeris antro,
Mors ubi dira fuit vita salusque patent.

[Quatrain composed for the gates of a market to
be erected upon the site of the Jacobin Club
House at Paris.]

I was sick—sick unto death with that long agony; and when they at length unbound me, and I was permitted to sit, I felt that my senses were leaving me. The sentence—the dread sentence of death—was the last of distinct accentuation which reached my ears. After that, the sound of the inquisitorial voices seemed merged in one dreamy indeterminate hum. It conveyed to my soul the idea of *revolution*—perhaps from its association in fancy with the burr of a mill-wheel. This only for a brief period, for presently I heard no more. Yet, for a while, I saw—but with how terrible an exaggeration! I saw the lips of the black-robed judges. They appeared to me white—whiter than the sheet upon which I trace these words—and thin even to grotesqueness; thin with the intensity of their expression of firmness—of immovable resolution—of stern contempt of human torture. I saw that the decrees of what to me was Fate were still issuing from those lips. I saw them writhe with a deadly locution. I saw them fashion the syllables of my name; and I shuddered because no sound succeeded. I saw, too, for a few moments of delirious horror, the soft and nearly imperceptible waving of the sable draperies which enwrapped the walls of the apartment. And then my vision fell upon the seven tall candles upon the table. At first they wore the aspect of charity, and seemed white slender angels who would save me; but then, all at once, there came a most deadly nausea over my spirit, and I felt every fibre in my frame thrill as if I had touched the wire of a galvanic battery, while the angel forms became meaningless spectres, with heads of flame, and I saw that from them there would be no help. And then there stole into my fancy, like a rich musical note, the thought of what sweet rest there must be in the grave. The thought came gently and stealthily, and it seemed long before it attained full appreciation; but just as my spirit came at length properly to feel and entertain it, the figures of the judges vanished, as if magically, from before me; the tall candles sank into nothingness! their flames went out utterly; the blackness of darkness supervened; all sensations appeared swallowed up in a mad rushing descent as of the soul into Hades. Then silence, and stillness, and night were the universe.

I had swooned; but still will not say that all of consciousness was lost. What of it there remained I will not attempt to define, or even to describe; yet all was not lost. In the deepest slumber—no! In delirium—no! In a swoon—no! In death—no! even in the grave all *is not* lost. Else there is no immortality for man. Arousing from the most profound of slumbers, we break the gossamer web of *some* dream. Yet in a second afterward, (so frail may that web have been) we remember not that we have dreamed. In the return to life from the swoon there are two stages: first, that of the sense of mental or spiritual; secondly, that of the sense of physical, existence. It seems probable that if, upon reaching the second stage, we could recall the impressions of the first, we should find these impressions eloquent in memories of the gulf beyond. And that gulf is—what? How at least shall we distinguish its shadows from those of the tomb? But if the impressions of what I have termed the first stage are not, at will, recalled, yet, after long interval, do they not come unbidden, while we marvel whence they come? He who has [never] swooned, is not he who finds strange palaces and wildly familiar faces in coals that glow; is not he who beholds floating in mid-air the sad visions that the many may not view; is not he who ponders over the perfume of some novel flower; is not he whose brain grows bewildered with the meaning of some musical cadence which has never before arrested his attention.

Amid frequent and thoughtful endeavors to remember, amid earnest struggles to regather some token of the state of seeming nothingness into which my soul had lapsed, there have been moments when I have dreamed of success; there have been brief, very brief periods when I have conjured up remembrances which the lucid reason of a later epoch assures me could have had reference only to that condition of seeming unconsciousness. These shadows of memory tell, indistinctly, of tall figures that lifted and bore me in silence down—down—still down—till a hideous dizziness oppressed me at the mere idea of the interminableness of the descent. They tell also of a vague horror at my heart, on account of that heart's unnatural stillness. Then comes a sense of sudden motionlessness throughout all things; as if those who bore me (a ghastly train!) had outrun, in their descent, the limits of the limitless, and paused from the wearisomeness of their toil. After this I call to mind flatness and dampness; and then all is *madness*—the madness of a memory which busies itself among forbidden things.

Very suddenly there came back to my soul motion and sound—the tumultuous motion of the heart, and, in my ears, the sound of its beating. Then a pause in which all is blank. Then again sound, and motion, and touch—a tingling sensation pervading my frame. Then the mere consciousness of existence, without thought—a condition which lasted long. Then, very suddenly, *thought,* and shuddering terror, and earnest endeavor to comprehend my true state. Then a strong desire to lapse into insensibility.

Then a rushing revival of soul and a successful effort to move. And now a full memory of the trial, of the judges, of the sable draperies, of the sentence, of the sickness, of the swoon. Then entire forgetfulness of all that followed; of all that a later day and much earnestness of endeavor have enabled me vaguely to recall.

So far, I had not opened my eyes. I felt that I lay upon my back, unbound. I reached out my hand, and it fell heavily upon something damp and hard. There I suffered it to remain for many minutes, while I strove to imagine where and *what* I could be. I longed, yet dared not, to employ my vision. I dreaded the first glance at objects around me. It was not that I feared to look upon things horrible, but that I grew aghast lest there should be *nothing* to see. At length, with a wild desperation at heart, I quickly unclosed my eyes. My worst thoughts, then, were confirmed. The blackness of eternal night encompassed me. I struggled for breath. The intensity of the darkness seemed to oppress and stifle me. The atmosphere was intolerably close. I still lay quietly, and made effort to exercise my reason. I brought to mind the inquisitorial proceedings, and attempted from that point to deduce my real condition. The sentence had passed; and it appeared to me that a very long interval of time had since elapsed. Yet not for a moment did I suppose myself actually dead. Such a supposition, notwithstanding what we read in fiction, is altogether inconsistent with real existence;—but where and in what state was I? The condemned to death, I knew, perished usually at the *auto-da-fes,* and one of these had been held on the very night of the day of my trial. Had I been remanded to my dungeon, to await the next sacrifice, which would not take place for many months? This I at once saw could not be. Victims had been in immediate demand. Moreover, my dungeon, as well as all the condemned cells at Toledo, had stone floors, and light was not altogether excluded.

A fearful idea now suddenly drove the blood in torrents upon my heart, and for a brief period I once more relapsed into insensibility. Upon recovering, I at once started to my feet, trembling convulsively in every fibre. I thrust my arms wildly above and around me in all directions. I felt nothing; yet dreaded to move a step, lest I should be impeded by the walls of a *tomb.* Perspiration burst from every pore, and stood in cold big beads upon my forehead. The agony of suspense grew at length intolerable, and I cautiously moved forward, with my arms extended, and my eyes straining from their sockets in the hope of catching some faint ray of light. I proceeded for many paces; but still all was blackness and vacancy. I breathed more freely. It seemed evident that mine was not, at least, the most hideous of fates.

And now, as I still continued to step cautiously onward, there came thronging upon my recollection a thousand vague rumors of the horrors of Toledo. Of the dungeons there had been strange things narrated—fables I had always deemed them,—but yet strange, and too ghastly to repeat, save in a whisper. Was I left to perish of starvation in the subterranean world of darkness; or what fate, perhaps even more fearful, awaited me? That the result would be death, and a death of more than customary bitterness, I knew too well the character of my judges to doubt. The mode and the hour were all that occupied or distracted me.

My outstretched hands at length encountered some solid obstruction. It was a wall, seemingly of stone masonry—very smooth, slimy, and cold. I followed it up; stepping with all the careful distrust with which certain antique narratives had inspired me. This process, however, afforded me no means of ascertaining the dimensions of my dungeon, as I might make its circuit and return to the point whence I set out without being aware of the fact, so perfectly uniform seemed the wall. I therefore sought the knife which had been in my pocket when led into the inquisitorial chamber; but it was gone; my clothes had been exchanged for a wrapper of coarse serge. I had thought of forcing the blade in some minute crevice of the masonry, so as to identify my point of departure. The difficulty, nevertheless, was but trivial; although, in the disorder of my fancy, it seemed at first insuperable. I tore a part of the hem from the robe and placed the fragment at full length, and at right angles to the wall. In groping my way around the prison, I could not fail to encounter this rag upon completing the circuit. So, at least, I thought; but I had not counted upon the extent of the dungeon, or upon my own weakness. The ground was moist and slippery. I staggered onward for some time, when I stumbled and fell. My excessive fatigue induced me to remain prostrate; and sleep soon overtook me as I lay.

Upon awaking, and stretching forth an arm, I found beside me a loaf and a pitcher with water. I was too much exhausted to reflect upon this circumstance, but ate and drank with avidity. Shortly afterward, I resumed my tour around the prison, and with much toil, came at last upon the fragment of the serge. Up to the period when I fell, I had counted fifty-two paces, and, upon resuming my walk, I had counted forty-eight more;—when I arrived at the rag. There were in all, then, a hundred paces; and, admitting two paces to the yard, I presumed the dungeon to be fifty yards in circuit. I had met, however, with many angles in the wall, and thus I could form no guess at the shape of the vault, for vault I could not help supposing it to be.

I had little object—certainly no hope—in these researches; but a vague curiosity prompted me to continue them. Quitting the wall, I resolved to cross the area of the enclosure. At first, I proceeded with extreme caution, for the floor, although seemingly of solid material, was treacherous with slime. At length, however, I took courage, and did not hesitate to step firmly—endeavoring to cross in as direct a line as possible. I had advanced some ten or twelve paces in this manner, when the remnant of the torn hem of my robe became entangled between my legs. I stepped on it, and fell violently on my face.

In the confusion attending my fall, I did not immediately apprehend a somewhat startling circumstance, which yet, in a few seconds afterward, and while I still lay prostrate, arrested my attention. It was this—my chin rested upon the floor of the prison, but my lips, and the upper portion of my head, although seemingly at a less elevation than the chin, touched nothing. At the same time, my forehead seemed bathed in a clammy vapor, and the peculiar smell of decayed fungus arose to my nostrils. I put forward my arm, and shuddered to find that I had fallen at the very brink of a circular pit, whose extent, of course, I had no means of ascertaining at the moment. Groping about the masonry just below the margin, I succeeded in dislodging a small fragment, and let it fall into the abyss. For many seconds I hearkened to its reverberations as it dashed against the sides of the chasm in its descent; at length, there was a sullen plunge into water, succeeded by loud echoes. At the same moment, there came a sound resembling the quick opening and as rapid closing of a door overhead, while a faint gleam of light flashed suddenly through the gloom, and as suddenly faded away.

I saw clearly the doom which had been prepared for me, and congratulated myself upon the timely accident by which I had escaped. Another step before my fall, and the world had seen me no more. And the death just avoided was of that very character which I had regarded as fabulous and frivolous in the tales respecting the Inquisition. To the victims of its tyranny, there was the choice of death with its direst physical agonies, or death with its most hideous moral horrors. I had been reserved for the latter. By long suffering my nerves had been unstrung, until I trembled at the sound of my own voice, and had become in every respect a fitting subject for the species of torture which awaited me.

Shaking in every limb, I groped my way back to the wall; resolving there to perish rather than risk the terrors of the wells, of which my imagination now pictured many in various position about the dungeon. In other conditions of mind, I might have had courage to end my misery at once, by a plunge into one of these abysses; but now I was the veriest of cowards. Neither could I forget what I had read of these pits—that the *sudden* extinction of life formed no part of their most horrible plan.

Agitation of spirit kept me awake for many long hours, but at length I again slumbered. Upon arousing, I found by my side, as before, a loaf and a pitcher of water. A burning thirst consumed me, and I emptied the vessel at a draught. It must have been drugged; for scarcely had I drunk, before I became irresistibly drowsy. A deep sleep fell upon me—a sleep like that of death. How long it lasted, of course I know not; but when, once again, I unclosed my eyes, the objects around me were visible. By a wild, sulphurous lustre, the origin of which I could not at first determine, I was enabled to see the extent and aspect of the prison.

In its size I had been greatly mistaken. The whole circuit of its walls did not exceed twenty-five yards. For some minutes this fact occasioned me a world of vain trouble; vain indeed! for what could be of less importance, under the terrible circumstances which environed me, than the mere dimensions of my dungeon? But my soul took a wild interest in trifles, and I busied myself in endeavors to account for the error I had committed in my measurement. The truth at length flashed upon me. In my first attempt at exploration I had counted fifty-two paces, up to the period when I fell; I must then have been within a pace or two of the fragment of serge; in fact, I had nearly performed the circuit of the vault. I then slept and, upon awaking, I must have returned upon my steps—thus supposing the circuit nearly double what it actually was. My confusion of mind prevented me from observing that I began my tour with the wall to the left, and ended it with the wall to the right.

I had been deceived, too, in respect to the shape of the enclosure. In feeling my way I had found many angles, and thus deduced an idea of great irregularity; so potent is the effect of total darkness upon one arousing from lethargy or sleep! The angles were simply those of a few slight depressions, or niches, at odd intervals. The general shape of the prison was square. What I had taken for masonry seemed now to be iron, or some other metal, in huge plates, whose sutures or joints occasioned the depression. The entire surface of this metallic enclosure was rudely daubed in all the hideous and repulsive devices to which the charnel superstition of the monks has given rise. The figures of fiends in aspects of menace, with skeleton forms, and other more really fearful images, overspread and disfigured the walls. I observed that the outlines of these monstrosities were sufficiently distinct, but that the colors seemed faded and blurred, as if from the effects of a damp atmosphere. I now noticed the floor, too, which was of stone. In the centre yawned the circular pit from whose jaws I had escaped; but it was the only one in the dungeon.

All this I saw indistinctly and by much effort: for my personal condition had been greatly changed during slumber. I now lay upon my back, and at full length, on a species of low framework of wood. To this I was securely bound by a long strap resembling a surcingle. It passed in many convolutions about my limbs and body, leaving at liberty only my head, and my left arm to such extent, that I could, by dint of much exertion, supply myself with food from an earthen dish which lay by my side on the floor. I saw, to my horror, that the pitcher had been removed. I say to my horror; for I was consumed with intolerable thirst. This thirst it appeared to be the design of my persecutors to stimulate—for the food in the dish was meat pungently seasoned.

Looking upward, I surveyed the ceiling of my prison. It was some thirty or forty feet overhead, and constructed much as the side walls. In one of its panels a very singular figure riveted my whole attention. It was the painted figure of Time as he is commonly represented, save that, in lieu of a scythe, he held what, at a casual glance, I supposed to be the pictured image of a huge pendulum, such as we see on antique clocks. There was something, however, in the appearance of this machine which caused me to regard it more attentively. While I gazed directly upward at it (for its position was immediately over my own) I fancied that I saw it in motion. In an instant afterward the fancy was confirmed. Its sweep was brief, and of course slow. I watched it for some minutes somewhat in fear, but more in wonder. Wearied at length with observing its dull movement, I turned my eyes upon the other objects in the cell.

A slight noise attracted my notice, and, looking to the floor, I saw several enormous rats traversing it. They had issued from the well which lay just within view to my right. Even then, while I gazed, they came up in troops, hurriedly, with ravenous eyes, allured by the scent of the meat. From this it required much effort and attention to scare them away.

It might have been half an hour, perhaps, even an hour (for I could take but imperfect note of time), before I again cast my eyes upward. What I then saw confounded and amazed me. The sweep of the pendulum had increased in extent by nearly a yard. As a natural consequence its velocity was also much greater. But what mainly disturbed me was the idea that it had perceptibly *descended*. I now observed—with what horror it is needless to say—that its nether extremity was formed of a crescent of glittering steel, about a foot in length from horn to horn; the horns upward, and the under edge evidently as keen as that of a razor. Like a razor also, it seemed massy and heavy, tapering from the edge into a solid and broad structure above. It was appended to a weighty rod of brass, and the whole *hissed* as it swung through the air.

I could no longer doubt the doom prepared for me by monkish ingenuity in torture. My cognizance of the pit had become known to the inquisitorial agents—*the pit*, typical of hell and regarded by rumor as the Ultima Thule of all their punishments. The plunge into this pit I had avoided by the merest of accidents, and I knew that surprise, or entrapment into torment, formed an important portion of all the grotesquerie of these dungeon deaths. Having failed to fall, it was no part of the demon plan to hurl me into the abyss, and thus (there being no alternative) a different and a milder destruction awaited me. Milder! I half smiled in my agony as I thought of such application of such a term.

What boots it to tell of the long, long hours of horror more than mortal, during which I counted the rushing vibrations of the steel! Inch by inch—line by line—with a descent only appreciable at intervals that seemed ages—down and still down it came! Days passed—it might have been that many days passed—ere it swept so closely over me as to fan me with its acrid breath. The odor of the sharp steel forced itself into my nostrils. I prayed—I wearied heaven with my prayer for its more speedy descent. I grew frantically mad, and struggled to force myself upward against the sweep of the fearful scimitar. And then I fell suddenly calm, and lay smiling at the glittering death, as a child at some rare bauble.

There was another interval of utter insensibility; it was brief; for, upon again lapsing into life, there had been no perceptible descent in the pendulum. But it might have been long—for I knew there were demons who took note of my swoon, and who could have arrested the vibration at pleasure. Upon my recovery, too, I felt very—oh! inexpressibly—sick and weak, as if through long inanition. Even amid the agonies of that period, the human nature craved food. With painful effort I outstretched my left arm as far as my bonds permitted, and took possession of the small remnant which had been spared me by the rats. As I put a portion of it within my lips, there rushed to my mind a half-formed thought of joy—of hope. Yet what business had *I* with hope? It was, as I say, a half-formed thought—man has many such, which are never completed. I felt that it was of joy—of hope; but I felt also that it had perished in its formation. In vain I struggled to perfect—to regain it. Long suffering had nearly annihilated all my ordinary powers of mind. I was an imbecile—an idiot.

The vibration of the pendulum was at right angles to my length. I saw that the crescent was designed to cross the region of the heart. It would fray the serge of my robe—it would return and repeat its operations—again—and again. Notwithstanding its terrifically wide sweep (some thirty feet or more), and the hissing vigor of its descent, sufficient to sunder these very walls of iron, still the fraying of my robe would be all that, for several minutes, it would accomplish. And at this thought I paused. I dared not go further than this reflection. I dwelt upon it with a pertinacity of attention—as if, in so dwelling, I could arrest *here* the descent of the steel. I forced myself to ponder upon the sound of the crescent as it should pass across the garment— upon the peculiar thrilling sensation which the friction of cloth produces on the nerves. I pondered upon all this frivolity until my teeth were on edge.

Down—steadily down it crept. I took a frenzied pleasure in contrasting its downward with its lateral velocity. To the right—to the left—far and wide— with the shriek of a damned spirit! to my heart, with the stealthy pace of the tiger! I alternately laughed and howled, as the one or the other idea grew predominant.

Down—certainly, relentlessly down! It vibrated within three times of my bosom! I struggled violently—furiously—to free my left arm. This was free only from the elbow to the hand. I could reach the latter, from the platter beside me, to my mouth, with great effort, but no farther. Could I have broken the fastenings above the elbow, I would have seized and attempted to arrest the pendulum. I might as well have attempted to arrest an avalanche!

Down—still unceasingly—still inevitably down! I gasped and struggled at each vibration. I shrunk convulsively at its every sweep. My eyes followed its outward or upward whorls with the eagerness of the most unmeaning despair; they closed themselves spasmodically at the descent, although death would have been a relief, oh, how unspeakable! Still I quivered in every nerve to think how slight a sinking of the machinery would precipitate that keen, glistening axe upon my bosom. It was *hope* that prompted the nerve to quiver—the frame to shrink. It was *hope*—the hope that triumphs on the rack—that whispers to the death-condemned even in the dungeons of the Inquisition.

I saw that some ten or twelve vibrations would bring the steel in actual contact with my robe, and with this observation there suddenly came over my spirit all the keen, collected calmness of despair. For the first time during many hours—or perhaps days—I *thought*. It now occurred to me, that the bandage, or surcingle, which enveloped me, was *unique*. I was tied by no separate cord. The first stroke of the razor-like crescent athwart any portion of the band would so detach it that it might be unwound from my person by means of my left hand. But how fearful, in that case, the proximity of the steel! The result of the slightest struggle, how deadly! Was it likely, moreover, that the minions of the torturer had not foreseen and provided for this possibility? Was it probable that the bandage crossed my bosom in the track of the pendulum? Dreading to find my faint and, as it seemed, my last hope frustrated, I so far elevated my head as to obtain a distinct view of my breast. The surcingle enveloped my limbs and body close in all directions— *save in the path of the destroying crescent*.

Scarcely had I dropped my head back into its original position, when there flashed upon my mind what I cannot better describe than as the unformed half of that idea of deliverance to which I had previously alluded, and of which a moiety only floated indeterminately through my brain when I raised food to my burning lips. The whole thought was now present— feeble, scarcely sane, scarcely definite—but still entire. I proceeded at once, with the nervous energy of despair, to attempt its execution.

For many hours the immediate vicinity of the low framework upon which I lay had been literally swarming with rats. They were wild, bold, ravenous— their red eyes glaring upon me as if they waited but for motionlessness on my part to make me their prey. "To what food," I thought, "have they been accustomed in the well?"

They had devoured, in spite of all my efforts to prevent them, all but a small remnant of the contents of the dish. I had fallen into an habitual seesaw or wave of the hand about the platter; and, at length, the unconscious uniformity of the movement deprived it of effect. In their voracity, the vermin frequently fastened their sharp fangs in my fingers. With the particles of the oily and spicy viand which now remained, I thoroughly rubbed the bandage wherever I could reach it; then, raising my hand from the floor, I lay breathlessly still.

At first, the ravenous animals were startled and terrified at the change—at the cessation of movement. They shrank alarmedly back; many sought the well. But this was only for a moment. I had not counted in vain upon their voracity. Observing that I remained without motion, one or two of the boldest leaped upon the framework, and smelt at the surcingle. This seemed the signal for a general rush. Forth from the well they hurried in fresh troops. They clung to the wood—they overran it, and leaped in hundreds upon my person. The measured movement of the pendulum disturbed them not at all. Avoiding its strokes, they busied themselves with the anointed bandage. They pressed—they swarmed upon me in ever accumulating heaps. They writhed upon my throat; their cold lips sought my own; I was half stifled by their thronging pressure; disgust, for which the world has no name, swelled my bosom, and chilled, with a heavy clamminess, my heart. Yet one minute, and I felt that the struggle would be over. Plainly I perceived the loosening of the bandage. I knew that in more than one place it must be already severed. With a more than human resolution I lay *still*.

Nor had I erred in my calculations—nor had I endured in vain. I at length felt that I was *free*. The surcingle hung in ribands from my body. But the stroke of the pendulum already pressed upon my bosom. It had divided the serge of the robe. It had cut through the linen beneath. Twice again it swung, and a sharp sense of pain shot through every nerve. But the moment of escape had arrived. At a wave of my hand my deliverers hurried tumultuously away. With a steady movement—cautious, sidelong, shrinking, and slow—I slid from the embrace of the bandage and beyond the reach of the scimitar. For the moment, at least, *I was free.*

Free!—and in the grasp of the Inquisition! I had scarcely stepped from my wooden bed of horror upon the stone floor of the prison, when the motion of the hellish machine ceased, and I beheld it drawn up, by some invisible force, through the ceiling. This was a lesson which I took desperately to heart. My every motion was undoubtedly watched. Free!—I had but escaped death in one form of agony, to be delivered unto worse than death in some other. With that thought I rolled my eyes nervously around on the barriers of iron that hemmed me in. Something unusual—some change which at first, I could not appreciate distinctly—it was obvious, had taken place in the apartment. For many minutes of a dreamy and trembling abstraction, I busied myself in vain, unconnected conjecture. During this period, I became aware, for the first time, of the origin of the sulphurous light which illumined the cell. It proceeded from a fissure, about half an inch in width, extending entirely around the prison at the base of the walls, which thus appeared. and were completely separated from the floor. I endeavored, but of course in vain, to look through the aperture.

As I arose from the attempt, the mystery of the alteration in the chamber broke at once upon my understanding. I had observed that, although the outlines of the figures upon the walls were sufficiently distinct, yet the colors seemed blurred and indefinite. These colors had now assumed, and were momentarily assuming, a startling and most intense brilliancy, that gave to the spectral and fiendish portraitures an aspect that might have thrilled even firmer nerves than my own. Demon eyes, of a wild and ghastly vivacity, glared upon me in a thousand directions where none had been visible before, and gleamed with the lurid lustre of a fire that I could not force my imagination to regard as unreal.

Unreal!—even while I breathed there came to my nostrils the breath of the vapor of heated iron! A suffocating odor pervaded the prison! A deeper glow settled each moment in the eyes that glared at my agonies! A richer tint of crimson diffused itself over the pictured horrors of blood. I panted! I gasped for breath! There could be no doubt of the design of my tormenters—oh! most unrelenting! oh! most demoniac of men! I shrank from the glowing metal to the centre of the cell. Amid the thought of the fiery destruction that impended, the idea of the coolness of the well came over my soul like balm. I rushed to its deadly brink. I threw my straining vision below. The glare from the enkindled roof illumined its inmost recesses. Yet, for a wild moment, did my spirit refuse to comprehend the meaning of what I saw. At length it forced—it wrestled its way into my soul—it burned itself in upon my shuddering reason.—Oh! for a voice to speak!—oh! horror!—oh! any horror but this! With a shriek, I rushed from the margin, and buried my face in my hands—weeping bitterly.

The heat rapidly increased, and once again I looked up, shuddering as with a fit of the ague. There had been a second change in the cell—and now the change was obviously in the *form*. As before, it was in vain that I at first endeavored to appreciate or understand what was taking place. But not long was I left in doubt. The Inquisitorial vengeance had been hurried by my two-fold escape, and there was to be no more dallying with the King of Terrors. The room had been square. I saw that two of its iron angles were now acute—two, consequently, obtuse. The fearful difference quickly increased with a low rumbling or moaning sound. In an instant the apartment had shifted its form into that of a lozenge. But the alteration stopped not here—I neither hoped nor desired it to stop. I could have clasped the red walls to my bosom as a garment of eternal peace. "Death," I said, "any death but that of the pit!" Fool! might I not have known that *into the pit* it was the object of the burning iron to urge me? Could I resist its glow? or if even that, could I withstand its pressure? And now, flatter and flatter, grew the lozenge, with a rapidity that left me no time for contemplation. Its centre, and of course its greatest width, came just over the yawning gulf. I shrank back—but the closing walls pressed me resistlessly onward. At length for my seared and writhing body there was no longer an inch of foothold on the firm floor of the prison. I struggled no more, but the agony of my soul found vent in one loud, long, and final scream of despair. I felt that I tottered upon the brink—I averted my eyes—

There was a discordant hum of human voices! There was a loud blast as of many trumpets! There was a harsh grating as of a thousand thunders! The fiery walls rushed back! An outstretched arm caught my own as I fell, fainting, into the abyss. It was that of General Lasalle. The French army had entered Toledo. The Inquisition was in the hands of its enemies.

EDGAR ALLAN POE

THE BLACK CAT

For the most wild yet most homely narrative which I am about to pen, I neither expect nor solicit belief. Mad indeed would I be to expect it, in a case where my very senses reject their own evidence. Yet, mad am I not—and very surely do I not dream. But to-morrow I die, and to-day I would unburden my soul. My immediate purpose is to place before the world, plainly, succinctly, and without comment, a series of mere household events. In their consequences, these events have terrified—have tortured—have destroyed me. Yet I will not attempt to expound them. To me, they have presented little but horror—to many they will seem less terrible than *baroques*. Hereafter, perhaps, some intellect may be found which will reduce my phantasm to the common place—some intellect more calm, more logical, and far less excitable than my own, which will perceive, in the circumstances I detail with awe, nothing more than an ordinary succession of very natural causes and effects.

From my infancy I was noted for the docility and humanity of my disposition. My tenderness of heart was even so conspicuous as to make me the jest of my companions. I was especially fond of animals, and was indulged by my parents with a great variety of pets. With these I spent most of my time, and never was so happy as when feeding and caressing them. This peculiarity of character grew with my growth, and, in my manhood, I derived from it one of my principal sources of pleasure. To those who have cherished an affection for a faithful and sagacious dog, I need hardly be at the trouble of explaining the nature or the intensity of the gratification thus derivable. There is something in the unselfish and self-sacrificing love of a brute, which goes directly to the heart of him who has had frequent occasion to test the paltry friendship and gossamer fidelity of mere *Man*.

I married early, and was happy to find in my wife a disposition not uncongenial with my own. Observing my partiality for domestic pets, she lost no opportunity of procuring those of the most agreeable kind. We had birds, gold-fish, a fine dog, rabbits, a small monkey, and a cat.

This latter was a remarkably large and beautiful animal, entirely black, and sagacious to an astonishing degree. In speaking of his intelligence, my wife, who at heart was not a little tinctured with superstition, made frequent allusion to the ancient popular notions, which regarded all black cats as witches in disguise. Not that she was ever *serious* upon this point—and I mention the matter at all for no better reason that that it happens, just now, to be remembered.

Pluto—this was the cat's name—was my favorite pet and playmate. I alone fed him, and he attended me wherever I went about the house. It was even with difficulty that I could prevent him from following me through the streets.

Our friendship lasted, in this manner, for several years, during which my general temperament and character—through the instrumentality of the Fiend Intemperance—had (I blush to confess it) experienced a radical alteration for the worse. I grew, day by day, more moody, more irritable, more regardless of the feelings of others. I suffered myself to use intemperate language to my wife. At length, I even offered her personal violence. My pets, of course, were made to feel the change in my disposition. I not only neglected, but ill-used them. For Pluto, however, I still retained sufficient regard to restrain me from maltreating him, as I made no scruple of maltreating the rabbits, the monkeys, or even the dog, when, by accident, or through affection, they came in my way. But my disease grew upon me—for what disease is like Alcohol!—and at length even Pluto, who was now becoming old, and consequently somewhat peevish—even Pluto began to experience the effects of my ill temper.

One night, returning home, much intoxicated, from one of my haunts about town, I fancied that the cat avoided my presence. I seized him; when, in his fright at my violence, he inflicted a slight wound upon my hands with his teeth. The fury of a demon instantly possessed me. I knew myself no longer. My original soul seemed, at once, to take its flight from my body; and a more than fiendish malevolence, gin-nurtured, thrilled every fibre of my frame. I took from my waistcoat-pocket a penknife, opened it, grasped the poor beast by the throat, and deliberately cut one of its eyes from the socket! I blush, I burn, I shudder, while I pen the damnable atrocity.

When reason returned with the morning—when I had slept off the fumes of the night's debauch—I experienced a sentiment half of horror, half of remorse, for the crime of which I had been guilty; but it was, at best, a feeble and equivocal feeling, and the soul remained untouched. I again plunged into excess, and soon drowned in wine all memory of the deed.

In the meantime the cat slowly recovered. The socket of the lost eye presented, it is true, a frightful appearance, but he no longer appeared to suffer any pain. He went about the house as usual, but, as might be expected, fled in extreme terror at my approach. I had so much of my old heart left, as to be at first grieved by this evident dislike on the part of a creature which had once so loved me. But this feeling soon gave place to irritation. And then came, as if to my final and irrevocable overthrow, the spirit of Perverseness. Of this spirit philosophy takes no account. Yet I am not more sure that my soul lives, than I am that perverseness is one of the primitive impulses of the human heart—one of the indivisible primary faculties, or sentiments, which give direction to the character of Man. Who has not, a hundred times, found himself committing a vile or a stupid action, for no other reason than because he knows he should *not?* Have we not a perpetual inclination, in the teeth of our best judgment, to violate that which is *Law,* merely because we understand it to be such? This spirit of perverseness, I say, came to my final overthrow. It was this unfathomable longing of the soul to *vex itself*—to offer violence to its own nature—to do wrong for the wrong's sake only—that urged me to continue and finally to consummate the injury I had inflicted upon the unoffending brute. One morning, in cold blood, I slipped a noose about its neck and hung it to the limb of a tree;— hung it with the tears streaming from my eyes, and with the bitterest remorse at my heart;—hung it *because* I knew that it had loved me, and *because* I felt it had given me no reason of offence;—hung it *because* I knew that in so doing I was committing a sin—a deadly sin that would so jeopardize my immortal soul as to place it—if such a thing were possible— even beyond the reach of the infinite mercy of the Most Merciful and Most Terrible God.

On the night of the day on which this most cruel deed was done, I was aroused from sleep by the cry of fire. The curtains of my bed were in flames. The whole house was blazing. It was with great difficulty that my wife, a servant, and myself, made our escape from the conflagration. The destruction was complete. My entire worldly wealth was swallowed up, and I resigned myself thence forward to despair.

I am above the weakness of seeking to establish a sequence of cause and effect, between the disaster and the atrocity. But I am detailing a chain of facts—and wish not to leave even a possible link imperfect. On the day succeeding the fire, I visited the ruins. The walls, with one exception, had fallen in. This exception was found in a compartment wall, not very thick, which stood about the middle of the house, and against which had rested the head of my bed. The plastering had here, in great measure, resisted the action of the fire—a fact which I attributed to its having been recently spread. About this wall a dense crowd were collected, and many persons seemed to be examining a particular portion of it with very minute and eager attention. The words "strange!" "singular!" and other similar expressions, excited my curiosity. I approached and saw, as if graven in *bas-relief* upon the white surface, the figure of a gigantic *cat.* The impression was given with an accuracy truly marvellous. There was a rope about the animal's neck.

When I first beheld this apparition—for I could scarcely regard it as less— my wonder and my terror were extreme. But at length reflection came to my aid. The cat, I remembered, had been hung in a garden adjacent to the house. Upon the alarm of fire, this garden had been immediately filled by the crowd—by some one of whom the animal must have been cut from the tree and thrown, through an open window, into my chamber. This had probably been done with the view of arousing me from sleep. The falling of other walls had compressed the victim of my cruelty into the substance of the freshly-spread plaster; the lime of which, with the flames, and the *ammonia* from the carcass, had then accomplished the portraiture as I saw it.

Although I thus readily accounted to my reason, if not altogether to my conscience, for the startling fact just detailed, it did not the less fail to make a deep impression upon my fancy. For months I could not rid myself of the phantasm of the cat; and, during this period, there came back into my spirit a half-sentiment that seemed, but was not, remorse. I went so far as to regret the loss of the animal, and to look about me, among the vile haunts which I now habitually frequented, for another pet of the same species, and of somewhat similar appearance, with which to supply its place.

One night as I sat, half stupefied, in a den of more than infamy, my attention was suddenly drawn to some black object, reposing upon the head of one of the immense hogsheads of gin, or of rum, which constituted the chief furniture of the apartment. I had been looking steadily at the top of this hogshead for some minutes, and what now caused me surprise was the fact that I had not sooner perceived the object thereupon. I approached it, and touched it with my hand. It was a black cat—a very large one—fully as large as Pluto, and closely resembling him in every respect but one. Pluto had not a white hair upon any portion of his body; but this cat had a large, although indefinite splotch of white, covering nearly the whole region of the breast.

Upon my touching him, he immediately arose, purred loudly, rubbed against my hand, and appeared delighted with my notice. This, then, was the very creature of which I was in search. I at once offered to purchase it of the landlord; but this person made no claim to it—knew nothing of it—had never seen it before.

I continued my caresses, and when I prepared to go home, the animal evinced a disposition to accompany me. I permitted it to do so; occasionally stooping and patting it as I proceeded. When it reached the house it domesticated itself at once, and became immediately a great favorite with my wife.

For my own part, I soon found dislike to it arising within me. This was just the reverse of what I had anticipated; but—I know not how or why it was—its evident fondness for myself rather disgusted and annoyed me. By slow degrees these feelings of disgust and annoyance rose into the bitterness of hatred. I avoided the creature; a certain sense of shame, and the remembrance of my former deed of cruelty, preventing me from physically abusing it. I did not, for some weeks, strike, or otherwise violently ill use it; but gradually—very gradually—I came to look upon it with unutterable loathing, and to flee silently from its odious presence, as from the breath of a pestilence.

What added, no doubt, to my hatred of the beast, was the discovery, on the morning after I brought it home, that, like Pluto, it also had been deprived of one of its eyes. This circumstance, however, only endeared it to my wife, who, as I have already said, possessed, in a high degree, that humanity of feeling which had once been my distinguishing trait, and the source of many of my simplest and purest pleasures.

With my aversion to this cat, however, its partiality for myself seemed to increase. It followed my footsteps with a pertinacity which it would be difficult to make the reader comprehend. Whenever I sat, it would crouch beneath my chair, or spring upon my knees, covering me with its loathsome caresses. If I arose to walk it would get between my feet and thus nearly throw me down, or, fastening its long and sharp claws in my dress, clamber, in this manner, to my breast. At such times, although I longed to destroy it with a blow, I was yet withheld from so doing, partly by a memory of my former crime, but chiefly—let me confess it at once—by absolute *dread* of the beast.

This dread was not exactly a dread of physical evil—and yet I should be at a loss how otherwise to define it. I am almost ashamed to own—yes, even in this felon's cell, I am almost ashamed to own—that the terror and horror with which the animal inspired me, had been heightened by one of the merest chimeras it would be possible to conceive. My wife had called my attention, more than once, to the character of the mark of white hair, of which I have spoken, and which constituted the sole visible difference between the strange beast and the one I had destroyed. The reader will remember that this mark, although large, had been originally very indefinite; but, by slow degrees—degrees nearly imperceptible, and which for a long time my reason struggled to reject as fanciful—it had, at length, assumed a rigorous distinctness of outline. It was now the representation of an object that I shudder to name—and for this, above all, I loathed, and dreaded, and would have rid myself of the monster *had I dared*—it was now, I say, the image of a hideous—of a ghastly thing—of the Gallows!—oh, mournful and terrible engine of Horror and of Crime—of Agony and of Death!

And now was I indeed wretched beyond the wretchedness of mere Humanity. And *a brute beast*—whose fellow I had contemptuously destroyed— *a brute beast* to work out for *me*—for me, a man fashioned in the image of the High God—so much of insufferable woe! Alas! neither by day nor by night knew I the blessing of rest any more! During the former the creature left me no moment alone, and in the latter I started hourly from dreams of unutterable fear to find the hot breath of *the thing* upon my face, and its vast weight—an incarnate nightmare that I had no power to shake off—incumbent eternally upon my *heart*!

Beneath the pressure of torments such as these the feeble remnant of the good within me succumbed. Evil thoughts became my sole intimates—the darkest and most evil of thoughts. The moodiness of my usual temper increased to hatred of all things and of all mankind; while from the sudden, frequent, and ungovernable outbursts of a fury to which I now blindly abandoned myself, my uncomplaining wife, alas, was the most usual and the most patient of sufferers.

One day she accompanied me, upon some household errand, into the cellar of the old building which our poverty compelled us to inhabit. The cat followed me down the steep stairs, and, nearly throwing me headlong, exasperated me to madness. Uplifting an axe, and forgetting in my wrath the childish dread which had hitherto stayed my hand, I aimed a blow at the animal, which, of course, would have proved instantly fatal had it descended as I wished. But this blow was arrested by the hand of my wife. Goaded by the interference into a rage more than demoniacal, I withdrew my arm from her grasp and buried the axe in her brain. She fell dead upon the spot without a groan.

This hideous murder accomplished, I set myself forthwith, and with entire deliberation, to the task of concealing the body. I knew that I could not remove it from the house, either by day or by night, without the risk of being observed by the neighbors. Many projects entered my mind. At one period I thought of cutting the corpse into minute fragments, and destroying them by fire. At another, I resolved to dig a grave for it in the floor of the cellar. Again, I deliberated about casting it in the well in the yard—about packing it in a box, as if merchandise, with the usual arrangements, and so getting a porter to take it from the house. Finally I hit upon what I considered a far better expedient than either of these. I determined to wall it up in the cellar, as the monks of the Middle Ages are recorded to have walled up their victims.

For a purpose such as this the cellar was well adapted. Its walls were loosely constructed, and had lately been plastered throughout with a rough plaster, which the dampness of the atmosphere had prevented from hardening. Moreover, in one of the walls was a projection, caused by a false chimney, or fireplace, that had been filled up and made to resemble the rest of the cellar. I made no doubt that I could readily displace the bricks at this point, insert the corpse, and wall the whole up as before, so that no eye could detect anything suspicious.

And in this calculation I was not deceived. By means of a crow bar I easily dislodged the bricks, and, having carefully deposited the body against the inner wall, I propped it in that position, while with little trouble I relaid the whole structure as it originally stood. Having procured mortar, sand, and hair, with every possible precaution, I prepared a plaster which could not be distinguished from the old, and with this I very carefully went over the new brick-work. When I had finished, I felt satisfied that all was right. The wall did not present the slightest appearance of having been disturbed. The rubbish on the floor was picked up with the minutest care. I looked around triumphantly, and said to myself: "Here at least, then, my labor has not been in vain."

My next step was to look for the beast which had been the cause of so much wretchedness; for I had, at length, firmly resolved to put it to death. Had I been able to meet with it at the moment, there could have been no doubt of its fate; but it appeared that the crafty animal had been alarmed at the violence of my previous anger, and forbore to present itself in my present mood. It is impossible to describe or to imagine the deep, the blissful sense of relief which the absence of the detested creature occasioned in my bosom. It did not make its appearance during the night; and thus for one night, at least, since its introduction into the house, I soundly and tranquilly slept; aye, *slept* even with the burden of murder upon my soul.

The second and the third day passed, and still my tormentor came not. Once again I breathed as a freeman. The monster, in terror, had fled the premises for ever! I should behold it no more! My happiness was supreme! The guilt of my dark deed disturbed me but little. Some few inquiries had been made, but these had been readily answered. Even a search had been instituted—but of course nothing was to be discovered. I looked upon my future felicity as secured.

Upon the fourth day of the assassination, a party of the police came, very unexpectedly, into the house, and proceeded again to make rigorous investigation of the premises. Secure, however, in the inscrutability of my place of concealment, I felt no embarrassment whatever. The officers bade me accompany them in their search. They left no nook or corner unexplored. At length, for the third or fourth time, they decended into the cellar. I quivered not in a muscle. My heart beat calmly as that of one who slumbers in innocence. I walked the cellar from end to end. I folded my arms upon my bosom, and roamed easily to and fro. The police were thoroughly satisfied and prepared to depart. The glee at my heart was too strong to be restrained. I burned to say if but one word, by way of triumph, and to render doubly sure their assurance of my guiltlessness.

"Gentlemen," I said at last, as the party ascended the steps, "I delight to have allayed your suspicions. I wish you all health and a little more courtesy. By the bye, gentlemen, this—this is a very well-constructed house," (in the rabid desire to say something easily, I scarcely knew what I uttered at all),—"I may say an *excellently* well-constructed house. These walls—are you going, gentlemen?—these walls are solidly put together"; and here, through the mere frenzy of bravado, I rapped heavily with a cane which I held in my hand, upon that very portion of the brick-work behind which stood the corpse of the wife of my bosom.

But may God shield and deliver me from the fangs of the Arch-Fiend! No sooner had the reverberation of my blows sunk into silence, than I was answered by a voice from within the tomb!—by a cry, at first muffled and broken, like the sobbing of a child, and then quickly swelling into one long, loud, and continuous scream, utterly anomalous and inhuman—a howl—a wailing shriek, half of horror and half of triumph, such as might have arisen only out of hell, conjointly from the throats of the damned in their agony and of the demons that exult in the damnation.

Of my own thoughts it is folly to speak. Swooning, I staggered to the opposite wall. For one instant the party on the stairs remained motionless, through extremity of terror and awe. In the next a dozen stout arms were toiling at the wall. It fell bodily. The corpse, already greatly decayed and clotted with gore, stood erect before the eyes of the spectators. Upon its head, with red extended mouth and solitary eye of fire, sat the hideous beast whose craft had seduced me into murder, and whose informing voice had consigned me to the hangman. I had walled the monster up within the tomb.

NATHANIEL HAWTHORNE

THE BIRTHMARK

In the latter part of the last century there lived a man of science, an eminent proficient in every branch of natural philosophy, who not long before our story opens had made experience of a spiritual affinity more attractive than any chemical one. He had left his laboratory to the care of an assistant, cleared his fine countenance from the furnace smoke, washed the stain of acids from his fingers, and persuaded a beautiful woman to become his wife. In those days when the comparatively recent discovery of electricity and other kindred mysteries of Nature seemed to open paths into the region of miracle, it was not unusual for the love of science to rival the love of woman in its depth and absorbing energy. The higher intellect, the imagination, the spirit, and even the heart might all find their congenial aliment in pursuits which, as some of their ardent votaries believed, would ascend from one step of powerful intelligence to another, until the philosopher should lay his hand on the secret of creative force and perhaps make new worlds for himself. We know not whether Aylmer possessed this degree of faith in man's ultimate control over Nature. He had devoted himself, however, too unreservedly to scientific studies ever to be weaned from them by any second passion. His love for his young wife might prove the stronger of the two; but it could only be by intertwining itself with his love of science, and uniting the strength of the latter to his own.

Such a union accordingly took place, and was attended with truly remarkable consequences and a deeply impressive moral. One day, very soon after their marriage, Aylmer sat gazing at his wife with a trouble in his countenance that grew stronger until he spoke.

"Georgiana," said he, "has it never occurred to you that the mark upon your cheek might be removed?"

"No, indeed," said she, smiling; but perceiving the seriousness of his manner, she blushed deeply. "To tell you the truth it has been so often called a charm that I was simple enough to imagine it might be so."

"Ah, upon another face perhaps it might," replied her husband; "but never on yours. No, dearest Georgiana, you came so nearly perfect from the hand of Nature that this slightest possible defect, which we hesitate whether to term a defect or a beauty, shocks me, as being the visible mark of earthly imperfection."

"Shocks you, my husband!" cried Georgiana, deeply hurt; at first reddening with momentary anger, but then bursting into tears. "Then why did you take me from my mother's side? You cannot love what shocks you!"

To explain this conversation it must be mentioned that in the centre of

Georgiana's left cheek there was a singular mark, deeply interwoven, as it were, with the texture and substance of her face. In the usual state of her complexion—a healthy though delicate bloom—the mark wore a tint of deeper crimson, which imperfectly defined its shape amid the surrounding rosiness. When she blushed it gradually became more indistinct, and finally vanished amid the triumphant rush of blood that bathed the whole cheek with its brilliant glow. But if any shifting motion caused her to turn pale there was the mark again, a crimson stain upon the snow, in what Aylmer sometimes deemed an almost fearful distinctness. Its shape bore not a little similarity to the human hand, though of the smallest pygmy size. Georgiana's lovers were wont to say that some fairy at her birth hour had laid her tiny hand upon the infant's cheek, and left this impress there in token of the magic endowments that were to give her such sway over all hearts. Many a desperate swain would have risked life for the privilege of pressing his lips to the mysterious hand. It must not be concealed, however, that the impression wrought by this fairy sign manual varied exceedingly, according to the difference of temperament in the beholders. Some fastidious persons—but they were exclusively of her own sex—affirmed that the bloody hand, as they chose to call it, quite destroyed the effect of Georgiana's beauty, and rendered her countenance even hideous. But it would be as reasonable to say that one of those small blue stains which sometimes occur in the purest statuary marble would convert the Eve of Powers to a monster. Masculine observers, if the birthmark did not heighten their admiration, contented themselves with wishing it away, that the world might possess one living specimen of ideal loveliness without the semblance of a flaw. After his marriage,—for he thought little or nothing of the matter before,—Aylmer discovered that this was the case with himself.

Had she been less beautiful,—if Envy's self could have found aught else to sneer at,—he might have felt his affection heightened by the prettiness of this mimic hand, now vaguely portrayed, now lost, now stealing forth again and glimmering to and fro with every pulse of emotion that throbbed within her heart; but seeing her otherwise so perfect, he found this one defect grow more and more intolerable with every moment in their united lives. It was the fatal flaw of humanity which Nature, in one shape or another, stamps ineffaceably on all her productions, either to imply that they are temporary and finite, or that their perfection must be wrought by toil and pain. The crimson hand expressed the ineludible grip in which mortality clutches the highest and purest of earthly mould, degrading them into kindred with the lowest, and even with the very brutes, like whom their visible frames return to dust. In this manner, selecting it as the symbol of his wife's liability to sin, sorrow, decay, and death, Aylmer's sombre imagination was not long in rendering the birthmark a frightful object, causing him more trouble and horror than ever Georgiana's beauty, whether of soul or sense, had given him delight.

At all the seasons which should have been their happiest, he invariably and without intending it, nay, in spite of a purpose to the contrary, reverted to this one disastrous topic. Trifling as it at first appeared, it so connected itself with innumerable trains of thought and modes of feeling that it became the central point of all. With the morning twilight Aylmer opened his eyes upon his wife's face and recognized the symbol of imperfection; and when they sat together at the evening hearth his eyes wandered stealthily to her cheek, and beheld, flickering with the blaze of the wood fire, the spectral hand that wrote mortality where he would fain have worshipped. Georgiana soon learned to shudder at his gaze. It needed but a glance with the peculiar expression that his face often wore to change the roses of her cheek into a deathlike paleness, amid which the crimson hand was brought strongly out, like a bas-relief of ruby on the whitest marble.

Late one night when the lights were growing dim, so as hardly to betray the stain on the poor wife's cheek, she herself, for the first time, voluntarily took up the subject.

"Do you remember, my dear Aylmer," said she, with a feeble attempt at a smile, "have you any recollection of a dream last night about this odious hand?"

"None! none whatever!" replied Aylmer, starting; but then he added, in a dry, cold tone, affected for the sake of concealing the real depth of his emotion, "I might well dream of it; for before I fell asleep it had taken a pretty firm hold of my fancy."

"And you did dream of it?" continued Georgiana, hastily; for she dreaded lest a gush of tears should interrupt what she had to say. "A terrible dream! I wonder that you can forget it. Is it possible to forget this one expression?—'It is in her heart now; we must have it out!' Reflect, my husband; for by all means I would have you recall that dream."

The mind is in a sad state when Sleep, the all-involving, cannot confine her spectres within the dim region of her sway, but suffers them to break forth, affrighting this actual life with secrets that perchance belong to a deeper one. Aylmer now remembered his dream. He had fancied himself with his servant Aminadab, attempting an operation for the removal of the birthmark; but the deeper went the knife, the deeper sank the hand, until at length its tiny grasp appeared to have caught hold of Georgiana's heart; whence, however, her husband was inexorably resolved to cut or wrench it away.

When the dream had shaped itself perfectly in his memory, Aylmer sat in his wife's presence with a guilty feeling. Truth often finds its way to the mind close muffled in robes of sleep, and then speaks with uncompromising directness of matters in regard to which we practise an unconscious self-deception during our waking moments. Until now he had not been aware of the tyrannizing influence acquired by one idea over his mind, and of the lengths which he might find in his heart to go for the sake of giving himself peace.

"Aylmer," resumed Georgiana, solemnly, "I know not what may be the cost to both of us to rid me of this fatal birthmark. Perhaps its removal may cause cureless deformity; or it may be the stain goes as deep as life itself.

Again: do we know that there is a possibility, on any terms, of unclasping the firm grip of this little hand which was laid upon me before I came into the world?"

"Dearest Georgiana, I have spent much thought upon the subject," hastily interrupted Aylmer. "I am convinced of the perfect practicability of its removal."

"If there be the remotest possibility of it," continued Georgiana, "let the attempt be made at whatever risk. Danger is nothing to me; for life, while this hateful mark makes me the object of your horror and disgust,—life is a burden which I would fling down with joy. Either remove this dreadful hand, or take my wretched life! You have deep science. All the world bears witness of it. You have achieved great wonders. Cannot you remove this little, little mark, which I cover with the tips of two small fingers? Is this beyond your power, for the sake of your own peace, and to save your poor wife from madness?"

"Noblest, dearest, tenderest wife," cried Aylmer, rapturously, "doubt not my power. I have already given this matter the deepest thought—thought which might almost have enlightened me to create a being less perfect than yourself. Georgiana, you have led deeper than ever into the heart of science. I feel myself fully competent to render this dear cheek as faultless as its fellow; and then, most beloved, what will be my triumph when I shall have corrected what Nature left imperfect in her fairest work! Even Pygmalion, when his sculptured woman assumed life, felt not greater ecstasy than mine will be."

"It is resolved, then," said Georgiana, faintly smiling. "And, Aylmer, spare me not, though you should find the birthmark take refuge in my heart at last."

Her husband tenderly kissed her cheek—her right cheek—not that which bore the impress of the crimson hand.

The next day Aylmer apprised his wife of a plan that he had formed whereby he might have opportunity for the intense thought and constant watchfulness which the proposed operation would require; while Georgiana, likewise, would enjoy the perfect repose essential to its success. They were to seclude themselves in the extensive apartments occupied by Aylmer as a laboratory, and where, during his toilsome youth, he had made discoveries in the elemental powers of Nature that had roused the admiration of all the learned societies in Europe. Seated calmly in this laboratory, the pale philosopher had investigated the secrets of the highest cloud region and of the profoundest mines; he had satisfied himself of the causes that kindled and kept alive the fires of the volcano; and had explained the mystery of the fountains, and how it is that they gush forth, some so bright and pure, and others with such rich medicinal virtues, from the dark bosom of the earth. Here, too, at an earlier period, he had studied the wonders of the human frame, and attempted to fathom the very process by which Nature assimilates all her precious influences from earth and air, and from the spiritual world, to create and foster man, her masterpiece. The latter pursuit, however, Aylmer had long laid aside in unwilling recognition of the truth—against which all seekers sooner or later stumble—that our great creative Mother, while she amuses us with apparently working in the broadest sunshine, is yet severely careful to keep her own secrets, and, in spite of her pretended openness, shows us nothing but results. She permits us, indeed, to mar, but seldom to mend, and, like a jealous patentee, on no account to make. Now, however, Aylmer resumed these half-forgotten investigations; not, of course, with such hopes or wishes as first suggested them; but because they involved much physiological truth and lay in the path of his proposed scheme for the treatment of Georgiana.

As he led her over the threshold of the laboratory, Georgiana was cold and tremulous. Aylmer looked cheerfully into her face, with intent to reassure her, but was so startled with the intense glow of the birthmark upon the whiteness of her cheek that he could not restrain a strong convulsive shudder. His wife fainted.

"Aminadab! Aminadab!" shouted Aylmer, stamping violently on the floor.

Forthwith there issued from an inner apartment a man of low stature, but bulky frame, with shaggy hair hanging about his visage, which was grimed with the vapors of the furnace. This personage had been Aylmer's under-worker during his whole scientific career, and was admirably fitted for that office by his great mechanical readiness, and the skill with which, while incapable of comprehending a single principle, he executed all the details of his master's experiments. With his vast strength, his shaggy hair, his smoky aspect, and the indescribable earthiness that incrusted him, he seemed to represent man's physical nature; while Aylmer's slender figure, and pale, intellectual face, were no less apt a type of the spiritual element.

"Throw open the door of the boudoir, Aminadab," said Aylmer, "and burn a pastil."

"Yes, master," answered Aminadab, looking intently at the lifeless form of Georgiana; and then he muttered to himself, "If she were my wife, I'd never part with that birthmark."

When Georgiana recovered consciousness she found herself breathing an atmosphere of penetrating fragrance, the gentle potency of which had recalled her from her deathlike faintness. The scene around her looked like enchantment. Aylmer had converted those smoky, dingy, sombre rooms, where he had spent his brightest years in recondite pursuits, into a series of beautiful apartments not unfit to be the secluded abode of a lovely woman. The walls were hung with gorgeous curtains, which imparted the combination of grandeur and grace that no other species of adornment can achieve; and as they fell from the ceiling to the floor, their rich and ponderous folds, concealing all angles and straight lines, appeared to shut in the scene from infinite space. For aught Georgiana knew, it might be a pavilion among the clouds. And Aylmer, excluding the sunshine, which would have interfered with his chemical processes, had supplied its place with perfumed lamps, emitting flames of various hue, but all uniting in a soft, impurpled radiance. He now knelt by his wife's side, watching her earnestly, but without alarm; for he was confident in his science, and felt that he could draw a magic circle round her within which no evil might intrude.

"Where am I? Ah, I remember," said Georgiana, faintly; and she placed her hand over her cheek to hide the terrible mark from her husband's eyes.

"Fear not, dearest!" exclaimed he. "Do not shrink from me! Believe me, Georgiana, I even rejoice in this single imperfection, since it will be such a rapture to remove it."

"Oh, spare me!" sadly replied his wife. "Pray do not look at it again. I never can forget that convulsive shudder."

In order to soothe Georgiana, and, as it were, to release her mind from the burden of actual things, Aylmer now put in practice some of the light and playful secrets which science had taught him among its profounder lore. Airy figures, absolutely bodiless ideas, and forms of unsubstantial beauty came and danced before her, imprinting their momentary footsteps on beams of light. Though she had some indistinct idea of the method of these optical phenomena, still the illusion was almost perfect enough to warrant the belief that her husband possessed sway over the spiritual world. Then again, when she felt a wish to look forth from her seclusion, immediately, as if her thoughts were answered, the procession of external existence flitted across a screen. The scenery and the figures of actual life were perfectly represented, but with that bewitching, yet indescribable difference which always makes a picture, an image, or a shadow so much more attractive than the original. When wearied of this Aylmer bade her cast her eyes upon a vessel containing a quantity of earth. She did so, with little interest at first; but was soon startled to perceive the germ of a plant shooting upward from the soil. Then came the slender stalk; the leaves gradually unfolded themselves; and amid them was a perfect and lovely flower.

"It is magical!" cried Georgiana. "I dare not touch it."

"Nay, pluck it," answered Aylmer,—"pluck it, and inhale its brief perfume while you may. The flower will wither in a few moments and leave nothing save its brown seed vessels; but thence may be perpetuated a race as ephemeral as itself."

But Georgiana had no sooner touched the flower than the whole plant suffered a blight, its leaves turning coal-black as if by the agency of fire.

"There was too powerful a stimulus," said Aylmer, thoughtfully.

To make up for this abortive experiment, he proposed to take her portrait by a scientific process of his own invention. It was to be effected by rays of light striking upon a polished plate of metal. Georgiana assented; but, on looking at the result, was affrighted to find the features of the portrait blurred and indefinable; while the minute figure of a hand appeared where the cheek should have been. Aylmer snatched the metallic plate and threw it into a jar of corrosive acid.

Soon, however, he forgot these mortifying failures. In the intervals of study and chemical experiment he came to her flushed and exhausted, but seemed invigorated by her presence, and spoke in glowing language of the resources of his art. He gave a history of the long dynasty of the alchemists, who spent so many ages in quest of the universal solvent by which the golden principle might be elicited from all things vile and base. Aylmer appeared to believe that, by the plainest scientific logic, it was altogether within the limits of possibility to discover this long-sought medium; "but," he added, "a philosopher who should go deep enough to acquire the power would attain too lofty a wisdom to stoop to the exercise of it." Not less singular were his opinions in regard to the elixir vitae. He more than intimated that it was at his option to concoct a liquid that should prolong life for years, perhaps interminably; but that it would produce a discord in Nature which all the world, and chiefly the quaffer of the immortal nostrum, would find cause to curse.

"Aylmer, are you in earnest?" asked Georgiana, looking at him with amazement and fear. "It is terrible to possess such power, or even to dream of possessing it."

"Oh, do not tremble, my love," said her husband. "I would not wrong either you or myself by working such inharmonious effects upon our lives; but I would have you consider how trifling, in comparison, is the skill requisite to remove this little hand."

At the mention of the birthmark, Georgiana, as usual, shrank as if a redhot iron had touched her cheek.

Again Aylmer applied himself to his labors. She could hear his voice in the distant furnace room giving directions to Aminadab, whose harsh, uncouth, misshapen tones were audible in response, more like the grunt or growl of a brute than human speech. After hours of absence, Aylmer reappeared and proposed that she should now examine his cabinet of chemical products and natural treasures of the earth. Among the former he showed her a small vial, in which, he remarked, was contained a gentle yet most powerful fragrance, capable of impregnating all the breezes that blow across a kingdom. They were of inestimable value, the contents of that little vial; and, as he said so, he threw some of the perfume into the air and filled the room with piercing and invigorating delight.

"And what is this?" asked Georgiana, pointing to a small crystal globe containing a gold-colored liquid. "It is so beautiful to the eye that I could imagine it the elixir of life."

"In one sense it is," replied Aylmer; "or, rather, the elixir of immortality. It is the most precious poison that ever was concocted in this world. By its aid I could apportion the lifetime of any mortal at whom you might point your finger. The strength of the dose would determine whether he were to linger out years, or drop dead in the midst of a breath. No king on his guarded throne could keep his life if I, in my private station, should deem that the welfare of millions justified me in depriving him of it."

"Why do you keep such a terrific drug?" inquired Georgiana in horror.

"Do not mistrust me, dearest," said her husband, smiling; "its virtuous

potency is yet greater than its harmful one. But see! here is a powerful
cosmetic. With a few drops of this in a vase of water, freckles may be washed
away as easily as the hands are cleansed. A stronger infusion would take the
blood out of the cheek, and leave the rosiest beauty a pale ghost."

"Is it with this lotion that you intend to bathe my cheek?" asked Georgiana, anxiously.

"Oh, no," hastily replied her husband; "this is merely superficial. Your
case demands a remedy that shall go deeper."

In his interviews with Georgiana, Aylmer generally made minute inquiries as to her sensations and whether the confinement of the rooms and the
temperature of the atmosphere agreed with her. These questions had such a
particular drift that Georgiana began to conjecture that she was already
subjected to certain physical influences, either breathed in with the fragrant
air or taken with her food. She fancied likewise, but it might be altogether
fancy, that there was a stirring up of her system—a strange, indefinite
sensation creeping through her veins, and tingling, half painfully, half
pleasurably, at her heart. Still, whenever she dared to look into the mirror,
there she beheld herself pale as a white rose and with the crimson birthmark
stamped upon her cheek. Not even Aylmer now hated it so much as she.

To dispel the tedium of the hours which her husband found it necessary to
devote to the processes of combination and analysis, Georgiana turned over
the volumes of his scientific library. In many dark old tomes she met with
chapters full of romance and poetry. They were the works of philosophers of
the middle ages, such as Albertus Magnus, Cornelius Agrippa, Paracelsus,
and the famous friar who created the prophetic Brazen Head. All these
antique naturalists stood in advance of their centuries, yet were imbued with
some of their credulity, and therefore were believed, and perhaps imagined
themselves to have acquired from the investigation of Nature a power above
Nature, and from physics a sway over the spiritual world. Hardly less
curious and imaginative were the early volumes of the Transactions of the
Royal Society, in which the members, knowing little of the limits of natural
possibility, were continually recording wonders or proposing methods
whereby wonders might be wrought.

But to Georgiana the most engrossing volume was a large folio from her
husband's own hand, in which he had recorded every experiment of his
scientific career, its original aim, the methods adopted for its development,
and its final success or failure, with the circumstances to which either event
was attributable. The book, in truth, was both the history and emblem of his
ardent, ambitious, imaginative, yet practical and laborious life. He handled
physical details as if there were nothing beyond them; yet spiritualized them
all, and redeemed himself from materialism by his strong and eager aspira-
tion towards the infinite. In his grasp the veriest clod of earth assumed a
soul. Georgiana, as she read, reverenced Aylmer and loved him more
profoundly than ever, but with a less entire dependence on his judgment
than heretofore. Much as he had accomplished, she could not but observe

that his most splendid successes were almost invariably failures, if compared with the ideal at which he aimed. His brightest diamonds were the merest pebbles, and felt to be so by himself, in comparison with the inestimable gems which lay hidden beyond his reach. The volume, rich with achievements that had won renown for its author, was yet as melancholy a record as ever mortal hand had penned. It was the sad confession and continual exemplification of the shortcomings of the composite man, the spirit burdened with clay and working in matter, and of the despair that assails the higher nature at finding itself so miserably thwarted by the earthly part. Perhaps every man of genius in whatever sphere might recognize the image of his own experience in Aylmer's journal.

So deeply did these reflections affect Georgiana that she laid her face upon the open volume and burst into tears. In this situation she was found by her husband.

"It is dangerous to read in a sorcerer's books," said he with a smile, though his countenance was uneasy and displeased. "Georgiana, there are pages in that volume which I can scarcely glance over and keep my senses. Take heed lest it prove as detrimental to you."

"It has made me worship you more than ever," said she.

"Ah, wait for this one success," rejoined he, "then worship me if you will. I shall deem myself hardly unworthy of it. But come, I have sought you for the luxury of your voice. Sing to me, dearest."

So she poured out the liquid music of her voice to quench the thirst of his spirit. He then took his leave with a boyish exuberance of gayety, assuring her that her seclusion would endure but a little longer, and that the result was already certain. Scarcely had he departed when Georgiana felt irresistibly impelled to follow him. She had forgotten to inform Aylmer of a symptom which for two or three hours past had begun to excite her attention. It was a sensation in the fatal birthmark, not painful, but which induced a restlessness throughout her system. Hastening after her husband, she intruded for the first time into the laboratory.

The first thing that struck her eye was the furnace, that hot and feverish worker, with the intense glow of its fire, which by the quantities of soot clustered above it seemed to have been burning for ages. There was a distilling apparatus in full operation. Around the room were retorts, tubes, cylinders, crucibles, and other apparatus of chemical research. An electrical machine stood ready for immediate use. The atmosphere felt oppressively close, and was tainted with gaseous odors which had been tormented forth by the processes of science. The severe and homely simplicity of the apartment, with its naked walls and brick pavement, looked strange, accustomed as Georgiana had become to the fantastic elegance of her boudoir. But what chiefly, indeed almost solely, drew her attention, was the aspect of Aylmer himself.

He was pale as death, anxious and absorbed, and hung over the furnace as if it depended upon his utmost watchfulness whether the liquid which it was distilling should be the draught of immortal happiness or misery. How different from the sanguine and joyous mien that he had assumed for Georgiana's encouragement!

"Carefully now, Aminadab; carefully, thou human machine; carefully, thou man of clay!" muttered Aylmer, more to himself than his assistant. "Now if there be a thought too much or too little, it is all over."

"Ho! ho!" mumbled Aminadab. "Look, master! look!"

Aylmer raised his eyes hastily, and at first reddened, then grew paler than ever, on beholding Georgiana. He rushed towards her and seized her arm with a grip that left the print of his fingers upon it.

"Why do you come hither? Have you no trust in your husband?" cried he, impetuously. "Would you throw the blight of that fatal birthmark over my labors? It is not well done. Go, prying woman, go!"

"Nay, Aylmer," said Georgiana with the firmness of which she possessed no stinted endowment, "it is not you that have a right to complain. You mistrust your wife; you have concealed the anxiety with which you watch the development of this experiment. Think not so unworthily of me, my husband. Tell me all the risk we run, and fear not that I shall shrink; for my share in it is far less than your own."

"No, no, Georgiana!" said Aylmer, impatiently; "it must not be."

"I submit," replied she calmly. "And, Aylmer, I shall quaff whatever draught you bring me; but it will be on the same principle that would induce me to take a dose of poison if offered by your hand."

"My noble wife," said Aylmer, deeply moved, "I knew not the height and depth of your nature until now. Nothing shall be concealed. Know, then, that this crimson hand, superficial as it seems, has clutched its grasp into your being with a strength of which I had no previous conception. I have already administered agents powerful enough to do aught except to change your entire physical system. Only one thing remains to be tried. If that fail us we are ruined."

"Why did you hesitate to tell me this?" asked she.

"Because, Georgiana," said Aylmer, in a low voice, "there is danger."

"Danger? There is but one danger—that this horrible stigma shall be left upon my cheek!" cried Georgiana. "Remove it, remove it, whatever be the cost, or we shall both go mad!"

"Heaven knows your words are too true," said Aylmer, sadly. "And now, dearest, return to your boudoir. In a little while all will be tested."

He conducted her back and took leave of her with a solemn tenderness which spoke far more than his words how much was now at stake. After his departure, Georgiana became rapt in musings. She considered the character of Aylmer, and did it completer justice than at any previous moment. Her heart exulted, while it trembled, at his honorable love—so pure and lofty that it would accept nothing less than perfection nor miserably make itself contented with an earthlier nature than he had dreamed of. She felt how much more precious was such a sentiment than that meaner kind which would have borne with the imperfection for her sake, and have been guilty of treason to holy love by degrading its perfect idea to the level of the actual; and with her whole spirit she prayed that, for a single moment, she might satisfy his highest and deepest conception. Longer than one moment she well knew it could not be; for his spirit was ever on the march, ever ascending, and each instant required something that was beyond the scope of the instant before.

The sound of her husband's footsteps aroused her. He bore a crystal goblet containing a liquor colorless as water, but bright enough to be the draught of immortality. Aylmer was pale; but it seemed rather the consequences of a highly-wrought state of mind and tension of spirit than of fear or doubt.

"The concoction of the draught has been perfect," said he, in answer to Georgiana's look. "Unless all my science have deceived me, it cannot fail."

"Save on your account, my dearest Aylmer," observed his wife, "I might wish to put off this birthmark of mortality by relinquishing mortality itself in preference to any other mode. Life is but a sad possession to those who have attained precisely the degree of moral advancement at which I stand. Were I weaker and blinder it might be happiness. Were I stronger, it might be endured hopefully. But being what I find myself, methinks I am of all mortals the most fit to die."

"You are fit for heaven without tasting death!" replied her husband. "But why do we speak of dying? The draught cannot fail. Behold its effect upon this plant."

On the window seat there stood a geranium diseased with yellow blotches, which had overspread all its leaves. Aylmer poured a small quantity of the liquid upon the soil in which it grew. In a little time, when the roots of the plant had taken up the moisture, the unsightly blotches began to be extinguished in a living verdure.

"There needed no proof," said Georgiana, quietly. "Give me the goblet. I joyfully stake all upon your word."

"Drink, then, thou lofty creature!" exclaimed Aylmer, with fervid admiration. "There is no taint of imperfection on thy spirit. Thy sensible frame, too, shall soon be all perfect."

She quaffed the liquid and returned the goblet to his hand.

"It is grateful," said she with a placid smile. "Methinks it is like water from a heavenly fountain; for it contains I know not what of unobtrusive fragrance and deliciousness. It allays a feverish thirst that had parched me for many days. Now, dearest, let me sleep. My earthly senses are closing over my spirit like the leaves around the heart of a rose at sunset."

She spoke the last words with a gentle reluctance, as if it required almost more energy than she could command to pronounce the faint and lingering syllables. Scarcely had they loitered through her lips ere she was lost in slumber. Aylmer sat by her side, watching her aspect with the emotions proper to a man the whole value of whose existence was involved in the process now to be tested. Mingled with this mood, however, was the philosophic investigation characteristic of the man of science. Not the minutest symptom escaped him. A heightened flush of the cheek, a slight irregularity of breath, a quiver of the eyelid, a hardly perceptible tremor through the frame,—such were the details which, as the moments passed, he wrote down in his folio volume. Intense thought had set its stamp upon every previous page of that volume, but the thoughts of years were all concentrated upon the last.

While thus employed, he failed not to gaze often at the fatal hand, and not without a shudder. Yet once, by a strange and unaccountable impulse, he pressed it with his lips. His spirit recoiled, however, in the very act; and Georgiana, out of the midst of her deep sleep, moved uneasily and murmured as if in remonstrance. Again Aylmer resumed his watch. Nor was it without avail. The crimson hand, which at first had been strongly visible upon the marble paleness of Georgiana's cheek, now grew more faintly outlined. She remained not less pale than ever; but the birthmark, with every breath that came and went, lost somewhat of its former distinctness. Its presence had been awful; its departure was more awful still. Watch the stain of the rainbow fading out the sky, and you will know how that mysterious symbol passed away.

"By Heaven! it is well-nigh gone!" said Aylmer to himself, in almost irrepressible ecstasy. "I can scarcely trace it now. Success! success! And now it is like the faintest rose color. The lightest flush of blood across her cheek would overcome it. But she is so pale!"

He drew aside the window curtain and suffered the light of natural day to fall into the room and rest upon her cheek. At the same time he heard a gross, hoarse chuckle, which he had long known as his servant Aminadab's expression of delight.

"Ah, clod! ah, earthly mass!" cried Aylmer, laughing in a sort of frenzy, "you have served me well! Matter and spirit—earth and heaven—have both done their part in this! Laugh, thing of the senses! You have earned the right to laugh."

These exclamations broke Georgiana's sleep. She slowly unclosed her eyes and gazed into the mirror which her husband had arranged for that purpose. A faint smile flitted over her lips when she recognized how barely perceptible was now that crimson hand which had once blazed forth with such disastrous brilliancy as to scare away all their happiness. But then her eyes sought Aylmer's face with a trouble and anxiety that he could by no means account for.

"My poor Aylmer!" murmured she.

"Poor? Nay, richest, happiest, most favored!" exclaimed he. "My peerless bride, it is successful! You are perfect!"

"My poor Aylmer," she repeated, with a more than human tenderness, "you have aimed loftily; you have done nobly. Do not repent that with so high and pure a feeling, you have rejected the best the earth could offer. Aylmer, dearest Aylmer, I am dying!"

Alas! it was too true! the fatal hand had grappled with the mystery of life, and was the bond by which an angelic spirit kept itself in union with a mortal frame. As the last crimson tint of the birthmark—that sole token of human imperfection—faded from her cheek, the parting breath of the now perfect woman passed into the atmosphere, and her soul, lingering a moment near her husband, took its heavenward flight. Then a hoarse, chuckling laugh was heard again! Thus ever does the gross fatality of earth exult in its invariable triumph over the immortal essence which, in this dim sphere of half development, demands the completeness of a higher state. Yet, had Aylmer reached a profounder wisdom, he need not thus have flung away the happiness which would have woven his mortal life of the selfsame texture with the celestial. The momentary circumstance was too strong for him; he failed to look beyond the shadowy scope of time, and, living once for all in eternity, to find the perfect future in the present.

PROSPER MÉRIMÉE

LA BELLE HÉLÈNE

1

Now, those of you who would hear the sorrowful tale of La Belle Hélène and her husband, Theodore Khonopka, gather round Jean Bietko, the finest *guzla* player you have ever heard. The finest that ever you will hear.

2

Theodore Khonopka was a courageous hunter who lived in the times of my grandfather, from whom I heard this tale. He married La Belle Hélène, who chose him instead of Piero Stamati, because Theodore was handsome and Piero was ugly and mean.

3

Piero Stamati came one day to Theodore Khonopka's house. "Hélène," he said, "is it true that your husband has gone to Venice, and that he needs to be gone for a whole year?" "Sadly true. And oh how painful it is to be left alone in this huge house . . ."

4

"No need to grieve alone and lonely, Hélène, when company is so near at hand. Let me sleep with you, and I will give you a handful of golden coins to put in your jet black hair."

5

"Get thee behind me . . . villain . . . ."Ah," said the cruel Stamati, "let me sleep with you and I will give you a velvet robe and as many gold coins as my bonnet can hold."

6

"Get thee behind me, villain. Or I will tell my brothers of your perfidy, and they will kill you." ....

Now you must know that Stamati was small and old, ugly and stunted, and Hélène was tall and strong.

7

Well for her that she was tall and strong.............. Stamati was thrown on his back. Weeping, he tottered back to his own house on trembling knees............

8

He went to a certain impious Jew and asked how he might avenge himself on Hélène. The Jew said, "Seek till you find a black toad that lives under a tombstone. Then bring me the toad in an earthen pot."

9

Stamati brought him a black toad found under a tombstone, and the Jew poured water over the beast's head, and called it "John." —What a dreadful blasphemy—to baptise a toad with the name of so great an apostle!

10

Well then, they scored the toad's skin with their daggers' points until a subtle venom oozed from the cuts. This they gathered into a vial, from which they forced the toad to drink. That done, they caused the toad to lick the skin of a lovely fruit.

11

And Stamati said to his servant lad, "Take this fruit to La Belle Hélène, and tell her that my wife sent it to her." The boy did as he was told, and took the fruit to Hélène, who ate it at once with the greatest pleasure.

12

Having eaten the lovely fruit, Hélène felt terribly sick, and it seemed to her that a snake was stirring in her belly...................

Now those of you who would know the end of this story [must] give a little something to Jean Bietko, the teller of the tale.

PART TWO

1

When La Belle Hélène had eaten the fruit, she made the sign of the cross, but still she felt that something was stirring in her belly. She called her sister, who told her to drink some milk. [She did,] but the snake-like stirring continued.

2

And now her belly began to swell, little by little; each day a little more........
The women said, "Hélène is pregnant; yet how can that be, since her
husband has been in Venice for more than ten months?"

3

And La Belle Hélène was deeply ashamed, and could not hold her head
high, nor think of going out into the street. She stayed indoors, and wept her
days and nights away. She said to her sister, "What will become of me when
my husband returns?"

4

When he had been gone for a year, Theodore Khonopka thought of
returning home. Taking a place on a gilded ship, he made a safe journey to
his homeland. His friends and neighbors came to greet him, dressed in their
finest clothing.

5

But no matter how closely he searched among the crowd, Khonopka could
not see La Belle Hélène and he inquired: "What has happened to my wife?
Why isn't she here?" His neighbors hid their smiles; his friends blushed; but
no one replied.

6

When he came to his house, he found his wife seated on a cushion. "Get up,
Hélène." She stood and he saw her belly—how it was swollen. "What is this?
Hélène, it has been more than a year since I slept with you?"

7

"My lord, I swear to you by the blessed Virgin Mary, I have been faithful to
you; but I have been bewitched in some manner that has caused my belly to
swell." But he did not believe her and, drawing his sabre, he cut off her head
with a single blow.

8

When he had cut off her head, he said, "I will take the child from her
perfidious belly and will expose it in the fields as if I meant it to die. Then its
father will come looking for it, and by this means I will recognize the man
who betrayed me, and I will kill him."

9

He opened her white, white belly, and lo! instead of a child, he found a black toad. "Alas, alas! What have I done?" he said. "I have killed La Belle Hélène who never betrayed me. She was indeed bewitched by means of a toad."

10

He took up his dear wife's head and kissed it. Suddenly, the cold head opened its eyes. Its lips trembled and it said, "I am innocent, but for vengeance's sake the sorcerers cast the spell of a black toad upon me.

11

"Because I was faithful to you, Piero Stamati, with the help of a wicked Jew who lives in the valley where the tombs are, cast the spell on me." Then the head closed its eyes; the tongue grew chill and never spoke again.

12

Theodore Khonopka sought out Piero Stamati and cut off his head. He also killed the wicked Jew; and he caused thirty masses to be said for the repose of his wife's soul.

May God have pity on them and on all this company.

NUCKELAVEE

Nuckelavee was a monster of unmixed malignity, never willingly resting from doing evil to mankind. He was a spirit in flesh. His home was the sea; and whatever his means of transit were in that element, when he moved on land he rode a horse as terrible in aspect as himself. Some thought that rider and horse were really one, and that this was the shape of the monster. Nuckelavee's head was like a man's, only ten times larger, and his mouth projected like that of a pig, and was enormously wide. There was not a hair on the monster's body, for the very good reason that he had no skin.

If crops were blighted by sea-gust or mildew, if live stock fell over high rocks that skirt the shores, or if an epidemic raged among men, or among the lower animals, Nuckelavee was the cause of all. His breath was venom, falling like blight on vegetable, and with deadly disease on animal life. He was also blamed for long-continued droughts; for some unknown reason he had serious objections to fresh water, and was never known to visit the land during rain.

I knew an old man who was credited with having once encountered Nuckelavee, and with having made a narrow escape from the monster's clutches. This man was very reticent on the subject. However, after much higgling and persuasion, the following narrative was extracted:—

Tammas, like his namesake Tam o'Shanter, was out late one night. It was, though moonless, a fine starlit night. Tammas's road lay close by the sea-shore, and as he entered a part of the road that was hemmed in on one side by the sea, and on the other by a deep fresh-water loch, he saw some huge object in front of, and moving towards him. What was he to do? He was sure it was no earthly thing that was steadily coming towards him. He could not go to either side, and to turn his back to an evil thing he had heard was the most dangerous position of all; so Tammie said to himself, "The Lord be aboot me, an' tak' care o' me, as I am oot on no evil intent this night!" Tammie was always regarded as rough and foolhardy. Anyway, he determined, as the best of two evils, to face the foe, and so walked resolutely yet slowly forward. He soon discovered to his horror that the gruesome creature approaching him was no other than the dreaded Nuckelavee. The lower part of this terrible monster, as seen by Tammie, was like a great horse with flappers like fins about his legs, with a mouth as wide as a whale's, from whence came breath like steam from a brewing-kettle. He had but one eye, and that as red as fire. On him sat, or rather seemed to grow from his back, a huge man with no legs, and arms that reached nearly to the ground. His head was as big as a clue of simmons (a clue of straw ropes, generally about three feet in diameter), and this huge head kept rolling from one shoulder to the other as if it meant to tumble off. But what to Tammie appeared most horrible of all, was that the monster was skinless; this utter want of skin adding much to the terrific appearance of the creature's naked body,—the whole surface of it showing only red raw flesh, in which Tammie saw blood, black as tar, running through yellow veins, and great white sinews, thick as horse tethers, twisting, stretching, and contracting as the monster moved. Tammie went slowly on in mortal terror, his hair on end, a cold sensation like a film of ice between his scalp and his skull, and a cold sweat bursting from every pore. But he knew it was useless to flee, and he said, if he had to die, he would rather see who killed him than die with his back to the foe. In all his terror Tammie remembered what he had heard of Nuckelavee's dislike to fresh water, and, therefore, took that side of the road nearest to the loch. The awful moment came when the lower part of the head of the monster got abreast of Tammie. The mouth of the monster yawned like a bottomless pit. Tammie found its hot breath like fire on his face: the long arms were stretched out to seize the unhappy man. To avoid, if possible, the monster's clutch, Tammie swerved as near as he could to the loch; in doing so one of his feet went into the loch, splashing up some water on the foreleg of the monster, whereat the horse gave a snort like thunder and shied over to the other side of the road, and Tammie felt the wind of Nuckelavee's clutches as he narrowly escaped the monster's grip. Tammie saw his opportunity, and ran with all his might; and sore need had he to run, for Nuckelavee had turned and was galloping after him, and bellowing with a sound like the roaring of the sea. In front of Tammie lay a rivulet, through which the surplus water of the loch found its way to the sea, and Tammie knew, if he could only cross the running water, he was safe; so he strained every nerve. As he reached the near bank another clutch was made at him by the long arms. Tammie made a desperate spring and reached the other side, leaving his bonnet in the monster's clutches. Nuckelavee gave a wild unearthly yell of disappointed rage as Tammie fell senseless on the safe side of the water.

JOHN KEATS

LA BELLE DAME SANS MERCI

I

O, what can ail thee, knight-at-arms,
   Alone and palely loitering?
The sedge has wither'd from the lake,
   And no birds sing.

II

O, what can ail thee, knight-at-arms,
   So haggard and so woe-begone?
The squirrel's granary is full,
   And the harvest's done.

III

I see a lily on thy brow,
   With anguish moist and fever dew;
And on thy cheek a fading rose
   Fast withereth too.

IV

I met a lady in the meads,
   Full beautiful—a faery's child,
Her hair was long, her foot was light
   And her eyes were wild.

V

I made a garland for her head,
   And bracelets too, and fragrant zone;
She look'd at me as she did love,
   And made sweet moan.

VI

I set her on my pacing steed,
   And nothing else saw all day long,
For sideways would she bend, and sing
   A faery's song.

VII

She found me roots of relish sweet,
   And honey wild, and manna dew,
And sure in language strange she said—
   'I love thee true.'

VIII

She took me to her elfin grot,
   And there she wept, and sigh'd full sore,
And there I shut her wild wild eyes
   With kisses four.

IX

And there she lullèd me asleep
   And there I dream'd—Ah! woe betide!
The latest dream I ever dream'd
   On the cold hill side.

X

I saw pale kings, and princes too,
   Pale warriors, death-pale were they all;
They cried—'La Belle Dame sans Merci
   Hath thee in thrall!'

XI

I saw their starved lips in the gloam,
   With horrid warning gapèd wide,
And I awoke, and found me here
   On the cold hill's side.

XII

And this is why I sojourn here,
   Alone and palely loitering,
Though the sedge is wither'd from the
    lake,
   And no birds sing.

JOHN KEATS

ISABELLA, OR THE POT OF BASIL

I

Fair Isabel, poor simple Isabel!
   Lorenzo, a young palmer in Love's eye!
They could not in the self-same mansion dwell
   Without some stir of heart, some malady;
They could not sit at meals but feel how well
   It soothed each to be the other by;
They could not, sure, beneath the same roof sleep
But to each other dream, and nightly weep.

II

With every morn their love grew tenderer,
   With every eve deeper and tenderer still;
He might not in house, field, or garden stir,
   But her full shape would all his seeing fill;
And his continual voice was pleasanter
   To her, than noise of trees or hidden rill;
Her lute-string gave an echo of his name,
She spoilt her half-done broidery with the same.

III

He knew whose gentle hand was at the latch,
   Before the door had given her to his eyes;
And from her chamber-window he would catch
   Her beauty farther than the falcon spies;
And constant as her vespers would he watch,
   Because her face was turn'd to the same skies;
And with sick longing all the night outwear,
To hear her morning-step upon the stair.

IV

A whole long month of May in this sad plight
   Made their cheeks paler by the break of June:

401

'To-morrow will I bow to my delight,
   To-morrow will I ask my lady's boon.'—
'O may I never see another night,
   Lorenzo, if thy lips breathe not love's tune.'—
So spake they to their pillows; but, alas,
Honeyless days and days did he let pass;

V

Until sweet Isabella's untouch'd cheek
   Fell sick within the rose's just domain,
Fell thin as a young mother's, who doth seek
   By every lull to cool her infant's pain:
'How ill she is!' said he, 'I may not speak,
   And yet I will, and tell my love all plain:
If looks speak love-laws, I will drink her tears,
And at the least 't will startle off her cares.'

VI

So said he one fair morning, and all day
   His heart beat awfully against his side;
And to his heart he inwardly did pray
   For power to speak; but still the ruddy tide
Stifled his voice, and pulsed resolve away—
   Fever'd his high conceit of such a bride,
Yet brought him to the meekness of a child:
Alas! when passion is both meek and wild!

VII

So once more he had waked and anguished
A dreary night of love and misery,
If Isabel's quick eye had not been wed
   To every symbol on his forehead high:
She saw it waxing very pale and dead,
And straight all flush'd; so, lisped tenderly,
'Lorenzo!'—here she ceased her timid quest,
But in her tone and look he read the rest.

VIII

'O Isabella, I can half perceive
   That I may speak my grief into thine ear;
If thou didst ever any thing believe,

Believe how I love thee, believe how near
My soul is to its doom: I would not grieve
   Thy hand by unwelcome pressing, would not fear
Thine eyes by gazing; but I cannot live
Another night, and not my passion shrive.

IX

'Love! thou art leading me from wintry cold,
   Lady! thou leadest me to summer clime,
And I must taste the blossoms that unfold
   In its ripe warmth this gracious morning time.'
So said, his erewhile timid lips grew bold,
   And poesied with hers in dewy rhyme:
Great bliss was with them, and great happiness
Grew, like a lusty flower in June's caress.

X

Parting they seem'd to tread upon the air,
   Twin roses by the zephyr blown apart
Only to meet again more close, and share
   The inward fragrance of each other's heart.
She, to her chamber gone, a ditty fair
   Sang, of delicious love and honey'd dart;
He with light steps went up a western hill,
And bade the sun farewell, and joy'd his fill.

XI

All close they met again, before the dusk
   Had taken from the stars its pleasant veil,
All close they met, all eves, before the dusk
   Had taken from the stars its pleasant veil,
Close in a bower of hyacinth and musk,
   Unknown of any, free from whispering tale.
Ah! better had it been for ever so,
Than idle ears should pleasure in their woe.

XII

Were they unhappy then?—It cannot be—
   Too many tears for lovers have been shed,
Too many sighs give we to them in fee,
   Too much of pity after they are dead,

Too many doleful stories do we see,
    Whose matter in bright gold were best be read;
Except in such a page where Theseus' spouse
Over the pathless waves towards him bows.

XIII

But, for the general award of love,
    The little sweet doth kill much bitterness;
Though Dido silent is in under-grove,
    And Isabella's was a great distress,
Though young Lorenzo in warm Indian clove
    Was not embalm'd, this truth is not the less—
Even bees, the little almsmen of spring-bowers,
Know there is richest juice in poison-flowers.

XIV

With her two brothers this fair lady dwelt,
    Enriched from ancestral merchandise,
And for them many a weary hand did swelt
    In torched mines and noisy factories,
And many once proud-quiver'd loins did melt
    In blood from stinging whip;—with hollow eyes
Many all day in dazzling river stood,
To take the rich-ored driftings of the flood.

XV

For them the Ceylon diver held his breath,
    And went all naked to the hungry shark;
For them his ears gush'd blood; for them in death
    The seal on the cold ice with piteous bark
Lay full of darts; for them alone did seethe
    A thousand men in troubles wide and dark:
Half-ignorant, they turn'd an easy wheel,
That set sharp racks at work, to pinch and peel.

XVI

Why were they proud? Because their marble founts
    Gush'd with more pride than do a wretch's tears?—
Why were they proud? Because fair orange-mounts
    Were of more soft ascent than lazar stairs?—
Why were they proud? Because red-lined accounts

Were richer than the songs of Grecian years?—
Why were they proud? again we ask aloud,
Why in the name of Glory were they proud?

XVII

Yet were these Florentines as self-retired
    In hungry pride and gainful cowardice,
As two close Hebrews in that land inspired,
    Paled in and vineyarded from beggar-spies;
The hawks of ship-mast forests—the untired
    And pannier'd mules for ducats and old lies—
Quick cat's-paws on the generous stray-away,—
Great wits in Spanish, Tuscan, and Malay.

XVIII

How was it these same ledger-men could spy
    Fair Isabella in her downy nest?
How could they find out in Lorenzo's eye
    A straying from his toil? Hot Egypt's pest
Into their vision covetous and sly!
    How could these money-bags see east and west?—
Yet so they did—and every dealer fair
Must see behind, as doth the hunted hare.

XIX

O eloquent and famed Boccaccio!
    Of thee we now should ask forgiving boon,
And of thy spicy myrtles as they blow,
    And of thy roses amorous of the moon,
And of thy lilies, that do paler grow
    Now they can no more hear thy ghittern's tune,
For venturing syllables that ill beseem
The quiet glooms of such a piteous theme.

XX

Grant thou a pardon here, and then the tale
    Shall move on soberly, as it is meet;
There is no other crime, no mad assail
    To make old prose in modern rhyme more sweet:
But it is done—succeed the verse or fail—
    To honour thee, and thy gone spirit greet:

To stead thee as a verse in English tongue,
An echo of thee in the north-wind sung.

XXI

These brethren having found by many signs
    What love Lorenzo for their sister had,
And how she loved him too, each unconfines
    His bitter thoughts to other, well-nigh mad
That he, the servant of their trade designs,
    Should in their sister's love be blithe and glad,
When 't was their plan to coax her by degrees
To some high noble and his olive-trees.

XXII

And many a jealous conference had they,
    And many times they bit their lips alone,
Before they fix'd upon a surest way
    To make the youngster for his crime atone;
And at the last, these men of cruel clay
    Cut Mercy with a sharp knife to the bone;
For they resolved in some forest dim
To kill Lorenzo, and there bury him.

XXIII

So on a pleasant morning, as he leant
    Into the sunrise, o'er the balustrade
Of the garden-terrace, towards him they bent
    Their footing through the dews; and to him said,
'You see there in the quiet of content,
    Lorenzo, and we are most loth to invade
Calm speculation; but if you are wise,
Bestride your steed while cold is in the skies.

XXIV

'To-day we purpose, aye, this hour we mount
    To spur three leagues towards the Apennine;
Come down, we pray thee, ere the hot sun count
    His dewy rosary on the eglantine,'
Lorenzo, courteously as he was wont,
    Bow'd a fair greeting to these serpents' whine;

And went in haste, to get in readiness,
With belt, and spur, and bracing huntsman's dress.

XXV

And as he to the court-yard pass'd along,
    Each third step did he pause, and listen'd oft
If he could hear his lady's matin-song,
    Or the light whisper of her footstep soft;
And as he thus over his passion hung,
    He heard a laugh full musical aloft;
When, looking up, he saw her features bright
Smile through an in-door lattice, all delight.

XXVI

'Love, Isabel!' said he, 'I was in pain
    Lest I should miss to bid thee a good morrow:
Ah! what if I should lose thee, when so fain
    I am to stifle all the heavy sorrow
Of a poor three hours' absence? but we'll gain
    Out of the amorous dark what day doth borrow.
Good bye! I'll soon be back.'—'Good bye!' said she:—
And as he went she chanted merrily.

XXVII

So the two brothers and their murder'd man
    Rode past fair Florence, to where Arno's stream
Gurgles through straighten'd banks, and still doth far
    Itself with dancing bulrush, and the bream
Keeps head against the freshets. Sick and wan
    The brothers' faces in the ford did seem,
Lorenzo's flush with love.—They pass'd the water
Into a forest quiet for the slaughter.

XXVIII

There was Lorenzo slain and buried in,
    There in that forest did his great love cease;
Ah! when a soul doth thus its freedom win,
    It aches in loneliness—is ill at peace
As the break-covert bloodhounds of such sin:
    They dipp'd their swords in the water, and did teas
Their horses homeward, with convulsed spur,
Each richer by his being a murderer.

XXIX

They told their sister how, with sudden speed,
　　Lorenzo had ta'en ship for foreign lands,
Because of some great urgency and need
　　In their affairs, requiring trusty hands.
Poor Girl! put on thy stifling widow's weed,
　　And 'scape at once from Hope's accursed bands;
To-day thou wilt not see him, nor to-morrow,
And the next day will be a day of sorrow.

XXX

She weeps alone for pleasures not to be;
　　Sorely she wept until the night came on,
And then, instead of love, O misery!
　　She brooded o'er the luxury alone:
His image in the dusk she seem'd to see,
　　And to the silence made a gentle moan,
Spreading her perfect arms upon the air,
And on her couch low murmuring, 'Where? O where?'

XXXI

But Selfishness, Love's cousin, held not long
　　Its fiery vigil in her single breast;
She fretted for the golden hour, and hung
　　Upon the time with feverish unrest—
Not long—for soon into her heart a throng
　　Of higher occupants, a richer zest,
Came tragic; passion not to be subdued,
And sorrow for her love in travels rude.

XXXII

In the mid days of autumn, on their eves
　　The breath of Winter comes from far away,
And the sick west continually bereaves
　　Of some gold tinge, and plays a roundelay
Of death among the bushes and the leaves,
　　To make all bare before he dares to stray
From his north cavern. So sweet Isabel
By gradual decay from beauty fell,

XXXIII

Because Lorenzo came not. Oftentimes
    She ask'd her brothers, with an eye all pale,
Striving to be itself, what dungeon climes
    Could keep him off so long? They spake a tale
Time after time, to quiet her. Their crimes
    Came on them, like a smoke from Hinnom's vale;
And every night in dreams they groan'd aloud,
To see their sister in her snowy shroud.

XXXIV

And she had died in drowsy ignorance,
    But for a thing more deadly dark than all;
It came like a fierce potion, drunk by chance,
    Which saves a sick man from the feather'd pall
For some few gasping moments; like a lance,
    Waking an Indian from his cloudy hall
With cruel pierce, and bringing him again
Sense of the gnawing fire at heart and brain.

XXXV

It was a vision.—In the drowsy gloom,
    The dull of midnight, at her couch's foot
Lorenzo stood, and wept: the forest tomb
    Had marr'd his glossy hair which once could shoot
Lustre into the sun, and put cold doom
    Upon his lips, and taken the soft lute
From his lorn voice, and past his loamed ears
Had made a miry channel for his tears.

XXXVI

Strange sound it was, when the pale shadow spake;
    For there was striving, in its piteous tongue,
To speak as when on earth it was awake,
    And Isabella on its music hung:
Languor there was in it, and tremulous shake,
    As in a palsied Druid's harp unstrung;
And through it moan'd a ghostly undersong,
Like hoarse night-gusts sepulchral briars among.

XXXVII

Its eyes, though wild, were still all dewy bright
  With love, and kept all phantom fear aloof
From the poor girl by magic of their light,
  The while it did unthread the horrid woof
Of the darken'd time,—the murderous spite
  Of pride and avarice,—the dark pine roof
In the forest,—and the sodden turfed dell,
Where, without any word, from stabs he fell.

XXXVIII

Saying moreover, 'Isabel, my sweet!
  Red whortleberries droop above my head,
And a large flint-stone weighs upon my feet;
  Around me beeches and high chestnuts shed
Their leaves and prickly nuts; a sheepfold bleat
  Comes from beyond the river to my bed:
Go, shed one tear upon my heather-bloom,
And it shall comfort me within the tomb.

XXXIX

'I am a shadow now, alas! alas!
  Upon the skirts of human nature dwelling
Alone: I chant alone the holy mass,
  While little sounds of life are round me knelling,
And glossy bees at noon do fieldward pass,
  And many a chapel bell the hour is telling,
Paining me through: those sounds grow strange to me,
And thou art distant in Humanity.

XL

'I know what was, I feel full well what is,
  And I should rage, if spirits could go mad;
Though I forget the taste of earthly bliss,
  That paleness warms my grave, as though I had
A Seraph chosen from the bright abyss
  To be my spouse: thy paleness makes me glad;
Thy beauty grows upon me, and I feel
A greater love through all my essence steal.'

XLI

The Spirit mourn'd 'Adieu!'—dissolved, and left
   The atom darkness in a slow turmoil;
As when of healthful midnight sleep bereft,
   Thinking on rugged hours and fruitless toil,
We put our eyes into a pillowy cleft,
   And see the spangly gloom froth up and boil:
It made sad Isabella's eyelids ache,
And in the dawn she started up awake

XLII

'Ha! ha!' said she, 'I knew not this hard life,
   I thought the worst was simple misery;
I thought some Fate with pleasure or with strife
   Portion'd us—happy days, or else to die;
But there is crime—a brother's bloody knife!
   Sweet Spirit, thou hast school'd my infancy:
I'll visit thee for this, and kiss thine eyes,
And greet thee morn and even in the skies.'

XLIII

When the full morning came, she had devised
   How she might secret to the forest hie;
How she might find the clay, so dearly prized,
   And sing to it one latest lullaby;
How her short absence might be unsurmised,
   While she the inmost of the dream would try.
Resolved, she took with her an aged nurse,
And went into that dismal forest-hearse.

XLIV

See, as they creep along the river side,
   How she doth whisper to that aged Dame,
And, after looking round the champaign wide,
   Shows her a knife.—'What feverous hectic flame
Burns in thee, child?—what good can thee betide,
   That thou shouldst smile again?'—The evening came,
And they had found Lorenzo's earthy bed;
The flint was there, the berries at his head.

XLV

Who hath not loiter'd in a green churchyard,
    And let his spirit, like a demon-mole,
Work through the clayey soil and gravel hard,
    To see skull, coffin'd bones, and funeral stole;
Pitying each form that hungry Death hath marr'd,
    And filling it once more with human soul?
Ah! this is holiday to what was felt
When Isabella by Lorenzo knelt.

XLVI

She gazed into the fresh-thrown mould, as though
    One glance did fully all its secrets tell;
Clearly she saw, as other eyes would know
    Pale limbs at bottom of a crystal well;
Upon the murderous spot she seem'd to grow,
    Like to a native lily of the dell:
Then with her knife, all sudden, she began
To dig more fervently than misers can.

XLVII

Soon she turn'd up a soiled glove, whereon
    Her silk had play'd in purple phantasies:
She kiss'd it with a lip more chill than stone,
    And put it in her bosom, where it dries
And freezes utterly unto the bone
    Those dainties made to still an infant's cries;
Then 'gan she work again; nor stay'd her care,
But to throw back at times her veiling hair.

XLVIII

That old nurse stood beside her wondering,
    Until her heart felt pity to the core
At sight of such a dismal labouring,
    And so she kneeled, with her locks all hoar,
And put her lean hands to the horrid thing:
    Three hours they labour'd at this travail sore:
At last they felt the kernel of the grave,
And Isabella did not stamp and rave.

XLIX

Ah! wherefore all this wormy circumstance?
   Why linger at the yawning tomb so long?
O for the gentleness of old Romance,
   The simple plaining of a minstrel's song!
Fair reader, at the old tale take a glance,
   For here, in truth, it doth not well belong
To speak:—O turn thee to the very tale,
And taste the music of that vision pale.

L

With duller steel than the Perséan sword
   They cut away no formless monster's head,
But one, whose gentleness did well accord
   With death, as life. The ancient harps have said,
Love never dies, but lives, immortal Lord:
   If Love impersonate was ever dead,
Pale Isabella kiss'd it, and low moan'd.
'T was love; cold,—dead indeed, but not dethron'd.

LI

In anxious secrecy they took it home,
   And then the prize was all for Isabel:
She calm'd its wild hair with a golden comb,
   And all around each eye's sepulchral cell
Pointed each fringed lash; the smeared loam
   With tears, as chilly as a dripping well,
She drench'd away: and still she comb'd, and kept
Sighing all day—and still she kiss'd and wept.

LII

Then in a silken scarf,—sweet with the dews
   Of precious flowers pluck'd in Araby,
And divine liquids come with odorous ooze
   Through the cold serpent-pipe refreshfully,—
She wrapp'd it up; and for its tomb did choose
   A garden-pot, wherein she laid it by,
And cover'd it with mould, and o'er it set
Sweet Basil, which her tears kept ever wet.

LIII

And she forgot the stars, the moon, and sun,
  And she forgot the blue above the trees,
And she forgot the dells where waters run,
  And she forgot the chilly autumn breeze;
She had no knowledge when the day was done,
  And the new morn she saw not: but in peace
Hung over her sweet Basil evermore,
And moisten'd it with tears unto the core.

LIV

And so she ever fed it with thin tears,
  Whence thick, and green, and beautiful it grew,
So that it smelt more balmy than its peers
  Of Basil-tufts in Florence; for it drew
Nurture besides, and life, from human fears,
  From the fast mouldering head there shut from view:
So that the jewel, safely casketed,
Came forth, and in perfumed leafits spread.

LV

O Melancholy, linger here awhile!
  O Music, Music, breathe despondingly!
O Echo, Echo, from some sombre isle,
  Unknown, Lethean, sigh to us—O sigh!
Spirits in grief, lift up your heads, and smile;
  Lift up your heads, sweet Spirits, heavily,
And make a pale light in your cypress glooms,
Tinting with silver wan your marble tombs.

LVI

Moan hither, all ye syllables of woe,
  From the deep throat of sad Melpomene!
Through bronzed lyre in tragic order go,
  And touch the strings into a mystery:
Sound mournfully upon the winds and low;
  For simple Isabel is soon to be
Among the dead: She withers, like a palm
Cut by an Indian for its juicy balm.

LVII

O leave the palm to wither by itself;
   Let not quick Winter chill its dying hour!—
It may not be—those Baälites of pelf,
   Her brethren, noted the continual shower
From her dead eyes; and many a curious elf,
   Among her kindred, wonder'd that such dower
Of youth and beauty should be thrown aside
By one mark'd out to be a Noble's bride.

LVIII

And, furthermore, her brethren wonder'd much
   Why she sat drooping by the Basil green,
And why it flourish'd, as by magic touch;
   Greatly they wonder'd what the thing might mean:
They could not surely give belief, that such
   A very nothing would have power to wean
Her from her own fair youth, and pleasures gay,
And even remembrance of her love's delay.

LIX

Therefore they watch'd a time when they might sift
   This hidden whim; and long they watch'd in vain;
For seldom did she go to chapel-shrift,
   And seldom felt she any hunger-pain:
And when she left, she hurried back, as swift
   As bird on wing to breast its eggs again:
And, patient as a hen-bird, sat her there
Beside her Basil, weeping through her hair.

LX

Yet they contrived to steal the Basil-pot,
   And to examine it in secret place:
The thing was vile with green and livid spot,
And yet they knew it was Lorenzo's face:
The guerdon of their murder they had got,
   And so left Florence in a moment's space,
Never to turn again.—Away they went,
With blood upon their heads, to banishment.

LXI

O Melancholy, turn thine eyes away!
   O Music, Music, breathe despondingly!
O Echo, Echo, on some other day,
   From isles Lethean, sigh to us—O sigh!
Spirits of grief, sing not your 'Well-a-way!'
   For Isabel, sweet Isabel, will die;
Will die a death too lone and incomplete,
Now they have ta'en away her Basil sweet.

LXII

Piteous she look'd on dead and senseless things,
   Asking for her lost Basil amorously:
And with melodious chuckle in the strings
   Of her lorn voice, she oftentimes would cry
After the Pilgrim in his wanderings,
   To ask him where her Basil was; and why
'T was hid from her: 'For cruel 't is,' said she,
'To steal my Basil-pot away from me.'

LXIII

And so she pined, and so she died forlorn,
   Imploring for her Basil to the last.
No heart was there in Florence but did mourn
   In pity of her love, so overcast.
And a sad ditty of this story born
   From mouth to mouth through all the country pass'd:
Still is the burthen sung—'O cruelty,
To steal my Basil-pot away from me!'

JOHANN WOLFGANG VON GOETHE

THE ERL-KING

Who is it that rides through the forest so fast,
While night frowns around him, while chill roars the blast?
The father, who holds his young son in his arm,
And close in his mantle has wrapped him up warm.

—"Why trembles my darling? Why shrinks he with fear?"
"Oh father! my father! the Erl-King is near!
The Erl-King, with his crown and his beard long and white!"
—"Oh! thine eyes are deceived by the vapours of night."

—"If you will, dear baby, with me go away,
I will give you fine clothes; we will play a fine play;
Fine flowers are growing, white, scarlet and blue,
On the banks of yon river, and all are for you."

—"Oh father! my father! and dost thou not hear
What words the Erl-king whispers low in mine ear?"—
—"Now hush thee, my darling, thy terrors appease:
Thou hear'st 'midst the branches when murmurs the breeze."

—"If you will, dear baby, with me go away,
My daughter shall tend you so fair and so gay;
My daughter, in purple and gold who is drest,
Shall nurse you, and kiss you, and sing you to rest."

—"Oh father! my father! and dost thou not see?
The Erl-king and his daughter are waiting for me?"
—"Now shame thee, my dearest! 'tis fear makes thee blind:
Thou seest the dark willows which wave in the wind."—

—"I love you! I dote on that face so divine!
I must and will have you, and force makes you mine!"
—"My father! my father! Oh hold me now fast!
He pulls me! he hurts, and will have me at last!"—

The father, he trembled; he doubled his speed:
O'er hills and through forests he spurred his black steed:
But when he arrived at his own castle-door,
Life throbbed in the sweet baby's bosom no more.

THE MARQUIS DE SADE

THE COUNT
DE GERNANDE

Episode from *Justine*

Thérèse (Justine), having escaped from the Benedictine monastery of St. Mary-in-the Wood in which she has been a prisoner of four infamous monks, is all but immediately captured by two men who bring her to the secluded home of the Comte de Gernande, fifty years old, huge and fat. "Nothing could be more terrifying than his face, the length of his nose, his wicked black eyes, his large ill-furnished mouth, his formidable forehead, the sound of his fearful raucous voice, his enormous hands; all combined to make a gigantic individual whose presence inspired much more fear than reassurance . . ."

The Comte adds Justine to his household staff and she is forced to participate in the Comte's sanguine pleasures . . .

Then he took one after the other of my arms, rolled my sleeves to the elbows, and examined them attentively while asking me how many times I had been bled.

"Twice, Monsieur," I told him, rather surprised at the question, and I mentioned when and under what circumstances it had happened. He pressed his fingers against the veins as one does when one wishes to inflate them, and when they were swollen to the desired point, he fastened his lips to them and sucked. From that instant I ceased to doubt libertinage was involved in this dreadful person's habits, and tormenting anxieties were awakened in my heart.

"I have got to know how you are made," continued the Count, staring at me in a way that set me to trembling; "the post you are to occupy precludes any corporeal defects; show me what you have about you."

I recoiled; but the Count, all his facial muscles beginning to twitch with anger, brutally informed me that I should be ill-advised to play the prude with him, for, said he, there are infallible methods of bringing women to their senses.

"What you have related to me does not betoken a virtue of the highest order; and so your resistance would be quite as misplaced as ludicrous."

Whereupon he made a sign to his young boys who, approaching immediately, fell to undressing me. Against persons as enfeebled, as enervated as those who surrounded me, it is certainly not difficult to defend oneself; but what good would it have done? The cannibal who had cast me into their hands could have pulverized me, had he wished to, with one blow of his fist.

I therefore understood I had to yield: an instant later I was unclothed; 'twas scarcely done when I perceived I was exciting those two Ganymedes to gales of laughter.

"Look ye, friend," said the younger, "a girl's a pretty thing, eh? But what a shame there's that cavity there."

"Oh!" cried the other, "nothing nastier than that hole, I'd not touch a woman even were my fortune at stake."

And while my fore end was the subject of their sarcasms, the Count, an intimate partisan of the behind (unhappily, alas! like every libertine), examined mine with the keenest interest; he handled it brutally, he browsed about with avidity; taking handfuls of flesh between his fingers, he rubbed and kneaded them to the point of drawing blood. Then he made me walk away from him, halt, walk backward in his direction, keeping my behind turned toward him while he dwelled upon the sight of it. When I had returned to him, he made me bend, stoop, squat, stand erect, squeeze and spread. Now and again he slipped to his knees before that part which was his sole concern. He applied kisses to several different areas of it, even a few upon that most secret orifice; but all his kisses were distinguished by suction, his lips felt like leeches. While he was applying them here and there and everywhere he solicited numerous details concerning what had been done to me at the monastery of Saint Mary-in-the-Wood, and without noticing that my recitations doubled his warmth, I was candid enough to give them all with naïveté. He summoned up one of his youths and placing him beside me, he untied the bow securing a great red ribbon which gathered in white gauze pantaloons, and brought to light all the charms this garment concealed. After some deft caresses bestowed upon the same altar at which, in me, the Count had signaled his devotion, he suddenly exchanged the object and fell to sucking that part which characterized the child's sex. He continued to finger me: whether because of habit in the youth, whether because of the satyr's dexterity, in a very brief space Nature, vanquished, caused there to flow into the mouth of the one what was ejected from the member of the other. That was how the libertine exhausted the unfortunate children he kept in his house, whose number we will shortly see; 'twas thus he sapped their strength, and that was what caused the languor in which I beheld them to be. And now let us see how he managed to keep women in the same state of prostration and what was the true cause of his own vigor's preservation.

The homage the Count rendered me had been protracted, but during it not a trace of infidelity to his chosen temple had he revealed; neither his glances, nor his kisses, nor his hands, nor his desires strayed away from it for an instant; after having sucked the other lad and having in likewise gathered and devoured his sperm:

"Come," he said to me, drawing me into an adjacent room before I could gather up my clothes, "come, I am going to show you how we manage."

I was unable to dissimulate my anxiety, it was terrible; but there was no other way to put a different aspect upon my fate, I had to quaff to the lees the potion in the chalice tendered to me.

Two other boys of sixteen, quite as handsome, quite as peaked as the first two we had left in the salon, were working upon a tapestry when we entered the room. Upon our entrance they rose.

"Narcisse," said the Count to one of them, "here is the Countess' new chambermaid; I must test her; hand me the lancets."

Narcisse opens a cupboard and immediately produces all a surgeon's gear. I allow your imagination to fancy my state; my executioner spied my embarrassment, and it merely excited his mirth.

"Put her in place, Zéphire," Monsieur de Gernande said to another of the youths, and this boy approached me with a smile.

"Don't be afraid, Mademoiselle," said he, "it can only do you the greatest good. Take your place here."

It was a question of kneeling lightly upon the edge of a tabouret located in the middle of the room; one's arms were elevated and attached to two black straps which descended from the ceiling.

No sooner had I assumed the posture than the Count steps up scalpel in hand: he can scarcely breathe, his eyes are alive with sparks, his face smites me with terror; he ties bands about both my arms, and in a flash he has lanced each of them. A cry bursts from between his teeth, it is accompanied by two or three blasphemies when he catches sight of my blood; he retires to a distance of six feet and sits down. The light garment covering him is soon deployed; Zéphire kneels between his thighs and sucks him; Narcisse, his feet planted on his master's armchair, presents the same object to him to suckle he is himself having drained by Zéphire. Gernande gets his hands upon the boy's loins, squeezes them, presses them to him, but quits them long enough to cast his inflamed eyes toward me. My blood is escaping in floods and is falling into two white basins situated underneath my arms. I soon feel myself growing faint.

"Monsieur, Monsieur," I cry, "have pity on me, I am about to collapse."

I sway, totter, am held up by the straps, am unable to fall; but my arms having shifted, and my head slumping upon my shoulder, my face is now washed with blood. The Count is drunk with joy . . . however, I see nothing like the end of his operation approaching, I swoon before he reaches his goal; he was perhaps only able to attain it upon seeing me in this state, perhaps his supreme ecstasy depended upon this morbid picture. . . . At any rate, when I returned to my senses I found myself in an excellent bed, with two old women standing near me; as soon as they saw me open my eyes, they brought me a cup of bouillon and, at three-hour intervals, rich broths; this continued for two days, at the end of which Monsieur de Gernande sent to have me get up and come for a conversation in the same salon where I had been received upon my arrival. I was led to him; I was still a little weak and giddy, but otherwise well; I arrived.

"Thérèse," said the Count, bidding me be seated, "I shall not very often repeat such exercises with you, your person is useful for other purposes; but it was of the highest importance I acquaint you with my tastes and the manner in which you will expire in this house should you betray me one of these days, should you be unlucky enough to let yourself be suborned by the woman in whose society you are going to be placed.

"That woman belongs to me, Thérèse, she is my wife and that title is doubtless the most baleful she could have, since it obliges her to lend herself to the bizarre passion whereof you have been a recent victim; do not suppose it is vengeance that prompts me to treat her thus, scorn, or any sentiment of hostility or hatred; it is merely a question of passion. Nothing equals the pleasure I experience upon shedding her blood ... I go mad when it flows; I have never enjoyed this woman in any other fashion. Three years have gone by since I married her, and for three years she has been regularly exposed every four days to the treatment you have undergone. Her youth (she is not yet twenty), the special care given her, all this keeps her aright; and as the reservoir is replenished at the same rate it is tapped, she has been in fairly good health since the regime began. Our relations being what they are, you perfectly well appreciate why I can neither allow her to go out nor to receive visitors. And so I represent her as insane and her mother, the only living member of her family, who resides in a château six leagues from here, is so firmly convinced of her derangement that she dares not even come to see her. Not infrequently the Countess implores my mercy, there is nothing she omits to do in order to soften me; but I doubt whether she shall ever succeed. My lust decreed her fate, it is immutable, she will go on in this fashion so long as she is able; while she lives she will want nothing and as I am incredibly fond of what can be drained from her living body, I will keep her alive as long as possible; when finally she can stand it no more, well, tush, Nature will take its course. She's my fourth; I'll soon have a fifth. Nothing disturbs me less than to lose a wife. There are so many women about, and it is so pleasant to change.

"In any event, Thérèse, your task is to look after her. Her blood is let once every ninety-six hours; she loses two bowls of it each time and nowadays no longer faints, having got accustomed to it. Her prostration lasts twenty-four hours; she is bedridden one day out of every four, but during the remaining three she gets on tolerably well. But you may easily understand this life displeases her; at the outset there was nothing she would not try to deliver herself from it, nothing she did not undertake to acquaint her mother with her real situation: she seduced two of her maid-servants whose maneuvers were detected early enough to defeat their success: she was the cause of these two unhappy creatures' ruin, today she repents what she did and, recognizing the irremediable character of her destiny, she is co-operating cheerfully and has promised not to make confederates of the help I hire to care for her. But this secret and what becomes of those who conspire to betray me, these matters, Thérèse, oblige me to put no one in her neighborhood but persons who, like yourself, have been impressed; and thus inquiries are avoided. Not having carried you off from anyone's house, not having to render an account of you to anyone at all, nothing stands in the way of my punishing you, if you deserve to be, in a manner which, although you will be deprived of mortal breath, cannot nevertheless expose me to interrogations or embroil me in any unpleasantnesses. As of the present moment you inhabit the world no longer, since the least impulse of my will can cause you to disappear from it. What can you expect at my hands? Happiness if you behave properly, death if you seek to play me false. Were these alternatives not so clear, were they not so few, I would ask for your response; but in your present situation we can dispense with questions and answers. I have you, Thérèse, and hence you must obey me. . . . Let us go to my wife's apartment."

Having nothing to object to a discourse as precise as this, I followed my master: we traversed a long gallery, as dark, as solitary as the rest of the Château; a door opens, we enter an antechamber where I recognize the two elderly women who waited upon me during my coma and recovery. They got up and introduced us into a superb apartment where we found the unlucky Countess doing tambour brocade as she reclined upon a chaise longue; she rose when she saw her husband.

"Be seated," the Count said to her, "I permit you to listen to me thus. Here at last we have a maid for you, Madame," he continued, "and I trust you will remember what has befallen the others—and that you will not try to plunge this one into an identical misfortune."

"It would be useless," I said, full eager to be of help to this poor woman and wishing to disguise my designs, "yes, Madame, I dare certify in your presence that it would be to no purpose, you will not speak one word to me I shall not report immediately to his Lordship, and I shall certainly not jeopardize my life in order to serve you."

"I will undertake nothing, Mademoiselle, which might force you into that position," said this poor woman who did not yet grasp my motives for speaking in this wise; "rest assured: I solicit nothing but your care."

"It will be entirely yours, Madame," I answered, "but beyond that, nothing."

And the Count, enchanted with me, squeezed my hand as he whispered: "Nicely done, Thérèse, your prosperity is guaranteed if you conduct yourself as you say you will." The Count then showed me to my room which adjoined the Countess' and he showed me as well that the entirety of this apartment, closed by stout doors and double grilled at every window, left no hope of escape.

"And here you have a terrace," Monsieur de Gernande went on, leading me out into a little garden on a level with the apartment, "but its elevation above the ground ought not, I believe, give you the idea of measuring the walls; the Countess is permitted to take fresh air out here whenever she wishes, you will keep her company . . . adieu."

I returned to my mistress and, as at first we spent a few moments examining one another without speaking, I obtained a good picture of her—but let me paint it for you.

Madame de Gernande, aged nineteen and a half, had the most lovely, the most noble, the most majestic figure one could hope to see, not one of her gestures, not a single movement was without gracefulness, not one of her glances lacked depth of sentiment: nothing could equal the expression of her eyes, which were a beautiful dark brown although her hair was blond; but a certain languor, a lassitude entailed by her misfortunes, dimmed their *éclat,* and thereby rendered them a thousand times more interesting; her skin was very fair, her hair very rich; her mouth was very small, perhaps too small, and I was little surprised to find this defect in her: 'twas a pretty rose not yet in full bloom; but teeth so white . . . lips of a vermillion . . . one might have said Love had colored them with tints borrowed from the goddess of flowers; her nose was aquiline, straight, delicately modeled; upon her brow curved two ebony eyebrows; a perfectly lovely chin; a visage, in one word, of the finest oval shape, over whose entirety reigned a kind of attractiveness, a naïveté, an openness which might well have made one take this adorable face for an angelic rather than mortal physiognomy. Her arms, her breasts, her flanks were of a splendor . . . of a round fulness fit to serve as models to an artist; a black silken fleece covered her *mons veneris,* which was sustained by two superbly cast thighs; and what astonished me was that, despite the slenderness of the Countess' figure, despite her sufferings, nothing had impaired the firm quality of her flesh: her round, plump buttocks were as smooth, as ripe, as firm as if her figure were heavier and as if she had always dwelled in the depths of happiness. However, frightful traces of her husband's libertinage were scattered thickly about; but, I repeat, nothing spoiled, nothing damaged . . . the very image of a beautiful lily upon which the honeybee has inflicted some scratches. To so many gifts Madame de Gernande added a gentle nature, a romantic and tender mind, a heart of such sensibility! . . . well-educated, with talents . . . a native art for seduction which no one but her infamous husband could resist, a charming timbre in her voice and much piety: such was the unhappy wife of the Comte de Gernande, such was the heavenly creature against whom he had plotted; it seemed that the more she inspired ideas, the more she inflamed his ferocity, and that the abundant gifts she had received from Nature only became further motives for that villain's cruelties.

"When were you last bled, Madame?" I asked in order to have her understand I was acquainted with everything.

"Three days ago," she said, "and it is to be tomorrow. . . ." Then, with a sigh: " . . . yes, tomorrow . . . Mademoiselle, tomorrow you will witness the pretty scene."

"And Madame is not growing weak?"

"Oh, Great Heaven! I am not twenty and am sure I shall be no weaker at seventy. But it will come to an end, I flatter myself in the belief, for it is perfectly impossible for me to live much longer this way: I will go to my Father, in the arms of the Supreme Being I will seek a place of rest men have so cruelly denied me on earth."

These words clove my heart; wishing to maintain my role, I disguised my trouble, but upon the instant I made an inward promise to lay down my life a thousand times, if necessary, rather than leave this ill-starred victim in the clutches of this monstrous debauchee.

The Countess was on the point of taking her dinner. The two old women came to tell me to conduct her into her cabinet; I transmitted the message; she was accustomed to it all, she went out at once, and the two women, aided by the two valets who had carried me off, served a sumptuous meal upon a table at which my place was set opposite my mistress. The valets retired and the women informed me that they would not stir from the antechamber so as to be near at hand to receive whatever might be Madame's orders. I relayed this to the Countess, she took her place and, with an air of friendliness and affability which entirely won my heart, invited me to join her. There were at least twenty dishes upon the table.

"With what regards this aspect of things, Mademoiselle, you see that they treat me well."

"Yes, Madame," I replied, "and I know it is the wish of Monsieur le Comte that you lack nothing."

"Oh yes! But as these attentions are motivated only by cruelty, my feelings are scarcely of gratitude."

Her constant state of debilitation and perpetual need of what would revive her strength obliged Madame de Gernande to eat copiously. She desired partridge and Rouen duckling; they were brought to her in a trice. After the meal, she went for some air on the terrace, but upon rising she took my arm, for she was quite unable to take ten steps without someone to lean upon. It was at this moment she showed me all those parts of her body I have just described to you; she exhibited her arms: they were covered with small scars.

"Ah, he does not confine himself to that," she said, "there is not a single spot on my wretched person whence he does not love to see blood flow."

And she allowed me to see her feet, her neck, the lower part of her breasts and several other fleshy areas equally speckled with healed punctures. That first day I limited myself to murmuring a few sympathetic words and we retired for the night.

The morrow was the Countess' fatal day. Monsieur de Gernande, who only performed the operation after his dinner—which he always took before his wife ate hers—had me join him at table; it was then, Madame, I beheld that ogre fall to in a manner so terrifying that I could hardly believe my eyes. Four domestics, amongst them the pair who had led me to the château, served this amazing feast. It deserves a thorough description: I shall give it you without exaggeration. The meal was certainly not intended simply to overawe me. What I witnessed then was an everyday affair.

Two soups were brought on, one a consommé flavored with saffron, the other a ham bisque; then a sirloin of English roast beef, eight hors d'oeuvres, five substantial entrées, five others only apparently lighter, a boar's head in the midst of eight braised dishes which were relieved by two services of entremets, then sixteen plates of fruit; ices, six brands of wine, four varieties of liqueur and coffee. Monsieur de Gernande attacked every dish, and several were polished off to the last scrap; he drank a round dozen bottles of wine, four, to begin with, of Burgundy, four of Champagne with the roasts; Tokay, Mulseau, Hermitage and Madeiro were downed with the fruit. He finished with two bottles of West Indies rum and ten cups of coffee.

As fresh after this performance as he might have been had he just waked from sleep. Monsieur de Gernande said:

"Off we go to bleed your mistress; I trust you will let me know if I manage as nicely with her as I did with you."

Two young boys I had not hitherto seen, and who were of the same age as the others, were awaiting at the door of the Countess' apartment; it was then the count informed me he had twelve minions and renewed them every year. These seemed yet prettier than the ones I had seen hitherto; they were livelier ... we went in ... All the ceremonies I am going to describe now, Madame, were part of a ritual from which the Count never deviated, they were scrupulously observed upon each occasion, and nothing ever changed except the place where the incisions were made.

The Countess, dressed only in a loose-floating muslin robe, fell to her knees instantly the Count entered.

"Are you ready?" her husband inquired.

"For everything, Monsieur," was the humble reply; "you know full well I am your victim and you have but to command me."

Monsieur de Gernande thereupon told me to undress his wife and lead her to him. Whatever the loathing I sensed for all these horrors, you understand, Madame, I had no choice but to submit with the most entire resignation. In all I have still to tell you, do not, I beseech you, do not at any time regard me as anything but a slave; I complied simply because I could not do otherwise, but never did I act willingly in anything whatsoever.

I removed my mistress' simar, and when she was naked conducted her to her husband who had already taken his place in a large armchair: as part of the ritual she perched upon this armchair and herself presented to his kisses that favorite part over which he had made such a to-do with me and which, regardless of person or sex, seemed to affect him in the same way.

"And now spread them, Madame," the Count said brutally.

And for a long time he rollicked about with what he enjoyed the sight of; he had it assume various positions, he opened it, he snapped it shut; with tongue and fingertip he tickled the narrow aperture; and soon carried away by his passions' ferocity, he plucked up a pinch of flesh, squeezed it, scratched it. Immediately he produced a small wound he fastened his mouth to the spot. I held his unhappy victim during these preliminaries, the two boys, completely naked, toiled upon him in relays; now one, now the other knelt between Gernande's thighs and employed his mouth to excite him. It was then I noticed, not without astonishment, that this giant, this species of monster whose aspect alone was enough to strike terror, was howbeit barely a man; the most meager, the most minuscule excrescence of flesh or, to make a juster comparison, what one might find in a child of three was all one discovered upon this so very enormous and otherwise so corpulent individual; but its sensations were not for that the less keen and each pleasurable vibration was as a spasmodic attack. After this prologue he stretched out upon a couch and wanted his wife, seated astride his chest, to keep her behind poised over his visage while with her mouth she rendered him, by means of suckings, the same service he had just received from the youthful Ganymedes who were simultaneously, one to the left, one to the right, being excited by him; my hands meanwhile worked upon his behind: I titillated it, I polluted it in every sense; this phase of activities lasted more than a quarter of an hour but, producing no results, had to be given up for another; upon her husband's instructions I stretched the Countess upon a chaise longue: she lay on her back, her legs spread as wide as possible. The sight of what she exposed put her husband in a kind of rage, he dwelt upon the perspective . . . his eyes blaze, he curses; like one crazed he leaps upon his wife, with his scalpel pricks her in several places, but these were all superficial gashes, a drop or two of blood, no more, seeped from each. These minor cruelties came to an end at last; others began. The Count sits down again, he allows his wife a moment's respite, and, turning his attention to his two little followers, he now obliges them to suck each other, and now he arranges them in such a way that while he sucks one, the other sucks him, and now again the one he sucked first brings round his mouth to render the same service to him by whom he was sucked: the Count received much but gave little. Such was his satiety, such his impotence that the extremest efforts availed not at all, and he remained in his torpor: he did indeed seem to experience some very violent reverberations, but nothing manifested itself; he several times ordered me to suck his little friends and immediately to convey to his mouth, whatever incense I drained from them; finally he flung them one after the other at the miserable Countess. These young men accosted her, insulted her, carried insolence to the point of beating her, slapping her, and the more they molested her, the more loudly the Count praised and egged them on.

Then Gernande turned to me; I was in front of him, my buttocks at the level of his face, and he paid his respects to his God; but he did not abuse me; nor do I know why he did not torment his Ganymedes; he chose to reserve all his unkindness for the Countess. Perhaps the honor of being allied to him established one's right to suffer mistreatment at his hands; perhaps he was moved to cruelty only by attachments which contributed energy to his outrages. One can imagine anything about such minds, and almost always safely wager that what seems most apt to be criminal is what will inflame them most. At last he places his young friends and me beside his wife and enlaces our bodies; here a man, there a woman, etc., all four dressing their behinds; he takes his stand some distance away and muses upon the panorama, then he comes near, touches, feels, compares, caresses; the youths and I were not persecuted, but each time he came to his wife, he fussed and bothered and vexed her in some way or other. Again the scene changes: he has the Countess lie belly down upon a divan and taking each boy in turn, he introduces each of them into the narrow avenue Madame's posture exposes: he allows them to become aroused, but it is nowhere but in his mouth the sacrifice is to be consummated; as one after another they emerge he sucks each. While one acts, he has himself sucked by the other, and his tongue wanders to the throne of voluptuousness the agent presents to him. This activity continues a long time, it irritates the Count, he gets to his feet and wishes me to take the Countess' place; I instantly beg him not to require it of me, but he insists. He lays his wife upon her back, has me superimpose myself upon her with my flanks raised in his direction and thereupon he orders his aides to plumb me by the forbidden passage: he brings them up, his hands guide their introduction; meanwhile, I have got to stimulate the Countess with my fingers and kiss her mouth; as for the Count, his offertory is still the same; as each of the boys cannot act without exhibiting to him one of the sweetest objects of his veneration, he turns it all to his profit and, as with the Countess, he who has just perforated me is obliged to go, after a few lunges and retreats, and spill into his mouth the incense I have warmed. When the boys are finished, seemingly inclined to replace them, the Count glues himself to my buttocks.

"Superfluous efforts," he cries, "this is not what I must have ... to the business ... the business ... however pitiable my state ... I can hold back no longer ... come, Countess, your arms!"

He seizes her ferociously, places her as I was placed, arms suspended by two black straps; mine is the task of securing the bands; he inspects the knots: finding them too loose, he tightens them, "So that," he says, "the blood will spurt out under greater pressure"; he feels the veins, and lances them, on each arm, at almost the same moment. Blood leaps far: he is in an ecstasy; and adjusting himself so that he has a clear view of these two fountains, he has me kneel between his legs so I can suck him; he does as much for first one and then the other of his little friends, incessantly eyeing the jets of blood which inflame him. For my part, certain the instant at which the hoped for crisis occurs will bring a conclusion to the Countess' torments, I bring all my efforts to bear upon precipitating this denouement, and I become, as, Madame, you observe, I become a whore from kindness, a libertine through virtue. The much awaited moment arrives at last; I am not familiar with its dangers or violence, for the last time it had taken place I had been unconscious ... Oh Madame! what extravagance! Gernande remained delirious for ten minutes, flailing his arms, staggering, reeling like one falling in a fit of epilepsy, and uttering screams which must have been audible for a league around; his oaths were excessive; lashing out at everyone at hand, his strugglings were dreadful. The two little ones are sent tumbling head over heels; he wishes to fly at his wife, I restrain him: I pump the last drop from him, his need of me makes him respect me; at last I bring him to his senses by ridding him of that fiery liquid, whose heat, whose viscosity, and above all whose abundance puts him in such a frenzy I believe he is going to expire; seven or eight tablespoons would scarcely have contained the discharge, and the thickest gruel would hardly give a notion of its consistency; and with all that, no appearance of an erection at all, rather, the limp look and feel of exhaustion: there you have the contrarieties which, better than might I, explain artists of the Count's breed. The Count ate excessively and only dissipated each time he bled his wife, every four days, that is to say. Would this be the cause of the phenomenon? I have no idea, and not daring to ascribe a reason to what I do not understand, I will be content to relate what I saw.

However, I rush to the Countess, I stanch her blood, untie her, and deposit her upon a couch in a state of extreme weakness; but the Count, totally indifferent to her, without condescending to cast even a glance at this victim stricken by his rage, abruptly goes out with his aides, leaving me to put things in whatever order I please. Such is the fatal apathy which better than all else characterizes the true libertine soul: if he is merely carried away by passion's heat, limned with remorse will be his face when, calmed again, he beholds the baleful effects of delirium; but if his soul is utterly corrupt? then such consequences will affright him not: he will observe them with as little trouble as regret, perhaps even with some of the emotion of those infamous lusts which produced them.

I put Madame de Gernande to bed.

ANONYMOUS

LORD RANDAL

1

"Oh where ha' you been, Lord Randal, my son?
And where ha' you been, my handsome young man?"
"I ha' been at the greenwood; mother, mak my bed soon,
For I'm wearied wi' huntin', and fain wad lie down."

2

"And wha met ye there, Lord Randal, my son?
And wha met you there, my handsome young man?"
"O I met wi' my true-love; mother, mak my bed soon,
For I'm wearied wi' huntin', and fain wad lie down."

3

"And what did she give you, Lord Randal, my son?
And what did she give you, my handsome young man?"
"Eels fried in a pan; mother, mak my bed soon,
For I'm wearied wi' huntin', and fain wad lie down."

4

"And wha gat your leavin's, Lord Randal, my son?
And wha gat your leavin's, my handsome young man?"
"My hawks and my hounds; mother, mak my bed soon,
For I'm wearied wi' huntin', and fain wad lie down."

5

"And what becam of them, Lord Randal, my son?
And what becam of them, my handsome young man?"
"They stretched their legs out and died; mother, mak my bed soon,
For I'm wearied wi' huntin', and fain wad lie down."

6

"O I fear you are poisoned, Lord Randal, my son!
I fear you are poisoned, my handsome young man!"

"O yes, I am poisoned; mother, mak my bed soon,
For I'm sick at the heart, and I fain wad lie down."

7

"What d' ye leave to your mother, Lord Randal, my son?
What d'ye leave to your mother, my handsome young man?"
"Four and twenty milk kye; mother, mak my bed soon,
For I'm sick at the heart, and I fain wad lie down."

8

"What d' ye leave to your sister, Lord Randal, my son
What d' ye leave to your sister, my handsome young man?"
"My gold and my silver; mother, mak my bed soon,
For I'm sick at the heart, and I fain wad lie down."

9

"What d' ye leave to your brother, Lord Randal, my son?
What d' ye leave to your brother, my handsome young man?"
"My houses and my lands; mother, mak my bed soon,
For I'm sick at the heart, and I fain wad lie down."

10

"What d' ye leave to your true-love, Lord Randal, my son?
What d' ye leave to your true-love, my handsome young man?"
"I leave her hell and fire; mother, mak my bed soon,
For I'm sick at the heart, and I fain wad lie down."

P'U SUNG-LING

THE PAINTED SKIN

At T'ai-yüan there lived a man named Wang. One morning he was out walking when he met a young lady carrying a bundle and hurrying along by herself. As she moved along with some difficulty, Wang quickened his pace and caught her up, and found she was a pretty girl of about sixteen. Much smitten, he inquired whither she was going so early, and no one with her. "A traveller like you," replied the girl, "cannot alleviate my distress; why trouble yourself to ask?" "What distress is it?" said Wang; "I'm sure I'll do anything I can for you." "My parents," answered she, "loved money, and they sold me as concubine into a rich family, where the wife was very jealous, and beat and abused me morning and night. It was more than I could stand, so I have run away." Wang asked her where she was going; to which she replied that a runaway had no fixed place of abode. "My house," said Wang, "is at no great distance; what do you say to coming there?" She joyfully acquiesced; and Wang, taking up her bundle, led the way to his house. Finding no one there, she asked Wang where his family were; to which he replied that that was only the library. "And a very nice place, too," said she; "but if you are kind enough to wish to save my life, you mustn't let it be known that I am here." Wang promised he would not divulge her secret, and so she remained there for some days without anyone knowing anything about it. He then told his wife, and she, fearing the girl might belong to some influential family, advised him to send her away. This, however, he would not consent to do; when one day, going into the town, he met a Taoist priest, who looked at him in astonishment, and asked him what he had met. "I have met nothing," replied Wang. "Why," said the priest, "you are bewitched; what do you mean by not having met anything?" But Wang insisted that it was so, and the priest walked away, saying, "The fool! Some people don't seem to know when death is at hand." This startled Wang, who at first thought of the girl; but then he reflected that a pretty young thing as she was couldn't well be a witch, and began to suspect that the priest merely wanted to do a stroke of business. When he returned, the library door was shut, and he couldn't get in, which made him suspect that something was wrong; and so he climbed over the wall, where he found the door of the inner room shut too. Softly creeping up, he looked through the window and saw a hideous devil, with a green face and jagged teeth like a saw, spreading a human skin upon the bed and painting it with a paint brush. The devil then threw aside the brush, and giving the skin a shake out, just as you would a coat, threw it over its shoulders, when lo! it was the girl. Terrified at this, Wang hurried away with his head down in search of the

431

priest, who had gone he knew not whither; subsequently finding him in the fields, where he threw himself on his knees and begged the priest to save him. "As to driving her away," said the priest, "the creature must be in great distress to be seeking a substitute for herself; besides, I could hardly endure to injure a living thing." However, he gave Wang a fly-brush, and bade him hang it at the door of the bedroom, agreeing to meet again at the Ch'ing-ti temple. Wang went home, but did not dare enter the library; so he hung up the brush at the bedroom door, and before long heard a sound of footsteps outside. Not daring to move, he made his wife peep out; and she saw the girl standing looking at the brush, afraid to pass it. She then ground her teeth and went away; but in a little while came back, and began cursing, saying, "You priest, you won't frighten me. Do you think I am going to give up what is already in my grasp?" Thereupon she tore the brush to pieces, and bursting open the door, walked straight up to the bed, where she ripped open Wang and tore out his heart, with which she went away. Wang's wife screamed out, and the servant came in with a light; but Wang was already dead and presented a most miserable spectacle. His wife, who was in an agony of fright, hardly dared cry for fear of making a noise; and next day she sent Wang's brother to see the priest. The latter got into a great rage, and cried out, "Was it for this that I had compassion on you, devil that you are?" proceeding at once with Wang's brother to the house, from which the girl had disappeared without anyone knowing whither she had gone. But the priest, raising his head, looked all round, and said, "Luckily she's not far off." He then asked who lived in the apartments on the south side, to which Wang's brother replied that he did; whereupon the priest declared that there she would be found. Wang's brother was horribly frightened and said he did not think so; and then the priest asked him if any stranger had been to the house. To this he answered that he had been out to the Ch'ing-ti temple and couldn't possibly say: but he went off to inquire, and in a little while came back and reported that an old woman had sought service with them as a maid-of-all-work, and had been engaged by his wife. "That is she," said the priest, as Wang's brother added she was still there; and they all set out to go to the house together. Then the priest took his wooden sword, and standing in the middle of the courtyard, shouted out, "Base-born fiend, give me back my flybrush!" Meanwhile the new maid-of-all-work was in a great state of alarm, and tried to get away by the door; but the priest struck her and down she fell flat, the human skin dropped off, and she became a hideous devil. There she lay grunting like a pig, until the priest grasped his wooden sword and struck off her head. She then became a dense column of smoke curling up from the ground, when the priest took an uncorked gourd and threw it right into the midst of the smoke. A sucking noise was heard, and the whole column was drawn into the gourd; after which the priest corked it up closely and put it in his pouch. The skin, too, which was complete even to the eyebrows, eyes, hands, and feet, he also rolled up as if it had been a scroll, and was on the point of leaving with it, when Wang's wife stopped him, and with tears entreated him to bring her husband to life. The priest said he was unable to do that; but Wang's wife flung herself at his feet, and with loud lamentations implored his assistance. For some time he remained immersed in thought, and then replied, "My power is not equal to what you ask. I myself cannot raise the dead; but I will direct you to some one who can, and if you apply to him properly you will succeed." Wang's wife asked the priest who it was; to which he replied, "There is a maniac in the town who passes his time grovelling in the dirt. Go, prostrate yourself before him, and beg him to help you. If he insults you, show no sign of anger." Wang's brother knew the man to whom he alluded, and accordingly bade the priest adieu, and proceeded thither with his sister-in-law.

They found the destitute creature raving away by the roadside, so filthy that it was all they could do to go near him. Wang's wife approached him on her knees; at which the maniac leered at her, and cried out, "Do you love me, my beauty?" Wang's wife told him what she had come for, but he only laughed and said, "You can get plenty of other husbands. Why raise the dead one to life?" But Wang's wife entreated him to help her; whereupon he observed, "It's very strange: people apply to me to raise their dead as if I was king of the infernal regions." He then gave Wang's wife a thrashing with his staff, which she bore without a murmur, and before a gradually increasing crowd of spectators. After this he produced a loathsome pill which he told her she must swallow, but here she broke down and was quite unable to do so. However, she did manage it at last, and then the maniac, crying out, "How you do love me!" got up and went away without taking any more notice of her. They followed him into a temple with loud supplications, but he had disappeared, and every effort to find him was unsuccessful. Overcome with rage and shame, Wang's wife went home, where she mourned bitterly over her dead husband, grievously repenting the steps she had taken, and wishing only to die. She then bethought herself of preparing the corpse, near which none of the servants would venture, and set to work to close up the frightful wound of which he died.

While thus employed, interrupted from time to time by her sobs, she felt a rising lump in her throat, which by-and-by came out with a pop and fell straight into the dead man's wound. Looking closely at it, she saw it was a human heart; and then it began as it were to throb, emitting a warm vapour like smoke. Much excited, she at once closed the flesh over it, and held the sides of the wound together with all her might. Very soon, however, she got tired, and finding the vapour escaping from the crevices, she tore up a piece of silk and bound it round, at the same time bringing back circulation by rubbing the body and covering it up with clothes. In the night she removed the coverings, and found that breath was coming from the nose; and by next morning her husband was alive again, though disturbed in mind as if awaking from a dream, and feeling a pain in his heart. Where he had been wounded there was a cicatrix about as big as a cash, which soon after disappeared.

JOHN MILTON

SATAN
AT THE GATES
OF HELL

Excerpt from *Paradise Lost,* Book II

Book II

Meanwhile the Adversary of God and Man,
Satan, with thoughts inflamed of highest design,
Puts on swift wings, and toward the gates of Hell
Explores his solitary flight: sometimes
He scours the right hand coast, sometimes the left:
Now shaves with level wing the deep, then soars
Up to the fiery concave towering high.
As when far off at sea a fleet descried
Hangs in the clouds, by equinoctial winds
Close sailing from Bengala, or the isles
Of Ternate and Tidore, whence merchants bring
Their spicy drugs; they on the trading flood,
Through the wide Ethiopian to the Cape,
Ply stemming nightly toward the pole: so seemed
Far off the flying Fiend. At last appear
Hell-bounds, high reaching to the horrid roof,
And thrice threefold the gates; three folds were brass,
Three iron, three of adamantine rock,
Impenetrable, impaled with circling fire
Yet unconsumed. Before the gates there sat
On either side a formidable Shape;
The one seemed woman to the waist, and fair,
But ended foul in many a scaly fold,
Voluminous and vast, a serpent armed
With mortal sting. About her middle round
A cry of Hell-hounds never-ceasing barked
With wide Cerberean mouths full loud, and rung
A hideous peal; yet, when they list, would creep,
If aught disturbed their noise, into her womb,
And kennel there; yet there still barked and howled
Within unseen. Far less abhorred than these

Vexed Scylla, bathing in the sea that parts
Calabria from the hoarse Trinacrian shore;
Nor uglier follow the night-hag, when, called
In secret, riding through the air she comes,
Lured with the smell of infant blood, to dance
With Lapland witches, while the labouring moon
Eclipses at their charms. The other Shape—
If shape it might be called that shape had none
Distinguishable in member, joint, or limb;
Or substance might be called that shadow seemed,
For each seemed either—black it stood as Night,
Fierce as ten Furies, terrible as Hell,
And shook a dreadful dart: what seemed his head
The likeness of a kingly crown had on.
Satan was now at hand, and from his seat
The monster moving onward came as fast
With horrid strides; Hell trembled as he strode.
Th' undaunted Fiend what this might be admired—
Admired, not feared; God and his Son except,
Created thing naught valued he nor shunned;
    'Whence and what art thou, execrable Shape,
That dar'st, though grim and terrible, advance
Thy miscreated front athwart my way
To yonder gates? Through them I mean to pass,
That be assured, without leave asked of thee.
Retire; or taste thy folly, and learn by proof,
Hell-born, not to contend with Spirits of Heaven.'
    To whom the Goblin, full of wrath, replied:—
'Art thou that Traitor-Angel, art thou he,
Who first broke peace in Heaven and faith, till then
Unbroken, and in proud rebellious arms
Drew after him the third part of Heaven's sons,
Conjured against the Highest—for which both thou
And they, outcast from God, are here condemned
To waste eternal days in woe and pain?
And reck'n'st thou thyself with Spirits of Heaven,
Hell-doomed, and breath'st defiance here and scorn
Where I reign king, and, to enrage thee more,
Thy king and lord? Back to thy punishment,
False fugitive; and to thy speed add wings,
Lest with a whip of scorpions I pursue
Thy ling'ring, or with one stroke of this dart
Strange horror seize thee, and pangs unfelt before.'
    So spake the grisly Terror, and in shape,
So speaking and so threat'ning, grew tenfold
More dreadful and deform: on th' other side,

Incensed with indignation, Satan stood
Unterrified, and like a comet burned,
That fires the length of Ophiuchus huge
In th' arctic sky, and from his horrid hair
Shakes pestilence and war. Each at the head
Levelled his deadly aim; their fatal hands
No second stroke intend; and such a frown
Each cast at th' other as when two black clouds,
With Heaven's artillery fraught, come rattling on
Over the Caspian, then stand front to front
Hovering a space, till winds the single blow
To join their dark encounter in mid-air:
So frowned the mighty combatants, that Hell
Grew darker at their frown; so matched they stood;
For never but once more was either like
To meet so great a foe: and now great deeds
Had been achieved, whereof all Hell had rung,
Had not the snaky Sorceress that sat
Fast by Hell-gate and kept the fatal key
Risen, and with hideous outcry rushed between.
    'O father, what intends thy hand,' she cried,
'Against thy only son? What fury, O son,
Possesses thee to bend that mortal dart
Against thy father's head? and know'st for whom?
For him who sits above, and laughs the while
At thee, ordained his drudge to execute
Whate'er his wrath, which he calls justice, bids—
His wrath, which one day will destroy ye both!'
    She spake, and at her words the hellish Pest
Forebore: then these to her Satan returned:—
    'So strange thy outcry, and thy words so strange
Thou interposest, that my sudden hand,
Prevented, spares to tell thee yet by deeds
What it intends, till first I know of thee
What thing thou art, thus double-formed, and why,
In this infernal vale first met, thou call'st
Me father, and that phantasm call'st my son.
I know thee not, nor ever saw till now
Sight more detestable than him and thee.'
    T' whom thus the Portress of Hell-gate replied:—
'Hast thou forgot me, then, and do I seem
Now in thine eye so foul?—once deemed so fair
In Heaven, when at th' assembly, and in sight
Of all the Seraphim with thee combined
In bold conspiracy against Heaven's King,
All of a sudden miserable pain

Surprised thee, dim thine eyes, and dizzy swum
In darkness, while thy head flames thick and fast
Threw forth, till on the left side opening wide,
Likest to thee in shape and count'nance bright,
Then shining heavenly fair, a goddess armed,
Out of thy head I sprung. Amazement seized
All th' host of Heaven; back they recoiled afraid
At first, and called me *Sin*, and for a sign
Portentous held me; but, familiar grown,
I pleased, and with attractive graces won
The most averse—thee chiefly, who full oft
Thyself in me thy perfect image viewing,
Becam'st enamoured; and such joy thou took'st
With me in secret that my womb conceived
A growing burden. Meanwhile war arose,
And fields were fought in Heaven: wherein remained
(For what could else?) to our Almighty Foe
Clear victory; to our part lost and rout
Through all the Empyrean. Down they fell,
Driven headlong from the pitch of Heaven, down
Into this deep; and in the general fall
I also: at which time this powerful key
Into my hand was given, which charge to keep
These gates forever shut, which none can pass
Without my opening. Pensive here I sat
Alone; but long I sat not, till my womb,
Pregnant by thee, and now excessive grown,
Prodigious motion felt and rueful throes.
At last this odious offspring whom thou seest,
Thine own begotten, breaking violent way,
Tore through my entrails, that, with fear and pain
Distorted, all my nether shape thus grew
Transformed: but he my inbred enemy
Forth issued, brandishing his fatal dart,
Made to destroy. I fled, and cried out *Death*!
Hell trembled at the hideous name, and sighed
From all her caves, and back resounded, *Death!*
I fled; but he pursued (though more, it seems,
Inflamed with lust than rage), and, swifter far,
Me overtook, his mother, all dismayed,
And, in embraces forcible and foul
Engend'ring with me, of that rape begot
These yelling monsters, that with ceaseless cry
Surround me, as thou saw'st, hourly conceived
And hourly born, with sorrow infinite
To me: for, when they list, into the womb

That bred them they return, and howl, and gnaw
My bowels, their repast; then, bursting forth
Afresh, with conscious terrors vex me round,
That rest or intermission none I find.
Before mine eyes in opposition sits
Grim Death, my son and foe, who sets them on,
And me, his parent, would soon devour
For want of other prey, but that he knows
His end with mine involved, and knows that I
Should prove a bitter morsel, and his bane,
Whenever that shall be: so Fate pronounced.
But thou, O father, I forewarn thee, shun
His deadly arrow; neither vainly hope
To be invulnerable in those bright arms,
Though tempered heavenly; for that mortal dint,
Save he who reigns above, none can resist.'
    She finished; and the subtle Fiend his lore
Soon learned, now milder, and thus answered smooth:—
    'Dear daughter—since thou claim'st me for thy sire,
And my fair son here show'st me, the dear pledge
Of dalliance had with thee in Heaven, and joys
Then sweet, now sad to mention, through dire change
Befall'n us unforeseen, unthought-of, know
I come no enemy, but to set free
From out this dark and dismal house of pain
Both him and thee, and all the heavenly host
Of Spirits that, in our just pretences armed,
Fell with us from on high. From them I go
This uncouth errand sole, and one for all
Myself exposed, with lonely steps to tread
Th' unfounded deep, and through the void immense
To search, with wand'ring quest, a place foretold
Should be—and, by concurring signs, ere now
Created vast and round—a place of bliss
In the purlieus of Heaven; and therein placed
A race of upstart creatures, to supply
Perhaps our vacant room, though more removed,
Lest Heaven, surcharged with potent multitude,
Might hap to move new broils. Be this, or aught
Than this more secret, now designed, I haste
To know; and, this once known, shall soon return,
And bring ye to the place where thou and Death
Shall dwell at ease, and up and down unseen
Wing silently the buxom air, embalmed
With odours. There ye shall be fed and filled
Immeasurably; all things shall be your prey.'

He ceased; for both seemed highly pleased, and Death
Grinned horrible a ghastly smile, to hear
His famine should be filled, and blessed his maw
Destined to that good hour. No less rejoiced
His mother bad, and thus bespake her sire:—
    'The key of this infernal Pit, by due
And by command of Heaven's all-powerful King
I keep, by him forbidden to unlock
These adamantine gates; against all force
Death ready stands to interpose his dart,
Fearless to be o'ermatched by living might.
But what owe I to his commands above,
Who hates me, and hath hither thrust me down
Into this gloom of Tartarus profound,
To sit in hateful office here confined,
Inhabitant of Heaven and heavenly born,
Here in perpetual agony and pain,
With terrors and with clamours compassed around
Of mine own brood, that on my bowels feed?
Thou art my father, thou my author, thou
My being gav'st me; whom should I obey
But thee? whom follow? thou wilt bring me soon
To that new world of light and bliss, among
The gods who live at ease, where I shall reign
At thy right hand voluptuous, as beseems
Thy daughter and thy darling, without end.'
    Thus saying, from her side the fatal key,
Sad instrument of all our woe, she took;
And, towards the gate rolling her bestial train,
Forthwith the huge portcullis high up drew,
Which, but herself, not all the Stygian Powers
Could once have moved; then in the key-hole turns
Th' intricate wards, and every bolt and bar
Of massy iron or solid rock with ease
Unfastens. On a sudden open fly,
With impetuous recoil and jarring sound,
Th' infernal doors, and on their hinges grate
Harsh thunder, that the lowest bottom shook
Of Erebus. She opened; but to shut
Excelled her power: the gates wide open stood, . . .

SCOTTISH FOLKTALE

THE MILK-WHITE DOO [1]

There was once a man that wrought in the fields, and had a wife, and a son, and a dochter. One day he caught a hare, and took it hame to his wife, and bade her make it ready for his dinner. While it was on the fire, the goodwife aye tasted and tasted at it, till she had tasted it a' away, and then she didna ken what to do for her goodman's dinner. So she cried in Johnie her sone to come and get his head kaimed; and when she was kaiming his head, she slew him, and put him into the pat. Well, the goodman cam hame to his dinner, and his wife set down Johnie well boiled to him; and when he was eating, he takes up a foot, and says: "That's surely my Johnie's fit."

"Sic nonsense! it's ane o' the hare's," says the goodwife.

Syne he took up a hand, and says: "That's surely my Johnie's hand."

"Ye're havering,[2] goodman; it's anither o' the hare's feet."

So when the goodman had eaten his dinner, little Katy, Johnie's sister, gathered a' the banes, and put them in below a stane at the cheek o' the door—

> Where they grew, and they grew,
> To a milk-white doo,
> That took its wings,
> And away it flew.

And it flew till it cam to where twa women were washing claes, and it sat down on a stane, and cried—

> "Pew, pew,
> My minny me slew,
> My daddy me chew,
> My sister gathered my banes,
> And put them between twa milk-white stanes;
> And I grew, and I grew,
> To a milk-white doo,
> And I took to my wings, and away I flew."

"Say that owre again, my bonny bird, and we'll gie ye a' thir claes," says the women.

[1] Pigeon.
[2] Talking nonsense.

"Pew, pew,
My minny me slew," etc.

And it got the claes; and then flew till it cam to a man counting a great heap o'siller, and it sat down and cried—

"Pew, pew,
My minny me slew," etc.

"Say that again, my bonny bird, and I'll gie ye a' this siller," says the man.

"Pew, pew,
My minny me slew," etc.

And it got a' the siller; and syne it flew till it cam to twa millers grinding corn, and it cried—

"Pew, pew,
My minny me slew," etc.

"Say that again, my bonny bird, and I'll gie ye this millstane," says the miller.

"Pew, pew,
My minny me slew," etc.

And it gat the millstane; and syne it flew till it lighted on its father's house-top. It threw sma' stanes down the lum, and Katy cam out to see what was the matter; and the doo threw all the claes to her. Syne the father cam out, and the doo threw a' the siller to him. And syne the mother cam out, and the doo threw down the millstane upon her and killed her. And at last it flew away; and the goodman and his dochter after that

Lived happy, and died happy,
And never drank out of a dry cappy.

ENGLISH FOLKTALE

THE WIFE OF USHER'S WELL

1

There lived a wife at Usher's Well,
  And a wealthy wife was she;
She had three stout and stalwart sons,
  And sent them o'er the sea.

2

They hadna been a week from her,
  A week but barely ane,
Whan word came to the carlin wife
  That her three sons were gane.

3

They hadna been a week from her,
  A week but barely three,
Whan word came to the carlin wife
  That her sons she'd never see.

4

"I wish the wind may never cease,
  Nor fashes in the flood,
Till my three sons come hame to me,
  In earthly flesh and blood."

5

It fell about the Martinmass,
  When nights are lang and mirk,
The carlin wife's three sons came hame,
  And their hats were o' the birk.

6

It neither grew in syke nor ditch,
  Nor yet in any sheugh;
But at the gates o' Paradise,
  That birk grew fair eneugh.

7

"Blow up the fire, my maidens,
  Bring water from the well;
For a' my house shall feast this night,
  Since my three sons are well."

8

And she has made to them a bed,
  She's made it large and wide,
And she's ta'en her mantle her about,
  Sat down at the bed-side.

9

Up then crew the red, red cock,
  And up and crew the gray;
The eldest to the youngest said,
  " 'T is time we were away."

10

The cock he hadna crawed but once,
  And clapped his wings at a',
When the youngest to the eldest said,
  "Brother, we must awa'.

11

"The cock doth craw, the day doth daw,
  The channerin' worm doth chide;
Gin we be missed out o' our place,
  A sair pain we maun bide.

12

"Fare ye weel, my mother dear!
Fareweel to barn and byre!
And fare ye weel, the bonny lass,
That kindles my mother's fire!"

CHARLES PERRAULT

BLUEBEARD

There was once upon a time a man who had several fine houses both in town and country, a good deal of silver and gold plate, embroidered furniture, and coaches gilt all over with gold. But this same man had the misfortune to have a Blue Beard, which made him so frightfully ugly that all the women and girls ran away from him.

One of his neighbours, a lady of quality, had two daughters who were perfect beauties. He desired of her one of them in marriage, leaving to her the choice of which of them she would bestow upon him. They would neither of them have him, and sent him backwards and forwards from one another, being resolved never to marry a man that had a Blue Beard. That which moreover gave them the greater disgust and aversion, was that he had already been married to several wives, and no body ever knew what were become of them.

Blue Beard, to engage their affection, took them with my lady their mother, and three or four other ladies of their acquaintance, and some young people of the neighborhood, to one of his country seats, where they stayed full eight days. There was nothing now to be seen but parties of pleasure, hunting of all kinds, fishing, dancing, feasts and collations. No body went to bed, they passed the night in rallying and playing upon one another: In short, every thing so well succeeded, that the youngest daughter began to think, that the master of the house had not a Beard so very Blue, and that he was a very civil gentleman.

As soon as they returned home the marriage was concluded. About a month afterwards Blue Beard told his wife, that he was obliged to take a journey into a distant country for six weeks at least, about an affair of very great consequence, desiring her to divert herself in his absence, to send for her friends and acquaintance, and carry them into the country, if she pleased, and make good cheer wherever she was: "Here," said he, "are the keys of the two great rooms that hold my best and richest furniture; these are of my silver and gold plate, which is not to be made use of every day; these open my strong boxes, which hold my gold and silver money; these my caskets of jewels; and this is the master-key that opens all my apartments. But for this little one here, it is the key of the closet at the end of the great gallery on the ground floor. Open them all, go into all and every one except that little closet, which I forbid you, and forbid you in such a manner, that if you happen to open it, there is nothing but what you may expect from my just anger and resentment." She promised to observe everything he ordered

445

her, who, after having embraced her, got into his coach and proceeded on
his journey.

Her neighbors and good friends did not stay to be sent for by the new
married lady, so great was their impatience to see all the rich furniture of her
house, not daring to come while the husband was there, because of his Blue
Beard which frightened them. They ran through all the rooms, closets,
wardrobes, which were all so rich and fine that they seemed to surpass one
another. After that, they went up into the two great rooms where were the
best and richest furniture; they could not sufficiently admire the number and
beauty of the tapestry, beds, couches, cabinets, stands, tables and looking-
glasses, in which you might see yourself from head to foot; some of them
were framed with glass, others with silver and silver gilt, the finest and most
magnificent as ever were seen. They never ceased to extol and envy the
happiness of their friend, who in the mean time no ways diverted herself in
looking upon all these rich things, because of the impatience she had to go
and open the closet of the ground floor. She was so much pressed by her
curiosity, that without considering that it was very uncivil to leave her
company, she went down a back pair of stairs, and with such an excessive
haste, that she had like to have broken her neck two or three times.

Being come to the closet door, she stopped for some time, thinking upon
her husband's orders, and considering what unhappiness might attend her
were she disobedient; but the temptation was so strong she could not
overcome it. She took then the little key and opened it in a very great
trembling. But she could see nothing distinctly, because the windows were
shut; after some moments she began to observe that the door was all covered
over with clotted blood, on which lay the bodies of several dead women
ranged against the walls. (These were all the wives that Blue Beard had
married and murdered one after another.) She thought that she should have
died for fear, and the key that she pulled out of the lock fell out of her hand.
After having somewhat recovered her surprise, she took up the key, locked
the door and went upstairs into her chamber to recover herself, but she
could not, so much was she frightened. Having observed that the key of the
closet was stained with blood, she tried two or three times to wipe it off, but
the blood would not come out; in vain did she wash it and even rub it with
soap and sand, the blood still remained, for the key was a Fairy, and she
could never quite make it clean; when the blood was gone off from one side,
it came again on the other.

Blue Beard returned from his journey the same evening, and said he had
received letters upon the road, informing him that the affair he went about
was finished to his advantage. His wife did all she could to convince him she
was extremely glad of his speedy return. The next morning he asked for the
keys, which she returned, but with such a trembling hand, that he easily
guessed what had happend. "What is the matter," said he, "that the key of
the closet is not amongst the rest?" "I must certainly," said she, "have left it
above upon the table." "Do not fail," said Blue Beard, "of giving it to me

presently." After several goings backwards and forwards she was forced to bring him the key. Blue Beard having very attentively considered it, said to his Wife, "How comes this blood upon the key?" "I don't know," said the poor Woman paler than death. "You don't know," replied Blue Beard, "I know very well, you were resolved to go into the closet, were you not? Very well, Madam, you shall go in, and take your place amongst the ladies you saw there."

Upon this she threw herself at her husband's feet, and begged his pardon with all the signs of a true repentance, and that she would never more be disobedient. She would have melted a rock, so beautiful and sorrowful was she; but Blue Beard had a heart harder than the hardest rock! "You must die, Madam," said he, "and that presently." "Since I must die," said she, looking upon him with her eyes all bathed in tears, "give me some little time to say my prayers." "I give you," said Blue Beard, "a quarter of an hour, but not one moment more."

When she was alone, she called out to her sister, and said to her, "Sister Anne," for that was her name, "go up, I desire thee, upon the top of the tower, and see if my brothers are not coming. They promised me that they would come today, and if thou seest them, give them a sign to make haste." Her sister Anne went up upon the top of the tower, and the poor afflicted lady cried out from time to time, "Anne, sister Anne, dost thou see nothing coming?" And sister Anne said, "I see nothing but the sun that makes a dust, and the grass that grows green." In the meanwhile Blue Beard, holding a great cutlass in his hand, cried out as loud as he could to his wife, "Come down presently, or I'll come up to you." "One moment longer, if you please," said his wife, and immediately she cried out very softly, "Anne, sister Anne, dost thou see nothing coming?" "I see," replied sister Anne, "a great dust that comes on this side here." "Are they my brothers?" "Alas! no, my dear sister. I see a flock of sheep." "Will you not come down?" cried Blue Beard. "One moment longer," said his wife, and then she cried out, "Anne, sister Anne, dost thou see nothing coming?" "I see," said she, "two horsemen coming, but they are yet a great way off. God be praised," said she immediately after, "they are my brothers. I have made them a sign as well as I can to make haste." Blue Beard cried out now so loud, that he made the whole house tremble.

The poor lady came down and threw herself at his feet all in tears with her hair about her shoulders. "This signifies nothing," says Blue Beard. "You must die." Then taking hold of her hair with one hand, and holding up the cutlass with the other, he was going to cut off her head. The poor lady turning about to him, and looking at him with dying eyes, desired him to afford her one little moment to recollect herself. "No, no," said he, "recommend thyself to God." For at this instant there was such a loud knocking at the gate, that Blue Beard stopped short of a sudden. They opened the gate, and immediately entered two horsemen, who drawing their swords, ran directly to Blue Beard. He knew them to be his wife's brothers, one a dragoon, the other a musketeer, so that he ran away immediately to save himself, but the two brothers pursued him so close, that they overtook him before he could get to the steps of the porch, when they ran their swords through his body and left him dead.

The poor lady was almost as dead as her husband, and had not strength enough to rise and embrace her brothers. Blue Beard had no heirs, and so his wife became mistress of all his estate. She made use of one part of it to marry her sister Anne to a young gentleman who had loved her a long while, another part to buy captains' commissions for her brothers, and the rest to marry herself to a very honest gentleman who made her forget the ill time she had passed with Blue Beard.

LUCIUS APULEIUS

THE VAMPIRE

Episode from *The Golden Ass*

When Socrates heard me rail against Meroe in such sort, he held up his forefinger to his lips, and, as half astonished, said; 'Peace, peace, I pray you,' and, looking about lest any person should hear, 'I pray you' (quoth he) 'Take heed what you say against so venerable a woman as she is, lest by your intemperate tongue you catch some harm.' 'What?' (quoth I) 'This hostess, so mighty and a queen, what manner of woman is she, I pray you tell me?' Then answered he: 'Verily, she is a magician, and of divine might, which hath power to bring down the sky, to bear up the earth, to turn the waters into hills and the hills into running waters, to call up the terrestrial spirits into the air and to pull the gods out of the heavens, to extinguish the planets, and to lighten the very darkness of hell.' Then said I unto Socrates: 'I pray you leave off this high and tragical kind of talk and away with the scenic curtain and tell the matter in a more plain and simple fashion.' Then answered he: 'Will you hear one or two or more of the deeds which she hath done? For whereas she enforceth not only the inhabitants of this country here, but also the Indians and Ethiopians and even the Antipodeans to love her in most raging sort, such are but trifles and chips of her occupation; but I pray you give ear, and I will declare of greater matters, which she hath done openly and before the face of all men.

'This woman had a certain lover whom, by the utterance of one only word, she turned into a beaver because he loved another woman beside her, and the reason why she transformed him into such a beast, is that it is his nature, when he perceives the hunters and hounds to draw after him, to bite off his members and lay them in the way, that the pursuers may be at a stop when they find them, and to the intent that so it might happen unto him (because he fancied another woman) she turned him into that kind of shape. Likewise she changed one of her neighbours, being an old man and one that sold wine, in that he was a rival of her occupation, into a frog, and now the poor wretch swimming in one of his own pipes of wine, and being well nigh drowned in the dregs, doth cry and call with croakings continually for his old guests and acquaintance that pass by. Likewise she turned one of the advocates of the court (because he pleaded and spake against her) into a horned ram, and now the poor ram doth act advocate. Moreover she caused the wife of a certain lover that she had, because she spake sharply and wittily against her, should never be delivered of her child, but should remain, her womb closed up, everlastingly pregnant, and according to the

449

computation of all men, it is eight years past since the poor woman began first to swell, and now she is increased so big that she seemeth as though she would bring forth some great elephant: and when this was known abroad and published throughout all the town, they took indignation against her, and ordained that the next day she should be most cruelly stoned to death; which purpose of theirs she prevented by the virtue of her enchantments, and as Medea (who obtained of King Creon but one day's respite before her departure) did burn in the flames of the bride's garland all his house, him and his daughter, so she, by her conjurations and invocation of spirits, which she uses over a certain trench, as she herself declared unto me being drunken the next day following, closed all the persons of the town so sure in their houses, by the secret power of her gods, that for the space of two days they could not come forth, nor open their gates nor doors, nor even break down their walls; whereby they were enforced by mutual consent to cry unto her and to bind themselves straitly that they would never after molest or hurt her, and moreover if any did offer her any injury they would be ready to defend her; whereupon she, moved at their promises, released all the town. But she conveyed the principal author of this ordinance, about midnight, with all his house, the walls, the ground and the foundation, into another town distant from thence a hundred miles situate and being on the top of a barren hill, and by reason thereof destitute of water; and because the edifices and houses were so close builded together that it was not possible for the house to stand there, she threw down the same before the gate of the town.'

Then spake I and said; 'O my friend Socrates, you have declared unto me many marvellous things and no less cruel, and moreover stricken me also with no small trouble of mind, yea rather with great prick of fear, lest the same old woman, using the like practice, should chance to hear all our communication; wherefore let us now sleep, though it be early, and after that we have done away our weariness with rest let us rise betimes in the morning and ride from hence before day as far as we may.'

In speaking these words, it fortuned that Socrates did fall asleep and snored very soundly, by reason of his new plenty of meat and wine and his long travail. Then I closed and barred fast the doors of the chamber, and put my bed and made it fast behind the door and so laid me down to rest; but at first I could in no wise sleep for the great fear which was in my heart, until it was about midnight, and then I closed my eyes for a little; but alas, I had just begun to sleep, when behold suddenly the chamber doors brake open; nay, the locks, bolts and posts fell down with greater force than if thieves had been presently come to have spoiled and robbed us. And my bed whereon I lay, being a truckle-bed and somewhat short, and one of the feet broken and rotten, by violence was turned upside down, and I likewise was overwhelmed and covered lying in the same.

Then perceived I in myself, that certain effects of the mind by nature are turned contrary. For as tears oftentimes are shed for joy, so I being in this fearful perplexity could not forbear laughing, to see how of Aristomenes I was made like unto a tortoise. And while I lay on the ground covered in the happy protection of my pallet, I peeped from under the bed to see what would happen. And behold there entered two old women, the one bearing a burning torch, and the other a sponge and a naked sword. And so in this habit they stood about Socrates being fast asleep. Then she which bare the sword said unto the other: 'Behold, sister Panthia, this is my dear Endymion and my sweet Ganymede, which both day and night hath abused my wanton youthfulness; this is he (who little regarding my love) doth not only defame me with reproachful words, but also intendeth to run away. And I shall be forsaken by like craft as Ulysses did use, and shall continually bewail my solitariness as Calypso'; which said she pointed towards me, that lay under the bed, and shewed me to Panthia. 'This is he,' quoth she, 'Which is his good counsellor, Aristomenes, and persuadeth him to forsake me, and now (being at the point of death) he lieth prostrate on the ground covered with his bed, and hath seen all our doings, and hopeth to escape scot-free from my hands for all his insults; but I will cause that he shall repent himself too late, nay rather forthwith of his former intemperate language and his present curiosity.'

Which words when I heard, I fell into a cold sweat, and my heart trembled with fear, in so much that the bed over me did likewise rattle and shake and dance with my trembling. Then spake Panthia unto Meroe, and said; 'Sister, let us by and by tear him in pieces, or else tie him by the members and so cut them off.' Then Meroe (for thus I learned that her name really was that which I had heard in Socrates' tale) answered: 'Nay, rather let him live, to bury the corpse of this poor wretch in some hole of the earth,' and therewithal she turned the head of Socrates on the other side, and thrust her sword up to the hilt into the left part of his neck, and received the blood that gushed out with a small bladder, that no drop thereof fell beside; this thing I saw with mine own eyes; and then Meroe, to the intent (as I think) she might alter nothing that pertaineth to sacrifice, which she accustomed to make, thrust her hand down through that wound into the entrails of his body, and searching about, at length brought forth the heart of my miserable companion Socrates, who (having his throat cut in such sort) gave out a doleful cry by the wound, or rather a gasping breath, and gave up the ghost. Then Panthia stopped the wide wound of his throat with the sponge and said: 'O, sponge sprung and made of the sea, beware that thou pass not over a running river.' This being said, they moved and turned up my bed, and then they strode over me and staled upon me till I was wringing wet.

When this was ended, they went their ways and the doors closed fast, the hinges sank in their old sockets, the bolts ran into the doorposts, the pins fell into the bars again. But I that lay upon the ground, like one without soul, naked and cold and wringing wet with filth, like to one that were newly born, or rather, one that were more than half dead, yet reviving myself, and appointed as I thought for the gallows, began to say: 'Alas, what shall become of me to-morrow when my companion shall be found murdered here in the chamber? To whom shall I seem to tell any similitude of truth, when as I shall tell the truth indeed? They will say: "If thou, being so great a man, wert unable to resist the violence of the woman, yet shouldst thou have cried at least for help; wilt thou suffer the man to be slain before thy face and say nothing? Or why did not they slay thee likewise? Why did their cruelty spare thee that stood by and saw them commit that horrible fact? Wherefore although thou hast escaped their hands, yet thou shalt not escape ours." '

While I pondered these things often with myself the night passed on into day, so I thought best to take my horse secretly before dawn and go fearfully forward on my journey. Thus I took up my packet, unlocked and unbarred the doors, but those good and faithful doors which in the night did open with their own accord could then scarcely be opened with their keys after frequent trials, and when I was out I cried: 'Ho, sirrah ostler, where art thou? Open the stable door, for I will ride away before dawn.' The ostler lying behind the stable door upon a pallet and half asleep, 'What?' quoth he, 'Do not you know that the ways be very dangerous with robbers? What mean you to set forth at this time of night? If you perhaps (guilty of some heinous crime) be weary of your life, yet think you not that we are such pumpkin-headed sots that we will die for you.' Then said I: 'It is well nigh day, and moreover what can thieves take from him that hath nothing? Dost not thou know (fool as thou art) that if thou be naked, if ten trained wrestlers should assail thee, they could not spoil or rob thee?' Whereunto the drowsy ostler, half asleep, and turning on the other side, answered: 'What know I whether you have murdered your companion whom you brought in yesternight or no, and now seek safety by escaping away?'

O Lord, at that time I remember that the earth seemed to open, and that I saw at Hell gate the dog Cerberus gaping to devour me, and then I verily believed that Meroe did not spare my throat, moved with pity, but rather cruelly pardoned me to bring me to the gallows. Wherefore, I returned to my chamber and there devised with myself in what violent sort I should finish my life. But when I saw that fortune would minister unto me no other instrument than my bed, I said: 'O bed, O bed, most dear unto me at this present, which hast abode and suffered with me so many miseries, judge and arbiter of such things as were done here this night, whom only I may call to witness for my innocence, render (I say) unto me some wholesome weapon to end my life that am most willing to die.' And therewithal I pulled out a piece of the rope wherewith the bed was corded, and tied one end thereof about a rafter which stood forth beneath the window, and with the other end I made a sliding knot and stood upon my bed to cast myself from aloft into destruction, and so put my neck into it. But when I pushed away with my foot that which supported me beneath, so that the noose when my weight came upon it might choke the passage of my breath, behold suddenly the rope being old and rotten burst in the middle, and I fell down tumbling upon Socrates that lay nigh me, and with him rolled upon the floor. And even at that very time the ostler came in crying with a loud voice, and said: 'Where are you that made such haste at deep night, and now lie wallowing and snoring abed?' Whereupon (I know not whether it was by our fall or by the harsh cry of the ostler) Socrates (as waking out of a sleep) did rise up first and said: 'It is not without cause that strangers do speak evil of all such ostlers, for this caitiff in his coming in, and with his crying out, I think under colour to steal away something, hath waked me, that was beside very weary, out of a sound sleep.'

Then I rose up joyful, as I hoped not to be, with a merry countenance, saying: 'Behold, good ostler, my friend, my companion and my brother whom thou being drunken in the night didst falsely affirm to be murdered by me.' And therewithal I embraced my friend Socrates and kissed him; but he smelling the stink wherewith those hags had embrued me, thrust me away and said: 'Away with thee with thy filthy odour,' and then he began gently to enquire how that noisome scent happened unto me, but I (with some light jest feigning and colouring the matter for the time) did break off his talk into another path, and take him by the hand and said: 'Why tarry we? Why leave we the pleasure of this fair morning? Let us go.' And so I took up my packet, and paid the charges of the house, and we departed.

We had not gone a mile out of the town but it was broad day, and then I diligently looked upon Socrates' throat to see if I could espy the place where Meroe thrust in her sword, and I thought with myself: 'What a madman am I, that (being overcome with wine yesternight) have dreamed such terrible things! Behold, I see Socrates is sound, safe and in health. Where is his wound? Where is the sponge? Where is his great and new cut?' And then I spake to him and said: 'Verily it is not without occasion that physicians of experience do affirm, that such as fill their gorges abundantly with meat and drink shall dream of dire and horrible sights, for I myself (not restraining mine appetite yesternight from the pots of wine) did seem to see in this bitter night strange and cruel visions, that even yet I think myself sprinkled and wet with human blood'; whereunto Socrates laughing, made answer and said: 'Nay, thou are not wet with the blood of men, but thou art embrued with stinking filth: and verily I myself dreamed this night that my throat was cut and that I felt the pain of the wound, and that my heart was pulled out of my belly, and the remembrance thereof makes me now to fear, and my knees do tremble that I totter in my gait, and therefore I would fain eat some what to strengthen and revive my spirits.' Then said I: 'Behold, here is thy breakfast,' and therewithal I opened my scrip that hanged upon my shoulder, and gave him bread and cheese, and 'Let us sit down,' quoth I, 'under that great plane-tree.'

Now I also ate part of the same with him: and while I beheld him eating greedily, I perceived that he wore thin and meagre and pale as boxwood, and that his lively colour faded away, as did mine also, remembering those terrible furies of whom I lately dreamed, in so much that the first morsel of bread that I put in my mouth (which was but very small) did so stick in my jaws that I could neither swallow it down nor yet yield it up; and moreover the number of them that passed by increased my fear, for who is he, that would believe that one of two companions die in the high way without injury done by the other? But when that Socrates had eaten sufficiently he wore very thirsty, for indeed he had well nigh devoured a whole good cheese, and behold there was behind the roots of the plane-tree a pleasant running water which went gently like a quiet pond, as clear as silver or crystal, and I said unto him: 'Come hither, Socrates, to this water and drink thy fill as it were milk.' And then he rose, and waiting a little he found a flat space by the river and kneeled down by the side of the bank in his greedy desire to drink; but he had scarce touched the water with his lips when behold, the wound of his throat opened wide, and the sponge suddenly fell into the water and after issued out a little remnant of blood, and his body (being then without life) had fallen into the river, had not I caught him by the leg, and so with great ado pulled him up. And after that I had lamented a good space the death of my wretched companion, I buried him in the sands to dwell for ever there by the river. Which done, trembling and in great fear I rode through many outways and desert places, and as if culpable of murder, I forsook my country, my wife and my children, and came to Actolia, an exile of my own free will, where I married another wife.

BOOK OF JUDGES

JAËL

CHAPTER 4

And the children of Iṣ'rā-ĕl again did evil in the sight of the LORD, when E'hŭd was dead.

2 And the LORD sold them into the hand of Jā'bĭn king of Cā'năan, that reigned in Hā'zŏr; the captain of whose host *was* Sis'ẽr-a, which dwelt in Ha-rō'shĕth of the Gĕn'tiles.

3 And the children of Iṣ'rā-ĕl cried unto the LORD: for he had nine hundred chariots of iron; and twenty years he mightily oppressed the children of Iṣ'rā-ĕl.

4 And Deborah, a prophetess, the wife of Lăp'ĭ-dŏth, she judged Iṣ'rā-ĕl at that time.

5 And she dwelt under the palm tree of Deborah, between Rā'mah and Bethel in mount E'phrä-ĭm: and the children of Iṣ'rā-ĕl came up to her for judgment.

. . . .

. . . .

. . . .

13 And Sis'ẽr-a gathered together all his chariots, *even* nine hundred chariots of iron, and all the people that *were* with him, from Ha-rō'shĕth of the Gĕn'tiles unto the river of Ki'shŏn.

14 And Deborah said unto Bā'răk, Up; for this *is* the day in which the LORD hath delivered Sis'ẽr-a into thine hand: is not the LORD gone out before thee? So Bā'răk went down from mount Tā'bŏr, and ten thousand men after him.

15 And the LORD discomfited Sis'ẽr-a, and all *his* chariots, and all *his* host, with the edge of the sword before Bā'răk; so that Sis'ẽr-a lighted down off *his* chariot, and fled away on his feet.

16 But Bā'răk pursued after the chariots, and after the host, unto Ha-rō'shĕth of the Gĕn'tiles: and all the host of Sis'ẽr-a fell upon the edge of the swords; *and* there was not a man left.

17 Howbeit Sis'ẽr-a fled away on his feet to the tent of Jā'ĕl the wife of Hĕ'bẽr the Kē'nite: for *there was* peace between Jā'bĭn the king of Hā'zĕr and the house of Hĕ'bẽr the Kē'nite.

18 And Jā'ĕl went out to meet Sis'ẽr-a, and said unto him, Turn in, my lord, turn in to me; fear not. And when he had turned in unto her into the tent, she covered him with a mantle.

19 And he said unto her, Give me, I pray thee, a little water to drink; for I

am thirsty. And she opened a bottle of milk, and gave him drink, and covered him.

20 Again he said unto her, Stand in the door of the tent, and it shall be, when any man doth come and inquire of thee, and say, Is there any man here? that thou shalt say, No.

21 Then Jā′ĕl Hē′bēr's wife took a nail of the tent, and took a hammer in her hand, and went softly unto him, and smote the nail into his temples, and fastened it into the ground: for he was fast asleep and weary. So he died.

22 And, behold, as Bā′răk pursued Sis′ĕr-a, Jā′ĕl came out to meet him, and said unto him, Come, and I will show thee the man whom thou seekest. And when he came into her *tent*, behold, Sis′ĕr-a lay dead, and the nail *was* in his temples.

23 So God subdued on that day Jā′bĭn the king of Cā′năan before the children of Iṣ′rā-ĕl.

24 And the hand of the children of Iṣ′rā-ĕl prospered, and prevailed against Jā′bĭn the king of Cā′năan, until they had destroyed Jā′bĭn king of Cā′năan.

CHAPTER 5

Then sang Deborah and Bā′răk the son of A-bĭn′ō-ăm on that day, saying,

2 Praise ye the LORD for the avenging of Iṣ′rā-ĕl, when the people willingly offered themselves.

3 Hear, O ye kings; give ear, O ye princes; I, *even* I, will sing unto the LORD; I will sing *praise* to the LORD God of Iṣ′rā-ĕl.

. . . .

. . . .

19 The kings came *and* fought; then fought the kings of Cā′năan in Tā′a-năch by the waters of Mē-gid′dō; they took no gain of money.

20. They fought from heaven; the stars in their courses fought against Sis′ĕr-a.

21. The river of Kīshòn swept them away, that ancient river, the river Kī-shòn. O my soul, thou hast trodden down strength.

22. Then were the horsehoofs broken by the means of the prancings, the prancings of their mighty ones.

23 Curse ye Mē′rŏz, said the angel of the LORD, curse ye bitterly the inhabitants thereof; because they came not to the help of the LORD, to the help of the LORD against the mighty.

24 Blessed above women shall Jā′ĕl the wife of Hē′bēr the Kē′nite be; blessed shall she be above women in the tent.

25 He asked water, *and* she gave *him* milk; she brought forth butter in a lordly dish.

26 She put her hand to the nail, and her right hand to the workmen's hammer; and with the hammer she smote Sis′ĕr-a, she smote off his head, when she had pierced and stricken through his temples.

27 At her feet he bowed, he fell, he lay down: at her feet he bowed, he fell: where he bowed, there he fell down dead.

28. The mother of Sis'ẽr-a looked out at a window, and cried through the lattice. Why is his chariot *so* long in coming? why tarry the wheels of his chariots?

29 Her wise ladies answered her, yea, she returned answer to herself.

30 Have they not sped? have they *not* divided the prey; to every man a damsel *or* two; to Sis'ẽr-a a prey of divers colors, a prey of divers colors of needlework, of divers colors of needlework on both sides, *meet* for the necks of *them that take* the spoil?

31 So let all thine enemies perish, O LORD: but *let* them that love him *be* as the sun when he goeth forth in his might. And the land had rest forty years.

APPENDIX

AUTHOR BIOGRAPHIES

Apuleius: 123–A.D. A Roman (Carthaginian) rhetorician and poet. *The Golden Ass* and Petronius's *Satyricon* are the only two Roman novels that have come down to us. The episode from *The Golden Ass* which I have included remains one of the best of the tales in the vampire genre.

John Milton: 1608–1674. The meeting of Satan with Sin and Death in *Paradise Lost* is a literary monument to the macabre.

Charles Perrault: 1628–1703. Long before film was invented, Charles Perrault designed his *Tales* with a film director's eye. In "Bluebeard," for example, the camera shifts skillfully from one dramatic focal point to another until we get the climactic and visually satisfying rescue scene at the end.

P'u Sung-ling: 1640–1715. A civil-servant manqué, P'u Sung-ling became a great teller of tales, some of which, like "The Painted Skin," can be violently bizarre.

Marquis de Sade: 1740–1814. Like Kafka's, de Sade's name has entered the dictionary: he spent much of his adult life in prison for sexual practices we now call sadistic. His major works of fiction, *Justine* and *The Hundred Days of Sodom,* elaborate the view that in a world without God, the powerful are almost duty bound to do what they like no matter what the cost in the lives or feelings of others.

Wolfgang Johann von Goethe: 1749–1832. "The Erl-King" creaks a little with age and is a little moist with German sentiment, yet it still has the power to stun its readers.

Frederick Marryat: 1792–1848. Known especially for his sea stories *(Masterman Ready),* Marryat has also created one of the earliest of the werewolf tales.

John Keats: 1795–1821. Though Keats is better known for his great lyrics ("Ode on a Grecian Urn," "Ode to a Nightingale"), he can also spin a neat terror tale.

Prosper Mérimée: 1803–1870. Mérimée has given us *Carmen.*
   "La Belle Hélène," the tale that follows, is taken from *La Guzla,* a collection of narratives purportedly sung by a Yugoslav bard accompanying himself on a guitarlike musical instrument—the *guzla.*

Edgar Allan Poe: 1804–1849. The *Petit Larousse* describes Poe as a "tormented genius . . . haunted by the 'angel of the bizarre.' " In Poe's work, reason and madness dance perpetually and warily around each other.

Nathaniel Hawthorne: 1804–1864. Hawthorne's fiction frequently broods over the question of pride. Here, in "The Birthmark," Hawthorne gives us another of the nineteenth century's overweening scientists who destroy what they seek to control.

James Malcolm Rymer: 1810–1879. Rymer was a prolific English penny-a-liner. Sensation was his specialty and gore his delight. His *Varney the Vampyre* is the most ebullient blood-sausage of a book ever made.

Sheridan Le Fanu: 1814–1873. Like Bram Stoker, Sheridan Le Fanu was born in Dublin. Le Fanu's genius ranged widely through the terror genre. His famous tales include "Uncle Silas," "Green Tea," and "Carmilla" (printed here).

Charles Baudelaire: 1821–1867. Baudelaire is best known for his *Flowers of Evil (Les Fleurs du Mal* 1857) and his prestigious translations of Poe into French. Victor Hugo said of Baudelaire that he "created a new shudder." In "A Carrion," we see what Hugo means.

Rosa Mulholland: 1841–1921. The unprepossessingly titled, but unforgettable, "Not to be Taken at Bedtime" is based on the magical power of the *burragh-bos,* the grimmest talisman ever devised.

Le Comte de Lautréamont (Isidore Lucien Ducasse): 1846–1870. *Les Chants de Maldoror* is Ducasse's nineteenth-century epic of self-loathing. The selection from it that follows is an early example of the literature of inner terror.

Bram Stoker: 1847–1912. Stoker's masterpiece, *Dracula,* has by now acquired the stature of a twentieth-century myth. "Dracula's Guest" is a deleted chapter from the masterwork. "The Squaw" is close kin in texture and feeling to Poe's "The Black Cat."

J. K. Huysmans: 1848–1907. *Là-Bas (Down There),* the novel from which the present selection is taken, was written in 1891 and was intended as a study in decadence; in it Huysmans interweaves episodes of contemporary satanism with the biography of Gilles de Rais, the fifteenth-century model for Bluebeard.

Guy de Maupassant: 1850–1893. In the history of fear literature, "La Horla" is a transitional tale in which "the horror from without" and "the horror from within" are both ambiguously present.

Lafcadio Hearn: 1850–1904. Hearn was an American journalist with a passion for world travel. He became enamoured of Japanese civilization and spent the last years of his life in Japan. His translations of Japanese folk tales are among the best we have in English.

Charlotte Perkins Gilman: 1860–1935. "The Yellow Wallpaper" is, like Poe's "The Black Cat," a study in monomania. More than that, it is an early—and horrifying—portrait of the subjection of women by the men who love them.

W. W. Jacobs: 1863–1943. "The Monkey's Paw" is by now a very old chestnut. However, the tale has lost none of its power to seize its first readers by the hair, or to shock with recognition readers already familiar with it.

Rudyard Kipling: 1865–1936. "The Mark of the Beast" is a particularly savage treatment of the "primitive curse" theme. H. G. Wells's "Pollock and the Porroh Man" which should be read in conjunction with it, is almost as appalling.

Edgar Lucas White: 1866–1934. Like Mary Shelley and Bram Stoker, who claimed to have dreamed the origins of their fictions, White asserted that "Lukundoo" came to him in his sleep. If ever there was a nightmare, "Lukundoo" surely is one.

H. G. Wells: 1866–1946. Wells is the master science-fiction writer of the twentieth century. Everyone knows his *War of the Worlds, The Island of Dr. Moreau, The Time Machine,* and *The Invisible Man.* "Pollock and the Porroh Man" nearly equals *The Island of Dr. Moreau* as a study in pain.

E. F. Benson: 1867–1940. Benson, the son of an Archbishop of Canterbury, made a reputation as a writer of light fiction. "Caterpillars" is anything but light fiction.

Algernon Blackwood: 1869–1951. Educated in England, Blackwood lived in the United States and Canada, working as a journalist. A prolific terror-tale writer, he was especially fond of haunted places and the lingering effects of ancient religions.

Saki (H. H. Munro): 1870-1916. "Sredni Vashtar" answers Blake's terrifying question about the tiger, "Did he who made the Lamb make thee?" with a deadly "Yes."

Stephen Crane: 1871-1900. Best known for his study of war in *The Red Badge of Courage*, Crane worked as a newspaper reporter who covered the expansion of the American frontier. "Manacled" is a rare example of Crane at his most macabre.

H. H. Ewers: 1871-1943. In his novel, *Der Vampyre*, Ewers tells the story of Frank Braun, a young German patriot in America during World War I who drinks the blood of his Jewish mistress to charge up his eloquence as a fund-gatherer for Germany. "The Spider" is a more traditional vampire tale.

T. F. Powys: 1875-1953. Like Robinson Jeffers, whose work he in some sense anticipated, Powys lived a reclusive life in England. "The Hunted Beast" makes a cruel judgment about human nature.

Sax Rohmer: 1883-1959. Rohmer was the creator of the unforgettable Fu Man Chu, one of the world's greatest, slyest, meanest, most whimsical, and most cultivated of ethnic villains. "Tchériapin," while not quite a Fu Man Chu tale, is just the same a vintage distillation of Rohmer's genius.

Lola Ridge: 1883-1941. Lola Ridge's spare, post-Imagist poems seem extremely fragile when one reads them today, but "My Doll Janie . . ." feels like barbed wire pressing against the brain.

George Langelaan: 1884-   . The Frenchman George Langelaan is best known to us as the creator of "The Fly." The 1958 film version of the story is notable for the episode in which the transmogrified man-fly, caught in a spider's web, cries out in the thinnest of thin voices, "Help me! Help me!" as the camera zooms in close.

Junichiro Tanizaki: 1886-1965. Tanizaki is a Japanese novelist who frequently deals with sadistic themes. The reader may want to turn to Ewers's "The Spider" for another dose of arachnid terror.

John Crowe Ransom: 1888-1974. Ransom was for many years editor of *The Kenyon Review*. He also wrote chastely formal poetry that elegantly expresses fear and trembling.

H. P. Lovecraft: 1890-1937. The night scribbler of Providence, Rhode Island, is famous as the creator of "The Cthulu Mythos," a dank cosmology in which evolutionary accidents survive to torment or to engulf contemporary humans. Despite his graceless style, Lovecraft has managed to acquire a cult following.

Ben Hecht: 1893-1964. Hecht was a journalist, playwright, and violin prodigy. In "The Rival Dummy," Hecht exploits that surest source of terror—the relationship between the ventriloquist and his inanimate alter ego.

Jorge Luis Borges: 1899-   . Edgar Allan Poe's and Kafka's anxieties meet in the Argentinian Borges's erudite and crystalline tales. Borges's fictions are based not so much on the conflicts between individuals as on the collision between destinies.

Richard Hughes: 1900-   . Hughes is best known for *A High Wind in Jamaica*, a book that Rebecca West called "a hot draught of mad, primal fantasy and poetry." "The Ghost," while far less ambitious in scope, works very much like an O'Henry story to induce surprise.

Langston Hughes: 1902-1967. In "End" Hughes, a major black American poet and essayist, reveals a capacity for horror rivaling that of Ambrose Bierce.

Helen Adam: 1909- . Helen Adam, a Scotswoman, came to the United States in 1939. Ten years later she moved to San Francisco where, in the fifties she wrote her disturbing play, "San Francisco Is Burning." She is also the author of *Ballads*.

Anthony Boucher: 1911-1968. For many years Boucher was a coeditor of *The Magazine of Fantasy and Science Fiction*. He was also a deft teller of fearful tales, as any "They Bite" reader will discover at once.

Julio Cortázar: 1914- . Cortázar is an Argentine writer who lives now in France. "Axolotl" is a tour-de-force study of fixation and its consequences.

Roald Dahl: 1916- . During World War II, Dahl was a fighter pilot in the Royal Air Force. Twice a winner of the Mystery Writers of America Edgar Allan Poe Award, Dahl is a busy writer of scary fiction.

Shirley Jackson: 1919-1965. "The Lottery" is a story that maddens and perplexes readers. "What does it mean?" is the usual cry of outrage. "It means what it says" is probably the best answer.

Ray Bradbury: 1920- . Bradbury is a prolific writer of swift, sharp, and frequently lyric stories of fear. "The Last Night of the World" is a typically poignant Bradbury tale.

Jerome Bixby: 1923- . Bixby has tried his hand at science fiction, western, and adventure writing. "It's A *Good* Life" is easily one of the most frightening stories about children ever written.

Richard Matheson: 1926- . "Born of Man and Woman" is a fit companion story to Bixby's "It's A *Good* Life." Both stories ask what constitutes a human being, and both offer a disconsolate answer.

Ursula K. Le Guin: 1929- . Le Guin, author of *The Left Hand of Darkness* and *The Dispossessed*, is considered one of the three or four major science-fiction writers of the second half of the twentieth century (the others: Robert Silverberg, Arthur C. Clarke, and Harlan Ellison). "The Ones Who Walk Away From Omelas" takes an unblinking look at moral passivity.

Jerzy Kosinski: 1933- . The selection from *Steps* included here is not terror fiction in the usual sense of the genre, but it is too stark and grim to be overlooked.

Harlan Ellison: 1934- . Like Hart Crane, Ellison was born in Cleveland, Ohio. "I Have No Mouth & I Must Scream" has shattered the nerves of an entire generation of science-fiction readers.

BIBLIOGRAPHY

ACKERMAN, FORREST J. *The Frankenstein Monster.* New York: Ace Books, 1969.

AESOP. *Five Centuries of Illustrated Fables.* Selected by John J. McKendry. New York: The Metropolitan Museum of Art, 1964.

AINSWORTH, WILLIAM HARRISON, ESQ. *The Lancashire Witches.* London: George Routledge and Sons.

ALLEY, RONALD. *Francis Bacon.* New York: Viking Press, 1964.

ANDERSEN. H. C. *The Complete Andersen.* New York: Limited Editions Club, 1949.

APULEIUS MADAURENSIS. *The Golden Ass.* Cambridge: Harvard University Press, 1915.

ARABIAN NIGHTS. *Thousand and One Nights.* Burton Club. Privately printed.

ARTHUR, ROBERT, comp. *Davy Jones' Haunted Locker; Great Ghost Stories of the Sea.* New York: Random House, 1965.

BABEL, ISAAC. *The Collected Stories.* New York: Criterion Books, 1955.

BADT, KURT. *Die Kunst des Nicolas Poussin.* Koln: Verlag M. DuMont Schauberg, 1969.

BALIKCI, ASEN. *The Netsilik Eskimo.* Natural History Press, 1959.

BANGS, JOHN KENDRICH. *Ghosts I Have Met and Some Others.* New York: Garrett Press, 1968.

BARCHILON, JACQUES. *Le Conte Merveilleux Français de 1690 á 1790.* 7th ed. Paris: Librarie Honoré Champion, 1975.

BARHAM, RICHARD HARRIS. *The Ingoldsby Legends.* London: Richard Bentley, 1858.

BARING-GOULD, SABINE. *A Book of Ghosts.* Freeport, N.Y.: Books for Libraries Press, 1904. Reprinted, 1969.

BAUDELAIRE, CHARLES. *Flowers of Evil and Other Works.* Edited and translated by Wallace Fowlie. New York: Bantam Books, 1964.

BEABLE, WILLIAM HENRY, comp. *Epitaphs: Graveyard Humour and Eulogy.* New York: Thomas Y. Crowell Company, 1925. Republished by Singing Tree Press, Detroit, 1971.

BECK, L. ADAMS. *The Ghost Plays of Japan.* New York: The Japan Society, 1933.

BENEDICT, STEWART H., ed. *Tales of Terror and Suspense.* New York: Dell Publishing Co., 1963.

BIERCE, AMBROSE. *The Collected Works of Ambrose Bierce.* New York and Washington: The Neale Publishing Company, 1909.

———. *Ghost and Horror Stories of Ambrose Bierce.* New York: Dover, 1964.

BINDMAN, DAVID, ed. *The Complete Graphic Works of William Blake.* London: Thames and Hudson, 1978.

BIRCH, CYRIL, AND ACKER, WILLIAM. *Anthology of Chinese Literature.* New York: Grove Press, 1965.

BLACKWOOD, ALGERNON. *Strange Stories.* London: Wm. Heinemann, Ltd. Reprinted by Arno Press, 1976.

———. *Tales of Terror and the Unknown.* New York: E. P. Dutton & Co., 1965.

————. *Tales of the Mysterious and Macabre.* London: Spring Books, 1967.

————. *Tales of the Uncanny and Supernatural.* London: Spring Books, 1962.

————. *The Doll and One Other.* Sauk City, Wis.: Arkham House, 1946.

BLAVATSKY, HELENE. *Nightmare Tales.* London: Thesephia Publishing House.

BLEILER, EVERETT F. *The Checklist of Fantastic Literature, a Bibliography of Fantasy, Weird and Science Fiction Books Published in the English Language.* Chicago: Shasta, 1948.

BLOCH, ROBERT. *Blood Runs Cold.* New York: Simon & Schuster, 1961.

————. *Pleasant Dreams-Nightmares.* Sauk City Wis.: Arkham House, 1962.

BOND, NELSON. *Nightmares and Daydreams.* Sauk City, Wis.: Arkham House, 1968.

BORGES, JORGE LUIS. *A Personal Anthology.* New York: Grove Press, 1976.

————, and ADOLFO BIOY CASARES. *Extraordinary Tales.* New York: Herder & Herder, 1971.

BOUCHER, ANTHONY. *A Far and Away.* New York: Ballantine Books, 1953.

————. *A Treasury of Great Science Fiction.* Garden City, N.Y.: Doubleday & Company, 1959.

BRADBURY, RAY. *Machineries of Joy.* New York: Simon & Schuster, 1964.

————. *The October Country.* London: Rupert Hart-Davis, 1965.

————. *R Is for Rocket.* Garden City, N.Y.: Doubleday & Company, 1962.

————. *The Vintage Bradbury.* New York: Vintage Books, Random House, 1965.

BREE, GERMAINE, ed. *Great French Short Stories.* New York: Dell Publishing Co., 1960.

BRENNAN, JOSEPH P. *Nine Horrors and a Dream.* Sauk City, Wis.: Arkham House, 1958.

BRIGGS, KATHARINE MARY. *Pale Hecate's Team: An Examination of the Beliefs on Witchcraft and Magic Among Shakespeare's Contemporaries and Successors.* London: Arno Press, 1962.

BULWER, SIR EDWARD GEORGE LYTTON. *A Strange Story.* Boston: Gardner A. Fuller, 1862.

BURTON, MAURICE. *Phoenix Re-Born.* London: Hutchinson, 1959.

BUSK, RACHEL HARRIETTE. *The Folk Songs of Italy.* London: Arno Press, 1887.

BUTLER, IVAN. *The Horror Film.* Cranbury: N.J.: A. S. Barnes, 1967.

CAILLOIS, ROGER, ed. *Anthologies du Fantastique.* Paris: Gallimard, 1966.

CERF, BENNETT A., ed. *Famous Ghost Stories.* New York: Modern Library. Random House, 1944.

CHAMBERS, ROBERT W. *The King in Yellow.* Freeport, N.Y.: Books for Libraries Press, 1969.

CHINESE ACADEMY OF SCIENCES. *Stories about Not Being Afraid of Ghosts.* Translated by Hsien-Yi Yang and Gladys Yang. Peking: Foreign Languages Press, 1961.

CLARENS, CARLOS. *An Illustrated History of the Horror Film.* New York: G. P. Putnam's Sons, 1967.

COATES, ROBERT M. *Wisteria Cottage.* New York: Harcourt, Brace and Company, 1948.

COCKCROFT, T. G. L. *Index to the Weird Fiction Magazines.* Lower Hutt, New Zealand: Cockcroft, 1962, 1967.

COHEN, DANIEL. *A Modern Look at Monsters.* New York: Dodd, Mead & Company 1970.

COLERIDGE, SAMUEL TAYLOR. *The Complete Poetical Works of Samuel Taylor Coleridge.* Edited by E. H. Coleridge. *Poems.* Oxford: Clarendon Press, 1912.

COLLINS, CHARLES M. *A Feast of Blood.* New York: Avon Books, 1967.

COMBE, JACQUES. *Jerome Bosch.* Paris: René Huyghe & Germain Bazin, 1946.

CONGDON, DON, ed. *Stories for the Dead of Night.* New York: Dell Publishing Co., 1957.

CONKLIN, GROFF, ed. *The Supernatural Reader.* New York: Collier Books, 1962.

CORTÁZAR, JULIO. *End of the Game.* Translated by Paul Blackburn. New York: Pantheon Books, Random House, 1963.

CRANE, STEPHEN. *The Complete Short Stories and Sketches of Stephen Crane.* Garden City, N.Y.: Doubleday & Company, 1963.

CRAWFORD, F. MARION. *Wandering Ghosts.* New York: Macmillan, 1911.

CREIGHTON, HELEN. *Bluenose Ghosts.* Toronto: Ryerson Press, 1957.

CROSS, JOHN K., ed. *Best Horror Stories.* London: Faber and Faber, 1963.

CURTIN, JEREMIAH. *Tales of the Fairies and of the Ghosts of the World.* New York: Lemma Publishing Corporation, 1960. Reprint of the 1895 edition.

DAHL, ROALD. *Kiss Kiss.* New York: Alfred A. Knopf, 1960.

———. *Someone Like You.* New York: Alfred A. Knopf, 1953.

DANIEL, HOWARD. *Devils, Monsters and Nightmares.* New York: Abelard-Schuman Limited, 1964.

DANIELS, LEE, ed. *Dying of Fright.* New York: Charles Scribner's Sons, 1976.

DAVENPORT, BASIL, ed. *Deals with the Devil.* New York: Dodd, Mead & Company, 1958.

DAY, BRADFORD M. *The Supplement Checklist of Fantastic Literature.* Denver: Science-Fiction and Fantasy Publications, 1963.

DERLETH, AUGUST. *Collected Poems.* New York: Candlelight Press, 1967.

———, ed. *Dark Mind, Dark Heart.* Sauk City, Wis.: Arkham House, 1967.

———, ed. *Dark of the Moon: Poems of Fantasy and the Macabre.* Sauk City, Wis.: Arkham House, 1947.

———, ed. *Dark Things.* Sauk City, Wis.: Arkham House, 1971.

———, ed. *Far Boundaries.* New York: Pellegrini and Cudahy, Publishers, 1951.

———. *The Mask of Cthulhu.* Sauk City, Wis.: Arkham House, 1958.

———, ed. *Over the Edge.* Sauk City, Wis.: Arkham House, 1964.

———, ed. *Portals of Tomorrow.* New York: Holt, Rinehart and Winston, 1954.

———. *The Sleeping and the Dead.* Chicago: Pellegrini and Cudahy, Publishers, 1947.

———. *Tales of the Cthulhu Mythos.* Sauk City, Wis.: Arkham House, 1969.

———. *The Trail of Cthulhu.* Sauk City, Wis.: Arkham House. 1962.

———, ed. *Travellers by Night.* Sauk City, Wis.: Arkham House, 1967.

———. *Who Knocks.* New York: Holt, Rinehart and Winston, 1946.

———, and H. P. LOVECRAFT. *The Shadow Out of Time.* London: Victor Gollancz, Ltd., 1968.

DE SADE, MARQUIS. *Three Complete Novels.* Translated by Richard Seaver and Austryn Wainhouse. New York: Grove Press, 1968.

———. *Oeuvres Completes, Volume II, Justine.* Paris: Jean-Jacques Pauvert, 1955.

DESLANDRES, YVONNE. *Delacroix: A Pictorial Biography.* London: Thames and Hudson, 1963.

DICKENS, CHARLES, et al. *Classic Ghost Stories.* New York: Dover Publications.

DOUGLAS, DRAKE. *Horror!* New York: Macmillan, 1966.

DOUGLAS, GEORGE BRISBANE, ed. *Scottish Fairy and Folk Tales.* London: Arno Press, 1901.

DOYLE, ARTHUR CONAN. *The Great Kleinplatz Experiment.* Garden City, N.Y.: Doubleday & Co., 1947.

———. *The Parasite.* New York: Harper and Brothers, 1895.

———. *The Complete Adventures and Memoirs of Sherlock Holmes.* New York: Clarkson N. Potter, Publisher, 1975.

———. *The Sign of Four.* Garden City, N.Y.: Doubleday & Co., 1974.

———. *The Return of Sherlock Holmes.* London: John Murray and Jonathan Cape, 1974.

———. *The Adventures of Sherlock Holmes.* New York: Harper & Row, 1930.

DUCASSE, ISIDORE. *Maldoror.* Translated by Guy Wernham. New York: New Directions, 1946.

DUNSANY, LORD. *Gods, Men, and Ghosts: The Best Supernatural Fiction of Lord Dunsany.* New York: Dover Publications, 1972.

ELLISON, HARLAN. *Alone Against Tomorrow.* New York: Macmillan, 1971.

———. *Deathbird Stories: A Pantheon of Modern Gods.* New York: Harper & Row, 1975.

ERNST, MAX. *Gemälde und Graphik 1920–1950.* Brühl: Lothar and Loni Pretzell, 1951.

EVANS, HILARY AND DIK. *Beyond the Gaslight.* London: Frederick Muller, 1976.

EYRIES, J. B. B. *Fantasmagoriana.* Paris: Chez F. Schoell, 1812.

FIEDLER, LESLIE A., ed. *In Dreams Awake.* New York: Dell Publishing Co., 1975.

FONTENROSE, JOSEPH E. *Python: A Study of the Delphic Myth and Its Origins.* Berkeley: University of California, 1959.

FRAZER, PHYLLIS AND WISE, HERBERT ALVIN. eds. *Great Tales of Terror and the Supernatural.* New York: Modern Library, Random House, 1944.

FREEMAN, MARY E. WILKINS. *Collected Ghost Stories.* Introduction by Edward Wagenknecht. Sauk City, Wis.: Arkham House, 1974.

FUSELI, HENRY. *Johann Heinrich Füseli.* Zurich: Gemälde und Zeichnungen, Kunsthaus, 1969.

GILL, WILLIAM WYATT. *Myths and Songs from the South Pacific.* London: Arno Press, 1876. Reprinted by Arno Press, 1978.

GILMAN, CHARLOTTE PERKINS. *The Yellow Wallpaper.* Afterword by Elaine R. Hedges. Old Westbury, N.Y.: The Feminist Press, 1973.

GIYEN, WILLIAM. *Ghost and Flesh.* New York: Random House, 1952.

GOODSTONE, TONY. *The Pulps: Fifty Years of American Pop Culture.* New York: Chelsea House, 1970.

GOULART, RON. *An Informal History of the Pulp Magazines.* New York: Arlington House, 1972.

GOULD, CHARLES. *Mythical Monsters.* London: W. H. Allen, 1886. Reprinted Singing Tree Press, Detroit, 1969.

GOYA Y LUCIENTES FRANCISCO DE. *The Complete Etchings of Goya.* New York: Crown Publishers, 1943.

———. *Les Desastres de la Guerre.* Paris: Les Peintres du Livre, 1966.

——— *The Disasters of War.* London: George Allen & Unwin, Ltd., 1937.

GRAVES, ROBERT. *But It Still Goes On.* New York: Jonathan Cape and Harrison Smith, 1931.

GROOME, FRANCIS HINDES. *Gypsy Folk-Tales.* London: Arno Press, 1899.

GRUBER, FRANK. *The Pulp Jungle.* Los Angeles: Sherbourne Press, 1967.

GUERNEY, BERNARD GUILBERT, ed. and trans. *An Anthology of Russian Literature in the Soviet Period from Gorki to Pasternak.* New York: Random House, 1960.

HADFIELD, JOHN, ed. *A Chamber of Horrors Unlocked.* Boston: Little, Brown, and Company, 1965.

HAINING, PETER, ed. *The Fantastic Pulps.* New York: St. Martin's Press, 1975.

————, ed. *The Gentlewomen of Evil: An Anthology of Rare Supernatural Stories from the Pens of Victorian Ladies.* New York: Taplinger Publishing Co., 1967.

————, ed. *Gothic Tales of Terror.* New York: Taplinger, 1972.

————, ed. *Great British Tales of Terror. Vol. I.* London: Victor Gollancz, Ltd., 1972.

————, ed. *The Hollywood Nightmare.* London: Macdonald, 1970.

————. *The Midnight People.* New York: Popular Library, 1968.

————. *Terror.* New York: A & W Visual Library, 1976.

HARTLEY, LESLIE P. *The Traveling Grave and Other Stories.* Sauk City, Wis.: Arkham House, 1948.

HAWTHORNE, NATHANIEL. *Complete Short Stories.* Garden City, N.Y.: Hanover House, 1959.

HEARN, LAFCADIO. *Kwaidan.* New York: Dover Publications, 1968.

————. *Some Chinese Ghosts.* New York: Modern Library, Random House, c. 1927.

HECHT, BEN. *Collected Stories of Ben Hecht.* New York: Crown Publishers, 1943.

HELM, THOMAS. *Monsters of the Deep.* New York: Dodd, Mead & Company, 1962.

HITCHCOCK, ALFRED. *Alfred Hitchcock Presents My Favorites in Suspense.* New York: Random House, 1959.

————. *Alfred Hitchcock Presents Stories for Late at Night.* New York: Random House, 1961.

————, ed. *Alfred Hitchcock Presents Stories They Wouldn't Let Me Do on TV.* New York: Simon & Schuster, 1957.

HODGSON, WILLIAM H. *Deep Waters.* Sauk City, Wis.: Arkham House, 1967.

HOFFMAN, ERNST T. A. *Weird Tales.* Translated by J. T. Bealby. Freeport, N.Y.: Books for Libraries Press, 1970. Reprint of first published edition, 1923.

HOLZER, HANS. *Gothic Ghosts.* New York: The Bobbs-Merrill Co. 1970.

————. *Hans Holzer's Haunted Houses.* New York: Crown Publishers, 1971.

HURWOOD, BERNHARDT J. *Vampires, Werewolves, and Ghouls.* Payson and Clarke, 1928.

HUYSMANS, J. K. *La Bas (Down There).* Translated by Keene Wallace. New York: Dover Publications, 1928. Reprinted 1972.

INGERSOLL, ERNEST. *Dragons and Dragon Lore.* New York: Payson and Clarke, 1928.

IRVING, WASHINGTON. *The Bold Dragon and Other Ghostly Tales.* New Amsterdam: Alfred A. Knopf, 1944.

JACKSON, SHIRLEY. *The Lottery, or the Adventures of James Harris.* New York: Farrar, Straus, 1949.

JACOBS, JOSEPH, ed. *Celtic Folk and Fairy Tales.* New York: G. P. Putnam's Sons.

————, ed. *More English Fairy Tales.* New York: Dover Publications, 1967.

JAFFE, ANIELA. *Apparitions and Precognition: A Study of C. G. Jung's Analytical Psychology.* New Hyde Park, N.Y.: University Books, 1963.

JAMES, HENRY. Edited by Leon Edel. *The Complete Tales.* London: R. Hart. Davis, 1962.

———— *The Ghostly Tales of Henry James.* New Brunswick, N.J.: Rutgers University Press, 1948.

JEROME, JEROME K. *Told After Supper.* New York: Charles Scribner's Sons, 1891.

JOHNSON, LEE. *Delacroix.* New York: W. W. Norton & Company, 1963.

JORDAN, DAVID K. *Gods, Ghosts and Ancestors.* Berkeley: University of California Press, 1972.

KEATS, JOHN. *The Poetical Works of Keats.* Boston: Houghton Mifflin Company, 1975.

KEAY, CAROLYN, ed. *Henry Fuseli.* New York: St. Martin's Press, 1974.

KIEJI, NIKOLAS. *Japanese Grotesqueries.* Introduction by Terrence Barron, Rutland, Vt.: Charles E. Tuttle, Co., 1973.

KINGSCOTE, HOWARD. *Tales of the Sun: Folklore of Southern India.* 1890. Reprinted London: Arno Press, 1978.

KINSLEY, DAVID. *The Sword and the Flute.* Berkeley: University of California Press, 1975.

KIPLING, RUDYARD. *Phantoms and Fantasies: Twenty Tales.* Garden City, New York: Doubleday & Company, 1965.

———. *Wee Willie Winkie and Other Stories.* Garden City, N.Y.: Doubleday & Company, 1923.

———. *The Writings in Prose and Verse of Rudyard Kipling: The Phantom Rickshaw and Other Stories.* Vol. 5. New York: Charles Scribner's Sons, 1899.

KLINGER, MAX. *Max Klinger Ausstellung.* Leipzig: Museum der Bildenden Kunste, 1970.

KNOWLES, JAMES HINTON. *Folk-Tales of Kashmir.* London: Arno Press, 1893.

KOENIG, GEORGE. *Ghosts of the Gold Rush.* La Siesta Press, 1968.

LAMBERT, R. S. *Exploring the Supernatural and the Weird in Canadian Folklore.* Toronto: McClelland & Stewart, 1955.

LARKIN, DAVID. *The English Dreamers.* Introduction by Rowland Elzea. Toronto: Peacock Press, Bantam Books, 1975.

LA SPINA, GREYE. *Invaders from the Dark.* Sauk City, Wis.: Arkham House, 1960.

LEACH, MARIA, ed. *The Thing at the Foot of the Bed and Other Scary Tales.* Cleveland: World Publishing Company, 1959.

LECLAIRE, ALGER. *Gaelic Ghosts.* New York: Holt, Rinehart and Winston, 1963.

LEE, VERNON. *Pope Jacynth and More Supernatural Tales.* London: Peter Owen, Ltd., 1956.

———. *For Maurice: Five Unlikely Stories.* New York: Arno Press, 1976.

———. *The Snake Lady and Other Stories.* New York: Grove Press, 1954.

———. *Hauntings: Fantastic Stories.* London: John Lane, 1906.

LE FANU, JOSEPH SHERIDAN, et al. *A Stable for Nightmares or Weird Tales.* New York: New Amsterdam Book Company, 1896.

———. *Best Ghost Stories of J. S. Le Fanu.* New York: Dover Publications, 1964.

———. *The Hours After Midnight....* London: Des Hickey and Leslie Freurir Publishers, Ltd. 1975.

LE GRAND, FRANCINE-CLAIRE. *Ensor, cet inconnu.* Mouseron: Renaissance-Art, 1971.

LE GUIN, URSULA. *The Left Hand of Darkness.* New York: Ace Books, 1959.

———. *Orsinian Tales.* New York: Harper & Row Publishers, 1976.

———. *Wild Angels.* Santa Barbar: Capra Press, 1975.

———. *The Wind's Twelve Quarters.* New York: Harper & Row Publishers, 1975.

LEIBER, FRITZ, ed. *H. P. Lovecraft: A Symposium.* Regina, Canada: Riverside Quarterly, 1970.

LEODHAS, SORCHE NIC. *Gaelic Ghosts.* New York: Holt, Rinehart and Winston, 1963.

LETHBRIDGE, THOMAS. *Ghost and Divining Rod.* London: Routledge & Kegan Paul Ltd., 1963.

———. *Ghost and Ghoul.* New York: Doubleday & Company, 1962.

LEWIS, C. S. *That Hideous Strength.* New York: Macmillan, 1946.

LINTON, E. LYNN, ed. *Witch Stories.* London: Chapman and Hall, 1861.

LONG, FRANK BELKNAP. *The Horror from the Hills.* Sauk City, Wis.: Arkham House, 1963.

LOPEZ-REY, JOSÉ. *Goya's Caprichos: Beauty, Reason and Caricature.* Vols. I and II. Princeton, N.J.: Princeton University Press. 1953.

LOVECRAFT, H. P. *At the Mountains of Madness and Other Novels.* Sauk City Wis.: Arkham House, 1964.

———. *The Dark Brotherhood and Other Pieces.* Sauk City, Wis.: Arkham House, 1966.

———. *The Dunwich Horror and Others.* Sauk City, Wis.: Arkham House, 1963.

———. *The Horror in the Museum and Other Revisions.* Sauk City, Wis.: Arkham House, 1970.

———, and AUGUST DERLETH. *The Shadow Out of Time and Other Tales of Terror.* London: Victor Gollancz, Ltd. 1973.

MCCOMAS, HENRY CLAY. *Ghosts I Have Talked with.* Baltimore: The William & Wilkins Co., 1937.

MACDOUGALL, JAMES, comp. *Folk Tales and Fairy Lore in Gaelic and English.* Edinburgh: Arno Press, 1910.

———, ed. and trans. *Waifs and Strays of Celtic Tradition Argyllishire Series Number III Folk and Hero Tales.* London: David Nutt, 1891.

MACHEN, ARTHUR. *The Children of the Pool.* London: Hutchinson and Company, Publishers.

———. *The Strange World of Arthur Machen.* New York: Juniper Press, 1960.

———. *Tales of Horror and the Supernatural.* London: John Baker, 1949.

MCNALLY, RAYMOND. *A Clutch of Vampires.* New York: Bell Publishing Co., 1974.

MANLEY, SEON, comp. *Ladies of Horror: Two Centuries of Supernatural Stories by the Gentle Sex.* New York: Lothrop, Lee & Shephard Co., 1971.

MAPLE, ERIC. *The Realm of Ghosts.* New York: A. S. Barnes, 1964.

MARGOLIES, JOSEPH A., ed. *Strange and Fantastic Stories.* New York: McGraw-Hill, 1946.

MARQUEZ, GABRIEL GARCIA. *Leaf Storm and Other Stories.* New York: Avon Books, 1972.

MENVILLE, DOUGLAS. *A Historical and Critical Survey of the Science Fiction Film.* London: Arno Press, 1974.

MÉRIMÉE, PROSPER. *La Guzla.* Paris: Heitz, 1926.

MILTON, JOHN. *Paradise Lost.* New York: The Heritage Press, 1940.

MOSKOWITZ, SAM, ed. *Masterpieces of Science Fiction.* Westport, Conn.: Hyperion Press, 1966.

———. *Explorers of the Infinite.* Cleveland: World Publishing Company, 1963.

———. *Seekers of Tomorrow.* Cleveland: World Publishing Company, 1966.

———, ed. *Strange Signposts: An Anthology of the Fantastic.* New York: Holt, Rinehart and Winston, 1966.

MUNRO, HECTOR H. *The Short Stories of Saki.* New York: The Viking Press, 1930.

MUNSTERBERG, HUGO. *Dragons in Chinese Art.* New York: China House Gallery, 1971.

MUSICH, RUTH ANN. *The Tell Tale Lilac Bush and Other West Virginia Ghost Tales.* Lexington: University of Kentucky Press. 1965.

O'CONOR, NORREYS JEPHSON. *Battles and Enchantments Retold from Early Gaelic Literature.* Freeport, N.Y.: Books for Libraries Press, 1922.

O'FLAHERTY, WENDY. *The Origins of Evil in Hindu Mythology.* Berkeley: University of California Press, 1976.

OLIPHANT, MARGARET O. *Stories of the Seen and the Unseen.* Freeport N.Y.: Books for Libraries Press, 1970.

ONIONS, OLIVER. *The Collected Ghost Stories of Oliver Onions.* New York: 1971.

PARKER, HENRY. *Village Folk-Tales of Ceylon.* 3 Vols. London: Arno Press, 1941. Reprinted 1978.

PARRY, MICHEL. ed. *Beware of the Cat.* New York: Taplinger Publishing Co., 1973.

PASINETTI, P. M. *Great Italian Short Stories.* New York: Dell Publishing Co., 1959.

PERRAULT, CHARLES. Edited by Jacques Barchilon and Henry Pettit. *The Authentic Mother Goose.* Denver: Alan Swallow Press, 1960.

PIRIE, DAVID. *The Vampire Cinema.* New York: Crescent Publications, 1977.

POE, EDGAR ALLAN. *The Complete Stories and Poems of Edgar Allan Poe.* New York: Alfred A. Knopf, 1946.

P'U SUNG-LING. *Chinese Ghost and Love Stories.* New York: Pantheon Books, 1946.

RABKIN, ERIC S. *The Fantastic in Literature.* Princeton, N.J.: Princeton University Press, 1976.

RADIN, PAUL. *Primitive Religion: Its Nature and Origin.* New York: Dover Publications, 1937.

RALSTON, WILLIAM R. S. *Russian Folk Tales.* New York: Arno Press, 1977.

RAMSEY, JAROLD. *Coyote Was Going There.* Seattle: University of Washington, 1977.

RANDOLPH, VANCE. comp. *The Devil's Pretty Daughter and Other Ozark Folk Tales.* New York: Columbia University Press, 1955.

REDFIELD, ROBERT. *The Primitive World and Its Transformations.* Ithaca: Cornell University Press, 1953.

REDON, ODILON. *Odilon Redon, Selbstgespräch.* Munich: Rogner and Bernhard, 1971.

RESTIF DE LA BRETONNE. *The Corrupted Ones.* London: Neville Spearman, 1967.

REYNOLDS, JAMES. *Ghosts in American Houses.* New York: Bonanza Books, 1955.

RUSSELL, JOHN. *Where the Pavement Ends.* London: Eyre and Spottiswoode, 1921.

RYMER, JAMES M. *Varney the Vampyre.* New York: Dover Publications, 1972.

SATTY, WILFRIED. *The Illustrated Edgar Allan Poe.* New York: Clarkson N. Potter, Publisher, 1976.

SCARBOROUGH, DOROTHY. *The Supernatural in Modern English Fiction.* New York: Octagon Books, 1967.

SCHAMONI, PETER. *Max Ernst.* Munich: Bruckmann, 1974.

Schilderijen: Jan Toorop, Charley Toorop, Edgar Fernhout. Leiden: N.V. Drukkerij, Groen en Zoon, 1972.

SCHNEIDER, MARCEL. *La Littérature Fantastique en France.* Paris: Fayard, 1964.

SERLING, ROD, ed. *Stories from the Twilight Zone.* New York: Bantam Books, 1964.

SHAW, JOSEPH. *The Hardboiled Omnibus.* New York: Simon & Schuster, 1946.

SHAW, LARRY T., ed. *Great Science Fiction.* New York: Adventure Lancer Books, 1968.

SIEMON, FRED. *Ghost Story Index.* San Jose, California: Library Research Associates, 1967.

SIKES, WIRT. *British Goblins.* Yorkshire, England: EP Publishing, Ltd. 1973. First published by Sampson Low, London, 1880.

SMITH, CLARK ASHTON. *The Abominations of Yondo.* Sauk City, Wis.: Arkham House, 1960.

———. *Other Dimensions.* Sauk City, Wis.: Arkham House, 1970.

————. *Tales of Science and Sorcery.* Sauk City, Wis.: Arkham House, 1964.

SPECTOR, ROBERT D., ed. *Seven Masterpieces of Gothic Horror.* New York: Bantam Books, 1963.

STARRETT, VINCENT. *The Quick and the Dead.* Sauk City, Wis.: Arkham House, 1965.

STEVENSON, ROBERT LEWIS. *The Merry Men and Other Tales.* New York: Charles Scribner's Sons, 1925.

————. *The Strange Case of Dr. Jekyll and Mr. Hyde and Other Famous Tales.* New York: Dodd, Mead & Company, 1963.

STOKER, BRAM. *The Bram Stoker Bedside Companion.* New York: Taplinger Publishing Co., 1973.

SUMMERS, MONTAGUE. *A Gothic Bibliography.* New York: Russell and Russell, Publishers, 1964.

————. *The Supernatural Omnibus.* New York: Causeway Books, 1931.

————. *The Vampire In Europe.* New Hyde Park, N.Y.: University Books, 1962.

————. *The Werewolf.* New Hyde Park, N.Y.: University Books, 1956.

SWEETSER, WESLEY D. *Arthur Machen.* New York: Twayne Publications, 1964.

SWYNNERTON, CHARLES. *Indian Nights' Entertainment; or, Folk-Tales from the Upper Indus with . . . Illustrations by Native Hands.* London: E. Stock, 1892.

TANIZAKI, JUNICHIRO. *Seven Japanese Tales.* New York: Berkley Publishing Corporation, 1965.

VAN THAL, HERBERT, ed. *Great Ghost Stories.* New York: Hill & Wang, 1960.

VARNEDOE, J. KIRK T., ed. *Graphic Works of Max Klinger.* New York: Dover Publications 1977.

VILLENEUVE, ROLAND. *Le Diable: Erotologie de Satan.* Paris: Pauvert, 1963.

VON FRANZ, MARIE-LOUISE. *Shadow and Evil in Fairy Tales.* Zurich: Spring Publications, 1974.

VON HOLTEN, RAGNAR, ed. *L'Art Fantastique de Gustave Moreau.* Paris: Pauvert, 1960.

WAGENKNECHT, EDWARD, ed. *Six Novels of the Supernatural.* New York: Viking Press, 1944.

WANDREI, DONALD. *Strange Harvest.* Sauk City, Wis.: Arkham House, 1965.

WERNER, ALFRED, ed. *The Graphic Works of Odilon Redon.* New York: Dover Publications, 1969.

WHARTON, EDITH. *Ghosts.* Appleton Century, 1937.

WILBERT, JOHANNES, ed. *Folk Literature of the Yamana Indians.* Berkeley: University of California Press, 1977.

WILDE, OSCAR. *The Picture of Dorian Gray.* New York: Heritage Press, 1957.

WILLIS, DONALD. *Horror and Science Fiction Films.* Metuchen, N.J.: Scarecrow Press, 1972.

WILSON, COLIN. *The Mind Parasites.* Sauk City, Wis.: Arkham House, 1967.

WISE, HERBERT A., ed. *Great Tales of Terror and the Supernatural.* New York: Random House, 1944.

YOVANSVITCH, V. M. *La Guzla de Prosper Mérimée.* Paris: Librairie Huchette, 1911.